ALL FOR A KING'S SHILLING

WILLIAM ATLAY

Published by

MELROSE BOOKS

An Imprint of Melrose Press Limited
St Thomas Place, Ely
Cambridgeshire
CB7 4GG, UK
www.melrosebooks.com

FIRST EDITION

Copyright © William Atlay 2005

The Author asserts his moral right to
be identified as the author of this work
Cover designed by Ross Hilton

ISBN 1 905226 25 X

All rights reserved. No part of this publication may be reproduced,
stored in a retrieval system, or transmitted, in any form or by any means
electronic, mechanical , photocopying, recording or otherwise,
without the prior permission of the publishers.

This book is sold subject to the condition that it shall not,
by way of trade or otherwise, be lent, re-sold, hired out or
otherwise circulated without the publisher's prior consent
in any form of binding or cover other than that in which
it is published and without a similar condition including this
condition being imposed on the subsequent purchaser.

Printed and bound in Great Britain by:
Bath Press Limited, Lower Bristol Road,
Bath, BA2 3BL, UK

ALL FOR A KING'S SHILLING

Chapter One
Watkins and a Russian KGB Man
Whitehall, The United Kingdom 1987

The most dangerous enemy is the enemy within.

What can one say about Mr Graham Watkins? Well, he was a nondescript man. A man whom most people passing in the street would not normally give a second glance as they continued on their way to work. Yet if they had but known it, he was one of the most successful spy catchers employed by MI5. He was not a large man; only about five seven and of medium build, yet he was a giant amongst his peers. His suit always looked as if he'd slept in it – a sign of a man who had been passed over for promotion. When he arrived for work each day he invariably had a small white powder mark somewhere on his face, which was habitually caused by the daily use of a styptic pencil with which he had tried to stem the bleeding after cutting himself shaving, something that he managed to do every day without fail. His staff subconsciously looked for the mark each morning when he walked into the office although they no longer commented on it. If he had ever arrived in the office without one, it is possible he'd have been arrested as an impostor.

His office, a small cog in a very large department of government, was larger than most people knew and those who did know were very reluctant to say so. It was a department which many Members of Parliament, especially those in the Labour Party, believed was completely out of control. Graham's office was like so many other similar offices scattered in and around London; it was an intricate part of the vast web of the secret service. A service that had grown out of all proportion to its importance, due mainly to the vagaries of the Cold War upon which it thrived, as well as the renowned civil service promotion system which favoured 'merit'; but also within the organisation was the old inefficient civil service system of empire building, a system that based promotion on the number of people you controlled. All you had to do to get your foot on the ladder was to convince your superiors that the work you had been given was too much for you. Talk them into giving you an assistant, and then a little while later another assistant and you were well on the way to being promoted. In other words, the system favoured inefficiency. Graham was just thankful that his department was divorced from the main office by a myriad of streets that some of his superiors wouldn't attempt to negotiate. His office was situated in one of the myriad of old buildings located within the old centre of London and he was very reluctant to tell a lot of people where it was.

Graham was the type of man who would possibly have looked more at home in a university town or city than an office in the centre of London. He was born in the early 1930s at Ambleside, in the County of Cumberland, now along with its sister county of Westmorland, for some reason called Cumbria. After completing his education at Durham University, he had drifted into, more than joined the Education Corps. From there, after a couple of years of trying to educate the Squaddies of various battalions of the British Army he had graduated, again more by accident than ambition, to the ranks of MI5.

He always described himself as a desk jockey, never as a spy catcher! Mainly due to his own lack of ambition, his life in MI5 had been a slow crawl from one desk to another. It wasn't promotion in the true sense, more a better class of desk from which to work. He attributed his slow rise to the dizzy heights of his present position to the fact that he had not gone to the right schools when a young boy, before attending a university. Even though he had attended the third oldest university in England, he still believed his earlier education had put him below a class which he couldn't surmount. Because of his outward impression of lack of enthusiasm for advancement, he was also not considered to be a threat to any of the many civil servants who came and went as his department head. People who were on their ever-continuous climb to the highest positions in the department offices within the civil service, collecting a knighthood and all the other honours that the top of the muck heap plonks upon their heads; of course 'Oxbridge' helped a hell of a lot. Hence the new expressions now very popular with the younger members of his staff, like 'you plonker', and 'what a plonker he is!' and 'be glad when he gets his gong and moves on'.

His success as a spy catcher though, well that was second to none and he attributed this success to his one belief that no person does anything for nothing, no matter who they are. There was always a reason for tyranny. Sometimes it was greed, sometimes jealousy and the desire to see some person done down, or the 'I'll show you' obsession. Occasionally personal stature was involved, or even, but normally unlikely, ideology. Find the reason, as Graham would say and you would find your man; something he was forever telling anybody who would listen, but unfortunately not very many people in the department did listen to him. You see he couldn't do them any favours in the promotion stakes; or perhaps they just thought of him as an 'old plonker'. Whatever it was he didn't take offence at them; after all, they were just starting out and had to make their mark somehow. Yet he was one of a small band of interrogators who never missed a trick even if it was just a movement of facial hair.

Graham was no high-flyer himself and for the last five years he had been overseeing the vetting of defectors mostly from the Iron Curtain countries. His main task was to weed out the people who were obviously sent to spy; also the decoys sent to cover the entry of the spies; to check out the poor persecuted despondent souls seeking only a quiet life. Finding the genuine people who arrived on our shores and were only trying to get away from years of persecution, well that was a much harder and more astute job. From a way of life, which they had eventually decided was too much to bear, and was far too high a price to pay and they were just looking for something better. Graham always thought it odd that significantly more Communists tried to get out from behind the Iron and Bamboo Curtains than ever tried to get in.

So when he walked into his office in the centre of London, on the 14th August 1984, he knew by instinct that something had happened. Something which his staff obviously thought was very important. They couldn't hide the flush of excitement from their faces. Nothing of any importance had happened in his office for weeks or even months, so much so that the word redundancy had entered the office vocabulary. The flow of defections from the Iron Curtain countries had now all but dried up; so it was all hands to the lifeboats. Some members of his staff were already on the lookout for transfers to more secure departments such as the exotic departments of the Treasury, the Home Office and the like, some were even considering DHSS, and that was a real surprise to Graham when he heard it.

It was precisely because of all the excitement that morning that he was soon to be introduced to a Russian defector called Boris! A meeting which he didn't know at the time was going to have a profound effect on his future. Comrade Boris Trovalov, as this defector insisted was his name, but Graham, well Graham was certain right from the first day that this wasn't his real name mainly because he had never heard the name before. Firstly, in all the years he had been dealing with the Russians, 'Trovalov' was a name he had never even heard. Over the next two weeks there were occasions when Graham caught him off guard a couple of times when he called him by the name 'Boris Trovalov!' instead of just Boris; the man was just that little too hesitant in his reaction to the name. His reaction wasn't instant as a well-trained defector's would have been, or it was a deliberate ploy to confuse Graham and his staff.

This Boris was for some inexplicable reason the biggest man Graham had ever met. There was no other way he could describe him. Oh, Boris was big in stature, but not out of the ordinary. Okay he was over six foot two, but it was just that when they were together, to Graham Boris appeared to be twice the size he physically was. The whole phenomenon was at first a little unnerving for him and was something he hadn't ever come across before.

It transpired that this giant of a man had walked into Paddington Green Police Station at about two o'clock that morning. There, he had asked the Desk Sergeant for political asylum. He had told the Desk Sergeant at the Station that he had really intended to go to America to defect. Unfortunately, as he had explained, he could not wait any longer as he thought that the KGB were already on to him.

"If you do not take me into custody, I will be dead by daylight," he had pleaded.

Later that day at their first meeting he told Graham, "I have been passing information to you British and the Americans for years."

Graham thought, yes Boris, you probably have and then again, maybe not, but he only said, "So you would have me believe, Mr Trovalov, but we will only get to the bottom of that later, when we have checked out your story! Your name, your surname is such an unusual surname isn't it, so you don't mind if I just call you Boris, do you?" Graham had asked him. Boris did what he was to do quite a lot during their sessions; he totally ignored the question.

Earlier Graham's superior, when he had briefed him, had given Graham very little information about how, or why Boris had defected to England in the first place; none of the standard reasons they normally put forward in these situations.

"We don't want you going to interview him with any preconceived ideas," he had told Graham. "It would be better if you could find out how he came to England to defect and why he chose us of all people? Then justify the reasons he gives you."

That man just talks a load of bullshit most of the time Graham thought as he left the meeting. To hear him talk you would think I'd never done anything like this before. Still, he is my superior, but he is so new to this game why the hell doesn't he let me get on with it. No doubt he sees this as a big chance to make his mark. Like all the Prima Donnas in the Civil Service, a good report and he would probably move on and ever upwards to the dizzy heights where with any luck he would disappear into outer space. Just like the proverbial Ouslam Bird, go round and round in ever-decreasing circles until he disappeared up his own backside.

So it was that Graham came to spend the next two weeks in the company of Comrade Boris Trovalov. They talked about his defection and he asked Boris Trovalov everything he could about the work he did in the Russian Foreign Service, of which he claimed he was a member. What is more important, he also asked him about his work in the KGB, because he was certain that Boris was a member of the KGB. When Boris first mentioned The KGB Graham hesitated in his questioning waiting for Boris to react to his pause, but Boris didn't, so Graham took it for granted that he was after all a member of the KGB. He was now very interested in hearing why Boris had decided to defect of all things at this time. From all the reports reaching the West, everything in Russia was improving and life was getting better for the average Russian; more so now as the tensions between the East and the West had started to recede and all the Russians could talk about was this unpronounceable word meaning 'everything has changed'. My sweet arse it has, thought Graham.

"So, why defect at all Boris?" Graham had asked, but Boris never did answer that question.

By this time there was no doubt in Graham's mind that Boris was a member of the KGB; moreover, that behind his defection there was some ulterior motive. Another thing that he wanted to know was what information Boris had passed to the British and American Intelligence Services during his so-called spying period. He also wanted to know when, how and to whom all this information had been given. He questioned Boris deeply about the KGB operating procedures, all the things in which he was probably just as well versed as Boris was. All the time Graham was probing and looking for something that he knew did not ring true, but Boris was very good. In his own mind he thought Boris was too bloody good to be true, with his bumbling answers and his portrayal of himself as the innocent victim in all of this he only convinced Graham more than ever that Boris was not who, or what he claimed to be.

Graham also kept plugging away probing all the time for any contacts, which he was convinced Boris would have in both the UK and America for that matter. Boris either said he had none, or kept very tight-lipped as Graham tried to probe deeper. For a man who made a big thing about having passed information to the West for so long it looked as if the man had surprisingly few contacts among the West's Intelligence Services. Now that little gem was something that made him all the more suspicious of Boris. For instance not one squeak or word of protest had come from the portals of MI6 about Graham's department handling all this. Now, if Boris was a spy for Britain or the United States, then it would stand to reason that some person in MI6 and also the US would be his handlers. Why were they not clambering at the door to get him back? Something had to be wrong with our Comrade's story. Something smelled and it wasn't a lavender pot!

During all the time Graham spent with Boris, the stature of the man never diminished. Well, not in Graham's eyes anyway. He, like others who had dealings with Boris, just could not get over the exuberance of the man. It was the only outstanding asset he had and without it he came across as a nobody, a man who would be considered a nonentity. Looks more like a wheeler-dealer than anything else, one of the office staff remarked one day, but Graham let the remark pass, even though he agreed with it.

After he had been debriefing Boris for some two weeks, to his credit Boris had eventually given him some good information, but he had also given some of the standard Russian rubbish, the type of stuff they all bring with them. The stuff the Americans keep calling disinformation, but all the time Graham couldn't get rid of the feeling that Boris was not who he claimed to be, and it bloody rankled him somewhat. Also more and more he had the feeling Boris was not here of his own volition. He was convinced Boris was here to do a job. Just what that job was, and if it was to be done here in the UK or in the States, he could not tell; nor could he get anything at all from Boris about it. Not even the slightest sniff, as they say.

By this time Graham felt he had got as far as he could, or was ever likely to with Boris. He still did not believe Boris was genuine, and told his superior as much. The only argument he could put forward was that as defections to Britain had all but dried up, he wondered why Boris had decided to make a break for it now. It did not sit right on the West versus the East situation as it was these days.

Still, Graham's superior was satisfied that Boris was genuine and he said Graham was reading too much into the situation. 'Things are changing,' he had said, 'and you must get rid of all your old superstitions; we are ready to pass Boris on to the Americans.' What is more, the Americans wanted to get Boris over to the States rather urgently.

Perhaps they were a little too keen to get their hands on Boris for Graham's peace of mind. He believed that there was something wrong. The problem was that he was unable to translate his feelings into facts, but something was ticking away at the back of his mind. He just hated the thought that he may have missed whatever it was Boris was really up to.

It had transpired earlier on during their talks that Boris had told Graham he had once worked in the Russian Embassy in Washington. No doubt the Americans would be eager to find out if Boris had told Graham anything about their CIA men in London because if anybody knew of any Americans spying in England, then you could bet your bottom dollar the Russians would not only know who, but they would know from where they operated and just what is was they were after. For his money the Americans were far too eager to get their grubby hands on Boris, just that little bit too keen, there had to be more to it, there had to be something more to Boris than he had found out to date.

Although not too happy about Boris's reasons for defecting, he had to go along with his superiors. To this end he was about to write the final chapter in the file and send Boris off to America and to be honest Graham thought the best of luck to all of them. It was during their final talk that for the first time Boris referred to a specific member of the British Embassy staff he knew working in Moscow. Alarm bells started ringing in Graham's head. Suddenly he was wide awake and very attentive. He had trouble hiding his excitement that his doubts had been justified. Now, he thought, we will get to the real reason for Boris being here.

Boris then went on to say, "I was very friendly with this clerk in your Embassy in Moscow. It was some years ago now, and I passed some very good information to him, information which I had been led to believe your people had been after for years. It was about a Britisher who was a prisoner of our KGB, a prisoner whom the KGB had removed from the GRU shortly after his capture. The KGB had taken this man and after interrogating him they had charged him with treason and espionage. He was later tried in an open court, you know one of the old show trials, and he was tried along with a Russian female accomplice. They convicted both of them of spying and they sentenced the man to death, which as you already know would be a certainty in that situation. His female accomplice, well, she received a twelve-year sentence and yes, before you ask I am certain she was a Russian.

"This Britisher was then taken from the courtroom to a yard at the rear of the court and shot; or so everybody was told when the gunfire had stopped. There was even applause in the court when it stopped, but I now know that the man didn't die; he actually entered the KGB prison system where he underwent further interrogation. Far worse than anything he had suffered prior to his trial and by god he had suffered then; how he came to survive the second spell of interrogation only goes to show the resilience of the man.

"Of course his execution had by this time already been promulgated and you know something that was odd, the woman disappeared too; really odd that, isn't it? The British Government couldn't do anything at all. A sort of fait accompli, you might say. Except perhaps ask for his body to be returned. That was something else, they never did try to recover his body. Don't you think that was also very odd? Anyway after some months or perhaps it was years, I'm not sure, but the heads of the KGB thought that as they had reported this man's death to the British Government and they were no longer getting any regular reports about him from their interrogation centres, then they had in their infinite wisdom concluded that the man must by then be dead. The problem of course was that this was probably not so. The man was in reality possibly still alive, if only just. By some power that the man had, perhaps with some help from a contact in the KGB, I don't know, but he had managed to defeat all their attempts to kill him off. I think that in the end the people in control just forgot about him and he was then marked in the big book in which the KGB maintains their records of prisoners who die and in which he had been mistakenly entered when his trial ended; well, in all truth that was what probably saved his life.

"You see, he had somehow got lost in the KGB network of prisons and interrogation centres. They have so many prisoners it is not uncommon for one or two to get lost in the system for a while. All the prisoners die in the end anyway, so nobody cares too much. The numbers allocated to the prisoners and their names are sometimes mixed up. So, when one of the prisoners dies what's the problem. If a prisoner is listed in the ledger as somebody else, so what? They all suffer the same fate in the end, inasmuch as they all end up in the correct pigeonhole, the one marked 'dead'!

"Not this Britisher, though; somebody somewhere along the line must have deliberately altered the books for him to remain alive. Of that I'm convinced, how else could the man have stayed alive and survived the worst prison system in the world? He wasn't in the best of health, mind you, but at least he was alive and had been well hidden in the system. When he was transferred from the KGB prison system into the normal Gulag system, then the man would have a chance of surviving. Not much of a chance, but he would have a small chance anyway. It seems that this man took every advantage of that lifeline thrown to him; but thrown by whom, I have no idea.

"But it was I, Boris, who discovered that the man was not dead. It happened when I visited a small settlement in the Russian Arctic. I managed to obtain some papers. The papers, which were reportedly written by this Royal Marine, were in the house of a young woman; I think they called her Sharon. Anyway, she had left the village and the others said she had gone to meet this man in London of all places. Can you believe that, from the Arctic Circle to London to meet with a half-dead prisoner?"

"A Royal Marine, Boris, are you sure of that?"

"Oh, I'm sorry, didn't I tell you earlier that he was one of your Royal Marines? But I thought you would know. Anyway, these papers were written a long time after his death was reported at the time of his trial and later by a KGB prison governor, his last KGB prison governor before he disappeared into the Gulag system. The papers, well they came into my possession when I visited the small village in the Arctic and the villagers let me use the woman's house where the man had stayed before they both disappeared. Fancy, I stayed in the house where this man was supposed to have spent the latter part of one winter and most of the next summer."

"Are you sure this story you are telling me is correct, Boris? I don't remember any reports of a Royal Marine being executed in Russia? From what you say, Boris, I get the impression that you have met this man, this Royal Marine whom you are talking about. Did you ever meet him, Boris?"

The 'Oh no' that Boris half shouted to Graham was an obvious lie and Graham was determined to follow it up, but Boris then went on. "If your intelligence service had any sense at all and if they had read the papers immediately, well, they would have been able, after reading the papers, to have known exactly what a certain British Major and a retired Lt Colonel were up to for years. Both the Major and the Lt Colonel are no longer alive and it is thanks to the inactivity of your intelligence organisations that it is probably too late for you to investigate just what did happen to them. Both of them died in strange circumstances within days of one another and I'm sure that it was thanks to this man, this ex prisoner, this Royal Marine who killed both of them. You see the Major and the Lt Colonel were both among the top men in British Military Intelligence. They had also been the most successful GRU agents in England ever. In fact, they had been officers in the GRU longer than either of them had been in British Military Intelligence. They had been schooled since childhood for the roles they undertook."

Graham just looked at Boris when he had finished his tale and studied his face for at least long enough to make Boris fidget a bit. He then made the decision that Boris was this time telling him the truth. Also that he was privy to a lot more top secret information than he was admitting to otherwise how did he know the two officers he talked about were schooled from childhood for their roles as spies? What was more, he thought he now knew why Boris was here in London. He was here to stir the shit and to even a score, he was here to avenge the killing of their two stars by this mysterious Royal Marine; but he just looked at Boris and finally said, "You realise I will have to tell my superiors about this, Boris? I'm afraid your trip to the States could possibly be postponed, but then you already knew that, didn't you, Boris?"

Boris then went on, "This prisoner is alive, of that I'm certain. I'm also convinced that he was responsible for the Major's death, but I'm not so certain about the Lt Colonel."

"Well, Boris, if you are so certain then that this unfortunate and allegedly dead British Agent is not a dead agent after all, that he has come to Britain and killed two top men in British Military Intelligence, both men whom you are saying were actually GRU agents; then perhaps you could tell me, firstly, their names and units, and secondly, where this supposedly dead Royal Marine is right now?"

At this Boris shrugged his heavy shoulders, closed his mouth tight-shut and said nothing.

"Then, perhaps, if you have read these papers that you had, you can tell me just why it was he thought he had to kill these two men? Surely he didn't just kill them offhand like that? He must have had a reason for selecting these two and their being two of yours?"

Again Boris just shrugged his shoulders and said, "I can only speak English, I am unable to read it."

At first Graham was a little perturbed at his last remark; perhaps the notes were written in Russian, he thought. He then asked Boris, "Tell me, Boris, have you read these papers yourself?"

"Yes!" was the curt reply that Boris snapped at him.

This turn of events set alarm bells ringing in Graham's head. It also cancelled out Boris's first story and his reason for defecting. He had just convinced Graham that he was here to stir trouble for the British Security Services in a big way. Boris had just confirmed Graham's worst suspicions that he had held from the start – he was not here to help the British or the Americans at all. Graham was now more certain than ever that Boris was here to even a score. Yes, he was here to either kill somebody, or to wind us or the Americans up to kill somebody. That was somebody whom his masters back in Russia had got the hump about. Graham thought, yes and that somebody was a poor sod who, unknown to any of us, had done the West a great service by eliminating two Russian agents, two bloody agents of whom we had no knowledge whatsoever, men who had penetrated our intelligence services or, perhaps worse, were possibly in charge of them. This good deed which the man had done for us now looked as if it would cause a god almighty scandal within the security services of the West.

He then put it to Boris. "It is most important that I get to know who the hell this Lt Colonel and Major, who according to you are now both dead, were. Also it is important I find out who this dead, or not so dead, ex-prisoner of the KGB really is? Is he still alive, or is he now also dead and lastly, who was the man in our Embassy whom you contacted?"

All For A King's Shilling

Boris just said, "It was all in the papers which were written by the agent. Written after he had been officially reported dead, I might add, to both the Russian and the British authorities."

Which Major, which Lt Colonel, and what's more important, which agent? These were the questions Graham had to find the answers to and Graham, as the Americans would say, was now in a completely new 'Ball Game'. There was one bright spot in this story though; he could hardly wait to see the look of panic which he knew would cross his boss's face when he told him what Boris had just revealed.

Over the next day Boris's story did not make much sense. There were plenty of reasons for this. Firstly, after tentative enquiries, no department would admit having lost anybody – not even a private, let alone a Lt Colonel or a Major, which in itself was not uncommon. So, if these two who were now dead were supposedly Russian agents, as Boris had implied that they were, then to reach the ranks of Lt Colonel and Major in British Military Intelligence it would follow that they held the same ranks within some Regiment, Corps or other organisation within the British Armed Forces. To Graham this was starting to smell just a little bit if, as was more than likely, the agents were British Nationals, and it looked increasingly as if they had to be. To have enabled them to reach such ranks in the armed forces, then they must be the sons of long-serving illegal immigrants, illegal immigrants or their children who had been in the country for years, perhaps from the start of the Russian State as we know it today. Boris had insisted, after further questioning, that the Major and the Lt Colonel were British, and not Russian illegal immigrants. God, Graham thought, it's all turning into a hell of a mess.

What was worse, Boris was also adamant for some reason he would not divulge that the Major was an Officer in the British Navy and a British National. He was also adamant that the Major had been eliminated by this allegedly dead agent, the dead agent who had allegedly been a prisoner of the Russians for some considerable time but now was no longer a dead agent. Now Boris was not too certain how the Lt Colonel had met his death; he only knew that it was within days of the Major meeting his.

It was no wonder Graham was walking the corridors of the office scratching his head. Until, that is, he realised that the ranks Boris was talking of would be the ranks the men held in the Russian Security Services and not the British forces. That was when it all became as clear as mud, as they say!

Boris would go no further with his story, but his story was too convincing for it not to be true. During his deliberations Graham convinced himself that Boris knew this allegedly not so dead ex-prisoner of the Russians personally. What was more, Graham believed Boris knew this alleged prisoner was still alive and where he could be found. Boris was to his mind some part of the whole operation. One other thing that he could not fathom out at the moment was why Boris referred continually to the Major being senior in rank to the Lt Colonel. Senior in whose bloody army, Graham had shouted in his office later.

It was the next day when Graham was clarifying this point with Boris that Boris told him to whom he had passed the papers. The man was a not too senior but not too junior clerk he'd met, who worked in the British Embassy in Moscow. He also gave Graham a good idea just where that man now lived. To Graham it seemed as if Boris now wanted him to get on to the right track straight away. Next, Boris told Graham when he had passed the papers to this clerk and how. Graham could not get any more names or dates or details of their meetings from Boris; he did, however, give Graham some very definite pointers that there were other members of the Embassy Staff who needed to be looked at. Boris seemed very aggrieved that the papers he spoke of had not been, or seemed not to have been, passed on by this friendly Embassy Clerk.

Next he told Graham, "I didn't say anything about these papers earlier, because I thought you already knew all about them. When you hadn't questioned me about the papers, then I knew that they must have been got rid of by somebody. Obviously by some person or person who did not want them to come out and had covered the whole thing up or even destroyed them. Then when I arrived here in England I heard from our Embassy that the Major had met with an unfortunate accident some time ago. Well, I believed that British Intelligence had at last resolved one of their problems and were putting their house in order. It's no wonder the KGB nearly caught me, if as you say, you knew nothing about this matter."

At this point Graham was starting to wish the KGB had caught Boris after all. He was a little afraid of the can of worms he might just uncover in this investigation. What had started out purely as a vetting problem now had the makings of a really good major spy scandal. It might just be that the ramblings of Boris were so disjointed in places that the whole of the West's security services could end the day with egg all over them. Graham's private thoughts on the matter were that Mr Boris Trovalov was a very clever man indeed.

Having completed his summary of the situation in which he pointed out his thoughts on the matter and his conclusion that Boris, if that were his real name, was here to cause as much embarrassment as he could for the British Secret Service. Graham reported all of this to his superior at their conference the next day. His superior, in his infinite wisdom, decided Graham would be the best person to clear this little matter up.

"Once you have satisfied yourself you have got to the bottom of this fiasco, then you should limit the damage done and pass Boris on to the Americans ASAP. You may just have uncovered a very unwelcome event so it is better we don't stir things up too much with the Americans rubbing our noses in it again. Don't take too long about it, either; I have already told the Americans we are finished with him."

Graham looked at him for a moment in complete disbelief and was about to say something, thought better of it, closed his mouth and without another word stood up and left the conference room. "The man is not living in the real world," he muttered to himself as he left the room.

As he walked back to his office he thought, it won't take me long to clear up Boris's story once I've located this bloody clerk, the one to whom Boris is supposed to have given the information. His step got lighter as he made his way along the corridors of the office, the corridors of the real power of the land, his part of the Secret Service! He also realised that he might just have a new boss soon.

It turned out as Graham had thought it would be, a job which took his jolly band of pilgrims less than half a day to resolve.

By four that afternoon one of his assistants came into his office and said, "We've got him."

"Good," said Graham, "I said it would be no big deal to check it all out." He thought thank the Lord after all we could have been on for bloody months trying to track this man down. If they had covered their tracks well we might never have found him, always assuming the man was a KGB agent, as Graham now seemed to think. It could have been far too bloody easy, finding the man so quickly.

Early the next morning, it was a wet, cold and miserable start to the day as Graham joined one of his erstwhile colleagues, a Mr John Knowles, another member of the office staff who, like himself, was not the slightest bit interested in climbing to the top of the heap. John was driving the department's one and only car left in their London office. The two of them were off to visit a Mr Donald Charles Cogan, retired, ex employee of Her Britannic Majesty's Foreign Office.

"We could be on a wild goose chase, Graham, probably another ruse – just something more to help Boris accumulate more Brownie points before his trip to America," John said as the car threaded its way through the early morning rush hour traffic, which was trying to enter the capital.

"If there is anything in this, then I'm afraid Boris will not be going to America for some considerable time to come," Graham replied.

With that, they both fell silent as the car headed west on the M4. Thank God for these motorways, thought Graham as the car moved at speed into the dismal gloom towards the West Country. At this time of year the weather always seemed to be reasonable until you were west of Swindon, then for some reason everything seemed to be cold, wet, miserable and overcast. Today was the exception; it was wet and overcast to start with, which seemed to settle like a gloom of doom over the pair of them. Then the farther west they went the brighter the day became.

It was gone eleven o'clock when they finally arrived at a thatched cottage in East Devon not far from Woodbury Common. The location of the place caused a wry grin on Graham's face. The British serviceman whom they were here to investigate was allegedly a Royal Marine. Now here, not twenty minutes drive from this Embassy Clerk's home on the other side of Woodbury Common, was the Royal Marine Commando Training Centre situated near Lympstone Village.

They had made good time in spite of the rain and mist and they both alighted from the car in front of the small cottage. It was the type of cottage one sees on the front of postcards and chocolate boxes but never really believes exists. They walked up the short footpath to the front door and John Knowles looked at Graham and then knocked on the ornate door knocker. He then stepped back and surveyed the door. The knocker he had just used was a cheap copy of the famous Durham Cathedral Door Knocker.

Sanctuary, Graham thought, as he too looked at the ornate grotesque knocker. He's going to need some sanctuary when I'm finished with him. The knocker itself was set in the middle of a rather heavy oak door and Graham remarked, "Perhaps he has found sanctuary." He then continued to stare at the replica knocker, the original of which he knew so well from his days at university and attending services in the Cathedral most Sundays during his university years.

After a moment or so the door opened. They were both taken aback a little at the man standing before them. He was a small and very dapper man; but it was his dress that had them agog for he was wearing a pair of silk trousers and a dark maroon velvet smoking jacket. On his feet he had a pair of ornamental silk slippers, the type one sees illustrated in children's books of the 'Arabian Nights' or 'Sinbad the Sailor'. Graham looked him up and down and concluded that here was a real 'Hello sailor man'. The man was very effeminate, to say the least, not only in his dress but in his looks as well. He was not Graham's kind of person at all. To Graham he looked and probably was a raving fairy if ever he'd seen one. He was a man to whom at first impression Graham took an instant dislike. Talk about prejudged convictions – Graham would have hanged the man without a trial. What is it they used to say in the Army? "March the guilty bastard in, Sergeant Major."

Still, you cannot let your prejudices influence your decisions my dear boy, as his boss would say. Again a smile crossed Graham's face as he pictured his boss having tea and crumpets with this 'Nancy Boy'. Birds of a feather, he thought, but in the end he just said, "My name is Graham Watkins, this is Mr John Knowles, my colleague; we are both from the Home Office and we wondered if we might have a word with you?"

At this point they were invited into the cottage and were shown into what could only have been classed as a study. Graham made a somewhat guttural sound as he looked the place over then, satisfied that he had missed nothing about the room, he at last sat in the chair which Mr Cogan had suggested he should use. They looked at each other for a minute or so, as if getting the measure of one another. Then, just as Mr Cogan was about to speak, before the man could utter a word, Graham started to explain why they were there.

"My colleague and I are sorry to trouble you like this, Mr Cogan, especially now you are retired. I think the department should really leave you alone to enjoy your retirement. Unfortunately, they have asked us to call and see you as we are in the area today to save sending someone down from London. They want me to ask you a couple of questions which seemingly cannot wait. I hope you don't mind, but I have to ask them."

"Fire away I'm all ears."

"Right, well, it concerns the time that you were in Moscow. Did you, when you were in Moscow ever come into contact with a Russian called Boris Trovalov? I suppose we should say when you were not only stationed in Moscow, but anywhere of the other places that you served in, for that matter?"

"Yes, I knew a Russian called Boris once, he was one of the KGB people who carried out surveillance of us during the time of my last stay in Moscow; but I never met him anywhere else, or should I say saw him anywhere else. I didn't know him well enough to know his surname, though but yes, I knew a Boris."

"Are you sure that you don't know this Boris's surname Mr Cogan?"

"Yes I'm certain of that; I have told you I didn't know his surname!"

Graham noticed the man had a little irritation in his voice. Ignoring it he then said, "Be that as it may, this man knew you well enough to know your surname. If it is the same Boris, that is. Isn't Boris a name as common in Russia as John is in England?" asked Graham trying to calm the man down a little, and it seemed to work because when he answered this time his voice was back to the same tone as when he had answered the door.

All For A King's Shilling

"Well I'm really not sure, but I suppose you could say it is; mind, as an Embassy surveillance guard then Boris would know my name, wouldn't he?"

"You know, I would be no good as an Embassy surveillance guard at all, having to know the names of all the staff and the like. That would be far too much detail for my small brain to comprehend. Still I'm not a much-travelled man, so I don't think I would fit in too well with people like you, people who have travelled the world. Here am I, coming up to retirement and the furthest I have been is Brighton, well Devon now after today. Can you believe it these days, with all the modern jet travel and such like? So this Boris you knew was an Embassy surveillance guard, was he?"

"No, you have got it wrong; he was a Russian KGB man who maintained surveillance of the British members of staff whenever we went out of the Embassy."

"Oh, I see, he was keeping tabs on you. That's how you came to know him? I see!"

At that moment John cleared his throat and Graham thought, I wish he wouldn't do that.

Looking at Cogan he went on, "You fellows from the Foreign Office, you are the ones to know all about that sort of thing. I suppose all your life has been spent travelling from one place to another, on the go all the time. Do you miss the travel and the excitement of all those foreign capitals now you have retired?"

"I most certainly do not. When you have seen one of them, you have seen them all really. I'm just glad to be back in England, and away from all the strain some of these places put you under."

Graham's ears pricked up, it was the word 'strain' and he thought, "I bet he has been at it." The Italians would just love you, pal, saying that Moscow was on a par with Rome or Florence, but he just said, "What sort of strain would that be? I've always been led to believe it is all cocktail parties and socialising for most if not all the time. At least some of your colleagues would have us Home Office types think that was what happened nearly every day on the Embassy circuit. Work from nine till twelve then off for drinks and 'brunch' at some party. Back to the Embassy for an hour or two's work then off to bed for a couple of hours. Then off to another do, dinner or dance or some such gathering. Talk about the life of Reilly!"

Graham's colleague cleared his throat again and Graham looked across at him. He thought, I will kill the sod if he does that again, I wish I had left him in the office or outside in the car.

He had half expected a tirade from Cogan, but the man said nothing. So chancing his arm he went on and asked Mr Cogan, "Perhaps you can tell me about this chap you knew, this Boris chappie. We will then see if he is the same man I've met, can you describe him to me?"

"Yes, that will be no problem."

Cogan then described Boris. The Boris he described didn't match the man whom Graham had come to know. It did not seem to be the same Boris at all. Oh, the description was of Boris, but perhaps the impression of size which Graham had of Boris seemed not to influence this Cogan in the same way it had influenced Graham.

"Did this Boris ever give you a package of any sort?"

"Oh, that old rubbish, how did you know about that stuff?"

William Atlay

When Cogan made that remark, Graham's eyebrows rose just slightly. He had trouble with the matter-of-fact way in which the man had come out with it. After all, he had half expected Cogan to make an outright denial about it all, but he managed to hide his surprise and said, "Tell me about it."

"It was nothing really, but yes he did give me a package of sorts, one night when he was pretending to be drunk and full of vodka. He was nearly always drunk but this time, for some reason best known to him, he just pretended to be drunk. It was one of the nights when he really was making a right pig's ear of himself. Yes, that was the night that he gave me the package; it was full of absolute rubbish. I took a lot of notice of it at first, I must admit. You see it happened about the time we discovered they were giving us a load of 'strange stories and of strange goings on', stories that in the end proved to be false, but they were trying to pass them off as good sound information. The Americans were on to them a lot quicker than us, they called it disinformation; yes, that is what the Americans called it, disinformation. Anyway, I was certainly not going to put my career on the line, not on the word of some drunken passed over KGB officer."

"How did you know that the man Boris was some drunken passed over KGB officer?"

"Oh, you can tell them as soon as you see them. We soon learned how to spot them a mile away. They start to drink too much, you know, more than they normally drink and they do drink a lot normally. It finally gets to them and in the end they do nothing more than follow Embassy staff around all day long. Oh, yes, you can spot them a mile away; you can take my word for it and you can also take my word that Boris had been passed over for promotion in the KGB."

Graham did not like the way Cogan looked down his nose at him as he made that last remark. He could see that this last remark and his look had also amused his colleague. You'd better not cough again he thought as he looked at John who, sensing trouble, immediately averted his eyes from Graham's gaze.

Turning back to Cogan he said, "Okay, now tell us a bit about this package, and how you got it, also what was in it, if you can remember that far back? You know the excitement of these things must be great. When I think of all the exciting places that people like you serve in and all the exciting jobs you people in the Foreign Office get up to, well, I must say I often wish I had gone in for that instead of the routine Home Office rubbish we get involved with all the time. An all out strike by a union is the most exciting thing we can look forward to, if we are lucky that is. So if you can just give us a run-down of what happened we will be on our way."

"Well this man Boris was one of the Russian Security people, the ones who watched us, that is. I'd got to know him pretty well; I used to go to this small bar cum cafe where I'd first met Boris some months earlier. It was one of the times when he'd had a little too much vodka, the one glass extra that changed him completely. Mind, I had eventually learned to recognise that point in the evening's drinking and I would depart before he reached that stage. Oh, I had reported to my bosses about my friendship with him, so everything was above board and okay, as okay as could be expected in the circumstances, I suppose. Anyway, one night when I was having a beer in this bar which was, as I said, just down the road from the Embassy, well this friend Boris, I suppose I could call him a friend in the most casual way, well, he turned up and came and sat at my table.

"We chatted about how cold the winter had been and I remarked to him that I for one was glad that the winter was nearly over. At least it was starting to feel a little warmer each day now. Mind, I was not looking forward to the return of the mosquitoes, but I preferred them to the cold. Boris being Boris he made the remark that I was like all the Embassy staff, soft as the underbelly of a fat pig. Well, I said to him, you are probably right when you say we are soft, but calling me a pig is a little bit off. Then I got a little bit rattled and told him I was never born to a Russian winter or anything else Russian. Believe me, I told him that I was very glad that I worked in a clean heated office during the day. Moreover, that I had enough warm clothes to wear when I went out at night for a drink, which was more than I could say for most Russians. Mind you it was only a couple of drinks – I never had more. Well, I was starting to get really indignant with him and I was about to tell him some home truths about good old Mother Russia when he interrupted me. It was at this point he began to tell me a tale about some Royal Marine. He just said to me out of the blue, 'You're not as tough as one of your Royal Marines I once met here in Russia'."

To which I replied, "The Royal Marines are a pretty tough lot, they are trained to be rough and tough. They are not the same as a common desk clerk like me. You must know I am only trained to push a pen and file papers. What is more, I am damned good at my job."

Graham fought hard to keep the grin from his face as he heard the remark, 'rough and tough'. God, that's why he had retired to this area. Talk about 'hello sailor', it's more like 'hello bootneck'.

Then he heard Cogan saying, "Yes, Comrade, I bet you are pretty damned good at your job Boris had taunted me; and I was pretty damned peeved with him when he said that. So I left the bar, saying aloud for all in the place to hear, 'Good God you cannot have a drink in peace, without they are pestering you', and I then walked back to the Embassy."

"Yes, quite right, Mr Cogan," Graham said, still having difficulty keeping the grin from his face as Cogan continued.

"The next time I saw my friend Boris after that he was a little worse for drink. They do have this terrible problem with their drinking in Russia, you know."

"Yes, I have heard they can knock it back a bit and that they have some dangerous drinking dens all over the back streets in their major cities. Still, with the life they have to face what else can you expect? I think we would have the same problem over here, that is if all we had to look forward to was the same as those poor creatures then I think we would have drinking dens all over the place. I'm not so sure that we don't, anyway."

Mr Cogan just ignored what Graham had said and went on. "I had, of course told the security officer at the Embassy about our last conversation and Boris mentioning the Royal Marines. It was his opinion that Boris was probably bragging or just the drink talking. After he had given it some thought he told me that the next time I saw Boris, I was to try and find out just whom this Royal Marine he was talking about was. He said that he did not think it could be one of the Embassy guards, but if it was, then it could spell trouble for all of us."

Graham was a little puzzled as he tried to work out why it was okay for one of the Embassy clerical staff to have a KGB man as a friend, but not so for an Embassy guard to do the same. Still, he said nothing because Cogan was again in full flow.

"So, I entered the same bar cum cafe at about eight o'clock a couple of nights later and ordered vodka. For the first time in my diplomatic career I was on a mission for the Intelligence Officer and I felt somewhat elated. So, having ordered my drink and acting as I thought the good spy would, I moved over to a table by the window."

Graham glanced over towards John, who was having great difficulty keeping his face straight at some of Cogan's remarks.

Cogan continued, "Well, I just sat and waited to see if Boris would come in. It was not my intention to be seen in the rear of the bar with any Russian, not even Boris after that night. I'd made my mind up that if I were going to meet with him from now on it would have to be in a light and open place, where everybody would be able to see us. I'd no intention of ruining my career just for a little chat with my local KGB man; and while I'm on the subject, I didn't trust our Intelligence Officer either."

Graham thought that it was an odd remark to make, that he didn't trust his own Intelligence Officer, but again he said nothing. He had decided that he would keep all these questions for a later date when he would have Cogan in his office.

By now Cogan's rambling was in top gear and Graham thought he'd be unable to shut him up if he had wanted to as the man continued, "Boris came in and made straight for my table, it was about ten minutes after I had arrived in the bar. He made a big show of telling everybody I was his friend from the Embassy. 'This is the capitalist pig that Comrade Brezhnev had told him to watch.' What bull I thought, they are no different from our own drunken servicemen either back home, or when visiting any of the countries that I have ever served in. You should see some of them in Exeter or Exmouth on a Saturday night.

"Anyway, after this characteristic outburst, Boris settled down for a chat, asking me if I found it warmer yet. Then he again made a big show of telling everybody in the place that I was a soft capitalist pig. One who could not stand the wonderful Russian weather. This remark, of course, caused laughter all round, but I had a distinct feeling that a lot, if not all, of the laughter was forced. Forced purely because of his presence in the place, it was my considered opinion that the laughter had left most of the people of Russia some years ago. It was at this point while looking at him that I realised Boris wasn't drunk. Yes, he had consumed some drink, because his breath had a smell of drink on it, but he was not drunk. He wasn't drunk with drink or any other substance, alcohol, drugs or anything else for that matter as far as I could see. No, I came to the opinion that he was as sober as a judge as they say. Looking at him, it crossed my mind that I would have to be careful and take the utmost care in my dealings with Boris that night. To say I could be in trouble if I were not careful was an understatement. Over the years I have come to learn that sober Russians who act drunk are very dangerous animals indeed."

Graham and John exchanged glances, but ignoring them both Cogan went on with his tale.

"Boris then proceeded to tell anybody and everybody who would or would not listen just what fools he thought all we Westerners were. I think all the people in the bar thought he was trying to provoke me into a fight. The tension in the place was electric. Every once in a while, in his well-acted drunken outpourings, he would look me straight in the eye. There would be a slight, ever so slight shake of the head, and a look in his eye that seemed to tell me not to take any notice of him. I must admit it was bloody hard even for a pen pusher like me, not to get up and punch the Russian fool on the nose."

Graham thought, I doubt you would have ever come home to tell us this story if you had, my friend, but again said nothing. He waited for the man to continue and Cogan needed no urging.

"After about a half hour of this, I eventually said to Boris, I've had enough of your insults for one day and I'm going back to the Embassy. I'm going to have a drink with some good old Capitalists. Western Capitalists! Who, if nothing else, have some good manners. With that I made for the door, a double entrance affair, like an air lock. You know the kind, open one set of doors before you open the others, thus keeping the warmth in the bar and the cold out. Well, he came storming after me, shouting that I was doing the same as the British had always done ever since the war, run away from everything. I must admit he did frighten me as he came for me in that confined part of the door. He was a lot bigger than me and he got right up close until I could hardly breathe as he pushed and shoved me towards the outer door. While he did so, he pushed something under the chest front of my coat. He then grinned and winked at me, saying in a hushed voice, 'Some evening reading for you, Comrade.' The next moment, he backed off shouting abuse about everything Western and staggered back into the bar.

"My mind was in a turmoil; I did not know what to make of him at all. He'd been drunk before, but he had never been sober and acting drunk before. He had never acted this way at all. At first, I just stood there, trembling with fright. Then I thought, if this is what the intelligence boys get up to, I am glad I am just a simple pen pusher. My heart could not stand much of this kind of going-on."

"Good Lord, what a life you have led. Please do go on; what happened next?" Graham asked, winking at John as he did so.

Cogan gave Graham a strange look, but he continued, "I did not know what to do, for the life of me I dare not have a look at what he had given me. It could have been a bomb for all I knew. At last I started to pull myself together after seeing all the people in the bar staring at me through the glass door. I pushed my way out of the outer door and into the street. Once outside, I realised I was in a cold sweat and I stood in the street trembling and wondering what to do when I heard footsteps behind me. Well! I thought, I'm going to die, but somehow I managed to force myself to turn around just as the footsteps behind me stopped. Standing there looking at me was another of their damned security men. He was just standing looking at me. So I told him to bugger off! I've had a belly full of you KGB men for one bloody night.

"You know, I never ever swear or use bad language, and here they had got me swearing on my first night as a spy. Because of that, I vowed there and then that I would never get myself mixed up with these intelligence officers again. Believe me I never did, I promised myself and I haven't, until you came here."

"Well, we're not, as I've already said, from the intelligence service, my colleague here and I, we are just like you were, as they say, 'gofers' and 'doers'. You know, 'go for this, go for that, do this and do that.' That is about all of us are good for, just errand boys and simple pen pushers, but please do carry on with your story. I think you are just getting to the good bit."

Cogan said nothing, but he had a petulant look on his face. So Graham said, "Now, where did you get to? Yes, you were telling us about the KGB man outside the bar. So there were two KGB men there watching you. They must have thought a lot of you, to have two men follow you."

"That's as maybe," Cogan now resumed his story, much to Graham's relief. "This other KGB man told me not to worry, 'Boris gets like that quite a lot you know. He means you no harm. He once served in Washington, you know, but it got too much for him. All the lovely young women and, of course, there were also all those beautiful young men. Now he thinks looking after you junior Embassy people here in Moscow, well it's a come down for him. So he drinks a little too much now and again, who can blame him; after all, he has been to Washington. You see, drinking helps him through his bouts of depression, thinking about all those good times he had in Washington and all those lovely women there, and the boys. Have you ever been to Washington, comrade?'

"So I told him. No! I haven't been to Washington, and it is nothing to do with you where I have been, when I wasn't in this wonderful country of yours! Oh, I told him, to which he just said, 'Well, I shall walk you back to the Embassy, so you need not worry any more'.

"That was it, that's how I got back to the Embassy that night. What the man meant when he was asking me about Washington I shall never know."

Graham thought no and pigs might one day fly, my fine floppy friend, but he didn't interrupt him.

"When I arrived back at the Embassy," said Cogan, continuing his tale of woe, "much to my surprise I hadn't exploded, and I thought okay, so it can't be a bomb that fool has stuffed inside my coat. Next I made my way to my quarters and gingerly I removed the item from under my coat front. It was a package, which was wrapped in rough brown packing paper and I put it on the table in my room and poured myself a drink. Then I sat and looked at the package for at least half an hour; I can't explain why, but I did. At last I thought in for a shilling, in for a pound and I opened it. Much to my relief all it contained were bundles of paper.

"There is no point asking me because I cannot say what was going through my mind as I started to open the first of the bundles. I have to admit that at first I thought perhaps I had been handed the most secret details of the KGB. After all these years just doing the mundane tasks of the Embassies, here at last I had something. Something big and now I would be famous, people would nudge each other at gatherings and say, he's the one who cracked one of the KGB's biggest spy rings. So, once I was famous it would be an automatic transfer to MI6 or some other exotic branch of the Government."

Graham thought, Oh! My God, why is it that I always get these bloody fairies to deal with? I wish to hell he would come to the point.

"Well, I had not! That is to say I had not been handed the most secret details of the KGB. It soon dawned on me that the most secret details of the KGB would not have been likely to be written on scraps of old thick, poor quality paper. The paper was so ancient that it still had small bits of wood in it for a start. Well, I settled down to

All For A King's Shilling

read the scribbling, because that is what it was, just scribbling. Before I had read the third page I knew that at best I had been handed the crazy scribbling of a madman. At worst, some of the disinformation which the KGB was putting out from time to time. I thought it was just possible the written work was from a British prisoner of the KGB. Oh, it was after all written in English, albeit poor English, but the kind of English that no foreign power can master; it was of the style of English only poor English schooling can produce. So I poured myself another drink and sat down to read the first bundle. I was still trying to make sense of it all when it started to get light. My first thoughts were, God, I have been reading this junk, and junk it was, all night.

"My second thoughts were I would look a right fool if my assumptions were right and the whole thing was a hoax. It was probably just something to send us off on some wild goose chase; or even a crazy story concocted by some fool in the deepest bowels of the KGB with a double daily ration of vodka in him. The whole thing seemed too fantastic to be true anyway. As I read more of the stuff, I became more confused than ever. For the life of me I couldn't see how it was possible for our Armed Forces or other Armed Forces to carry out the actions this supposed prisoner had described in these bundles of paper. It was such a fantastic tale I would have thought it was impossible and, had anything gone wrong (as the tale suggested that it most certainly had!) then surely the Embassy staff in Moscow would have known about it. No, there was no way the scribbling could be true. I could not see the Russians letting us get away with this little lot. Not without rubbing our noses right in it by telling the whole world what we had tried to do.

"No, Sir, I wasn't going to tell anybody about this. It could affect my retirement. They would say I'd 'lost a screw or something'. I was also worried that perhaps my friendship with this KGB man 'Boris' might be looked upon in an unfavourable light, especially if I was to draw attention to myself. The last thing I needed at that moment was a scandal. I was too close to my pension to get involved in any of that sort of stuff. It was because of these facts that over the next two nights I just read and reread the bundle of papers and made my decision to forget the whole episode, just to get on with my life at the Embassy. You see I had, in other words, decided it was one of those childish stories which people with lots of time on their hands dream up. It is reported that they do have a load of people who are part crazy and locked in the bowels of the KGB headquarters; in America they call them film scriptwriters.

"Once I'd finished and made my decision, I just put the bundles of paper the story was scribbled on into the back of a drawer, and forgot all about them. To be honest, I just completely forgot all about them. More to the point, I never left the Embassy compound again. Not until it was time for me to leave the place for my journey home. The next time I laid eyes on the papers was when I was packing to come home some two years later. Even then I debated if I should 'shred the lot', or bring them home with me."

Hell! Graham thought! The daft sod has got rid of them.

"Then I decided on the latter, and so it is I still have them."

At that moment, Graham could have given him a kiss, then on second thoughts, maybe not.

William Atlay

"Would you like to see them? It will only take a second for me to get them for you?" Without waiting for an answer he left the room and they could hear him rummaging around in another room at the back of the cottage.

Graham said nothing; he just exchanged glances with John and waited in silence for Cogan to return. This he did holding a rather large brown paper parcel in his hands. "When I heard of my friend's defection I remembered these, but I didn't even think they would be needed. Still, as I have said, I do not think they are of any importance or I would have called you and told you all about them. In the end I would have told you what Boris had done, you know. The last thing on my mind was that he was an MI6 agent, or CIA, or whatever they call themselves these days. I do know that you people cause a lot of trouble and suspicion abroad. It makes the work of proper civil servants in Embassies around the world so much harder and so difficult for them to do their jobs properly. What is more, I still think that this whole story is a load of rubbish!"

When he had finished both Graham and his colleague exchanged glances and just shrugged their shoulders and they both looked at him, standing there with the package clutched tight against his chest. Not the action one would expect from an innocent man, holding the package so close and tight to his chest. Graham was getting a feeling about this retired Civil Servant and had already decided that once this episode with 'Boris' was concluded he would just take a long-in depth look at Mr Cogan. After all the years he had been in the service, and he talks and acts like a naive new boy. He must have known it was wrong to hold on to this lot and not inform his superiors and how the hell did he know Boris had defected to the UK? There was more to this one than he had thought.

Graham then asked him, "Could you give me the package, sir?" He thought, you say no, my friend, and I will not be responsible for my actions. What is more, I will turn the house upside down, and enjoy doing it.

With that Mr Cogan just leaned forward and handed the package to Graham, who then asked him, "Do you mind if I just take a quick look to see what it contains; perhaps we could have a cup of tea while I do so?"

As he said tea, Graham thought I bet he gives us the usual crap about green, Indian or some other stuff they are always going on about. Before Cogan could say anything, Graham told him any old tea bag would do. "Milk and no sugar for me, please," he added as an after thought.

With that Cogan turned and went into what Graham assumed was the kitchen. As he did, Graham asked him, "Is your wife out, or is she hiding in the back somewhere?"

Both his colleague and he were taken aback with the venom in Cogan's voice as he growled from the kitchen, "I have never been married, sir," adding that remark a little too quickly and also a little unnecessarily to Graham's mind. "I am not bent, if that's what you think." To Graham's mind he added it just a little too quickly. "I never got round to getting married, always being abroad and not meeting the right gal."

With that exchange over, Graham then settled down and spent the next half hour or so reading through the first few pages of paper in one of the bundles and then just glanced at others. He was inclined to agree with Cogan about the standard of the writing. It really was very bad quality. The writing was very patchy and faded and the writer had used an old-fashioned ink pen on some of the pages. On others he had used a pencil and as he had progressed and the pencil had grown blunter, the writing became very heavy. The English was so bad in places that Graham had to read each passage he looked at twice or more before it eventually made any sense. As he read and drank his cup of tea, concentrating on the faded pages of paper, he came to the conclusion that if the papers had been written by an Englishman as Boris claimed, then the Englishman was illiterate. As a Royal Marine NCO that couldn't be possible because of their high standard of education; or the poor sod had been through and was still suffering from at the time of writing one of the most horrific ordeals it was humanly possible to survive.

While he was reading the papers his colleague spent the time asking Mr Cogan about his time in the Foreign Office; Embassies he had served in over the years and the posts that he had held in those Embassies; where he'd been and when he'd been there, just general things like that about his career, and taking notes all the while.

After a half hour, Graham told Mr Cogan, "These are going to take some time to read and digest; I can now see why you took all night, could I take them with me? My colleague will give you a receipt for everything. Mind, I cannot say if you will ever get any of it back again."

Cogan agreed to all this and said, "Really, I am glad to be shot of it all at last. It is all a load of disinformation you know; you will see I am right when you have read it all," were his last words as they left him on his doorstep.

As they drove away, Graham's colleague asked, "What do you make of that? He is a very bitter man, Graham; it looks as if he has been passed over for every plum post he applied for, and I think he is very bitter."

"Tell me, John, what made him think it was his friend Boris who had defected? We haven't published anything yet, have we? That fool of a department head of ours hasn't made a press release, has he?"

"No, Graham, he hasn't published anything at all."

"Mind you, if you ever dare to cough again when I am lying my bollocks off to a person I am questioning, I will implicate you, up to your bloody neck, in whatever it is I'm looking into at the time. Now pull over and let me get in the back of the car, then shut up and drive, while I read some of this disinformation he has given us. Let us see just how misinformed the man has been."

Some time later as the car was humming along the M4 on its way back to London, Graham was now a little wiser, but not much, as he sat back and thought about the things he had just read. Looking out at the lights of Swindon as the car sped on its way he realised that he had arrived at a conclusion. That was, that the bundles of papers resting on his lap were going to take a lot longer to read and digest than he had at first thought. Having skirted through the notes, which he found very difficult to read, mainly because of the type of paper that the man had used, but also due to his use of one of those indelible pencils that were all the rage a few years ago, even so, he now had an inkling that a couple of officers in Military Intelligence had, some two years or so earlier, met their deaths in or around London. He now had names and facts to go on and whether these were correct or not they would all have to be checked out to get at the truth.

Simply because of the nature of undercover work a lot of cover-ups would have to be uncovered. That would cause a lot of resentment in some quarters but it would have to be done and he would in the end get there. He had a feeling that he didn't like at all, but that would not detract him from his task. It looked as though he would have to cause a lot of embarrassment around the corridors of Government to get to the bottom of it all. It could be that he had some of the details about one of the biggest espionage stings of all time. God alone knew how many illegal agents the Russians had managed to infiltrate into the country and beyond, because he was sure the Russians wouldn't waste an opportunity like this and all with the help of our own armed forces.

Later that evening he entered his office and told his staff he was not to be interrupted on any account. Not until he had read and digested the papers, anyway. The bundled papers which they had watched him unfold and lay in a neat pile on his desk. Next, he made himself a mug of strong black coffee, turned on the desk light and then turned off the main light in his office. He then took a sip from his first mug of the many mugs of coffee that he would consume that night. He settled down to read the scraps of paper; the scraps of paper which he had been given earlier that day, this time taking notes as he read. Graham started by rereading the pages he had already read. He needed to think through and digest all he had read so far, now he needed further time to read and digest the rest of the scraps of paper.

Chapter Two
Start of Written Story at Sharon's Insistence
Pentland Firth, Scotland 1957

Join the Navy and see the World
Join the Marines and scrub your way round it.

There is a young lady in this village called Sharon who has been an angel of mercy to me. Of all the people I've met she is the one who has restored my sanity. It is she who has helped me overcome the worst horrors of these past years. To help me further to overcome the rest of this small problem, it was she who suggested that I should write it all down. "Get it out of your system, empty your mind of it all, get it down on paper, then you can tear it up and forget it forever." I asked her just how I could do that, write it all down that is, considering that I hadn't the means so to do, and that in the part of the world that we were in there was no chance of getting any paper, pens or even pencils. At that, without a word, she just turned around, left me and went into her room in the cabin type of house that we shared.

A few minutes later she returned with some really rough looking and poor quality paper of varying sizes and shapes. She also had one of those indelible pencils, the type that shopkeepers in the good old days of the bad old times that were England in the thirties, used all the time. They would lick the end every so often as they added up the bill before putting the final figure on the slate, with very little or even no hope of ever collecting the money; and no chance of ever being able to rub out whatever it was they had written down. It was of course sensible economics on their part. If the people couldn't afford the groceries they were selling, then they would in the end have to throw most of their stock away when it had gone rotten. By running a slate there was always the chance that some might pay up, if not all they owed, then some. So it wasn't all a total loss to them.

When Sharon gave me the paper I just looked at her and she stood there, with her hands on her hips, one foot slightly forward of the other and tapping it on the floor with the impatience of some frustrated schoolmistress, which by the way she had been in the last village in which she had lived. A schoolmistress, that is, but I wouldn't know if she'd been frustrated at the time. Then with both hands on her hips she adopted that stance, feet slightly apart and hips thrust slightly, but distinctly forward, which I know she knew accentuated her sexuality. While we eyed one another up I had the first stirrings of sexual emotion that I'd had since I was in Katrine's house all those years before. Then she broke the spell and in an irritated voice insisted that I just start at the beginning.

I wasn't quite so sure about what beginning she meant so, to stop me making a fool of myself and standing up and approaching her with my first sexual stirrings, I decided to get on with the writing, which was of course the furthest thing from my mind at that precise moment in time. With a little embarrassment I picked up the pencil and placed a sheet of paper on the table in front of me. Looking at the blank piece of paper I couldn't help myself, I just grinned at it and then just sat staring at a point in the centre of it. I know that she knew exactly the effect she was having on me, and after watching me squirm for a little while longer, she turned and with a smile on her face she finally left the house.

For the first time since I'd arrived, I finally knew just how much of a woman she was, she really fulfilled the expression I'd often heard others say of women, "She's all woman, that one!"

Unfortunately, taking her advice to start 'at the beginning' was something that I could not do. Not just yet, anyway; I was not ready to talk about my life prior to the Marines. I thought I should start this part of my troubles in the week that I qualified for the rank of Sergeant in the Royal Marines, but then again I thought I should start with the reason why I joined the Royal Marines in the first place.

So here we go. Looking back at the events I now feel like the proverbial Marine who has been shit on from a great height; not by his mates, but by some people who were supposed to be his superiors. These very people, who by the traditions of the service are supposed to look out for the best interests and welfare of their men. Then again these superiors, supposedly Royal Marines or Royal Navy, but who really come from units that are not part of this great Corps that I joined so I could evade a trip to gaol for evading National Service in the Army.

When I joined the Service I was just a young green lad and I took the King's shilling in a dingy back room of the recruiting office in a building situated in Westmoreland Road, Newcastle-upon-Tyne. It was the autumn of 1949. I do not think that I knew too much or understood too much about what was happening to me, or what I was letting myself in for at the time.

There were eight of us all standing in a row in that room with our right hands stuck up in the air in a half Nazi salute. We were facing a man who was dressed in what looked like an out of work SS officer's uniform. He was reciting some gibberish from a card he held, about King and Country, his Heirs and Successors and people that he placed over me, so help me God; and what a sorry looking lot we were, as we repeated verbatim after him every word he uttered. Although why I needed 'God's help' I wasn't at the time sure. But I was soon to find out that I needed not only 'Gods help', but I was going to need anybody else's help I could get before I was finished.

What was going through the other lads' minds I have no idea, but all I wanted at the time was for the man to get on with it and get it over. I had been dodging conscription for a while now and I knew that the Newcastle Police had a warrant out for my arrest. So, the sooner I was enlisted the better. I half expected the Police to barge in, as is their wont, and arrest me at any minute during the ceremony.

No person in that room was more pleased than me when the officer said. "You are now all members of His Majesty's Royal Marines." For the first time that day and the only time I smiled. This man who looked to be wearing an ex SS man's uniform then said to all and sundry, "You will now be sent by train to the Royal Marines Depot, which is situated in Deal, Kent. The Sergeant Major will give you each a ten shilling advance of pay for the journey, but don't spend it all as you will need most of it to buy boot polish, blanco and soap."

Buy things like soap and polish. I had been led to believe that when I joined the Forces it was 'all found,' and here was this man telling me that out of my three shillings a day I was going to have to buy my own polish, soap and this Blanco stuff. I wondered at the time what other ideas they had for my three shillings a day. Little did I know that we were expected to buy our own uniforms out of our own pocket!

The Police never did turn up at the recruiting office and as the time drew near for us to leave I began to think that I might have been a little hasty in what I'd done. I was about to have a chat with one of the sergeants there and ask if I gave them the ten bob back would we be able to forget it all and maybe I could just slip away out of the back door. Before I could say anything this sorry looking specimen of an SS man returned and he told us, in no uncertain terms, "Right lads! You are now under military orders, and I am giving you all a direct order to report to Royal Marine Depot at North Barracks Deal by sixteen hours tomorrow." I wondered what would happen if the trains were late but before I could ask he went on, "Anybody who fails to arrive will be classed as a deserter and!" here he paused and slowly looked each and every one of us in the eyes and finally said, "as the British forces are on active service in various parts of the world that means anybody who fails to arrive could on conviction of desertion be shot!"

There was absolute bloody silence in that room as slowly we looked at each other with that dumbstruck look, the look that only comes when you realise you are really in the shit, way up over your head, and I mean shit, the real brown stuff.

Bloody hell! I thought while I looked at the others; if you get caught dodging conscription you get four years in your local nick! Go missing with this lot on your first day and when they catch you, the bastards are just likely to shoot you! I just knew from that day on I'd have been better off doing the four years in Durham Nick! Hell's bloody bells, I thought, just what have you let yourself in for? I decided that asking the sergeant that if I gave them the ten bob back I could withdraw my application and go home was not the best thing to do in the circumstances. Mind you, none of the others was saying much; they too looked to be in the same permanent state of shock that I was in.

Some time later we were all seated on bench-type seats in the back of a well-used military truck and driven to Newcastle Central Station, there to catch a train to London's Kings Cross Station. From there we were to go to Charing Cross Station and then onwards to Deal in Kent. At least I hoped that the Deal in Kent was the right one. There could only be one Deal where they shot young recruits who'd got lost.

The train on which we had been put left Newcastle at about three thirty in the afternoon on its way to London. Eight of us sat in the same compartment and I must say we had arrived in York before anybody said a word to anybody else. It was about 9.00 a.m. the next day when we left London and started the long slow crawl to Deal on a train that seemed to be intent on stopping at every station in that county. We were all still hanging on to our ten bobs, having only had a cup of railway tea since leaving Newcastle Central Station.

When the train finally arrived at what turned out to be Deal Station there were some men in blue uniforms walking, well I was soon to learn that they called the kind of walking they were doing, 'marching'. Anyway they were scurrying along the platform shouting, "All Royal Marines, out of the train now!" It took a minute or so to realise that the Royal Marines bit was meant for us.

So it was I arrived at Royal Marines, Deal. We were all ushered along the platform, as countless hundreds must have been before us, being shouted at and bustled towards a man in a blue uniform wearing a bright red sash over his shoulder and with a stick under his arm, which I was soon to learn was called 'a pacestick'. I was surprised to see that the man was human; he checked our names off. From his demeanour I assumed that the ones rushing about the platform swinging their arms like windmills must be a lot more important than the man checking our names. Ha! Ha! How stupid can one be, for Heaven's sake?

I was to learn later that all this shouting by the windmill gang was the first part of the disorientation required to brainwash us into dying for King and Country; and only a 'God' carried a pacestick. Well I had news for them, the dying bit wasn't in my contract, mind, they have frightened me a few times since then though. Anyway this man ticked our names off a list he had on what I was to learn was called 'a clipboard'. "Why is it called a clipboard?" I once asked. "Because it has a clip on the top you bloody moron!" I was promptly told. Ask a stupid question?

We, the new arrivals that is, were ushered out of the station into a rickety old blue bus. You could actually see where they had painted over the top of Navy with a darker blue and then painted Marine over the top of that; the 'Mari' being on the newer darker blue paint and the 'ne' of Marine on the older blue. That was when I realised that I had joined a Corps that was the poor relation of the Navy, and like all poor relations, it got the 'hand me downs' and never the new equipment. What is it they say, 'always the bridesmaid, never the bride'?

Once we were all aboard the bus it took us through some terraced streets and then into The North Barracks of Royal Marines, Deal. What happened next? Well, I can't remember too much about that, but I do know that I never stopped running around until nine that night, by which time I and the rest had been issued with most of the kit we would be getting. Nine o'clock was the time I and the other seventy-seven new raw recruits with me were in our beds. At nine thirty exactly some swine turned the bloody lights out at which some of us shouted, only to be told in no uncertain terms from the darkness at the end of the room to "Shut-up!" Something which we promptly did!

Next morning we were to meet the toy soldier with the red sash whom we had seen at the station, the one we thought wasn't too bad, again! During the night he had gone through some sort of metamorphosis and turned into a screaming maniac. At precisely 6.00 a.m. while we were all asleep and everything outside was black dark, the lights in the room suddenly came on again and there was this apparition standing at the end of the room. We all looked at him and just as we were about to grumble about what he thought he was doing, the remarks we were about to make died on our lips as he started shouting and screaming at us, in the loudest voice I have ever heard in my life. He was shouting things like 'Rise and shine' and 'Hands off cocks and on socks'. Another favourite of his, we were to learn, was 'Out of bed this instant you horrible stinking slime'. Looking at him as his screaming grew louder while he approached me, tipping beds over as he came, I realised that two days earlier I'd made the biggest mistake of my life! I knew in an instant that I would have been better off in Durham Nick serving the four years for dodging National Service. Along with some others, I was asked by men who had joined three weeks earlier if we had met the screaming scull yet. Before we could answer another one said, "Of course they have, can't you see they are still shell shocked?"

We were to spend thirteen weeks in Deal, 'tick-tocking' around the barracks from 8.30 a.m. until 4.30 p.m.. There were inspections at 8.30 and again at 2.00 p.m., with equipment not considered clean enough being cast in all directions around the parade ground (God's Little Acre) accompanied by hours of verbal abuse. Of course it never was clean enough and once they remembered your name, your life became one constant stream of abuse. There was one lad in our squad who had come down from Newcastle with us. He was from the dark depths of the back streets of that illustrious city. He spoke a language that no person in Deal had ever heard before. When asked a question he would adopt the broadest accent of the backstreets of that fair city that he could and answer. It was the only time in the whole of my time in the service I've seen Officers and SNCOs walking around not knowing if they had been insulted or not.

After the parade was dismissed each day there was a break for tea. Then after tea it was 'stand by your beds, clean this, and wash that, polish this and scrub that, spit on your boots, but don't you dare spit on the parade ground. Polish the floor, clean your locker, polish your greatcoat buttons', then things like 'wash your clothes again, you haven't washed them properly'. Then, every night it was into bed by 9.00 and lights out at 9.30 p.m. on the button. By week three we had all been fitted out with our walking out dress, uniform number one. It was around this time we got a lecture on our kit, we were told that now we had our full kit we would be well-advised to look after it very carefully indeed because from now on we would have to buy any replacements we would need. When one of the lads said that he had been told by his pal in the army that uniforms were replaced when worn out, we were all told, "No, in the Royal Marines we now buy our uniforms." When I asked if that was why we used 'second-hand transport', I found myself on three days Confined to Barracks for insubordination.

Now we had our full kit they duly gave us 'shore leave'. That was when I learnt that Marines don't 'go out'! No, Marines always 'Go ashore'! Even if they are already 'ashore living in barracks', when they step out of the barrack gate, they 'Go Ashore'!

I had teamed up with a couple of the lads who had travelled from Newcastle with me and one lad who came from the Midlands. We duly left the Barracks at 6.00 p.m. and by 8.30 two of us were being escorted back to Barracks having the shit kicked out of us in the back of a small truck by members of the shore patrol. We were of course under close arrest, but even then I thought two overweight old soldiers sitting on me in the back of a truck surely wasn't really classed as close arrest, but you live and learn, as they say. To cut a long story short my pal from the Midlands and I were given fourteen days confined to barracks and the other two, one of whom had started the fight in the first place, had got off Scot free; here endeth the lesson. In my first three weeks I had amassed a total of twenty days CB.

"Off to a good start, aren't we?" remarked the CO as he lashed me up to the fourteen days.

That little episode changed my whole stay while at Deal and in the Corps. Firstly, I never attempted to go ashore again while I was there and I was determined that I would never do CB again as long as I was in the Corps. Instead I became a moneylender. I did quite well at it, thank you very much! Oh, had I ever been caught that would have been big trouble, but I was lucky that way. I had to black a couple of eyes and kick the shit out of a trained soldier once, but after that they all paid up on the dot, in full. I could say that when I left Deal all debts except one had been settled. The exception was a corporal who left on draft thinking he was clever, but a few years later we met in a bar in Malta and after a little altercation everything was sorted, including interest.

Even though it was against Military law to lend money I figured I was owed something for the fourteen days Confined to Barracks I'd got for what I believed was helping someone who was being beaten up by some civilians, all I was doing was trying to prevent the fight getting worse. That was why I had two civilians in neck-holds, I told the CO. Anyway, if they hadn't squirmed so much they would not have nearly been strangled now, would they? But he saw it in a different light. At the time I didn't think the CO at Deal had any esprit de corps, as they say.

By week seven we were all 'tick-tocking,' around the barracks like zombies. Then at week eleven we all came to life once more as we realised that we would be out of the place in a couple of weeks. Also, the fact that we were, believe it or not, starting to feel fitter in ourselves had put us in a better frame of mind.

So it was, as we were to learn, all good things come to and end and we departed from Deal and arrived in RMB Eastney, Portsmouth, having made the jump from the frying pan into the fire. We got off the train in the dockyard station from where we travelled by truck and bus to a street about a quarter of a mile from the Royal Marine Barracks. There we formed up into three ranks and marched into the Barracks. We marched up the road at the rear of the drill shed, between the drill shed and the Signals School, passed the galley and then we wheeled right, and right again into the drill shed. Then when the drill instructor shouted the order for us to halt! we halted in a fashion that would have made any serviceman proud. Our feet came to the halt as if they were fastened together as one. Then it happened, the drill shed floor was so highly burnished with a century and a half of marines' hobnailed boots crashing to a halt on it that we took off like a bunch of skaters who had lost control on the ice. This performance had been laid on they said afterwards to test our standard of drill. I have always believed that it was laid on to humiliate us. We discovered over the next eight weeks that keeping one's feet when marching in that drill shed was an art. The problem was that the way they treated us that first day, with no warning that the surface was dangerous, meant that a couple of our members suffered back injuries that eventually caused them to be dismissed the service as medically unfit for the armed forces due to back injuries sustained whilst on duty.

My stay at RMB Eastney was the worst eight weeks of my training; I had believed that the first thirteen weeks spent at RM Deal had been the worst, but Portsmouth took the cake. Some of our squad liked it, which I found hard to understand, but I hated every day of it. We were there to learn the basics of naval gunnery, from 'sixteen inch calibre naval guns' down to 'four inch calibre' naval guns. As a gunner on a ship you were known in the Marines as a twenty-five mile sniper. Not only were we to do all the Naval Gunnery bit, but we were also to spend two weeks living on a cruiser tied to a buoy in Portsmouth Harbour, learning all about seamanship and how to sleep in a hammock. Talk about big ships, for me it was pure undiluted 'hardships', and I was delighted when we left Portsmouth and travelled to the Infantry Training Centre (ITCRM) at Lympstone, Devon, on the banks of the Exe River halfway between Exeter and Exmouth.

There we completed sixteen weeks of infantry training and the most sadistic bunch of instructors we'd ever met were the gunnery instructors who were sick, but this lot; well, this lot were what I'd always imagined the guards in German concentration camps must have been like. There was one slogan they incessantly shouted at us whenever the going was hard, which was daily, "Blood, sweat and tears save lives." None of us ever had the courage to ask just whose blood and whose tears were saving whose lives. We knew, of course, whose sweat and tears they were talking about – ours. The main thing about the training was that for most of the squad, which included me, this was the stuff we had joined to do. Ha! Ha! When I left Lympstone I just knew that I was a fountain of knowledge about infantry warfare. Just shows how green I was, about as green as the grass of Devon and grass doesn't get much greener than that.

Our next port of call was the RM Commando School in Northern Wales. I have never understood why it was called a school. Perhaps Borstal, detention centre, prison, hard labour camp, and even concentration camp, all of which seem more fitting names for the hell of that place. When I was at Lympstone I had thought that the instructors there were 'evil sadistic sods', but this bunch were nothing less than 'sadistic masochistic bastards'. The difference between the instructors at Lympstone and the ones in Wales was that the men in Wales not only took a delight in inflicting pain on us but also enjoyed watching us suffer to the point of near death. They did however do everything themselves that they insisted we did; but they never let us die though. Because death would have spoilt their fun, I don't think that they would have suffered any consequences if anybody had died, but their pride might have been hurt.

I still remember so vividly my first day at the Commando School; we did all sorts of physical things, like doubling everywhere. There was no walking or even marching in that place. We were taken on a short run around the assault course, then at a double to the galley for dinner. Next we had a lecture on the do's and don'ts of the camp. A visit to the sickbay for a medical inspection followed; I'm not so sure the man who stood at a door as we filed past him naked was even a doctor. Anyway, whoever he was, he pronounced us all fit to do the course. Then it was line up again and we had jabs in each arm. Once that was over we were ordered to dress and parade outside in two minutes. Now you may argue that a man cannot get fully dressed in all his clothes and full fighting order in two minutes, well I can vouch that when you are as frightened as we were well, yes you can; some may even have time to light a fag and have a quick drag as well.

More to the point of all this hustle and bustle, we hadn't even been shown where our barrack rooms were or where our kit was, apart from the stuff we were wearing. Then at 4.00 p.m. they took us out on a four-mile speed march, still wearing the full fighting order in which we had left Lympstone. March a hundred yards, then double a hundred yards; that is speed marching at its purest and from that day on speed marching became a way of life for me. Years later when I had nothing to do in the evenings I went bloody speed marching. If that's not being brainwashed I don't know what is. At 4.30 that first day as we were marched back into the camp and on to a group of barrack huts away from the rest of the camp, we were inspected and all given an extra parade for being dishevelled and dirty, then they dismissed us. Looking at one of my pals I said, "You can fuck this for a game of soldiers. I think I'll go big ships after all." There was one thing that the instructors in that place made certain I would do, and that was that I would pass that course first time, there was no power on this earth that would make me do that course twice. Failure was just not an option in my case. I always remember later when Brian London had been flattened by Rocky Marciano and was asked about a rematch, his words said it all, "You don't make mistakes like this twice!" That was how I felt about the commando course. I knew for certain that if I didn't pass it first time I was going 'walk about'.

So it was six weeks later that I and the thirty-two men remaining of the seventy-eight of us who had joined at RM Deal that lifetime ago were marched on to the parade to be presented with our green berets and we were now all Royal Marine Commandos. When we paraded to leave the place we all had a shot in the arm and our morale rocketed as we observed a sergeant by one of the huts. He was the animal who used to scream at us those first few weeks we were in Deal to get out of bed at 6.00 a.m.. Well, he was standing among a group who all looked like old men. They were complete in 'cap comforters', the badge of all trainees on commando courses. I asked our instructor, who by this time had taken on the mask of a human being and was somewhat approachable, with care that is, what the sergeant was doing there. "He's here to do the commando course. He has only ever served on big ships as a Marine since he joined, he spent the rest of his time at Deal, and now everybody in the Corps has to do the commando course, he's among the first batch." I was minded to ask our instructor to make the bastard suffer, but something in the way he was looking at his fellow sergeant told me I needn't bother.

We left the camp and found ourselves in RM Plymouth, where we were to spend two weeks on the parade ground relearning all the drill skills we'd lost since leaving Deal. At the end of the two weeks we paraded as The King's Squad in front of an army general and were passed for duty as fully trained Royal Marines. At the same time one of our original group was awarded the King's Badge as the best all-round recruit.

It seemed that it was with indecent haste after that that most of us found ourselves living in the bowels of a rusting hulk of a troopship called 'The Lancashire', which was to take us all to Singapore and overland from there to join one of the three

All For A King's Shilling

Commandos – Forty Commando, Four-two Commando and Four-five Commando – stationed in Malaya; the three units which made up 'Third Commando Brigade RM'. We shared the ship with a Regiment of what I think were Lancers. Anyway, they were nicknamed the Cherry Pickers, which was something to do with picking cherries in cherry orchards instead of charging the enemy during the Napoleonic Wars; it also had something to do with the colour of their hats.

It was some months later that we arrived in Singapore, having stopped for a couple of hours in Malta, Port Said, and Colombo. We disembarked in Singapore and immediately headed up into Malaya to join our units which had only arrived from Hong Kong a short time earlier. For the next two and a half years I did some things I didn't believe that I would ever do, and I saw some things that I hadn't ever dreamed I'd see. While I was there, an officer joined half way through my time in the unit. He became my troop commander and for some reason – I never knew why – he took a shine to me. It all started when a couple of us had a little too much to drink one afternoon when we had been detailed off for night guard. They locked us up and we got dressed in out best bib and tucker the next day to see the CO. Well, he gave my pal fourteen days CB and he dismissed the case against me. I should have known that there was a warning in there somewhere, but I was just relieved to come out of the CO's office with a clean sheet as I was a candidate for promotion and a charge of guilty would have had me struck off the candidates' list. I was just glad and I didn't see anything in it, "Arsehole that I was!"

It was after two and a half years of this Commando service that the people in 'head office' decided that I, along with the rest of the men who had joined with me, had done our penance and they sent us home, this time we travelled on the 'Empire Windrush'. When we arrived in Commando and Holding Company, situated in Royal Marine Barracks Plymouth and were all sent on seventy-two days leave with seventy-two days' pay.

So there was I, a young man with a dark brown suntan and a pocket full of white fivers and with a railway ticket to Durham and nowhere to stay. I had no civvies and I was in a blue uniform that had just spent two and a half years in the bottom of a kit bag in the Far East. It took me twenty hours to reach Durham, and why I picked Durham I shall never know, but I did. So, when I got off the train at 8.30 that morning it was first things first; I had to find myself a lodging house and then buy some cheap civvies. After about five weeks of this I had no money left and I'd lost my return ticket, so I went to the Police and told them that I'd lost it and they gave me a travel warrant to be charged against my pay account and I headed back to Plymouth.

There they put me in a transit room and I spent the rest of my leave in Barracks dodging authority and getting mates to smuggle me sandwiches out of the dining rooms that were situated in the base of each block. I used the time to swat up on the things I'd need to know for the Junior NCOs course I was to attend when my leave was over.

The day came when my leave was over; I duly turned up in the Commando and Holding Company Office, from where I was sent to join the JNCOs Cadre, which was situated at the other side of the parade ground; a little too near the officers' mess for my liking. When it ended, much to my and my instructor's surprise I had passed with a superior, and I was dispatched to 'Dodge City', Portsmouth to do my SBS course.

Now passing that course was I believe the start of my troubles. Oh, it was great for a few years and I really enjoyed it, but I was to fall into bad practices when I was pushing for promotion to the rank of sergeant. That I believe was when it all went wrong.

I suppose it all started back in the later half of the fifties when I inadvertently got myself diverted from being a good old-fashioned honest Royal Marine Corporal, in brackets, into a modern day newly fashioned fool. More commonly referred to as, "what a sucker!" Then again perhaps a more expletive expression like the one more commonly used in the form of a question, "You stupid bastard, why did you go and get mixed up with those twats?"

Enough of that, perhaps I should start with the training that I had, which turned me into this fully fledged fool.

Now take the word 'Training', boy that is a good word if ever I heard one. An NCO I knew in the old days told me that you can train anyone to do anything; just like a circus animal. At the time I thought he was a bloody fool, but as always seems to happen to me I have over the years had to change my mind, because he was so damned right! (Who's a pretty boy, then?)

Now it is my belief that the average citizen of an average European country is under the illusion that their servicemen train for every eventuality that may, or may not, confront their homeland; 'not a chance, mate!' At most, a serviceman will do a spell of basic training, learning how to march and to some people the most important bit; that of learning how to salute the officers.

As I've already said, other than being taught the basics of marching and not forgetting, of course, the most important bit of the whole soldiering game, that was how to salute officers correctly, a man is only trained in the very basics of warfare. Mainly his trainers want to make sure that when he sees an enemy, he can do at least two things, first that he can shoot at the enemy or at least in his general direction. It doesn't matter if he can't shoot too straight just so long as it is in the right direction. He will eventually succeed in doing something even if it is to frighten some of the enemy and he may even hit somebody, hopefully one of our enemies. Secondly, they hope that he won't run away for a few hours at least and that he stays long enough to frighten the enemy more than the enemy frightens him. My problem when in action has always been a dread that some bespectacled utterly useless soldier shooting at us and being such a bad shot while aiming at somebody else, might hit me by accident. Soldiers, the world over, are renowned for shooting somebody else and not the person they aimed at. Some even aim at the wrong targets on the ranges they train on. One only has to look at the newsreel pictures of some of the new enemy we have these days to see some fool pointing a gun around some corner and firing off thirty or more rounds in all directions. We all know that if he were to kill anybody it would be purely by accident and not design, but I digress again. It is a long time since I have watched any newsreels and I often wonder if I shall ever see a cinema screen again.

Any army about to engage in a battle, be it an army defending its homeland or the army doing the attacking, is a very volatile organisation. There comes a point just before any battle starts when no person, from the commander downwards, can tell, or know, just how the army of which he is a part will react.

All For A King's Shilling

The stress caused by fear of the unknown, the bravado of the canteen heroes leaving these stalwart, brave and trusted veterans of the beer bar, as the realisation of the sudden and sometimes not so sudden death that is possibly awaiting hits them. It is when the fog of the beer fumes starts to clear and the absolute fear of dying finally hits that life takes on a new meaning for them. Well, all these things will have an unforeseen effect upon them. The thought of the sights of mutilation that some of the men they call mates will suffer in a battle; it all has an effect on them and can, if not squashed by good leadership, cause trouble for them all.

I've seen over the years dozens of men practising taking out a packet of cigarettes, then opening the packet and taking a cigarette from it; then lighting the cigarette using a match from a box of matches. I have watched men practising all of these skills while only using one hand and sometimes standing on one leg – it has to be seen to be believed. You can see some men standing on one foot for a long time, then after a while seeing if they can walk with only one leg, holding the other good leg behind them, and it is always the bottom half of the left leg if they are right-handed and, of course, the right leg if they are left-handed. All of these things one will see, in what men believe are private moments in private places; but there are no private places in armies about to go to war. None of these men is going to get killed – wounded maybe, but killed, never! Oh, they may lose a limb, but none is going to die so they try to find out what it is going to be like with only one limb. Also it is never going to be their right arm if they are right-handed or their left arm if they are left-handed. I have even seen men reading with one eye shut. It is all human nature because if there was the slightest chance they would get killed they just wouldn't bloody be there now, would they? I mean, would you? They know some men will die, but it's not going to be them, if they are lucky they will only get a wound they can live with and satisfy their honour. By thinking this way they know they are going to make it, but even so all these things have an effect on their morale.

"Surviving your first battle is the way you become an old soldier," at least that was the information an old soldier kept telling me every time I bought him a pint in the canteen. He was of course right; he was an old man, of at least twenty-three years of age, so he had survived five years of battle or so I thought. He told me all this when I was about to go into battle for the first time as a young sprog Marine. I held the man in great respect those first few weeks in the unit. We talked at length just before we left for one of his many battles and my first encounter with a serious enemy. By serious enemy, I mean an enemy who, I was very soon to learn, was intent on inflicting on me the same bodily injuries that I had been ordered to inflict on him. Unfortunately for my morale I was to learn only too soon that it wasn't only my first battle, but my hero's first battle also, but unfortunately for him he didn't follow his own advice. He didn't make it! He froze with fear at precisely the wrong moment, but his advice to me was so good that in the end I didn't begrudge him the beer at all. I only hope he died easily.

Ever since then, though, I have realised that old soldiers are able to suss out an inexperienced Officer, NCO, or come to that a big mouthed useless Squaddie. Sometimes they follow, sometimes they help, but mostly the only help they give is the odd bit of sarcastic advice, spoken from within a group, which sometimes you would be a fool to ignore. Mostly, though, they just silently watch, as the Officers or their NCOs make complete arseholes of themselves. Perhaps I have always kidded myself that in the past they have helped me, but I never had any illusions about it, for I have always considered myself to be a right arsehole anyway. If I wasn't, I would not be in the situation I'm in right now, or have been through the hell I have suffered these last few years.

I remember some years before when I, along with six or seven hundred other men, had a Commanding Officer who had the most infuriating habit. Whenever he saw you, no matter who you were he would open the conversation with, "Gosh lads," then he would add some stupid remark like "Gosh, good here isn't it?"

It doesn't take too much of a stretch of the imagination to know he was soon known only as "Colonel Gosh"! There was an operation I was involved in when some men of another unit had been ambushed in the Whadi Matra, which was in the Radfan Mountains in the Aden Protectorate. My Company was on standby and we were waiting to take off in helicopters to go to their rescue. The problem was the RAF refused to fly as they hadn't had breakfast yet (allegedly). Nearly all the NCOs and Officers of the Company were standing with the Company Commander 'chewing the fat' as you do. A Corporal who was facing the Company Commander said, "Here comes Gosh, three Goshes and we'll be airborne." The Company Commander just grinned at the Corporal. Then because none of us facing him was grinning, he started to turn, but before he could a voice from behind him said, "Gosh, lads, are you still here; why haven't you left yet?" Before anybody could say anything the Corporal said, "The bloody hairy fairies haven't had their breakfasts yet, Gosh!"

You could see everybody in the group cringe and I do believe not one officer or NCO in the group knew what to do next. The Commanding Officer, with an astonished look on his face, just said, "Oh, haven't they? Well, we'll soon see about that," and he stormed off towards the place where the RAF had their control tent. Within minutes of him entering, the helicopter crews were running to their aircraft and the Corporal winked at the Company Commander and said, "What did I fucking tell you? But I was wrong, it only took two Goshes this time."

"Get your bloody men in that bloody helicopter, Corporal. I'll see to you later," was the only reply he got.

Enough of the good old times, I'm too far ahead of myself by far. I suppose you could say that my 'fight for survival' started years ago when, as a Corporal, I was stationed in the Royal Marine Barracks, Eastney, Portsmouth. It was a fight which I never in my wildest dreams would have expected to last for so long. Had I known the heartache and sorrow that it would bring me, I would have deserted there and then, but I hadn't a bloody clue what fate had in store for me. I'd just arrived back in RMB Eastney after qualifying for the rank of Sergeant at ITCRM and I was awaiting orders to return to my branch of the service. It had moved to a camp in Poole in Dorset, some couple of years earlier. So it was no surprise when within the hour I was on my way to Royal Marines Poole in a small Morris pickup, which in no stretch of the imagination could be called a truck. I was deposited at the main gate of the camp at about six o'clock that evening by the pickup driver, with my kit hanging around me like 'a bloody Christmas tree', or so the guard commander told me.

At first I had visions of being promoted the next day to the rank of Sergeant. As it was it took them many years before they saw fit to promote me to the rank of substantive Sergeant, and permanent membership of the Sergeants' Mess with all the privileges that entailed. I was for years puzzled why it took them so long to make such an obvious substantive promotion.

There is an expression in the services that really does annoy me and it is used by people who give orders or make decisions that they cannot logically explain and they use this expression. They give answers like, 'and here comes the lie', 'How can I say what the powers that be want?' Sometimes it's, 'Because the powers that be want it done that way.' It is all bloody lies and weakness covering up their own bloody inefficiencies as leaders of men. I was always given the stock answer, 'It's up to the powers that be' when I queried why my promotion hadn't come through. It is always, 'the powers that be'! Bullshit, it wasn't the powers that be, it was those bastards who had put the black ball on me because I was considered to be a 'Bolshie Commie kind of bastard'. It did take such a long time for them to come to their senses.

The thing is that my troubles started the next day after I arrived in RM Pool, and they started in earnest. It all kicked off after the morning parade was dismissed. I was standing outside the squadron office in my best snivelling dress and mode, when the Squadron Sergeant Major arrived. He looked me up and down and as he did so I thought you won't find anything wrong with my turnout mate! I'm sweeter than a 'shit-house seat on a frosty morning', but I didn't like the smile he gave me when he'd finished. I didn't like that look of his at all; it should have warned me, but I was flushed with the excitement that I would soon be off to change into my best blues to see the Commanding Officer. When he came back out of the office and told me to report to the Adjutant, well I just knew I'd be having lunch time drinks in the mess and the sergeant major and I would be on first names before the afternoon parade. 'Sergeants' Mess', here I bloody come!

My service life had been a load of bollocks for years and this day was no different. I was still the same old arsehole I'd been when I was dropped at the main gate the previous evening. Looking back I really should have deserted there and then. Instead of going to the Adjutant's office I should have just marched out of the main gate and kept going, but then I never did have any sense. Oh, I had lots of CDF, but no bloody sense whatsoever.

The Adjutant was one of those evil bastards whose parents couldn't do anything with him and sent him off to school at a very tender age. Whatever happened to him there I don't know, but he was determined to make everybody he ever came across suffer for it. That day it was I who had drawn the short straw. The bloody way he looked at me sent a shiver through my spine and I hadn't even said who I was by then and the expression 'Fucking Hell, what have I done now?' came to mind, but instantly disappeared as he snapped, "What do you want, Corporal? You are a Corporal, aren't you? The state of those stripes on your arm would make one think you didn't want to be one!" A short pause as he looked at me from head to foot. "Well, don't stand there like a spare prick at a wedding, what do you want?"

I was minded to say 'an honourable discharge, but you wouldn't give me one'. Instead, being the coward I am, I simply croaked out, "You sent for me, sir!"

"You must be Johnstone; it is Johnstone isn't it?"

I was about to say no! it's fucking Johannson and I'm off home to bloody Sweden, but I just said, "Yes, sir, Johnston, but without the 'e' sir!" Then I pondered why I'd said that bit about the 'e'. I'm becoming a real bloody fool, I thought, and I then said a silent prayer, 'God, please help me get away from here.' Little did I know my prayer was at that moment being given priority consideration in Heaven!

There was dead silence for a while as he looked at me as if I was something that needed standing on. Me, well I looked at a point about two feet behind him on the wall of his office. Finally I sensed him relax, more than seeing him do so. I felt a little safer then, but even so I didn't relax one little bit. After all, you don't relax your attention when in a room with a hooded cobra looking you eyeball to eyeball now, do you? His next utterance floored me completely, "The RSM!" – I love the way they always blame somebody else – "The RSM has put your name forward" – here comes the big lie – "as the best person to take charge of the men who are going on an exercise somewhere in Scotland, or maybe it's" – here he hesitated, it had got to be a lie, and he'd forgotten what he meant to say. Remembering his plot, he then said. "Well, it's up north somewhere. You will need sixteen sets of diving gear, you'll know what you need better than I do. The whole thing should be over in a couple of weeks. Oh yes, I've been told to tell you that if you do a good job then your third stripe might be on the end of it. So, keep up the good name of your squadron and do a good job; all right, that will be all. You had better get a move on; you have a train to catch; no good wasting time standing around here."

It was all so sudden and I was so deflated trying to take in all he was saying that I wasn't really listening to the swine. Therefore, I didn't have any time to think of a good reason why I should not go on this exercise. It was no good saying my wife was ill, because I didn't have one. So that was the standard excuse out the bloody window. Oh, I'd got the gist of it, but it wasn't until he said in a rather loud voice, "Go on man, you're dismissed!" that I was so flustered I was unable to call him all the names I'd been getting together in my mind. Instead of committing a heinous crime of gross insubordination I just saluted the bastard and left his office. That was my second and possibly my biggest mistake. I should have done time for the bastard. Instead I went like the lamb to the slaughter, and I turned on my heel and marched out of the Headquarters Block. Yes, I thought, and you have just made your first mistake selecting me for this bloody exercise or whatever it is that you're sending me on.

With a huge amount of luck and some help from people who normally wouldn't give me the time of day I managed to catch the train to Waterloo. As my train meandered its way through the southernmost counties of England I was stuck in a train without a corridor and my sixteen sets of top secret diving equipment were in a guard's van with a Dorset bloody turnip looking after them; and I had no means of being able to check on them. I had visions of arriving in London with the diving gear on a platform. Somewhere on a country platform in between Poole and bloody London

At Waterloo Station I was met by one of the Navy's finest. There waiting for me on the platform was a Chief Petty Officer of Her Majesty's Britannic Navy. He had with him four 'other ratings' but better still he had a Bedford three tonne truck standing just beyond the barrier. In no time at all my stores were transferred from the guard's van on to numerous platform trolleys, then as if by magic the whole lot were through the barrier and transferred on to the truck that was waiting outside. It seemed that I hardly had time to sit down in the back of the truck, before we arrived at King's Cross Station.

The rest of the lads who had been picked to go on this 'exercise' were waiting there for us. My Royal Naval guardian angel and his men loaded our stores into the special van that had been tagged on to the back of the train. I managed to get the rest of the group together and after checking that all those on the list were there I sent a couple of the corporals to find the carriage we were to travel in. While they were doing that I told the rest of the party what was going on. Well, that presented a bit of a problem really and after messing up my words for about the fourth time I asked if any of them knew what was going on. To that enquiry I only got some baffled looks and a couple of remarks like, "You're supposed to be in charge, you tell us."

I looked at them for a minute or so and said. "So, we all start from the same point. We all know nothing, so unless anybody tells you otherwise we are going to ride this train until it hits the buffers at the other end. If any civilian passengers ask what you're doing, tell them that the Russians have invaded Scotland and we are the advance party of the force that is going to push them back into the sea. When we find them that is, okay!" As I turned to see where the two corporals were I did notice some funny expressions passing between the men. Good, I thought, they now look as happy as I do.

Just then the Naval Chief Petty Officer arrived and directed us to the coach in which we were to travel. It was plastered with bits of paper marked 'Reserved for Military Personnel Only'. The two corporals I'd sent to find it were ensconced in the compartment at the rear of the coach and both of them were sitting reading. When I appeared at the door of the compartment they didn't even look afraid of me. One of them said, "With all the bloody paper saying it was our coach we knew you'd find it all right."

"Okay, smart arse, you two can now go and check all the men into the other compartments while I put my gear in here." Once they had gone, I moved their gear to the other side of the compartment. Then I put my gear on to the racks above the two window seats and settled myself down with my backside on one seat and my feet on the facing seat and waited for their return.

A couple of minutes later they returned. They both stood and looked at me then at their kit and then they came into the compartment and sat down. After about five minutes sitting in stony silence, finally they both looked at me and one of them said, "Okay, you are the boss. So it won't happen again!"

"That's right, it won't happen again. We will work together; from now on any grumbling about whatever there is to grumble about will be done in private between us; no more trying to get one over on anybody and I mean the rest of the men as well. I haven't a bloody clue what it is that we are going to do, no more than you do. So we all stick together from now on. If you don't want to work that way, then get off the train now before it leaves!"

They didn't get off, so I let it go at that. For my part I'd marked my territory and that was the end of it.

I got up then and went to each of the compartments where the men had settled themselves and checked that all was well. During my talks with them I asked each of them where they had come from. I was a little surprised when I found that all had been selected from Royal Marine establishments from Chatham and Deal in the South East of England to Plymouth and Bickleigh in the South West. All the marines and corporals had just recently qualified for the branch and all had been hoping to join RM Poole once the branch he settled in at its new base. I began to wonder what sort of exercise I'd been sent on with all the men newly qualified as divers. In my mind I knew that I wasn't experienced enough to be in charge of any type of exercise with newly trained men. It did make me wonder just what the hell was going on. I had heard that exercises, which the branch considered were suspect, have been filled with raw and inexperienced men before. Sometimes if they then turned out to be a success, the people in charge had risen rapidly in the branch. My first thoughts were that I hoped to God this wasn't one of those types of exercises.

While I was talking to the last two marines, who were in the compartment of the coach that was at the opposite end from my seat, the train left Kings Cross. When I finished and I was satisfied that I now knew who my men were, I made my way back to my own seat. The other two Corporals were now settled down and both were reading books. Once I'd sat down I thought I'd give them a shock and I took out my New Testament bible that I had been issued with from King George the Sixth and started to read it. As I read I kept glancing in the window, which because of the overcast sky outside acted as a kind of mirror. In it I could see the two of them exchanging glances and snatching looks at me as I read my bible. Yes, you pair of so and so's, I'll give you something to think about. I'll put money on it that by the time we get off this train I shall be known as 'a religious nut', something that was further from the truth than they would ever know.

While I held the book in front of me turning the pages at regular intervals I was thinking of the way we were being spirited away in the night. We had been gathered from all over the south of England. To be honest I didn't think anybody in any of the different establishments that we had come from would associate the sixteen men travelling on this train as having come from their establishments. It seemed a little odd really and I began to think that there was something going on that nobody was prepared to tell us about. By now the other two had put their books away and settled themselves down to try and sleep. Later, after about half an hour I took another walk along the corridor to check if the rest of the men were settled all right. In each compartment there were men sleeping in the most unusual positions, or trying to get to sleep. When I returned to our compartment the other two were asleep and I settled down to do the same.

At each stop during the journey I got up and checked just to make sure that no civilians entered the compartment. I wasn't disappointed because at York a man – and I presume his wife – boldly marched into the coach and told a couple of the lads to get up and let them sit down. Fortunately, I managed to get there before they were too rude to them. The man was all right and was prepared to leave, but the woman, oh boy, was she a problem. She was either thick and hadn't ever learnt to read or she was the most arrogant woman I've ever met. Even after one of the other corporals had leaned out of the carriage door window and removed one of the 'Reserved for Military Personnel' stickers she still wouldn't move. By now she had woken everybody up and some of the remarks coming from other compartments were terrible.

All For A King's Shilling

There was nobody more relieved than I when the train ticket inspector entered the coach; and she couldn't get out of the carriage fast enough. When I asked him what he told her he just said, "I told her you were all crawling with lice and crabs and you were on your way to be deloused."

I then had to stop the rest of the lads filling him in. So he left as fast as she did; only he gave us the 'V' sign at the end of the corridor and it had nothing to do with victory.

The next morning we arrived at Aberdeen after a very uncomfortable night, at around 8.30 in the morning. Not only were we tired, but we were all hungry as well. Once we had managed to disentangle ourselves from the train I went to see the station master, who incidentally was fast approaching us along the platform. Just as I spotted him one of the Marines spotted the guard's van containing our gear being dragged from the back of the train and out of the station the way we had entered. I immediately set off in pursuit of it only to be stopped by the station master. He told me that everything was okay, the van was being shunted on to the train that was to take us to our destination. Still apprehensive I watched the bloody van getting further and further away. Turning to the station master I said, "I'm not so fucking sure, that thing is getting a fair head of steam up and if it doesn't stop soon it'll be back in bloody London before lunch time."

At this point I noticed another of Her Majesty's finest standing looking at me; not only was he looking at me he was looking down his bloody nose at me. "What's your problem, Jack?" I asked him.

The venom in my voice took him a little aback and he said, "I'm here to meet you and show you to your next train."

"Oh yeah, well, Jack, if that bloody van that just disappeared out of this station isn't attached to our next train I wouldn't give much for your chances of finishing your time in the 'Andrew', mate!"

"It will be on the next train."

Next I turned to one of the corporals and told him to fall the men in and I told his mate to check that everything had been removed from the coach. "Check under the seats and in the racks, toilets, the bloody lot, no gash to be left, okay?"

Without a word they were both off. The station master then said, "Here you are, your train with the van attached is just pulling into the platform at the back of the station. If you come with me I'll show you how to get there."

Looking back along the platform I saw that the men were in three ranks and the corporal checking the coach gave me the thumbs up so I told the other one to bring the men along behind us. The matelot never said a word as we made our way to our next train. Now this was something else. It was a baby train, an 0-4-0 or something I think they are called. Anyway it had one coach; it didn't have a corridor; it also had no toilets and once it was going there was no way of getting from compartment to compartment and due to the lack of toilets, looking out of open windows was a dangerous occupation. Still, it was comfortable and as soon as we had closed the last door it was away.

We had hardly cleared the end of the platform before both of the corporals with me were once more fast asleep. I was leaning against the window looking out at the Scottish countryside as we moved relentlessly onwards, heading all the time northwards. Watching the countryside that we were passing through, I decided that it looked the most bleak and inhospitable I'd seen for a long time. It had started raining and I noticed for the first time that the rain here fell horizontally. I did wonder how far it travelled before it fell to the ground. The rain acted on me like a hypnotist's watch and very soon I was zonked out.

The train, at some stage during my sleep, must have left the coast and headed into the 'Bonny Heather'. I have often wondered if the man or woman who coined the phrase 'Bonny Heather' for that part of Scotland has ever been there. The part that my friends and I now found ourselves in, well it was pure bloody bog.

Not to put too fine a point on it the train came to a stop with a screech of locked wheels and a final jerk and bump as it ran into a set of old buffers at an old and decrepit station. Well, it may have been a station in days of yore! Now, if you could call a large grassy bank with a set of old rusty buffers at one end a station, then this was a station!

The bump more than the screech was what woke us all up. It was just after midday and the weather was atrocious. I dropped from the carriage and was immediately hit by a blast of wind and rain. It was like being a 'sandblaster'. The rain was coming at me in a nearly horizontal position and it stung like grit as it hit my face. I was about to shout and tell the lads to stay in the carriage when this full of life, jolly red-faced guard came and told us in a broad Scots' burr, "This is your stop lads, out you bloody get!"

Just as I was about to tell him that I was the one who gave the orders around here, he bellowed, "Come on lads, this is the end of the line. When you have got all your stuff off we shall be on our way back to civilisation!"

As we started to get our kit from the train a voice with a broad Cockney accent shouted, "So, you'll be off back to Kings Cross then, Jock, save me a seat."

He had no answer to that and as the last pack was thrown out of the carriage the train immediately started back the way it had come, only this time the train was pushing the carriage backwards instead of pulling it. God! I thought, what a bloody journey going backwards all the way to Aberdeen in that driving rain.

Once we had got our gear off the grassy bank that doubled as a platform – and we had a hell of an amount of gear – it was as if from nowhere, up popped another, but this time a larger and bigger mouthed matelot. This one was a lot bigger mouthed than the one we had just left at Aberdeen. This one 'had a mouth like Tynemouth', as they say. The only redeeming thing about him that stopped him getting thumped was the fact he had two very important things with him. Firstly he had a pair of trucks, but more important than the trucks, much more important than the trucks, he also had a load of bag ration meals, which he hastily distributed amongst us. Mind you he did so as if he was waving a magic wand, playing the great benefactor. I hate matelots with an attitude and this bastard had an attitude. Still, we got two bag rations each, one for the breakfast that we had missed and one for lunch, which was only an hour or so away anyway.

We managed to get our gear loaded into the trucks, and then we all clambered into what little space was left at the rear of them. He, the one with the big mouth that is, then drove off into the wide open spaces of the northernmost part of this wonderful, but one of the most inhospitable parts, of the British Isles. He was followed by his mate, driving the second truck.

After about an hour of bouncing around in the back of his truck we eventually arrived at what looked to be crossroads. Well, more like a set of crossed sheep tracks to be honest about it. We were in what looked to be and soon proved to be the middle of bloody nowhere and in the middle of a bloody bog, not to put too fine a point on it. It seemed we had left any resemblance to tarmacadam miles behind. When we got down from the rear of the trucks, much to our amusement and surprise there were already some servicemen there. There were some Royal Engineers and some Royal Electrical and Mechanical Engineers, but they were not the source of our amusement. It was the other group of men who were standing a little way from the army lads that were the source of our amusement. They were, judging by their dress, what could only have passed for a group of recruits, except for the fact that their ages were so varied. They would more likely have passed for the old and bold of Chelsea, or the old and bold of the Home Guard, or perhaps its predecessor, the LDV, Local Defence Volunteers! At the time they were more commonly known as the 'Look, Duck and Vanish' brigade. All of these men were sitting around on various lumps of baggage and boxes that we all presumed contained their personal equipment.

The strange thing about it all was that we all just stood around looking at one another, like a bunch of great big black puddings. Then just as things were starting to become a little unbearable a car was observed approaching us from the east of the tracks, the track it turned out along which we had all come. This car caused quite a stir of conversation among the older group and this was the first time anybody had spoken since we had arrived.

When the car stopped out popped the gem of all gems; he had on a khaki beret but no Regimental badge. The beret, which could not have been out of the clothing store for more than a day, was perched on the top of his head and he looked as if somebody had placed a model of a khaki aircraft carrier on his head. I watched him as he looked around the groups as if sizing us up, then he uttered his first words, which were, "Right, chaps!"

I looked at one of my Marines, a lad of about twenty-three called Nobby Clark, but before I could say anything he said, "I thought they shot all those bastards after Dunkirk."

Another Marine standing near us piped up.

"Could be one of them had a son?" somebody else said.

"Okay, okay, that's enough, let us see what he is about," I chipped in.

Trying to look as if he had not heard any of this his next utterance was, "Grab your gear and let's get going."

"Just one minute there," not knowing if I should address him as sir or not, I said, "go where?"

"With me."

"Right, and just who are you?"

"I am your guide."

"Okay, I'll buy that, but a guide to where?"

"Oh! Just over there, a little way," he said, pointing in a northerly direction.

"Right, and just how little a way is just over there?" I asked.

"Haven't measured it, but it's not very far."

"All right, I'll tell you what, we Royal Marines will come with you, but I doubt if we or any of the others here will be able to carry all this equipment, not in one trip that is. Not over that ground anyway, it looks like pure bog to me. That is going to need either more men, or vehicles of some sort, or we will have to make more than one trip."

"That's right, and how far is it to this house we are to be staying in?" said one of the look, duck and vanish group.

"House," our guide said, "there are no houses out here. You will be living rough, very rough indeed."

First, I looked at Nobby Clark and then at the rest of my happy band of pilgrims, who did not look too happy at all, and I said. "Come on, so what's new, it looks as if things are just back to normal."

"I agree," Nobby answered.

Turning back to our young guide I said, "Just how far is it to this rough house we are to live in for the next few weeks or so, you must have some idea?"

"Well, I think it is about four miles in that direction." Again he pointed in a northerly direction.

"Okay, then, how about we take all but two men from each group with us now? We carry our personal kit plus one piece of our other equipment now. We can see the place, have a look at the situation and then we can decide how we are to get the larger bits of equipment which all of us have with us out to or into this so-called house?"

I'm not sure if he knew what I was getting at, but he turned and struck off at a fair rate of knots across the bog. The man was jumping like a bloody goat from one lump of tussock grass to the next.

"Just hold your bloody horses there one minute," I shouted after him. "We have to sort some loads out yet, and also we need to get our personal equipment on. More to the point I think you should be carrying a load as well."

This stopped him dead in his tracks and he sat on a large lump of tussock grass, and I do believe he sat there and sulked, while we sorted our kit into loads. When the other groups had eventually agreed who was going and who it was they were leaving behind, we then hoisted a load each upon our backs along with our personal gear, and with the other items loaded as best we could over our shoulders we left the track. When we reached our guide he looked up and was about to say something, but before he could Nobby Clark and I dumped a large kit bag that we had been carrying between us on his lap. Looking down at him I said, "That's yours, mister guide, now lead on fine fellow that you are." By the look on his face I knew then that he was no officer or NCO for that matter.

We all suffered some pain carrying the stores we had with us, mainly because we did not have the proper load-carrying equipment with us. I'd left two of the Royal Marines with what bits of our diving equipment we couldn't carry and taking all except two men from each of the other groups we headed out into the heather and bog. While we were struggling along, I noticed for the first time there was an officer amongst the Royal Engineers and a sergeant. There were also two sergeants with the REME outfit and here was I, a simple Royal Marine Corporal, taking charge. Still, nobody had objected so far, so I said nothing.

All For A King's Shilling

The journey across the moor or bog, call it what you want, was one hell of a bloody trip I can tell you. I for one, even though I considered myself to be very fit was damned pleased when we eventually arrived at our destination. The tussock grass in this part of the world has this habit of growing just too far apart for even me, a six-footer, to be able to step from one tuft to another, a fact that led us all to end up at least once, and some of us a lot more than once, up to our armpits in the bog. These men then had to be extracted by the rest of the group before we could all go on. Although it turned out it was only a couple of miles to the place to which we were going, the trip took us quite a considerable time. We Marines were not exhausted when we got there, but we all knew we had been on a hell of a walk. When at last we arrived at a group of rocks protruding from the heather and situated on an inland facing slope about fifty feet below the ridge, our guide called a halt.

"Hear that noise? It's the sea. So that's what we need the diving gear for?" Remarked a young Marine I was to learn was called Nobby Clark.

I turned to the other Marines in the group. "The wisdom of this man is beyond me. We are all frogmen and he has just realised why we have our diving gear with us."

Then I turned, looked at Nobby, and told him, "I had not expected to be doing any diving in these bloody bogs, mate."

When I turned around again, our intrepid guide had disappeared from view.

The Royal Engineer officer came up to me and much to my relief asked. "Where the hell has that idiot gone off to now?"

At that moment he reappeared from a gap in the rocks. "Just lighting the lamps, now if you can all follow me please this way, gentlemen," he said, as he disappeared into the hole again. The man was starting to give the impression of a bloody Jack Rabbit.

"I am going to get great pleasure in doing him in," one of the Marines muttered. "He is starting to get on my bloody nerves; I was just about to address him as Sir, until one of the lads said he was a bloody National Service man, and a bloody Lance Jack (Lance Corporal) at that."

"Probably some square-headed sod from a university," one of the other lads remarked.

"Can it, that's enough," I said.

With that, one by one we made our way in through the hole after the intrepid Lance Jack. It was a bit of a tight squeeze to get in the place, but once inside the first thing one noticed was the stillness. There was no wind in there at all, which helped to make life a lot easier after the constant wind and rain outside. The only problem was that the lamps our guide had lit gave off more smoke than they did light.

"Put those bloody lamps right somebody," I said.

Marine Clark stepped forward and he immediately got two of the lads to help him trim the wicks and relight them. When they were alight once more we could see a little better what sort of place we had entered. Most of the 'look duck and vanish' brigade were still outside at this point and I told some of the lads to help them.

Meanwhile, I gave the place we were in the once-over. We were in a small area just inside the hole through which we had entered. It was about fifteen to twenty feet in width, twenty feet in length and about seven feet in height. The floor sloped slightly downwards in what I believed was the direction of the ridge and against the slope of the hill that we had climbed to get here. At the side opposite the hole through which we had entered, the roof tapered down towards a narrow passage that was about five feet in height. I remember thinking, I wonder what delight awaits us down there. Then just as my eyes were getting accustomed to the light in the place, a man popped out of this passage into the area we were now in. I had a distinct feeling that he had been watching us all the time from the darkness inside the passage.

"Christ," I blurted out before I could stop myself.

"Christ," repeated the man who had appeared from the passage. "Still using the man's name in vain are you, Johnston? I'll give you Christ! Get your bloody men together and get on down this passage."

Turning to the Royal Engineer Officer I said, "You're on your own now, sir, I shall be leaving."

To the men I said, "Right lads get your gear and follow me." Then I set off in a half crouch, down the passage.

As we were making our way down the passage Nobby, who seemed to have attached himself to me, asked, "Who is he mate, he seemed to frighten you?"

"He'll frighten the shit out of you too before this little shindig is over, mate!" I replied, and then went on. "One bit of advice though, always remember one thing, if he swears at you, you are okay. If he doesn't, you are for the high jump; he will throw the book at you. Who he is? Well, he is a passed-over Captain and he has a chip on his shoulder big enough to sink the bloody KGIV and the Anson. It is said he owns half of Scotland, the half that we just happen to be in right now, the top half; and for my money, he's bloody welcome to it."

We picked our way down a rather steep slope, which was very slippery underfoot. Then eventually we came to the end of the passage and came out into a large cave, and I mean large! Somebody had set up about ten floodlights around the walls of the place, which were powered by what looked like a small generator. The cave was really large and it also looked to be quite dry for a cave under or alongside a Scottish bog. Something to do with the type of rock it was in. Looking at the rest of my men I said, "Remember the house those guys were talking about, well they could put two or three houses in here and I somehow think that means hard bloody work for us."

Before anybody could reply, a stern voice behind me told me, "You always did have too bloody much to say for yourself, didn't you, Johnston?"

I turned and looked our illustrious Captain straight in the eyes; I thought that it was better for my men's' sake that he and I had this out, right now. So, after a second or two of eyeball to eyeball contact I asked him. "Is it going to be like this all the time, sir, or will you be having a go at somebody else as well as me?"

"Unfortunately for you mister, you are the only one whose name I am familiar with at the moment and don't you forget that it was I who selected you for this job in the first place."

"Well, sir!" I said. "You can just as easily deselect me if you want to; I will even make my own way back to Portsmouth if it is your wish, sir."

"Watch it, mister," he hissed as he turned and walked to the group of LDV bods who had now arrived in the cave.

Looking back on that moment I should have known then that all was not as it should have been. If everything had been above board and normal, then he would have slapped me in irons and had me carted off for a court-martial. He would have had me sentenced to death or some other unbearable punishment for insubordination; but he didn't, and I never asked why! Like the fool I was I thought I'd got away with back-answering an officer. Fool, nobody ever gets away with back-answering officers. We all have to pay the piper some time! Just then my thoughts were interrupted by Marine Clark.

"You and he old friends, I see," Nobby said as Captain Brown started chatting to the Look Duck and Vanish bods."

"Oh yes," I said. "You can watch it too mister!" at which we both laughed.

I was beginning to like this guy. "I'll tell you one thing, Nobby. He will bloody kill me when he finds out it was I who decided to leave some of the diving gear and the other blokes behind. By the way, his name is Brown. He is a Lord Shit, some shit or other, but in the Corps he is just plain old Captain Brown; most people refer to him as 'Haggis Brown'. To his face, I usually call him sir, but I'll not repeat some of the other names those who know him have for him."

As it turned out, that cave was to be our home for the next six weeks, during which time it changed from a bare floodlit cave to a rather respectable home. I once read somewhere that some French people had taken to living in caves in Southern France; they reasoned that it would be the best place to be just in case the Russians decided to drop a few atomic bombs on France. Mind you, this living in caves does have a lot going for it. Provided you all take good care of your personal hygiene then everything should be okay, but there is hell to play if you have a crabby, dirty bastard with you. As I have already said, we were to live in the place for a couple of months, but some of the others may still be there for all I know. You see, much to all our surprise we were all there to set up an underground base; a base from which the specialists would be able to monitor the sonar buoys.

What kind of buoys, you may well ask? They were the ones that the British and American Governments were in the process of laying across the North Atlantic. A string of sonar buoys that were supposed, by being connected to one another on the sea bed like a load of bloody 'fairy lights' to warn us every time the Russian submarines crossed into the Atlantic. Now I'm just a silly old Royal Marine Corporal, but I fail to see why we should worry about Russian submarines entering the Atlantic with their atomic missiles. You see even I knew in those days that the bloody Russians could hit any part of the United Kingdom they wished from Eastern Europe. So why should we bother about the Americans' sonar buoys? Anyway I'd been told, along with most other people in the British forces, that the bloody things didn't work.

So I believed the idea was to let the Russians think that everything was well with these sonar buoys and that they really did work. The Russians would know all about them anyway; some bloody two-faced person in the know would have already told them that they didn't work. So it was obvious that the way to deceive the Russians into thinking that the buoys were working would be to tell lies to the people in London. That way the spy would tell them that they did in fact work, and confirm that we would have to build a control post, base, call it what you like to monitor the damned things. I reasoned that was the only explanation why we were there, to get the cable from the sea bed and bring it ashore. This I reasoned would be done in full view of any Russian fishing boats that would be following the vessels laying the buoys from Iceland to bonny Scotland along the sea bed. Oh, boy, was I in for a bloody shock!

Why was I in for a shock? Well, my friend Brown, Captain Brown, he had thought up a better plan than that. We were to have one hell of a time doing the work that he had thought up for us, he had far better plans than that for us to do in that hole in the ground. He hadn't told us so far, but he had thought up the exercise of all exercises. Not only were we to bring the cable ashore, but we were also going to have to bring all the equipment needed to build the base ashore. Not from landing craft, as we at first thought they would. Oh no, that would be too easy. We were expected to collect the vast amount of stores needed to build a base from the actual sea bed. As things stood, there wasn't the slightest chance the items required to build the type of place he had planned for the cave could be brought into the caves the way we had arrived. No, sir! Well, not without making a bigger hole on the surface of the hill, and laying a road of some sort over the bog, which would give the precise position of the monitoring base away to the watching Russians. Because they would be out there watching, they would watch every move we made once we got started on the task we had been given. I believed that the Russian fishing boats would already be out on the twelve-mile limit waiting, just waiting for the whole fiasco to start. I have always believed that some stupid fool in the Admiralty sent them copies of our orders as a matter of course. Because the Russian trawlers always managed to appear in the right place just as the task we'd been given started. Judging by the weather, then God help them. Oh yes, they'd be out there sitting on the three-mile limit in their fishing boats waiting for us.

During the next few weeks, as soon as any RFA or other type of small cargo vessel came within a thousand yards of our operation, one of the Russians would come up to have a look at what we were doing. They would try to see whatever it was that the ships were slipping into the water, as the ships passed by the cave entrance. Quite a good game really, except it could get a bit on the 'scary side' to say the least. Mind you, I did not envy the young Russians the weather that they had to endure. It can become very rough up there off the northern coast of Scotland. Even at the best of times the weather is not so good, but in the autumn, well it can get quite horrendous. I have seen some of those fishing trawlers seem as if they were standing on their sterns with three quarters of the boat out of the water, only to come crashing down bow first into the trough between the last wave and the next one; waves rolling in from the Atlantic Ocean that had travelled three thousand miles across the open water with nothing to break them up or to slow them down. I didn't envy them remaining on station in their little fishing boats in all weathers. We had it rough, but boy, they must have been the most dedicated of seamen and to this day I take my hat off to them. Mind, they had nowhere to go; they couldn't get off the bloody things anyway. Captive heroes one might say.

We retrieved the remainder of our gear from the crossroads and managed to get it into the cave. The whole group of us then gathered in the main cave and Captain Brown started to tell us why we were there and what it was all about.

He started by telling us the usual story, 'a load of bullshit' most of it as was usual. I sometimes wonder how they think it all up. Anyway off he went. "The American and British Navies have completed laying the sonar buoys, well, nearly completed.

All For A King's Shilling

We, and by we I mean you lot, have one month to get the place ready. Ready for the installation and connection of the undersea cable to the equipment needed to monitor the sonar buoys. This place has to be transformed into an operational station ready to monitor the buoys as soon as possible after the connection has been made and I stress, as soon as possible. All I can tell you gentlemen is that the whole setup has to work first time. There will not be a second chance; all the buoys are tested before they are submerged and again once they are on the bottom. So far, all the tests have gone well."

The other NCOs among us Royal Marines were like me a little taken aback by all of this to say the least. As I've said earlier it was but a month or so ago that I'd attended a briefing about these sonar buoys before I left to do my Sergeants' exam. It was a briefing given by a staff officer from London which I had attended along with the rest of the NCOs and Officers in our Squadron. He had told us the sonar buoys didn't work properly and to date the whole operation had been a very expensive failure. The feeling amongst the 'powers that-be' in London was that as the Yanks were funding the operation, then it was no great loss to us if it didn't work anyway.

So you can imagine I for one was a little puzzled about Brown's remarks that after all, once we completed this job we would all be able to sleep happily in our beds. Now we had these buoys to guard us against the hordes of Russian submarines lying in wait in the North Atlantic ready to attack us. I was minded to ask about the buoys between Scotland and Norway. Questions like how do we check those out; but I thought better of it because obviously the Yanks didn't know about the eastern side of Britain having a coastline and that there was a sea called 'the North Sea' between us and the coast of Europe, that is. It looked, as far as I could tell, as if they didn't intend to lay any of these buoys across from Scotland to Norway. Therefore, there was nothing to stop these hordes of Russian submarines going down the North Sea and out into the Atlantic by way of the English Channel to 'Nuke' the shit out of America. Anyway once these submarines had crossed our row of fairy lights, how the bloody hell did we know where in the Atlantic they were? It's a bloody big ocean, isn't it? I believe they should have hung Columbus when he got back from finding America because we have had nothing but trouble ever since then.

Next our illustrious Captain Brown started into the how and wherefores of doing the job that my merry band of pilgrims and I had been allocated. It seemed that I and my happy band had the unenviable task of collecting the stores that we would need – from of all places – the seabed. At first we just sat there and looked at each other, our mouths hanging slightly open like dead cods on a fishmonger's slab.

The mind boggles at the fact that some foolish idea put forward by some stupid jerk in MoD was to be put into practice just to impress some bloody Yank or Russian. For my money, the buoys were American, then the 'boys' of the 'American Seals' should have been doing this job, not us. They would be better off getting cable and wireless to do the bloody job, but if they did get cable and wireless, then everything would work first time; and we and the Yanks wouldn't be able to lie about it, would we?

At this point we learnt that the stores we were going to collect from the seabed were to be dropped into the sea from passing Royal Fleet Auxiliaries (RFA) or any other vessels, such as coasters, and would you believe it, fishing boats, which the

Ministry of Defence could press into service. So I thought the Russians will be pleased to know that they and the Yanks aren't the only ones with barmy Admirals. I didn't think even the Russians could have thought this one up, not in a million years, and I bet Nelson was now well on the way to finishing that bloody barrel of brandy that they stuffed him in.

One wise guy from the boffins, because that is who the civvies that looked like the look, duck and vanish brigade were, asked Captain Brown. "I say, can you get some of these chaps of yours to bring in the equipment which we brought with us from the crossroads? Also, will you please ask them to be careful with it?"

"Now, yes, to your equipment," Captain Brown had said. "I'm afraid you will have to take it to the beach yourselves. The beach you can use is about eight hundred yards away from here. Corporal Johnston and his lads will then recover it from there and bring it in here for you."

"Well, I have no idea how you intend to recover our equipment from the beach, but I shall go with them to make sure they don't damage anything or worse still, get it wet."

I could see the slight twitch which appeared in times of stress and bad temper in Brown's face give that first little flick of movement to an otherwise granite face. Then his eyes started to show more white around the pupils and I knew he was getting ready for take off, all engines burning and turning as the 'crab hats' say

Just then another of the intrepid boffins said, "I shall go as well with these Marines. I want to make sure they handle the stores carefully as they carry them to the beach. If the way they handled their own stores coming here is anything to go by, I dread to think what damage they will do."

By now the twitch in Brown's face was flickering like a dodgy light bulb and he was having great difficulty as he tried to control his speech. I just loved it when somebody over whom he had no military jurisdiction got him going like this. I nudged the Royal Engineer Officer sitting next to me and whispered, "He'll be airborne any minute now."

"No sir, I think not!" By now Brown's twitch had gone into overdrive, but he was still keeping a tight rein on his voice.

"Come on, go get them, Brownie my boy," I muttered to myself as I watched him suffering. So keen was I to exploit the uncomfortable position that he was in that I was about to throw a little fat on the fire, but he interrupted me before I could get the words out of my mouth. He must have seen my mouth opening and realised that I was about to say something witty that would inflame the situation a little bit more. I felt cheated again as Brown went on in a more controlled and settled voice.

"No, sir, I think not!" He then went on, "You see, the entrance to this cave is about twenty feet below the low water mark." His voice rising to a crescendo on the word "mark", and he stopped again, then took a deep breath and settled himself. I realised that the fun was over as he went on in his normal voice, "You will have to get your own stores from the crossroads to the beach yourselves. What's more, it will be your own responsibility to see that your stores are waterproofed before Johnston and his bunch of hooligans get their hands on them. I have my doubts if Johnston and his men even know what, 'waterproof' means. Their wet suits probably leak like sieves anyway, isn't that so Johnston?"

All For A King's Shilling

Before I could answer him, a boffin piped up. "I have not come here to act as a labourer, I am a scientist, and as such I demand respect. You may not think it, but I am not without contacts, my man."

"Oh shit!" was all I said.

God I thought, the sparks will fly now, my hopes revived that we would witness the high-pitched screams as Brown blew his top. I felt the first smile of the day crossing my face. I knew I was about to watch a massacre.

"It is quite out of the question for you to go with them, isn't it, Corporal Johnston?"

Oh shit, I thought, the bastard is dragging me into this little exchange but before I could answer he again went on.

"Anyway, Johnston and his men will be bringing your equipment into this cave by the underwater passage. Even if you can dive, Johnston doesn't have any equipment to lend you. Everybody will have their work cut out doing their own thing, as you lot will be doing your own thing that is. No, sir, Johnston and his men will have too much work to do themselves without doing your work for you. What is more important, I don't care how many bloody contacts you have, so get on with it, do you understand?" Oh, shit, I thought as Captain Brown turned on his heel and stormed off into another passage leading from the cave, a passage none of us had even noticed before he entered it. Looking at his back as he disappeared I thought, hell he has turned into a damp squib. Either that or he has lost his bottle, or worse still there's something not right here?

"What a bloody letdown," I muttered to myself as the smile had slipped from my face. "The sod must be getting soft in his old age, or did this boffin have the contacts he said he had?" Whatever it was, Brown had been a letdown, not the ball of fire and brimstone I'd come to expect from him.

It was then that the penny – or should I say pennies – started to drop and I saw the first glimmer of what I thought was going on and why we were here. All that shit about the sonar buoys working and everything going to plan! I didn't buy that bullshit. If that was so then why not go the whole hog and build a bloody road over the bog to this area, then build a blockhouse to house these bloody boffins and their precious equipment and be done with it? It had to be something more than that. That was when the penny dropped that this had to be a rehearsal for something else. We were here to try out the feasibility of setting up a post somewhere else and that somewhere else had got to be on an enemy coast. "That's it," I said aloud.

"That's what?" asked Nobby Clark.

"Nothing; I shall tell you later when you have a weekend to spare."

With that I then sank back into my own thoughts. I'll bet the only reason that this was being done was to see if it were possible to recover from the seabed the vast amount of stores an operation of this type would require. It was bugger all to do with bloody sonar buoys. Meanwhile, all this activity here would help to convince the Russians that all was well with the original scheme of laying the sonar buoys, but more important that they were, after all, working. From now on it seemed the Russians would have to find a new route to deploy their submarines into the Atlantic. The logical conclusion was that the Russians would never be sure if the buoys worked, or if they didn't, from this day forward, would they? Crafty bastards these

Yanks, aren't they? I wondered if they had made any allowances for the people on both sides of the Atlantic who would practically be breaking their bloody necks to tell the Russians the truth about what was going on.

So certain was I in my reasoning that I would have put a year's pay on it. More to the point, I doubted very many if any of the groups in the cave at that precise moment really knew what the hell was going on there anyway. My summarising came to an abrupt end and with a start, when I noticed Lord Shit Brown had returned to the cave and had his beady eye on me.

My attempts to look busy were not very convincing and Brown had a face that looked like a 'busted boot'. He did not look a very happy man at all. His progress towards me was interrupted when the Royal Engineer's Officer asked him, "Just what is it we are to build in this cave? I need maps, plans, anything, but I need directions of some sort. As for the stores I will require, will they arrive in the correct order in which I will need them? About these boffins, how are they to be employed during this building phase?"

I think we all looked aghast when Captain Brown told him. "The building will eventually cover the whole floor of the cave. It will be two stories high – in some places three – and Captain, as for the stores starting to arrive, well, they already have started to arrive; as to your plans, you and I will go over them shortly. Then you can see your exact task, and you will also see the order in which your stores are to arrive. I think you will find everything alright."

"God," I said. "Two to three stories high; that's a hell of a lot of stores to haul off the seabed and into this place."

"Yes, that is true, but you will manage to do it, won't you Johnston? You only have to bring the stores to the underwater entrance and attach the hawsers, which the Royal Engineers will have lowered to you. They will then do all the hard work of hauling everything up to the lower cave level, using their cliff haulage equipment. Then while you are out there in the sea enjoying yourselves, getting more stores, the engineers will be hard at work hauling them up here. When the stores arrive here they will be unpacked and be put together like a giant meccano set and the work will go on twenty-four hours a day, until it is finished."

"Oh, great," I said. "When and how will they get their haulage gear in here?"

"That is already on the seabed, waiting for you to stop delaying things and go and collect it. If that is all right with you that is, Johnston?" he growled.

I knew right then that I should have kept my big mouth shut, but instead I went for broke and what happened next should have got me court-martialled. If I had been court-martialled then I'd never have been put through all the madness that I have endured these last few years; but he didn't court-martial me and I have been taking part in the full unabridged madness of it all ever since. That was when I mouthed off at him. "This whole setup is a shambles. There are no feeding arrangements, all any of us have had since leaving our bases in the south is two bloody bag rations, what is more there are no sanitation arrangements; and just where do we get our drinking water from, sir?" I said. "You're not going to tell me that's coming in from the seabed as well, or do we have to go back to the track each day to hump four-gallon bloody jerry cans in here every day as well as diving in the sea for twenty-four hours a day? Tell me sir, just where are we going to get all the other stores and things we need to make the bloody 'exercise' work?" Believing I'd said enough, I turned my back on him and slowly walked away from them all. I was waiting for the screaming and the 'insubordination and the direct order shit' and the 'I'm placing you in close arrest shit' but none of it came; and that threw me somewhat! However, it did confirm my suspicions that something was wrong here and it was serious stuff, I just wished to God I knew what it was that was wrong. I knew that it was so serious that he dare not bring it into the open by arresting and court-martialling me. Had I know then what I know now, then I'd have been out of there faster than a bloody weasel, mark my words I would. It would have been 'Colchester oh Colchester, here I bloody come, and you can stick your stripes up your arse, all bloody three of them!'

So, it looked as if I was not going to be shipped out of all the madness after all. Because madness is what I believed it had all been, right from the bloody start, complete and utter bloody madness! But all that bloody Brown did as I walked away was laugh at my back. The other servicemen in that cave were all standing or sitting with their bloody mouths open looking at me. So I turned on them and told them I thought it was about time we all got to bloody work instead of prancing around like a bunch of fairies looking for a toadstool to hide under. "There is a lot of work to be done in here before we can start to build anything. So look busy. Even if you have nothing to do look as if you are doing it in smart parade ground fashion. You all heard the Lord High Admiral command, so get on with it!"

At that, not to be outdone, Brown shouted after me just as I was about to enter the passage, "You will go off to the end of that passage to get your diving equipment ready. The Royal Engineers will start to survey this place. The rest of you are all to make your way back to the road to form a humping party to get all your personal kit and whatever else you decided to leave there." (A daggers drawn look in my direction I've been told as I continued on and took no bloody notice of him. Of course, I was acting the usual fool that I was because Brown had a punishment far, far worse than any court-martial up his bloody sleeve for me.)

Brown by now was rambling on like a bloody parrot. "Once you have got all the stores that will fit through the entrance into the cave, you will all help the boffins to get their remaining stores and any other items which are too large to be brought through the entrance, down to the beach."

Long pause, while looking all around, and then he went on again, by which time none of the servicemen were listening any more.

"From where Johnston and his group will take them and bring them in through the underwater entrance which we have already discussed. We will be working round the clock once we get things a little more organised. So, off you go Johnston, and the rest of you get bloody moving, we have wasted half a day standing around talking already, so move, time is of the essence. We have a deadline to meet."

His tirade was one of the longest and most uninteresting that I had ever heard from him in one go. I remember thinking it must be important to him if he was going to go on like this and not lock me up after what I'd just done. So I decided it might just be to my advantage if I was to keep a low profile and stay out of his sight until I found out why he was acting in the way he was. Because something was terribly wrong. I should have been shot at dawn for what I'd just done.

While the lads were checking the diving equipment, I took Nobby Clark with me and went to the lower level of the cave as detailed by Captain Brown to have a look around and do what? Well, I didn't know what I was supposed to do! When we arrived there, the Royal Engineer's Officer and his Troop Sergeant were right behind us and the Sergeant was giving the place the once-over.

The officer told me they had both been keeping a low profile back in the cave as they were not keen to become witnesses in a court-martial. "I hope you don't mind me asking, Corporal, but do all NCO's talk to their officers in your Corps the way you talk to him?"

"Oh no, sir! It's just that here he has got a little out of his depth, so to say. You see, he knows nothing about diving and the risks involved and he hasn't a bloody clue if we can recover the stores he has had dumped on the seabed already. He knows that if I say there is no diving then there will be no diving and he cannot do a damned thing about it. No, sir, I'm hoping that is what is going on because by now I should be in the tightest closet arrest you can think of! I only hope I'm right and that we are not involved in something we shouldn't be doing."

The RE Officer looked at me for a moment and then said, "What do you mean not doing?"

"Aiding and abetting an enemy for one!"

"Oh, I think not, Corporal! Anyway, at the moment we are more interested in working out how and where we are going to rig up our haulage gear."

We all looked at each other for a second or two, and then I said, "There is one thing that worries me about my men, sir, and that is that we all came from different units. Until we met at Kings Cross none of us had ever met before. Then there is one more very important point; the Petty Officer who met me at Waterloo and transported me to Kings Cross with all the stores was in my experience of a naval PO dealing with a Royal Marine, far too efficient. He didn't ask my Marines to unload his truck; he and his men did that. He also gave me some stores that I didn't have when I left my base."

The Royal Engineer Officer again broke the silence and said, "I know I should not say this, but you amongst all of us seem to know this man best; is he mad?"

"Well, like you say, sir, I shouldn't say this either, as I don't know you any better. At the moment I'd say that you are trying to change the subject, but yes, Captain Brown is right off his bloody head, mad as a March hare. The problem is, he used to be damned good at what he does, or so he has kept telling me every time I've met him, but come to that I'm not really sure what it is he does. If we do succeed here and make this plan of his work, then we may all look back at our time spent here and thank him. You will thank the bastard for making your life hell for however long it takes you to do the job. You will thank him because you will have learnt something from the experience. What you will have learnt I don't know and nor will you, but you will go away thinking you are a wiser man and you probably will be. You will go to war with him if he asks you, knowing in your heart you are mad for so doing. To be truthful I've already been to war with him, but I'll give you a bit of advice, beware if he doesn't scream and use bad language when he gives you a bollocking, that is. He'll be worse on you, sir, than he will on anybody else; except on me, that is; I'm his prime target for the moment and I have been since my days as a young Marine."

All For A King's Shilling

God, I thought as soon as I'd stopped talking, what a load of bollocks I talk at times; I'm sure it doesn't impress anybody.

"Wait a minute," the officer said and motioned me away from his sergeant . He then told me his situation was the same. He said he knew his sergeant, but the rest of his men he'd never seen before. "By the way, what do you mean, if we are to succeed?"

"Oh, don't let me worry you, it's just that if we do not succeed in building this place then we can all kiss any promotion ideas we have a fond farewell, that 'bastard', if you'll excuse the expression, has that kind of power. I've seen generals make a fuss of him as if he were the king, or more likely the queen. Me, well I just openly bloody hate the bastard and I don't trust him as far as I could throw him. He's meant nothing other than trouble for me every time we've met. Then again I shouldn't be saying this to another officer should I, sir?

"Mind you, I think this is just a rehearsal to see if this kind of thing can be done. We have to make it look real because of the Russian trawlers which are by now permanently fishing in these waters. Not that they ever catch anything though. I doubt if they would know what to do with any fish if they caught any. They do try to catch one or two of us now and again, though."

"What do you mean, never catch anything other than trying to catch you?"

"Well, occasionally they try to net us while we are out swimming. When they see us they cast their nets and make a trawl after us and it is a bloody dangerous game, I can tell you."

Just then that voice which I had always dreaded for years every time it crept up on me, but now after our earlier confrontation no longer frightened me, rang out.

"Johnston, this is not an Irish Bloody Parliament. You've always got too much to say for your own bloody good, haven't you? By now you should have been in the bloody water, and out there getting some of the stores into here."

"Yes, sir!" I replied with an exaggerated emphasis on the 'sir'. Out of the side of my mouth I muttered to the RE Officer, "See what I mean, hasn't a bloody clue."

With that, I went back up the passage with Nobby Clark in tow, but no longer as fast as the slippery slope and my little legs would let me. This time I took it easy. As it was we had the gear ready within minutes without any rush and all the lads were down in the cave standing by the shaft in the cave floor. This shaft which led down to the entrance of the tunnel which Brown had assured us debouched on to the Pentland Firth. It was my plan that all of them should be there when my team and I went in, just in case anything did go wrong. I'd decided to take Nobby Clark, and a young lad called Mick Smith with me initially. The rest of the group had banded into three teams of three and one of four, without my having to organise them.

The cave we were in was nowhere near the size of the main one, but large enough to rig the Royal Engineer's hand winch over the shaft. The shaft was about twelve feet wide and it looked very dark down there inside it. We could hear the sea more than see it in the darkness of the shaft. You could also feel the pressure of the swell as the sea surged in and out through the underwater entrance to the cave; I knew by instinct that controlling loaded pallets of stores in that tunnel was going to be very, very dangerous. We were yet to discover how wild it could get in that damned tunnel; or how bloody dangerous the work was going to be getting into the cave from the sea or out into the sea of the Pentland Firth from the bloody tunnel. There were times when the tightness of my wet suit was the only thing that stopped me shitting myself.

I will never as long as I live forget the first time I entered the water in that tunnel. The Engineer Sergeant had produced a guide rope above the shaft using a hook, which he had somehow secured to the roof of the cave. I dropped the rope into the shaft and kind of abseiled into the darkness without knowing what to expect. Much to my surprise the water seemed to be a good fifteen feet from the floor of the cave and about the same from the floor of the tunnel. Leaving the bulk of the rope at the bottom of the shaft for my two partners to follow me, I took the end of the rope and started out towards what I believed was the open sea. As I made my way along the tunnel I dragged the rope out with me as I swam. Within a minute or so I could feel the other two holding the rope and following me along the tunnel.

Having been underground in the cave and out of the wind for some time I hadn't realised just how rough the weather and therefore the swell of the sea had become out there off the north coast of Scotland. The surge of current in that tunnel was quite violent and getting worse all the time; so, when I saw the water starting to get lighter, and visibility around me getting better, I knew I was nearly out of the tunnel. Once I had cleared the cliff face I looked up towards the surface and then I looked at my depth gauge. One glance at it and I came to the conclusion that Captain Bloody Brown was talking out of his arse when he had said how deep the cave was. The next thing I did was to check the seabed. I had decided that if the tunnel entrance was not level with the seabed and there was the slightest height, even just two feet, from the seabed to the floor of the tunnel, then Captain Bloody Brown could kiss his exercise goodbye, but not for the first time I was 'pissed off' as they say. The bloody entrance to the tunnel sloped down in a gentle slope to the seabed, so I couldn't go back in and call the diving off over that now, could I?

It still took me quite a bit of hard reasoning at that point to stay where I was. My basic instinct was to return immediately to the tunnel and to head back in. Not because of the entrance, but because I was to say the least a little worried. My main worry was about other safe diving practices. The thought uppermost in my mind was that I didn't know of any decompression equipment within miles of the place. For some reason, and I don't know why, I decided against it. Later I thought that's just how much that man Brown's bullying tactics were affecting my tactical assessments. Oh, I'd given him some lip and got away with it, but that had been calculated bravado on my part. It was certainly not a very happy working environment in which we had found ourselves, yet I had no real case in disobeying his orders, except on the grounds of unsafe practice. If I did we would be in the realms of 'calculated risks', and I wasn't ready yet to face all the consequences of the full-blown court-martial that direct disobedience would bring down on my head. I knew that any objections by me would in the long run be construed as direct disobedience. Good old insubordination I could face, but as the group leader direct disobedience would be verging on mutiny and that means a hanging if proven, or maybe worse. So I just stayed where I was and I have to admit that as an agnostic I prayed and hoped nothing would go bloody wrong. Already I had been told that things must progress at a certain rate each day for it all to work and chances might have to be taken. I did however decide that when

I got back I would try and engineer a written order from him, just to cover my own arse.

The weather could not be allowed to hold up the work, so we had been told and with that in mind I decided that I'd done all the reasoning I needed to do so far and I readied myself to rise to the surface to check the surface weather. As I swam around I couldn't help but realise the enormity of the position in which we Marines now found ourselves. Doubts returned as I made my way along the seabed, because even down here on the bottom the current was quite strong. If that stupid bloody Brown thought for one minute that my happy band of pilgrims and I were going to get close to his bloody ships when they dropped their loads; then he had better think again. As good a soldier as he used to be, those days seemed to be over and he was not a frogman and once we were in the water then I'm afraid I would be in charge. So stuff you, Lord Haggis bloody Brown, out here I say what goes. He would have me shot at dawn if he ever knew I even thought like that; dumb insolence they used to call it; but I had to get this obsession out of my head and pay attention to what we were doing. I made myself a promise that none of my men were going to get killed on this job.

By this time the other two were alongside me and eventually we located some of the stores which Brown had mentioned were already on the seabed. They were secured to pallets and were lying on the seabed about three hundred yards out from the cliff. They were right opposite the mouth of the tunnel in the cliff that we had just left. At the time I thought it was bloody good shooting, for a blind drop that is. Nobby tied some cod line to the safety rope we were still using and connected the other end to these pallets and then the three of us made our way to the surface. I arrived on the surface first and a few minutes later Nobby and Mick came up alongside me. Nobby was shaking his hand and pointed to his watch and then upwards suggesting he thought I'd come up a little too quickly, but I just shrugged; it could only have been seconds, but it did set me thinking about a decompression chamber. I was certain that there wasn't one within a hundred miles of the place. In fact, we shouldn't be in the water at all if that was the case. Still it was more ammunition for my next round of sparring with Brown. I thought I'd been worrying too much about Brown and not paying enough attention to my drills. That's how you die, my lad, and very painfully, I thought. So get it bloody right from now on!

They both looked okay to me, but they both gave me the thumbs down, and shook their heads, that way indicating that neither of them liked the look of the job we had been given. Yes, I thought, yes mates I know it is going to be bloody dangerous here and we had all better be very careful from now on. If we had had an officer in charge he would have probably stopped the whole charade there and then, but we didn't have an officer and I hadn't the bottle to confront Brown just yet anyway.

Mick next pointed to the coast and as we rose and fell in the swell we could see the members of the other groups piling stores in small heaps on the beach. As we were watching the men on the beach the three of us noticed at the same time the old familiar beat of a ship's engines, also the unmistakable noises that ships' propellers make when they are rising clear out of the water in the swell. We turned to look out to sea and there, not more than half a mile away and heading straight towards us, was a small coaster of about six to eight hundred tonnes. It was really pitching and tossing. At times it looked to be standing on its nose, displaying the whole upper deck as if we were looking down on it. The next moment as we watched in awe we could see nearly its entire keel as it rode out of the top of the wave. There it seemed to hang for a moment or two before it went pitching down into the valley between the highs of the swell with its decks again fully visible to us. God, it was one hell of a sight and one I don't think I shall ever forget. As we watched I thought I'm not so sure if I'd like to be on board, or here where I am now. Here, I thought in the end, was the better place to be. I don't suffer seasickness in this kind of swell when swimming, but on board that thing I'd be throwing my insides over the side of the ship.

The lookout on the bridge must have seen us because he pointed in our direction. How it did it I shall never know, but the boat then manoeuvred itself until it was parallel to the coast and heading straight for us. Then when it was about twenty-five yards from us, the crew slipped a couple of pallets into the water from off the top of its one and only hatch. As the pallets passed us I thought, shit, if they snag this rope I have tied to my belt with their propellers it will be the end for me.

As I grabbed for the rope that was still attached to my waist, I turned to look and see where it was, only to find Nobby grinning at me from his mask. He was holding a piece of rope in one hand and his knife in the other. At first I thought I will kill the sod. Then I thought thank God he had the presence of mind to cut the bloody rope anyway.

When I turned back to look at the coaster, I saw the skipper was pointing to his starboard rear and he was shouting something. God knows how he expected us to hear what it was he was shouting and lip-reading in those conditions and at that distance was out of the question. So I just waved and gave him the thumbs-up signal as he sailed on and as he passed I could see him wave his arms as if in frustration.

Once he had passed us though, we saw immediately what it was he had been shouting about. Bearing down on us was one of the famous Russian trawlers, the ones that I have already mentioned, which was bristling with so many aerials that it looked like a cable and wireless station. Some bloody fishing boat, I thought, it is probably after flying fish. Just as I was about to give the other two the order to dive, I remembered what I had told the Royal Engineer Officer earlier. So better to be safe than sorry. I looked at the Russian again and sure enough he had a beam net over the side and near the surface. As the boat pitched in the swell, the fishing net kept coming clear of the water.

We were not certain at the time if he was after us or the stores that the coaster had just slipped. The thing was I could only hazard a guess and I assumed he was after the stores. He could not have seen us before he made his trawl so it had to be the stores. Signalling the other two to stay on the surface and swim towards the beach, I started to swim out to sea. After I had reached a position slightly to the north of the Russian course, I turned to face him. Next I took a red flare from my waist belt and after making sure he was still heading towards the drop, I sank below the surface until I was about ten feet down, then I fired the flare in as vertical a position as I could out of the water.

This red flare procedure is used by all NATO submarines when on exercise. They use it to record hits on enemy ships and I knew the Russian Skipper would know this; I was hoping he would think there was a submarine protecting the dropping site. He would therefore stop his trawling actions and clear the area.

All For A King's Shilling

Much to my relief, and I found out later to the relief of those lads who had been watching from the beach, that is exactly what he did. I didn't see it, but they said that he slipped his trawl and once he had done so he turned away from the area the three of us were in and made his way out to sea. As he went away from us he increased speed until he was outside the territorial limit. Nobody was more relieved than I; that he in his ultimate wisdom was returning to the three-mile limit.

Once I'd resurfaced I saw that he was on his way, and I was rejoined by Nobby and Mick, who had dived after the pallets. They had fastened the rope we had used as a guide rope on to the pallets that the coaster had just dropped. These pallets now hadn't very far to go before they reached the seabed. I indicated to the pair that we should follow them and it only took a little while before we sighted them. At first we all tried to influence their descent to the seabed, but without any consultation between us of how to proceed I realised that we were courting disaster so we gave it up and made our way along the rope to the ones we had found earlier. Then, after much 'huffing and puffing' as the expression goes, we finally managed to float and lever the first pallet we had found to the entrance in the cliff face of the tunnel from which we had earlier exited and which led back to the shaft in the lower cave. Leaving the pallet there, we swam back along the tunnel and surfaced into a bright floodlit shaft.

The Royal Engineers, who it seemed had been busy recovering some of their stores from the road, had also with a little bit of the old brute force and ignorance managed to get most of their equipment into the cave through the small entrance on the hillside. The Engineer Sergeant took great delight in telling me that he had managed to enlarge the entrance somewhat. He assured me this deed had made him just as much of a target as me in Captain Brown's eyes.

Amongst the boxes and bags he had managed to push through the cave entrance was one containing a small but very powerful generator. This he had used to light the passage leading to the cave area, where the shaft to the underwater tunnel was situated. So the whole area we were to work in around the shaft was well lit. I was relieved because the lighting made the work less hazardous for us. While we were bobbing up and down in the hole with the surge of water as it pushed in and out of the tunnel, the Royal Engineer Sergeant explained all of this to us. I then asked him to get the rest of the Royal Marines to come to the shaft area again and be ready to dive when told. While we were waiting for them to join us the Engineer Sergeant also explained how his winch system worked.

When my lads arrived I explained that I needed three more men in the water right now and the rest of them were to be ready and rigged to come to our rescue should any of us need rescuing, God forbid! I then explained the situation about the depth of water and water conditions on the seabed as well as on the surface. Oh, and I told them about the bloody Russian and what he was up to. Then I said that if any of them didn't fancy the dive I'd understand.

When I finished briefing my lads, I then told the Engineer Sergeant that we had managed to get the first pallet to the mouth of the tunnel. As soon as we got his winch cable we would go back out and connect it to the pallet. He and his boys could then haul it into the bottom of the shaft here. He nodded agreement to this and handed me the cable.

"But there is one snag!" I said as I took the winch cable from him. "That is there's no way whatsoever that I or any of my men will be able to guide this pallet or any of the pallets along the tunnel; that would be just too bloody dangerous. So we will have to hope it doesn't snag up on anything won't we? But if it does, then we will need to have some method for you to inform us first that you have turned your winch off and that it is no danger to us and, secondly, that it is safe for us to enter the tunnel to clear any snarl-up that may have occurred."

"It will probably make a hell of a mess in the tunnel and disturbance of any sediment will only make things worse, but as you say it would be bloody daft to try and help the pallet along. You'll just have to get used to swimming in thick, muddy water."

"That's no problem, I just don't want any of my men in that tunnel when your winches are working, all right? For the moment we'll use the line that is already in the tunnel. You give it a bloody big yank and continue doing so until we yank it back. Then stop your winch until we let you know we have cleared any obstacle by giving the rope three distinct pulls."

With that Nobby, Mick, and I and three other divers who had joined us in the water set off to bring the rest of the stores we had found to the tunnel mouth. As my team and I returned with the next pallet, the water in the mouth of the tunnel was as black as night, no vision whatsoever. It seems that the Engineer Sergeant had been right, because they had hauled the first pallet into the cave with a hand winch and it had scraped the floor of the tunnel and the sides of the shaft as well. This action had disturbed a lot of sediment from the floor and broken a lot of rocks from the sides of the tunnel and the shaft as they manhandled it up out of the water. As a result a lot of muddy water had been stirred up. The surge of the sea in and out of the tunnel was now dragging this out into the sea around the cliff where the mouth was. Looking at the mess, I was only glad we hadn't attempted to guide the pallet in by hand. We were also lucky we had the safety rope to work with; otherwise I hate to think what could have gone wrong trying to find the mouth of the tunnel. In all it took some ten hours, and all sixteen of our group had been in the water before we managed to get all the pallets out there off the seabed and into the cave.

As I hauled myself out of the water in the early hours of the next day a thought suddenly hit me. It was like a bombshell right between the eyes. I had been in the water when the coaster had dropped its load over the side. A point that I'd thought of at the time was that these pallets didn't hang around on the surface at all. They descended to the seabed in a rather fast fashion. Yet in all the hours we had been out there shifting those we had found and moving the gear from the beach, we hadn't given a thought to the fact that another coaster or ship of some sort might just as easily have arrived and dropped some more bloody pallets on top of us. I was going to have to reorganise my work groups or get a bloody timetable when these ships or whatever would be dropping stuff on top of us. I concluded we had been very lucky that first day, so I also decided in my wisdom that the less Brown knew about our progress the better.

We were sixteen very tired and worn-out divers when we made our way back into the main cave that night. What didn't help was to see that the only people who had done any unpacking of pallets were the Royal Engineers. None of the others had done

All For A King's Shilling

a stroke of work; they hadn't even unpacked their own kit that we had hauled from the beach for them. When I located Captain Brown I told him, "I am calling off diving for at least ten hours, sir."

"I am the one who says when diving will stop, Johnston. So you can get back in and get the rest of the gear in here, do you understand me?"

One of the other corporals was about to tell him that we had cleared the stores from the seabed, but when he saw my expression he shut his mouth and said nothing.

"Oh, yes, I understand you, sir, I understand you only too well, sir!" I replied.

There was an uneasy silence among the others as they watched the two of us eyeing each other up like two prancing gladiators. I watched him so closely as he tried to work out why I was so confident in my manner, but before he could guess what it was that gave me such confidence in my insubordination I got in before him. When I saw his throat moving I knew the tirade was about to come, so I got in first.

"Tell me, sir," (I was minded to say, "Tell me, kind sir," but thought better of it). Instead I went on, "And just what is it that we are supposed to breathe while we are down there in that cold black water then, sir, can you tell me that? Another thing, while we are on this subject of who tells who what to do. Have you made any provision for refilling our tanks? No, sir! You haven't given it a moment's thought, have you? Also, have you alerted any of the local authorities to the fact that they may receive some men with diving problems 'like the bends' for instance! It could all happen in the next few hours or the next few weeks. No, I bet you never gave it a thought, sir! There isn't a decompression chamber within hundreds of miles of this place, is there?" Then I thought, shit I'll bet there's one at Scapa Flow, but he didn't say anything. So now I had a full head of steam I thought I'd go for broke and stuff his bloody court-martial. I was about to go on and tell him some real home truths but as I was getting my first sentence together in my head he cut me short. He used the stock answer that they all use when confronted with any problem they don't understand or know the answer to.

He threatened that if I ever spoke to him in that manner again he would have me court-martialled for insubordination.

I looked at him for a moment or so, I'd expected more from him than that old standby, but I just said, "You do that, sir, but you will have a hell of a job explaining what qualifications you have to control diving activities. You would have got away with it a few years ago, but since the recent deaths in the branch due to unqualified men being in charge, I wouldn't give tuppence for your chances. There is one thing that is certain, sir, none of my men will enter that water again unless I deem it safe for them to do so. I don't care how many times you court-martial me, sir! You are breaking every rule in the book and you know it just as well as I do. I wonder just who it is who would come off worst at my court-martial, sir! I do know I'd do time and I'd lose my stripes, but that's nothing. As we all know NCOs are two a penny, but you'd kiss any advancement goodbye and you'd end up the oldest Captain in the Corps, or you would make the biggest gift to the Corps' silver fund ever, and as a parting gift at that, sir! Socially, sir, you'd be dead and you know it. So I expect that some sort of mobile decompression chamber will be parked somewhere near here by tomorrow, sir!"

With that he grunted and stormed off up the passageway. I was told later by the Royal Engineer's Officer that as he did so my shoulders visibly relaxed as I let out a large gasp of air.

Once Brown was out of sight I turned to the lads and told them to check all their equipment and what was left in the tanks. Captain Bloody Brown did not even know what was in the tanks. For all I know to this day I think he thought it was pure air. It never crossed his mind how it was that when we were in the water we never left any trace of bubbles.

When everything had been checked and we had replenished our tanks with oxygen from the oxygen tanks we had brought with us, and the return valves had all been cleaned and replenished each team checking each other's equipment to make doubly sure everything was alright, we all made our way into the rear of the large cave. Once there, we marked out an area for ourselves and collected our personal gear. Next we sorted out our sleeping areas and then we set to and started to cook ourselves a meal from items of compo food that I had had the good sense to bring with me from Poole. We had withdrawn from the rest of the people in the place and from that moment on we became a tight-knit little unit, keeping ourselves to ourselves and just getting on doing the job we had gone there to do. The only outsiders we had any contacts with were the Royal Engineers who were the only ones who dared approach the area we had picked out for ourselves; the rest we kept at a distance. We were a small self-contained unit and everybody fitted in well. This was to stand us all in good stead in the years to come and throughout the events that followed.

There was one incident that caused some amusement while we were cooking our meal. Nobby Clark was the first one to mention that we had some visitors. When I looked up, standing a few feet away were a group of the look duck and vanish lot. It seems they had sat in a huddle with their bits and pieces not speaking to anybody all the time the Engineers and ourselves were working, getting the stores into the place. Now the smell of food cooking had moved them to approach us with what looked like tin plates in their grubby little hands expecting no doubt 'a three course' spread.

Realising that I was the one who was going to have to tell them the facts of life I stood up from stirring a large tin of tea that I'd just made and asked the nearest one what he wanted, only to be told they had come to get their food.

"What food would that be then?" I asked him.

"The same as you are having," he replied without batting an eyelid.

Well, being still wound up over my altercation with 'Brown' I looked at them standing there and explained. "Look, the food we were cooking is our own food. It is food that I brought with me from our squadron stores. It is food we had left over from previous operations and we keep it for just such emergencies as this. If I hadn't seen fit to bring it with me then we would be in the same boat as you in a bloody cave somewhere in Scotland; being led by a, well you should know by now who and what the man is, who is leading us. So, gentlemen, as we only have enough to feed ourselves I'm afraid you had all better start looking for worms and grubs, because if we had no food that's what you would see us doing right now. Oh, and maybe you might even see a couple of us pinching some of his lordship's grouse or other birds that he keeps up here."

I was greeted with remarks like, 'that is our food just as much as it is yours'.

"I'm afraid not, gentlemen, this is food that my squadron had left after our last exercise and it is all we have until the man in charge of this little escapade decides to feed us. You no doubt heard me having a go at him about there being no food or fresh water here so you'll just have to wait; there is nothing I can do for you!"

At this point a rather angry man stepped forward and demanded some food.

The first thing that happened was that my men picked up all the food and moved away from where I was standing and starting to snort a little. The man must have looked into my eyes for the first time because he looked a little taken aback, and then he started to shake a little. "Look, mister, I don't know who you are, but you talk to me in that tone of voice again and I'll stick that plate, mug, knife, fork and spoon right up your arse. Now bugger off!"

While I stood looking at him and hearing the lads shuffling their feet behind me, I realised that if I did strike the man, I would be ostracised by the rest of the Marines for being a bully. So instead I repeated an old Marine saying I first heard about twenty minutes after joining the Corps and I said, "Look, mister, there is an old saying we have in this Royal Corps of mine and it goes like this.

"I care not for your predicament, Jack, for I am on the boat."

"More commonly expressed as, 'Fuck you Jack, I'm inboard', one of my men said.

Looking around the boffins I saw the look of disappointment on most of their faces, and seeing the Royal Engineer's Officer and Sergeant watching, I told the lads to see what food we could spare and I also asked the Engineers if they had anything to spare. Anyway, between us we managed to give everybody a hot drink and a small snack to eat.

About an hour later everybody had settled down and I set about the task of making our life a lot easier. I organised our group into four sections, each comprising four men. I then planned our work rota so that only one section would be in the water at any one time. One section would be the standby section and they would be situated in the area of the entrance to the underwater tunnel leading to the open water. The other two sections would be in our small base area. One of these would have their wet suits on, but would be resting. The fourth section would be completely stood down sleeping after just having come out of the water. These changeovers were to take place even if there were no stores to collect because we were waiting for a drop. I had while checking the area out found a ledge about a hundred yards from the tunnel entrance and about six feet above the high water mark. I told the men who were on duty in the water to spend their time there if we had cleared all the pallets from the seabed. They were on no account to tell anybody except the RE Sergeant when the seabed was clear and then make their way out to the ledge. There was no doubt that if my friend Brown found us out of the water with nothing to do he would have us doing the other group's work; and I was having none of that at all.

This way we were able to work a routine that was simple. As one section completed its time in the water and came into the complex, the standby section would take over their duties. The resting section in the base area would then replace the standby section and the sleeping section would then become the resting section. The section which had just left the water would then become the sleeping section. This way, everybody would get a fair amount of rest and just as importantly, would have time to keep themselves clean and their equipment clean and in good working order. We would then not be inclined to make the simple mistakes that tired men make and which nearly always cost lives. Always it seemed it would be some other poor sod's life.

So it was we went to work collecting stores from the seabed to build an underground control centre, a control centre into which the boffins would install all the equipment that was to be used to monitor the sonar buoys recovered by us from the seabed. The other men were the ones who were to help build the place and listen on the equipment for the Russian submarines as they crossed our line of sonar buoys. The sonar buoys stretched all the way from America to Scotland, by way of Iceland. They were the very same sonar buoys which I and others in the service had been told didn't work.

If the sole purpose of this charade was simply to hoodwink the Russians into thinking that all was well and the sonar buoys worked, therefore the great western technology really did work after all, well, why not just enlarge the entrance to this bloody cave? Build a tarmac road to it and ship the gear in overland. Much the same as they had already done with the early warning station at Fylingdales in North Yorkshire. The Russian fishing boats would be able to see what was going on, just as they had in Yorkshire. It would have the same effect as the project in Yorkshire, telling them the whole project worked okay. Secondly it would not be as dangerous as the episode we'd had out there off the coast of Scotland on the first day, but no it had to be done the hard way. So, the way my simple Corporal's mind worked, there had to be more to it than they were letting on, whomsoever 'they' were. I was convinced of this and certain that something else was going on. I believed some other game was being played, or was about to be played, and I was worried that I was becoming an integral part of it.

We had some frightening times up there on the north coast of Scotland. The sea in that area can change in a moment with no warning whatsoever. One minute all would be smooth calm and the next moment all hell would arrive and it would be the beginning of a hurricane type of storm then there would be mist and fog coming in from nowhere. The swell would rise more than twenty feet in less time than it takes to tell. Sometimes this rise in the swell would be followed by rollers up to fifteen feet high. It was only because of our excellent training, comradeship and the determination not to let our mates down that we did not lose any men or have anything drastic go wrong with the work we were doing. Even to this day I still marvel at the things we did up there and more importantly 'got away with', and 'getting away with' being the operative words. To me it was some of the best work I have ever done. We were of course very fit when we started and I must be honest, we did get fitter as the time passed. Then there was to come a time later when, like all fitness fanatics, we discovered we had overdone it.

To the surprise of all concerned we managed to fulfil all our tasks and we recovered every one of the loads that had been dropped off the various types of ships, ships that paid us unrelenting visits in all kinds of weather! After my first brush with Captain Brown that first night he was okay with us, but I kept a wary eye on him from that night on just the same. I always felt he was just waiting his chance to rip into us again, but to my relief he also kept his distance.

All For A King's Shilling

The Russian trawlers tried a couple of times more to net some of the stores, but thank God, each time they failed. The nearest they ever came to success was when they tried to net a couple of my divers. It was a very worrying moment for the two concerned, but in the end they just did a dolphin act and came out of the water over the top of the net and back into open water. They then swam as fast as they could for the rocky coastline. I was of a mind to go after the Russians with a couple of limpet mines, but I couldn't because we didn't have any. So as usual it was only my big mouth making hot air and blabbing off again. After that little incident, they must have thought better of it or so I thought; because they didn't try again; it just never entered my thick old head that they just may have been warned off.

The Engineers had more problems getting the stuff put together than we had collecting it from the seabed. After the first couple of drops we found it best to follow the loads to the seabed, then deal with them on the bottom, rather than to try and influence them during the descent. They did tend to make very erratic trips to the seabed anyway, swinging from side to side. We all decided it would be better for all concerned if the pallets made that trip themselves. We also came to the conclusion that whoever it was who was loading the damned things had no sense of balance or weight distribution. Just load the things in a factory, and send them on their way. Out of sight out of mind, it was also possible nobody had told the packers that their handiwork was being dropped in the sea off the northernmost tip of jolly old Scotland either.

Once the loads had reached the seabed we used a couple of balloons we had shaped from bits of equipment and tarpaulins; these we fashioned into balloon type parachutes and secured to a pallet, or depending on their size, maybe two pallets. Next we filled these balloons with air, using the tanks supplied to us on the second day.

Our guide who showed us to the place that first day turned up at the cave the very next day with a supply of oxygen and a compressor for our tanks and these new air tanks. So it was obvious that some planner somewhere had given some thought to this work, more so than one certain Captain who was not too far removed from us.

Anyway each time we used our mini parachutes we used just enough air to raise the pallet from the seabed. Once it was clear of the seabed we then moved the load gently through the water until we reached the cave entrance. There, we hooked up the engineers' cables and they hauled the items to the bottom of the shaft leading up to the cave. We had a line attached to the cable so when the Engineers had uncoupled it they gave it a good tug and we hauled the cable back to the entrance to the tunnel. This way none of us had to go into the tunnel until we had to change tanks or our spell in the water was over and it was time for a change-over. The Engineers took charge of the loads once they reached the end of the tunnel and hauled them out of the water while we went looking for the next pallet.

The only problem that did arise was that all the disturbance in the tunnel caused the water in it to be very dirty. Therefore, as the tide went in and out, eventually it created a large dirty stretch of water off the coast, making the entrance to the cave something that everybody in the area could see from the land, the sea or the air. Still, Brown was supposed to know what he was doing. I wonder how he explained that little lot away but then he was probably never bothered about it anyway.

William Atlay

Our part in the whole operation was over in the month they had allowed for it. This only went to give us a false sense of how good we were. I think we would have learnt more if we had encountered trouble in dealing with some of the tasks we had been given. Apart from the first couple of pallets we recovered, before the Royal Engineers had their haulage gear operating, everything went just fine. Still, we had been working in the cold waters off Northern Scotland for a month, and that in itself was an experience not to be forgotten. Also, none of our group suffered any illnesses that are worth mentioning and that was very good considering some of the things we have to do occasionally inside our wet suits.

The longer we worked at the task given us, the stronger was my opinion that from the start to the finish this whole operation was just a rehearsal for a more serious operation, something else the whiz kids of the security service had dreamt up for us. You see, when we finished and all the stores that had arrived were in the cave, although not built, we, the Royal Marines that is, were told we would be leaving in a couple of hours' time. It seemed to us that we were leaving the place with what seemed to be indecent haste. As it was, the ship or ships that were supposed to be carrying the underwater cable to the sonar buoys hadn't yet arrived. I kept asking myself who was going to bring the cable in through the tunnel now that it was all over for us. In the end I just gave up trying to fathom it all out and packed my kit ready to leave.

Before I left, I went to see the RE Officer. "Remember what I said the first day sir, that we'd all learn something. Well, I think we have both learnt something here this last month wouldn't you say?"

"Oh, yes, a month ago I thought we were on a fool's errand with a crazy RM officer and a mutinous bunch of Marines. I didn't believe that the task we had been given could be done and I believed that your men had been asked to commit suicide. Yet just look at that building and every bit of it lifted off the seabed. I do know that if we were allowed to tell anybody about this they wouldn't believe us." He then shook my hand and said, "Take care, Corporal, he'll get your stripes off you one day."

Maybe, sir, and then maybe I'll have his pips instead. I'm not as stupid as some 'tinkle peep I am'. With that I saluted him, turned on my heel and left the place.

Naturally, we thought we would at least be able to wangle a few days' leave out of it all and a bit of CO's leave would not come amiss, but that was not to be. We were all moved away from the place and back to the cross tracks taking all our gear with us. When we arrived at the tracks we embarked on to a couple of four-ton trucks and left in a westerly direction, a fact that caused a few discerning looks amongst us as we all knew the railhead by which we had arrived was the other fucking way.

Captain Brown addressed us before the trucks departed, telling us, "You have completed your part of the operation; you have said your farewells to your newfound friends. I would advise you to forget you have ever met any of these people. You lot are all off to better things, even a spot of leave maybe."

We had ribbed the others as some of them had helped us get our kit out of that bloody hole. Had they done the job they were sent to do right from the first as we had, then they would all be going on leave with us, we had chided them as we left to make our way to the track.

All For A King's Shilling

The month had been a rough old month and we had all been through some very hard working conditions, so not long after the vehicles set off, we were all sound asleep in the back of them. It could have been the fresh air that sent us to sleep, but whatever it was we were all out like the proverbial lights. We arrived not at a place to catch a train to Pompey or Guz as we had expected, but at a broken-down old army prefab camp. This camp was situated in the grounds of an equally broken-down old Scottish castle. A feeling of doom swept over me as I looked the place over when I alighted from the truck.

Captain Bloody Brown was there to meet us and he had with him one of his minions whom none of us had seen before and showed us to a building at the back of the castle. The building could not be seen from the road but at least it was habitable.

I've always hated that in the service you knew some smart arse officer would send you off in your trucks and then when you arrived at your destination, the same smart arse officer would be standing there to greet you. I think it is part of their trying to make out they are magic or something. A pain in the arse is all that they are really, why they do it I shall never understand. They think it has something to do with keeping the men's morale up. Somebody ought to tell them the only thing it does is get up our bloody noses.

The building contained the usual army beds and coir hair mattresses and it also had a pot-bellied stove in the centre of the room. We picked our beds, unpacked our personal kit and stored our diving gear in another room leading off the opposite end from where we had entered. Beyond that was a washroom with wash basins and two showers. We immediately started doing our dhobi and washing and showering. By the time we had completed all our ablutions and put on clean uniforms, it was supper time; we all ate a good meal of steak, egg and chips. This was followed by the old favourite 'Navy Cake and runny custard' washed down by strong sweet tea. By nine o'clock we were all sound asleep again. The stodginess of the Navy Cake was working well but not before I thought where did that bloody navy cake come from? Navy cake is made from leftovers from a previous meal. So where had it come from? Then I was sound asleep as were the rest of the men.

Next day we mustered in one of the rooms of the main castle once they were satisfied none of us had done a bunk during the night. A Captain, another person whom none of us knew, then told us, "You have all done a good job and maintained the Corps tradition."

Boy oh boy, what bullshit they manage to come out with at times like this. The problem is they have this twisted notion that we believe the silly so and so's.

"Bully, bully and jolly old hockey sticks, does that mean we will get an extra week's leave out of this?" one of the lads said.

Ignoring the remark, the Captain went on, "You have just completed a very hard and difficult job. In fact not only have you done well, but you have done an excellent job in very adverse conditions. What's more there are a lot of experts, some in your own branch of the Corps, who said it was impossible to do what you and your men have just completed. That was why we chose you young lads instead of the old hands."

I looked at Mick Wilson sitting on my right and whispered, "We were expendable. The bastards, there had better be an extra two weeks' leave here, mate."

"Not quite," said the Captain who was now talking again. "Maybe later you will get some leave, but not yet awhile. Well, not for you, Corporal Johnston; we have another small job for you and some of the others, eleven of you in total. Captain Brown has made a selection of the men he wants for the next phase of the operation. He wants you as the Sergeant in charge of the group, Corporal Johnston. So you will see the Commanding Officer after this briefing to be promoted Acting Sergeant and the following Corporals and Marines will be going with you."

He then read out the names of the others who would be going with me wherever it was that I was about to go. That was how the final group were chosen, but looking back I'd be inclined to say we had been railroaded. Three teams of three men in each section and another two as reserves in case anybody should drop out. Eleven in all as the man said. At the end of it all you could have heard a pin drop in that room. As for the lads who had not been chosen to take part in this next phase, well, they really looked most upset at being left out. That is until you looked in their eyes then you saw they were really laughing their bloody heads off.

The Officer who had told us all this good news looked at me and said, "You must have impressed old Brown; he has never asked for anybody by name before."

I just thought, oh shit! Why is it always me? He bloody knows I hate his bloody guts and still he picks me for the task.

Once the Officer had left the room, I was given the usual ribbing about how I got the promotion. Remarks like 'who's got a brown nose then?' and 'who has had two fingers up?' are some remarks that spring to mind along with the usual piss-taking which occurs in these circumstances.

What happened next was very predictable. The group of us who had been selected for greater and better things were immediately confined to camp for the next two nights. All we did after a complete check of our equipment was to submit a list of stores and parts required to bring everything up to operational standard, then it was heads down, there being nothing else to do. The other lads had left and I presumed had gone back to our base in the south of England. On the third morning we paraded in the courtyard where they issued us with some strange bits of kit. Small, fountain pen-sized items, which we had little time to look at or become conversant with. When you looked into the open end of them there was a meter type of scale at the other end. They told us just to put them away and not to lose them. We then immediately loaded our stores and set off for the north coast of Scotland again. As we were making this trip the thought occurred to me that no one had given any consideration to the fact that the others, who had gone south, if asked where we were, would tell whosoever was listening where we were and exactly what we were doing.

That part of service logic has always bemused me. We were being held incognito so to speak and the others who were not selected to do the job, but knew every little part of it, were being released to the world at large. I'm one of those people who believe that the person who is going to give the game away is not one of those going on a mission. Would you for instance tell an enemy that you were about to attack him or infiltrate his territory? No, sir!

No, it is more likely to be somebody in the backup, or at worst one of those not chosen to go who for some reason takes his not being selected as a slur on his ability. It could even be somebody who probably knows more than he or she should and just to gain personal stature more than anything else, tells all. The person opens his or her mouth in a bar, dance hall, cafe or whatever. It could also be that he or she just wants to achieve fame and standing among his mates, always giving others the impression that it is he or even she who is the fountain of knowledge, the trusted one and therefore knows all that is going on. Sometimes they are just showing off to others, or in some cases it is just plain old-fashioned greed that drives them. For fame or money the person talks too much or in the presence of the wrong people, but enough of this depressing subject. Again, I wasn't thinking too deeply at the time.

There is one point I'd like to make here. Neither I nor any of the men who stayed in Scotland with me ever to my knowledge saw any of the men who went south again. I never heard of them or met anybody who had met them or served with them after that time. Now I found that odd over the years; until later, that is, but I should have seen it.

Anyway, after what seemed like hours in the back of the truck, we arrived at a small cove on the coast. In the darkness we could just make out a couple of typical crofters' homes situated on the top of the cliff. At the bottom of the cove on the right-hand side was a small jetty. A path led to the jetty down the left of the cove and then about half way down it crossed over to the right-hand side of the cove. This path was about three feet wide and it was new. The jetty itself was about six feet wide, and had been cut out of the side of the cliff. It also was newly constructed. The whole setup did not look as if more than a couple of months had passed since it was built, if that! We carried all our gear down from the truck; that took us two trips to achieve, then we just sat and waited on the jetty. Nobody said anything at all, not a bloody word was spoken as we sat there. It was as if a sense of foreboding had come across us. We all just sat there, each with his own thoughts, not even looking at one another.

I was wondering just what I had got myself into. Captain Brown had promoted me Acting Sergeant back at the camp, but I was beginning to think I would have probably been a lot better off just waiting for my promotion in the normal way. After all, once I had completed whatever job it was they had for me and my usefulness to them was over they would put me back to Corporal in the blinking of an eyelid.

When we had been there for about an hour just sitting and dozing on our kit deep within our own thoughts, we heard the chugging of what I thought was the engine of a whaler. Looking up I nudged Nobby and Mick and the three of us looked out into the cove. Rounding the east point of the cove was this rather unkempt looking whaler, with a solitary matelot in the stern as it continued to chug its way up to the jetty. Once the whaler had arrived a couple of the lads took the lines that this matelot threw to us and secured the whaler to the jetty.

This matelot then looked up from the stern of his boat and had the audacity to say, "Right, you lot, let's be having you, we haven't got all day, you know."

He looked a little taken aback as a voice from within the group said, "If you want to live much longer, Jack, you will have all the time in the world, okay?"

"You can cut that kind of talk, you big rough and tough Marines don't frighten me," he said.

"If you had any sense, then these ones would," the officer replied.

"Oh, sir," the matelot said, "I didn't see you there, sir!"

I just looked at the two of them and said, "I don't see what his being an officer has got to do with it, Jack!"

All I got was a grunt and a rather stupid look, which I think he thought was his tough look. The young officer looked at me and said, "I trust you will not harm him."

"He will be all right, sir, we've all eaten once today."

Within a couple of minutes all our gear was loaded and the whaler was cast adrift from the jetty; and our matelot took us out to sea in what I believed was not a very seaworthy boat. I stood in the boat and watched the young officer on the jetty until we rounded the headland and he disappeared from view. Mick had been watching me as I did this and he asked. "Do you think that officer knows something we don't?"

"Yes, I think he knows a lot more than any of them have thought fit to tell us, I think we have landed ourselves into something too big for any of us, and far too bloody dangerous mate. I'm beginning to get just a little worried about it all and I'd advise you to keep alert from now on. It looks to me as if it is nearly time to find out where the nearest sick bay is, a few days' light duty would not come amiss right now, mate."

Most of the lads heard me and after exchanging glances with one another they were silent for the rest of the trip.

After another half an hour on a sea that resembled a mirror we came across a dockyard ocean-going tug. This we were told was the vessel which was to take us to our new destination. Once the whaler was secured alongside the tug in no time at all we had transferred our gear to the waist of the vessel and climbed aboard ourselves. Then when we were all aboard, the whaler cast off and without a word the matelot sailed off into the darkness of the night and that was the last any of us ever saw of him. He disappeared back into the darkness of the night from which he had come. I thought there goes a person who crossed our path this once and he will probably never be seen or heard of again by any of us. He had made no impression whatsoever on any of us; he could have been the Bloody Flying Dutchman for all we knew. For his sake I hoped it stayed calm until he reached land in that thing that he called a whaler, or he would be in deep trouble.

After he had disappeared into the darkness I turned to Nobby and Mick and said, "You know that silly bloody matelot has no navigational lights on that whaler of his."

"That's his fucking problem," they both said in unison and that was the end of the conversation about him, but to this day I marvel at how he found that bloody tug at all in the total darkness of that night.

We then spent the rest of the night trying to get what sleep we could in and around the tug's superstructure; most, if not all of us, were wrapped around the hot air vents around the superstructure.

The next morning the tug arrived off the Island of South Ronaldsay, which I think is in the Orkneys. We arrived there just before dawn and the crew did us proud. They provided us with a really good breakfast and they let us use their heads and showers with stacks of good hot water. After that I felt a lot better and I had thrown the feeling of doom off by the time we disembarked in a small cove to set up a base camp. The tug had a load of stores for us and we now had fresh food, tents, cooking

All For A King's Shilling

equipment and a rubber boat complete with an outboard motor. So, with all these stores we built a camp just up from a beach on the rocky south coast of that lovely Island. Once everything was set up, we took it in turns to do some practice dives in our sections. We didn't do too much that first day, mainly just practising working together, improving on the work skills that we had been using at the last place we had been. Working in groups of three instead of the teams of four which we had worked in took a little time to sort out. Although by night time we had things pretty well sussed, we had all been fed and I briefed them on a guard roster for the night. "Can't trust these bloody Vikings, you know," and then I thought to myself, if you lot only knew the half of it.

It was during the next day that the great and lordly Captain Brown arrived. He told us, "You have all worked excellently on your last operation."

So the exercise! has now become an operation, was the remark that crossed my mind. I wondered why all the pussyfooting had gone on. Why could they not call it a bloody operation from the start? Still, an exercise is to see if plans work, an operation is when you find out they fucking well don't.

This praising thing was something he had already done more than once and I had to admit I was getting a little worried about him; it wasn't like him to keep making a point of praising us, or anybody else for that matter. Let alone this harping on that he was doing now. What is it they say about Greeks bearing gifts, 'beware', well, if its officers be doubly aware, because the bastards are certain to be out to screw you!

He went on, "You are now going to practise some of the finer points in which you will need to be proficient for the next part of the operation."

It turned out that was his way of saying that we were to spend a couple of weeks practising getting in and out of submarines.

I promptly informed him, "Sir we all know how to get in and out of submarines, we do most of our work from submarines, getting in and out of them is old hat to us, so what's new?"

I could tell by the way he looked at me that I might just have lit a very dangerous fuse, but he went on. "You do not normally operate the way you will this time. This time you are going to have to enter and leave the submarine while it is submerged, not at deck level on the surface and it may also be under way when you are getting in and out of it."

They told me my mouth fell open at that, as did theirs; even so, I managed to say what had flashed through my mind to him and anybody else interested, "That's a bloody dangerous way of making a living sir, one I'm not too happy about. Shouldn't we have been given a choice in this matter?"

"No," was the only reply I got.

"Well sir, if we have no choice in the matter, then the sooner we get started the sooner we all get killed, the sooner you will know what it is you are up against, won't you?"

"I'll have those stripes off your arm if you don't watch it Sergeant!"

"I'm sorry sir, it must be the tiredness; did I get my words mixed up!"

"That's the spirit," he said.

Spirit! Spirit! Is it shit the spirit? I thought. I was rapidly going off this 'operation' as he now kept calling it. Not a bloody exercise any more, now it's a bloody 'operation'. To some people I might be splitting hairs and being pedantic, but I'm a pedantic hair-splitting bastard by nature. To me an exercise has always been just that, a practice to make sure your battle drills work. 'Operation' – well to me an operation means fighting, possibly to the bloody death and all that shit to me spelt bloody trouble, big bloody trouble. We were not even at bloody war, so why the fucking hell was he talking about 'operation'! I'm bloody missing something here and these bloody men with me are like a set of bloody sheep.

Looking at Nobby and Mick I tried to get some sort of reaction from them and I said, "Operations take place in two places, battlefields or bloody hospitals. We are not at war with anybody, are we? There are no hospital cases amongst us yet are there, apart from the fact that the lot of us should be in bloody Netly. So why does he keep talking about an 'operation'? Just what the fuck is going on, what is this 'operation' bit he keeps talking about? I left Poole to go on an exercise, not a bloody operation. I know now that I should have deserted half way between Poole and London!"

They just looked at me shrugged their shoulders and said nothing.

"Bloody great help you two are." I growled at them.

"You're the bloody Sergeant, you tell him to get stuffed!"

That's when I shrugged my shoulders. I'd decided to go along for the ride. A thought did cross my mind. I could out-swim the lot of them so I should have grabbed as many bottles of gas and air as I could carry and jumped into the bay and fucked off to Norway or Sweden, but I cast it aside as the stupid idea that it was. I'd probably only get half way and some silly bloody Scots fishing boat would rescue me, knowing my bloody luck of late.

So, reluctantly, bloody reluctantly, we started two weeks of embarking on submarines and sailing out to sea and disembarking, but it wasn't quite that easy though. First, the submarine would submerge and then make a run for the shore, once it was in a position the skipper thought safe! Safe! Shit, we were never safe getting in and out of their bloody submarines even in harbour, never mind at sea. We then had to swim to a designated spot on the coast. There we had to recover a small piece of equipment from the shore, return to the submerged submarine and re-enter it under water. This we would do three or four times each day, each team taking it in turns to practise the drills. The remainder were fully kitted out at alert stations just in case anything went wrong, which thank God more by good luck than good management, it never did. The problem, however, was that we were in our bloody wet suits all flaming day long with all the problems that entailed. Some days the smell in the compartment we occupied was just about bearable.

Come the second week we started to do much the same, with just one slight, but very frightening difference. Because of supposed enemy activity the submarine would be on the move as we launched from it. Once we were clear of the sides, the black hulk would disappear into the dark murky waters of the sea. My worst fear during this time was being run down by one of the bloody black monsters. We now had two of them playing silly buggers with us and in the same area at the same time.

Not satisfied with the way they dumped us in the sea we, the arse holes of the outfit that we were, well, we would then have to try and find the submarine and re-enter the bloody thing again under water. This had to be done not while she was stationary on the bottom. No, sirree, just to make it more exciting, we had to re-embark while the bloody thing was under way. It was the most dangerous and stupid training I have ever done and to my mind it was pure madness. Of the two submarines with which we were working, one skipper who must have thought along the lines that I did said it was madness to expect us to find the submarine after it had moved. The other skipper just said we were useless if we could not find his submarine after it had moved.

And a bloody Merry Christmas to the two of you as well; I bet the bastard who thought this little lot up has never been near water; no nearer than his own bloody bath, playing with his little yellow rubber ducks or little coloured something else.

After the two weeks of this playing silly buggers with them had passed and after we had had to surface several times because our tanks were becoming contaminated, I asked Captain Brown if he, the two submarine skippers and I could have a little talk just to get it all ironed out as tempers were getting a little frayed and some poor bastard just might get killed; a suggestion to which – much to my surprise – he agreed. During our little conference it came to light that the submarine skippers were, like Captain Brown, non-swimmers. That is, non- swimmers compared to the way my men and I are classed as swimmers, but worse still, neither of the skippers had worked with frogmen before.

After some bickering around the table, I asked if I might put a suggestion to them and they agreed. So I said, "If the submarine we are working from has to move its position because of enemy activity once we have launched from it, then it follows it would be rather stupid for me and any of my men to be swimming around looking for it." Before anybody could make any comments I went on, "Both of you tell me you are confident an enemy with all the complicated equipment he possesses cannot find you. Why is it that for some unexplained reason you both believe that we Marines who don't have any equipment more sophisticated than a field torch (and to my knowledge the Marines have never had any equipment more sophisticated than that) can find your submarines when you have moved them to a new position?"

The sympathetic submarine skipper nodded agreement with me, so I became really brave and suggested, "Perhaps it would help to eliminate the problem if we hung around near the surface, or even went to ground on land, for that matter, when we see any enemy activity in the submarine's area. The submarine could wait until all was clear and once everything had settled down again and the danger had passed it could then make its way back to the approximate area where it had been when we had left it. We could then meet up with it again when the coast was clear. Even if this took two days or more, it would be far better than trying to catch a submarine that was dodging enemy hunters while we were swimming around like demented cod looking for it. We are not talking about catching a train on the London Underground, you know," I concluded.

When I'd finished I watched them. I could see their minds tick-tocked through the idea. The thought came to me that I could be the first Corporal to be promoted to the rank of Sergeant, then in the short space of two weeks to be demoted to the rank of 'Sub Mariner'. There must be a Corps record in there somewhere. To my surprise they both accepted the plan, but being who they were could not resist making one or two little refinements to it just to assert their authority. I didn't care. No, that's not right; I didn't give a shit really, just so long as we stopped the stupid way we had been going on before some poor bastard got killed.

Well, we tried the system out over the next couple of weeks and it all worked surprisingly well. Each time the submarine moved, we went to ground on the island, and after an allotted time we set off again to make the rendezvous. Each time it went very well; nine out of ten times it worked first time. The next thing was that Captain Brown brought some other troops on to the island to look for us when we were stranded ashore waiting for the submarine to return. This was when it all developed into some of the most realistic training for an operation that I have ever done. At the end of the six weeks' training – the period to which it had been extended – Captain Brown and the troops he had brought in never knew if we were on the island, in the water or in the submarines.

I don't know about anything else, but I know the whole episode set me, and perhaps some others, wondering just how often well-trained men from other nations – for instance, the Eastern Bloc of countries – were perhaps landing on these island shores of ours without anybody knowing anything at all about it, because if we could do it so easily, then to me it was obvious others could do likewise. It also made a mockery of all the wartime shit about the Germans never landing spies or anybody else for that matter on our shores before or during the Second World War!

That, of course was a problem for other more senior people than me to fathom out. It wasn't a job for the likes of me. Like the rest of the rank and file of the armed forces I would probably become involved in guarding the coast. I didn't want to spend hours on end wandering up and down the shore looking for bloody Russians or anybody else for that matter. If the authorities in London ever did decide to do something about it, well to my way of thinking, that would be time enough to get involved, once the 'powers that be' decided to act and not before. I'm just a silly old Acting Sergeant, not an admiral, general or politician.

Once the training ended we returned to Portsmouth on one of the submarines. At Portsmouth we were taken off the submarine out to Spithead under cover of darkness. It looked to me as if Brown really was bloody serious this time. From there, we were taken first to a camp that was along the coast from the Royal Marines Barracks at Eastney. The next day we were moved to the South Downs in covered vehicles to a large country house, there they kept us incommunicado for nearly a week. We had all the facilities of any camp except we had no contact with any other people outside our own group at all. Even the staff in the house didn't talk to us. The food was very good and the sleep and rest, well, they were really welcome. It was of course too good to last and it was on the fifth day that the great and lordly Brown deigned to visit us. When I saw Captain Brown I turned to Nobby and Mick and said, "I am really beginning to detest this bastard; he is starting to cause us too much pain and bloody suffering every time we meet him, I wonder what plans he has for us now?" I would soon learn that this was another missed opportunity to desert!

Chapter Three
Off To God Alone Knows, But My Money Is On Russia!
Russia, The Arctic Circle 1958

"Train arriving at Platform Seven is not for Normal People."
The above announcement was made on the public address system at Plymouth North Road Station, in 1989, when a Troop Train arrived at platform seven and 45 Commando Royal Marines were about to board. The said train was en route to Northern Ireland when the troubles in that part of the UK had once again reared their ugly head!

The eleven of us arrived back in Northern Scotland in the cold and dark one night in the third week of September, where we were met by a very officious Naval Rating who then proceeded to take charge of the move from the station to a small fishing village. As I looked at him it occurred to me that the Navy for some reason best known to itself must have transferred all the offensive ratings it had to land-based jobs in Scotland.

When we at last arrived in the small fishing village we immediately began to embark along with all our kit on to a small coastal type of tug. This time we had two sets of diving equipment each. We had also been issued with a load of extra Arctic clothing, survival equipment and most frightening of all, full first line ammunition. Playing silly buggers is one thing, carrying live ammunition to boot; well that is an entirely different ball game, and I at last accepted that it was definitely an 'operation' and no longer an exercise.

This large and very unfit sailor even had trouble getting in and out of the cab of the three-tonne truck that he had ridden in, and here he was chivvying us to load the extensive amount of gear that we had with us, on to the tug. The man really was large and fat; moreover it seemed to me that he had a large, fat, useless mouth. He had no respect for his fellow man, regardless of who that man was. He would no doubt soon be retaking his annual swimming test if he continued shouting his mouth off for much longer; an event which would be sooner rather than later, if one or two more of the lads had anything to do with it.

I was about to 'put him in the picture' and to tell him that he should pay more respect to my men; men who in my mind were a lot more important to this country's defence than he would ever be; men who were headed for God knows what, and fully loaded with live ammunition to boot, while he would remain at home in his cosy little job. Whatever that job was didn't interest me, but I bet he had a couple of pints in his local every time a door opened. Then back home to his little wife who probably thought he was an admiral, but in the end I thought better of it and said nothing. Which was just as well really, for just then one of my lads dropped one of his Sterling submachine gun magazines. As the magazine clattered to the ground, a couple of live rounds fell out of the magazine and these ended up between this matelot's feet. He looked down at them for a moment, then his mouth fell open and for the first time I realised what the expression, 'A picture is worth a thousand words' really meant. He was, not surprisingly, extremely quiet from that moment on; gone also was all the bombast he had shown earlier.

Perhaps I should point out that I have developed some very strong and evil thoughts about matelots. I've always thought that they have three sixes tattooed on their bodies somewhere. It has been my belief for years that once they finish their basic shore training, they should then be placed on ships and kept outside the three-mile limit until their demobilisation, a tactic used by ships' captains that used to be widespread during the days of sail. Perhaps Nelson had the right idea all along.

Once we had got our gear aboard the tug, we tied it down as best we could on the rear deck as the tug cast off. It then set sail into the darkness of the night, to the west of the Pentland Firth. Again the sea was quite calm, rather like a millpond. Not as rough as it had been only a short time earlier, when we had been up here working out of the cave.

Eventually we arrived alongside a submarine belonging to our gallant Royal Navy. This was the submarine we had come to join, along with all our gear. So, with a little help from the crew we managed to get all our gear on to the deck casing and scrambled aboard ourselves. Again we were chivvied along, this time by a member of the crew, as it was too dark for me to make out who the big mouth was I had to button my lip; but that day just hadn't been a very good day for me. I was starting to foster a feeling of even greater hatred for the members of Her Majesty's Britannic Navy. I might add that in my case this was a prolonged dislike of all things 'Navy' and it stayed with me for a long, long, time.

At last, when my merry group of pilgrims was safely aboard the deck of the submarine the tug cast off. The fat sailor with the large mouth who had chaperoned us disappeared into the night along with the tug and its crew. It is possible, and most probable, that the man lived his life out getting on the nerves of just about anybody and everybody he ever met; he was just that kind of man. Perhaps he was like the characters in the 'BO' adverts. 'Nobody ever told them'. So, there was another lesson I'd learnt about life, even if you shout your big mouth off very few people will ever remember you; but I was getting sick of seeing matelots disappearing into the night. I don't know why, but it was always at bloody night. For some reason best known to them the authorities who organised these moves always seemed to organize them to take place during the night. Every time I have been sent anywhere it is always at night. I've sailed to the Far East at night, I've flown out of Heathrow again at night, always bloody night time.

The submarine we had joined was it seemed much to our disgust to become our home for the next week or two or so we thought. The moment I put my feet on the submarine's deck I had a premonition that night that some of us would have suffered some very frightening experiences before we saw the last of that particular bloody submarine. Frightening experiences which most of us would rather not have had to suffer in the company of a submarine's crew. For my part I would have preferred for us 'Royals' to have had all our frights on our own, thank you very much.

We had barely got in the damned submarine before the Captain was playing holy hell and hurrying us to stow and lash our kit securely as he wanted to get under way. Lying still in the water like this was to him hazarding his boat. So he made encouraging remarks like, "If you don't get a move on, I'll leave it and the lot of you floating in the sea."

My first reaction was to tell him I didn't give a shit anyway. I'd just put his name on the G10-998 to write off the stores. Then he would be the one who would have to explain why he had left us and the stores floating in the Pentland Firth; but life in the services isn't like that; in no time at all we were all below decks and all the hatches we'd used were secure. So I failed to see what all his huffing and puffing was about.

It has always been my belief that all that puffing and posturing is no more than a means to exerting their authority. To let us mortals know that we weren't welcome at all in their bloody boat. They treat you as an intruder in their special world, and they are the kings of all they survey and they really are kings of all they survey. There is something Masonic about submarine crews, their closeness and the rituals which they live by. One thing that never seems to enter their tiny minds is that perhaps, just perhaps, we don't want to be in their bloody submarine anyway. It is their own little Masonic world and for my part they can shove it!

Mind you, I have always found that the first few days you arrive anywhere in the service people in authority always seem to be like that, belligerent towards you. Perhaps it is something to do with the pecking order of the life that they have established. People think for some obscure reason that newcomers are likely to take away some of their standing. The problem is that these strange environments nearly always cause you to get agitated and then you perspire. You feel unsure of yourself and it is normally at that critical point that some person from that new environment which you have entered knocks you off balance. Normally by making some silly, stupid and irrelevant remark that has nothing to do with why you are there in the first place. This I have always found is at the most critical time for anyone joining a new environment, especially for NCOs. It is not really the sort of thing you need to happen to you, at least not when you think you are about to put your life on the line. Not that any of us thought that we were about to put our lives on the line, that is. Still, when they issue you with first line ammunition just before you leave your base to go on an exercise, oh, sorry, I mean operation, it does help to 'concentrate one's mind' somewhat.

From experience though, I have found that the best way to deal with these people is not to argue with them at all. Just put on a blank expression and remain quiet then as they say in Yorkshire 'say nowt'. They will always come round in the end, first they try the chat-up line to find out who you are. Then, when they at last realise you are not trying to usurp or knock them from their little perches they will try to find out why you really are there.

They will ask the obvious questions like, "Why are you travelling with us, mate?"

Notice you have suddenly become a 'mate'.

"Where is it you are going, mate?"

Again the "mate" is added.

"What it is you are going to do once you get there, mate?"

Again notice the "mate"!

It is as if the word 'mate' is the key to all doors they want to open.

There is one thing you can bet your last dollar on; the Captain will not have briefed them on your exact mission if he has even briefed them at all.

There is always some smart arse matelot who will reckon he knows it all though. He will make out that he knows all there is to know about you; why you are there, what it is you are going to do and why you are going to do it. He will be miles off the mark of course, but within hours he will have most if not all the lower decks believing him, with his nudge, nudge, and wink, wink attitude. Now this is the point where you have got them. Don't tell the bastards anything. It really grits the shit out of them having to remain in the dark. Each one of them has this unsatisfied, built-in desire to be the one who knows the real reason for your presence. Mainly so he can strut and parade around the place as the only one who knows what is really going on. The 'confidant' of the 'embarked force' whom all outsiders entering their close-knit community become known as.

We had been at sea for a couple of days when we at last surfaced in a fjord on the northwest coast of Norway. During the voyage we had done as many checks on our equipment as we could in the cramped conditions of the after torpedo compartment … a task which was difficult due to the restrictions of space imposed upon us because of the members of the ship's company who were working in the place. The main reason we did this check was just to make sure nothing had been damaged in the rush to get aboard the submarine and get our kit stowed.

After the submarine had surfaced in the fjord, the Skipper let us go up in our section groups to the deck space just to the rear of the conning tower. Once there, we could get some fresh air and the smokers amongst us – who numbered about six – could have a smoke. We could see the lights of the town of Harstad in the distance and it looked deserted, but of course it was in the middle of the night. 'See, everything was being done at night again.' Even so it was still not as dark as I felt the Captain would have preferred. It was that half light, half dark situation you get a few weeks before the full onslaught of the darkness of deep winter. I'd returned below and it was about half an hour later that I was called to the conning tower, this time by the Captain. That would have been about an hour after we had first arrived in the place.

When I arrived on the bridge nobody spoke to me and I was starting to think I shouldn't be there. After about five minutes my eyes had become accustomed to the dim light and the Skipper told me, "We have called here to pick up your Commanding Officer; he is in that Norwegian cutter, which is about to come alongside. Your Commanding Officer, Sergeant, has flown from England with the final orders for

All For A King's Shilling

this operation and once we have him aboard we shall be sailing immediately. From this moment on, we will all be working under very strict orders. All ranks from the moment we dive will be under strict active service discipline."

I was about to say that I always worked under very strict orders, but changed my mind and just nodded.

"In fact Sergeant," he went on. "We are from the moment we slip completely on our own, incommunicado! If anything goes wrong from here on in our Government will deny all knowledge of us."

"Tell me something new!" I nearly said, but managed to stop myself in time. Then I nearly committed suicide as I was about to ask him if 'incommunicado' was one of Gilbert and Sullivan's, but instead I finally said. "Very good, sir!" I couldn't think of anything else to say and I hadn't understood why I was up there anyway; what's more I really am not one for making small talk with submarine skippers anyway or any other type of skippers. Looking back in hindsight I should have become immediately insubordinate and got myself locked up and court-martialled and put away for years, but I didn't, being the arsehole that I am. Dangle a third stripe in front of me and I'm like a horny recruit outside a brothel. I'll do anything to get it.

During the two days since I had joined the submarine I had looked everywhere for some of the ratings whom I had got to know on the two submarines that we had worked with in Scotland, thinking that this was one of them. I'd spent a little time looking for them, but I didn't see any of them, not even the cook whom I'd got to know quite well. A main priority that, for people serving in units like the ones I served in; but I didn't see any of the men I'd got to know in the other two submarines. The ones in which we had done our training off Ronaldsay; but as soon as I'd got a good look at the Captain when we were in Harstad I knew why. This was a different boat; submarines to me are all the same, black on the outside and smelly on the inside. The only pronounced difference in them is that the crews are different. The skipper on this boat struck me as a man out to make a name for himself, which to my mind could only mean that we were in dead trouble. When you serve with men like 'this leader of men', you normally end up with medals; the only problem is that mostly they are posthumous.

The problem that I believed we had when I realised that we were on another boat was that all the time we had spent, and so much time at that, practising being launched from, and being recovered by the other boats underwater off South Ronaldsay Island, was now of no avail. We were now operating from a different boat altogether and it was doubtful this boat's skipper knew anything about our recent training. It makes one wonder why we bother training to get drills honed to perfection, because they must have known all along that we were in the end going to have some other commander who didn't know what drills we had practised and perfected to make the plan work, whatever that plan was. At that moment I remember that I felt really dejected and worried, worried for my own life as well as my men's lives. What I would have given to have been in the Middle East right then, getting a good tan and serving in one of the three Commandos.

Once our Commanding Officer was aboard, true to the skipper's word the submarine headed for the open sea. To this day I never have understood why he called me to the conning tower that night we picked up my OC. All that happened was that I stood looking over the side as he disappeared into the base of the conning tower. When we sailed we did so on the surface and yes! you guessed it. When we had cleared the fjord we turned and sailed south on the surface. I had the feeling that if the Skipper's brains were ever to function fully, he would be bloody dangerous. Any fools observing us pick up an officer, who had just flown into the Norwegian Air Force base at Bardufoss from England, and a man dressed in a uniform that was not a Navy uniform, Norwegian or English, but a man who was wearing a 'para' smock, well I ask you? Would an officer fly all the way from the UK, just to hitch a lift home on a bloody submarine back to the UK? I do not think so!

God, there are enough people living in this area who have friends and relations over the Russian border. All this information will get back to good old Mother Russia before we get out of the fjord. Just what kind of dimbos do our people take the Russians in the GRU and the KGB to be? Well, I ask you, what is it they say? "The patients have taken over the mad house." Still, that's about par for the course so far!

Eventually we did submerge and turned again on to a course that would take us north and finally we rounded the North Cape and into our operational area. During the duration of this part of the trip I had been hunting my new OC, the one who had just joined, but it was a fruitless task. Then completely by surprise I caught him alone outside the wardroom. I really was impatient to ask him some questions, not least of which was, 'who the hell was he'? Except that I had no intention of phrasing the question in that manner.

We stood in the passage just outside the wardroom and I assumed the skipper was still in the control room. So after I had introduced myself I asked him, "Who are you, sir? I've not seen you around the squadron before. Have you just joined the branch?" Before he could answer I went on, "Why sir, are we on a different submarine? Neither this Captain nor you for that matter have even been involved in any of the rehearsals for this, dare I say it, 'operation' which I take it we now seem to be embarked upon; why is it that we have two new people in command?" Just who, I wondered, were these two who were now in command?

He did not look at me directly, but he seemed to be avoiding eye contact with me, but he eventually said, while looking at the bulkhead behind me, "Before I left to join you Captain Brown told me that you would kick up shit about all that. I'm afraid that the other submarines you worked with have now been rescheduled to do other tasks. Don't worry though, Sergeant Johnston, this Captain knows these waters where we are going like the back of his hand. The Admiralty therefore considered he was the best man for the job, if it is to succeed at all, that is. As for me ,well I am here because I am the only one who knows the area in which we are to operate ashore, I also have contacts in the area and that is all you need to know."

I looked at him in disbelief not only about his explanation but at what Brown was supposed to have said. "With respect, sir, the Skipper of this submarine, you and Captain Brown have no knowledge at all about the routines and drills which we perfected with the other skippers. Routines to embark, disembark, or what drills we would carry out if the submarine had to move for any operational reason. To put it bluntly, sir, the three of you haven't got an idea what battle drills we have perfected these last few weeks. So I fail to see how the three of you can make qualified decisions about the tactics required for this operation. Whatever this operation might be and now after what you have told me, then I'm dreading ever finding out what this 'operation' is all about. You also said you had contacts in the area. Well if you don't mind, sir, I'd like to know what nationalities these contacts of yours might be, sir?"

"Now, Sergeant, I am the Officer in Command of the Marines on this boat and as it happens, you and the rest of your Marines will operate as I say you will. Is that understood? What is more if you insist on this bickering, then I shall have no alternative but to have you charged with insubordination, and you will be disciplined by a ship's captain; and you know what that means for you; do I make myself clear, Sergeant?"

"Yes, sir," I answered. "Yes, sir, you certainly do, there's no ambiguity about that sir!"

He looked at me as if he wasn't sure whether I was being insubordinate again, or not. For an officer not to know what I'd meant worried me somewhat. While he thought that one out I decided that any shit from him and all we Marines would do when we left the submarine would be to sit on the bottom until it was time to return to the boat. 'I'll teach the bastard,' I thought. But he had said something very odd. No Royal Marine Officer would have referred to us as Marines! He would have said, "The Royal Marines on this ship," or perhaps he would have referred to us as "The Royal Marine Detachment"! Other countries refer to their 'Marines' as Marines, but with the British, you see 'marine' is a rank as is 'private' in the British Army. Just as I was getting my teeth into this momentous discovery, a voice from behind the curtain covering the wardroom door said very authoritatively (the kind of voice of authority one can only learn at Dartmouth Naval College) "Now, Sergeant, I am the Captain of this boat and what I say is acted upon immediately. What is more if you two don't stop this bickering then I will have to step in and sort your command structure out. Do I make myself clear?"

"Yes, sir!" I said; no facetious remarks to this man; he'd know the bloody difference I'll bet.

"Right, now perhaps we can arrange a time tomorrow when the three of us can get together and discuss how we intend making a success of this operation, right!"

Neither the young officer nor I said a word. We just looked at one another and stood there in the passageway like two spare pricks at a wedding as they say.

"All right, as both of you have lost your tongues, we will meet at 10.30 tomorrow morning in the wardroom. By 'Tot time', we should have everything sorted and you can all get the rest you need before we start the operation proper."

I looked at my young OC, and I didn't like what I saw. So without a word, I just turned and made my way back to the rear torpedo room where the rest of the lads and I had been billeted. When I arrived there, the lads looked at me and Nobby was the first to speak.

"You look a bundle of joy, mate, things not going right?"

"You have got it in one, I have found some bastard I hate more than bloody Lord Captain Bloody Brown."

"Like that, is it mate?"

"Yes it bloody well is."

"You will not believe it, but this new OC we have just been lumbered with has got his own bloody contacts in the operational area. I'll bet all our pay that they are bloody Russians to boot. Now that might not worry you, but it frightens the shit out of me. I've never heard of them ever being able to turn a Russian, well, not one who wasn't a double agent already? So grab a hold of that mate!"

"You really have got a shitty on about this haven't you," said Mick.

I was, over the next few days, to change that opinion dramatically about the Submarine Captain. As I said it had been shortly before my encounter with the Captain that the submarine had submerged and turned north, from then on it steadily made its way to the North Cape. It sailed on taking us steadily and relentlessly northwards, carrying us to our date with destiny. The die was cast and although we did not know it then we were about to partake in a phase of military activity which would have such a profound effect on our lives that before it was completely over it would see most of us dead within the next few years or so, ten of us at least! Ten out of thirteen is not really very good odds I can tell you.

I realised at the briefing the next day that the Submarine Captain did know these waters very well. It was then he explained why it was his boat and not the others we were on.

"While you, Sergeant, were practising your drills off the Island of Ronaldsay, we have been tracking Russian ships up in the operational area. The area that we are now heading for; the other Skippers kept me informed of all developments, and the drills which you worked out. I have here the précis on everything you and your men did; I know all that went on off and on the Island. Also I'm sure I can get you into the operational area without any problems. I'm confident I could stay there for as long as it takes for you and your men to get established." He then added as a sort of afterthought, "ashore."

As I saw no point in contradicting him I just nodded and kept my big mouth shut for once. I'd realised that my bickering and belligerent attitude wasn't going to help my lads at all. For that reason I had promised myself that unless anything really stupid was suggested by either of these two I'd try and keep my big mouth shut.

"Now, down to the nitty gritty, as they say," the skipper said.

I looked at him and bit my lip as I realised my promise was going to be hard to keep.

"First," he said, "our orders are to enter Murmansk Bay without attracting any Russian attention. Which goes without saying really. Once in the Bay you and your detachment are to reconnoitre the whole of the operational part of the bay. At the same time, you are to reconnoitre the coast and I'll give you all the details you will need later. So, you are to reconnoitre the coast with a view to establishing a base similar to the one in Scotland. The aim of the base will be, with the help of sonar buoys, to monitor all ships entering and leaving the Kola Peninsula; paying particular attention to the movement of submarines and surface warships."

Why, I thought, do we have to look out for warships above or below the waves. I thought he told me he had spent the time we were training in Scotland doing just that. 'This bastard is taking the piss', I concluded as I looked at my OC to see what his reaction was, but he was on his way to the clouds.

The skipper was burbling on. "If such a place can be found then you are to collect and retrieve all stores that will be delivered by Merchant ship, from the seabed," was all I got from his last mouthful.

All For A King's Shilling

"Secondly you are to construct and make a habitable place, which will withstand the rigours of the winters in the area; for the installation of monitoring equipment and habitation for the crews who will operate them.

"You are to lay the cable required for the sonar buoys. You are then to test the sonar buoys and make sure that everything is in working order ready for the crews who operate them. These men will join you some time next spring."

When he had finished I was a little speechless to say the least. I looked at him and before I could say anything he asked, "Any of that give you a problem, Sergeant?"

"No, sir, it doesn't cause me a problem; to be honest it frightens me to death."

"Well, I'm glad about that, Sergeant, because if it didn't I'd be a little worried about you."

"There are just a couple of points I would like to clear with you, sir."

"Go ahead and ask," he said in that bored way only skippers of ships can do.

"Well, sir, as it seems we are going to invade Russia, perhaps we should have been given the choice or luxury of at least volunteering for this task, operation, suicide mission or whatever else you want to call this stupid ill thought-out pantomime."

"Now, Sergeant, you are bordering on the court-martial insubordination again. I thought we had cleared that up yesterday."

"That, sir, was before I knew for certain I was being asked to commit suicide. I am not so sure the court-martial wouldn't be the better option."

"You would be well advised to give that argument really long and deep consideration, Sergeant. Now, what was your second point?"

My new OC during all this time hadn't uttered a word either in support of me or in support of the Skipper. When I looked at him I had an idea he was on another ship, trip or even another planet.

"Time, sir," I said "That's my next point. We all know that the coast up here freezes over soon. It doesn't leave us much time to get the stores ashore and construct a control post. Also we are going to have trouble laying these sonar buoys once the ice has started to form along the coast."

"Yes, Sergeant I agree, you and your men will have to work that much harder won't you. Have you any more grouses while you are at it? If not we will get on with the briefing."

The Skipper then started into his second message of doom.

"Once you get yourselves established on the ground all submarine support will be withdrawn. You will, gentlemen, be on your own. When you have completed construction of this post and it is operational and everything works okay, then you may be withdrawn by submarine, but that is by no means hard and fast as yet!"

"I'll not be asking for questions as I think you, Sergeant, have covered the only one we expected. You seem to have made such an impression on the big wigs in the Ministry Sergeant that I think you are the only reason why we are here in the first place."

'Ah! Ah!' I thought, that's why he has been so hostile towards me. Then I thought, what a load of bollocks. 'Impressed the big wigs, my arse', but before I could protest he picked up his bit of paper and walked out of the wardroom. He left me looking at the empty space of the wardroom doorway as he just disappeared behind the curtain that covered it.

William Atlay

So, he really was blaming me for being here, no wonder he was antagonistic towards me. I must admit though that he did impress me with his briefing. I should coco! I'm as wise now as I was when I boarded the train at Poole all those weeks ago. Oh he had been short and to the point but there was no real information on how all these tasks were to be accomplished. No wonder they called us the mushroom Commandos 'fed on shit and kept in the dark'! Because when he had finished, well I felt no more confident in the operation because I knew no more than when I'd entered the wardroom. Looking at my new OC whom I didn't like the look of at all, I just collected my bits and pieces and said, "Oh, shit, with all of this I'm off for my bloody 'Tot'."

With that I got to my feet and left the wardroom after the Skipper. Then I made my way to the place the chiefs called their mess where I was mustered in for my tot! While making my way there, I thought it is going to be very hard trying to keep my resolution not to be belligerent.

The first hold-up came when the weather took a turn for the worse and it was another day before we could start to creep into the bay. This bay led to the river that was part of the Murmansk Military area and thus to the Russian submarine bases on the Kola Peninsula. It took quite a long time and much nail-biting before we were able to get in there. They have this fantastic shipping control system there, not unlike the highway system in America. They also have this traffic cop system as well, something we were soon to find out about.

This was when the skipper of the submarine showed what he was made of and I believe that all of us on board from the first officer down were, if not scared, then very frightened. You could see it on people's faces as he just kept edging the submarine in. From where I stood I could see a young lad whom I believed was the submarine's sonar operator. He was a spotty-faced young lad and he looked as if he should still have been at school because he looked more like a schoolboy than a submariner. This lad was listening to his equipment with an intensity which belied his years and he looked as if he was in a world of his own, in the single-minded way he was concentrating. I stood by the open hatchway and surveyed the scene before me. It was then that I realised for the first time that all the orders were being whispered. They were being passed along a line of men who had formed a line from the control room to wherever it was the orders were going. The sonar operator was reporting all the contacts he had to the skipper, again in whispered tones. One of Her Majesty's submarines was running as they say, 'silent, but I think not running so bloody deep'.

I soon realised that what the skipper was doing was a task which I am now certain was the Naval equivalent of being a lookout in a forward position. The problem, of course, is that the position is way out in front of your own front lines, and much too near the enemy for comfort. The sort of situation which at night, when the enemy is active, is akin to having taken an overdose of a very good instant laxative or to having consumed too many bottles of German lager is another comparison that springs to mind! I believe that due to the shape of the seabed in these parts, there were places where we were not able to run deep at all.

It was just before we commenced the 'exercise' of entering the waters off the entrance to Murmansk that we were told we had to put on the equipment we had been given in Scotland. 'The hollow pen things', which we now had to wear always in or

All For A King's Shilling

out of the submarine and not to get them wet. We had to check them four-hourly and that was regardless of where we were, in or out of the submarine. I would just love to know how we were to check them when we were in the water and not get them wet. When outside the submarine if any of us received readings above a certain level, we were to return to the submarine immediately and report to the navigation officer our exact movements. It was at that point I realised that they knew nothing at all about how frogmen work, what with 'don't get them wet' and then the 'exact movements' bit! Well, I thought 'exact movements, my arse'! When you know an area of seabed, yes, when you have laid out a grid on the seabed, yes, but when you don't know the area exact movements are not a part of the art, not mine anyway. Well, even if I know an area exact movements are not a forte of mine.

I learned from the Jimmy (the First Officer) that these new pieces of pen-like equipment were called Geiger counters and I felt like asking him if that meant they were a kind of calculator. Because I thought I could find a use for one of them, but like the rest of the officers on the submarine he had no sense of humour either. I must admit though that the pen things did frighten all of us. A visible enemy we can handle, but the invisible enemy whose only presence can be measured on a bloody glorified fountain pen, well, that was something else. It was obvious that if we had to wear them all the time then somebody thought there must be a danger of us getting a dose of radiation of some kind. I wondered just what it was that the Russians were doing in these waters and just what it was that they were discharging into the sea anyway.

The skipper having negotiated the sea lanes without any problems and having avoided the mined area, eventually put the submarine on the bottom, just off to one side from the mouth of the river, the eastern side that is. We were at a point approximately thirty-three degrees thirty-seven minutes east, sixty-nine degrees eighteen minutes north, which was under the coastal shipping lane or so the man said! So, finding the submarine would be easy, just follow any eastern-bound freighter and we'd be home and dry. It was at this point we divers really started to earn our keep. There was one point of order which became very apparent from the word go and this was that the Captain would stand no nonsense about noise from anybody at all, regardless of rank or favour. The first sign of any person in that submarine making a noise and I believe that he would have fed the person concerned to the fish personally via the skipper. He gave me the impression that he thought every Russian on the Peninsula was sitting on the coast, each armed with one of the old trumpet hearing aids, sitting on the shore just above the high water mark, with one end of the trumpet in the water and the other end stuck in their ears. Just sitting there listening for us. For my money he just might have been bloody right. I don't think I have ever been as scared in my life as I was those first few days I spent in that godforsaken place; but it is surprising how blasé one becomes. When after the first few days the Great Russian Bear hasn't gobbled you up, one tends to relax one's guard and caution that was practice on the first few days and standards can slip. Luckily for us nothing untoward happened, but that was due more to luck than to good management. The distrust felt towards our officers didn't help us any.

The submarine had been on the bottom for only about two hours when the Skipper suggested in a not too delicate way that, "Now is as good a time as any for you underwater specialists to start carrying out your orders. I want your first team ready to launch in fifteen minutes to start reconnoitring the bay and the area surrounding the submarine. Also, I want two teams in the water at any one time. The other teams will remain here on a very high state of readiness just in case of trouble. I'd have thought you'd all have been champing at the bit to get out of my submarine after the things you have all been saying about my boat."

I didn't rise to the bait, but being a taxpayer I did think I had a share in 'his bloody boat', but I didn't say so and so it was, without any choice in the matter, I took my first look at 'Mother Russia'. I believed then – and more so now – that Russia is perhaps the cruellest mother of all mothers. How anybody in their right mind can love the Godforsaken place beats the hell out of me, but they do. God knows they do, but more to the point they are bloody fanatical about it, and that my friends was what was worrying me about my new OC and his supposedly Russian friend.

We eventually returned to the submarine, a task in itself which was not without trauma; because we had big, big trouble finding the damned thing. At first we thought that the Captain (being the comedian that he was) had perhaps moved his bloody submarine just to let me know that he had read the report of our South Ronaldsay training. In the end we realised that he hadn't moved his submarine at all, it was just that we had got caught as we nearly all of us do when we go into that frozen part of the world for the first time. You see compasses react in an erratic way when they are close to the Magnetic North Pole. They are too near to the magnetic North Pole; too near home for comfort and the pointers swing around a lot. Judging by the amount of scrap metal we'd seen on the bed of the bay which suggested a rather large number of wrecks or dumping of scrap, this didn't help matters either. I was amazed that the skipper hadn't put his boat down on top of any of them when he had placed it on the bottom; but that may have been due to the expertise of the spotty young lad who was operating the sonar.

The compasses had us swimming around like the proverbial goldfish in a bowl, but in the end we managed to sort it out and made it back. Albeit with little oxygen left and a couple of trips to the surface to try and spot some landmarks, but for me the margin was too close for comfort and I told the man so, when I got back in, because we did get back into his damned submarine, we were not only very close to being out for the count, but very close to exhaustion. Our first dive in such cold waters hadn't helped our morale much either.

To make it worse, the Captain gave us a rollicking for returning late. At first I was all for giving him a mouthful, but as I glanced at our young OC I realised I was now on my own. There was no way that he would back me up in anything I said and I also knew that there was no way that I could bamboozle the skipper of this submarine the way I had bamboozled Brown and the rest of them in Scotland. Anyway it was obvious my OC was going to be no good in any kind of confrontation that I might have with the skipper about operating procedures. He also worried me somewhat as he showed no interest in the fact that our trip could have ended in a total disaster. Either he didn't know how close we had come to disaster, or worse still, 'he just didn't give a shit'. If anybody had asked me I would have had to admit I'd not developed any feelings of loyalty for this new OC of ours, if anything it was the complete opposite. I distrusted him completely and I didn't know who he was or where he'd come from. The man had just appeared out of the darkness of a Norwegian fjord and not one of us knew him. Not one member of the team had seen him or even heard of him before, now for a close-knit branch of the service like ours that's not on. It is most unusual to say the least. I was beginning to wonder from which direction his plane had come when it landed in Norway. Yet again, I kept my big mouth shut, which was something that I seemed to be doing quite a lot since I became an SNCO and only a bloody acting SNCO at that. It looked as if I was acting the fool more frequently than was good for me or the lads these days.

I know that the SNCOs of the Royal Marines Deal put on a Christmas Pantomime every year for charity. The way I was carrying on I think that I must qualify for the role of principal boy.

To make it worse not only for me, but for my lads as well I, was being thwarted at every turn and I didn't like it one little bit. Worse still though was the lack of response from our OC; he didn't talk very much at all and talking to him was like pulling bloody teeth. I wondered more than once if he could speak English very well at all. A couple of times I tried to put my worries to the test, but a yes, no and a yeah! just didn't give me a chance to test the man! So I never knew for certain if he was what I thought he was.

It is really surprising how quickly people settle into new environments though and we had been in the bay for only a few hours and when we returned to the submarine here were all those submariners, settled into what they called a silent routine. They were moving around the boat with what looked like bloody great big bedsocks on their feet that looked more like padded wellie boots than anything else. They seemed quite cheerful, although the first one to make any noise at all would, in the Captain's own words, "Be fed to the fish, and Russian fish at that." To this day I never did discover whether the crew loved their Captain, or if they were just plain terrified of him. I don't know what hold he had over them, but he ruled them with a rod of iron and they seemed to enjoy it. I think they were all masochists. By now I had realised that there was no mileage to be made in taking him on. He really was 'god' in the situation in which we now found ourselves.

As it was, things went very well that first couple of days once everybody had begun to calm down a little. Things only got better after that first trip out on the day when we arrived in the bay. It was fair I think to say we were all a little scared and we did have one hell of a scare when a bloody big Russian submarine, which was far bigger than ours, passed within a couple of hundred yards of us.

Did I say a little scared? Hell's bells, we were all scared shitless. Even so, in no time at all we came to know the side of the bay we were in like the back of our hands. The first two days were spent familiarising ourselves with the operational area and we all spent quite some time out of the submarine swimming all over the bay.

I'd just returned from one of the longest dives I had made to date; apart that is from the first one when, dare I say, we had got lost. This time though I'd been out with one of my section leaders. When I emerged from the diving lock I was confronted by our young OC, who was standing there with a face like a busted boot. Nobby Clark was with him and he looked very agitated to say the least.

"You are to get ready to go out again with me, we have to see the skipper for a briefing in an hour's time and we are to leave about one hour after that." Then without another word he turned and left both Nobby, the section leader, and I standing there with water dripping off us. Our mouths were hanging wide open and we were just looking at one another.

Then I said to Nobby, "He doesn't know too much about the diving game, Nobby?"

"You can say that again, Sarge, he must have known you would be going with him before you left on this dive. Surely he could have sent somebody else instead of you."

"If I were you I'd refuse to go, you'd be in your rights. Hell, man, neither of us knows the condition we are in. Any of us could come down with the bends in no time at all. I don't think the Russians will lend us a decompression chamber if we need one, assuming they have one up here."

My recent diving companion said, "Yes I know, but regardless of what you or I think, the one man who could suggest to the skipper that some other person should go has just turned his back on us. So, I think I will have to go along with it now."

One hour later I arrived at the wardroom door and the Captain indicated I should sit. When I had settled myself at the table he then began his briefing for the next phase of the operation. He started by telling me, not my OC, but me, "You will need to wear some warmer clothing under your wet suit this time Sergeant. The two of you are to go to this beach here (pointing to a map of the bay). There, you will be met by one of our agents who will approach you. Under no circumstances, and I repeat, under no circumstances are you to approach him. You are to leave it for the man to contact you."

"Who is this agent, is he an Englishman, or is he Russian?" I asked.

"He is a Russian who has worked for us for many years now, since the war in fact," the skipper replied.

"So, I take it you have been given all the details about this man covering the years you say he has worked for us, sir? You are sure of this man or have you just been informed of his existence, sir?" I asked.

Before the Skipper could answer my questions my young officer answered as if irritated by my questioning the loyalty of the man, or woman for all I knew. "Yes, I'm certain of his standing, he is one of our best Russian agents."

"Well, well he would have to be, one of the best that is sir! Wouldn't he?" I said with a sarcastic tone in my voice, because to me it was a question of; is he Russia's best agent or Britain's best agent. To the Skipper I asked, "Why is it we have to meet this man now, sir?"

The Skipper who was by now looking a little agitated as well said, "I don't think I like the insinuations in your voice Sergeant, I'll not tell you again to watch your manner. Now to answer your question this man has found us a place where you and your men can build your little house. He has been searching the area for months now and he has found the perfect place."

I could see the look in the Skipper's eyes, and I knew he was not happy. He was daring me to say what was in my mind. Then I thought, shit, why not. "You, sir, must know as well as I do there is no such thing as the perfect place. Not in this game we are playing, anyway, and more to the point we never have had a successful Russian agent. It is me who is likely to be tortured to death and then buried in the frozen land hereabouts. If they do catch me I'll tell them all about you and your submarine. No,

All For A King's Shilling

we have never had a successful Russian agent either here or in any part of Russia or the world for that matter."

It was many years later I learnt that we had one really true Russian agent working for us, but as far as I know he was or is the only one who ever did.

"Right, Sergeant, you have gone about far enough, I agree there is no such place as the perfect place, but this is the nearest anybody has ever come to it. What is more I'm told by the highest in my service that this man is a true agent and friend to us and I have to accept that, do you understand?"

"Yes, sir, I understand, sir, but I don't believe it, not a Russian agent. No, sir!" I mumbled to myself.

The Skipper just looked at me and said, "Yes, a Russian agent, Sergeant. Now perhaps we can get this show on the road, can we?"

My OC got up and left the wardroom and I waited until he left and then I looked at the Skipper and I eyeballed him as I said, "I'll tell you this, sir, if he squeaks the wrong way he'll not be a British agent for much longer. I don't care what you or your highest authority says. If I decide he is a danger to me and my men I'll slit his bloody Russian throat from ear to ear and you can court-martial me, hang me, shoot me and hang draw and quarter me if you like, but I'll kill the bastard! That's how far I'm prepared to go, sir!"

Before he could say a word I turned on my heel, made my way back to the mess deck and started to get ready. It was with great difficulty that I managed to get two pairs of Arctic long johns and vests, also a stoker's boiler suit, under my survival suit, which was as tight as a French letter on an elephant. Just as I was trying to get my wet suit over the top of that, the skipper came into the compartment. Nobby and Mick were sweating their bollocks off trying to get my wet suit down over my chest and it was also a skin-tight fit with all the bloody things I was wearing underneath it.

I thought he had come to put me under arrest for insubordination, but he said, "I am sorry that you have been chosen to go ashore with your OC. The problem is you seem to know more about what is required than anybody else. The orders to meet this Russian came in while you were out swimming. It specifically said you were to go. I am sorry." He then turned and asked the other two lads to step outside the compartment and once the lads had left he continued. "Look here, Sergeant, I know what you meant back there in the wardroom. So for God's sake take care when you land and please no dead Russians unless it is a last resort to avoid capture. I don't want you going on a killing spree and causing an International incident."

"Don't you think us being sat on the bottom of the bay at the entrance to Murmansk is an international incident then, sir?"

He looked at me and I was certain he was going to say something, which I was praying would be, 'you are under close arrest', but he didn't, and I wasn't. Instead he just turned on his heel and left with a curt, "Good luck, Sergeant!"

As he left I thought, so you don't trust the bastard either, but I heard myself saying, like the stupid shit I am, "That's all right, sir." Then I thought what a snivelling arsehole that third stripe has turned you into. Nobby and Mick came back in and I said as they looked at me, "Like trying to fit a quart into a pint pot, isn't it lads?"

It took the combined strength of the three of us to complete the job of getting me into my wet suit and then I could hardly bloody move. I just hoped that I'd still be able to swim, but at least we were now going to look for a site for this post that we were here to set up. So, now the real game was afoot as they say. Mind if anybody had asked me to swap duties, I would have; I must admit, I had butterflies in my guts this time. Similar to those great big bastards you see in the jungles of South East Asia. Lying off good old Mother Russia in a submarine, and going for a swim in her sacred waters was one thing. To land, well, that was another kettle of fish altogether. As I looked at the faces of my friends, I thought shit, not one of them is going to volunteer to take my place. Still if the boot was on the other foot I wouldn't bloody volunteer either.

That was how one day, so long ago now, with great reluctance and trepidation I exited from the submarine. I was with my new, but not trusted and not yet tried young officer and gentleman. What lay ahead of us was not the great mystery I had believed that it would be. No, it was what I have come to know over the years as stark bloody fear. It wasn't fright really, it was a feeling that went way beyond fright or even stark fear. It's a feeling that cannot be described, but anybody who has experienced it will know what I mean. I have also discovered since that night that the feelings one has at these moments don't come any easier with time. No matter how often one is in that situation, one never gets used to the tightening of the gut and fearful apprehension; or the mental and physical concentration to stop the backside popping open every once in a while; or the inexplicable feelings surging through one's body in case things go wrong in a big way. But that night was for me the granddaddy of them all.

As we left the submarine both of us stayed very low during the swim to the mainland. For my part I had believed we would make for the western side of the bay, but I was wrong. The place we had been ordered to make a landing was the eastern side of the bay, which was about a mile away. We eventually made a landfall on the eastern side about half an hour or so after we had left the submarine having changed direction a couple of times. We finally landed on a rocky shore that sloped gently upwards from the high water line. I lay in the water looking the beach over to check for any untoward movements and the like, but my young officer, well he immediately stood up. Then with splashing noises that would have done a herd of elephants justice marched straight up the beach. Using expletives the most polite of which was, "Shit," I leaped to my feet and stormed after him. After covering about a hundred yards of beach we came to a cliff, which was about one hundred or so feet high and nearly vertical. It was by this time getting dark and it was a little difficult to see things.

Considering the state of my nerves, which by now were tighter than a duck's arse and that I'm told is watertight, the most frightening happening occurred next. Something, I might add, that became the first of many incidents that were to cause me near fatal heart attacks. Although I could see some things around us and outlines of others, you could have laid me out with a feather when this gruff Russian voice from the shadows said, in that hesitant English only Russians use, "Good evening gentlemen. You are a little late, my friends!"

Late! Late, you bastard, you're bloody lucky I didn't kill you, any more frights like that and I'll bloody kill you. Well, that is what I had intended to say, but I didn't. God, they were really playing on my hopes of keeping that third stripe.

It turned out that we had been met by the Russian agent. No James Bond, this fellow, he was more like an overweight ugly sister from some bloody pantomime. He hadn't approached us, but he had frightened me to bloody death. That was not what I was told he would do at all. The problem was I did not expect him to be at the exact spot from which I had crawled out of the water. To me that smelt of collusion of some sort and I was not enamoured of it at all. He was standing just by the base of the cliff and in the only shadow there was.

With hindsight I should have recognised the warning signals that early in the operation, but I didn't. I was worried 'yes', but you see it was the last thing in the world I had ever expected to happen. An agent who was not pretending to be a Russian but was the genuine article. Standing at the base of a cliff, at the exact point from which we had just climbed out of the water. No, it was too good, too bloody good to be true and something was wrong, I was certain of it. I had the strangest feeling and I just knew that this Russian agent didn't have my health and prosperity uppermost in his mind. God, but I was getting terrible. I was reading disaster into everything and everybody I met.

This person we met was without doubt Russian. He was about five feet six inches in height and about, or looked to be about, fifteen to sixteen stones in weight. It was after we had removed our lead weights and diving equipment at the foot of the cliff where my OC and this man had just met; they then went into the first of several intense whispered conferences they were to have. The man then led us up a track in the cliff face as we made our way to the top. I do not think we would have found that track, even if we'd looked all night for it. Next the two of them got themselves into another huddle and the whispering started all over again. First this one and then the other would whisper, pointing this way and that way. I was scared about it all. I just didn't like the setup one little bit and I had a strange feeling about the whole affair. I was being blanked out of all the discussions these two were having, and I was supposed to be the king fish in this pond.

While this meeting was going on I did the thing I was best at doing, I was interested in orienting myself with the lay of the land. To tell the truth I was looking for bloody bolt-holes and the quickest way back to my diving gear. I wasn't happy about leaving my diving gear behind. For all I knew some Russian kleptomaniac could be down on the beach not believing his luck at what he'd found there right now. My study of the ground though was something that was to stand me in good stead some years later. It was at this point I noticed the ground fell away from the top of the cliff. It sloped away until it reached a point where it could only have been about ten feet, if that, above sea level. I kept looking back at the beach and then back at the depression. I had spent a little time studying the ground with my head swivelling like a tuppeny budgie. It wasn't very long before I concluded that the depression could not be seen from the water. Looking from the sea one would have to be very high to have seen into the depression. Higher than any crow's nest I'd ever seen on a ship.

After this last little conference with the Russian, we then took off inland. My OC never once told me what he was about to do and I just had to follow him like a bloody pet dog. He uttered not one sodding word to me at all of what his actions were going to be. He and his new-found friend just up and off, not even a 'follow me boys' from the bastard. To say I disliked him would be an understatement, but far worse than that I didn't like the way he was sucking up to the bloody Russian. I had this feeling that we were no longer the masters of the situation and I was becoming a bag of nerves the way things were going, my imagination was running bloody wild.

We seemed to go quite a distance, but later on I realised that we had been going very carefully, and it was no great distance at all. Eventually we came to a small clearing, situated in some trees that were on the far side of the depression. By the roots of one of these trees was what looked like a hole in the ground. The OC gave his first order then, deciding that I should keep watch while he and this Russian gent went down this hole around which the three of us had been crouching.

I must admit that I was starting to feel more comfortable now I'd been ashore for a little while, and the big Russian bear had not yet gobbled me up. The cold was starting to make its presence felt even though it was not yet anywhere near winter. It was a coldness that I was never to forget, the coldness of that place. For a long time afterwards I felt that terrible chill whenever I opened a fridge or upright freezer door and the coldness fell out on to my feet.

It has been my experience in the past that when you are left alone in a strange place for the first time you start seeing all sorts of things, some of them very frightening things. Sounds are new and unaccustomed to your ears and when you hear a noise you look quickly towards it and you convince yourself that you have just seen something move or just glimpsed someone diving behind a bush ... I believe that you are so keyed up, your imagination runs completely amok.

So, considering the state my nerves were in you can well imagine that in no time at all I was a raving nervous wreck. Then when I felt a hand on my shoulder, well, I nearly filled my pants. Then I reasoned that any person who was going to kill me wouldn't have put his hand on my shoulder. At this point and with a concentration I didn't know I possessed, I managed to squeeze my backside tight enough so as not to embarrass myself or my Corps.

Then with all the decorum I could muster at the time I turned to see who it was who had given me such a fright. There in the darkness half in and half out of the hole was the bloody Russian. He pointed to the hole which was filled at that precise moment by his huge body. Then he grunted some unintelligible remark which I took to mean that I should join him and my boss down the hole. Something which I was only too pleased to do; the sooner I was out of sight of anybody or anything who might be watching me (as I knew only too well they were, ducking and diving from bush to bush getting ever closer to me all the time) the bloody better. I had reasoned when my imagination was running wild that there was at least a company of Russians out there watching me.

Once inside the cave I got quite a surprise as it was a lot larger than I had expected. It crossed my mind many times afterwards, just how in the hell did he discover the cave anyway. The skipper told us at our next briefing, after I'd asked him, that the Russian had spent ages looking for the place.

I didn't believe him; I mean how anybody could find a hole in the ground the size of that hole. The man was telling us that as one of our agents he had wandered around this area looking for a cave and finding a cave like this one, the entrance to which is at the base of a tree and is hidden in the natural rubbish one finds under the trees growing in any wood or forest for that matter. Well, I mean how bloody many trees do you have to rummage among the roots of before you find what you are looking for at the base of one of them anyway. Not only was he looking on the coast, but on an Arctic coast and one of the most heavily guarded coasts in the Russian Arctic? No, here was a hole that led into a cave that was exactly what we needed and in exactly the right place. That's what got me; it was in exactly the right place for our purpose, not a foot out either way; there had to be a rabbit off somewhere. Give me a bloody break!

The cave which I had entered was large enough to build an American-style Ranch House in. Again I had doubts about the place and the main thing that worried me somewhat was how in the hell can a person go wandering around this heavily guarded place like this while looking for a bloody hole just like this. For anybody to wander around this part of Russia without arousing at least some sort of suspicion beats the hell out of me. To do so with the patrols the Russians would have in this area, well, I didn't see how he could have done it.

No, I believed I had a bloody good reason to be scared shitless, there definitely had to be a rabbit off somewhere and I had no intention of becoming that rabbit and I don't mean bloody greyhound bait either! It even crossed my mind that they may have dug the place ready for us, and then I thought. 'You stupid arsehole, you really are being silly now' and cast the idea from my mind; not because I didn't believe it but because I reasoned that if they had gone to this effort there had to be a reason for it and my men and I would be safe so long as our being here satisfied their needs. Having settled my mind with that I knew I would be able to sleep now.

At first glance the cave had three chambers leading off a large main chamber. My young OC and this Russian had some lights going. They had lit two hurricane lamps and a Russian equivalent of the good old British Tilley lamp. None of the lamps were as good as their British equivalent and the Tilley lamp was a damned sight noisier than its British counterpart. It sounded more like a bloody hydro cooker. Not only was the place large, it was also a lot warmer in there than it had been on the surface. We were one sorry looking trio I might tell you. I would not have fancied our chances, if we had been apprehended by any of the Russian security forces in this area. Away from this area, well we may have made it, but this highly sensitive area of Naval and Military establishments, not a chance. There were the two of us, both six feet tall, both young, and reasonably fit. With us we had a Russian, five feet nothing. The man was thickset (thickset being a kind way not to say fat) and Russian, whose motives for helping us even I was finding very suspect at best. His motives, well, they were the one thing about him that I didn't dare to contemplate. Had I known as much about him then, I don't think I would ever have closed my eyes for the rest of the time I was up there. No, this was definitely a case of, "What you don't know, could get you killed!"

I must admit though I was a damned sight happier now that I was down in the cave than I had been when they had left me up on the surface to keep watch. It wasn't only because it was warmer in the cave either. The OC told me to have a good look round and get to know the place. He then told me that I was to study the place to create a firm secure position inside the cave. It seemed my young OC was full of ideas of things for me to do. He didn't seem to have the slightest enthusiasm about doing any part of the task we had been given by the submarine Skipper. All he wanted to do was chat to this Russian whom he had said was one of his contacts and it looked to me as if they had much gossip to catch up on. Because to me they looked as if they were long-lost buddies, or was the Russian briefing him on something else.

Their friendliness really did worry me, but I felt that I was perhaps starting to get a bit paranoid about it all. So without any more thought on the subject I took the largest of the hurricane lamps and off I went to investigate. As I went I was doing what I seemed to be doing best these days, chuntering on and on about my discontent and distrust of the two of them and moreover about everything Navy. Both the Russian and my OC acted as if I wasn't there at all and settled into a close huddled conference. I was definitely getting paranoid about those two and I intended to make my feelings known to the Skipper when I got back to the submarine, if I were ever to get back that is!

Even though the next hour or so was like being a kid again, scrambling around underground in this rather large cave, I still did the job that I'd been sent to do. First I made my way towards the part of the cave which was nearest to the coast. The cave on that side went for quite a distance before the floor and the roof both started to slope downwards; the roof sloping more than the floor at this point. Where they did so, I went farther in until there were only three or four feet between the floor and the roof. At this point I was on my belly and I stopped so that I could study the floor. It was a gravel type of substance, and looked to be frozen; yet I noticed that it was quite damp in places on the vertical wall and looked to have been recently disturbed. The digging out of the place flashed across my mind again, but I cast it from my mind. What was more, when I sniffed this dampness it was definitely salty and not fresh water that was causing it. As I crouched there, I could feel the pressure of the sea swell as it came into the shore and then rolled back again. I suppose this was to be expected, being so close to the sea, but I decided to have a close look at all the walls, especially near the hole through which we had all entered the place. The saltiness of the dampness of the lowest part led me to believe that it if it was not below the high water mark, then it was just above it. I could not be certain of course, but I was reasonably sure of that.

As I made my way back to the others, I made some calculations and continued to plan how we should build a control room in the place. Already I had decided that we would have to build a substantial wall at the back of the place, which would be the seaward side. The flanking side walls would need to be substantial as well and we would also have to build some of our escape routes out of the place behind those walls.

When I got back to the main part of the cave system I was surprised to see my OC and the little fat Russian were still whispering to one another. The two of them had some maps and papers spread around and they were huddled over a lamp studying these. So, I approached them to see what they were up to, but they covered whatever it was they were looking at before I got there. Muttering to myself I then took off to see what else I could find. The cave system was quite big and I think if anything it was too big for what we had in mind. This cave had a lot bigger floor space than the one in Scotland, but was not as high. As I looked around I thought we are going to have our work cut out building a control centre in this place. If it was going to be manned all the year round as I think it just might be, it was going to take some bloody heating to allow the occupants to survive an Arctic winter. Straight away I realised that the amount of heating required would give it away immediately once the winter had set in. I pondered what would happen if the heating required for the occupants' survival started to melt the surrounding frozen earth.

The place was after all not too far away from a very active military area. One chance sighting from the air by a Russian spotter plane or passing helicopter of any variation in the snow and ice cover and that would be the end of everything. Of course there was an alternative, which would save time and effort and that would be to build a house within the cave. Okay it would take some materials that we had not yet thought we would require. Wood would be the best medium to use in this climate, not only would it be easier but it would in the long run be warmer than a concrete shell. We might be able to get enough timber from our Russian friend and maybe he had some other friends of his who like himself, were able and willing to help us. Who knows, he just might at that! Like a Russian engineer battalion perhaps?

The main thing was that sarcasm apart I was beginning to form a picture of what I thought we would need to make this crazy scheme succeed. Wood of course would be the best and the easiest material to use so I settled for wood. Not only was it in plentiful supply hereabout, but it was also the quickest and easiest medium to work with. I thought that there would be problems with concrete in these circumstances. The main one was the amount of sand, cement and aggregate needed would be vast. Another drawback was that none of us were experts in the mixing and setting of the stuff, which would be difficult to do in these parts. We would still have to use double the amount of timber to make the shuttering required for the concrete building than for a wooden one. We would also need god knows how many miles of reinforcing steel rods and double the amount of wood would be needed than if we were to build the thing completely of wood anyway. So when one came down to it, wood would be a lot warmer for the men who would have to man the thing, and I had for some reason convinced myself that this would be an all round the year job. If extra protection were to be needed then it could be lined with some form of flexible sheeting, like perhaps tarpaulins, and backed up with earth.

So it was that I started to paint a picture in my mind's eye of what the place would look like when it was built. Next, I set off around the complex, taking measurements, pacing things out. Calculating in my head the areas, volumes and the capacities of the cave; all the details I would need to make my plan. Then when I had all the measurements I needed, I sat on a small mound to start and work out the plan for the post. To my surprise the mound collapsed the way a heap of gravel on a building site in England would have done. I got to my feet and looked at it for a moment. Then after shaking my head I sat down on the cave floor to continue drawing my plan.

I had decided on a three-room complex as the best option. One would house the monitoring equipment and another would be sleeping and living quarters; the third would be for the stores and cooking equipment. That way, duty personnel wouldn't interfere with the personnel who were off duty relaxing, resting or sleeping. Time passed so quickly and it was not until I started to feel tired and hungry that I realised just how long we had been ashore in the place. Also, I realised I hadn't eaten since breakfast. When I looked at my watch I saw that it was now five hours since we had entered the place. My past training started to tick away in my head and told me tiredness and hungriness are the first signs, which are soon followed by cold, and then you have exhaustion. This told me that it was time we were not here because exhaustion in this region equals death. So, it was time to make our way back to the safety of the submarine. It also worried me that if it was light now, then our diving gear might have been spotted at the foot of the cliff. I put my hand down on the cave floor to raise myself to my feet and I realised that the floor was frozen, so I wondered why the mound that collapsed hadn't been frozen. The problem caused me to give the floor of the cave a closer look. I couldn't be certain, but I had the feeling that the floor had been flattened some way or other. The more I saw of this setup the more I disliked it, but my problem was who would believe me and if I mentioned it to the pair in the place with me I might not make it out.

There was one last thing to work out before we left though, which I believed to be the most important of all, escape holes, one of which I had already decided upon, but I did believe that there would be a requirement for more than one. In my calculations I had planned a strong wall at the rear of the cave, by rear I meant the seaward side. Next I had looked at the possibility of leaving space along to the flanks. I had come to the conclusion that if the position was ever located then all these possible escape routes would probably be found before any attack was launched against the position. Any commander worth his salt would have taken such escape routes into consideration and would have built them into any attack plan against the post.

So because of this I planned three obvious bolt-holes and two secret ones. Of the latter I eventually built one into the design of the place, but the second one I told nobody about, a decision which I came to be very pleased about some time in the future.

When I rejoined my young OC in the main cave he was still in deep conversation with his new-found Russian friend. For my part I wouldn't class either of them as a friend. What they had to talk about for all that time I could not understand. One thing I had overheard at an earlier part of the proceedings worried me, as I had heard him tell the Russian we were from the submarine. I did not think it would be wise to tell the Captain of the submarine he had said that, though, because he would only deny it and I would have given away the fact that I understood Russian.

To say I was not sorry to leave that place or that particular Russian was to say the least a little bit of an understatement. I just did not like the look of the man one little bit and I was rapidly going off my OC as well. Something about the pair of them did not ring true. It was something about the way they conversed together, which worried me a lot. There was no way I could bring myself to believe the Russian was a dissident, spy or any other kind of person who would betray his country. It was just something about his manner and his stature that did not ring true to me. He did not match my picture of a Russian dissident, or a crook for that matter. He did however represent my idea of a KGB man, yes, but a dissident, no! I think not! Also I didn't like the way I occasionally caught him looking at me. The man worried me quite a lot and when we emerged from the cave I was frightened to bloody death. It was full daylight and the weather was fine, nice sunshine clear skies and cold as hell, if that's not a metaphor! When we had arrived in the dark of the previous night we had moved tactically from the beach to the cave entrance. Now it was full daylight and a sunny day here we were just strolling along as if we were out for a daily walk. We walked to the top of the cliff, the Russian and my OC chatting away like long-lost friends not worried one jot about the situation we were in. At the bottom of the cliff I was into my diving gear in record time and into the water while my OC was still chatting to the Russian. My idea was that the sooner I was under water the better I'd like it.

By the time we got back to the submarine I don't know about my OC; I was not only exhausted, but a gibbering hopeless wreck. It had been a long time since I had made my first dive earlier that day, or was it the day before. I was also for the first time since we had arrived there, starting to feel the shadow of doom about me. We had only been back in the submarine for about ten minutes and had hardly managed to get out of our kit. Never mind me regaining my composure I had this urgent desire to rush to the skipper and tell him to get his submarine 'the hell out of there'. Before I could a Petty Officer arrived and told me to go to the control room to make a report about our escapade to the Captain. Escapade, I thought, what the fucking hell is wrong with this bloody lot.

The Captain then took one look at me and decided that I needed sleep, more than I needed debriefing. So he sent me off to eat and write up my report. Then I was to rest while he studied my report. Mind I could not for the life of me see what my OC would have to report about and that was probably why he wasn't there, but I was tempted to put in my report what I observed him and his Russian chum had been up to. After much thought that is what I did. What good it ever did me I never knew. The Skipper also told me that the first phase was over and he was withdrawing his submarine to deeper water. He then told me he would discuss my report with me later once he considered his boat was out of any danger.

So off I went and after I'd handed my report to the Skipper I had my first real sleep for God knows how many days. It is really strange how one loses all track of time when you are awake for long periods. Of course interrogators make great use of this disorientation caused by tiredness. The other members of our group, who had remained on the submarine while we had been ashore, told me they hadn't slept much at all either. If they were telling the truth then I do believe that they worried about me, when I was out there for so long. Mind you, they could not have done anything had something untoward happened to me anyway. My OC and I had really been on our own as I could not see the Submarine Commander risking his boat, or letting any of the divers come after us.

It was while they were asking what had happened ashore that I learnt they had a new name for our OC, the lads told me he was known as, 'Bonzo'. I asked why they had nicknamed him Bonzo. They just shrugged and said he looked like a Bonzo. I dared not ask them who or what I looked like, but I had a feeling they had thought up some derogatory names for me also.

Once the submarine had withdrawn from the northern coast of Russia and settled at a reasonable depth in safe waters the Captain eventually sent for us. We met him in the space which they will insist on calling the wardroom and there he listened to our story.

When we had finished our reports he said, "Right, Sergeant, you can give me your list of stores, the ones which you think we will need to do the job."

"Yes sir I can let you have that. I shall need time to draw my plans and list the stores we need, but yes, I can let you have a list."

"Good," he said, "I'll get it off to the Admiralty, but I do not think it will happen you know."

"Sir, do I take it that you have not been told we have already built one of these in northern Scotland?"

The answer I received was not the type one would publish in Admiralty Fleet Orders. A sexual expletive meaning the occupants of a 'funny farm' whose parents were unmarried, I think was the most polite way one could describe it.

I had a strange feeling that he thought the whole thing was a load of stupid rubbish and I must admit that although I had thought the same before northern Scotland, now I believed that if the sonar buoys in the Atlantic didn't work then this place was the only place where we could monitor the Russians. So, I had come to the conclusion it had to be done because after all we were at war with them, albeit a cold one. Mind you I certainly had no intention of ever being one of the people who would have to man the damned monitoring post. Building it is one thing, living in it for six to twelve months on end, no sir. That was not for me.

Suddenly my OC, who until then had seemed to be in a dream during the meeting with the Skipper, looked at me and asked me to produce a list of all the stores that we would require to get the place operational.

The Submarine Captain gave him a strange kind of look, then he looked at me with what I think was his 'what did Horace say?' look. Then my young OC said, "Oh, but sir, Sergeant Johnston has already built one of these places. He knows all about building these posts, don't you, Sergeant?"

"No I'm afraid you have it wrong, sir," I said. "I only retrieved the stores from the sea bed; the REs actually did all the construction. What is more there had better be some REs arriving with any stores which do find their way up here as well."

I do think the Captain was going to have an attack of some sort. He looked at me for some considerable time; so long it was becoming embarrassing. At last he seemed to calm down and turned to my young officer and said, "Young man I have just asked your Sergeant to give me a list of stores, and he has just told me that although he was involved in the building of this type of place he was only involved in gathering the stores from the seabed for others to establish the place. So can you tell if any of your superiors really know what it is they are doing? The sooner you cowboys are off my boat the damned better," he concluded.

I was on the point of jumping and shouting, "I concur with you, sir!" Then I thought better of it and said nothing but looked quite deliberately sheepish. Do you know I'm certain to this day that he knew exactly what I had thought as I looked at the skipper and then trying desperately to change the subject I said, "Sir, at the risk of being insubordinate I would suggest you do not leave these waters until you get an answer to your signal, the one about stores that is."

"Please God, save me from underwater fishermen," was all he said as he stormed out of the wardroom. To which I muttered is there any other kind seeing how the fish live in water. Then I said an instant prayer hoping he hadn't heard me, but judging by the shrug of his shoulders I do believe he had. So the man may have a sense of humour after all?

I just looked at my OC who looked as if he had gone off into orbit again and I shrugged my shoulders. What else could I do? From that moment on I believed I was no longer in control of any of the events unfolding around me. It was as if my days of being in charge of the men were well and truly numbered. That was a point that was about to be brought home to me with very, very grave consequences and very, very soon!

My list took me the best part of the day to get ready and then I did not show it to my OC. Instead I went to the 'organ grinder and bypassed the monkey' and gave the list to him.

He said, "You really are serious, aren't you?"

"Oh, yes, Sir, never more so in my life. It's a game I am forced to play; they are the only cards I've been dealt."

"Well, Sergeant, if that is the case, we had better let my Chief Engineer have a look at it with us just to make sure you have covered every eventuality."

It was on my mind to ask, first, if he was taking the piss? As I had not presumed to help him and the Royal Navy design and build this submarine, why should they have anything to do with the job I was now doing? I therefore did not think it would be necessary for his ship's engineer to check the plans for my building.

Instead I just looked at him and asked, "How many underground control posts has your Chief Engineer been involved in of late, sir?"

These Submariners do not have much of a sense of humour, especially when their superiority over their fellow man is challenged.

At first I thought I may have finally overstepped the mark, but at last he looked at me and said, "I do believe you are just mad enough to know what the hell you are doing, Sergeant."

With that he called the Yeoman to his cabin and the list was encoded and sent.

We were all (and that included the skipper) taken aback with the swiftness of the reply which we received from Naval HQ to our stores' list. Mind, one person in the submarine who obviously knew what was going on was not at all surprised. I will not give you any guesses as to who that was. My young OC; I now decided he was too dodgy to be true. Something was wrong. I didn't like him one little bit and I could see all of us ending up in a Gulag before long.

The Captain did have one surprise for us, though; he told us we were to be transferred the next morning to another submarine. All of us, that is, except our OC and the two reserve divers. This new submarine would then take us back into the bay ready to receive stores from a freighter, which would be arriving a few hours after the transfer had been completed.

At this information I looked at the Submarine Captain and said, "You will be glad now you did not head back to England. These stores have been on their way long before our list arrived. You know, sir, I bet those stores were dispatched and loaded on to the freighter about the time we left Harstad in Norway. If your submarine had been sunk then the skipper of the freighter would have slung the stores overboard somewhere along the Norwegian coast."

He just grunted and said, "We have an added problem, Sergeant, the sea is starting to get a little rough, and we will be making the change-over in daylight."

The Captain wasn't amused by my idea at all, of that I'm certain. I could also see why he was so much against us. The operation we were about to do would put him and his precious submarine at what he considered an unnecessary risk! He had considered us to be hazardous to his boat, right from the moment that we put foot on the damned thing. Now he was going to have to expose his boat in the dangerous waters off Northern Russia to enable this transfer to take place. I did feel a certain amount of hatred towards him as it would be my men and I who were going to be in serious danger more so than his tin can.

As the Captain had said, the sea was starting to get quite rough and he left me to plan the change-over of my men and I from one submarine to another. It seemed now that our young OC was not to go with us; he did not even want to play any more. Any normal officer of our corps would have been in at the planning and if necessary would have done all the planning for the transfer. Not this young man though, he was something else, which made me even more suspicious of him. I was very glad that we were at last parting company.

Later that day our submarine made contact with the replacement submarine without any problem. If he had any problems in contacting the other submarine then I would have been very alarmed. When at last the two submarines did make contact, well, that was when it began, one of the worst ordeals I was ever to suffer in the whole of my life. The Captain of the new submarine decided he would control the procedure.

I put it to the skipper that as we were all divers and had had plenty of practice getting in and out of submarines, we had no fear of the water, in it, on it or even under it. Then I thought perhaps the best method would have been to put a line across to guide us, and then just let us swim over. Because of the rough sea up top and the hazard to the two boats all the lads and I were prepared to try to make the transfer that way.

The skipper just said, "No, it has to be by rubber boat."

From experience over the years I have come to understand one thing in particular. That is, when an officer and a gentleman puts forward a 'stupid idea' to solve a problem and this 'stupid idea' doesn't work, somehow it is never their 'stupid idea' that is the problem. Oh, no it is always some silly peasant who failed to make their 'stupid idea' work. The peasants are the ones who are the problem, wouldn't you know! It's sad, but in all the countries around the world, be it the capitalist West or the Communist East, it is always the same bloody breed and class who are the officers and gentlemen, and it is always the same poor sods who are the peasants. Occasionally a peasant makes the jump from peasant to officer, but never ever to gentleman. It has always been my belief that the ordinary people of both the West and the East put up with the same shit from these people. People, I might add, who consider themselves to be better than the rest, a superior breed, then it's God help us lowly souls!

I have yet to come across any ordinary workers, from East or West, who have betrayed their countries with the gusto of the officers and gentlemen of the upper classes from the Eastern and Western worlds. Can you imagine it? After all, what have us peasants got to offer the other side, we are only the workers, the commoners and the cannon fodder. Or, in the words of Lord Wellington at Waterloo when he visited his troops before the battle, "The scum of the earth." That, 'me hearties', puts us right where we belong, and we should never forget it. When the world is at peace we are a nuisance because we breed too prolifically and when the world is at war we cannot breed fast enough for their killing machines. If you don't believe me, look up the battle plans of World War One!

All For A King's Shilling

Well, that is my grouse over for the moment (I hate all bloody officers, as anyone still reading this will by now have gathered). There are very few officers I've ever saluted out of respect and I hadn't seen any of them around for a while. Very disheartening, I might add.

There is a system used by submariners to recover men from the sea. It is a very simple procedure and requires no real concentration on the part of the submarine skipper. We get in our rubber boats and head for the rendezvous. We then wait with a line attached from the bow of one boat, which is attached to the other. The submarine skipper, having located us, as they always manage to do, then comes along at periscope depth and picks up our rope with his periscope; he then tows us to what he thinks is a safe place. Once there he stops and slowly rises in the water to deck height. We load our stores on to the deck and while some are putting those stores below with the help of the crew, we deflate the boats and stow them below. Simple, nothing could be simpler. Well, that all depends on the submarine skipper as I was going to find out. Simplicity can just as easily turn into disaster.

So it was, I can tell you, with great trepidation that later that day we launched from the submarine that had been our recent home. Once the submarine lowered his deck and we floated away from him, we started to paddle away with all our might towards the submarine which had now surfaced about two hundred yards away. This submarine we had been led to believe was now going to become our base for some considerable time to come. The sea swell by now was running at about ten feet and it was also starting to break into white-topped waves. The conditions were, to say the least, becoming very nasty indeed. We were of course still far too close to the northern coast of Russia for comfort and we were in a very vulnerable situation indeed.

The two captains seemed to fear that if we did use any propulsion to power our boats as we covered the distance from one submarine to the other we would give our position away to the Russians. Especially if there were any Russian submarines, or for that matter any Russian surface ships in the area, then the game would be up for all of us or so they would have us believe. A logical question about the whole thing that to this day has caused me great consternation is, if the Russians could detect the outboard motor of our rubber boats, why couldn't they detect the two bloody submarines' engines?

There was no way round it; the pair of them insisted we cross by rubber boats and that exercise, due to the sea that was running, as my father would say was like, "Pissing against the wind!" We were as you might well imagine in no time at all completely and utterly exhausted and so wet that our gear weighed a ton. The boats had water in the bottom of them and the cold was so bad that it sapped our strength so quickly in those conditions we all thought we would die in the boats. If we hadn't been lashed together we'd have drifted too far apart to have been able to join up later and god knows what would have happened to us. But what did happen to us was bad enough anyway.

While watching us through his periscope, as we floundered around getting nowhere, the captain we had just left came up with a bright idea. Wonders will never cease, and this idea was that it would be better for all concerned if he were to leave the area. Then the captain of the relief submarine could bring his boat to us, which was the usual practice anyway. We would then be less exhausted and might just have enough strength to haul ourselves on to the casing of the new boat. I had a better idea at this stage, I thought it would be better for all concerned if we were to start our outboard engines, leave the area and head for Norway or Russia for that matter. It would to my mind be safer for us and then those two could play silly buggers as long as they wanted.

I was to learn later that all this was decided as we were still pulling our hearts out with the paddles, getting absolutely nowhere and after the captain we had just left threatened to report the one that we were trying in vain to reach, to the Admiralty. The first we had known of it was when my radio crackled into life in its waterproof bag.

So, while we were still struggling in the sea swell trying to reach the other submarine by which time we were completely exhausted and all our kit was soaking wet, we were now in a situation which made everything twice as heavy and with ice starting to form on most of it and us. We all watched the first submarine's periscope as it slowly edged away from us. As it did, it took all our combined strength, what little we had left, to hold the rubber boat still in the water and stop it being dragged after him. We had to row even harder and I thought it would probably have been a lot better if he had just submerged instead of sailing away from us. Still at last we were free from his drag, and he was about two hundred yards away from us.

At this point one of the lads nudged me and asked where the other submarine was. We ended up sitting in the boat looking around in all directions too scared to stand up in the boats because of the sea that was running; we must have looked like the 'fuckarewe tribe', the little men who live in the long grasses on the African plains and spend most of the day jumping up above the grass looking around and saying, "Where the fuck are we?" As we looked neither of the submarines was anywhere to be seen. So we rode from the troughs to the highs of the swell, each time we crested the swell we looked in all directions trying to locate a submarine, but not a bloody trace of them anywhere in sight. My first thoughts were that the pair of bastards had done what I'd wished and done a runner, fucked off and left us, but I was about to be put right on that score very rudely.

It was while I was struggling with the waterproof bag holding my radio. I had now decided to call on the radio the captain we had just managed to get clear of. My intention was to ask the sod if he knew what was going on. I was getting the radio from its waterproof covering and I was just about to drop the antenna into the water when I had this premonition that something terrible was just about to happen; and it bloody well did.

The stupid bastard captain of the relief submarine, which we were trying to join, had submerged and he was now coming up right underneath us. We were in a ten-foot plus swell, we were totally exhausted and we did not have the strength to even hold on to this damned rubber boat any more. Now to make matters worse this stupid bastard of a captain was coming up right underneath us. Not only was he coming up, but he was also, would you believe it, under way as well.

The next few minutes were utter pandemonium. First we were lifted by the pressure of the bow wave from the submarine as it rose underneath us. From the bow as it rose out of the water we crashed backwards on to the forward deck carried by the water of the bow wave. The bow, which by now was at an angle of about thirty degrees protruding from the sea, was standing up in front of us. The next moment we skidded along the deck grating and smashed into the front of his conning tower, which was still rising out of the water. Within seconds the rubber boat I was in was cut to shreds as the bow plunged back into the sea and then the next wave came racing over the deck towards us. This next ten to fifteen foot of swell then lifted us all up and over the front of the conning tower. We then continued up and over the top of it. For a second or two what remained of our rubber boat got hooked on to something between his periscope and some other thing protruding from the bloody thing. By now our equipment had been thrown from what did remain of our rubber boat and scattered on to the deck of the submarine. It crashed across the steel casing of the deck and off over the side of the black monster and disappeared into the depths of the Arctic Ocean.

At this point, our rubber boat was deflated and hanging down the rear of the conning tower with us clinging on to the rope straps for fear of death. The remains of the boat then got itself caught on some of the extrusions, which where welded on to the sides and the top of the bloody conning tower. The other rubber boat was by now hanging from the other side of the conning tower, having already spilled all the men and their gear into the ocean.

Instead of sliding down the rear of the tower, the two rubber boats, or what was left of them, hung there like some deflated party balloons. The men who had been in my boat were now like me all too exhausted to hang on any more and we all descended the sides and rear of the conning tower without the rubber boats. By now they were well and truly fixed to the top of the conning tower on to something sticking out of the top of this fool's damned submarine. As I crashed on to the grating of the rear deck I finally landed on my back.

While I was looking back the way I'd just come I saw one of my men speared in the back of his head. He had been hooked by some other obstruction on the rear of the bloody submarine's conning tower. He had no chance at all, as the submarine slowly started to disappear back into those dark murky waters from whence it had come like some dark ancient monster of the deep. I looked on in horror as he was dragged in by his head, which was still firmly attached to the black bloody monster submerging once more under the surface of those black icy waters. Before I could get myself pulled round to help him, the next wave was rushing past the tower and I thanked God he could not have suffered for very long, poor sod.

At that moment I had an overwhelming desire to kill Submariners, Captains, Petty Officers and other ranks, and any other submariners that I came across; the desire flooded over me at this point in an uncontrollable rage. I'm sure to this day that had I had a limpet mine about my person I'd have sunk the bastard there and then. Things were happening too fast though for me to dwell on thoughts like that. The next moment it was me who was being bounced over the rough grating of the deck and across the edge of it. Then I was sliding down the rounded side of this black monster and into the cold dark waters of the ocean. The next I knew I was being bashed and bumped against the side of the monster by the sea swell and waves as it sailed on past me. That was when I realised that I was getting too close to the rear of the bloody thing for comfort. While I was sliding along the side of the submarine as it relentlessly sailed on by me I received some more knocks. As each wave receded I could still see my young Marine hanging by his head on the side of this black monster being twisted and turned by the wash from the conning tower as it went relentlessly sailing on.

Then self preservation eventually took control and I thought, hell man if you do not do something fast you are going to die. You are going to get yourself sucked into the propellers of this bloody crazy bastard's submarine. With strength and energy I managed to get from somewhere, I know not where, I at last managed to kick myself clear of the side and managed to swim clear of his slipstream and far enough away to avoid his propeller wash.

When I next looked round the submarine had gone, it was as if the thing had never existed at all. All was quiet, except for the wind as it howled and whistled over the swell. When I eventually pulled myself together, I looked around to see if and how many of the others had made it. The cold was like having a toothache in every part of every bone in your body as the wind lashed the sea spray into my face. I finally managed to get my brain in gear and it was telling me to 'Remember your training', for god's sake, man, remember your bloody training! Come on you shit! For heaven's sake shout something even if it is only 'goodbye'.

So I did just that, I started shouting as loud as I could above the noise of the wind and the surf that was now breaking on the top of the waves and blowing heavy salt foam into my face, which stung with the intensity of bee stings. Raising my arm as I did, I shouted for all I was worth, my legs going like a dog trying to get away from a vet with a knife. Then, one by one the survivors did the same. We swam together and got ourselves into a tight circle. When I did the head count, two of my men were missing. One I already knew about, but the other lad's fate is to this day a complete mystery.

I shouted to the others, "I hope that the crazy bastard has got lost. With a bit of luck we might get rescued by a Russian ship, it would probably be much safer." On that point I could see them nodding their heads in agreement, but I knew we were done for. Even with our survival suits on, we would start dying any moment now and I gave us three to four minutes at best.

We were by now all really starting to feel the cold. Even our survival suits under our wet suits couldn't save us, now we could see all of us starting to suffer. I didn't know how long we had been in the boats, but I knew then that they all realised that a few more minutes in this water and we would all be dead. Strange as it may seem the pain I was suffering was starting to disappear. If we had had diving gear on then we could have got down from the surface and we may have stood a chance. Up here on the surface it would be certain death for us all very, very soon. It was then that we heard the submarine coming again. So, I thought we must have become expendable and he was coming back for another go at us. I knew that if I made it out of this, my grandchildren would never in a million years ever believe I'd been run over by a fucking submarine and an English one at that.

As I looked at the others I thought the bastard is out to kill us all. To this day I still thank God it was not the replacement submarine which surfaced alongside us, but it was our previous host. He surfaced a short distance from us and in seconds we had all drifted alongside him. The next thing we were being hauled back on board by the eager hands of the crew we thought we had seen the last of.

All For A King's Shilling

Once the members of the crew had dragged one of us from the sea, they immediately took that person down below. They didn't wait to help others; as soon they had one of us they hurried below with that person. It was a drill that saved our lives. Once below they provided us all with a drink of hot sweet tea laced with neat rum, which with hindsight wasn't the best of drinks to give us. At this point most of us were physically beyond being able to stand, sit or even swim. They half carried us to the Chief's or PO's quarters and helped us to take our wet suits and survival suits off. They then rubbed us vigorously with large white towels; then they helped us into warm woollen clothing and wrapped us in blankets; they also had large multiple bar electric fires. I don't think the crew knew what had happened, but they soon spotted we were two down.

The Captain came into the after torpedo room, which was where they had put us once we had recovered from our initial exhaustion. He told us he was making a report to Admiralty and he said he was going to make a suggestion to them that would for the moment put everything on hold. "You need time to recover from your recent ordeal in the ocean. At least two days' rest for you and your men because none of you are in a fit state to continue with anything they want you to do."

"I'd rather you had said cancel the bloody operation, sir. We have just lost two good men out there, and all because of that submarine Skipper's incompetence." At my last remark there was a deathly silence from the submariners who were helping us. It was broken after about a minute, because at that point our OC put in his first appearance of the day. The bastard hadn't helped at all in our rescue, he hadn't come to see us once the crew members had got us below decks. He had totally ignored us and reminded the skipper the first Merchantman was due to arrive shortly with the first load of stores. He then said, "Perhaps you should be making a run back into the bay to mark the drop place, and get the men back into the water to start the operation."

"Sir?" I said.

Now I know that at times I'm inclined to suggest in a 'telling sort of way' things that I think officers should do, but there was one thing I had learnt since joining this tub. Nobody tells this Skipper what to do in any way, direct, nicely or even in a roundabout way. I thought my OC was about to be fried. I didn't believe the Skipper would fry him in public, but he would fry him at some later date, of that I was sure.

I had not liked the Captain of this submarine when we arrived on board and I never did get to like him very much. There is no law in the service which can order you to like your officers. Personally I believe it is best that you don't, but he was the best Submarine Captain I ever worked with.

Firstly, he looked at us, and then he looked at our OC and just said, "I will have to think about it for a while, there is no way I can put any divers back into the water in this condition."

That is not true I thought, so ever the optimist with a chance to drop an officer in it, I said, "Excuse me, sir, but there are two men and an officer aboard all of whom have been well rested. They could do the job of marking the drop; it would be no problem for them. Then once we have rested we could take over again; that is if we had any diving gear."

William Atlay

The Captain looked at me for a while, then a slight smile crossed his face, but he just shook his head and left us. If looks could have killed, the one I got from my OC would have done for me there and then. He then turned and followed the skipper from the compartment. I watched him go and when I turned to look at the lads everybody including the submariners were giving him the 'V' sign and it had nothing to do with victory.

The Captain then took his submarine into the Norwegian port of Batsfjord and laid off in the middle of the fjord. We who had survived the ordeal of the transfer then settled down to a night's, or perhaps it was a day's sleep. By this time I did not know if it was night or day anymore. Getting a good night's sleep on a submarine is not really possible until you have done a few trips anyway and I remember waking occasionally. I did have a bad dream of the lad going under the water attached to the submarine, which did not do a lot for my morale at the time.

The PO medic did offer us something to help us sleep, but I for one did not want any truck with that sort of stuff. Although I was young and daft in those days even so I wouldn't touch the drugs that he offered me. I had seen what had happened to lads who got involved with that sort of stuff. Memories of days in the jungles of Malaya some time earlier always came to mind. Those days it was common for the lads to take pills to stay awake during patrols and ambushes. The problem came when it was all over and the rest of us were asleep, back in our base. They would be walking the camp unable to sleep and stressed out to the limits. No sir! They were not for me, so I declined the offer and took my chance at getting to sleep in the normal way. As their leader though, I did make a mental note of those lads who did take something from the submarine medic; but that was a complete waste of time, like most things at that time.

Before very long, a matelot moving through the compartment awakened me and thinking that I had only been asleep for some half hour or so, I was not in too good a frame of mind. As I awoke, I was prepared to give whoever it was who had awakened me a piece of my tongue then I realised that whoever it was had just disappeared into thin air. It was at this time I noticed that everything around me was that horrible red of action stations. I had been on this damned thing long enough to know that we were running at action stations. With the top open by the smell of salt air which was pervading all around the place.

Chapter Four
We Were Off Again, My Money Is Back On Russia
Murmansk, Russia

Back into the dark dangerous waters

It was probably the fresh air that had awakened me because when I looked around and there was nobody in sight I realised that I had awakened naturally. So I lay back and just took in the sounds of the submarine and thought of all the events that had happened in the last few hours, or perhaps it was days?

It was some half hour after I had awakened that a petty officer came to tell me that the Captain wanted to see me now and that I should make my way to the control room ASAP!

Without saying a word to him I arose, got dressed and made my way to the control room as requested. I'd learnt from experience that submarine captains did not like to be kept waiting, even for such a hero as myself. When I arrived in his, the Captain's kingdom that is, he greeted me with a smile. I also noticed that a few heads that did turn my way as I entered were also smiling. At that moment I became very, very wary of them all. 'Hello, I thought to myself" and just what have I done that would cause this man and the others to smile at me? 'Beware of smiling submarine captains'. They have got to be worse than Greeks bearing gifts. I have always believed that any man who takes a delight in operating a submarine on the surface or under it, in open seas or enemy waters, is some kind of nutcase! They must have a strange way of getting their kicks, but when that nutcase smiles at you, then beware. This smiling 'nut', while still smiling at me invited me to the wardroom to have a talk about the situation. I do not think I have ever felt so nervous in my life. To me, the man was acting all out of character. For a start we did not like each other at all and here he was grinning at me like a bloody Cheshire Cat. No, I thought as I followed him to the wardroom, it is time I was off your bloody boat, mister. You are, not to put too fine a point on it, starting to frighten me somewhat!

"Come!" he said as he held the curtain open that divided the wardroom from the rest of his castle.

When I was seated in the wardroom he then poured me a cup of coffee and placed it on the table in front of me. Another warning sign I thought as I watched him. Then he asked me, "Did you have a good sleep?"

To which I warily replied, "Yes, sir, at least I think I did, thank you."

"Do you know Sergeant, that you have slept for over thirty hours and some of your men are still out for the count?"

Yes, I thought to myself, and I bet I can tell you which ones they are. It did surprise me though to hear I'd been out for thirty or more hours.

"Is there anything wrong with you Sergeant, you look a little fidgety at the moment?"

"Well, yes, sir, there is, I don't like the way you keep smiling at me. It makes me feel the way the Christians must have felt while they were waiting to be introduced to the lions in the arena."

This brought the first full throated laugh I'd heard from him and when he at last stopped, he said, "All right, are you ready for the bad news first? Or would you care for the good news first?"

"If it's all right sir, I can't see there being any good news now. Only two variations of bad news like, 'oh, what bad luck' news and the really bad, like 'oh shit not that' type news. So I'd prefer the 'oh, what bad luck' news first. That they have cancelled the whole silly operation rather than the 'oh, shit not that' news, that we have to stay on this submarine for a month or more."

"Unfortunately for you Sergeant the operation will go ahead as planned. That is the 'Oh shit!' news as you put it. The bad news is that the only difference to the plan is that I will take you back into the bay. There I will put you and your men ashore to start work. Your young officer and I have been talking to the Captain of the ship which has your first load of stores. This Captain is going to slow his ship down to about four knots and he is going to invent some engine trouble. This we hope will give us time to get you and your men back into the bay."

The Captain looked at me for a moment and then asked, "Are you okay to go on with this or not?"

"Oh, yes, there's no problem there, do I have any choice like?"

"You already know the answer to that question, Sergeant."

"Right, sir, but what about our young officer, sir, what is he going to be doing while all this is going on, sir?"

"Well, I'm afraid he will not be taking any more part in the operation with you. We put him ashore in Norway off Veranger Fjord when we collected all the replacement diving gear which you lost during the attempted change-over from this boat to the other one."

Hello, I thought, he's back to normal. I love the point he slipped in that it was I who lost all that bloody diving gear during the fiasco of the attempted change-over of boats. Not a sodding word out of him that it was his bloody opposite number in the other boat. Nothing at all about the two of them who perhaps might have had a hand in the loss of all the equipment, my bloody equipment, which had gone sailing over the side of his mate's bloody boat and into the depths of the Arctic Ocean.

Before I could ask him about the disaster he said, "It is all right, we have made our reports and the other submarine has left the operational area. I can only say I am sorry for what happened, but what happened has happened and that's the end of it for now. For your own sake don't dwell on it for now."

I sat in his little wardroom and looked him in the eye. Sorry, I thought, I'll give you bloody sorry, before this little lot is over. You'll wish you had never been born by the time I'm finished with you. If you think sorry will be enough for the men I've lost because of the bloody game you and your mate played, then you have a lot to learn, Mister Submarine Skipper.

Finally I broke the silence and said, "Okay, that's in the past for now as you say. So, why can't the two who stayed on board cover this drop and then leave when you do?"

He completely ignored my question and I thought as he went on to give me the details of the drop, the man hadn't let his guard drop for long and we really were back to normal. He was blabbing on about the rendezvous point where we were to meet the ship. Then he told me how we were to mark the drop which the ship would make as it made its way into Murmansk.

When he had finished dictating his orders I finished writing my notes. I looked up from my notepad and it was the first time I had caught him looking at me with his guard down. He had what looked to me the nearest look of pity that I have ever seen in any officer's eyes. I sat looking at him and thought there is something you are not telling me, Mister Submarine Man! Well, I'll give you something to think about, mate.

"Sir," I said. "I'm afraid there is one small point I'd like sorted right now. Do you really want me to start putting marker buoys on the surface of the coastal shipping lane in the bay? Marker buoys for every Russian in the area to see as he goes sailing by? Hey comrade the English are down here!"

He completely ignored my question, something he often did and asked me, "Do you have any more questions?"

At first I was going to say, "No sir." Then, on second thoughts I said. "Yes sir, I have. First if you put my young OC ashore in Norway, why didn't his relief join us with the stores you collected? Also what is to happen about the fact I'm two men short? Third and last sir, I must ask again, do you really want me to place marker buoys on the surface of the inshore shipping lane? Marker buoys for all the Russians and anybody else who happens to be sailing by muttering the English are back?"

"Are these the only three questions or do you have any more you would like to add to the list?"

I said nothing and just fiddled with my papers and maps as I looked at him. I knew as I looked at him that I had missed something somewhere down the line, all was not right. So, ever the optimist I said, "Something is wrong, isn't it, sir?" Once more he ignored me.

At last he said, "Your new OC is on the cargo vessel, the one with the stores which is following up behind us. Once it has docked, and if everything goes to plan, he will join you in the proposed base overland from Murmansk."

He looked at me and said, "No problem there is there? What else was there? Oh, your two men, well the two who were to go back didn't; they are still aboard this vessel."

I was about to ask him if the ship our new OC was on was called the 'USSR Lybianka'? But all I did was to push my point about the marker buoys!

"Look Sergeant, don't labour the point. It is up to you how you mark the bloody drops. I've just told you what I was told to tell you, satisfied?"

"Oh yes, sir, I am satisfied, do you get the feeling the KGB might have a hand in all this fiasco? Buoys would certainly make their job easier!"

"Now you are being stupid Sergeant!"

"You're probably right sir, but if you won't tell me what to do about this marking of the drop sites, perhaps you could advise me. After all I'm just a lowly Acting Sergeant!"

Again, all I got from him was the blank face and silence. No bloody wonder they call it the silent service. Hell it's like drawing bloody teeth talking to him. Everything was so vague; but I noticed that he didn't pass any comment about the KGB! Anyway I then went on to the subject of his fellow Submarine Commander. "Just what is going to happen to that pal of yours, the one we nearly met the other day? What is going to happen to him, sir?"

"Oh him – well the Admiralty has decided that he should go and patrol some other area of operation. The submarine that will relieve him is of a different type altogether. It will not be on station for at least three to ten days." He then added more as an afterthought than anything, "I think you should get rid of any of those ideas, you should put them out of you mind Sergeant."

To which I just said, "I am sorry sir but I do not even know what you are talking about. What's in the past is in the past, don't you agree, sir!"

As we stared at each other, I knew he did not believe a word I had said. Still, why should I worry about his thoughts on the subject; some day I would settle that score with the two of them and in my own good time. My men would not have died in vain.

(It is strange how time and the adversities of life change one's aspects on revenge. To this day I haven't sought out these two skippers to exact any revenge on them. I'm not even sure any more how I'd react if I came across them unexpectedly. Still, that is something I will have to think about later.) For the moment I must return to my tale as at that time we were going back into Murmansk.

So the die was cast and we returned to that hell-hole of a place, Murmansk Bay. Everything went as planned; the Captain again edged the submarine back into the bay. None of my men or the crew of the submarine were tensed up this time as we headed back. We were not screwed up inside as we were the first time we entered the place. To this day I never found out if it was because we were more confident in ourselves, or if we were just plain tired and fed up. My two mates, Nobby and Mick, and I were too busy getting into our survival and wet suits to think too much about it all anyway. While we were struggling into our gear a stoker came through the compartment we were in and he was carrying a rather large sort of spanner. I looked at him and asked if they had a doctor on board?

"No!" he replied. "Why?"

"Well Jack, if you had I was going to ask you to break my legs with that bloody spanner. I need a spell in the sickbay and then some leave."

The stoker looked at me and shook his head, then walked on his way.

All For A King's Shilling

When the submarine neared the place where the cargo boat was to drop its load of stores, the three of us left it by the forward escape hatch. That exercise was quite a hairy experience I might add. Leaving by the rear escape hatch I don't mind, but the front hatch can get a little scary, plus it's a little squashed with three fully-equipped divers in there. Even when the submarine is underway, albeit very slowly, if visibility is practically non-existent it's worse still; nevertheless we made it, and then slowly we made our way to the surface, which I might add was not very far. That crazy Submarine Captain could have only been just below periscope depth.

When we surfaced, I thought we would have a while to wait for the cargo boat, but I was wrong. I was just going to signal the other two to gather close to me, when I saw Nobby pointing at something to my rear. I turned to look and see what he was pointing at. I first felt and then I heard the beat of a large ship's engines coming up behind me. Immediately, I swam like hell to my left, the ship's starboard. I only hoped the other two were doing the same as me I thought, as I swam. I wonder which of the bloody submarine captains is trying to kill me, or have all the captains involved in this taken a dislike to me. Perhaps they are all working on orders from on high, and I do not mean the "Admiralty" in London. I was now getting bloody paranoid about this whole operation, including the KGB and the GRU.

Well, I had just managed to get clear of this bloody cargo boat that was bearing down on me when the next thing I knew, I was forced out of the water and up into the air. I was in mid-air completely clear of the water wondering what the hell was happening. The next moment, I was looking into the face of some awe-stricken bloody merchant seaman on the rear deck of the cargo boat. They had slipped the stores from off the top of the forward two hatches. These pallets had then landed in the sea, one each side of me. The force and pressure of them hitting the water had caused such a large displacement of the water that I was treading that this pressure was strong enough to catapult me clear out of the water to about deck height.

The splash and noise of all this had drawn the attention of a cook, or perhaps a stoker, I'm not sure which. Whoever he was, he was out on the deck for a smoke or a breath of fresh air. He had a pot mug in one hand and a lighted cigarette in the other. As he turned to look and see what it was that had caused the noise of something falling over the side all he saw was a frogman. This frogman was looking at him from about five feet clear from the side of his ship. This goggle eyed monster that was now looking at him, eye to eye, had risen from the depths of the icy waters of Murmansk Bay; like some monster of old, in an old mariner's tale from the last century.

I have often wondered what he thought as he sailed on by me and I again sank back down into those dark murky cold waters of the bay. Looking back now, I only wish that I'd had the presence of mind to salute him.

Mind you with all the near misses that I was having these last few days, it was no wonder I was starting to think that perhaps I should change my service trade. Perhaps I should become a clerk or perhaps a tech store man. To say I was starting to get a little bit of a mood on about it all was an understatement.

As the ship cleared the position, I looked around the area to see if the other two were all right. To be honest, I must admit that I was somewhat relieved when I saw those two heads bobbing up and down close to me. I had a distinct feeling that both Nobby and Mick were laughing at me. It was just after this incident they christened me 'Torpedo Johnston'. Later they told me that it was to do with the way that I had shot out of the water when the stores had landed in it. In years to come we would all have some good laughs about it. We also had some fights when outsiders became too familiar with the nickname. It was one of those private things that bond men together.

The stores had by this time started to sink to the seabed, so I signalled the two of them that it was time we were down there with them. It was important that the stores did not drift too far away from this point. We had learnt from our experience in Scotland it was better if we just let the stores descend themselves. We would keep an eye on them and let them settle themselves. The only time we would get involved was to try and keep them away from very rocky parts of the bottom.

To drop the stores for us, the merchant ship had made a detour from the course allotted to it by the Russian authorities. Not much, but a drift of a few hundred yards or so, to where we were. This would allow it to drop the stores away from the centre of the main shipping lanes. The last problem we needed while we were trying to recover these stores was half the bloody Russian Navy sailing up and down over the top of us; with their bloody sonars ping ponging at us.

We managed to catch up with the two pallets after they had cleared the surface. I have to admit that we did try to influence their descent, even though we knew it wasn't a very wise action to take. The reason we did so was because the coast where we were going to have to drag these pallets ashore, was a good distance away. As we had already learnt in Scotland, it was a useless game. These pallets were far too big for us to handle. The other and most important point was we were just likely to end the exercise with somebody getting hurt. Damage to our wet and survival suits out here would be fatal. So I signalled the other two that we should leave the pallets to sink on their own. I felt sure we would find them again quite easily, so I pointed to the surface and the three of us made our way back up to the surface.

Again we had only been on the surface for a few minutes when we heard another ship approaching the area. Shit, I thought, it is starting to get like Piccadilly Circus around here. We trod water as we kept watching the area where the noise seemed to be coming from. Then out of the greyness we eventually saw the lights and silhouette of a small Russian coastal patrol craft approaching us. Our first reaction was that we thought the Russians had discovered us and I remember thinking, oh shit, it is going to be one hell of a swim from here to Norway. What's more we are not fit enough to swim that sort of distance underwater or on bloody top for that matter.

Then, gathering my composure and remembering how hard it is to see anybody or anything in the sea at night, a ship is bad enough let alone three heads, I reasoned it would be pure bad luck if they even spotted us. With this in mind I signalled the other two just to stay where they were and to remain still for the next two to three minutes. We just trod water and watched the Russian craft go on by. During my time in the bay I saw the same situation happen often. If a ship strayed off its allotted course then one of these patrol boats would be on it like a shot. This one I thought must be after the ship that had just dropped the stores off for us. Surprisingly this was the closest they ever got to catching any of our stores as they were dropped in the bay. I was to learn years later that these boats had another purpose in that bay.

All For A King's Shilling

The area we were operating in was a channel between the main shipping lane and the east-bound, coastal shipping lane. The area we were in was out of bounds to fishermen and according to the charts we had, was mined. During all the time we were there, we didn't come across any mines in the marked areas. There were plenty of them scattered elsewhere, but not where the charts said. The unexpected items we did come across, however, were hundreds of heaps of scrap, which the Russians had dumped all over the area. We also learnt now why we had been given the pen looking things they had given us in Scotland. They checked the 'gamma rays' that we were being bombarded with.

I decided we had given the stores long enough to reach the seabed and off we went to join them. All three of us were glad to be away from the surface again and felt a lot safer now we were again under the water. It took us a couple of minutes to locate the pallets as they settled on the seabed and it looked as if they had survived the trip to the bottom without any damage. All we needed now was for a bag of cement or other such material to bust out of its container. That would more than likely stain the water in this area from seabed to surface, but all was well, as nothing seemed to be damaged. Satisfied all was well we selected three items from one of the pallets. I selected a jerry can of paraffin oil. Nobby managed to find a pack of compo rations attached to which were two packets of Tommy cookers and solid fuel. Mick then collected two Jerry cans of fresh water and the three of us made our way to the shore. We swam for the point where I'd met the Russian with our newly departed OC a few days ago. I could not help thinking that this operation had been a long time in the planning. It is not automatic for the first pallet to arrive to contain cans of fresh water, food and smokeless fuel, which is what the Tommy cooker fuel was. Water, food and smokeless fuel were exactly what we required right then to set the ball rolling. Soon we would have eleven men ashore to be fed and watered so to speak. Somebody had given more thought to this operation than the one in Scotland.

By the time we did make it to the shore the three of us were, to put it mildly, shattered. Unlike the last time I had been on this beach we lay in the water resting our loads on the bottom as we looked the place over. If anybody had seen us we must have looked like the pictures one sees of seals looking at the shore. There was no way I was going to get out of the water the way my OC had the last time I'd landed on this beach.

Instead we spent a good half hour watching and listening for the slightest unusual sound or movement. At last I was satisfied all was well; I signalled the other two that they were to follow me once I had cleared the beach. Much to my surprise I'd stiffened up lying in the cold water and I was a little clumsy as I got myself out of the water and made a hobbling type of dash for the cliff face. I must have looked a real arsehole as I hobbled over the beach. Any Russians watching must have thought that Fred Carnoe's army had invaded them.

Finally I arrived at the cliff face quite puffed out, which surprised me a little at first. I flattened myself against the cliff and took a couple of deep breaths. Well, more deep rasping gasps than breaths. A few seconds later I felt quite relieved when the other two caught up with me. They were in a worse state than I was, gasping and puffing like old steam engines. I just hoped to god that the Russians didn't have any patrols in the area with the amount of noise we were making.

We stayed at the foot of the cliff for a little while, mainly to check all was well, but ostensibly to get our breath back. As there were still no nasty surprises waiting there, we started the scramble up the cliff. We tried not to leave any trace of having passed that way and we finally made it to the top. God, but we must have been living in fairy dairy land if we thought we could hide all traces of our passing and not leave any trace on the cliff face. Still when we did arrive at the top of the cliff we lay down in a defensive half circle, with our backs to the sea. This was also another ploy to rest our weary limbs and we lay there for about fifteen minutes before we started the scramble towards the cave.

If the Russians had been waiting for us while we were in our 'defensive half circle' there was very little we could have done about it anyway. Except perhaps to slide down the cliff and back into the sea and hope to catch the next submarine home! I wondered how often they ran.

As we lay there, I briefed the other two how we were to make it to the cave. I told them we had to be most careful not to leave any tracks from here to the cave at all. We had to be certain there were no tracks whatsoever as we made our way from the cliff through the trees to our destination. Then, moving very cautiously I led the way from the cliff top to the old tree, my brand-new silenced sterling submachine gun in one hand and a four and a half gallon jerry can of paraffin in the other. Both Nobby and Mick took so much care and time obliterating all trace of us having passed that way that at one stage I thought I'd lost them. A little panic ensued before they caught up with me again.

We at last arrived by the tree where the entrance to the cave was. I could sense their disbelief as I slipped into the hole at the base of the tree. Then I popped my head back out of the hole and told them to hand me the stores and equipment, then get themselves into the place. Once they had lowered their equipment and stores into the cave and were dropping in, I took my torch and located the hurricane lamps that the Russian had left when I was last there.

When I'd lit one of them and held it up to give off more light I said, "There now, it's not such a bad place, is it?"

They just looked at one another and said, "You must be bloody joking, Sarge." Then they started to take the rest of their equipment off.

While we were doing this, I think we all realised that we were if anything starting to feel the cold. We had got ourselves a little overheated with the effort and the fear we all felt as we had made our way here from the beach. So, sorting our priorities out, we decided that hot food was number one in that situation. The three of us started to get ourselves some sort of a hot meal before we did anything else. We needed hot food inside us otherwise we might not last the night out. I think I can truthfully say that by the time we had our food that night we were out on our feet. To be honest we were probably feeling the effects of our ordeal when we tried to change submarines both physically and mentally.

Our saving grace was that we had managed a hot drink and a good-sized hot meal of tinned steak and tinned vegetables. About an hour later we made some piping hot cocoa. Nobby and I had collected some deadwood and some leaves from outside while Mick was doing the cooking, and we soon had a fire going. I just hoped as we sat round the fire that we were not pushing smoke out of this place like an old steam engine going over Shap Fell. Still the choice was easy, a fire or freeze to death! It was now dark outside and unless somebody was to smell the fumes of the fire then we should be all right. By this time I was too comfortable to worry about it anyway. Tiredness plus the first effects of hypothermia were taking hold; only we hadn't recognised them yet and that showed just how much our standards were slipping. When one of a group starts to suffer from hypothermia the others see it and something can be done. Unfortunately when you all are suffering, then who's to see it?

A little later when we settled down, it was obvious that none of us was too worried about being caught. With that frame of mind rampant we laid our weary bones down to get some rest. No thoughts of posting sentries or anything like that, just sleep (classic hypothermia symptoms). It was an event the full implications of which could have cost me my life years later if I hadn't learnt from it. This time we got away with it, but only because Mother Nature intervened.

We had as I said at least managed to get ourselves the hot drink of cocoa. The tinned food, well that was another story but it was warm. Even though we had heated the tinned food it was really not hot enough but we did, I'm afraid, make pigs of ourselves with it. We had all overeaten and now while we slept I know what I'd eaten lay heavy in my stomach, and it turned out Nobby felt the same even if it didn't affect Mick. Still everybody knew he had the constitution of a horse. The food did I think save our lives in the end.

When we had been settled for I think about half an hour or so although, as it always does in these circumstances, it felt like about six hours, suddenly I grew wide awake because I had heard or smelt something different. What it was I did not know, but something had brought me wide awake. I was wide awake and bushy-tailed, as they say. First I looked towards Nobby and I could see he was in the same state as I was. He was lying on the opposite side of the fire from me, his eyes wide open and his ears waving around like radar dishes. We just looked at each other across the embers of the fire. Every nerve in our bodies strained to hear what had aroused us and whatever it was it was getting closer to us by the second. It seemed as if a lifetime passed while we lay there. Our nerves tingled with excitement and I might add, fear, but it could only have been seconds. We cleared the kit from off our bodies. We had been using it to help to keep us warm. Then we readied ourselves for action of some sort or other.

It was then we heard it again; the same noise only nearer. It sounded rather like heavy breathing, combined with a shuffling noise. Both Nobby and I saw the damned thing at the same instant. Standing upright on its hind legs just out of the circle of light caused by the hurricane lamp and the fire not six feet from Mick was a bloody great big Russian Brown Bear. Together we uttered the well-known phrase that one utters in these situations, "Oh, shit!"

Now the experts do tell us that "these bears will not eat humans". Oh yeah! "Well, not normally," they always add as a proviso and then they make the stupid statement, "Well, only as a last resort." Ho, ho, ho, and a merry bloody Christmas to you too! As far as I was concerned, and I didn't quite know what Nobby had in mind, I did not intend to give the bear the option of a choice.

I do believe it turned out that Nobby must have been of a similar train of thought because we both lunged for the bear at the same instant. At any rate, as the bear turned, we both arrived on his back at the same moment. We then started to grapple with him trying to gain a hold around his neck. That we intended to kill the bear was without doubt. At least that was what I had in mind. It was at that point the three of us, Nobby, the bear and I all fell on to Mick. Mick, who until that moment was still sound asleep; well Mick being Mick was very annoyed at being woken up this way and he was very, very verbal about the whole thing.

This bear was certainly a strong bastard because as we struggled with him he managed to stand upright again without too much bother. So now the three of us, Nobby, the bear and I, were doing a sort of tango around the cave. It was at this point I felt a sudden searing pain in my left arm. My left arm being the arm I had clamped firmly around the bear's neck. My first thought was he has bitten me and he's got the taste of blood. Now we are really going to have a fight on our hands and I'm a goner for a start.

Then I heard Mick say, "What are you two silly bastards playing at now, for god'ws sake can't I get any sleep?"

That was when I thought, shit, it's all a bad dream and I will wake up in a minute. I did have the presence of mind at the time not to let go of the bear though.

It was just as well really, because I felt another searing stabbing pain in my left arm. It was then I realised what was going on and I shouted to Nobby. "Nobby! Why don't you try killing the fucking bear, instead of sticking your fucking knife in my arm? I know I'm more dangerous than this bear is, but could you please stop sticking your fucking knife in my bastard arm?"

To which I was promptly told, "Get your bastard arm out of the way then."

"So be it," I said, and without any more ado I withdrew from the conflict. Clasping my injured arm I sat down and tried to see just what damage that sod Nobby had done to it. The next few minutes were hilarious if not downright comical or would have been if it had not been for the pain in my bloody arm.

There was Nobby now doing a Boston Two Step round this bloody cave with the Russian bear. The two of them were being ignored by both Mick and me; Mick was seeing to my arm, because that stupid bloody Nobby in his attack on the bear had cut two deep wounds into my left forearm. While Mick was attending to my arm I watched the bear and Nobby. I assumed that Nobby was getting a little tired now, because he was at last calling to us to help him. To both Nobby's and my astonishment, Mick shouted to him, "Hold the bloody thing still."

"That's easier said than done, you bloody fool," retorted Nobby.

Mick then picked up his Lanchester sub-machine gun, which like all our weapons was fitted with a silencer, and shot the bear. It was as simple as that really, and the whole bloody episode was over. I looked at Mick and asked him why he didn't shoot the bear earlier before that maniac Nobby stabbed me? He just shrugged his shoulders and finished dressing my arm. You bastard I thought!

Mind you we now had enough fresh meat to last us for ages and as the bear was now dead I told Nobby. "Perhaps you could now take a look around and see if this damned animal had a mate in here with it who may just start to look for its second half?"

"No problem," he said, "they always hibernate on their own."

All For A King's Shilling

As I looked at him, I said, "Remind me to do the same in future, you are far too bloody dangerous mate. It would serve you right if I have you barred from carrying a knife for ever."

"Oh, you know you don't mean that Sarge, do you?" he said as he turned and left us.

So, as Nobby went off to explore the place and see if there was anything else we should worry about, Mick finished dressing my arm. By now it was very painful and I only hoped for Nobby's sake that it didn't turn septic. I knew that Nobby kept his knives spotlessly clean, but you could never tell.

Shortly after Mick had finished dressing my arm, Nobby returned to the area where we were. He had, he said, checked the whole of the cave completely and he reported, "Gentlemen, we now have this delightful residence to ourselves for one night only and there are no other squatters or uninvited guests in the place."

He then said to Mick, "Hey you should see the size of this place, Mick. We will be able to play football in here."

With that we built up the fire again to try warming us up while we tried to get what rest we could. One thing was certain, I would not be doing very much swimming for a while. Not with the kind of water temperatures which were prevalent in the bay. I would become a real casualty in the water in a very short time. It would even be dangerous trying to get me out to the submarine the way my arm was. Still that would be a question for tomorrow, whenever tomorrow may be. So we settled down to get what sleep, if any, we could manage before the first of the other members of our expedition arrived from the submarine and our new OC from Murmansk. We were expecting him to arrive from Murmansk itself at some point the next day.

That was when despite all my efforts I started to drift off into sleep, then ever so slowly at first I started to feel a slight throbbing and pain in my arm. It was just a twinge to start with and then as always happens with these situations you start to think about it. Rather like a toothache when you continually touch the offending tooth with the tip of your tongue, then you give it a good suck. The pain then gets slightly more intense each time and, before you know it you are off into a case of raving, searing pain. Well, I did not get to that stage, but I was in a rather bad way after about an hour. Mick then decided to give me a shot of morphine and after that I settled down. While I lay there the pain was subsiding a little. I went through all the events that had happened since we had first arrived in Scotland, but I knew none of it made sense. I just couldn't draw it all together yet, but there was something that wasn't right. Against all my better judgement I was refusing to accept what I was certain was going on; I just could not bring myself to believe that the Corps that I was so proud of being a member of would do this to us. It never ever crossed my mind that perhaps, just perhaps, they didn't know a bloody thing about what was happening.

Things at that point started to become very hazy, maybe it was because of the morphine with which Mick had injected me, but I soon felt drugged up to the eyeballs. Even though I was under the influence of morphine there was one factor which kept ringing through the whole thinking. For some reason, and I didn't know why, I believed some person somewhere was fitting all of us up. A voice in the back of my mind kept shouting 'Sucker, sucker, you silly sucker', over and over it went, laughing all the time, 'Sucker, sucker, sucker!' It's got to be the morphine that was scrambling my brain and causing me this trouble I thought. Then I thought this feeling is not so far removed from Friday night on pay week when the pubs are shut and some bloody landlord has all your fortnight's money in his till; at last I lapsed into a deep and troubled sleep. Mick told me later that I had passed out with the morphine taking hold. Whatever it was I promptly forgot all about the thoughts that had bothered me so much. It was some time later when everything came flooding back to me and it all fitted into place.

The next memory I have of the cave was some time later, when I awoke to see the medic from the submarine standing over me. He was telling me that I had a couple of nasty cuts in my arm, that I should be more careful in future. To which I suggested that if they disarmed that bloody idiot Nobby then we might all be able to live more easily.

He was a fountain of wisdom and pronounced that I was suffering so much pain because of the coldness. Something I was already fully aware of anyway. He then went on to say that although I did not have an infection the cold was the main problem. 'Three cheers for Jack the medic'.

Because the swim to the submarine would cause me excruciating pain I would therefore not be moved to the submarine. I'd have to stay where I was to recuperate. This hole in the ground of good old 'Mother Russia' was to be my emergency ward ten for the moment.

He packed his bag ready to leave and I looked at him and then said, "Why couldn't you tell me something I didn't know, Jack?"

He looked me up and down as matelots do when they are being supercilious and said. "You lot make me sick. You are nothing other than a bunch of arseholes."

"Well, Jack, you may have a point there, but I will get better one day and it is possible I will meet you ashore one day. So beware, Jack, we will meet again on neutral ground then we will see just which one of us is the arsehole."

He just grinned and left the cave and that was how I became a semi-permanent resident of the cave. By the time I was fit again I had come to know it quite well. All of which was to turn out to be to my advantage some time later.

From that day onwards the building of the post continued apace without anymore mishaps. Surprisingly, everything went along without a hitch. There were those of us who thought it all went along too bloody well. We didn't have one alert during the whole time we were building the place. Not one Russian, either flying or walking, ever strayed into the area; it was all too uncanny to be true, as they say. It was as if the Russian patrols had completely stopped entering the area we were in. The way we were able to move around without any Russians seeing us was uncanny. To some of us it looked as if the Russian patrols were banned from the actual area that we were operating in. It was all very, very strange indeed and somewhat frightening. We were all on edge and for a while conflicts would arise over the smallest word, glance or action. I had my work cut out keeping the peace, but more importantly keeping the work on schedule.

Everybody concerned in the project was most surprised at the pace with which the work went along. It was always and still is my belief that there was an underlying reason why the work we were doing was completed so quickly. We all wanted to get the hell out of there and most if not all of us thought the place had the feeling of doom about it. Nobody mentioned it, but all of us felt it, I know I for one wanted to get the hell out of there ASAP. The situation was a 'too good to be true situation'. There was a time at first when all we ever talked about was bumping into a Russian patrol. Then there came a time when even to mention a Russian patrol was taboo. You see nearly all of us believed that the Russians knew we were there. At first it was an unspoken thought then one by one we all came to the same conclusion. The Russians knew we were there, they had to know. That was the thought which had most of us on edge all the time and was the true reason behind the bickering that kept surfacing every now and then.

It was no time at all before the sonar equipment and radio equipment started to arrive. It was all packed in waterproof containers. These containers were difficult to get ashore, but with many tears, sweat and blood we eventually made it. Then two bespectacled and pasty looking naval technicians arrived from Murmansk off the same ship. They arrived the same way our present OC had. Along with our first OC's Russian friend, he brought them from Murmansk to within a few hundred yards of the post by vehicle. These two caused some consternation when they told us that they had arrived here by vehicle from Murmansk. The news caused quite a flurry of whispering and fear amongst the rest of us. This was because of the implications it could have for all of us, I can tell you. I mean creeping around the coast is one problem, but riding around in Russian vehicles, well that is another ball game. Anyway these two men were to install the monitoring equipment and then test it. Mind there was a catch with that statement. The installation of the bits that went underwater, well that fell to my happy band of pilgrims. I had been back in the water and swimming all over the bay for some time now, back to full operational duties, P1 I think they call it nowadays; I think it used to be A1.

I was also starting to develop an evil dislike of our so-called leader, our OC. More so now that I had learned he had access to a vehicle. Yet surprisingly everything progressed without incident so, like the fool I was, I put all my worries down to stress.

Then one day this sailor arrived, again from a merchant ship docked in Murmansk. I was by now starting to get a little paranoid by the number of men who were getting off British ships in Murmansk. The worry was that to my knowledge no other men were then re-boarding the ships to replace the men who had disembarked when the ships sailed. I just couldn't understand the Russians allowing this to happen; it didn't look right.

Anyway, this sailor boy arrived and he informed me that he was to be in charge of the setting up of the base from now on. Really you could see at first glance that he was not the best type to have on this kind of operation. To this day I do believe he thought he was still in 'HMS Nelson' in Good old Pompey or in some hole in the ground just along the coast from there. The man's first words when he walked in were, "Where is the senior rates' mess?" He made the unfortunate mistake of asking Nobby this question as soon as he entered the place.

"Silly Bastard," Nobby said, and before the Petty Officer could react Nobby walked away from him. From that day on Nobby kept referring to the Petty Officer as "The silly bastard". For the rest of the time we were there, "Where is the silly bastard?" Nobby would ask when he was looking for the Petty Officer, or "Tell the silly bastard we are just leaving." I know I should have stamped it out, but I felt the same way about the silly bastard myself.

Mick never did say anything at all about him or to him. He totally ignored the man's chattering on, but he watched him like a hawk. This Petty Officer, because that was all he was, even though he acted as if he was The Admiral of the Grand Fleet, Well, he had the cheek to ask one of the lads, "Where are my sonar buoys?" His face when he was told that they were somewhere on the seabed, was a picture. "They are about two miles offshore," the lad took a great delight in telling him. At that point we all thought the Petty Officer was going to have an attack of apoplexy and the young lad was telling everybody to come and have a look at the 'Admiral having a fit'. At that point I had to step in and tell them not only to 'wrap it in' but to keep the bloody noise down. "We are still in bloody Russia in case you have forgotten." This did shut them up and I took the Petty Officer aside and told him a few home truths. If he took any notice of me I don't think I will ever know.

Our OC eventually calmed him down and told him that a team of our divers was at that very moment bringing them ashore.

Next day we all gathered in the area of the post that had now become the operations room of this Petty Officer cum Admiral! Well, he gave us lessons on how to deploy his sonar buoys; mind you, they were now his 'sonar buoys' would you believe. After we had all had a go at connecting his bloody buoys to the cable, he then came out with the funniest remark he was ever to make in that place. It was then that he announced to all of us," You will all have to have at least three practices doing this underwater before you can go to lay them, 'practice makes perfect' lads."

This caused smiles among the lads, but his next remark, "Then before you lay them for real I will test you and see if you are capable of laying them correctly, as I've instructed you to, it is most important." This last remark brought the house down.

When the laughing stopped, he asked, "What's so funny about that, lads?"

Before anybody else could say anything I was surprised by Mick who said, "Look, Petty Officer, we will only have one chance to lay your stupid sonar buoys. So, when the teams detailed to lay these buoys leave here they will do just that. They will lay the buoys and that is what they will do. No practice runs, no testing as you put it, just lay them. Of course if you think we are not up to it, then maybe you would like to don a wet suit and lay them yourself. Oh, by the way do we get a badge if we qualify?"

Nobby then butted in with, "I'm certain our illustrious Sergeant will lend you one of his wet suits if you are that keen. If you ask him nicely, I'm sure he'll lend you one. He's forever pissing in them and a few times he's shit in them so they may smell a little." Then, as an afterthought he added "Silly bastard."

At this point our OC intervened. He had come alive for the first time since he had arrived. His interruption was so unexpected that we all turned and looked at him. Since his arrival here the man had hardly found the time to talk to any of us. He told Mick and Nobby to "Shut up". Then he turned to the Petty Officer and told him, "Petty Officer, the reason you are here is to show the men how to lay the buoys. You are not in anyway in charge of, nor are you in anyway in control of this operation. You are just another cog, and a not too important cog at that in this operation. So you should forget your delusions of grandeur which you seem to have acquired since leaving England."

His outburst had as I've said taken most of us by surprise. It was the most he had said in one go since he had arrived from the Merchantman; the one that had brought our first two pallets of supplies. He had spent most of his time talking with the Russian, the one whom I'd met the first night when I had come ashore with our old OC. That and the other pastime that seemed to fill most of his time when his Russian friend wasn't in the place, that of forever polishing those bloody brown boots he wore. He was talking to the Russian, polishing his boots or bloody well eating. He ate two men's rations every day and I wasn't the only one in the group who worried about what was going on. I believe we all had visions of a visit to a Russian concentration camp when we had completed this little lot. None of us trusted the man.

Still he went on to tell the Petty Officer, "After the men have completed laying the buoys and the day comes to switch them on, if anything is wrong, then that would be the time to go out and put them right. Now there isn't too much time left for the men to lay the buoys, Petty Officer. The conditions out in the bay are deteriorating by the hour." I wondered how he knew that, but he went on. "It is so cold now that before long we will have to travel some distance over ice to reach open water. We now have a fight against time and the onset of winter. You are just lucky that Sergeant Johnston had the presence of mind to lay the cable before you arrived here. So now get on with it man!"

I couldn't resist putting in my twopenny worth so I piped up, "In a few more days there will be very little open water left. So we have to get those buoys connected to the cable out there while we are still able to reach the shore. That means, Petty Officer, when we do leave to lay the buoys, it will be the one and only chance this year that we are going to get."

The OC then told him. "Any tactical decisions that need to be taken about the work in the bay, Petty Officer, they are in fact Sergeant Johnston's province. Even I would not interfere with any of his decisions about any of the diving."

I'm certain none of this went down well with our little admiral. Although we gave the impression we were not taking his instructions in, we had, believe me, not missed a word of his very detailed instructions. So when we did set off to lay his little sonar buoys we made a very good job of it even if I say so myself. The main reason for this of course was that we didn't believe in doing the work twice.

By the next night we had laid all of the buoys except for the last three on the west side of the bay and we intended to see to those the next night. Nobby, Mick and I left earlier than we had intended to because the weather closed in and we took advantage of it to get an early start. We intended to reach the other side before it got dark and we could also take advantage of the full moon, if the sky cleared that was. We left from our side of the river mouth and moved in a north westerly direction. We swam at a steady pace until we reached the coast on the other side of the bay. From there we made for a point at or about thirty-three degrees eighteen minutes east and sixty-nine degrees nineteen minutes north. There we should if our calculations were correct, pick up the end of the cable where we were to lay the last of the buoys. The line of the buoys then passed about a mile to the north of the Island of Ostrov Toros. The idea was to stop any Russian submarines slipping by and making it out to sea by way of the western channel of Mys Lopskiy.

It was while Nobby, Mick and I were at this point of this our last trip that we ran into trouble and I mean trouble with a big 'T'. We had successfully found the end of the cable and I left Nobby and Mick checking it and connecting the end buoy there. While they were laying the last buoy, I edged my way towards the coast of the small island. This island was to the north of Ostrov Toros. It was there on an earlier trip that I had located a Russian buoy that did not show on our maps. I'd decided to check it out and see if there was any build-up of ice at that position. Much to my surprise there was and I swam up to the ice face and inspected it; satisfied with what I saw I decided to return to my two pals.

That was when I hit the trouble, and it was big trouble. It was just as I turned to go back to the others I found myself looking into the face of a Russian frogman. He was about two feet away from me and his diving gear was very old and worn looking. He looked me up and down as if he was appraising my wet suit and equipment. Then he made that signal all divers know only to well. He signalled for me to go to the surface! Well, I figured I had to think fast, but the cold wasn't helping very much. It was funny though he somehow seemed to me not to be hostile, if that makes sense. Meanwhile my immediate thought was, "Oh shit! This is the bloody end."

Exactly what happened next is still to this day very confusing for me to understand. I don't know why, but for some reason, and as I said I don't know why, I did the same as he had; I first looked him up and down as he had me. All the while I was wracking my brain about what to do. Try as hard as I did nothing came to mind. So, I looked back at his face and gave a little shrug of my shoulders. I don't think I looked past him, but it may have been just my subconscious thought to look and see if the others had been caught. If that were the case, I still don't know why I did it. Because there was no way I would have been able to see them in those dark waters, even with a full moon and the visibility was just a few yards.

To my absolute and utter amazement I could not believe my eyes, when he turned his head; I think it was to see what if anything I had looked at. Realising that it was the only chance I was going to get and like the virgin sturgeon I needed urging, as the saying goes, as he started to turn back towards me, my knife was entering deep into his throat just above his collar bone and with my left hand I removed his mouth piece. The poor sod did not stand a chance, but it was the look in his eyes behind his eye mask that affected me the most. It was the look of, "Why did you do that, I meant you no harm look?" It affected me so much that I had to turn his body round so as not to look into them. As I held him with my left arm with his body half turned away from me I wondered what the hell I was going to do with him.

My guts were in a mess and I would have thrown up; but managed not to as I'd have died in my own vomit, within my regulator. That was when I noticed he had a piece of what looked like cod line hanging from the weights on his waist belt. It looked rather like the lariat used by cowboys in the wild west. So, I used this to anchor him to some rocks on the seabed just clear of the ice. Then I swam back to see what the other two were up to. Discretion is the better part of valour, so they say, and I approached them very cautiously indeed. As I approached them I could see the tell tale bubbles of somebody diving on air. When I got close enough to see them clearly

All For A King's Shilling

I saw that they too had a visitor. So there were two Russian divers in the area, I had half thought there might be. Nobby and Mick were just staring at him as if transfixed. The Gods were on my side that day because I was able to dispatch him in roughly the same way that I had his friend only this one never even saw me coming. Funny really, but while I held him with the other two watching I knew that should we ever get caught in Russia, then I was a marked man from now on.

It did cross my mind that they must have been amateurs, it was the only explanation I could think of. I could not understand why two divers who were patrolling an area and had come across three possibly enemy divers should do what they had done. Having come across three suspicious divers and then to do what this pair of divers did well, they had to be green and untrained men. They must have watched the three of us split up with me going off on my own and then they did the same themselves. They separated and tried to apprehend the three of us on a one to two and one to one basis. They must have been mad or as I say, young and green. Whatever it was it cost the two poor sods their lives; I have never understood the logic of what they did. There was another point, of course; why was it when they were breathing air and leaving a trail of bubbles a mile wide, that we didn't see them first?

Having one big fright a day is enough for me. So, I suggested to my two team mates, that it was time we were long gone from this side of the bay. We checked that all cable and buoys were well covered and hidden. Once satisfied, I went back and collected the first Russian. While I did this Nobby and Mick took charge of the second of the two divers I'd had to dispatch. Then, with our two dead charges in tow, we started the long two and a half mile swim back to the other side of the bay.

It was a long swim back across that bay and I do not know what was going through the other two's minds. Nor did I want to know, but it was my belief that when these two we had in tow didn't surface, well, we could be in deep trouble, and I mean deep, deep trouble. The bay would be alive with divers and patrol boats shortly and I just hoped we would be out of it before they started any search in earnest.

As this was the first contact we'd had with the Russians, except that is for the little fat so and so friend of our OC, I was wondering how it was they had come across us now, just as we were finishing our work here. My mind has never worked overtime the way it did on that long swim, as we returned to base with two dead divers in tow. At last nearly exhausted and nerves tingling like bloody fairy lights we arrived at the edge of the ice and spotted our marker. The marker looked to be closer to the edge of the ice now than when we had left. It probably was my imagination, but I wasn't sure. My mind was full of all sorts of ideas then. Because of the belief that the ice was thickening up by the minute I decided to anchor the two dead Russians further out in the bay. So having spotted a large heap of twisted girders and what look like the remains of an engine of some sort, I signalled to the others what I intended to do, and together we managed to wedge and anchor them in amongst the girders where we tied them as securely as we could with the cod line. As we started to leave them, I looked back and watched as they swayed in the tide, and the first one I'd killed was still looking at me. It was one of the eeriest sights I have seen in the whole of my life and caused me some nightmares. The thought crossed my mind that I too might just end my days in the same way as these two had.

We then made our way back to the base and this time we were very cautious getting out of the water. Next with the adrenaline surging through our veins we gingerly crossed the ice and open ground as we made our way to the base. As we entered, that bloody Petty Officer started to ask questions immediately. Mick had recently started to refer to him as Petty by rank and Petty by nature, which I must admit the man was.

"You three are late back, where have you been all this time?" he asked as we entered the place.

Mick turned on him, "Shut it, Mr Petty Officer, we have a problem and it has nothing to do with you. What's more we can take as long as we bloody well like when we swim around the bay, it has got sod all to do with you."

The Petty Officer looked at me and said, "What the hell is going on? My sonar buoys are the most important part of this operation, and don't you forget it."

Following Mick's outburst I turned and said with all the composure I could muster, "For the last time Petty Officer, as Mick has just told you, we have a very serious problem out in the bay. We may all find ourselves in a bloody Russian prison camp before the bloody day is out. Digging bloody coal, chopping down trees, digging salt or whatever it is they bloody well do in Russian prison camps these days. So shut it please, because if it isn't sorted soon that is where we will all end up. So, Petty Officer all will be revealed in good time. We will give you all the details that you will need to know to allow you to complete your job here. Concerning your request to know more about the work we do out there, well, you will get those details as and when the time is right, but only on a need to know basis. At this very moment in time Petty Officer, you don't need to know anything, so can it please. The least you know about what we get up to the better the Russians will treat you if or when they catch you."

We then made our report to the OC. This did not worry him too much at first and I was a little puzzled about that to say the least; but then after a little thought he said, "Yes, I agree, they will eventually be missed. Mind, if they acted as you said they did then they must obviously be new trainees on their first dive. It is possible they were on their first dive and yes, that is it, their non-appearance after the dive would go down as another of their training accidents; one more statistic for their records. Life for them is very cheap you know."

I looked at him in amazement and I thought 'what the fucking hell does he know about their training and statistics and values of life', but I said. "What do you mean, just another statistic, sir? I cannot see even the Russians sending down two green divers together on their first dive, especially not in these conditions and in these waters. The fact I could so easily dispose of the one who followed me just tells me that the more experienced of the two took on Nobby and Mick. Again, the fact that I was able to creep up on him, and dispatch him also, was pure bloody luck."

"Oh I think you do yourself an injustice saying that, Sergeant."

"Well, Sir, that is your opinion, but I think that the time has now come for you to put on a wet suit and come and have a look at them. With your expertise, which you obviously have, once you have had a look at them perhaps you will be able to say whether they are experienced divers or not. We have them anchored just off the edge of the ice and because of the speed with which it is forming I think you had better not wait too long. It will not be many days before they are completely encased in it. I'm certain they will be out looking for their two men and I just hope to God they do not find them or our cables and equipment. You see sir, the cables lead right into this little setup here. Right into the back door of this so nice and so cosy little setup we have here. So, the next knock on the door sir could be the KGB or the GRU. Speaking for everybody here we would appreciate it therefore, if you do not leave this place to make another trip into Murmansk, not until a reasonable time has passed, Sir!"

He was quite taken aback with that last request, and looked a little flustered to say the least.

"Well Sergeant," he said, once he had overcome his shock. "I see no reason for me to go out into the bay to see these dead Russians. No, I shall take your word for it that they are secure, no there's no need for me to go."

I looked at him at this point and he had that little boy not interested look one sees when chastising children. His eyes had a glazed over look in them, a look which worried me somewhat. Shrugging my shoulders I went on, "Some of the lads are a little concerned by the fact you have never once put a wet suit on."

For some reason I had the feeling that he saw the point I was making. He agreed to what I had suggested without a word or hint of any objection; something which I found very odd and disturbing.

That was when the Petty Officer, who obviously could contain himself no longer, then burst into our meeting.

"I demand to know what the hell is going on," he asked in a very agitated voice.

"Well, Petty Officer, while we were out in the bay laying the last of your bloody precious sonar buoys today, well, we had a bit of a problem. We were joined by two Russian frogmen. With a lot of help from Lady Luck, I was able to overpower them, so for the moment everything is all right."

"Where are these two Russians now?" he asked.

Nobby, Mick and I looked at one another just a little surprised at the question and Mick got in first. "They are out in the bay just past the ice, why?" he asked the Petty Officer.

"How long do you intend leaving them out there, they will freeze to death in these temperatures?"

Again we looked at each other in disbelief. This time it was Nobby who got his two-pennyworth in first.

"Oh, I don't know, we will probably leave them until next year when the ice thaws."

"They will die out there; you are nothing other than a bunch of sadistic murderers."

Nobby was in like a flash. "That is something you may do well to remember for the rest of your life Petty Officer." Then pointing to me he went on. "He really is a sadistic bloody murderer. As for the Russians, they are already dead, and you can thank him for that you silly bastard!"

"That is enough, Nobby," I said.

To the Petty Officer I said, "Look we are in for a few very tense days, the last problem we need right now is a screaming crazy Naval Petty Officer. So, for your own good if you do not want to join the Russian frogmen out in the bay, you would be well-advised to adopt a low profile and keep very quiet, but more importantly keep out of my way. For once you would do well to just wind your bloody neck in real tight, all right?"

Funnily enough I had no further trouble with him for the rest of his time with us.

We then devised a routine by which we kept a permanent watch out on the cliff top looking out over the ice. We also improved our lookouts on the landward side of the setup even more so. For the first three or four days everybody was 100 per cent alert. Then as time passed it became obvious that the post had not been compromised and if it had then it was obvious by their non activity that they did not intend to do anything about it; not yet anyway. So, after a reasonable time had passed, everything again settled down and we started to relax. So it was that something which could have wrecked the operation passed off without any further incidents. The encounter with the Russian frogmen started a train of thought in my mind which in the end was even too much for my little brain to comprehend. I wasn't certain what I was thinking was right, and I couldn't have changed anything anyway. So I did the next best thing, I just cleared all the thoughts out of my mind and forgot it. But it would not go away. I would have flash backs over the next year or so.

There was now a new urgency in our work after the incident with the two Russian divers. It is surprising how such an event helps to concentrate the mind. Especially after getting a little over confident because the work had gone so smoothly, and without any incidents; now everything was different. We, or more to the point I, thought that I had killed two Russians. Everybody in the place was on edge, looking over one's shoulder became the name of the game. Hands, fingers and legs worked with a dexterity that they had not shown since the second week after we had arrived here.

In no time at all after that all the underwater work was completed. I got the impression that none of us wanted to be in the water for very long. Some of the others remarked that they now felt as if they were being watched all the time that they were out of the base. I had to admit I had a similar feeling myself every time I stuck my nose out of the place. One thing I was sure of, we had all regained the efficiency which we had had when we started this mission. So, once the work in the bay was finished we only had to wait for the bay to open again once the thaw had set in. That was when the first operators would arrive and we could then leave for good old Blighty ourselves.

We spent the rest of the winter putting the finishing touches to the place. All the stores we required for the job were now in the place. We never did get any stores from the Russian in Murmansk. Something that worried me quite a bit along with some other events that happened then. It was some years afterwards when it all made sense to me and I knew that I had made a terrible, terrible mistake when I killed those two divers in the bay.

Still, we now set about building the accommodation for the men who would man the place. By the time the ice had started to melt we had completed the living quarters. We had also built a galley, a rest room and an eating room. We used most of the old crates and packing cases used in the transhipment of the stores to make chairs, tables and bunks. Other bits and pieces which were left over were used to line the place for more warmth. I'd been quite busy myself. The submarine's chief engineer had made me a hatch. This I had managed to get ashore before the submarine had withdrawn earlier on. Mick and I got it ashore one night using a rubber boat. Some of the submarine's engineers had helped us. For them, the trip to shore had been a big adventure on which I think they managed many free drinks in later years. The main thing was, I had managed to get the thing ashore and none of the people in the cave knew anything about it other than Mick. I had decided some time ago, the first night I was ashore doing the reconnaissance, that I might just need an escape hole of my own some day. I don't know what it was that set me off making this escape plan, but I used all the spare time I had putting it in place.

Most of the winter I had spent digging and securing my escape hole in the back of the cave. It was behind the deepest hut, at a point where the roof of the cave came down in a rather steep slope. I had a gap which was large enough for me to get into with comfort. Once in the gap, I found I could wander around the area between the huts that we had built and the cave's natural walls. While I did none of the people inside the huts could see or even hear me.

The entrance to the cave, which I had used with the Russian and my old OC through the tree, now led directly into a small hut. From there, entry to the main complex was gained along a short passage. This small passage meant the remainder of the cave outside the huts was completely sealed from the area in which I roamed around while I built my escape hatch. This suited me down to the ground. None of the rest ever asked me where it was I used to disappear to every afternoon and most evenings.

When I dug the hole in the back wall of the cave in which I intended my hatch to go, I came to an ice filled kind of tunnel. It was like looking up the bottom end of an ice cream cone after you have bitten the end off. Just a wall of ice surrounded by a hard rock and gravel surface; after a little while I came to the conclusion that it had to be an underwater tunnel. In the end I decided to pick away around the ice at the hard gravel surface and the result confirmed that it was a frozen sea water tunnel. Satisfied I then set to and began to sort of wedge my hatch into the hole I'd made. After the loss of much sweat and tears, I at last managed to get the hatch fitted into place.

The next problem was harder to overcome. Eventually, using what cement and sand I could steal from the stores and the gravel I'd dug out of the face of the cliff, I managed to concrete the hatch into the hole. The mixing of the concrete was the biggest problem. I finally overcame this by using Tommy cooker fuel and melting water that had frozen. When the water was just hot enough for me to put my hand in I quickly used it to make a batch of the mixture and built it around the hatch. Once the hatch was held in position to my satisfaction I built a thick rim of my concrete mix around it. I hoped it would be sufficient to stop any water leaking around or through the hatch. The last thing I needed was to flood the place and drown the lot of us when the thaw set in. This work kept me busy nearly all winter, along with the other chores I had to perform. Like the everyday one of stopping the men killing the Petty Officer.

As for our OC, well he just went to sleep for the duration, which suited me down to the ground. Most of all I was pleased he had stopped his wanderings to Murmansk. I have never really trusted the bastard and the way he acted was exactly the way people from the far north do in the winter. They go to sleep, and this only caused me more worry.

I remember I asked a Norwegian Officer one time when I was on an exercise in Norway. "What do you lot do in the winter?"

To which he replied. "Oh, we go to bed and make love and maybe sleep a little."

So I countered him by asking. "So what do you do in the summer when it is light twenty-four hours a day?"

"Oh, we just make love!" was his bland reply.

Well, I thought at the time I can't remember my grandparents acting that way during my stay with them in Oslo during the war, but this sounds like the place for me. Now I've been up here in this incessant cold for so long I'm not so sure.

Eventually it started to get warmer. Then Mick, Nobby and I along with the other divers were able to take to the water again. We started by moving out over the ice until we found a gap. We then secured a line to the ice and then took it in turns to go in and check what we could of our last season's work. Everything on the whole looked okay, so we began to believe the plan might just work after all.

Then the day came when one of our submarines re-entered the bay; it was quite a day for us. We all packed up our gear and readied ourselves to embark; this was our way out. The first team would arrive in a week. This team would arrive by freighter and our gallant leader and his Russian friend would meet them in Murmansk. This Russian, the one whom I had met the first night I had been here had now reappeared on the scene. Next to come was the bombshell, which landed two days before the operators arrived.

It was decided that Nobby, Mick and I would stay to help with the testing of the equipment by the operators. The argument was that should any of the sonar buoys have developed a fault over the winter, they would need a team of divers who knew the exact location of the buoys men who could take the replacement divers out into the bay to repair or change them. The three of us were to be that team. The reason he picked us, he said, was because we had installed most of them on the bed of the bay anyway. Therefore we would be the best ones to stay behind. It was a task none of us was very keen on doing. We still had very vivid memories of the incident that had happened when we laid the last of the damned sonar buoys.

There were still two reminders of that dive – the two Russian divers who were still standing like sentries out in the ice. I'd hoped to be miles away from Russia when they broke loose. You see at that time we all still thought that the two divers we'd encountered were Russians. There was nothing at all we could do about it; we also thought the decision to kill them was tactically correct. The problem with that was why had our OC not been worried about it all; did he know something about Russian divers that we didn't?

It just wasn't right for all of us to pack our bags and leave the place when the operators arrived from the UK. For one thing they would not all be swimmers but mostly technicians. We knew they would need help in tuning the damned buoys out in the bay. Even if there were a couple of swimmers with them they would need to know where and what it was they were to work with. To be honest it would have surprised me if there were not more than two or even four swimmers among the operators. So it was I spent a further week in that Godforsaken hole in the ground with my two mates and our OC, whom by now I detested. Because I was certain in my own mind he was a bloody Russian, as certain as I had been about his predecessor.

Well, the day finally dawned when the operators arrived and, what's more, they arrived right on time. They arrived on the first British merchant ship to make Murmansk that spring. The idea was they would come ashore to shop and such. Their place aboard the merchant ship would then be taken by our lads as they moved around the town. As for me, who had turned into the old Doubting Thomas of the outfit, well, I didn't like the plan one little bit. You try that game in good old Portsmouth or Plymouth and the Security guys would latch on to you before you could blink an eye. What right had we to think that the Russians were not as smart, or even smarter?

Still, like everything else about this operation it went like clockwork. That was another problem that gave me cause to worry about my shiny brown-booted friend. Yet, by last light, all the new guys were ensconced in their beds. More to the point, all our guys were safely back on UK territory. The British freighter in the docks of Murmansk represented UK territory. All, that is, except for my trusted two, Nobby, Mick and of course myself; oh, and not forgetting our dutiful boss.

Next morning the excitement of being in a foreign country illegally and not yet being in prison had started to wane and we started the briefing by telling them of the situation in the area. The conditions under which they were now going to have to live for the next few months, if not a year! It was easy to see that nobody had told any of them the enormity of the situation in which they now found themselves.

Once they had assembled, I started the briefing and I particularly did not like the look that came over their faces. Especially when I told them about the two Russian frogmen we had anchored out in the bay. At first I told them that they would have to dispose of the bodies at some time very soon. I made a point of telling them, "If those two bodies anchored out in the bay were to break loose before you get a chance to bury them, then if a Russian patrol boat was to pick them up while they still have the ropes on their legs, or the marks which the ropes will have left on them, or worse still, if the Russians see the wounds in their necks; well, this side of the bay will become a hornets' nest. So you will have to get the bodies out of the water and bury them, burn them, or some other drastic action, it is up to you. Once the ice has started to thaw in that area of the bay where we have them anchored, then they will be in danger of breaking loose. I'm sorry to leave you with this problem, but it is a fact of life you will have to live with and sort out."

It all helped to enforce and bring home to them that this was not a bloody exercise in the good old training areas of the British Isles. I could see the situation was starting to sink in when I said. "This isn't Lulworth Cove, lads, this is trespass of the worst kind; it is trespass as in 'invasion' or worse still as in 'spying'!"

To be truthful, at first I wasn't really too confident about leaving the setup in their obviously capable hands. Even I could see that some of them were not the material for this kind of operation. As I looked them over, I had serious doubts about some of them being cooped up in this cave for any length of time. At least any of them who were swimmers would get a break in the monotony of being cooped up for perhaps six months to a year or even longer. Looking back now I really didn't give a shit about it all. I just wanted to get the hell out of the place.

During the week before they arrived I made a model of the bay. Now I pointed out the exact position of the sonar buoys on the model. Once the operators were fully settled in I spent quite some time briefing the four swimmers in the team. While Nobby and Mick spent time briefing the others I kept going through the locations of the buoys with the swimmers. Over and over I told them about the most likely places for Russian activity and the places to stay clear of because of underwater currents, fishing and, of course, the mined areas. Moreover, I warned them of all the problems we had encountered during the tide runs.

If I briefed them once about the Russian divers we had left in the bay I must have told them twenty times. I repeatedly told them to the point of boredom that they had to get rid of those bodies once the ice thawed. To this day I do not know if they ever did the job, or if they did, did they do it properly?

The third day after their arrival we took them out and showed them the actual buoys themselves. On that day, once we had donned our wet suits and we were ready to go, they had one last look at the model. I then proceeded to destroy it completely. The lead swimmer watched in amazement then at last found his voice and asked me.

"What are you destroying the model for Sarge?"

My reply changed the look on his face to one of anxiety, when I said. "Under no circumstances is there to be a model, map or anything else relating to the 'buoys' out there in the bay. Their positions and their existence out there are to be 'non licit' in this location."

Then and only then did I get the impression that the "word" had sunk in. Finally the seriousness of the situation that he and his colleagues were now in had at last got through to his brain.

As we left the cave and made our way across the ice he asked me, "Why haven't you got an entry point to the water, more undercover than this?"

"If you had listened at the briefing, you would have realised the ice hasn't as yet thawed enough to swim through it. Now would you please shut up, this is not Brighton Beach. Any local around here won't take kindly to hearing a British accent out here on the ice, let alone seeing a British serviceman."

With that he at last shut up. Over the next day or so we showed them all the routines that we had worked out for them. Routines so that they would have some sort of starting point to set up their own routines; I must admit that one or two of them were starting to settle very well. As I watched them I began to think if the rest of them settle down, then perhaps the operation might just after all work out in the end.

Then the day came when it was time for the four of us to make that trip out. The one we had made when we came in. There was no chance of us leaving the way our other lads had gone either, as no more men were coming in on freighters. Therefore it would be far too hard if not impossible to get on to a British freighter in the harbour. So it would have to be a long swim for us, as there was no submarine either. It had only lain off the bay as an emergency in case we had to be withdrawn before the others arrived. Only now everything was established and up and running, it too had been withdrawn. So it would be just one long drag all the way across the bay and then across the Poluostrov Peninsula. Once we had crossed that hurdle, it would be the open waters of the Barents Sea, then on to the Norwegian coast.

All For A King's Shilling

Well, the day finally dawned and it was time for us to leave. There were the four of us, in our wet suits with the rest of our kit, like the extra tanks of fuel for our rubber boat. We also had extra rations and extra Tommy cookers and fresh water plus Arctic boots and Parkas. Everything was lashed in what we hoped were waterproof bundles in the bottom of the Gemini craft. It was my belief that somebody had planned for us to leave this way. Otherwise why had this craft miraculously arrived along with the last load of stores to be delivered by merchant ship.

Finally with all this paraphernalia we made our way out over the ice, dragging the Gemini behind us and heading towards the open water. There was quite a thick damp fog over the place and for some reason best known to him our OC was loaded down with all his gear. We couldn't understand why he insisted on carrying it when it could have been in the bottom of the rubber boat. He had some extra bits and bobs with him, 'In case we ran into trouble', he said, but it was bloody hard going for him and he really was struggling as we crossed the ice. He kept continually stopping and looking around after taking a couple of strides. At first I thought he was nervous about having to do any swimming if we ran out of fuel for the Gemini.

The man was starting to piss me off somewhat and it was after the third time he stopped I'd had enough. I turned on him and said, "Look, sir, we had better get a move on as we have a long way to go before we meet up with the people waiting for us in Norway. We will at least be in safe hands once we get there so let's get on. Don't forget there are people waiting over there to meet us, and they will only wait for so long. So come on sir, let's push on, we haven't a lot of time you know."

He looked at me with the first sign of irritation I'd seen in his face and said in a very abrupt manner. "I think you are leading us the wrong way Sergeant."

Oh, shit, I thought here we go, but I said, "Sir, I have crossed this ice a thousand times I know I am on the right track. So please come along, we have to keep moving, sir."

"You are wrong!" he shouted, and with that, he turned to his right and moved off to the north in the direction of the North Pole and god knows what.

I was just about to say stuff him to the other two when all of a sudden he disappeared through the ice. One second he was there, the next he had gone. We ran as best we could dragging the Gemini behind us to the place he had gone through, but there wasn't a trace of him. Not even a bloody air bubble and I just looked at the other two, my mouth hanging open like a fish out of water.

"He could be anywhere." Mick said.

For a moment or two we just looked at the hole, then I said, "Come on, we can't waste time here looking for him. We still have a hell of a long way to go before we will be safe."

So, we turned and made our way to open water. I thought about what had just happened and I think that if we had had a more loyal feeling towards him, if it had been one of us who had fallen in, then we would have gone into the hole after him. We would have found him and then fished him out. As it was, none of us felt it was worth delaying our departure and risking our own lives any further. Especially for a man we suspected of, if not being a Russian, then an Englishman who was a Russian agent serving in the British Forces. Therefore I don't believe any of us as we continued on our way had any regrets at what we had just done.

Eventually, we made it to the edge of the ice, and launched the Gemini into the water. Once it was in the water we clambered aboard and with bated breath we started the Johnson outboard motor. When the engine did spring into life the noise which broke the peace and quiet was deafening; then after a few minutes and the local KGB agents hadn't pounced on us we pointed it out into the bay. With a great deal of hope and trepidation we set off across the open water towards Poluostrov Rybachiy Peninsula, which was to be our next landfall.

It was to be the longest and most tiring of journeys any of us had ever made in one of this type of craft. The trip started well enough keeping the engine on low revs to save fuel, because we believed fuel was our biggest problem. At first we made steady progress, but the tide flow was affecting our position constantly. First it kept carrying us offshore and then later inshore. So we were forever having to correct our course.

It was some time before we realised that the low revs we were using were not enough to counteract the tide. Finally the penny dropped that by not using more revs we were actually making the trip longer. We were having to cover the same bit of sea over and over as the tide affected us, pushing us in and out at will. Although we didn't know it at the time, our situation had become very tenuous indeed.

It was important we kept the coast of the peninsula in sight all the time. This we were able to do by aiming at the lighthouse situated on the northernmost tip of the peninsula. We also had to keep back-checking our position with the light on the island of Kildin, which was where I think our OC had intended to lead us and perhaps spend a spell in a Russian labour camp?

The trip also showed as we progressed across the bay just how unfit we had become by being in that cave for so long. I for one did not realise just how unfit we really had become. The state of our fitness finally hit us as we tried to hang on to the boat, which was buffeted around in all directions by the waves. All the time as we progressed towards the peninsula I was thinking about those two Russian frogmen swaying in the water like sentinels guarding an underwater kingdom. I could not help thinking all the time I could end up like that one day and that was something else we had not talked about. I had no way of knowing what the pair of them thought about it, or how it had affected them.

We had been going for what I thought was hours when the engine stopped and I looked around to the back of the craft. All I could see was Mick who was acting as coxswain of the Gemini. He was frantically shaking the fuel cans in the bottom of the craft and looking around. I turned back to try and get a fix on the light we were making for. To my dismay I could no longer see the light which we had been heading for. It was Nobby who next spotted the light on the coast and it looked as if a craft of some sort had passed between the light and us. We all watched it for a while, but could see or hear nothing other than the waves.

Then I looked at the two of them in the dark and said. "We have got to get ashore now or we will be done for. If we drift around out here in this thing for long it will not be too long before some bloody Russian KGB man asks us in for breakfast and a few years' hard labour."

"Okay," they said in unison and without another word we donned our tanks and flippers. Mick and I hauled the outboard motor into the boat and lashed it to the bottom planks. The three of us then slipped over the side of the boat and secured our waterproofed bags to our waists, hoping that they wouldn't sink and drag us down with them. Next we started to stab the living daylights out of the inflated tubes that made up the sides of the Gemini. Slowly they started to collapse and eventually after about half an hour it started to sink. Well, it lay just under the surface for a while and that was good enough for me. It did improve my confidence in the Gemini as I realised they were bloody hard things to sink.

Having decided we had waited long enough for it to go, by now I thought it was more important to reach land. There wasn't time to worry about this bloody rubber contraption sinking. So, as I have said, once I was satisfied it had started to sink I signalled the others to 'follow me boys'. What an overworked expression that is in the services of the world. 'Follow me boys' – the order you give when you haven't a bloody clue what to do or say.

Anyway I set off at a steady pace for the headland. 'Australian crawl' I think they call it. More like, 'let's get the hell out of here crawl' I'd say. I reckoned the headland was about two miles away as I could just see the cliffs on the coast above the sea. So, we just kept putting one arm over the other and kept our eyes on the light. At this point nothing else mattered, just the light. "Fix your eyes on the light and we will be all right," was all the wisdom that came out of me at that time as we then swam for the light on the cliffs.

With the current running the way it was the swim would take a little while, but I didn't tell the other two what I was thinking. That by the way time was running out any reception party which should be waiting in Norway would by now have packed up and gone home.

Eventually, in a very tired and nearly exhausted condition we made a landfall on the coast of Poluostrov Rybachiy. We landed well to the south of the lighthouse on a very rocky shore. We hauled ourselves on to the rocks and made our way up to a point which we thought was above the high water mark. We found what we needed in no time at all, a fold of the cliffs. This we managed to squeeze into and pulled our equipment across the entrance to keep some of the cold out.

We decided to stay in this fold until we got some circulation and some energy back. Our first priority now was to get some sustenance inside us and we must have eaten about four or five bars of chocolate each while we sat there. We took care to re-pack all the wrappings from the chocolate away in our kit again. We didn't want to leave any trace of our having been there. While we were eating our chocolate, Nobby had collected some water from a large lump of ice a little to one side of the place we were in. Using a Tommy cooker and some hexamine fuel blocks, which he produced from his kit, he boiled the water up and made a mug of hot tea. This he laced with sugar and we shared it amongst the three of us.

The tea and the chocolate had put some life back into us and the heat from the Tommy cooker had warmed us a little. So, we donned our Parkas and boots, then picked up all our bits and pieces. Once we were satisfied all was clear and we hadn't left any incriminating bits we set off cautiously to cross the peninsula. We were now heading for the western side of the peninsula and hopefully home.

There was a ridge to our south that looked to run due west. Slowly and painfully I led them to the top of it. Even though it was still dark we could see the valley to our right, which had the lighthouse at its highest point opposite us. We half sat and rested our loads against a rocky outcrop just below the crest of the ridge we were on. At this point we each ate a couple of boiled sweets. Not a word passed between us as we rested here just below the crest of the ridge. We kept our own counsel for a little while as we rested there. Then without a word being said we rose, loaded up our gear and set off, heading in a westerly direction; always we head in a westerly direction. All my life I have headed in a westerly direction, perhaps it has something to do with the way the world spins.

The going was hard, more so because of the exhaustion we were all suffering from. We had to stop more often than we would have liked, but we had to conserve as much energy as we could. There was no point flogging ourselves at the start. We had another long swim ahead of us once we got to the other side of this peninsula. I had worked it out that we had about fifty kilometres to go before we reached open water and the Barents Sea. To be perfectly honest I didn't think we had a snowball's chance in hell of ever seeing the coast of Norway again. Let alone the United Kingdom of Great Britain; but we would be giving it our best shot.

We stopped twice during that journey to have a meal and get some sleep. Sleep was a very dangerous pastime due to the state we were in. Once asleep we might not wake again, but there are limits to how long one can go without sleep in these conditions. We therefore took it in turns for one of us to sleep while the other two kept watch.

Three times during the journey we heard people's voices. It was a little unnerving really. We had spent all that time over on the eastern side of the bay and never heard anybody in the area. Now we were on our way out in a more inhospitable place and we kept hearing voices, which we deemed to be Russians talking in the area. When at last we heard the sea washing against the shore our hearts lifted a little at first because we had made it thus far; but then sank again with the realisation that we still had one hell of a long swim ahead of us before we reached the relative safety of Norway. We stopped at a place just under a cliff overhang about two hundred feet above a rocky beach. There we rested for a while and took turns to snatch a little sleep. We then pooled what little food we had left, cooked it on the last of our Tommy cookers, ate it and washed it down with a mug of hot tea each. We packed our parkas away in our bundles and shared the last of our chocolate between us before we descended the ridge down to the water. We never thought to keep any food or water to have when we reached Norway, mainly because none of us thought we would ever make it. Once there we checked all our kit to see just what we had left. It was a pitiful sight really; among the three of us all we could muster was a little tea in a little fold of paper, a small fish paste size tin of condensed milk and a small compo tin opener all the chocolate had just been shared out and had been devoured.

After some serious discussion we decided to make our last brew with the tea, eat what remained of the condensed milk, and drink the tea. It was Nobby who said, "What the hell, lads, we might as well have a feast now as we're never going to bloody make it anyway." So you could say we had our Christmas dinner or maybe it was to be our last supper about two feet above the water of Varanger Fjord.

A little later as we stood on the western coast of the peninsula we nodded to each other and we waded into the waters of the Varanger Fjord and at the time we thought possibly oblivion. We started strongly enough at first, and it was good to be back in the water. We made good progress as the tide carried us out, first in a north westerly direction and then in a westerly direction. This we thought was just what wanted. We were going to make it no problem, but then the tide turned and we were in deep, deep trouble. The race of water was carrying us back towards the coast of Russia. It was bloody terrifying the speed at which we were being dragged back into the Russian coast.

Before long we were back to an area about six miles south from the place where we had entered the water and only about three miles out from the Russian northern coast. Panic was starting to set in as we gathered in a circle with our arms hooked together. We trod water for a little while as we waited to see if the tide was going to cast us ashore. It was Mick who decided we were no longer drifting towards the shore. "Look you two, we haven't moved for at least five minutes"

"Suppose you're right Mick, then it is time we started to head west again. We might yet make it," I said.

"Which way is west?" asked Nobby

"Fucked if I know mate, just keep up with us," I said as we set off again towards what we thought might be Norway.

We must have been on the top of the tide because for the next hour or so it didn't seem to be affecting our movement. As we pressed on all our spirits started to lift and we really thought it was going to be easy from here on in.

The next sign of trouble was when Nobby who, like Mick and me had been keeping an eye on the coast, pointed out, "that headland over there, in front us. Well, I think it is the one that we were opposite a few moments ago and it is now in front of us again. So, we are swimming backwards again folks."

"I've had enough of this shit for one day lads. I don't care if it is Russia, Norway or bloody Timbuktu at the moment. To be honest I can't say if that land over there is Norway, or Russia. What I can say is if we do not get out of this water soon, we will never get out of it alive."

I looked at them and they both nodded in agreement, so we set off for the coast, perhaps to imprisonment, death or heaven knows what.

It took longer than we thought it would. Well, it took longer than I thought. God, I haven't a bloody idea how long it took. It could have been a week, but eventually, completely exhausted I managed to haul myself on to the rocks of a small headland. Then I turned and gave my two mates a hand as I hauled them out of the water. At that precise moment I had the greatest feeling of comradeship I think I have ever experienced in my life. We lay there exhausted for some minutes and I was starting to doze off to sleep. Then a little voice in the back of my head started telling me to 'get up you big daft bastard, you are going to die if you stay here'.

Mick I think had the same idea for we both sat up and the two of us grabbed hold of Nobby. He by now was in a really bad way and he had just about passed out. Mick and I half carried and half dragged him off the headland and further inland. When we were clear of the exposed headland we half dragged and half carried Nobby into the shelter of some small saplings a little way off in amongst some rocks. Once in amongst them and about two hundred yards from the sea we laid him down. The two of us then set about collecting as much wood and dead leaves and the like as we could find. In no time at all we had a fire going. We really didn't care if we were in Norway or Russia by this time just so long as we could get warm. The cold was like toothache in every nerve and bone in our bodies.

Some half an hour later when we had started to warm up it was when we started to worry about the fire we had lit which by now was burning quite well. Even then it was not the thought of capture that worried us most. It was how the hell we could warm our backs at the same time as we warmed our fronts. We would get warm in front, turn to warm our backs, and in no time at all our fronts were cold again. We started to dance around the fire trying to keep the blood flowing in our limbs. I was starting to have murderous thoughts towards Nobby, the pain in my left arm where he had stabbed me was killing me, and I could hardly refrain from screaming.

After about half an hour of this we decided to look around and see if there was anything we could use to make a hide of some sort. While we were doing this Nobby, who had regained his composure, came across a small dugout. Its shape was not unlike the places the shepherds use when they are out at night lambing in the hills of Scotland and Wales. The place had three sides, which had a type of lean-to roof over it. Really it was just a hole in the ground caused by the constant action of the ice, wind and snow, a recess in a small bank that some passing traveller had covered with saplings and turf.

The thing was it was large enough for the three of us to lie in with our backs to the rear of it. We decided to build another fire in the front of it. Once we had got everything ready, I then went to get a piece of burning wood from the other fire. It was then I saw Mick had now passed out, or perhaps he was just asleep. If he was as tired as I was then he probably was just asleep, but we could not wake him. Even though he was shaking quite a bit we couldn't get him awake. So, wasting no time in getting him into the place we had just found, I lit the second fire in front of it. In no time at all I had a large blaze going. This time the heat from the fire was then trapped in the shelter we were in. Mick, whom we had between us, and the two of us could now get the full benefit of the heat from the fire.

We lay in the hollow with Mick in between us and we had enough wood to keep the fire going for some considerable time. What is more important, Mick slowly stopped shaking and then he started to breathe more evenly. I think both Nobby and I felt a little better then. How long we were there, we have no way of knowing. What I do remember is both of us had to go and look for more wood at least a couple of times each and Mick never came round all the time we were there. We were really getting very weak when Nobby nudged me and said he thought he could hear some people coming.

When we had first got into this hollow, we made plans to defend it. When the time came, we would just have to pick up our weapons and look to our front. Then we would shoot any bastard who appeared in front of us. Some bloody plan! That shows just how far gone we were.

We listened for a little while then suddenly from nowhere there were four people in what looked like military winter clothing standing looking at us. I for one did not have the strength to pull the trigger of my gun so I just looked at them and felt a right arsehole. My mind was telling me to shoot the bastards, but the orders were not reaching my trigger finger. I think I had what the signallers call a breakdown in communications, or my body had mutinied or it just didn't want to know.

All For A King's Shilling

The next recollection I had was of floating up and down as I was carried, first by a big man, at least I thought he must have been big, because the ground looked a hell of a long way down behind him. I remember looking in wonderment as a pair of heels kept rising up alternately and disappearing under my head. Then before I knew it I was on a stretcher, looking up the arse of another man. He farted with every other step he took. Vodka and beans, I thought, the fucking Russians have got us. Next I was in a truck and that was when I thought we are all right! The fucking Russians would have kicked us up on to our feet and made us walk to the bloody truck.

The only memory I have of this is of blankets as they were tightly wrapped around me; even so I was still very cold. The pain I had in my left arm was, to my surprise, gone. That could have just been because my arm had died on me. At first I thought the lack of pain was a good sign. Next I had second thoughts and panic set in. Shows how much I knew, it was while I was starting to panic that I succumbed and went to sleep. They told me later I had passed out due to hypothermia. They were going to tell me that my arm, which I had been screaming about as they lifted me, was after all, all right, but I went out before they could.

Who were they? They were Norwegians of course. We had against all the odds made it, but only just. If we had remained drifting in the water for a further ten minutes then we would have ended our days in a Russian Gulag or worse. If there is anything worse than a Russian Gulag that is; well I cannot imagine anything worse really, can you?

Some time later when we had made a partial recovery from our ordeal one of the group who had rescued us gave us all the details of the rescue. He said he was one of Carl's men, the men who had found us. He was a member of the Norwegian intelligence staff who had learned about the group of Englishmen who had set up a camp on the coast a few kilometres from the Russian border. As no Englishmen had permission to be so close to the Russian border, Carl and his men had been sent to see what they had got up to.

They had been informed by the locals who lived in the area that the English were waiting for some men to land from a submarine. When the men hadn't arrived from the submarine, they had left. All the same luckily for us the Norwegian intelligence had sent Carl and his men to see what if anything had happened. They were about to give up when they saw the smoke from our fire only a couple of miles from the Russian border. That was how they had found us.

It seemed it had been a 'touch and go' situation if any of us would survive. The three of us had nearly died of exposure, and in truth we should have died. Had we not made for the shore when we did we would have been well and truly in Russia or floating belly up in the sea. It was some time later the penny dropped and I realised they did not know we had come from Russia. They had believed the story they had heard that we came from a submarine. What our Government told them about us we never did find out. The Norwegians gave us the impression that they believed we had come from a submarine. At least that was what their questions hinted at.

I often wondered how it was the submarine skipper had got all the replacement diving gear for us after the mishap when we were transferring boats the year before. He said he had picked it up from the coast of Norway. I was beginning to wonder about it all.

William Atlay

The Norwegians kept us in a hospital in Tromso and we were there for the best part of a month. It was during this period that I had a visit from Carl, only to discover that I knew Carl very well indeed. It was very difficult talking to him in the presence of my men. I think we were both worried that we might give the game away. Carl suggested that he hand it all over to another agent; to which I said it might be too obvious if he were to do that. Better I think if we just carried on as we were and let them think we met at some skiing competition. That way we could honestly say that we had met some years earlier. During one of our walks in Tromso we started talking about our youth. I was the one who mentioned that before the Second World War I had visited an aunt in Stockholm with my father; and I think that was when we first met and found out we were from the same tribe of noggins. If you remember she dragged us across the border into Norway to see her sister, your mother?

I didn't see Carl for a couple of days after that and when I first asked another of their men where he was, I was just told he was on two days' leave. So, I thought, I wonder what he is up to. You can well imagine my surprise when two days later Carl returned to Tromso and while we walked in the grounds of the hospital he handed me a photograph.

Immediately I saw the photograph my suspicions were confirmed; I knew if it got out, I could be in trouble. The photograph which he showed me was of a group of people standing in a small garden, the type one sees in lots of big towns. As I looked at it I sat down on a bench near the door we had just come out of. You see I had seen that photograph before and it wasn't in Norway.

After a while Carl said, "Well what do you think of that, Bill?"

Pointing to a young boy of about ten years old I said, "That, Carl, is you.

"That tall man is my father and the woman with the long hair next to your mother is our aunt; it was my mother who took the picture; the girl with the dark hair is my sister. I remember when that photograph was taken, Carl. It was the summer of 1939, the time we visited our aunt in Stockholm as my sister and I had come to stay with our grandparents there."

It was at this point I got a bit worried and suggested that we walk. The two of us then walked for quite some time without saying a word. I had the photograph in my hand and every now and then I'd have a look at it.

It was Carl who at last said, "You know our fathers knew each other from childhood, Bill. Although they were not related they were the nearest to brothers any two men could be. They attended university in Stockholm together and when the First World War started they both entered the Swedish secret service."

"I know all about the work my father did during the First World War, Carl. One thing, I wonder if you know that the man who ran the whole bloody setup was in fact an Englishman."

"Well yes we all know that now Bill, but neither your father nor mine knew that at the time."

With that we both fell silent for a while. I was about to tell him what I had been up to then thought better of it. I did not divulge anything about my work or how we happened to be in Norway. To my surprise, he did not ask. However, as it transpired he knew both our fathers were members of the Swedish secret service during the First and Second World Wars. My father was a field operative and his was a type of operational secretary back at base. Now he was also a member of the same secret service and I did have the distinct feeling that he knew all there was to know about me. I'm sure he knew we had not been up to any good wherever it was we had just come from. Over the next few weeks we renewed our friendship from my days in Sweden with my grandmother and as I said we really got on well together. He never once asked me to compromise the other two or myself. For that I respected him very much. He used to visit us daily and we all got on well together. When we knew that we were to leave Tromso and head back to England it was I who suggested we should keep in contact now we had met up again. I had made the choice of my own free will. Then he said a strange thing; he said he would have to get it authorised. I told him I wasn't so sure they would do that for him.

In the end we exchanged addresses and I told him that I still carried my Swedish passport; why I told him that I don't know, but it just seemed right to do so. We said we would keep in contact and of course we did keep in contact, very much so. On the surface it was just two servicemen in NATO corresponding, but he had become my mentor as well as my greatest friend and handler. Carl used to turn up in some of the most bizarre places you could think of. I think he was forever popping up in my life, but more about Carl later.

We had been in the Tromso hospital for a couple of weeks before any of our people arrived from London. We had one hell of a job trying to assure them we had told the Norwegians nothing. As I told them when they eventually arrived, because they didn't see any urgency in coming to our rescue why should we worry about their little problems. Mind it was not until everybody was satisfied they had got the truth out of us. They eventually booked us on a ship for home. For two reasons I will always remember the day we sailed. The three of us stood on deck as the ship cast off in the early morning light. While it edged its way from the jetty it was then I noticed Carl standing by a shed on the side of the docks, hands in his pockets, hat pulled down over his forehead watching our departure. I was to see him in that sort of stance many times in various parts of the world after that. The second reason troubled me quite a bit more than I was prepared to tell anybody yet.

Captain, now Major Brown, who had been the driving force behind the whole setup, hadn't shown his face at all; he was probably swigging back the pink gins having finally become a Field Officer, except the only fields he would see were in bloody Sussex somewhere.

So it was that another chapter in my life of service to Crown and Country had ended or so I thought. All I needed now was a relaxing period to get over the whole episode. My aim was now to forget any nagging doubts I had about the safety of those poor sods, the men whom we had left in that hole in the earth, the earth of good old Mother Russia.

Chapter Five
Quick Trip To Russia, Then Off To Singapore For A Rest
Singapore, The Far East 1963

"Hardships, Old Ships, New Cap Badge"

Nothing untoward happened in my life for some time after that. I carried on doing my duty as they say. I served in a couple of commandos, but my name and future in my branch was shit. Five years later, however, in the early nineteen sixties, I was involved as a guide in the insertion of a replacement team into the observation post, the one situated in the Murmansk area of Northern Russia and it was my first visit to the place since we had constructed it. The idea was that my team would land from a submarine and once ashore we would meet the replacement team, arriving by British Merchantman outside Murmansk. From there we had to escort the new team into the base, no mean task. They were to be escorted to the position in groups with two or three men in each group. Then after a handover period we would escort the outgoing team to the ship, which would be about to sail from Murmansk Harbour.

Our task would not be complete until we had got the outgoing team safely aboard the British Merchantman, a large bulk carrier alongside the commercial dock. From there, we were to get them safely on to another Merchantman, which was due to sail within an hour or so of the men arriving. Once they were safely aboard we were to rendezvous with the submarine, which would by then have returned to a position just off the coast. We didn't know at the time, but the authorities had another task for us to complete on Bear Island before we returned to the UK.

The condition of the men we brought out shocked me somewhat. I had expected them to be at least somewhat elated at being relieved and to be heading home. They were not, they looked rather like soldiers who had just lost a major battle; they didn't carry themselves as military men do. Even when tired and exhausted, military men have a distinct way of walking. It is of course marching, but it looks so easy and coordinated without the pomp and circumstance yet well disciplined, looks relaxed and easy and takes years of square bashing to achieve. These men reminded me of those pictures one sees of men who have spent long periods of time lost in the wildernesses of the world and not in any shape or form did they have the stature of British soldiers. Their condition set off warning bells in my head, but due to the circumstances which followed I was true to form and when it was all over I forgot all about them.

We had seen these poor souls on to the Merchant ship and eventually made our way in groups of two or three men leaving Murmansk at ten minute intervals. In our groups we made our way to a position which was about a mile from the place where we had hidden our rubber boats. Because of the tight time table the submarine was working to, any group who was late would more than likely be left behind. Any unfortunate group that was left would have to make its way to Norway alone. Having made that trip once before I was determined not to be left behind this time. Come what may my group and I would be on that bloody submarine, or we would be dead.

All the groups made it to the place, with one group arriving just as we were about to leave. When we had all collected our gear together we then left as one unit, moving in a group to the beach. From where we were, we had to launch our rubber boats and hopefully rendezvous with the submarine, which we hoped was waiting for us a little way out. As we moved we automatically adopted a semi-tactical formation for our own protection. The thing which we all dreaded the most, an 'ambush', happened just as we were nearing our departure point.

Some Russians troops ambushed us, and it was lucky for us that we were all together when it happened. Had we still been travelling in our small groups, or if one of the groups had not made it to the rendezvous, then I'm sure that we would have been wiped out to a man, but luckily for us we were nearly on equal terms with them. There were only about three or four more of them than there were of us, which wasn't bad odds, all things considered.

There followed a short and a very vicious fire fight. It was only after the initial bursts of shooting we did as we'd had drilled into us so often in training that we immediately closed with these Russians who had the temerity to ambush us and that movement alone gave them a bit of a fright. Once we had closed with them we then became involved in some nasty hand to hand fighting. My old pal Nobby Clark, who had now risen to the rank of Corporal; well, he and I became involved in a very nasty bout of hand to hand fighting with four of these Russians. As the thing drew on, it reminded me, albeit in slow motion, of the practice sessions we used to have back in base. At one point I was struggling with a rather big Russian over the possession of my gun. It was at that point through the fog of memory I heard my old instructor saying. "If he wants your gun, then fucking give the man your bloody gun, then as he stands back in shock at receiving it, kill him!" It worked and then I recovered my gun from him, I turned and saw the next Russian coming at me, sidestepped and bayoneted him in his right side as he stumbled past me.

Then as quickly as it had started, it was over as we regrouped, and I did a quick head count. As I was doing that I remember thinking, these Russians were not your ordinary Russian soldiers, no, these guys, they were specialists. Now that it was all over and we had come out on top we all felt elated. The only problem was that a couple of my lads had been rather badly wounded. In the confusion that followed, I do not think they got the best of first aid as they should have had and which we could have given them. The Russians who we thought at the time had stumbled across us, were all killed. When everything had settled down and the dust had cleared I took Nobby to one side; there I asked him as I looked at the dead Russians, "Nobby, did you think it odd that those four Russians who attacked you and me were trying to capture us and not kill us?"

"Well, now you mention it, Bill, they didn't seem too keen to kill us and one of them could have killed me early on in the tussle. Shit, Bill, I hope this doesn't mean what I think it does, after all you and I are the only two here who were in the original group."

"I hope we are wrong Nobby, but the sooner we get on that bloody submarine the better."

"I'll drink to that, Bill!"

Next I made my way to speak with the young officer who had insisted on coming with us. He was from the post and he had refused to go on the Merchantman when he had left the post. It was against all the rules but I had brought him with me rather than having a row with him and leaving him wandering around Murmansk. Anyway before I got to him one of the lads called me over to see our lads who had picked up a couple of nasty wounds each. I told him to do what he could for them and as I turned he pulled at my sleeve and said he had something to tell me.

"Go on," I said, "spit it out man, we haven't got all day."

"It's that officer, Sarge, he hid behind those bushes during the punch-up we've just had. Also I think he was a little surprised when it ended and he came out, to see we were not all dead or prisoners."

"Shit! That's all I need to make my day. Get everything together and let's get the hell out of here, so take two of the lads and go and get the boats ready to launch. We'll be along in a minute, right!"

Next I approached very cautiously the young officer we had acquired."Sir!" I said, "I think it could be very dangerous for us and disastrous for the people we have just left if we leave these dead bodies and they are found before we and the men on the Merchant ship are well clear of Russian territorial waters."

"Oh!" he said, "and why would we be in trouble Sergeant?"

"Well, sir, I hope you don't take offence, but I think that if we leave dead bodies around the place, the locals might just get a little bit upset about it. By locals I mean the Local Military. After all we are in one of the most heavily populated Military areas in the world."

"Yes I suppose you are right, but what do you think I should do about it Sergeant?"

I looked at him and thought shit he is the officer and I'm just one of the bloody Indians. I may have a few more feathers than the average, but I am still just an Indian and not a chief, so what does he mean by that question, "What do I think we should do with them?"

Instead I just said. "You sir, well, you won't have to do anything. You see you are just a passenger on this trip sir. It is I who will decide what we do and sort that thing out. I'm purely informing you out of courtesy that I intend to take these dead Russians with us. At least we are now very close to the launch point. So we do not have to carry them too far, but I'm also afraid you are going to have to carry one of them."

He looked at me for at least a full minute before he said, "Well I suppose it will be better if we don't leave bodies all over the place."

Too bloody true it was mate, I thought, as I turned and told the others to load up with a body each and move out.

So, the die was cast and along with our wounded and the dead Russians we eventually made it back to the submarine. When we got inboard I was called to the control room to see the Skipper.

He told me, "Your young officer has already given me a brief outline of the problems that you have caused ashore Sergeant."

I just looked at him with my mouth open. "Problems I've caused ashore, and young officer," I said, "you know I don't have a young officer with me. I have a member of the team who came out of the post and refused to go on the Merchant ship, but he's not one of mine sir."

"Well, who the hell is this young man?" the Skipper asked, pointing to the officer who had come with us.

"He is the man I've just told you about; he is from the listening post. He refused to board the Merchant ship and came along with us instead. Another thing, sir, we were ambushed by a group of very professional soldiers; they were some of the best troops I have come across for a very long time. What I would like to know is how they came to be waiting for us just where they were, sir?"

"All right, Sergeant, save us from the war stories. You realise that we can no longer go on with the next part of the operation."

I thought, really sir, I don't give a shit about that, but I said. "I have two very badly wounded men and I would like to go and see how they are, if you don't mind Sir!"

He looked at me for a second or two and then his stance relaxed and he said, "Yes of course you must go and see to them, but I want you back here as soon as you can make it."

I made my way to the small space they call a sickbay on the submarine. There, I had a word with the medic they had on the boat, a Chief Petty Officer. He told me, "One of your lads has died, and I do not think the other one can last the day out."

As I looked at him he said, "I do not have the facilities on here; these men needed a major operating theatre. All I've got are bandages and pills, which is all we ever carry; I am very sorry mate."

"That's okay. Just do your best, let me know as soon as you can if my other lad dies. I've got to get back to the control room now, so thanks anyway."

Then I made my way to see Nobby who was with the rest of the lads in the forward torpedo room. I asked him if they had found any radios amongst the Russian bodies. I was most surprised when he told me they had not. So, I thought if they had no radios and none of them had got away from the fight then it stood to reason that their superiors might think they had not yet made contact with us. It was then that I had the idea we could bury the dead Russians at sea so that they would not be found. My point was the Russians would not yet know a contact had been made. They might even think they had a group of deserters on their hands, which was highly unlikely and I didn't really believe either. My belief was that they would not be looking for us yet or the men we had left behind in the listening post. All of which just went to show how naive I was about the whole operation. I was now starting to have doubts about the whole setup and I was starting to wonder just a little bit how it was we had been able to move around one of the most heavily guarded military areas in the world without question.

When I returned to the control room the Skipper asked me how my men were and I told him, "One is dead, and the other will probably not see the day out."

To which he said, "I am sorry to hear that, but we must press on, we have other more immediate problems at the moment. We have just picked up a contact on the sonar. I am not happy with it and unfortunately we are going to be very busy here for a while. So you and your young officer had better leave the control room and get some rest while we go about losing this Russian."

It was about seven hours later that I was awakened by a young matelot who told me the Skipper would like to see me now. When I arrived in the control room the Skipper immediately said. "It would be best if we take these bodies back to base along with the two of your lads who have died of their wounds."

I disagreed and said, "If we do, sir, there is always the chance of more people than is good for the operation finding out about it. It is always easier to keep something secret, the fewer the number of people who know about it."

While the Skipper and I were talking I noticed, but paid little attention to, the young officer who had been in charge of the party we had brought out. He should have been on the Merchantman, but was somehow on the submarine. I did notice though that he was taking a rather intense interest in our conversation.

In the end the Skipper and I had quite an argument about the problem of the dead Russians, but he eventually saw that I was right. The point which finally convinced him was that he would have one hell of a job explaining to his immediate superiors why it was he had a group of dead Russian servicemen on his submarine when he returned to his base on completion of his patrol, by which time we would have all left his submarine.

At last the Submarine Skipper decided to give them all a decent burial at sea. Once that had been done he made arrangements to put us ashore at a prearranged place. It was always the policy that if things should go drastically wrong, we would be put ashore at night and at the first opportunity. Preferably he was to put us ashore in an area where British Land Forces were exercising. So it was that three nights later we all turned up in the middle of an exercise battle area in Scotland. We found ourselves amongst part of the Highland Division of all people.

That was something else. At first, I thought the Skipper of the submarine had taken revenge on me by putting us ashore back in bloody Russia. It was one of the most unnerving things that ever happened to me. We appeared in the middle of the night amongst this bunch of heathen camouflaged devils who spoke a language no self respecting 'Englishman' would deem to learn. Not only could we not understand a word they said to us but they made out or pretended not to understand us. Another thing I do believe the Skipper delayed his signal to London that he had landed us as arranged in the predetermined area. I believe it was just to get even with us for spoiling his next exercise in the area of Bear Island. I suppose that I should have looked at it as a forerunner to the troubles that I am suffering at this moment. But then at that precise moment I did not intend ever to get into this situation. Still we live and learn.

The signal from the shadowy people in the bowels of 'Whitehall' who run these operations eventually reached these heathen bastards. I think they thought they had captured some German Second World War paratroopers. Not to put too fine a point on it, I think I am right in saying that we were all extremely pleased to be away from them. They live in a different world from you and me. You know to them it is a glorious world of poor 'Bonny Prince Charlie' and how he was double-crossed by the same people who kicked them off the land to make way for sheep!

The main thing was the listening post we had left was to everybody's surprise, well to my surprise, up and running as normal. It seemed that everybody who was anybody was happy, and really pleased with themselves. For my part I was just pleased to be away from it all; I believed we had pushed our luck just about as far as it would go. My mind was made up, wild bloody horses would not be able to drag me back into that damned place again and I said as much in my cups that night. We all went on the town that night before we dispersed to better things and better places. This last trip had taken a hell of a lot out of us all and to tell the truth we had all had one hell of a fright.

Not to put too fine a point on it, from now on as far as I was concerned any trips to the north were taboo. I was due to join a commando unit in Plymouth for what I hoped would be a long and quiet summer. It can be beautiful in that part of the country in the summer. Running around on Dartmoor playing silly buggers, and taking part in exercises organised and run by non-combatants and lying in the heather with the sun beating down on one's back, while pretending to play soldiers. What with trips around the sound to Jennycliff, runs ashore in Union Street or even the Barbican in the old Scrumpy Dens, and make and mend every Wednesday afternoon. Hell, what more could a man ask for.

So, with much enthusiasm, the next afternoon I caught the train to Plymouth from Paddington. So it was that within a couple of hours of arriving and seeing the movements non-commissioned officer in The Royal Marine Barracks Stonehouse, I was off to join 43- Commando, stationed in those Barracks in Plymouth. Good old 'Guz'.

When I joined 43-Commando in the Barracks I had expected to be there for at least eighteen months; what a fool I turned out to be. I hardly had time to settle in when I received a pier head jump to join a unit in the Far East. It was natural for me to think they must require my expertise out there. God! What a load of cobblers that turned out to be. I could not come up with any really good plausible reason or excuse why I should not go. So I did what all good little soldiers in all armies do; I packed my knapsack and off to war I went. Not quite like the first time I had been out there in the Far East, like the proverbial 'lamb to the slaughter'. No, I did have a little more off than that this time; because I had after all been trained in a certain kind of job that required some sense of reality since my first trip to the Far East.

They do not after all send people like me to such places as the Far East without a reason and that would not be to sample the delights of the flesh spots that those parts of the world offer our young men for a price. Well, they wouldn't send me there without a job of work for me to do, or so I consoled myself. So it was that I left the cold and wet summer of Southwest England and that Early Warning System of attack against our beloved England which was safe in the hands of a dozen or so men, men who were buried deep in the ground just off the left-hand side of the river mouth leading to the Russian northern port of Murmansk! Oh! Sleep well in your beds, you stalwart men of England in the knowledge that you are safe. I knew that I was off to a far safer place than you even if there was a war going on out there. In other words "I care not for your predicament, Jack, for I am in the boat" or to be more precise, "'F' you, Jack, I'm safely inboard".

I arrived in Singapore, only to find that the unit which I was to join had left for Borneo some few days before. As is the dream of all of us who join units that have just left to go on exercise, or to war even, it looked like 'Ceremonial Duties' for me. At last my dream had come true and I believed that I had for the first time in my professional life made the dreaded 'Rear Party'. The high life of those unsung heroes, 'the Rear Party', at last I'd made it; my cup it runneth over, as the man said. Mornings spent lying around some company store or office, drinking tea, coffee or Cokes and the like, contemplating the evening entertainment. Afternoons getting my head down and the evenings spent checking on the lonely talent left behind, boy oh boy what a hell of a posting!

Well, that idea was short-lived if anything ever was. Within a couple of hours of the aircraft landing at Changi International Airport, I arrived at Burma Camp in Johore. The mess steward showed me to a cabin and then told me I would have to vacate it in the morning. "Why?" I asked him. He told me that I would be flying out to join the unit in Borneo the next day. That was the first of many surprises and one that I hadn't expected at all. You could have knocked me out with a feather when he told me I was to fly out and join the unit in Borneo. Well, I did expect to do that anyway, but the next day. That was a bit of a shit house move if I ever saw one.

I had believed Corporal Jenkins, the movements clerk in Barracks back in Plymouth, when he told me that the unit was going to be re-deployed to Borneo. He said that would not be for a couple of months yet. So when the driver who collected me from Changi movements told me they had already gone well, I thought I was looking good for 'the Rear Party' for a week or two at least, but it was not to be. Still I would at least get my jungle training in a realistic manner. I'd expected to be sent to Borneo as soon as they could get me on a flight, but tomorrow!

So having accepted the inevitable I had a shower and settled down to write to my wife before supper. To say I was not in a very good frame of mind was a bit of an understatement if ever there was one. I was also a little worried as I thought that my bad temper may have been transferred into the letter I was writing. After about four tries at writing a letter to her, I gave up the idea of writing at all and made my way to the mess.

When I entered the mess at suppertime there were only two other mess members there. They looked a couple of surly sods to say the least. They made no move to even acknowledge I was there so I introduced myself to them. They then told me the rest of the rear party SNCOs were all men who had their wives out here with them, which figured. The three of us therefore had the mess to ourselves. At one point I had toyed with the idea of getting a taxi down to Singapore alone because they were not very good company. Then I thought, what I really need is a good night's sleep; it would really be better for me than a night on the town. Nothing worse in the world than having a hangover when you are on a flight in an RAF transport plane to make you feel on top of the world. More so if the flight is taking you to join a unit which is on active service in one of the biggest jungles of South East Asia.

As I was about to retire for the night the bell to the front door of the mess rang. One of the men whom I had met earlier got up and sauntered to the door to answer it. He returned to the bar a couple of minutes later and said, "There is a man at the door to see you. Says he is an old friend of yours; he is dressed in civilian clothes, but he says he's a Naval Commander or something."

When he had completed his little speech he just stood there looking at me. I don't know why he did that, perhaps he expected me to jump through a hoop or something. From the look on his face I could see that he disapproved of sergeants who fraternised with Naval Officers. If he did but know it on that point I agreed with him.

With reluctance I got up and went to the door. Sure enough standing there was a man dressed in the obligatory cream linen suit worn by all officers abroad. This one said he was a Naval Commander and he was standing there a little too fidgety for my liking. He was no old friend of mine either. I had never seen the man before in my life.

"Colour Sergeant Johnston?" he asked.

"Yes," I replied, giving him my nonchalant couldn't care less look.

"Oh! Good, I am Commander Fitzsimmonds, I'm with the Foreign Office, and I need to talk to you in private."

Oh shit here we go again, but I stood just inside the mess door looking at him, and said nothing; for a brief second or two I had a great impulse to close the door in his face. My bloody basic training took over and I didn't, but I had a strange feeling that this man would mean nothing other than grief for me. I just felt bad about him. He had an air of doom about him, my bloody doom! He also had the deepest voice that I have ever heard.

Instead of following all my instincts I said, "You had better step inside, sir, while I get clearance for you to enter the mess."

To which he said, rather too quickly. "No, we need to talk more privately than that; perhaps we could take a walk around the camp."

"We'd better take a turn round the parade ground then, hadn't we, Sir?"

With that we set off to find the parade ground and I thought I must be bloody mad. I had never been in this camp before. I didn't have the slightest idea or clue where the bloody parade ground was. While we were wandering aimlessly around the camp looking for the parade ground, I spotted a young Marine who was carrying what looked to be a pick handle. To me he looked as if he was a wandering patrol type of sentry, but I wasn't sure. When I asked him where the parade ground was he looked at me as if I had just landed from Mars. He did point us in the right direction though, but most surprising he never checked our identity. Perhaps it was because of the linen suit the Commander was wearing.

Finally we found the parade ground and the Commander stopped under a lamp post, which was by the entrance to 'God's Little Acre' as they call it. He then said,

"I have some things to show you. It is better we stay by this light then we can take a walk when you have seen them."

With that he produced a batch of photographs, he handed them to me saying, "Have a good look at these."

They were all pictures of groups of men. As I studied them I noticed there were in all of them two men; a thin man who was about five foot eight in height and another one about six foot two. In some of them the thin man looked reasonable, but in others he had the look of a hunted man. He was a man whom I knew and for whom I had no feeling of comradeship at all; I only had feelings of hatred.

The Commander then said, "As you can see, two men are common to them all."

I just nodded; in a couple of them he was in uniform, but in others he was wearing civilian clothes. In some he was with a couple of others; in others he was with anything from two to twenty companions. In one he was with a large group at some sort of protest march, on all the photographs there was one more thing – he was the one doing all the talking. This was common to each of the groups of photos. It was obvious in all of them that he was the leader.

I handed them back to the Commander and we moved away from the circle of light. As we did so, I asked him, "Has your man got the photographs of us, which he was taking, all right?"

"Probably, after all he is quite good."

"Good, but being photographed talking to me may not have been the wisest move you have made so far. Now can we get on to why you are here?"

"Do you want to check my identity?"

At first I was going to say no, but changed my mind and said. "Yes, as I don't know who you are sir. I would rather check it before you start to tell me what it is you want with me."

"Right," he said as he produced his ID card, "did you recognise anybody in the pictures I have just shown you?"

"Well yes, I did, I'd be a bit thick if I hadn't spotted anybody because I'm in two of them myself."

"Right, now do you know which of the men in those pictures I am interested in?"

"Well if it's not me then, yes, I do. He is the only other one who is in them all."

"How long have you known him?"

"Well, I first met him in the Suez Canal Zone in 1953 when I was a young Corporal serving in a Commando there. We were stationed in the 156 Transit Camp in Port Fuad. He was an RCT driver in an RCT Transport Company, which was stationed over the Canal in Port Said; in those days he called himself Geordie Merchant. We used to spend most of our time escorting the RCT's company trucks around the Canal Zone. I got to know him and most of the other drivers in the company quite well. The man was an out and out Communist, but then you already know that, don't you?

"We met up again later, when I was on a detachment to the Home Office. Both of us had different names by then. I think he was really original in his choice; he called himself Smith, I mean Smith! You would have thought he could have thought of a more original name than that."

All For A King's Shilling

Then I went on. "You know he thought I went to gaol with the rest of them. As you probably know, I did go for a time, just long enough for it to look convincing. He never really worried me you know. No, it is that rat who is his minder. That's the man who puts the willies up me."

"You must tell me about him some time, but I have a more important problem just now," he said. "Did you know your friend Merchant or Smith, whatever he calls himself, is occasionally here in Singapore?"

"Oh, is he and just what has that to do with me?"

There followed a pause and he eventually said, "I, well we, would like you to renew your acquaintance with him."

"Why?"

"Well, I cannot tell you that until you agree."

This time it was I who took time to answer. "I am not going in cold or alone, not with that minder of his around. He is an evil bastard and I know I can take Merchant out any day, on a one to one basis, if you ask me to. The problem, as you may have noticed, if you have followed him around, is that he is never alone; his minder is always there in the background."

"He has always been alone when we have watched him" the Commander said.

I knew Merchant or Smith, or whatever he now called himself, had never operated alone in his life. I looked at the Commander in disbelief. "All I can say to you Sir, is your men are not very good. If you believe that he is always alone, I wouldn't mind betting Merchant and his man have got every one of your men pegged. So the answer I'm afraid has got to be no, I will not go in. You see they will also have hired local heavies to cover their tracks. Out here that means if you make a mistake you will have some local Triad members on your back before you can wink an eye and those bastards play for keeps. So, I'm afraid it has got to be no, in these circumstances."

He paused for a while and then said. "What if we can put a team together whom you know, then will you do it?"

"With my partners, well maybe, but with your men who haven't spotted his backup yet, it has still got to be no way! It is all immaterial anyway because none of the men I normally work with are in this part of the world. So, it seems the operation you have planned is a no-go, as far as I am concerned isn't it, Sir?"

"They warned me that that might be your answer, so I have already arranged for one of your partners to go in with you."

"Who is that then?"

"Corporal Smith, he is in my car waiting for us, he is on if you are."

"What about Corporal Clark, have you managed to get him?"

"I am afraid not, but I have some good men with the team."

After looking at him for a while, I at last said, "Okay sir, you are on. I'll give it a whirl on two conditions. First you had better clear it with this unit's CO before we go any further. I don't think I'm exactly flavour of the month in this man's army at the moment. So I need to see his authorisation before I do anything with this. Secondly, if Corporal Nobby Clark is not there then I'll call it off; and if I don't think you or your men are up to it then I shall have the liberty to call it all off! You can go ahead and play silly buggers as long as you like but we will not take any part in it, okay, Sir?"

"Well, I have already got clearance from your CO, and yes you can quit as and when you want."

I wasn't surprised by this and said. "Good, but I would like to see all of that, the authority and your okay for me to call it off. If or whenever I feel the job has become too unsafe, in writing, sir."

"Let us go to my car," he said.

"No sir, if you don't mind, I will read it under the lamp post over there. If it is in your car, then you must go and get it."

With that we walked over to the lamp. He handed a paper over to me, which he took out of his pocket. So he had had it with him all along. My trust in him did not increase in the slightest with that move. Sure enough, it was from the Commando's Commanding Officer saying I was to be seconded to this Commander's unit for as long as required, to complete their operations in Singapore.

"All right, now let us add the first and second proviso to the bottom of this piece of paper. Then I'll get some things from my cabin and I will be right with you."

When he had entered the provisos to the form and signed them I folded the paper up and took it with me to my cabin to collect a couple of changes of clothes, a couple of knives that I thought I might need, knowing the man I was about to get involved with. Then with one last look around the cabin I went out and got into the back of the Ford car, which was now waiting at the front of the mess. I climbed in the back seat, and looked at the man already sitting in the back of the car and said, "How long have you been out here mate?"

"A week, all right. I only hope you know what the hell we are getting into."

"You tell me, it seems you signed up first! So what line of shit did he spin you then?"

The drive down to Singapore was quiet; after our tête-à-tête nobody in the car spoke at all. It was an uncomfortable drive to Singapore and finally when we arrived at a small office block situated in Ophir Street later that evening I was a little worried. The offices were in the three floors over a tailor's shop, in the down town area of Singapore. The Commander suggested that both of us should have a look at Bugis Street, before we turned in for the night. Get to see the lie of the land before we started the operation in the morning, he said.

"Why, has it all changed since I was here in fifty-one on my way to join the Commando who were stationed at Batu Gajah?" I asked him.

"No, but I would rather you looked over the area where the operation is to take place. So I think it would be best if you have a look at the area now."

"All right, but get me some street maps of the area and some coffee and leave Mick and me alone for the next couple of hours."

"Look I am the one who is running this operation and you will do as you are told."

"That's all right by me; come on Mick, we will make our own way back to our units. Good night sir, best of luck with what you have in mind. Just get a couple of your own men to carry out your orders; we are off."

"Just a minute, I am in command and I say what happens, you are now seconded to my unit and you will both do as you are told."

All For A King's Shilling

I was about to say you would be a wise man not to place any bets on that assumption mate, but in the end I kept quiet. Which was really just as well because the next moment from the doorway came that resounding voice, which sent shivers down both Mick's and my spines, as Major or perhaps by now it's Colonel, god knows what he is now, bloody Brown spoke his words of wisdom.

"I would suggest you listen to what the Colour Sergeant says," the voice from the doorway said. "You see Commander, if you are going to ask these men to risk their lives, the least you can do is let them work out for themselves how."

"Sir," the Commander said, "you said this was my part of the operation."

My ears pricked up when I heard this Naval Commander call my old pal Brown "Sir!" It wasn't normal for a Naval Commander to call a Major Sir, what with the Commander being senior to the Major that is.

Oh yes, that bit," Brown said, "but that was before you got this bum Johnston on your team and I don't think you quite know him. You may have read his file, but that will only tell you the good bits. He doesn't care if you have him court-martialled you know, he knows you will be the loser. So let him do it his way just this once, just to please me, I will see he stays on the straight and narrow for you. If he is to be court-martialled, then I promised myself some years ago that it would be I who would have the pleasure of hanging the bastard."

"I see he still loves you , Bill," said Mick

"If I had known you were involved sir I would not have touched this lot with a barge pole. I just can't take this bloody name-calling these days."

"Now then simmer down Colours, there's a good man. What do you intend doing with the maps?"

Giving him my 'what an idiot you are look' I said, "Well, what I had intended sir was for Corporal Smith and I to have a good look at the street area, and memorise my way around before I get out there. Tomorrow when the place is busy and going about its normal business, then Mick and I will go out and check the ground we have memorised this evening."

"That sounds okay to me! So, Commander you had better organise some coffee for them as well because I think they may be in for a long night."

I looked at Mick, but his face had that not in this world look and I thought there is a rabbit off somewhere. Looking back at Brown I came to the conclusion he had either retired or he had been promoted. Mick had me worried a little and I wished to hell Nobby had been here as well, but he wasn't so I'd better make the most of it.

"We would also appreciate a complete run down on what you really want us to do. Once we have satisfied ourselves about the area, that is, if it is okay with you, sir." I asked the Commander. With a curt nod of his head he gave his agreement, but it was obvious he was reluctant so to do. He appeared to be irritated by the way things had gone since old Brown had turned up.

Mick and I spent the next three hours memorising the street maps of Singapore. We were tracing our movements around the place on the maps backwards and forwards around the place. We were planning short cuts from one street to another, routes that we would test out the next day when we got out on to the streets. We had to know our way round the place, side streets, back streets, alleyways and even short cuts through people's houses; and studying how to get around by using all these back streets and alleyways was one way of losing a tail or staying with a target.

The Commander returned with some coffee, but most importantly he had some aerial photographs of the area. He also had with him some photographs of normal daytime street scenes. The street scenes showed the changes that took place when the area became an entertainments' centre at night. We thanked him, and continued with our studies. It was around two o'clock when we decided we had accomplished all we could at that point. So, I went looking for the Commander and I found him in a small kind of operations room. This room was a little farther down the passage from the room we were working in. It contained some quite sophisticated radio gear in it, also a couple of items which I could only think were computers and a teleprinter. As I looked around the place to my surprise I saw somebody whom both Mick and I knew. A man I had not seen for some years; the last time was when we were doing the trial run up in Scotland; he was one of Brown's sidekicks. He had left the place in Scotland the same time as us, but he had not been one of our men and he had not been to the camp to which they took us. He hadn't been any part of the operation so far as I knew, but he knew a hell of a lot about it. That he was one of Brown's men I was certain and by the same token, as a Royal Marine, I believed he would help us if we asked him to; that he would eventually tell Brown went without saying.

I made my way over to him and said, "Hi! Long time no see; what's your part in this crazy operation?"

He then went into a rigmarole about the job he had, which was all Double Dutch to me, it seemed he had progressed into the base planning side of operations. Then I asked him, "Tell me, can you keep an eye on the reports of people's movements which may come in later? I believe we will not be given all the information we need, being the outsiders that we are?"

"That's okay, no problems, I'll keep my eyes open."

"Don't let any of the others know, mind, it's just that I don't want to be caught with my pants down. As you will remember I don't trust old Brown, because it's his back that he looks after first, and this Commander guy, is he really for real, or what?"

"No problem, Bill, I'll keep a good watch out for you." His reply made me think a little and wonder just how much loyalty some weeks spent together in Scotland would buy! Also a short spell in the same 'Mob' normally buys a little help these days, but as usual I said nothing.

Just then the Commander arrived at my side, I do not know if he had heard any of our conversation or not, but I turned to him and said. "We are happy so far with the area, but we intend to do some leg work tomorrow. We need to know every part of the place before we commit ourselves. I would feel a lot better about it all if you could tell us what it is all about. Then we will be able to go to work in the morning, knowing exactly what you require of us."

"Yes, Colour Sergeant, you are right. The time has come for all to be revealed." Then to the room in general he said, "So if you would all like to make your way into the conference room we can make a start with the briefing. I'm afraid there is one problem, somebody will have to man the communications' room, while the rest are being briefed."

All For A King's Shilling

At that the man I had just been talking to volunteered and he was immediately given the job of watching the shop as they say. He just nodded to me as we left the room and we followed the others to their conference room; as we left I caught the glance between the man I'd been talking to and I realised then that I would not really be able to trust anybody or anything these anybodies told me from now on.

When everybody had gathered in this small room they called a conference room, which was along the landing at the rear of the building, the Commander, after all the silly chattering that was going on had stopped, introduced all his staff to us. Mick and I were both relieved when he declined to give our names to the gathering.

He just told them, "These two men are from 3 Commando Brigade. They are now part of the team for the duration of this operation."

I wasn't too happy with some of the grins and smirks which I saw that bit of information greeted with. As I looked around the assembled group I wasn't too happy with either their dress or their haircuts. Something didn't look right with this little lot. No, very few of them to my mind had the mannerisms that I would associate with British servicemen. Something was definitely not right here, but what was it, what was wrong?

There was a slide projector on a stand and a sixteen-millimetre film projector on the table which was at the rear of the room. In this room when we entered was a man whom neither Mick nor I had ever seen before. The Commander omitted to introduce him, but I knew the moment the man opened his mouth it would have a slight and nearly untraceable American accent. All he needed was his porkpie straw hat, his Frank Sinatra trench coat and he would be set. Talk about CIA and the like, hell they have the imagination of budgerigars. Well, this was the one who gave us a presentation on the situation as our intelligence or should I say the CIA saw it.

It was obvious from the start that my friend from the old days in the Suez Canal Zone was the target in the whole affair. It turned out that he had done his time inside after we had all been arrested some years earlier. It was also obvious that his time in gaol hadn't reformed the man at all; he was still a true traveller. All it had done was to put him out of circulation for a while. He had upon his release continued his way as the traveller that he was. To tell the truth he had probably spent most of his time inside just studying his 'cause', which was socialist world domination, still further.

It was this continued activity that had, it seemed, brought him to the notice of our American friends which would account for the man with the very slight American accent being there. The last part of the film they showed us was of my old friend and he was in amongst the tables and crowds of Bugis Street. At this point I was looking at the film intently.

"Can you stop this film, wind it back and replay the last few frames, then put it on hold when I ask you? I want to have a look at it a few frames earlier if I can?"

"No problem, I can stop it at any point. You just give me the nod and we will stop it for you" the American said.

When they next stopped the film I pointed to a man in the crowd and asked. "Is this man one of yours?"

I knew before they answered that he was not, but to my surprise a couple of them replied rather hesitantly that he was. Then I pointed to another man and asked them if they knew him; again to my surprise they said yes.

At that point I said. "Well, folks that changes everything, because if they are your men I'd really be surprised. What is more if it is true and they are your men then I'm going to be on the flight to Kuching. So can somebody get me a fast black to take me back to Burma Camp? I need to collect my gear."

That was when they all gathered round the picture being projected on to the wall and peered at the faces which I had pointed out. The first one I had pointed out I knew as McDonald Ferguson, who worried me more than anything, or anybody. The description I used of rat face was perfect once you had seen him, but he was the most evil man I knew. He killed for pleasure; friend or foe, it made no difference to him; when the urge to kill came over him he did just that, he killed!

The Commander said, "He just looks like a merchant seaman on a run ashore, so what is odd about him?"

"That maybe so," I said from the door, "but the point is you said he was one of yours. So rewind the film for a few frames then play it through in slow motion if you can, and watch him."

This they did and eventually the penny dropped as to just what the rat-faced man was up to; I heard one or two gasps from the rest of them. The one who was the field section leader said. "We had confused the man you pointed out with one of our own men, who just happened to be standing next to this man you have pointed out."

"Just happened to be standing next to," I said, "hell what have we let ourselves into Mick? I don't know about you, but I'm off to Borneo tomorrow, or is it today. You stay if you want to."

They stepped back from the screen and decided to find out who this man was. "No need for that, it will only show him as deceased. You see he was supposed to have been killed in a car crash some years ago in England. God knows who was in the car; whoever it was he fitted this toerag's description to a tee. His real name in case you want to know is McDonald Ferguson. That is the name he has always used in the past, what he calls himself now I have no idea."

God I thought why am I still standing here talking to these fools? If I had any sense I'd be in a fast black by now on my way to Burma Camp. That was when I realised that I had to do this thing; I owed some of my pals from the Home Office days that much. Years before I'd said I would make sure they would not have died in vain. Some day somewhere I'd get the little shit that had killed them. Yes, I had a date with that bastard Merchant, a date I would now be able to keep. I had vowed then I would kill the pig of a man one day. This looked to be the first and only chance I was ever going to get to do just that. So I would stay, that was why I was still standing in the room and not in a fast black heading for the causeway.

I looked across at the Commander and I studied him for a moment and satisfied he had no idea of my reasons for staying, I said. "There sir, I told you there would be a back-up covering your man, but you said no. Yet, here you have a film of the whole setup. The other man I pointed out is not one of yours either, that I know also. All of you look at these pictures of yours, and you only see the target and your own men. You are blind to what is going on around you. Know what that is, sir? It's the sign of amateurs. What you need to do now is to check out every person in the film. You need somebody who knows what he is doing to analyse the whole crowd; an expert will be able to tell from the film just who is watching whom. Then and only then can we venture out into the street with any degree of certainty that all aspects of the job are covered. Now, after this carry on I do not really think any of you are being very professional about this. So I think my friend and partner, well, we will just withdraw our services from this little charade. Until everything is sorted out.

"If you want a couple of mugs to have a go at these two as things stand now, well then there are plenty of servicemen in this area who would jump at the chance of a good fight. Mind, I think the possibility of death for Queen and Country or is it Uncle Sam and America would be the last thing on their minds. For my partner and me, well the answer at the moment is no. Get things sorted by morning and we may re-enter the fray. You see these men you have filmed are not your common or garden criminals. They are the serious type of 'fellow travellers', they are not to be messed with. Not that is, unless you feel as strongly about your own cause as they do about theirs and perhaps you are prepared to die for it. Because they are prepared to die for their beliefs, every day they wake up they are prepared to die that day if needs must for the cause! "

I looked at them for a minute or so then said. "The way your vibes are coming across to me, well I'm not too sure any of you know just how serious, and I mean, deadly serious this thing you are now involved in really is. What is more, with you lot covering my back I know I would not feel safe or secure out there. Not with a bunch of amateurs backing us up. No sir, you can deal us both out of this game until you get your act together. These men you are following are not your normal international revolutionaries. They are not your twisted self-righteous college Communists. No sir these men fight to the death; they have left people who were a lot better than us at the job dead in dirty gutters all over the world. These men are your dedicated travellers of the cause and the cause is more important than any one of them. I do believe I speak for both of us," and I looked over at Mick and he nodded his approval, "when I say until you get your act together count us out!"

At that point I had a distinct feeling I had thrown a cat in amongst the pigeons and with that both Mick and I rose and left the room.

We had not gone more than two steps down the corridor when the guy with the American accent came out of the room. "Can I have a word with you two?" he asked.

As I looked at him I thought this guy just isn't right in this setup. Then I looked at Mick and he just shrugged his shoulders. "It's up to you Bill," he said.

Why not? I thought, I have no intention of leaving now. Not when I have an old score to settle. So, I turned to the American and said, "Okay, but tell me what rank are you in your secret army?" He looked a little taken aback at first then getting his act back in gear he said with a deeper American accent, "that's none of your business, but what rank are you, the way people run after you I don't believe you are a Sergeant?"

"No, my man," I replied, "I'm a Captain, a captain of the heads."

"A captain of what?" he asked.

"The bloody heads, man; I clean up all the shit that fools like you leave everywhere and embarrass your governments while you play silly buggers! Now whatever story you have to tell us, it had better be a bloody good one."

He showed us into another room to the left of the passage.

When we were inside he closed the door behind us. My friend Brown who had saved us from the Commander earlier was already in the room. I looked at Mick and said, "I do not like this one tiny bit, I think we are being railroaded mate!"

The American opened the conversation, "You are not being railroaded as you put it and yes it has been a very amateur operation so far." He then went on before I could get a word in, "Your friend here," nodding in Brown's direction, "assured me everything would change once you two arrived. By the way, should there not be three of you?"

Just as I was about to say yes, I thought and what the hell has it got to do with you how many of us there should be. Then I looked at Brown and back again to the Yank, and I finally said. "How about we cut the crap, as you Yanks say and just get on with what you called us in here to tell us." I didn't like this Mr America at all and I could see Mick wasn't too enamoured of him either.

"Okay," he said, "it is like this. My name is John Smith, and I work for the American Government."

Both Mick and I looked at each other in astonishment and I said, "He isn't even original in his choice of a name is he, John bloody Smith indeed, any relation of yours Mick? Sorry mate but it looks as if we are knee deep in Smiths at the moment."

A hurt expression crossed the Yank's face, but he just said, "If you don't mind I will continue." He then launched into a tale of woe the Americans were going through, which broke my heart folks, it really did.

He told us, "The Vietcong were getting many sophisticated weapons of late and we believed this Smith, Merchant or whatever he calls himself, has something to do with it."

"How would that be?" I asked.

"I am coming to that," he said and went on. "It seems your friend, Geordie Merchant, as you call him, was released from a gaol in Scotland soon after you were released, Colour Sergeant. He turned up in London and while he was there he caused the death of an undercover agent. Or at least that's what your people think, that it was him who caused the man's death. The next we heard of him he was working out of Gdansk as a crew member of an ocean going Polish collier. It is our belief he is the ship's political officer. It is because he is a member of the crew that your people in London started to take an interest in the ship and him."

"That would figure, but what has this to do with you, Vietnam and us?" I said.

He continued, "Well, it was shortly after he joined the ship, it started sailing for the Far East and it always called in at Singapore. It always spent three days here and three days is a long time for a ship to bunker at Singapore which is not very cheap these days. Don't get me wrong, the bills are always paid on time, there are no problems there. It is strange, but when the ship calls here your friend is the only one who is allowed ashore. The Skipper never comes ashore here and that is unusual to say the least. He must be the only Skipper who has never set foot in Singapore."

"Tell me," I asked him, "does McDonald Ferguson come ashore with him as well?"

"We always thought he was alone so we always thought he came ashore on his own. It was not until you pointed Ferguson out we even knew he was here. Or that he was in any way connected with your old friend."

All For A King's Shilling

I looked at Mick, but he just shrugged.

"Okay," I said, "go on, but I would need to know both men's movements and what happens when they come ashore. What they do, where they go and who do they see? "

"Well," he said, "he, Merchant that is, goes to the office of the shipping agent who looks after their interests. Nothing odd there, we have a man in the office."

"Hold it a minute, did I hear you say you had a man in the shipping office? A man in a shipping office that handles Communist ships and details manifests and the like and you need our services. What is wrong?"

"Don't worry, everything in the office is above board. Anyway after visiting the office he goes and does some shopping, buys some shirts and things. Sometimes he buys cameras, watches and radios. Sometimes he buys other items, items which are attractive to people behind the Iron Curtain and ready cash for him when he returns. All of these we think are either for the crew, for their own use, or maybe for sale on the black market back in Poland. Anyway he returns to the ship at about four o'clock each day he is ashore."

"If what you tell us is correct, how is it some of those photographs were taken at night?" I asked.

"I am just coming to that."

"Somehow I thought you might be, but you still haven't answered my query about your man in the shipping office," I said.

Again he didn't enlighten me on the shipping office, but went on about Merchant leaving the ship again.

"At about 9.30 he leaves the ship and," he said, "again he is on his own when he comes ashore. He visits one or two clubs and hotels around the docks' area. It is mostly the seedy joints in the area. Then when it gets to midnight he makes his way to Bugis Street. The street is just coming to life then and he sits alone in the middle of the street, always in the middle of the street. Spends his time talking to the girls, and the boys! If you can tell the difference that is; I for one can't tell the difference between the boys or the girls in that place."

That bit over he went on in his flat monotone voice, which was becoming a bit of a drag to listen to. "Normally at about two in the morning he goes off to one of the dosshouses which abound along the side streets. He always takes one of the young boys with him, never a girl and never one of the boys dressed like the girls, always a young boy."

The Yank for some reason seemed a little touchy about this, so I said, "Hasn't changed his habit much then I see, he always was a dirty bastard. A trait he picked up in the old days in Port Said."

The Yank looked a little disgusted at that, but he continued, "He is normally away about three quarters of an hour and when he returns he is always alone. The boy he goes with, well he will not normally return at all. He then sits at a table until dawn and when the street starts to return to its normal business as a street market, he makes his way back to the ship. The ship then sails about three hours later, on the third day, that is. Never more and never less, always three days, and always the same routine, always the same," he repeated.

I looked at the two of them and said, "So far you have told us nothing which requires our attendance. It is just a normal port bunkering visit. Communist ships do not normally let their crews off their ships, not in places like Singapore anyway; they may not get the blighters back again. A bit like our Royal Navy was, a couple of hundred years ago you know. If you care to check into the young boys then you might be on to something. You said the boys never come back to the street; is that never, never or only that night never? You see you perhaps could just get the Singapore police to arrest him as a child murderer. If the boys do appear again then that's no good. So, just what is the punch line, Mr America?"

Again I noticed he got a little touchy when I mentioned the young boys, but he went on. "We're getting to that. The ship which we are talking about is one of the three which are supposedly carrying coal to China. The manifest says it is high-grade furnace coal."

"Well what is wrong with that, may I ask?"

"For one thing," said my old friend Brown who was obviously getting a little irritated, "it is only a few years since Britain and America were going to import high-grade furnace coal from China. So why should China import the bloody stuff now, when they are bloody smothered in the damned stuff?"

"That's not all," the Yank butted in before I could answer. "The ships leave here and then have a bunkering stop in the waters off Hanoi. Now Hanoi is not renowned as a bunkering port; more to the point if these ships can sail quite comfortably all the way from Poland to Singapore, with only one stop in Angola. How come they cannot make it to China from here without a further stop and a four day stop at that in Hanoi of all places," he said. "No, we believe there is a link between the three days here and the four days in Hanoi. After spending the four days in Hanoi, they are a lot higher in the water when they leave. We think they are transporting arms to the Vietcong," he concluded.

"Okay, I'll buy that." I said, "But where do Mick and I fit into this? The sale of arms to North Vietnam is not illegal is it? You Americans, you sell millions of tons of arms to the South Vietnamese, so what is illegal about the North Vietnamese buying arms from like-minded governments to defend themselves. Anyway I seem to remember a time when Ho Chi Minh was your ally, don't you?"

The Yank looked at Brown and asked, "What is with this guy?"

"I'll reply to that one sir, if you don't mind," I said. "You see, Mr America, it's like this; it may not seem right to you that a country you are at war with, and you are at war with it even if it is only by proxy at the moment, has the right to buy arms to defend itself against aggression. Or even to carry the war to you. There is no international law which says America can sell arms to whomsoever it wants, but no other country can do the same for America's enemies. No sir," I said, "if you want my friend and me to risk our lives to do something for you well you had better come up with a better reason than you have given us so far!"

Now I could see that he was not very happy about this last bit, so ever the optimist I added, "before you say any more, Mr America, I am not nor is my 'oppo' a bloody Commie bastard. As a matter of fact if anything we are Royalists, but then you would not know what a Royalist is, would you?"

I could see my friend Brown was getting a little hot under the collar by now and it looked as if I might have pushed my luck to the limit. So I said to him, "What is your involvement in this affair then, sir?"

He looked at me for a while, and then said, "None really we are just trying to help an ally out. We hold political sway in this area, so we said we would try and help. Short of having American servicemen here, that is."

I asked him if the Singapore Government knew what was going on. "Their Prime minister would not be very pleased if he knew what you are up to."

Brown looked at the Yank and said, "Didn't I tell you he was an argumentative bastard? If you want him to go and take a look at the bloody ship and see what cargo they are really carrying, well, you had better come up with something better than you have so far."

"So, now we have it," I said "You want Mick and me to go and board a foreign ship in a foreign port to see if the cargo manifest is correct. Is that it, Mr America? Why not use the port authorities? God, you've got some bloody nerve, I'll give you that. Why don't you just stop and search it on the high seas like you do around Cuba?"

"We have tried the port authorities and we have had them open the hatches, and all there was in them was coal, and for god's sake will you stop calling me Mr America."

"So," I asked, "what the hell makes you think we will find anything other than coal? What is it you really want us to do, that the port authorities cannot do? Dig through the bloody coal until we reach the keel?"

"We need proof rather than circumstantial evidence. We don't want an incident on the high seas unless we're sure of our ground. So we would like you to have a look under the coal. Otherwise, if we stopped it on the high seas and found nothing, we would only look like fools," he said.

I looked at Mick in amazement and asked with some sarcasm, "So what is new, Mr America? You are a group of bloody fools, but you seem to want to make us the silly buggers this time. No I'm out of here unless you come up with something better.

"Oh yes, and just how is it we are going to have a look under this coal? I suppose we are talking thousands of tons of the bloody stuff. You know I was only joking when I asked you if you wanted us to dig through the bloody stuff, Christ, man, you can't be serious."

"I take umbrage at the remark that we are fools and yes, now you mention it, we are talking thousands of tons of coal and as you now ask yes, we are serious about digging into it, but I shall leave you to work out that part of your task. They say you are the best they have got. Now bloody prove it."

"Just wait one pigging minute there, Mr Stars and Stripes. They may say I am the best and perhaps I am, but I'm not bloody daft to boot. Anyway I'm only good when I am working for my own country. Not your bloody Bill of Rights, but just supposing I take you up on your request," I said, "when is the next time my old friend will be here?"

He looked at his watch and said, "Well you happen to be in luck. He has been here two days already, he is already ashore tonight. If he stays true to form he will be back again tomorrow and in Bugis Street tomorrow night. You can renew your friendship with him any time you want tonight, or tomorrow."

I looked at the Yank and said, "I am going off you, very quickly." He just grinned at me knowing he had trapped me into doing his job for him. I'd planned on killing Merchant in Singapore, but this swine would have me on this Polish ship and that was a different ball game. Digging coal, hell I'll not be digging any coal unless it is to bury some evil bastard in it.

A moment later I said, "It's perhaps time you left Mick and me to have a little chat."

They both agreed to this and left the room.

As they left the room old Brown turned at the door and said, "Best of luck to both of you Colours."

Once the door had closed and they were out of the room and we were alone in there I looked at Mick and told him. "This will be bloody dangerous Mick. I am not so sure we have an obligation to help the Yanks. There is no way I will do this if you don't think it's a goer. Mind I do owe that Communist bastard a visit."

Mick said, "If you think it is okay, then I am in. How do you intend to play it?"

"Well I've an idea or two, but I will have to run them past you as things progress today, and tomorrow morning. It has to be tomorrow, or not at all."

"Okay," Mick said, "let's do it."

I thought, you haven't given this much thought Mick, my lad, you look as if you are running on automatic at the moment. What is it you are not telling me?

Then I got up and went to the door and popped my head outside and told the Yank and Brown, "We'll do it."

"Right," the Yank said, "let's talk over how you propose to tackle this task."

"Now just slow down there a little bit, Mr America, off you go again all bright-eyed and bushy-tailed about getting involved in the job. There's more to this little charade than you think. So it would be better for all concerned if you leave the mechanics to us."

He was about to object, when Brown interrupted him.

"The Colour Sergeant is right, John, it would be better for all concerned if you stay out of it at this point. They are the operators, John, so let them operate."

To Brown I said, "I will work out the details and it really is best if none of you know, not even you, sir, just how we intend to carry out the task."

Turning to the Yank I said, "If things do go wrong, and I thought it was through anybody talking out of line, I will come after everybody who is in on it. So it is best you don't know anything from now on. I wouldn't want to spoil the American/UK relationship now, would I? That special relationship which seems to only work one way these days, eh! Still, if I need any assistance from your satellite system which you can give me, I will ask you for it. That would be the only part of the plan you would be told about."

"Suits me, Colour Sergeant, but my name is John Smith and not Mr America."

This I ignored and spoke to Brown, "I do have something I need from you though, sir. I'll need backup right from the word go, but this time I want McDonald Ferguson covered, and at the right time picked up and put under wraps. Just what wraps you put him under is up to you, but I do not want him stalking Mick's or my back, once this thing is over. The last thing I need is to spend the rest of my life looking over my shoulder to see if Ferguson is behind me."

He agreed with me and we returned to their conference room where I then outlined what I needed from the group.

"At some stage during the next evening I shall be making contact with Merchant, probably after his tête-à-tête with whatever boy he picks up. Now I shall need information on everything that happens during his trip ashore tomorrow. It is important that I know what he is up to, whom he sees and moreover everywhere he visits – shops, market stalls, bars and cafes. Most of all I need to know what Ferguson is up to and what time the two of them spend together. Where and for how long? I do not intend to have him behind me once I move in. He and any local thugs they have must be taken out before I move in. Ferguson always knew I was not the person whom Merchant thought I was. By that I mean the rat knows I am not a committed renegade like the rest of them. I'm working on the principle that he has not told anybody about me. It is hard to believe, but I am hoping that they have not discussed me, thinking I was still in jail somewhere. They must have contacts somewhere in the system because by my reckoning they should still be incarcerated in a jail somewhere in the UK."

At this I heard a bit of a snigger from one of the young men at the back. So I stopped talking and looked at them all. "I've only one thing to say to you lot," I said. "This is not a game you are involved in; some of you could die in the next few hours; these two men have killed more than twice the number of men there are in this room. Also I might add men who were better at their jobs than any of you lot seem to be. They are dedicated men and they have a cause they are fighting for. A cause which they are quite prepared to kill for. Dedicated men are dangerous men, but dedicated men who have a cause to fight for are lethal men. Now if any of you think that our way of life is not worth fighting and dying for, then I would suggest you let me know and leave this operation immediately."

Looking across at the Yank I said, "I think we need to sort this crowd out right now. They have been watching this man for god knows how long. Yet they never spotted the most dangerous man in the whole setup, Ferguson! The one man whose whereabouts it is imperative I know and also what he is up to! It is of paramount importance that he is taken out of circulation totally, before I make any contact with Merchant. Otherwise, gentlemen, if this man isn't taken out, the whole deal will be off."

"Don't worry," he said. "I shall see to it myself."

"Well, Mr America, I don't think you are the man to do it if you don't mind me saying so! You see you don't have the authority to arrest the man here in Singapore. No, it has to be done by the MPs in conjunction with the Singapore CID. It's my bet that he is living under an assumed name and is here without a work permit. Once the plan I have is in motion, if I don't get the proof that he is in a secure cell then I will abort the operation.

"Also, I want that man over there kept off the streets until the whole thing is over," pointing to the man to whom I had talked earlier. "Give him the job in the operations room of collating all the messages coming in from your men on the ground. I've worked with him before and he knows how I operate. So, until it is all finished I want him to sort out the important reports from the not so important. Because my partners and my life will be resting on him reading the correct assumptions into the reports as they come in. So, until it's over one way or another he stays in the ops room."

"Done," said the Yank.

"Now, I want men in the following places from 8.00 p.m. onwards. One man to be at the junction of Rochor Road and Victoria Street. One man in each of the following places, first man at Malabar Street, second at Hylam Street, third at Malay Street. The fourth at North Bridge Road, fifth at Victoria Street, and lastly two at the junction of Rochor Road and North Bridge Road. Also, you must have a snatch party standing by to lift Ferguson at a moment's notice." I then gave a rough outline of the plan of how I meant to contact Merchant. Only a rough outline, there were many things I had no intention of telling them. To be frank about it I didn't trust too many of them if I trusted any. I'd also kept things from Mick; something was wrong with him and I didn't know what it was. I was minded to send him on a wild goose chase once things were up and running, I didn't want his blood on my hands at all!

Everybody was to keep the players in the game, Mick and me, Ferguson and Merchant, under observation all the time. When Merchant took off with his young male paramour, then Ferguson was to be lifted. He was to be taken into safe custody. "If I were you," I said to Commander Fitzsimmonds who had just been standing all the time in the doorway, "I would make that permanent custody. In fact I would go so far as to give him a military funeral."

The seriousness of what we were embarking on finally seemed to sink in and he looked at me aghast, "This is getting beyond a joke," he said. "I cannot do that, it is out of the question. All this lifting people and putting them in custody is rubbish. You are living in an unreal world, Colour Sergeant."

I looked at him for a minute or so, and said, "Yes, sir, you are probably right. It is Corporal Smith's and my lives which are going to be on the line out there sir. We would both I think feel a lot safer if you were nothing to do with this. So, if those are your instructions and you are adamant about them, well, I think that for Corporal Smith's safety and mine it is now time to call the whole charade off."

He looked at me and I thought he was going to explode. Instead, he said, "All this talk about killing and such, nobody is going to get killed. You are far too dramatic, Colour Sergeant. You need to see a psychiatrist; I think you are off your head to put it bluntly. This is real life, not some stupid spy film."

I looked at the Yank and said, "Well, that is it then, I shall be going back to my unit now. Can you get somebody to get a 'fast black' to take me back up to Burma Camp in Johore?"

"Just a minute," Brown said from behind me.

I could see the effect he had on Mick's face. Oh shit I thought the last thing we need right now is a bloody set to with him.

Then Brown lowered his voice just a little and said, "Right Colour Sergeant, I will see you and Corporal Smith upstairs right now. You can then tell me what it is you have decided to do. It will be I who says if it goes ahead or not, all right? Upstairs with you now laddie."

All For A King's Shilling

"Yes sir," I said, and did just that. As we left, I could feel the tension building in the room as we did so. Next I heard Brown saying to them all, "Haven't any of you lot got any work to do?"

Both Mick and I made our way to the next floor and waited in the passage. We heard the firm steps of a very confident man coming up the stairs. We looked at one another and we both shrugged. He arrived at the top and motioned the pair of us to follow him into an office. There were a desk, several telephones, and a couple of chairs. "Sit," was all he said and it was enough. We both sat.

"Well, I see you are up to your old tricks again, Colour Sergeant," he said, "taking bloody charge of officers again. See a weak officer and you are like a bloody ferret after a rabbit."

Then he added. "I knew, I bloody well knew, the way you were talking to the American earlier, that I'd let you go too far and you'd got too bloody cocky for your own good. So I'm going to have to take charge of you before you run wild like the headless chicken you are."

"I may be lots of things sir, but a chicken is not one of them, headless or not."

He turned on me like a wild bull and stared at me. Whatever it was he was going to say he changed his mind and said nothing.

So I just looked at him with that blank expression one learns very early in one's career.

At last he said, "Now what is your plan? Spill it out laddie and let us see if your brains really are still scrambled or not."

Bloody hell, I wish I was in Borneo, I thought, but I then went through the plan I had made, I told him of the contingency plans we had worked out. Also I told him why I had made a point of not telling the people downstairs all the parts of the plan, stressing to him that I had only told them the parts that they needed to know for them to do their jobs. "After all Sir you are the one who always told me to keep certain parts of my plans to myself. Only tell people what they need to know, to enable them to do the job required of them."

"All right," he said, "I know I have to take the blame for some of the harebrained schemes which you keep coming up with. Telling a Naval Commander to murder some Communist agitator is going over the top. I must call a halt to you there. Naval Commanders don't go round murdering people, not on purpose anyway. I'll deal with that part of your plan. He'll be satisfied if he thinks he has won that point. I will go along with your plan, and I will run things from this end once it gets under way. Do you agree?" he asked.

"Yes, sir, but I must insist that Ferguson is removed and held securely while Corporal Smith and I are away."

"Well yes, that goes without saying. I'll now go and brief the rest; you and Corporal Smith had better go over your timings, and make sure you have all the equipment you need. I shall see to things at this end."

"There is just one thing sir," I said, "is that American for real?"

"He is the real McCoy that one, Colours – the coat, Frank Sinatra hat, the trench coat, everything, the complete works."

"Right, sir, the other thing is, once I go in I need to be with a group of other men. We need to take over a table near to our target. I would suggest you send some men in early. Then when Ferguson has been lifted I shall move in and join them. From there I'll play it all by ear as to how I'm going to make contact with our target."

"What about Corporal Smith, what will he be doing?"

"I've a job for him, do not worry, he will be fully occupied. He will be doing a close support job for me."

"I insist on knowing what that job will be Colours."

"Well sir, you are not going to get to know. You are asking me to go out and board a foreign ship in a neutral harbour, a ship which you think is doing something that upsets our American friends. That something, which to all intents and purposes, is not a crime at all. I do not think a man with such a sense of duty as you needs to know just what my partner or I will be doing. It may cause you to have a fit of conscience later sir if that is at all possible."

He appeared to accept this. "Get about your business, Colour Sergeant," was his curt reply.

As he left the room I thought that is the first time I've given him a load of shit and he has taken it. He'll kill me when he finds out I've only told him half of my plan. Still I'd got one over the sod and I don't think he was unhappy, but I didn't give a damn anyway.

With that Mick and I then left to get some sleep for a couple of hours then the game would be afoot. When we were back downstairs I asked the Yank if he had a place Mick and I could rest up for a while. He led us to a flat above the offices we had been in. There, we had a shower, and breakfast. Then we retired to the bedrooms at the back and went to sleep. We both slept well and were feeling refreshed when we were wakened by the Yank. For some unexplained reason Brown was with him. We all had a cup of tea, and the Yank said, "Well the game is afoot, as you say Colours. Your friend Merchant has this moment just landed from his ship. We are watching him and the men have reported for the first time that Ferguson is watching him as you said he would. I cannot understand how we have missed him all this time."

"I can," I said. "You either weren't looking properly, or you are just a bunch of wankers."

At that point the Yank stormed out saying, "I'm not staying here to be insulted like this."

Brown got up and followed him out. At the door he turned and pointing the index finger on his right hand at me the way kids do to imitate a gun, he then gave me what I think he thought was his 'devil eye' look, and left the room. At that precise moment in time I did not grasp the significance of that action, but it was soon to become very clear.

He left us and again I gave him my version of a Churchillian salute. "F*** you too," I muttered under my breath.

Then I gave Mick fifty dollars and told him, "Mick I want you to go out and buy two complete sets of clothes. Identical clothes, mind you. Everything must be the same and get some black hair dye, enough for both of us. When we go out from here to start this operation we must look like twins at first glance. It may perhaps just save our lives, in the long run."

He went off to do the shopping just as the Commander came into the room. "Are you going to join the men on the streets?" he asked Mick.

All For A King's Shilling

To which Mick just said, "No sir!" and shut the door.

The Commander looked a little taken aback, but said nothing. To me he said, "Everything seems to be going to plan, Colours, our target has not deviated at all from previous trips. It is silly to make so much out of all this. So, I have sent the person whom you asked to be given a job in here out on the streets with the rest of the lads."

I looked at him and just said, "If that man is not back in this building within ten minutes, then the whole thing is off."

"You cannot do that Colour Sergeant." He said.

"That is where you are wrong sir, I can do just that," I replied then went on. "I do not think any court-martial will look kindly on a Naval Commander who helped a couple of Royal Marine NCOs to board a foreign ship in a free port. A ship which was not committing any offence, just because some unknown American said the ship was probably carrying weapons to North Vietnam. You'd not last too long in the Navy, and I'd not look to those two for help sir. If anything goes wrong, they will both disappear into the woodwork from which they have just crawled out."

"Now, Colours, that is a bit rough," Brown, who was standing in the doorway again, said.

"Oh! Maybe it is a bit rough sir, but you know it's true sir."

"Yes, I suppose so; you see, Commander, the good Colour Sergeant is right. You would be left holding the can if it all goes sour. Better get the man off the street now, there's a good man."

So that bit was settled and I felt happier when I saw him enter the offices below us.

When Mick came back, he put the gear he had bought into the two bedrooms that we were using. Then I asked the Yank, "Let us know when the target is back on the ship and McDonald Ferguson has gone back to ground. As for McDonald Ferguson, I want him watched at all times. Do not let him out of your sight at all from now on.

"If he goes to ground, I want the building ringed. I do not intend to be on the street when he pokes his nose out again."

"No problem," he said.

"You still intend lifting the man once the operation is under way tonight?" I asked.

"Yes, that is all in hand," Brown replied.

It was about three that afternoon when Ferguson went to ground in a hotel near the Brit Club. Mick and I set off to do our reconnaissance. Mick left first then I left a few minutes later. We had both dyed our hair in a rather reddish brown, but we were not yet wearing our identical sets of clothes; that would come later. Then I walked around the area that I intended working when night fell. Next I checked out all the streets I had memorised and walked the area four more times. Until I was confident I knew the place well enough to move around without any problems. Later that afternoon, satisfied with my plans, I made my way back to the office block where we were staying.

When I got back Mick was already there. I asked him, "How did you get on mate?"

"Okay Bill, I lost you twice but I managed to pick you up again immediately by taking the short cuts we had talked about."

"Good," I said; out of the corner of my eye I could see the Commander was quite interested in our conversation. He was breaking his neck to ask what we had been doing, but in the end he managed to keep his own counsel. Which was just as well for his sake as for some reason that I still hadn't decided I was starting to feel an overwhelming distaste of the man.

Next I asked Mick about the other thing that we had discussed and he said, "That's all arranged."

"Good, now for some rest. We have a long night and perhaps a long day ahead of us. Let's both get some sleep."

The Commander could hold himself back no longer. "What have you two been up to?" he asked.

"Well, we have been making our contingency plans for tonight." Before he could ask anything else, I went on. "You remember the person who was lifted the other year in London sir, the one who was passing Ministry files to the Russians?"

"Yes," he said.

"Well, you could take a leaf out of that report. Here you are following one man and you do not know half of what he is doing. The reason for it is you do not have enough men. These people you are following are professionals. They will spot a person they see twice as a threat. In London we had over four hundred people to keep tabs on one man."

"I could never get that many men to do the job," he said.

"No, but then you already have that many and more if you did but know it. Look, sir, you know his routine, so all you have to do is to find out how many service personnel are in the area at those times. They may be going to work or they may be out shopping and they do not have to work for you. All they do is to just tell you that they saw the man you are interested in and he was doing so and so. That way you keep tabs on him, you see his pattern of movements. When he does anything that is out of the ordinary, that's when you move some of your own men in to check it out – easy really!"

Before he could start a debate about it all I said. "I need to get some rest now. I've a long and maybe a very dangerous twenty-four hours facing me. Perhaps you should ask Brown about it, he will tell you how it is done because he thinks he is the expert at following people. It was a picture watching him trying to follow Mick today."

"I got there in the end," Brown said from the doorway.

"Oh yes," I said, "but you may have missed the most important part of the whole walk-about; you never saw me once."

"Go and get some bloody rest," was all he said.

It was nearly ten when I awoke and got dressed. I put on the clothes Mick had left for me, and then I headed down to the offices below. There I saw the guy I had had them pull off the streets earlier in the day. He was sitting in the operations room. The Commander was in there as well. It was obvious the Commander was not going to move; he seemed set for the night, and it looked as if he intended to control things from there.

All For A King's Shilling

So I stood for a while taking the scene in and then said, "Well I can't hang around here all night." With that I turned to the man I had made all the fuss about earlier and asked him, "Has the Yank gone out, John?"

"Yes, and Brown has gone off just as you thought he would also."

"Okay, fine, now you know how to get hold of me if things do not go right."

"Yes, Bill," he replied. The Commander was looking at me as if I had flipped my top.

He was about to open his mouth, but before he could say a word I said. "I would rather you ask John here any questions sir, I have a rather urgent appointment to keep right now." With that I turned and left the room; I went into the corridor and hesitated. I heard John saying, "It's a long story sir, I will tell you all about when this lot is over. The main thing is we keep a close watch on what everybody is doing tonight. Bill's and Mick's lives may depend on what we read into the reports as they come in."

At that point I had heard enough and I went along the passage, down the first stairs and hesitated at the door for a second or two. Then I touched the hilt of my knife settled in the hollow of my spine and resigned to what I was about to do, I stepped straight out into the throng of people. The Chinese, the Malaysians and the Europeans (mostly English) were the main peoples who made up the cosmopolitan city of Singapore and they were all out in force as was normal and I knew I would blend in without any trouble. So firstly I walked along the street for about forty paces, then stopped and turned right into a small corner shop on the corner of Ophir and Victoria Streets. A shop that sold mainly watches, but some other types of jewellery as well. I walked to the back of the shop. There I turned and stood with my back to the back of the shop and looked at what can only be described as the front shop door. The owner looked up from a customer he was serving and just grinned. He offered me a Coke and turned back to his customer. I waited for what seemed an eternity, but could only have been seconds. There he was, my old friend 'Major Bloody Brown'.

What game is this we are playing, sir? He obviously thought I had turned the corner and continued along Victoria Street. So, I then left the shop and headed across the road to the corner opposite the watch shop, which faced the offices Brown and his Yank friends were using. Once there I stood under the veranda of the shop on this corner and looked down the road that Major Brown had taken. He had obviously just realised I was not in front of him because I could see him looking first to his left across the road. Then he was bobbing his head from side to side, to see if I was after all ahead of him. As I watched him, I waited until he was in a bit of a mess at having lost me. It was then I stepped back into the shop and spent the next few minutes pretending to look at the wares that were on display for sale. At the same time I was taking note of everything going on in the street outside.

I did not have long to wait; next I saw three men I had not seen before arrive in a fast black. They got out and two of them took up positions on the corner opposite the shop which I was then in. The other went down the street and talked to Major Brown. I was still watching them when Mick came in from the rear of the shop.

When I pointed the three men out to him, he said, "I know two of them, but not the one with Brown. The two over there are just foot soldiers in these new recce type troops. That other guy, I don't know who he is. What I do know though is that I don't like the look of him."

"Neither do I, he looks an evil bastard doesn't he. I'm sure he is no bootneck though so let's get the hell out of here," I replied.

With that, both of us went to the rear of the shop, gave the owner ten dollars and left by the rear. The back of the place was like a rabbit warren. The alley was only wide enough for one of us to walk down at a time. We made our way back the way Mick had come in. It was the best part of ten minutes before we were out on the street again. When we were halfway along the block, in the opposite direction from the one taken by Brown, we were on Rochor Road, just opposite Malabar Street. There, we got into the cab Mick had hired before he came to the shop. We then made our way to the steps in Keppel Harbour where our man was to come ashore. We told the driver to park by a large pile of timber which was waiting to be loaded onto lighters ready for transporting to a ship laid off in the roads.

We spent the next half hour working out exactly how we were to carry out the task given us. I had purposely kept the main part of my plan to myself until this moment. I thought it best only the two of us should know it. I was certain we could get away with it if we were the only two who knew the full details, mainly because I did not trust the Yank or the Commander and I never trusted bloody Brown at any time in my service career to date or any of their bloody staff. I could not get my head round this shit about arms from Poland to North Vietnam; no, I thought, we had been invited to a three-headed execution, the three heads being mine, Mick's and Merchant's; I didn't like this little setup at all and who were these blokes who had just turned up tonight?

This plan was quite simple really, I would make contact with our target, like long lost buddies, which I suppose you could with tongue in cheek say we were. Then I would stay with him until he was due to go back to his ship and hope to get an invitation back to the ship. In the meantime Ferguson would hopefully have been removed. I then told Mick, "I had a talk with John before I left."

"Good," he said.

"Only problem, the Commander was there at the time." Mick did not seem too happy about that bit. "So I told him not to worry, John would be on the other end listening to the reports coming in. If Ferguson was not lifted, he would let us know immediately."

"I bloody hope so," added Mick.

For some reason I had the feeling he was not too happy at all. Looking back, I should probably have kept my mouth shut. Still, it was too late now. So I then told him how he should cover me on the trip to Keppel Harbour should I get an invitation back to the ship.

"It is important, Mick, should Ferguson get away, then the taxi I will be travelling in with Merchant must be stopped, and I have to be arrested, to maintain my cover. You are to arrange it and make sure it happens."

He said, "Don't worry mate, everything will go to plan."

We kept going over the plan. I was to get back to the ship. Mick was to take one of the boats that plied the harbour and get to the place in the 'Singapore Roads' where the ship which Merchant was on was lying at anchor. He had to get there before Merchant and I arrived. He was to wait until I went on board. Then he was to try and board the ship as well. With us both dressed the same we should be able to move

All For A King's Shilling

around without drawing too much attention to ourselves. One of us would look in the forward hatches, the other in the rear. We hoped to be off the damned thing before it sailed.

I asked Mick, "Are you all right Mick?"

"Yes, I'm as well as can be expected, you and your bloody big mouth. You could have trusted John to act on his own initiative. The fewer people who know this setup the better."

"Okay," I said, "I made a mistake, but it will be all right."

Mick just looked at his watch and said, "It's time you were off Bill, I'll see you on this Polish rust bucket of a ship shortly. See you."

With that he took off into the darkness and I knew then that he had one of the boats that plied around the roads ready. Then I got back into the cab and told the driver where to drop me.

I paid him off when he dropped me at the bar a few minutes later. For a while I stood checking the street scene in front of me. The whole of the main thoroughfare before me was now laid out as one giant bar and restaurant. From each side of the street for a good two hundred yards there was nothing but tables, full of people drinking. Some were British servicemen stationed in Singapore and there were a few Yanks on R and R from Vietnam. Some of them were from ships and some were just tourists come to gaze on this renowned street of delights.

Then I spotted some members of the surveillance team in the throng of people drinking amongst the tables. The drinkers were mostly servicemen and the people serving on the tables were all Chinese. Then I saw the target and I didn't think time had been too kind to him. He had aged quite considerably, more than his years. I saw Ferguson sitting on the edge of the throng and he was watching his charge all the time. A team member 'accidentally' bumped into me and muttered, "He has just got back."

"Good," I said, "now tell that boss of yours to get rid of Ferguson."

It was as he swayed off into the crowd pretending to be drunk I heard a commotion coming along the street leading into Bugis Street. When I looked up I saw a group of Chinese who were coming along it waving knives and axes in the air. I thought shit, that's all I need, the bloody Chinese to go on the rampage at this time. Most Europeans in the area were scampering into taxis and beating a hasty retreat. Bugis Street is not the best place to be when the Chinese have got a bastard on and have gone on the rampage.

Most of the tourists by this time had gone and most of the servicemen in their drunken state were all for taking the Chinese on and having a fight. As it turned out, the Chinese were after a bloody twelve-foot snake, which must have come across the causeway. Anyway in the end many of the servicemen in the area joined in the great snake hunt. I don't think the bloody thing stood a chance. It in fact worked well for us, because during all the commotion they lifted Ferguson. Again I looked around once it had quieted down and that was when I made a point of catching my old friend's eye. Immediately I made a big show of looking at him, looking away and then quickly back again. Then in a noisy boisterous way I stood up and hailed him across the tables. He stood up, looked a little apprehensive, then at last as he recognised me he smiled. I staggered across to him holding my glass high above my head. The great test of the drunk, I knew as he watched me that if I spilled any he would know I was shamming and not drunk!

We embraced each other like long lost friends and I got the feeling he needed friends. He was shaking as we embraced so I pushed him away and said. "Let me look at you mate, hey what in hell's name are you doing in Singapore?"

He said, "And you too you old fraud?"

I didn't hesitate with my answer. "Well," I said, "I decided to give England the push. There is nothing left for me there. As an ex con I could not get a job. So I took off for Australia, but it seems they do not let old English cons in there any more. Bloody hell mate," I went on, "they all used to be old cons once. Now the bastards won't even let us in. The pigs deported me. So I ended here. I only got out of the airport earlier today. They have given me two days to get myself sorted and find a job or I will be deported from here as well."

He looked at me and said, "Christ man you never change, do you?"

"Well, that's life anyway, so what the hell are you doing here?" I asked him.

"Oh, I'm in the Merchant Navy now and I'm on a ship that has just called in for a couple of days. We sail tomorrow so let's have another drink, what are you drinking?"

"Tiger bloody beer mate," I said.

He flicked his fingers and a Chinese waiter immediately appeared, as if by magic; he ordered the beer for me and whisky for himself. We chatted over old times and what had happened to us. I then asked, "How did you manage to get into the Merchant Navy with your record?"

"No problem," he said. "Why don't you join?"

He made no mention that it was the bloody Polish Merchant service he was in, but I just said. "Hey, that's a great idea, why don't I? You can tell me what to say and I will be in in no time." Then I said, "I shall join as soon as I get back to England."

"No need to wait," he said. "I know you well enough, and we need a cook on the ship I am on. It will get you in, and then if you fancy doing deck work, once you have your ticket you can move on to another ship without any problems."

I just looked at him with my mouth open, I hadn't thought it would be that easy. Here was I trying to find a way of getting on his bloody ship and here he was, offering me a bloody job on it. "Are you all right?" he asked.

"Well yes, I'm just a little bit shocked, I started the day with no hope of anything, and stranded in Singapore. Now I have met you, whom I haven't seen since we were in court together. You have fixed me up with a job just like the old days; you know I always felt great around you."

"It is great seeing you again. Drink up and I'll take you back and introduce you to the skipper."

"Great!" I said. With that we downed our drinks and headed off to the taxis. As I walked along with him, I was thinking this is easy, it's far too bloody easy, there's got to be a rabbit off here somewhere. I could be just walking into a bloody trap, but I was committed now and I thought I'd take it a bit further.

We arrived at the jetty where the boat from his ship was waiting for him. The crewmen looked a little surprised to see me with him. He said something in Polish to them and that seemed to settle them. I asked him, "What language was that you used?" He muttered something about only being able to get foreign nationals to work for the rates of pay his company paid.

"Hey," I said keeping up the old pals' act, "I expect I will get better paid being an Englishman and being a friend of yours."

His answer was rather sharp, "You will get what you are due."

Ding! Dong, bloody dong! The first alarm bell rang in my head and I did not like that one little bit. I had a feeling he was perhaps getting a bit suspicious of me. Then he noticed I was thinking about that and laughed and he slipped back into his old lost pals' act. I still didn't feel any happier, and I had a feeling he had let his real feelings slip and I tried really hard to go along with his act. Anyway as the boat bobbed along on the waves I touched the hilt of my knife once more for reassurance.

It took us a good twenty minutes to reach his ship. We did not chat all the way. I tried to keep a conversation going, but it was hard work and I gave it up when we must have been half way there. His attitude was starting to seriously worry me, but I reasoned that I couldn't pull out at this point and would have to keep going.

We at last arrived at the ship, which was a lot bigger than I had been led to believe. It looked to be one of the new types of bulk carriers that were starting to appear on the main shipping lanes. It certainly was no bloody coastal collier, which travelled the North Sea, occasionally crossing to Europe with the odd cargo. No, sir, this was one hell of a size coaster. We climbed the ladder and as I was going up I glanced at the bow. I thought I do not envy Mick his task of getting up that anchor chain. I hope to God he has, or has had no trouble scaling it. Christ I thought as I looked at it, how in hell's name, are we going to search this thing in the time we have?

At last we arrived on the deck. The first thing I saw was an armed guard. I looked at my old pal and said, "Hey, what's with the man with the shooter, old pal?"

He muttered something about pirates in these waters and that they took no chances.

Then I asked him, "Will I have to carry a gun?"

He just laughed and said, "God, you with a bloody gun. No chance, we would all be in danger if we gave you a gun."

I adopted a hurt sound in my voice and said, "Hey, there is no call to be like that. Remember all the times I guarded you with my trusty musket, all those years ago. God it seems like a lifetime ago?"

"Look, old pal," he said, "I'm getting pissed off with your constant use of 'Hey', if you say it again I will not get you this job."

Just then an officer came up to us and he muttered away in Polish to this old long lost pal of mine. He then turned and looked at me, saying in English, "So you are to be our new cook. Jock will show you to your quarters, then first thing tomorrow we will show you your place of work."

His English was good, but he had a slight accent; this officer was no Englishman. With that he left and Jock told the guard to show me to the quarters forward and he left saying over his shoulder that they would deal with me in the morning.

As the guard and I moved forward on the port side of the deck, he kept to the inside of me close to the hatch covers. He was also just that little bit behind me, just enough for me to be unable to jump him. I began to think it looked increasingly likely that I had been set up.

William Atlay

We were halfway past the second hatch from the bows, when I saw a slight movement on the end of the hatch we were passing. I started to ask the guard how often they got ashore, and had he had a good run in Singapore. He started to answer me in broken English. It was just enough to put him off his guard, his trying to concentrate on speaking English to me. This caused him to miss the movement of Mick rising and coming at him from the side and slightly to his rear.

Before I had time to turn, the guard was cut off in mid-stutter, just as he was trying to say "No shore leave for other ranks". As he fell dead on to the deck, I thought it odd he should use the word 'Ranks', it was also his last, poor sod. Still, we had to get rid of the body now. We were both sweating like hell by the time we got the corner of the hatch open and his body in under the coal.

We then entered the hatchway leading to the crew's forward quarters. Once in we made our way as far down the ladders as we could. We ended up five decks down. There, we stopped and crouched under the ladder. It was I who spoke first and I said to Mick, "I think we are in deep trouble Mick. It's my belief they knew we were coming and we'd better make this as fast as possible and then leg it back to shore. I'm not happy with this setup at all," I concluded.

Mick looked at me, "You want to know something, mate? They were waiting for you, they knew you would be coming. There were three of them on the deck just after I got here. I had just managed to get my breath back, after climbing that bloody chain, did you see it?" I nodded, indicating I had. Then he added, "Well I had just got myself sorted out when a fourth one arrived to say you and Jock had started on the trip back. As your boat came alongside all of them except the guard left the top of the ladder and stood back under the side of the bridge. Once you were on the deck one of them stepped out to talk to you. He is the boss man."

I looked at Mick, "I think we had better look around and then get the hell out of here."

"I agree and the sooner the bloody better."

With that we stood up and were going to make our way back on deck looking for any way into the holds. We had been standing on a large hatch, and as we started to climb the ladder, Mick saw the clips moving. Shit I thought we will have to gallop up this lot to hide from whoever is coming through there. It was at this moment I heard somebody start to descend the ladders. I looked at Mick, he looked at me and we both looked around and then spotted a small hatch in the bulkhead. We broke all records as we managed to get it open and climb through.

We found ourselves in a small duct of some sort. It was dark, but there was light coming into it a little farther along. So we lay still for a few minutes until all was quiet in the ladder way behind us. I whispered for Mick to get back out of the duct, and keep watch. Then I would slide forward and see if I could see anything through the grid through which the light seemed to be coming.

Mick got back out and kept the hatch just ajar and I edged forward to the grid. It was quite difficult, but I could make out some detail of a hold. As it was, I did not get a good view of the place through the grid, but what I did see made me suck the air back into my mouth. As I just lay there and looked in stunned surprise, I could see some men working in what one could only describe as an aircraft hangar. They seemed to be assembling aircraft; I could hardly believe my eyes and I looked as

All For A King's Shilling

best I could to the right and left. Everywhere I looked it was a hive of activity of aircraft being assembled; both helicopters and fixed wing aircraft were being bolted together.

Now I had a problem; it was obvious that I needed more information. It was important that I see just how big this hold was and if the other holds were set up for the same work. I decided it was time I went looking for entrances to the other holds and I started to edge myself back to the hatch.

When I let myself back into the ladder way, Mick was nowhere in sight. I looked around and decided my best bet was to get back on to the main deck. It took me only a couple of minutes to reach the deck and I hid behind the forward hatch covering and tried to steady myself. It took a minute or so for my eyes to get accustomed to the light, then I saw Mick lying by the edge of the deck. My heart leapt into my throat; I thought he had been killed as he was lying so still. My first instinct was to rush to his side and see if he was dead, but I realised that if he was or wasn't there was nothing I could do for him either way now.

So I wedged myself into a corner of the hatch top and took a little more time to check the area very carefully. I had a feeling I was not alone; something felt wrong. The hair on the nape of my neck was standing on end, but I could not see any reason why this should be. In these situations I never ignore any signals I get from the back of my neck. So I shook myself and looked around again; I spent the best part of ten minutes looking all around. I was worried about Mick and hoping he was playing possum. Still if he was alright, he must have seen me come out of the forward hatch. If he had he did not let on and I had to find out why he was acting the way he was.

I was just about to move to him, when I caught a glimpse of a movement. It was at the very edge of my right field of vision. At first I thought my eyes were playing tricks on me, but I very slowly turned my head round. It was then I saw a man standing in the shadows of the hatch out of which I had come. For the life of me I could not understand why he had not spotted me coming out of it, perhaps he was looking the other way when I exited. So he would not now know where I was. He was obviously waiting for something or other. However, I could not afford the luxury of waiting much longer. If Mick had been injured and was not dead, but unconscious, then it would be criminal for me to sit here for much longer, to save my own skin.

So I decided it was time for me to make a move. What is it they used to say on the promotion courses, in moments of indecision? "Do something lad, even if it is only to say 'Good-bye'."

I thought fast as I felt the adrenaline start to pump around my body. As far as I could see, there was only one possibility – I had to get rid of the watcher. I hadn't seen anybody else and now that I'd identified the danger, the hair on the nape of my neck settled back down. A sign I took to mean there were no more of them around. So, I very slowly edged my way back along the deck glued to the side of the hatch and the deck, trying as much as possible to make myself invisible as I moved along half under the lip which is so common on modern ships' hatches these days.

It took me a few minutes of careful movement and then I was far enough along the forward edge of the hatch to stand up. When I got to my feet and as there wasn't a hue and cry, I made a dash to the starboard side of the ship. Once there, I took stock of the situation; I needed to get a lot closer to the man before I could do anything about him. First I had to scramble over a pile of winching gear and the like, the type of stuff that covers most cargo ships' bows; this was a nightmare on its own. It was hard going, but I made it and finally I arrived just behind the man. He had not made a move and was intent on watching Mick, who lay on the deck in front of him. I was now no more than eighteen inches from him.

Now I didn't hesitate at all and in seconds I had my arm round his lower face and my knife in under his ribs to the hilt. He never made a sound as I felt him go heavy in my arm and his head nearly slipped through my arm and I knew he was dead. Gently, but only so I didn't make any noise, I laid the man on the deck, then turned him over to see who it was I had sent to his maker. To my surprise and amazement it was my old mate Jock Merchant.

So, I'd finally done something I had promised myself a few years ago that I would one day do. As I looked at him I could hear myself telling Dave, one of my team mates those years before as he had slumped dying in my arms, that I would put the bastard under one day – today was that day.

As I crouched there I looked around the bows and studied the layout. Mick was still lying on the deck, but worse he was not moving. So, after checking around again and as everything looked clear I made my way over to him. When I reached his side without any more trouble, I thanked God as I felt his chest, that he was still alive. Although he was in a state of semi-consciousness I pulled him over to the side of the hatch and into the darkness of the shadows. As I did, the movement must have helped him because he started to come round and I put my hand over his mouth. The last thing I needed was his groaning alerting any of the rest of the crew. Somehow I managed to keep him quiet and at last he slowly came around. I do not know what Jock had hit him with, but whatever it was it had raised a hell of a lump on the side of his head. When I thought he was able to understand me, I told him what I thought we should do next.

"Now Mick, listen to me. I want you to get back to your boat and wait there. Soon you will hear two splashes when I throw the two dead bodies over the side. You are to wait two minutes then start your outboard engine. You are to leave the area immediately and make as much noise as you can so that they can hear you and hopefully see you. With luck you will be seen and as we are both dressed alike, they will think it is me who is doing a runner from them. This should leave me time to have a look at the other holds and then go over the side myself."

Mick weakly protested that we should both stay and look together.

"No, it is better we do it this way, you are in no condition to help me now." He eventually agreed to go along with the plan. So I told him, "Once you do go, get out of sight of the ship and wait to pick me up when I come over the side."

Reluctantly he agreed to all of this, so I kept a look out while he made his way to the forward anchor chain and started his descent. Once he was out of sight I got the two bodies, Jock's and the other man whom Mick had killed earlier, from the hold. Then I tied them together with some rope I found in a locker near the first hatch. Next I tied two spare links from a large chain to the middle of the rope, which took some doing as the links were bloody heavy. I'd found them on the fo'c'sle lying next to a windlass. Next I put the links over the side of the ship and then propped the two bodies against the railings ready to drop them overboard.

All For A King's Shilling

As I watched, Mick made his way slowly, and in what looked to be a very painful way, down the anchor chain. As I crouched on the deck and watched him descend the chain I felt as if I were standing on the centre spot at Wembley Stadium. It felt as if I was in front of a full house. With the flood lights all on me, I was shit scared. "Come on Mick get a bloody move on," I kept muttering to myself. At last he made it to the bottom of the chain and into the boat that he had left tied to it. When he was in the boat he turned and gave me the thumbs up. I breathed a sigh of relief and pushed the two bodies over the side and stood and watched until they hit the water. The links of chain then pulled them quite quickly under the surface. Then I gave Mick the signal to start the outboard engine. As he did, I could hear footsteps coming along the deck and I slipped in amongst the winding gear and other things they had stowed on the fo'c'sle.

Next I heard them shouting in Polish, which I assumed from their actions were things like "over there" and "there he goes"; another one of them shouted for the guard to come up and shoot the English pig, which he did as Mike disappeared into the night out of sight.

By this time Mick had disappeared into the darkness. Even so they still fired off another couple of rounds in the general direction of the noise that Mick's outboard motor was making. Then they moved back along the deck towards the gangway, which was just forward of the superstructure.

When all had settled down again, I gingerly made my way back down the starboard side of the ship. I was looking at the hatches to see if there was any way I could get into them. It wasn't long before I got the feeling I was wasting my time and I was also getting uncomfortably close to the Bridge structure. So I tucked myself in under the outer lip of the hatch and studied the situation which I was now in for a few minutes. Finally I decided I could not get past the superstructure to the rear of the ship. I wanted to see if there were any more hatches to the rear of it, but unable to do so I moved forward again. I'd returned to the forward hatch when I heard a bell sounding and the crew were called to sea stations. Hello! I thought, I did not know merchant seamen were called to sea duties in the way the military navies of the world are. Because I was certain that I had heard the Polish equivalent of hands to sailing stations, etc, etc.

Now I was at a loss what to do when I remembered there was one place I could probably hide and that was this place where I had seen the aircraft earlier on. It was at this point I made my second mistake; the first one was me being there in the first place. Still being the fool that I am I made my way down to the hatchway from which I had entered the ventilation shaft earlier that night! It took me but a couple of minutes to get myself into it and I made my way to the vent which I had looked through before. It seemed that now everything was in darkness. Perhaps they had finished their work for the night, I did not know, but I did think it strange. When I had been on deck and just about to enter the hatchway I'd heard them come out of this hangar type place, which had to be under the coal. The problem was that they had not come out on deck. So there had to be some way of getting from this part of the ship and into the crew's quarters to the rear of the forward hatches. There had to be a passage under the coal, probably some passage such as Burma Way, which is situated under the hangar deck on all our aircraft carriers. This passage runs the length of the ship and I thought that had to be the answer.

After making that deduction I settled in my mind and decided to make my way further along this vent to see where it led to. As I inched my way very carefully along it I was thinking I might still be heard. I didn't know what was above or below this ventilation shaft so I edged my way forward with the utmost caution and eventually made it to the next wire-covered opening. The sweat by now was dripping off my face and running into my eyes from my forehead. Hell's bells, I thought, I must be bloody unfit so I lay there for a little while taking a rest and just listening. By now I was feeling very tired and the warm air which was flowing along the ventilation shaft that I was in was sending me to sleep. It was then I realised just how tired I was and I thought there was not much I could do at that moment in time. When I looked at my watch, I was surprised to see it was nearly 4.30 in the morning. There was nothing I could do right then and I needed to have a little rest before I went on. So, fool that I am, I made myself comfortable and lay back against the side of the ventilator shaft and unfortunately I closed my eyes for just a moment.

When I awoke it was with a start and I was shivering. This was because I was in a blast of cold air and as my senses returned, I realised the ship was at sea. Now I could feel the gentle rise and fall of the ship as she drove through the swell of the open sea. Looking at my watch, I saw it was just after seven o'clock and I thought, God I wonder how long they have been at sea. Now I really started to panic, god did I panic. I looked through the wire vent. There was some dim lighting and I could now make out what appeared to be boxes of ground to air missiles. At that point I decided I had seen enough and I was getting off this tub come what may. There was no way I was going to Hanoi on this bloody thing for that matter, so I made my way back along the shaft. When I reached the place from which I had first looked into the hold it was in total darkness. From that I presumed that they must only work when the ship was in harbour. That would explain the reasons for the three days' stopover in Singapore. I'd discovered all I wanted to and my priority now was to disembark as soon as I possibly could. They could get someone to watch the thing being unloaded to check the number of whatever it is they have in here as they unload them in Hanoi. That way they could get an idea of what amount of military hardware each ship was carrying. So how much coal was it carrying? Well I was starting to come to the idea that I didn't think it ever got unloaded. For the time being I had many other things on my mind, foremost of which at that moment was getting off the ship.

Slowly I now edged myself to the entrance to this ventilation shaft. When I arrived there I half sat and half lay and listened as I tried to hear if there was anybody moving around in the ladder way. Trying hard to find out what if anything was going on. The way things were I would have to get out feet first and all I needed then was for somebody to be out there. I waited for a few minutes and then thought I could be here for hours if I was too careful. At last I took the bull by the horns and opened the hatch and got out.

To my relief I was alone and I went up the ladders in leaps and bounds. It was good to be out of that confined space and I made the deck hatchway without incident, I looked out and saw the deck was clear. First I felt the fresh sea breeze on my face then I looked to the right, but I could see no sign of land where Singapore should have been. Then I stepped out on to the deck and as I did I felt the wind of something pass at great speed by the side of my head. Whatever it was, it hit the hatchway door behind my head and ricocheted out to sea. It was then that I heard the report of the rifle. The old 'crack and thump' shit, which all we servicemen learn about in our basic training. The crack was about a foot and a half from my right ear and thump told me where to look for the rifleman and that was in the area of the bridge.

So I looked up at the bridge and there he was, the rifleman I'd seen last night and now taking aim at me for a second shot. That was when I thought, "Oh bollocks to this for a game of cards, these bastards are a downright nasty bunch of pilgrims if ever I saw any." At that point I decided to bail out and I had made a dash for the ship's rails. I'd only taken a couple of steps when I felt another bullet strike my left heel. At first I thought I had been hit, but right then I didn't have the time or inclination to stop and check, so I kept moving. It was as I put my left foot on the deck that I realised I'd lost the heel off my left shoe. With another bound I dived over the rail and cartwheeled into the sea, feet first. It seemed to take minutes and all the time I felt I was a sitting duck for the guy on the bridge. My feet and arms were beating the air as I tried to stay upright, but it was useless.

At last my feet hit the water. I went under and started to strike out at right angles from the side of the ship. My common sense told me I needed to get away from the ship's propellers, as well as that bloody murderer with the gun. When at last I came up for air, I was three quarters of the way along the length of the ship, and about ten to fifteen yards clear of the side. When I turned my head and looked up I could see the man with the rifle. He was now on the main deck, had spotted me and was taking aim to have another pot shot at me. He had bloody moved to get down from the bridge on to the main deck as quickly as that.

Again I dived and as I did, I saw a streak of bubbles as a bullet ripped past my head. This sod is not going to give up that easily, is he, I thought. This time I stayed down until my lungs felt ready to burst and I was now in white water. All this would mean a certain and a messy death if I were sucked into the propellers. At last I made the surface and took a massive gasp of air. I looked round and I could not believe it. The sod was now on the stern of the ship, taking aim again. Why didn't the bastard give up? I was likely to drown out here anyway, but down I went again. The next time I surfaced I knew I was safe; because the rifleman was walking back around the side of a structure that looked like the galley. As I watched him go I thought I'd put money on that bastard saying he got me.

Now I started to tread water and I raised my right hand and gave him a Churchillian salute as the ship sailed away from me. All I had to do was see which direction Singapore was and swim for the shore. Slowly I looked round as I scanned the horizon. That was when I had a deep sinking feeling in my gut. I had half expected to see some land, but I could see nothing. There was nothing but the stern of the ship that I had so hurriedly departed under a hail of bullets only a moment ago. To lighten my load I kicked off my shoes and thought, you are really in Shit Street this time you bloody fool. Again I looked around very carefully. I was trying to see the direction in which Singapore could be. It could not be too far away, but I saw nothing. Next I checked my bearings as best I could in the circumstances – ever tried using a watch to find north whilst treading water? Assuming the ship was on a course for China or Vietnam it would have to be heading into the South China Sea. Then my best bet was to swim in a north westerly direction. Then with Brown's words, "You really are an arsehole Colours" ringing in my head I set off looking for Singapore. Well, to be honest any bloody 'Pore' would do, just so long as it was 'Terra Firma' type of 'Pore'.

After I had been swimming in a very leisurely crawl for about half an hour I paused to take stock. I must be honest about this, but I didn't have a clue if I'd been swimming in the right direction; or for that matter if I had just been going round in circles. It was then that I noticed some cloud formations ahead of me, which suggested land of some sort. Perhaps it was Singapore or one of the many islands which make up the state of Singapore. The cloud was in the right direction, or so I thought, it never once crossed my mind that I might just be on my way to South America. Anyway I set off again at a leisurely pace towards the clouds. When I say leisurely, I mean a pace which I knew I could keep going for some time.

I do not know how long I was in the sea, because my watch had given up the ghost shortly after I had left the ship. Now as I swam I had all sorts of thoughts running through my mind and I was nearly driven crazy by some of them. That was when I decided to go into automatic mode. Anybody who has done the famous fifteen mile speed marches the Royal Marine Corps of ours keeps insisting that we all must do from time to time will know what I mean; they say the pain only goes after the first five miles and everything is easy-peasy after that as you are by then completely comatose!

Some time later when the light was starting to lose its intensity I realised I was getting sore on my face and forearms. When I looked at my arms I saw I had been burnt rather badly by the sun and salt. That's just great, I thought, that is all I need, a bloody dose of sunburn. Strange as it was it was at that point I thought why the hell hadn't Mick followed the ship to sea? He must have known I was still on the damned thing and would be over the side at the first chance I had. Then I thought, silly bastard you did go to sleep for some three hours. Then I thought he must have given up and returned to the shore. After all, the boat he had was not the type you go to sea in, not if you have any bloody sense that is!

Perhaps I drifted off into some other state of mind after that. Because the next thing I remember, it was dark and I was being pushed in and out by the waves over a sandy beach. Although I am not a religious man, I did offer up a small prayer of sorts like thanks, oh and I think god came into it also. It must be night as it was dark or I'd gone blind with the sun and water. I looked at my watch before I remembered it was useless, but better still I could still see it; strange that even when close to disaster some habits remain. Checking the time that is, so important to a diver, time! Eventually I managed, with great effort, to get to my feet and made it to the trees which I could see at the back of the beach. My first thoughts were that I was somewhere on the shore of Singapore Island. So I looked around to see if there were any lights and I also listened for the noises that you can hear over almost all the Island. It was all dark and it was deadly silent.

Next, I decided I had to rest as I felt totally exhausted, so I knelt down and made myself a small scrape in the sand just a few feet from the trees at the rear of the beach and lay down in it. My digging in the sand must have disturbed some insects that immediately identified me as food and I spent most of the night slapping myself to kill the little biting sods. I did get some rest, but not much. It seemed to me that the little sods took a great liking to my arms and face, which had been cooked out at sea.

The next morning I was awakened by voices. Somebody was calling me and I thought I was dreaming. Then with great difficulty I managed to open my eyes, which were encrusted with salt and sun blisters. The only thing I could see was a grinning Malay fisherman about fifty years old. He was so close to my face and looking directly into my eyes I could feel his wispy beard touching my face. I smiled and said "Good morning, Mr Fisherman" and at the same time I raised my arm to look at my watch. I wanted to see what time it was. He gave a chuckle and said, "About eight o'clock" in 'pidgin English'. Then I saw my watch had gone, but I could see it was in good hands as it was on his arm. Well, it'll be right twice a day for him, I thought. The strap was much too big for him and I was just going to say I needed it back, when I heard somebody shuffling their feet behind me.

As I turned my head I felt the skin on my face and neck splitting with the tightness of the blisters, which I believed covered my face and neck. Eventually I managed to make it and standing behind me was a much younger man. He was not a Malaysian fisherman or any kind of Malaysian; he looked more western than Asian. To him I said, "Good morning" also. It was then I gave up any thought of getting my watch back there and then. He was not hostile, but there was something about him that made me forget my watch. Looking at him I thought the watch will probably never be of any use again after my swim the day before.

It was then I decided to stand up and even though I say it myself I almost made it. Unfortunately I fell back down as my legs gave out on me. What humiliation I thought, I bet Captain Cook never had problems like these. It must be cramp after all the time I spent in the water yesterday. Again I looked at the old man and said, "I'm sorry sir, but it seems I am unable to stand at the moment. It won't be long though; once I get the circulation going I shall be okay you will see. I had a bit of a long swim yesterday, but I will be okay in a minute." With that I started to rub my legs vigorously.

Then the younger man spoke for the first time. "Don't do that," he said, "It will only make things worse. You have been bitten badly, very badly, and you have also been poisoned."

"Well," I said, after I had got over the shock of what he had said. "You have a very tactful way of putting things my friend, but I'm not too keen on your bedside manner at all."

"That is as maybe, but I would shut up if I were you," he said. "You have a lot of pain coming in the next few hours. If you are going to make it at all you will know in about eight hours or so. We are going to take you to the village just a little way from here. The old man will look after you and doctor you. If you make it, I will talk to you tonight."

With that he turned, said something to the old man in Malay and left. He walked away from where I lay and I watched his back as he walked along the beach. Then I turned to the old man and said, "Is this Singapore?"

To which he just grinned, and said, "No!"

"Where is it then?"

He just grinned at me and then his face went all blurred as I fell backwards. To this day I am sure I fell backwards for at least a day or two, falling, falling, all the time falling.

The next thing I knew was my mind was as clear as a bell. I had come awake and I was soaked in my own sweat, but my mouth and my throat were as dry as a desert. As I looked around, I saw an old woman sitting watching me. I asked her for a drink, and she just shook her head saying no. Mad as hell I shouted, "You silly old cow, it's a drink I need." I made to get up to get one myself, but fell flat on my face, and everything went black.

The next time I came round the old man was there; at least he gave me a drink. It was disgusting, but felt good once I'd managed to get it down my throat, which felt as if a rasp had been pushed down it. When I tried to talk it was really sore, and my voice sounded like a croaking old frog. Then I lay back on the cot which I was now in and just relaxed a little. I think I may have dozed off a bit for it seemed to get dark very soon.

The old man came back and offered me some more of the horrible drink, this time my throat was not as sore. He also gave me some rice and what I think was fish and I must admit I felt much better after I had eaten and I settled down again and within a couple of minutes the young man whom I met on the beach came in.

We looked at each other for a while, and I think we were sizing each other up. It was I who spoke first. I started by saying, "Thank you for having me looked after so well, I would have probably died had it not been for you and the old man."

"Yes," he said, "you would have died if it had not been for the old man's medicine."

Then I asked him, "Just where am I?"

"You are on a small island off the coast of Singapore; it's called Riouw. Are you from Singapore?"

"Yes, I am and I need to get back as quickly as possible."

"You will not be able to leave until tomorrow and only then if I decide you are fit enough for the journey to Singapore. Maybe I will go to Singapore then and you would be welcome to come with me, if I go that is. Is there any reward for finding you?"

I looked him up and down before I answered him because I knew my life might depend on it. Then with the most casual laugh I could muster I said, "I don't think that is very likely, honestly do I look the kind of person people pay rewards for?"

We eyed each other up for a moment then he laughed and agreed with me as he said, "No I think not."

He asked me then, "How did you come to be on our island then?"

Remembering my interrogation training, which is to tell the truth because it is always the easiest story to maintain under torture, that is what I did.

"I fell overboard from my ship and I drifted all day in the sea." Of course I didn't mention which ship, or that I had been swimming for most of the day.

He said, "I only asked in case you were one of the others who use the island as a resting place when they are travelling to the Malaysian mainland."

All For A King's Shilling

I hoped that my ears had not pricked up too much when he said that, but I only said, "Oh!" Then I waited a reasonable time and then asked him, "Are they fishermen who rest here on the island then?"

His answer rather surprised me. "Oh no," he said. "They are soldiers, they come in from the west in big boats and spend a couple of days here; some of them leave at night in smaller boats. The rest of them go back to the main island to the west in the larger boats. Then after a few days they return and then the ones in the little boats come back. They then load everything on to the bigger boats and go back to an island to the west, which island I do not know."

I looked at him for a while and said, "Would I be correct if I said you are talking about Indonesians?"

"Yes, you would."

"Okay, but I don't look anything like an Indonesian so why did you think I might be one of them?"

"Sometimes they have white men with them when they come here. They are in charge giving orders and organising things," he replied, his face expressionless.

"Tell me, how often does this happen, and would I be right in assuming the smaller boats go to Singapore, or Malaya?"

"You would be right and they come once or sometimes twice a month."

So, I thought, the Indonesians are using this island to infiltrate the mainland of Malaya; no wonder they knew all about what the Malaysians were up to, military movements to and from Borneo, unit strengths and such...

After thinking it over I said, "Well I am not certain, but I think I know a man who would pay you for that information. Provided you could prove it so I think you and I should go to Singapore together tomorrow, do you agree?"

"I'm not keen to leave here for too long. I would have to return within a couple of days, but if there is money in it I may just take you."

"Okay it's agreed then we leave tomorrow?" I did not say so but I believed that they may have been thinking of selling me to the Indonesians. I would feel a lot happier when I was off this island and heading back to Singapore if telling him they would pay for this information might just help. These people lived so close to the line between life and death that I understood that if some poor bugger landed in their lap they would just sell him to the highest bidder. I could accept that!

It was just after dark the following day when we landed in Singapore. Without too much trouble I managed to get a fast black just off the jetty and I bundled my friend in. When we were both seated in the back of it I gave the driver the address of the office that I had left all those hours and miles ago. Because of the traffic it took about fifteen minutes to get there. Then I took my newfound friend by the arm and told the driver I would get the fare for him and went up into the office. It looked as if I were just in time as they were in the process of packing everything up.

When I walked in you would have thought I had just come back from the grave, but unperturbed I looked around the room and said, "Hey, everybody, it's me, the old proverbial bad penny. I've come home." Then I turned to Mick who was standing with his mouth open. "There is a fast black downstairs, the driver needs paying, can you do the honours?" He just nodded and left.

Then I marched my friend into the office at the rear where I found Major Brown. Looking at him I said, "This gentleman has a story which may interest you. He is going to need paying for this information though and I think you had better pay him well and agree on a figure up front before he says anything."

"How much do you think it is worth?" Brown asked me.

"It sounded really bloody valuable to me; it may even win us the war, sorry, confrontation. Mind he may take equipment for his people rather than money," I said.

After some bartering with the man Brown agreed to pay him money up front, but only if the information was really good. Then he would throw in some fishing gear, nets and things and a load of rice and other food. Knowing Brown it would probably be out of date British army rations.

Only then did I turn to my companion and say, "Go on, tell him what you told me." To Brown I said. "I'm starving, so while you two talk I am going to have a meal over the road and just maybe, just maybe I'll have a can or two of Tiger."

With that I was off before Brown could stop me. I needed to see Mick. I needed to find out what had happened, particularly what happened to my backup. I also wanted to find out why he looked so surprised to see me. Alright, I know it had been hard out there. Also that it had been close, but why was he so dammed surprised to see me walk in? I had to know.

First I tried to find him in the building, but I had no joy, he was nowhere to be seen. So I went across the road to the café where I had told Brown I was going to get a meal. I half expected him to greet me as I entered, but he was not there. So I sat down and ordered a steak and all the trimmings and to drink I ordered a can of Tiger. The beer came and I sat at the table sipping it while trying to work the whole thing out. The beer tasted horrible and as I sat there thinking about the last few days none of it made any sense at all. Where had Mick gone? Why was he so surprised to see me? What had gone on while I had been missing? As I was still trying to get to the bottom of it, the steak arrived and I noticed everybody was giving me some very strange looks. Feeling embarrassed I settled to eat my steak and I took one look at it and felt I was going to be violently sick. It took all my concentration to stop myself throwing up, even before I had eaten any of it.

I was still trying to stop making a fool of myself wondering what the hell was going on, when Brown came into the cafe and sat down opposite me. He said, "You have done very well, Colours. It was a bonus, you finding out about the gunrunning via the islands. Especially after you both found nothing on the ship."

You could have knocked me out with a feather with that remark. I looked at him for a minute and then said, "Just what did Corporal Smith tell you about the ship, sir?"

"Well," said Brown "He didn't tell me anything, but I gather from our American friends that all was normal and the ship was really just loaded with coal; that is right, isn't it."

I looked at him long and hard. Then I said, "Yes, if that is what Mick told you. By the way where the hell is he?"

"He has gone off for a drink, and then he is going to rejoin his unit; the American is paying for the drinks. He has given you up as a bumbling idiot. Then he would after what Corporal Smith told him wouldn't he? By the way, Colours, I'd see the doctor soon if I were you, you look bloody awful man. What the hell have you been up to?"

As I looked at him, I thought the bastard is telling me pork pies. Mick doesn't drink, he is TT not Grog. More to the point why the hell hadn't he asked how I came to be on the island. We just stared at each other, eye to eye and at last I said, "I want to return to my unit now sir if that is all right by you."

I needed time to sort this little lot out. I could not for the life of me understand what had got into Mick. We had been through so much together, yet he had abandoned me. I just could not believe it. No, I said to myself, making excuses for him, he is as I am very, very tired.

With that thought in mind I let Brown get me a car, and I heard him say, "Take the Colour Sergeant back to his unit, he is finished here. He will be flying out to join the main party in Borneo tomorrow or the day after." As I looked at him I thought I'm getting far too bloody old for this type of thing. Also I hate it when the Americans get involved, with all their smart-arsed CIA shit. They are the biggest load of plonkers on God's Earth. Shit to them all and why were they all surprised to see me still alive? With that the car left for the causeway and Malaya and I thought oh, bollocks to the lot of them. All I needed was a good night's sleep and then off to Borneo.

Chapter Six
Off To Borneo To Do Some Real Commando Work
Borneo, Far East 1963-64

I hate Young Sergeant Majors and Sprog Officers

My arrival in Kuching was about as uneventful a day as you could think of, no hero's welcome in this unit. I must admit that I had a feeling that History was being made all around me. Just showed what a shit I had turned into. I'd started to believe I was an important person in this man's army, but did they have a bit of a surprise for this little Colour Sergeant!

When I reported to the Movements' Office of the unit, it was full of the hustle and bustle of dispatching men all over the place. Some men to the border outposts, some back to the UK. I would be prepared to bet serious money that they had a hand in putting a man in space, they were that efficient. With choppers taking off every few minutes it was like being in the centre of the Universe, or is it the 'Poolyverse'. The thing was, I truly believed that I would be sent for to be briefed on my obviously important mission in this mudbath, otherwise why was I there. In this obviously important place of course only I knew I'd be sent for, as and when the Commanding Officer had time.

How wrong can one be! The Movements' Sergeant literally just told me, "You had better go and find yourself a bed for the night and report back here tomorrow." The Second in Command of the unit was there and as I knew him of old we had a chat.

So being the good Royal Marine that I am I made a beeline for the best-looking building in the place, which I just knew had to be the 'Crab Hats' Sergeants Mess', the RAF Senior Non-Commissioned Officers' Mess to be exact. Once there, I was able to get myself fixed up with a bed and returned to the mess bar. There I introduced myself to the mess president who gave me a better welcome than I'd had from my unit. I ordered a can of Tiger beer from the bar and put one in the wood for the mess president. Then I made my way to the mess veranda, from where I watched in comfort the activity going on around and all over the airfield from the comfort of the mess veranda, my cold Tiger beer in my hand. The longer I watched it all, the more

I marvelled at this hive of activity. Of course I'd fallen into the trap that all base wallahs set for people like me.

It is funny how the more hustle, bustle, and puffing they do, ordinary types like me think they are so indispensable. What is the saying about the 'indispensable man'? "Put your hands in a bucket of water;

Splash them about as much as you want.

When you take your hands out of the water,

The hole that remains in the water is the measure

Of how much you will be missed

When you're gone!"

While all this was going through my mind I failed to notice the Royal Marine SNCOs, a Provost Colour Sergeant, and another two Colour Sergeants arrive in the mess. The first I noticed was when one of the mess men pointed to me. Then they made their way towards my table, in a rather determined manner. Now, that was when the alarm bells should have started to ring, but they didn't. For I was still so full of my own piss and importance, I could only think that they were paying me a courtesy call, a welcoming party with greetings from the CO. I wouldn't have been surprised if they had hailed me as Caesar; but the look on their faces should have told me otherwise.

"Are you Colour Sergeant Johnston?" the Provost Colour Sergeant asked.

"Yes. That's me. Pleased to meet you," I said as I offered him my hand.

He refused my hand and started into that old shit all provost staff recite before breakfast like a bunch of Buddhist monks! "I am placing you in cabin arrest for being absent without leave."

I rose to this with a magnificence I was proud of. "Just hang on there just one pigging minute there; I left Singapore as soon as my detachment was ended. I arrived here not two hours ago. What is more I didn't even have a run ashore before I left Malaya. When I arrived here I was told by the movements' SNCO to find a bed for the night so here I am. Like all good Marines I found a bed for the night."

As I looked at them, I thought, why did I make that stupid reference about no run ashore, they must think I am a bloody great big OD, if they could think that is! Mind, my protestations did not stop them doing what they came to do. They arrested me; I did for once in my infinite wisdom, decide that an RAF SNCOs Mess was not really the place to sort out Royal Marine affairs and kept my mouth firmly shut from that moment on about such things as seniority of rank. For instance if the two Colour Sergeants were junior to me they could not act as my escort or jailers; but I reasoned that talking that talk might just piss my new CO off a little bit more than he seemed to be already by having me arrested.

Unfortunately I spent the night locked up in a tent on the edge of Kuching Airfield. The tent was like a Turkish bath what with aircraft coming and going all bloody night long, some bloody cabin arrest this, I thought. What a start to my new life in a new unit. I had decided at about 3.00 a.m. I would give this Commanding Officer a piece of my mind but by morning I thought it through a bit more and decided against such tomfoolery; I calmed down a bit and decided I would wait to get the lie of the land first.

I was wakened at first light from what little sleep I had managed to get by one of my escorts. He, bless him, said. "You are to get ready to fly to Commando

Headquarters which is at Serian. Once there, you are to be arraigned before the Commanding Officer, as soon as possible after our arrival. If the unit parade is over by then, that is."

I thought, what kind of bloody unit have I joined, what kind of a unit holds parades when in a war zone? Looks as if Lord Haig hasn't died after all, but I only said, "Did I hear you right when you said 'parade'? I thought that sort of stuff went out after Waterloo?"

Again it looked as if I had made a faux pas. Because the look he gave me spoke volumes, like have you just landed from Mars or some other distant planet?

That was it I thought, I will only take so much mister; and I asked him what his date of seniority was. When he told me I started to laugh and he gave me a filthy look. "Well, my young Acting Colour Sergeant you are actually not qualified to escort me no matter what offence I'm supposed to have committed. You may like to go and tell the Provost Sergeant that as the third most senior Colour Sergeant in this jolly old Corps of ours he may just have a problem getting enough men senior to me to form an escort for me? Oh, and by the way he doesn't qualify either!"

After explaining that little blunder I was told to go to the RAF Mess and have my breakfast, much to the amusement of the older ranks in the unit; who had realised that it was me that they were trying to march around the place. The Provost's head started turning like a parrot's head when a voice rang out from a stores complex, "I see they finally got you under arrest Colours, I never thought I'd see that happen. Lost your touch, have you?"

To which I replied, "Not fucking yet young man!" and back came the reply "Don't let me down, Colours, I've got fifty bucks on you being out by lunchtime!" My simple reply was, "Money in the bank young man, money in the bank!"

Then with that fiasco over, the Provost Colour Sergeant marched me off to the tent which housed the movements' office. From there I was, shall I say no longer marched, but guided to the helicopter which was to fly me to Commando Headquarters, where provided they'd finished Trooping the Colour on the jungle parade I would be marched in front of the Commanding Officer.

When eventually the circus arrived at Commando Headquarters, the Provost SNCO hero of the revolution that he was, tried to march me to the CO's office; but regular changes of stride and step had him hopping around like a cat on a hot plate. The CO's office was situated on the only bit of gravel road in the place. There, the RSM subjected me to a lecture about my loyalty to the Corps.

Right smart arse he turned out to be. "You did not act in a correct and Royal Marine manner, when you went and got yourself established in the RAF mess instead of joining up with the Commando's own SNCOs Mess," he barked at me for all to hear.

To this outburst I was going to ask just where the hell that mess was, but changed my mind and said nothing. It had been some years earlier that I had learnt that the best defence, once you know the charge is wrong (as it looked as if I was going to be charged under section 69) is simply to keep your bloody big mouth shut.

One of my old mentors had told me a long, long time ago now, "If you tell them that the charge they are using is wrong before they read it out in front of the adjudicating officer, then the bastards will change the charge."

All For A King's Shilling

So I took the RSM's tirade directed at me. Despite my natural instinct and built-in bolshiness to fight to the bitter end, I kept my bloody big mouth well and truly shut.

They had planned the whole charade well, because it was two hours after the helicopter flight, and a wait in the Headquarters' tent. This could have passed for a Turkish bath without any problems as well. During the two hours and because of the humidity I had a good sweat on. My appearance was no longer as smart as it had been when I had started out on this charade; then I had been as smart as any Drill Instructor. I had intended to make a good impression and I could not have been smarter. They had taken me round the camp to be seen by the unit doctor – of all things to see if I were fit for punishment – fit for punishment, I ask you. Later, when he told me to bend over I told him that I knew all about him and if he put a hand on me I'd claim he had homosexually abused me; after a short pause in the proceedings the doctor moved away from behind me, he told me to get dressed and walked to his desk. There he then signed a piece of paper, which he duly handed to the Provost Sergeant passing me 'fit to be flogged'. He then wished me 'good luck' as I left his office. When we left the Provost Sergeant asked me what had happened between the doctor and me. I just said it was known as covering your arse where that 'Bones' was concerned. All he said was "So the rumours are right then?" I just nodded. By this time I must admit I was starting to look like a bag of wet shit, tied in the middle with a white web belt! To this day I think the delay was all part of the plan to make me look like some dirty, slovenly, and ill-disciplined SNCO when I was marched in front of the CO. So when the RSM got two sergeants to stand either side of me as escorts, the Provost Sergeant whispered something in his ear and that something must have had something to do with seniority; because everything seemed to change and I was left standing facing the CO's door all on my own. When at last I was marched in front of the Commanding Officer, I looked like a right shit.

After all that 'Left right, and left right again' the 'halt, don't salute' rang out loud and clear. It's the crap they bawl and shout and it makes them important. Don't get me wrong, some of the RSMs I've met are the salt of the earth. There isn't a rank in the services can touch them, but like all professions you occasionally get the arsehole.

Well by the time I'd halted the RSM bawled out the charge, because in no stretch of the imagination did he read it out; I think that the Indonesians over the border must have heard him. I had lost all interest in creating a good impression by now and was wondering if the Indonesian were sympathising with me. They were probably waiting with bated breath to hear the outcome of the proceedings.

"Colour Sergeant Johnston," he started, "You are charged under section sixty-nine of the Manual of Military Law. In that you, contrary to good order and military discipline, did bring the Corps into disrepute by seeking accommodation in the Kuching RAF SNCOs mess when you had been ordered to report to your new unit, to whit, Forty Commando Royal Marines."

Even I knew enough about military law to know that the wording was incorrect and that alone would nullify the charge. You see I had reported to, to whit, Forty Commando. If I hadn't reported to Forty Commando Royal Marines, then what the bloody hell was I doing in front of its Commanding Officer?

Next the Commanding Officer asked, "Do you understand the charge, Colour Sergeant?"

(Oh! I understood the charge all right. For some reason beyond my comprehension, I was being framed. That worried me, because who would gain from framing an arsehole like me.)

But I just replied, "No, not really, sir, I don't!"

The Commanding Officer either didn't hear what I'd said or he ignored it. Possibly because his unit's posting to such an outpost of the Empire had just meant he was promoted to god! He then ordered the RSM to march in the first witness. After much bawling and shouting, with a 'left right and another left right', in marched an SNCO whom I had never seen before in my life. The RSM then shouted, "Halt, salute, make your report to the Commanding Officer."

It was then I learnt he was the unit PWI, to whit, the unit Platoon Weapons Instructor. The RSM's whipping boy.

This goon then gave out, "Sir I am PO14710 Sergeant Anderson Unit Platoon Weapons Instructor." He then proceeded to perjure himself by saying, "At approximately 2.30 yesterday I was present when Colour Sergeant Johnston was told by the Movements' SNCO to report to the SNCOs Mess."

So there was the proof of the order that I had disobeyed.

When the Commanding Officer then asked me, "Do you have any questions you would like to ask this witness?"

"Yes, sir, I do."

"Then you must ask them through me."

So I said, "Sir, could you ask Sergeant Anderson who it was who gave me the order to report to the SNCOs Mess, and when did that person give me the order?"

To my surprise Sergeant Anderson replied, "I gave him the order myself."

"Does that answer your question, Colour Sergeant?" the Commanding Officer asked.

"No sir. First, I don't take orders from anybody junior to me unless it is an order relayed to me by a person of higher rank and sir, how could Sergeant Anderson have given me an order to report to the SNCOs Mess when he has just told you it was the Movements Sergeant who told me to report to the SNCOs Mess? Anyway, sir, even if he wasn't lying about the Movements SNCO, I've never seen this SNCO in my life before, sir, I've never laid eyes on the man before now."

"I gave you the order when you arrived yesterday at Kuching," he blurted out.

The Commanding Officer then asked me, "What has all this to do with the fact that the Sergeant gave you an order which you saw fit to disobey?"

"Well, sir, I have never seen this SNCO before in my life. In fact, sir, I reiterate that this is the first time I have ever laid eyes on him; I fail to see how he could have given me any orders of any sort, sir, and I do believe he is lying to the extent that I request that all evidence be given under oath…"

The first look of surprise came into the Commanding Officer's eyes. I heard the RSM suck air through his teeth. Then the unit PWI started to fluster as he tried to find words to explain what he had just said. He tried to say something, but got all tongue-tied and nothing but grunts came out.

He then blurted out, "I have known Colour Sergeant Johnston for years, sir. In fact I was in the same squad as him when we were recruits."

All For A King's Shilling

Before any of those present could get themselves into a frenzy of any sort, the Commanding Officer asked, "What do you have to say to that?"

"Well, sir, a simple check of the regimental numbers of the witness and myself on the charge sheet would prove the Unit Platoon Weapons Instructor had joined the Corps at least ten years after me. If my memory of the regimental number system is correct, that is, sir, which further explains why I request all evidence be given under oath."

To this, the Commanding Officer just grunted and told the RSM to march the witness out. Next there came the evidence of my arrest in the RAF mess. When asked if I had anything to say I looked the CO in the eye and thought somebody is out to get me; and my life in this unit is going to be hell, so it was going to be in for a penny then in for a pound. "Yes sir I do, my arrest at the RAF SNCOs mess was an illegal arrest, sir! To place me under arrest I should have been placed in cabin arrest or equivalent and not in a hastily constructed tent at the end of the runway, which was padlocked at each end. There was no camp bed or anything else in that tent, sir, and I had no protection against any of the insects flying or crawling that came to spend the night with me. Secondly, sir, the arresting officer and the escorts he had with him were not senior to me or of a higher rank." I was going to stop there because the CO was in a rather strange way and colour, but being me I thought shit you want a fight you're going to get a bloody fight! "I think, sir," I went on, "because of the way this whole episode is going I believe it is in my best interest to request a trial by court-martial. I would also like to put in a request to see the next visiting general about a grievance." The Adjutant was trying to whisper something to him and the RSM was about to explode, he was having trouble breathing and his face was puffing up like a 'puffer fish'.

The Adjutant and the CO had a little conflab then and the RSM was asked to leave. The CO then looked at me and said, "What am I to do with you?"

It seemed to me that with great control he did manage to restrain himself and stopped himself. He did though have the good sense to ask me, "What have you to say for yourself, Colour Sergeant Johnston?"

"Sir," I said, "I think this charade has gone too far and I do believe that you cannot deal with this case. By the Manual of Military Law you have to seek advice from a higher authority." I didn't like the look he gave me, but I went on, "When I wasn't in the water counting fish sir, I studied Military Law. With a personality like mine that is essential studying sir and this whole charade is a fit up by people who have said when my draft came out to this unit that they would teach me what serving in a real Commando is really like. Well for the record sir I have served six and a half years in Commando service all of which was on active service which is more than any other SNCO in this unit!"

"Colour Sergeant is right sir; I do have his file here and I think it is important that you read it sir."

"Can I call my own witness Sir?" I interjected at that point.

"Witness, what witness have you got, that you can call?" the Commanding Officer asked.

"The Unit Second in Command, sir; he has agreed to give evidence for me.

A rather long pause followed, during which I interjected, "Major J P Smithers, sir."

"I think you will find I know my Second in Command, Colour Sergeant," the Commanding Officer replied.

"I believe he will also clear this mess up, sir. He will confirm my story, sir. That I reported to the Movements' Office when I arrived in Kuching; as he was the most senior man there when I entered the tent, then I naturally reported to him. It was he who told me to go to the RAF mess and make myself scarce. That is, until today, when I should report to the Movements' Office. Then I would be brought here to see you, sir, he had told me. You would interview me and tell me which company I was to join, and the job I was to do, sir!"

I must admit that the pause this time was so long that I did think of asking if everybody was all right. The CO then did a strange thing, he asked me to go with the Adjutant and he would see me later. With that settled the Adjutant handed the CO what I took to be my file and told me to follow him and we left the office by another door.

Some time later when everything seemed to have settled down the Adjutant took me back into the CO's office by the main door outside which the RSM and his PWI were chatting to the Provost Sergeant.

The Commanding Officer then blurted out. "It is not good enough; you must realize that discipline is the essence of a good unit. We cannot have people like you running wild and doing just what you want, even if you are used to working on your own and making your own decisions. It has got to stop, now that you are in an operational commando unit.

"I see by your file that you have had a chequered career. It says here that you swam over forty miles to reach land after having been washed overboard in the Straits of Malacca. It also says that the lumps and pockmarks on your face are the results of your being bitten and stung by insects which could, had you not been treated as quickly as you were, have killed you. Well I can promise you that I shall be watching you very closely. If you do step out of line from now on all this past glory won't ever help, do you understand?" He then just said, "Posted to Alpha Company, and oh, don't lecture me on Military Law again. Now get him out of here, Adjutant."

"Salute, about turn, quick march," the Adjutant said, and out I went to the left right, left right charade again. Outside the RSM latched on to me and said, "Well, Colour Sergeant, you seem to have been extremely lucky this time; but it will be the last time you will ever get away with anything again I shall be watching you very closely from now on."

To this day I never have cottoned on to what it was all about. When they had all said their piece I just wandered off looking for a way to get to "Alpha Company's" location. The sooner I was away the better; I did not wish to spend too much time in this madhouse, it might be catching. So I did the most obvious thing and headed for the air traffic controllers' abode. I was lucky, I had only just entered the building when I saw an old friend who had graduated from the mess drunk to a crewman in these new troop carrying Wessex Mk5 choppers.

All For A King's Shilling

He just burst out laughing when he saw me. "It was my impression that they had locked you up and tossed away the key. Have you managed to escape already, should we recapture you or something?" he asked.

"No bloody chance of that. No, I need a bloody lift out of this bloody place as fast as you can mate."

"Hey, don't you call me a mate. Mates of yours are always getting into serious trouble. Sometimes it is the dead type of trouble," he added.

"It looks as if it is getting too hot for my well-being in this bloody place. I wish I knew what the hell was going on. So, now I am calling in a favour you owe me, I need a lift to Alpha Company's location, wherever that might be, as soon as possible."

I really was in luck now. I heard a voice from the air briefing room just down the corridor ask, "Have they let that big bastard out again, Chief?"

"That's right, sir. God almighty is the only one who knows how the hell he does it, but he's bloody done it again!"

"Never mind my bloody life history, sir, can you get me out of this place today?"

"You could just be in luck my son, it seems that I'm always lifting you out of the shit somewhere with my little HE-LO- Copter doesn't it!" he replied.

Within half an hour I was in a helicopter, along with a load of stores heading for God knows what, but at least I was away from those HQ bastards who seemed for some reason best known to themselves to have taken a violent dislike to me even before they had met me. I spent the rest of the flight just thinking about that.

When at last I arrived in Alpha Company, at a place called Tapan, it was not long after midday. My arrival was, to say the least, not overpowering, no fatted calf for me. It felt as if I had in fact arrived like a dose of the pox. I don't know what stories had gone around ahead of me, but they didn't like me at all. Do not believe anybody who tells you that there is no ice in the Far East. That company made their own in those times. Still, I was away from those dangerous bastards in Kuching and Serian. That in itself took a load off my mind.

The fact that "A" Company was in reserve and therefore not up on the border also set my mind at rest. The unit was deployed from Sungaibatu to the coast. They held a series of outposts along the border. With Alpha Company being in reserve that would give me time to get my act together, and perhaps find out why everybody seemed to have taken a violent dislike to me. For the first time in my life I felt that I was being treated like an outcast, in my own Corps. The fact that I did not know why worried me a little. Why did I say worried me a little? It worried me a bloody lot, but I was going to find out, by shit I was!

It was three weeks after I had arrived in this Company, and I must admit, things were starting to look up. Now I was no longer being treated like a leper, and the lads, who were quite a good bunch, seemed to have accepted me. I was starting to feel at home again, I had proved that I did know a lot about jungle warfare. So the Company Commander and the other SNCOs started to accept me as well. The men would take you for a ride if you let them, but then what bunch of British servicemen wouldn't, given half a chance?

We had been carrying out patrols in the rear areas of the two forward companies. The Indonesians had this sneaky habit of coming over in strength, trying to wipe out one or more of the local kampongs, then hitting one or other of the forward companies' positions from the rear, on the way back over the border. Our job was to patrol the area in the rear of our two forward companies, to discourage the Indonesians and let them know that we were around. I was not quite sure how we were to discourage them, or how to let them know we were around. Unless, of course, we bumped into them one fine day which was always possible as things sometimes heated up a bit and some officer was out to make a name for himself!

Still I suppose they had quite a few friends located in the villages that we visited, of that I have no doubt; and if we started to set up a pattern of patrolling, they would certainly hit us one fine day as sure as eggs were eggs.

My troop was out on one of these patrols when my life took another turn for the worse. Mind I did not know it at that time. The realization of that useful point of information only dawned on me some long time later.

We had made our way through the jungle for a couple of hours on the third day of a six-day patrol. All was well, there was no untoward activity in the area and it was a nice day, as days on patrol go, that is. The smell of the kampong for which we were heading was getting stronger, we could hear the sound of dogs and people. I thought, we will be able to stay in this area long enough to cook our main meal of the day. It will not be noticed in the smell of the kampong cooking.

We were about half a mile away from it, when the radio started to make those noises which only mean one thing. Some bastard with nothing better to do had probably decided to send us off to see if the water in a stream ten miles away was drinkable. You may well laugh, but that is the sort of thing some of these young officers think up, mainly to impress the CO.

I remember some years before when I was in Cyprus during the emergency there in the fifties; I was stationed on Mount Olympus in the Troodos Mountains. My section and I were sent out a distance of nearly seven miles to see in which direction a stream half way up the south side of Mount Olympus flowed. It may be that all the military maps of the area still show the stream flowing upwards towards the crest; because that was the direction that I reported the stream flowing.

This time I was wrong, the message was that we had to make it to the kampong in a few minutes, as a helicopter would be calling there. We had to meet it there, and protect it whilst it was on the ground.

I said to my young officer. "I have never heard of anything so bloody stupid, we will have to throw caution to the wind, and run to get there in time. All the training and patrol discipline, which we have just perfected, will be lost. It will take some poor bastard to get killed before these useless sods learn all about jungle warfare. Ah, but it's not a war, is it. No sir, it's just a bloody confrontation. Isn't it?"

I thought I only wish some sod would tell the Indonesians that. To them it is war, and it is a war that we mean to win!

If we win, it will only be by luck, and not at this moment in time with the political aim that the generals have to work to. Still, enough of my grousing; last one in the kampong stinks! To anybody who has been to a kampong there is a pun there.

As we were making our half mile dash to the kampong we could hear the chopper getting closer overhead. My young officer seemed determined to get there before it did. He was in full flight down the track, when he went 'arse over tit' and nearly killed himself with his own bloody rifle. If he thought that he was going to get any sympathy, he was in the wrong man's army. I had one hell of a job not splitting my sides with laughter, let alone stopping the lads just about falling over themselves.

When we at last got to the kampong, the chopper was about to land. After a minute or two I managed to get the locals out of the way and some sort of defensive perimeter established, just as the chopper touched down. Then I ran into the side of the chopper to talk to the crewman and see who, and what, all the fuss was about. As I got there and the dust cleared, I saw a familiar face in the back of this monster of a bird. As I looked at him I thought, well this is what it is all about. If Nobby is out here, then my reason for being here is obvious and I knew at once the chopper was here to pick me up.

The first man out of the chopper was the Assistant Adjutant; he came across to where I had moved back to. He told me, "We have received orders for you to report, along with Corporal Clark, to Brigade Headquarters." He then said, "The Commanding Officer has said that I am to go with you, and I am to keep him informed as to what is happening to Corporal Clark and yourself."

I thought, you don't expect me to swallow that shit surely, but I just said, "As we are going to have to evacuate my young officer by air because of his injuries, then sir perhaps, as the only officer here, you should now take command of the patrol?"

"No, Colour Sergeant, that I cannot do."

He simply got on the radio and ordered an airlift to take them and the Troop Commander out, and back to base. With that we were all on our way to Brigade Headquarters.

I was unable to talk to Nobby, because of the noise in the helicopter. As I looked at him I did not feel like letting this young officer know that we did in fact know one another. For the first time since arriving here I must admit that I was pleased to see somebody to whom I could really relate. At least I knew that there was one person that I could trust in this godforsaken place. I'd already trusted my life in his hands more than once.

The trip took about three quarters of an hour, and like all servicemen the world over, both Nobby and I dozed off to sleep. We remained in that half awake state, which allows instant response to whatever may happen suddenly. I was not sure just what it was the young Assistant Adjutant got up to, nor was I interested in knowing. He was the same as all young officers I suppose. Every assignment given him by his Commanding Officer must lead to nothing other than Glory. He'll get wise some day, and then the Commanding Officer will just replace him. He will get another one from the box they seem to be forever popping out of, and so it goes on. As one gets wise, so another of the little blighters pops up out of the box to take his place.

We eventually arrived at Brigade HQ to be met by (guess who was there to meet us?) that's right, the same two who arrested me at Kuching when I first arrived in this bloody place. They told me, "We are to take yourself and Corporal Clark to the Brigade briefing room."

The Assistant Adjutant then said, "I am in charge of this party, and we will all be going to the briefing room."

The larger one said, "That is as maybe, sir, but we only have orders to take the Colour Sergeant and the Corporal to the briefing room, not you. So, I'm sorry, sir, you will have to make your own way there!"

They then ushered Nobby and me into a Land Rover, and we departed from the landing site leaving our young Assistant Adjutant all alone on the airstrip; even the aircraft had also departed. The last thing I saw as we left, he was heading towards a Land Rover parked by one of the airstrip gun positions. I thought then, you've got to give him his due. He was either frightened to death of his Commanding Officer; or he had got a lot more guts than was good for him, and perseverance, or he is just plain 'thick'. I think it is probably the first.

Seeing these two sods in Brigade did not do very much for my morale I might add. Nothing had been said about arrest or such things, but I still felt a little uneasy about these two. It's funny really, but the longer I have thought about it, that was the first time I had the feeling that things were not as they should be. The feeling that I was being used came over me; and like the fool I am I just shrugged my shoulders and thought that perhaps I was getting a little too old for this type of thing.

As we entered the Brigade briefing room guess who pushed past me, and made a bee line straight up to the Brigadier. Yes, that's right, our Assistant Adjutant. He threw the Brigadier an officer's parade ground type salute and promptly announced, "Sir, Lieutenant Wills, Colour Sergeant Johnston, and Corporal Clark reporting for duty, sir!"

The golden rule of all young officers, and non-commissioned officers for that matter, is if you are going to make an arsehole of yourself then for god's sake do not do it in front of the Brigadier. Definitely do not do it in front of other officers and the men; but definitely, do not include the Brigadier in your cock up! The Brigadier's face was a picture. All he said was, "You are probably right young man." To the Brigade Major he said, "Please see this young officer gets back to his unit."

You see it seems the Brigadier was not expecting anybody other than Nobby and me. He was not amused; he did not even know the young officer; but the Brigadier was a gent; he would not have embarrassed the young officer in front of anybody, he was that kind of officer. The last I saw of that young man that day was when we came out of the briefing. He was fidgeting from foot to foot as the Brigade Major was having a real heart to heart with him.

Our briefing was, to say the least, a little on the vague side for the type of operation this whole thing turned into. The Political Officer for the area had been given some information from his trusted servants and spies (servants who had no problem working both sides of the border). The information was the Indonesians had moved into the border area with two divisions. They were getting ready to push us into the sea, drive us out of Borneo for good.

On the strength of this 'garbage' Nobby, myself and I had assumed, Corporal Mick Smith, were required to go and check it out. Go and check out information that the Political Officer's own people could not do. Not only that but none of them would be accompanying us. They said it was too dangerous for them. It was then that I should have realised that things were not what they ought to be. Looking back, it was the second time that I should have called a halt to the whole thing and deserted.

Then I received the next 'gem' of information when I asked the Brigade Intelligence Officer where my other team member was.

"If you mean Corporal Smith," he said, "I'm sorry to inform you that he was killed; he was in a car accident in Singapore two weeks ago."

Well when I heard that you could have knocked me over with a feather. Then after the initial shock I asked, "What happened?"

The Intelligence Officer said, "He had been in Singapore on R and R. It seems he had gone ashore, had too much to drink, and stole a car. He then crashed the car on the Thompson Road."

I was dumbfounded, and I just could not make any sense of it. As I looked at the Brigadier, all I did was say, "No, sir, not Mick, that can't be, he was 'TT', he never touched drink. He would not be drunk, you see, sir, the man didn't ever drink; he really was a real teetotaller, he was one of Aggie Weston's most adherent followers!"

Then I was just about to say some more, when I saw the way Nobby was looking at me, and ever so slowly he moved his head from side to side. It was with great difficulty I managed to keep it all back, and I just said to the Brigadier, "I can hardly believe he would be drunk, sir."

"I know, Colour Sergeant, I know, but these unfortunate accidents happen from time to time," was all he said.

The rest of the briefing seemed to go over the top of my head. I just could not get over the news that I had been given. The briefing consisted of the usual stuff about how well we were doing and how badly the enemy was doing. If that were so, then what in hell's name were we doing here; being briefed to go over the border, just to see how badly these two divisions really were doing? I asked myself.

You see not all the British armchair generals were in England, some of the bastards must be out here with us. It seemed that the Indonesians had decided after all this time that the gods were with them at last and it was time to drive us into the sea. To achieve this glorious aim they had amassed a couple of divisions just over the border in the area opposite brigade. The way they put it was to me, quite funny!

"I want you to go over and have a look-see; should only take a couple of days at best. More of a swan, than anything else, it will just be like being on Woodbury Common again." It was on the tip off my tongue to ask where that was. But I kept my mouth shut.

Mind I did get a bit hot under the collar when they started on about the signals part of the briefing. They said that they would call me on the hour, every hour, and that these times had to be strictly followed. They said I was to keep a listening watch on the radio at all times.

I complained bitterly about this, and said, "It is against all procedures. We, my team and I, may not be in a situation to call every hour on the hour. We may be in a fire fight with the enemy, or we may be in a situation where we are creeping around inside one of his camps so to start broadcasting would give our position away and be certain torture and a long lingering death. What is more, we would have to get rid of all our equipment to make room for all the batteries we would have to carry."

Then the signal officer said, "Be that as it may, you will remain on listening watch all the time."

I asked him, "Are we using a new type of radio, or have you found a way of supplying us with new batteries while we are over there? Surely we should do as we have always done in the past, sir? It would be better for your men, who are in stationary secure positions, to remain on listening watch. We would call and check with them as and when it was best so to do."

He told me, "That is not possible and you will do as you are told." I was by now beginning to hate this man, to the extent that I was subconsciously fingering the handle of my knife; and to think that perhaps they did not like me in this outfit either. First it was my own unit, with that fiasco at Kuching, and now this bloody jumped up grammar schoolboy. God they ruined this Corps when they let any Tom, Dick or Harry with five 'O' levels join with aspirations of a Queen's Commission. So I decided that perhaps a change of subject would be of benefit to us all. So I asked, "Is there to be a third man in the team, and if there is, why isn't he here for this briefing? I'd like to meet the third man I'm to take with me, could I meet him?"

This little shit of a Signals Officer then said, "I have personally picked one of my best men to go with you as your operator, he will also be in command. He has already been briefed; in fact at this moment he is gathering together the stores which he will need, ready to be loaded on the chopper. He will have everything ready for you when you take off, if you two can be ready in time."

"That's good," I said, "Just who is this man? I'd still like to meet him."

I then turned and asked the Brigadier, "Excuse me, sir, but your staff seem to have everything under control. So why are Corporal Clark and I here? It seems to be so well organized as a signal section swan, from this end; perhaps, sir, this mission doesn't need anybody of Corporal Clark's or my expertise?"

I could see by the looks on certain faces that at last I was getting the upper hand in this conversation.

The Brigadier said, "Now, now Colours, do not be so facetious, there is only one person who will be in charge on this little trip and that is you, as you know full well."

He turned to the Signals Officer then, and said, "I think you have overstepped the mark telling your signaller all that rubbish about being in command. Also I would advise you to stop him drawing any stores; you will find the Colour Sergeant will know exactly what he requires. What is more he is right about the signal procedure. He has not got the manpower to carry all the batteries he would need to follow your plan."

So, I thought to myself, I'll grind this little bloody Signal Officer's best man into the deck. Had I been a gambling man I would have bet the Signals Officer was a mate of that little shit that came with us in the chopper earlier, probably from the same batch of young officers.

I must admit I did feel much better now. The Brigadier had just confirmed who was in command; not that it was ever in question, but he had put them all in their places. He then cleared everybody out of the briefing room except for himself and me! As Nobby was leaving, I told him, "Go and sort the stores out, you know what we want, don't forget coloured smoke either."

Nobby just grinned and said, "Yes, Colour Sergeant," with a slight bow of his head!

All For A King's Shilling

The Brigadier then gave me some orders, which were for him and me alone. He also gave me a word of warning. "I want you to be extra careful" he said, "and trust no one, and I mean no one. Once you leave here, not even him, nodding to the door Nobby had just exited. I am relying on you, so don't foul up on this one. Remember what we have just been talking about. Oh, I'm sorry that you had to go through all that shit when you joined Forty, your CO told me you created havoc in his orderly room!"

"So it was all put up then, sir, why?"

"Because this would not work if we were to use our lads; we had no guarantee we could keep it secret and if you were to uncover anything untoward over there our men would have to ask for guidance before they acted and the cat would be out of the bag. Most importantly you know that once the go-ahead is given there will be no stopping it; so you'd better get it right before you give me the all clear."

"Okay sir but what about the Signal Corporal, sir?"

"Especially not the Signal Corporal you have been lumbered with as your third man; use him as a mule only, if you can dump him somewhere safe we will pick him up later. I'm sorry it has to be like this but nothing here is secure so take care and do your best as I know you will, so good luck!"

The remark about Nobby was a little over the top I thought, as I could see no reason not to trust Nobby, but I said nothing. "Of course I will do my best to carry out your orders, but I will need time to get everything ready."

"Do not worry. I have had all the charges you will need made up by one of your old sparring partners. They will work first time. I've also been advised that the direction beacons will work perfectly first time."

"I hope so, sir, otherwise it's going to be one mad scramble to get back over the border."

He looked at me and then told me, "For you that may not be an option, if it all works I'll get you out, but now you should go to the market in the town before you leave. You will see an old friend of yours who will be helping you even if it is only from a distance." With that the briefing ended, and he said, "You had better be on your way, and for god's sake, be extra vigilant; and again good luck!"

Then I did as the Brigadier had said, I went to the local market, which was just outside the camp. Once there, I took a walk down among the vegetables piled up like the old piles of cannon balls one sees on Plymouth Hoe. At one pile of oranges I picked up some of them, and was having a good old haggle with a young man about the price being far too high. Just as I thought he was going to drop his price, an old wizened man took over the bargaining. As I turned to look at him, for a second or two I hesitated, and then said, "I know you, you silly old fool, don't I?"

"Yes and I know you too, big shit," was the only reply I got.

Then we looked each other straight in the eyes, and I said, "You are uglier now than the last time we met, you little shit face."

"You big ugly bastard now, big shit!"

"Not much, have I?" I said, "Are you the shit face I am to meet here?" I asked.

"Yes," he said, "I shall be over there before you. I will see you when you get there. Now you want fucking oranges or not."

"Yes I said, but at my price."

With that he just grinned and said. "I still see you off, big shit."

So I took the oranges and left. As I turned, I was sure I caught a glimpse of somebody whom I knew to be dead. As I walked back into the Camp I thought, you are getting past this type of thing. This has got to be the last time I'm starting to see bloody ghosts now. A good old number looking after some company stores in Plymouth Barracks would do you just right when you get away from here, I thought. Then I turned and made my way back into the Headquarters Camp.

I decided when I got back to Camp that now seemed as good a time as any to meet this third member of our team. I must admit, I knew I was going to dislike the bloke right from the start. If only because of the way he had been picked and planted on us. The Brigadier's remarks had not endeared him to me either. I was just at the door of the briefing room when it was pushed open, and in he came. He was all bright-eyed and bushy-tailed, flushed with the excitement of his first operational command. As all base wallahs normally are when they get the chance to do what they believe to be a doddle, and thus help them up the ladder to greater and better base wallah posts.

"So you are one of the blokes who are coming with me, are you? You really should have a bath you know, you stink."

That was as far as he was ever going to get. The Brigadier, who had returned to the briefing room, looked at me and said, "I will leave it up to you to tell him Colours, and don't forget, take care this trip." With that he left.

I just said "Yes, sir."

I turned to the Signal Corporal, but before I could say anything, he said, "You did not salute the Brigadier, you will have to change your ways when you are with me, laddie."

I immediately thought I've been called that once too often and I looked him eyeball to eyeball and taking my knife out of it sheath and holding its tip about half an inch from his nose I said, "If you still want to be wearing this nose when we get back, if we ever do get back that is, you had better change your attitude; first I am the third senior Colour Sergeant in this Corps of ours and that means you have no option but to obey every order I give you from this moment on understand!

"No! I did not salute him, did I and don't you ever call me laddie again?"

Then I said, very quietly, "It is time you knew the truth, Corporal, you see I am the one who is in charge of this little operation. You are here only because the man who has been my signaller for years has just been killed. Secondly, maybe I'm not the best Colour Sergeant in the Corps, but I have about sixteen years' experience in undercover operations under my belt. Now I don't care if you want to live a long or a short life, but if you do not do exactly what you are told, when you are told, then I can promise you it will be a short one rather than a long one. It seems to me you may have had your head inside your radio earphones for too long. So first I'm the Colour Sergeant, you are the Corporal. It therefore follows, you are the one who is coming with me as my radio operator, I give orders, and you obey them. What is more I smell of the jungle and that is how I stay alive. By the time the helicopter takes off later today you will also smell of jungle even if you have to roll yourself around in the undergrowth in the jungle or you will not be coming with us. Well I may take you with us and throw you out of the helicopter before we get to the border!

All For A King's Shilling

"When I am on a run ashore, I do smell much the same as you do. Right now we are not going on a run ashore, we are going to venture into enemy territory. The enemy will pick up any poncey smells like the ones emitting from you, up to a mile or more away. So you are to go and get rid of whatever it is that makes you smell like some Chinese prostitute's flip-flop. Do I make myself clear?"

He started to say something, then thought better of it, and said something altogether different. He said, "I was told that there would be three Corporals going, and as the signaller I would be in charge."

"Well, that is a problem you will have to live with, but we are leaving very shortly, I haven't the time to stand and argue the point. Unfortunately I do believe, my friend, that I have to take you with us. Be that as it may, if you do not smell like Nobby and I do by the time the helicopter takes off, as I said I will personally throw you from it. Once we get out of sight of this Camp and base area that is. I do hope that I make myself clear to you?"

"I am going to see my Signal Officer about you."

"If I were you, I'm sure I would do the same. Now I'm going to see Corporal Clark and check the stores out, the ones that you in your infinite wisdom have decided upon. You in the meantime can go and see who you want, but you had better get rid of that smelly soap, aftershave and talcum powder you have so liberally covered yourself in. You see, I don't care if you get killed when we are out there, but I'll not have you endanger our lives, okay!"

With that he stormed off in one direction, still muttering something about seeing his OC, and I took off to find Nobby who was in the back of the QM's compound. He was chatting to one of his old three badge cronies, a friend from some other time and some other place no doubt. He introduced me, but even to this day I can't remember who the hell the man was. I took Nobby over to one side to have a heart to heart with him. As we settled down, he pulled a couple of cans of Tiger beer from his pack, and offered me one. I didn't think that we really had time to drink beer, we had some other things to discuss before we went any further.

"To say that I'm not too happy with this situation, is the least I can say. What do you know about Mick's death, Nobby?"

Again I should have seen the warning signs then, but I must have been 'running a brain in for an idiot at the time'. After the way things had turned out between Mick and me a few weeks ago, I should have connected it all.

"I only heard about Mick's death today. The unit Signals Officer told me, just as I was about to leave on the chopper which brought us both here."

"Did the man tell you what had happened?"

"Only the same as you were told in the briefing. That Mick had got drunk, stolen a car and crashed it."

"But for god's sake Nobby, Mick was such a fitness fanatic, he wouldn't touch drink, and both you and I know that. So how the hell can Mick have died in a car crash, stoned out of his mind with drink? No Nobby, I don't like this one little bit. I think that there have been dirty deeds done. I'll tell you something Nobby, once this little lot is over, I'm going to get to the bottom of what has happened to Mick. Have you seen him recently, Nobby?"

"Yes I have. I saw him in Singapore before he came over here, but that was all. We had a run ashore together, Mick drinking lots of fresh orange juice, as was normal, and I got pissed out of my head. You know he has never touched drink."

"Did Mick say anything to you about the job he had been involved in with me in Singapore recently?"

"Mick did not mention anything."

"Funny, you know Mick and I were involved with the old firm in Singapore for a couple of days."

"No! I didn't know, what was that all about then?"

Looking at him I couldn't read anything in his expression, so I let it go.

We were both silent for a while, thinking our own thoughts, then finally I said, "It is about time we got moving my friend."

I thought to myself, are you still my friend, Nobby? I would dearly love to know, and just what you are thinking about. What I do know is I was sinking into really deep thoughts about Mick. The type of bloke that he was, and the unreality of him being involved in a car crash; as a drunken driver, that is, and his strange reaction to my return from the dead in Singapore just a few weeks ago! I was still wrestling with that, when Nobby broke the silence.

"You are right, it is time we got moving. We have to check out these stores which the Brigade Signals Officer's wonder boy has picked out for us."

With that we rose and made our way back to the QM's compound; as we went I asked Nobby, "What do you think of this wonder boy, as you call him?"

"Not much," was the terse reply.

"Perhaps we should leave him behind when we leave from the forward base. It might be better if we do the whole trip on our own?"

I knew that he would not be keen on that. We would still have to take all the equipment with us, and it would mean the loads being split two ways instead of the three if we took wonder boy with us. If we did meet trouble on this trip we would need a third man to give us some ability to move. Using the old fire and movement we servicemen are so prone to doing, you need a minimum of three men for any success.

So that was it, as we made our way to see the stores, the die as they say, was cast. Both of us had accepted the situation, and we had a new partner. What was more the game was afoot.

I did not expect the stores which our newfound partner had selected and drawn for us would be right for the job in hand. It was a foregone conclusion that, even before I saw them, I would reject them out of hand. So I then really did feel a right fool when I did reject them anyway. He had drawn all sorts of bloody things. He had even drawn a petrol cooker. As I handed the QM's storekeeper a list of the things we would need, he said, "I have already issued the stores for this operation, and you had better see the bloke in charge, Corporal West."

That was the point when Nobby said, "Oh shit! Here we go again."

At this point I started to lose what little sense of humour I had left. I told the QM's storekeeper, "I am the one in charge as you put it, of the patrol. It is a patrol, it is not, and I repeat not, a mission or a bloody operation. A patrol, a bloody stinking patrol, of which I am the leader, that's all it is. As for the stores which you have issued, you can,

All For A King's Shilling

as far as I am concerned, stuff them up your mission leader's arse. In the meantime you could save yourself a hell of a lot of heartache and pain if you just got the list which I have given you ready."

As I left to find the so-called leader of the mission again I heard him ask Nobby, "Just who the hell does he think he is, the Brigadier?"

With that I turned round and headed back into the stores.

As I entered, Nobby was at the door. "Okay;" he said, " I'll sort it, Colours, we don't have too much time and you'd better collect our new partner and any new orders before we go."

"All right, but you had better tell that arsehole in there that I may just ask for him to come with us. Then I really will have somebody else to throw out of the fucking chopper, instead of just the so-called mission leader."

It was half an hour later, and we were back in another helicopter heading for a company position close to the border. According to the report we had, the position was within a few hundred yards of the border. We were led to believe that it would be quite easy to cross the border at this point. There was only one thing about this part of the plan which worried me. If the Indonesians were, as had been reported, massing over the border to attack us, then how the hell was it we could slip across to their side without any problems. Mind once I got away from the restrictions of Brigade Rules and Standing Orders. I would have the freedom of decision and movement which are so necessary on an operation of this kind.

The trip took us some forty minutes; I was very busy checking our position as we flew over the jungle. I noticed Nobby was pretending to sleep, and missing nothing. He was if anything taking a big interest in the two bundles my old engineer pal Pete Harrison had put in the chopper just as we were taking off. Corporal West was too excited to know what the hell he was doing. I thought, 'Shit, what have I got myself into this time'.

We eventually arrived at our destination; we quickly unloaded our gear and when we were clear of the chopper the pilot and the crewman got out and waved me forward. As I talked to them they told me to take care and not trust anybody; the pilot said he would see me when I needed lifting out and to take bloody care.

As the chopper lifted off it flew towards the border and then did a small turn just before it got there, then it set off back the way we had come. After it had gone I reported to the OC of the camp and from him I gathered none of the occupants were very keen to have us. The first question was, how long were we staying.

The Brigadier had given me a story which I then told the Company Commander; which was that we were going to set off after dark to check out the withdrawal route should there be a full-scale attack over the border by the Indonesians. "Oh I see, shouldn't some of my men be with you, as we would be the ones using it?"

"I don't know about that, sir," I said. "We have just been told to reconnoitre the route. I think it is more a feasibility study than anything else. Maybe it is to find out how long it would take the Indonesians to get to Brigade, if they overrun you." He seemed satisfied with that. Anyway he left us alone from then on.

We then set about trying to get the information I had suggested we needed to glean from them before we had boarded the helicopter. Nobby then set off to wander the perimeter of the camp, and I went to the Operations Sangar. To see what I could find out, without raising any suspicions, that is.

I told Corporal West, our new member, "Go to the Signals dugout, on the pretext of checking wavelengths, and swapping dead batteries. I want to know all their operating wavelengths, okay."

"My batteries are not flat."

"No, is that so, well you can check them out anyway."

He told me later, "I cannot understand how it is possible that half my batteries were dead."

To which Nobby told him, "I can, when you've been in this game a while you'll know."

While this little exchange was going on, I set to and repacked my rucksack, packing away the contents of the two bags Pete Harrison had given me. I had to pass some items over to Nobby and he packed them away without a word. As we did this I could see Corporal West was dying to ask what we were doing, but he kept his peace.

It was half an hour later when we got together in an open part of the camp overlooking the Indonesian border. Then I asked Corporal West, "You are sure your batteries are okay now?"

"Yes, but I had to change half of them."

"What about their signal setup?"

"They have a funny signal set up here altogether."

"Well I never, odd don't you think?"

"Well," he said, "they have the usual links of a rifle company, a link to Regimental Headquarters, one to Brigade Headquarters. They also had one to a fire support base, one to the helicopters, and then one rather large and a more powerful set, of a type which I could not recognize."

"Good," I said, "You have done well. We will make a fighter of you yet."

"How did you get on, Nobby?"

"Well, they have quite a bit of fire power here. They have cut the jungle down for killing grounds, a lot further out than is normal. I made a note of their fixed line machine guns. The other thing is the camp does not look right, too new for the area of jungle which has been felled. I don't know what it is, but it is not like your normal border outpost."

"With that, I do agree."

It was then that I told them what I had found out. "After some snooping around I have been able to locate their DFSOS target, and also their other DF tasks. It is now that I would like to point out that I am not happy with the plan to get us over the border. So as you can guess I have made some amendments to it."

"First if we were to leave here the way the Brigade Intelligence Officer had told us to, well, we would be walking right through their DFSOS and DF tasks and possibly I think an ambush."

They both looked at me, and Nobby said, "Surely you are joking."

"I only wish I was, Nobby, but I'm not joking at all, I am bloody serious."

"Well what do we do now?" asked Nobby.

"We are going to leave the camp, and head to the rear once we start. I will then pick a course to get us over the border when I think it is right for us to cross."

"Bit dodgy that isn't it?" said Nobby.

"Yes, so if anything happens to me, you are to abort the mission at once, and do just what I had told the Company Commander we were here to do anyway. You are to make your way back to Brigade and you, Nobby, are to report exactly what happened to the Brigadier alone, okay?"

They had some questions, and once they had been gone through we settled back to rest before it got fully dark. There was no chance of us sleeping; we just sat with our own thoughts for the next half hour before we were told it was time for stand to. We had better muster at the rear of the Operations Sangar. This we did, and we remained there until it was time for us to leave.

Chapter Seven
Still In Borneo, But The Commando Bit Has Gone By The Board
Still Borneo, The Far East 1963-64

Did I ever tell you I'm scared of snakes?

As we moved out of the camp, we headed out to the left rear of it. After about two hundred yards Nobby said, "It is time we moved towards the border, we will make better progress in the area of the camp which has been cut for their fields of fire."

I looked at him as best I could in the dark, but I just said, "Not just yet Nobby, before stand to I saw some movement outside the camp on the outer edge of the cleared area. The reason I did not say anything before was that I did not want you both to start looking towards the place. It seemed to me that they had an ambush laid out there and nobody thought fit to tell us about it. I don't want to walk into it; I also don't want to walk too far down this track just in case they have another one out here as well!"

Then I told them both, "That's what I was trying to tell you about when I asked you back there if you'd seen all their defensive positions and located their DFSOSs. When you said 'yes' I thought you had spotted the place I am talking about."

"I didn't see anything mate, but then I had no idea what you were on about."

"Well I saw the ambush Nobby, because that's what I think it is and if I did not know you better, I'd say your brains have gone all mushy on you and you're not as alert as you should be."

At this point for some obscure reason Corporal West decided to make a radio check, the noise he made when he did this frightened the shit out of both Nobby and me. It was then that I realized the man didn't need a bloody radio, the way he shouted into the mouthpiece just about everybody in Borneo must have heard him.

He was still trying to talk into it as I reached out and ripped the headphones off his head, and the mouthpiece from his hands.

All For A King's Shilling

"Shut that bloody racket mister if you want to live for the next ten seconds, that is. You have got up my nose ever since I met you, understand! Now turn that bloody radio off. I've already told you that you are only to switch it on as and when I tell you. For God's sake man can't you do anything you're bloody told to do. Do you understand me?"

He just gave a little whimpering sort of sound as I handed him the headphones back.

When I had settled my nerves down, I motioned them to follow me and I moved off the track into the jungle. Once inside the jungle edge I pointed to Nobby and indicated he was to bring up the rear, with that I moved off at the best speed I could.

If you have ever moved in thick jungle at all, you will know it is not recommended as a night time occupation. As you can perhaps imagine, if the jungle is dense it will be black dark, you will not be able to see your hand in front of your eyes. This jungle we had just entered, well, it was an understatement to say it was dense. So it was very hard going for some time, and in no time at all we were wringing wet with sweat. We were not making very fast progress at all. We must have been going for about four hours before it started to thin a bit. It was about a half hour later we came across a type of trail. I did not know if it was an animal trail or what it was. Neither did Nobby, and superman, well he was a washout. The main thing was it made our progress through this jungle a little easier, as long as the track headed in the direction we needed to go.

Many times that night a recurring thought kept crossing my mind that perhaps, just perhaps, I was getting too old for this type of thing. Also I promised myself that if that bloody Signals Corporal uttered the phrase once more, "Do you really know what you are doing?" I'd give him a mouthful. If he was an expert, God save me from the rest of you people. It was with great difficulty I kept my cool which I did for some time longer than I would normally have managed in these circumstances, but eventually he got to me and within a flash the next time he started to say it I had him by the throat against a tree with the tip of my knife prodding his gut, "Knock it on the head son or I'll open you like a cod!"

That seemed to do the trick and we stumbled through the jungle for quite some time and if he had even squeaked I would have laid into him as I was at the point of exploding. That was when I heard that unmistakable pop of a mortar being fired and it definitely came from the camp we had just left. Well this was it I thought, we would know soon if I had made the right decision to move off into the jungle as I had. So I told the two of them to stand still and keep their mouths open, as we waited. Then I heard another sound; this time it was the rapid machine gun fire of a General Purpose Machine Gun; it fired a burst of about twenty rounds. It started just as the first mortar bombs landed; they were quick off the mark I thought. As I had expected, the next thing was rapid small arms fire from the place where I'd seen the movement which I had assumed was an ambush position. It seemed as if all the fire was directed to the area we would have had to cross had I not changed our course.

I didn't have time then to explain, but I told them, "This is where we throw caution to the wind my friends. Follow me at the bloody rush because I intend for us to get as far away as possible from this area and across the border as soon as we can.

It is my belief, I may be wrong, but I think we will be a lot safer once we are over the border and really into enemy territory."

"I am certain you are mad, Colour Sergeant," Corporal West piped up.

"You are perfectly correct," Nobby said, "If you want to stay alive, you would be well advised to do exactly as you are told. You don't only have the enemy to worry about now mate, you have him and he could be the biggest fucking danger to your life you will ever meet."

"Will you two shut your bloody gabbing on and get bloody moving, or do I have to shoot one of you to enforce discipline, now bloody move!"

It was getting close to dawn when I stopped our headlong dash. I told them, "While you two rest here, I am going to have a look around and scout out the land."

Nobby asked, "Do we eat now?"

"Yes, cold, I don't want any fires."

Turning to the signaller I said, "Set your radio up, but do not, and I repeat do not under any circumstances make any calls on it. If they call you, you are to make a note of any messages they may pass but otherwise ignore them. You tweak that bloody handset once and you are a dead man. Do I make myself clear?"

"Yes, Colour Sergeant."

"Good! Let us all become the professionals we keep telling people that we are."

I turned to Nobby and said, "Make sure he does as he is told Nobby."

"No problem."

With that I moved off into the jungle. My main problem now was trying to see if we had managed to make it over the border or if we were still on our side. Also, I wanted to see if we had landed in among the thousands of Indonesians they told us were over here. We had for the last couple of hours been climbing steadily, puffing and panting like a couple of Courage's old dray horses. So provided we had not gone round in circles we should at least be over the other border and the thousands of Indonesians would probably know exactly where we were.

Dawn was already breaking over the canopy of the jungle as I scouted around. It was getting lighter and I was starting to see things a lot more clearly and realised we had in fact made it over, we would have to be bloody careful from then on.

I turned to go back to the others, and nearly died of fright. There, not two feet from me with a bloody machete raised was a little wrinkled old man; standing not more than four and a half feet tall, his face no bigger than my fist. Yet a man who had in his day probably put the shits up more men than I had ever done. The man was a headhunter, your genuine Borneo headhunter, and I should know.

"Christ," I said, "I wish to hell you would not do that, you little black shit."

His face opened into the biggest grin you ever did see, all mouth filled with shitty brown filed teeth that looked like rusty nails in a piece of rotten wood. "I get you one day, you big shit," he said.

Then he put his hand to his face and signalled me to be quiet and move into the under growth. He signalled to another person standing nearby, whom I had not seen either, and called him in to talk with us. The three of us sat in a sort of den he had constructed in the undergrowth. I was to learn later he had the bloody things all over the area. He could appear and disappear like a bloody well-greased jack rabbit up the jacksy.

All For A King's Shilling

The three of us then settled down in the bushes and he said. "They nearly get you last night, big shit."

"Yes," I said, "But not quite yet mate."

So, the old man thought it was my little party they were after with the mortars. I was becoming very puzzled about the whole bloody setup now; what with the warning the Brigadier had also given me if only I could put it all together. Still I had too much on my mind just then to worry about that!

He then told me, "This other old man is my brother; he was in Malaya the same time as me, but he was at Ipoh with Forty Commando. It would be best if my brother kept a watch on you, and I keep a watch over all of you. Then I will only contact you when I think you should know something I have found out."

When I had listened to all he had to say, I told his brother, "I am honoured to meet you and work with you. What is more, I hope our work together will be as rewarding for you as it will be for me. Your brother and I have always had a good relationship, and I hope ours will be the same."

"Thank you for your good words, and I will be looking forward to my reward."

"Shit," I thought, and just what have I promised this little sod? I hope he doesn't think my head on his belt is his reward. In the past I never trusted these little bastards, but I said, "We will be heading into the valley to the south, can you tell me how many Indonesians there are in the valley?"

"There are lots of Indonesians in the valley, too many for you to fight; even if you are as big a fighter as my brother says."

"Thank you for you the help you are going to give me, but I have to get back to my friends now, so I will look for the usual signs which your young brother and I used in Malaya."

Again I thanked them both, but I never did tell them all my plans. I had not expected to meet two of them, and I would rather it had just been the old man, the one who had been in Malaya with me. Then again those two little bastards didn't tell me all they knew and I knew they had a couple of surprises lined up for me; it was all tests with them but before I left, I asked them, "Do either of you know the Political Officer who works on the other side of the border?"

"Yes," said the older brother.

Then I said, "Wish I had seen him before I had left, at least he could have thrown some more light on the situation over here. It all came up so fast, and I am still very much in the dark. You see I have just lost a partner, in very strange circumstances, and I am not concentrating enough."

When I looked at them, they were both looking at one another in a funny way. I thought, they don't understand what I am talking about and I don't either for that matter.

Then when I made ready to leave them the old man said in his clipped way, "You need think hard then you may just stay alive, big shit!"

I had cause to think long and hard on that remark over the next few days.

My little black friends then gave me an update of all the people in the area. Of the Indonesians, how many, and so forth. They also told me of two other groups in the area. One group was composed of all white men. "The same as you," they said. "The other funny slit eyes, all black clothes same, same, as the thieves in the market."

Well, I thought, this is a totally different ball game. I wondered who these two groups could be. The white ones could be Yanks; and the others could only be Chinese!

Next I asked them, "How many of the men in your village will be willing to help us?"

The old man said, "Only our sons, and maybe a friend, but better you work alone."

"It is up to you. I think I will need all the help you can give me before it is over. As to your family I do not want to meet them just yet though. It will only bring trouble on their heads."

Then I turned to the brother and said, "Don't forget, if you give me the usual signs I will be grateful."

"Like old day Malaya?" he said.

"Yes," I said, "Just like old Malaya."

With that I left them and headed back to the place where I had left my two stalwart buddies.

To say I was a little surprised that I was able to approach the place without any trouble, without even being challenged, would have been an understatement. Nobby had made no attempt to protect himself and the signaller from any hostile approach or attack. What was more I could hear that stupid bloody signaller talking over the radio to Brigade, as if he was on Woodbury Common. I could hardly believe my ears. When I got to them I ripped the earphones off the signaller's head and for the second time since we had met I kicked his bloody radio over.

Then I laid into him, "I am sick to the back teeth with you, mister. I told you, didn't I bloody well tell you that you were under no circumstances to talk to Brigade; or anybody else for that matter and as soon as my back is turned, you start to broadcast like a bloody budgie?"

"They called us, so I had to answer them," he said.

"They called us," I mimicked. "They called us, so you stupid bloody fool that you are couldn't resist the temptation to cackle on. Don't you know, hasn't your wonderful Signal Officer told you? The Indonesians have some of the best and most sophisticated listening devices you can get, over here. Better than anything we possess. Two sodding minutes on the air and they will have you pinpointed. How long have you been broadcasting?"

"They are not that good, Colour Sergeant."

"Yes they fucking well are, you dozy bloody fool! Pack your bloody kit right now, the pair of you, we are moving off. I don't intend sitting here waiting for the bastards to arrive, okay."

While they packed up, I said to the signaller, "Look I'll say this for the last time. You will only turn the bloody radio on as and when I tell you to and then you will only use the whisper control to transmit when using voice, but mostly you will be using Morse. So why was your radio switched on when I specifically told you yesterday not to turn it on? "

He started to get a little noisy in his reply shouting, "I have a job to do. I was given orders to keep in contact with Headquarters at all cost. I shall do that Colour Sergeant regardless of what you say."

"Have you never heard of the system in the Corps that says you must obey the last order you are given?"

"Yes I have, Colour Sergeant!"

"Well I'm a Colour Sergeant and I'm giving you that last order; do not under any circumstance whatsoever turn that fucking radio on, your last order, Corporal, because if there is a next time you are dead, do I make myself clear?"

It was at this point I heard sounds that were nothing to do with the dawn chorus, or the row going on between the signaller and myself. Or any other jungle noises, no, these were human noises. Nobby at last came alive, as he should have been hours ago.

"Holy shit," I snarled at him, "you silly bastard, the Indonesians haven't got any good listening or direction finding gear, have they? You incompetent bastard, who do you think is making that bloody noise?" He didn't know what hit him! There was no time to explain what was happening, so with a good right upper cut I just laid the stupid bastard out cold.

Nobby and I just managed to get him and his equipment under some undergrowth, and then we took off towards the noise which had disturbed our argument. I just hoped and prayed that the fool stayed out as long as possible, or as long as it took to sort this little lot out.

We made it to the edge of a little clearing, in the opposite direction to which I had been earlier. Running through the clearing was a track, not a large track but a well used one. We were about twenty feet from it and in quite thick undergrowth. The sounds we had heard were coming from the left, and moving towards the border or what we thought was the border, back the way we had come during the night.

Next I looked to see where Nobby had positioned himself, for the first time in years I was getting just a little bit worried about him. The noise which was coming up the track was quite loud now and getting louder by the second. It crossed my mind that we were just a little too close to the track for bloody comfort. I'd just made up my mind to move back from the edge of the clearing, when the first two of the people making the noise came into view. They were Indonesian soldiers all right, but they were dressed more like their Marines. Not a chance to move now, we were in it, a shit or bust situation. We both very, very slowly, released our safety catches. So I thought if this is where it is all going to end, then so-be-it.

I was a little surprised at the state and age of these soldiers who were now coming into the clearing. They were loaded down to their knees with cooking pots and all sorts of paraphernalia. What was more they looked more like a troop of American boy scouts at summer camp than a group of 'gung ho' soldiers. There was one thing that did worry me more than a little, and that was that they were all armed with the latest American Armalites.

As they moved through the clearing, it was as if they were just out for a stroll and I was a little surprised with their attitude. They were deep in conversation with each other and not in the least interested in their surroundings. Also I do believe that had the pair of us stood up they would probably not have seen us anyway. The other disturbing thing about the patrol, if it was a patrol, was the number of them. There were at least one hundred and fifty of them, about a company in strength, but I couldn't get over the casual way they were going about their business. They must have felt terribly safe. Here we were, creeping around over the other side of the border, and there they were, out for a picnic.

When they had passed and all had gone quiet again we looked at each other and very slowly made our way back to where we had left our stalwart radio operator. He was sitting looking at his radio, and looked as if he was still in a daze. Even so he had that 'I must transmit' look on his face. A sort of glazed look which seems to affect most signallers when they see a radio, a must get on the air syndrome!

His first words though when he saw me were, "I am going to have you court-martialled for striking a junior officer. It is illegal to strike a junior rank. You will be locked up for this, just wait and see."

To which I promptly replied, "I am getting a bit pissed off with you mate, and if you do not shut your bloody big mouth, I was going to put a couple of bullets in your radio but I think I'll just shoot you, right here and now instead! Then Nobby and I can get on with the job we have come over here to do. You have nearly got us killed once, so from now on, no talking, only signs. It looks as if we are surrounded by Indonesians, and we will be lucky to see the day out without getting shot."

His reply was a gem, "What are all these signs you are on about?"

I just looked at Nobby, "You better talk to him before I shoot the bastard."

Nobby just looked at me and said, "This last couple of days haven't been your best, Bill, have they?"

That was when I walked away and took up a position behind a tree, some distance from the two of them. When I had settled and my temper had subsided somewhat, I gave Nobby the sign I was moving off in another ten minutes, and I would be looking for somewhere safe to settle down and get some rest. I think I was sulking a little bit. Mainly because I felt I was no longer in control of things. I was having to lead and explain things as we went along. The type of thing you only do in training when putting a new outfit together. Out here everything should run like clockwork, everybody should know how each member of the team was going to react to a given situation. Not the crap way the three of us were carrying on. Nobby was acting like a bloody great big OD and I was starting to think that he had lost it. Then I thought that that was exactly how Mick had acted back in Singapore!

At that point I was about to wash my hands completely of the idiot Signal Officer's 'best man'. What I also needed was to have time to think; it looked to me as if the Political Officer's tales had been right after all. Had I known we were being watched at that precise moment, I would have been a damned sight more worried than I was. As I was to find out later, it was not my old friend or his brother who were watching us either.

Nobby was talking to the signaller, and I heard him say, "I am telling you mate, if you don't wind your bloody neck in he will kill you. He will kill you as soon as bloody look at you."

"He can't go around shooting people on his side, surely?" the signaller said.

"The way you are acting mate, you are giving him grounds to think you are not on his side. Forget all the shit your Signal Officer gave you. You are with a raving nutcase now, but a nutcase who is at his best in this type of job, that's certain. I've worked with him for years now and I've owed my life to him more than once. So if it comes to it, I am on his side; if ordered to do so, I might just shoot you myself."

All For A King's Shilling

The conversation ended there. I think they talked some more, but I was too busy sorting things out in my mind to hear them. It took about ten minutes to clear all the damage we had done in our little altercation earlier. To me that was too long.

We eventually moved off into the thickest part of the jungle slowly without leaving any trace of our passing. Bending each branch or twig in our way individually, so as not to break them and make any noise or leave any sign of our having passed that way. This way we moved deeper and deeper into the jungle away from the track and the border. The deeper the better I thought. By mid morning we had not moved very far at all but we were in my mind far enough away from the track to be able to rest and feed ourselves. We set up a little cave-like structure in this thick undergrowth and eventually we had a position in which we couldn't have been seen if somebody had passed the place two feet from it. I would not allow any cooking, so we ate our rations cold and in dead silence.

Looking at the two of them I thought we had certainly got off to a bloody good start this trip. Hadn't we just? I was the first one to break the silence when I started into the situation we were now in.

"As I see it, we are in the middle of the whole bloody stinking Indonesian army."

Nobby seemed to nod his approval of that.

Next I asked our illustrious signaller, "What do you think?"

To which he said, "I do not care, but if we have found out what we came for, shouldn't we call up on the radio and tell them? We can then leg it back tonight, and the Brigadier will be able to make his plans accordingly."

"Well," I said, "on the face of it yes, but it is not quite that simple. First the sighting of an Indonesian company moving towards the border without taking any precautions did not mean the whole Indonesian army was here. It simply confirmed the Brigadier's suspicions that the enemy did not think we would ever break the rules of our own Government and cross the border.

"Remember," I went on, "we are committed not to carry out any aggressive action over the border. So the Indonesians think they are as safe as houses over this side. Mind you they become very tactical and professional once they cross the border.

"Secondly, we would look right Charlies if we did go back with this tale. The whole of our reserves would then be committed to this area, the Indonesians could then cross else where with impunity.

"No. We need to have a little bit more of a look-see as your boss says." That was when I saw Nobby was now taking more of an interest in what I was saying.

With this thinking aloud done I then suggested we get some sleep and I told Nobby, "Set up a position a few yards away, in the direction of the track. We will keep the usual watches. Wake me next, I don't want our signaller on watch on his own, he might start cackling on his bloody radio again."

Once that was sorted I settled down and Nobby went off to keep first watch. When he had gone I decided to have a heart to heart with our new partner; like it or not we were now in not too good a situation.

. So I said to our signaller, "We know the Indonesians are all around us and I do believe there are large numbers of them. Just how large and what kind of troops they are, well that is one of the most important things we need to find out. We are all tired after our night's march so I have decided we shall get some rest, taking turns to keep watch. Then once we have rested and regained some of our composure we will take a little walk further into their territory. We will see just what they are up to."

He said, "I have to make radio contact with my Signal Officer at Brigade Headquarters every hour, or they will write us off as having been killed."

"Okay, but just who was it who told you we would be written off if you didn't make the hourly calls?"

"My Signal Officer," he replied as if in disbelief that I didn't know that!

"Well I am going to let you into a secret which may frighten you, young man. The minute we climbed into the helicopter in Brigade Headquarters, and it got off the ground safely and could no longer be heard it was at that point that the Brigadier wrote us off his strength and reported that one of the helicopters was overdue."

I watched him for a second or two and then as the information began to sink in, I said; "Yes, Corporal, the Brigadier has written us off already. To him we are already dead; he has probably already written his letters of condolence to our next of kin to be posted at a later date if it all turns to shit. He may even say we pinched the helicopter and have deserted. Haven't you asked yourself why it was they have seen fit to give us so little information?"

"Well," he said "I never gave it a thought; my boss gave me a very good briefing anyway."

"Yes he did, if you say so, Corporal; his briefing has nearly got us killed a couple of times before we even got really started. What I can tell you though is, the least you know the better for you. You see my young friend you don't want to know about the real reason why we are here. The less you know about it the less you are likely to tell your captors anything when you are being tortured if, or more likely when, you are captured that is. They will you know, torture you if they catch you. No, your officer hasn't been any great help to you, I am afraid."

He was about to say something else, but changed his mind.

"I think you had better get some sleep lad; when we move watch Nobby, and stay with him, he will look after you. All you have to do is to start to remember the basic training you had, and do as you are told as and when you are told. I will not give you an order that would endanger your life if at all possible; your life will at times depend on your prompt reaction to what I tell you to do. So don't let us have anymore of you go your way and I'll go mine, from now on we all go my way and we might, just might get away with this little charade. You will see some things happen from now on and they will not be pretty. What is more you will also have to do some of these things yourself. There'll be times in the next few days when we will unfortunately have to kill some Indonesians; if we don't then they will kill us. It is very simple; we will have to kill to stay alive. You can take it as read, Nobby and I will probably be too busy defending ourselves to look after you. We do not have the time to train you for what we may encounter. So from now on my young man it is 'standing room only'. I do hope you know what that means. Now if you do get back you might like to tell your officer just what sort of walk you have had and how very different from Woodbury Common this jungle really is. Now get some sleep." With that said I closed the conversation and got my head down.

All For A King's Shilling

Nobby woke me halfway through the day and I took over the task of keeping watch. It was quiet for most of the day, and it was close to dark when I woke them. The signaller had slept all day; he seemed in a better frame of mind when he woke. The first thing he did when he woke though was to get hold of his radio. It was as if he was addicted to the bloody thing; I looked at him and shook my head. He then settled back into the back of the basha we'd built.

When I was on watch, I had heard a lot of movement on the track, during the day, even though we were a fair distance from it. There was no way of knowing if it was the lot we had seen that morning coming back, or perhaps another lot returning from a position they had relieved, if indeed they had relived any post or position. It was something I did intend to find out over the next few days or sooner if possible. We had another cold meal and then both Nobby and I surprised our newfound friend by taking green lichen from the bark of the trees. Then after covering our faces and arms with it, we checked each other for leeches. He was a little taken aback, as we suggested to him he should do the same. By the time we had finished this it was nearly dark. We just had enough light to make it back to the clearing and the track.

Now came the real nervy bit. Nobby had protested earlier when I told him what I intended to do. That was to go down that bloody track. I just didn't believe the Indonesians would have any ambushes on it. I reasoned that the way we had seen them earlier, and the noises which I had heard during the day meant they were not at war this side of the border.

Once we got to the clearing from which Nobby and I had observed the Indonesians earlier, I told Nobby, "Take care of our unwanted partner, and follow me down the track. Keep well back, and if any hand lands on your shoulder further down the track, it will be mine. Do not let that bloody gun you are carrying go off."

With that said and satisfied that I was now back in charge of the operation, I took off; well 'took off' is not the phrase really; I moved very, very carefully and very precisely down the track. It is going to be a long, long night I thought; but I pressed on with something approaching caution like being in a haunted house I suppose.

All went well to start with. When I had covered about a mile I thought I heard some movement ahead, whichever the way ahead was that is. It was so bloody black I couldn't see anything, only the tree next to me, or the track right in front, and that was all. My nerves were on fire and I think I was a trembling wreck, but I pressed on. I wanted to get this part of the job over with. So far I had had enough of the whole setup. That bloody signaller was getting through to me again now I was all tensed up and out front on my own; and Nobby was also acting like a bloody green recruit, all professional one minute then acting like a recruit again the next. As for myself, well I was constantly thinking of Mick being killed in Singapore, drunken driving my arse. Then these men with black clothes, and the white men same, same as me! About whom I'd been told by the old man; it was all starting to get too much for me.

As I was still pondering on all this, the next thing I knew I was standing in the open and I came back to my senses bloody fast I might tell you as I dived back into the jungle out of which I had just stumbled, panting like a bloody knackered cheetah that had just run a mile for nothing. It took a few moments to realize what lay before me. I'd walked out on to a cultivated plain and it was a rather large area; what was more it seemed to have four or five or even more villages on it; there were lights flickering all over it. Once back under cover and I'd just started to get my wits about me when I thought shit, Nobby will be here in a minute or two. So I turned and started to walk back a little way into the jungle and settled by a tree at the side of the track to await them.

After I had been there for about two minutes, I thought they should have joined me by then. It was starting to give me the creeps, why hadn't they come? I was hoping to hell they had not come across any of these people in black clothes, but just as I was starting to get really worried, I heard a noise very close to me, it was Nobby doing his 'commando one' bit, with our intrepid signaller hanging on to him by the back of his belt. My first thought was to let them pass by, and then touch the signaller on the back. Then I thought better of it, he had a loaded gun. The thought reminded me that I did a similar stupid thing like that some twelve or more years ago whilst serving in the Suez Canal Zone. That time I saw an intrepid soldier of her newly crowned Majesty's army, discharge thirty-two rounds of Sten gun ammunition into the air via his stomach. No sir I thought, not again!

When I tapped Nobby on the back he stopped dead in his tracks. Then I said, "It's okay mate, it is only me."

As I said it, I could see a visible relaxing of his shoulders, and I thought oh shit!

"Is anything wrong with you mate?"

"No, I'm okay, Bill." He had a slight tremor in his voice as he spoke.

Here was I out in enemy territory with a stupid signaller and now the only man alive I could trust was cracking up on me. I would like to know what the hell was going on. A minute ago I should have been looking down the barrel of a gun or feeling the steel blade of his knife at my throat. But no he just froze. He had acted the same as Mick had a few weeks earlier; so what the hell had gone on with these two.

There was no way we could move very far tomorrow, not until I had done a recce of what lay ahead of us, so I motioned them into some deeper cover, and told them of the situation.

Once settled I told them, "The jungle ceases not more than fifteen yards down the track. It opens out into a fully cultivated plain; I think there are four or five what look like villages out there, and it is quite a large area indeed. As you may gather I do not intend moving out into it, not until I have seen just how large the place is. Or how many villages there are and what sort of problems they would present to us whilst trying to cross it to the other side. So, I propose we stay here for a while. Nobby, you and I will have a look around and select a little hide just under the canopy and set up an observation post. We can then have a good look at the countryside before we make any move at all."

To Corporal West I said, "One thing more before I leave, do not under any circumstance touch that bloody radio."

Then as an afterthought I told him, "You get yourself into a good fire position, stay down, and do not in any circumstance fire that bloody weapon you have there."

Nobby and I then moved off a few yards from the signaller, and I said, "Nobby, you and I have been mates for a long time now, what bloody gives? It would have been so easy to slit your bloody throat back there, on the track. Okay I know we're all a little bit on edge. I know I am, especially after the news of Mick's death. Christ man, we are now over the border and we are in the thick of God knows what. You are acting like a spare prick at a wedding, for your own sake man, get your bloody act together, or we will both cop it this time."

He sat for at least ten minutes before he answered me. When he did I was not really expecting what came out. He said, "You know I saw the Political Officer back in Headquarters. They told us he wasn't around, but he was. I saw this geezer talking to another officer when I was going to the stores. I thought I recognized him, but could not seem to place him. His face was familiar, but I could not for the life of me think where I had seen him before."

"So," I said, "he arrived too late for the briefing, not so unusual that is it?"

"No. But you would still expect him to come and see us before we left wouldn't you?"

"That would have been the norm."

"It was when we were about to leave the camp, the penny dropped. Remember the time we had to swim out of the base in Murmansk? And remember our boss the bastard who panicked and disappeared under the ice and we thought he died?"

"Yes, I remember the sod, him and his bloody brown boots."

"Well, he is the Political Officer, the officer who was our last OC in the post in Russia. Well he is the bloody Political Officer. How many times did we go in that bloody frozen place, and the only time we have trouble is during our last trip. Shortly after we hear Mick has been killed, and who do I see, the bastard we thought died years ago. Now here we are, on a harebrained stupid arsehole of a mission, with a bombed out bloody fool of a signaller for our third partner; and I'm not so sure he is as stupid as he makes out he is. Everything is going wrong and it is this Political Officer's mission we are on isn't it? I believe the mortar fire was directed at us last night mate and the sooner we divorce ourselves from the whole bloody setup the better."

"You are right about the mortar fire but why in bloody hell's name are you telling me all this now? Why did you not come out with it last night? At least we could have stayed over the other side of the border and holed up for a couple of days until we got it all sorted out; before we even crossed over to this side. Now we are here we are going to have to make the best of it and stay alive. Because what you are really saying is that the Political Officer is out to get us. We must assume he has agents working on both sides of this war if what you say is true. You know, Nobby, that now Mick is dead we are the only two of the original group still alive, you do know that, don't you?"

"Yeah, well I mean, if you and I are the only two left alive who else knows anything about Murmansk? Just suppose we were the ones to be killed in that skirmish as we came out of Murmansk the last time we were there. We were too good for them and got away, taking their men with us. Just suppose all the others left in the place had been taken out, and replaced by Russians. We are the only two left who could blow the gaff on them. It would mean we are the only two who could stop them feeding our lot a load of duff information about their submarine movements."

"God I wish to hell you had not brought all this up at this moment in time. We have enough to worry about right now without some deep GRU intrigue reaching right over here. Okay, I admit we do have a problem to worry about, we have to stay alert 100 percent from now on. Do not trust anybody, Nobby. You watch my back and I will watch yours. If it comes to a sort out, forget our illustrious signaller and leave him to sort his own troubles out. You and I need to stick together, no matter what. Now let's get ourselves into a good hide mate, I do not see us moving from here before tomorrow night. We're going to put our new partner at ease, so he can pull himself together before we move on. Also I need to find a good hide back in the jungle. Let's just make ourselves secure here for a while."

About an hour before full daylight we moved back into the jungle from the place where we had spent the remainder of the night. Nobby spotted a good position in a little hollow in amongst some thick undergrowth and it was about five hundred yards from the forward edge of the jungle and about six hundred from the track which we had come down the night before.

We cleared a small place in the undergrowth and we settled to making our breakfast. I stood guard as Nobby made his and my breakfast and Corporal West struggled to make his. I noticed that Nobby had to stop every now and again to help him with it, but at last all was ready and Nobby handed me mine then went back to eat his.

When we had finished eating and all traces of the meal had been cleared away Nobby came and took over as lookout. Once more I briefed Corporal West. He was a sorry sight as I looked at him and I thought he is going to have a mental breakdown any moment now, but I had to say what I knew was never in a million years ever going to enter his head. It was for the first time I realized that he didn't have the mental aptitude to accept the sort of work we were involved in. I'd just have to keep plugging away at him hoping that perhaps a little of what I was saying to him would sink into his mind beyond the wall he had built round his mind of what he thought were injustices perpetrated on his body and mind by me.

"Corporal West, I'm going to have to insist once more, under no circumstances are you to use the radio. You are not even to switch it on. We are in a very dangerous situation now and the Indonesians will home in on you within two minutes if you attempt to transmit. Now Corporal Clark and I are going to a place we have found on the forward edge of the jungle and we will be away all day. Do not move an inch from this position at all and once again I can't stress enough, do not switch on the radio. Do you understand me?"

When I'd finished I looked at him and I knew he hadn't taken any notice of what I'd said. So without saying another word I removed the headset and the handset from the radio and I was about to leave when I caught the look in his eye and I turned and removed the Morse key as well.

Just after that Nobby and I moved off through the jungle to the forward edge. We left our now reluctant signaller in a frame of mind neither of us could understand. It was my opinion that he thought he was now in a position where he would remain for the rest of the operation and he had washed his hands of the whole bloody escapade. His actions led me to believe he now thought he was on an exercise, and not a dangerous operation behind enemy lines so to speak. I honestly think he withdrew from taking any further part in the proceedings from then on. If it was not for the fact that I hate to lose men, I would have washed my hands of him right there and then. He seemed quite happy in his own little world when we left.

All For A King's Shilling

"As long as you don't move around, you should be all right." I told him, as Nobby and I left. It did not occur to me to tell him I had his handset, headset and Morse key from his radio; even though he saw me take them I'm sure he hadn't realized that I did have them with me.

Nobby and I, as I said, made our way to the forward edge of the jungle. We found the hide we had selected the night before, but the view was not as good as we had hoped so we looked around and at last found a place with a good view over the whole of the plain. It was quite a large plain which we had come across, an area of about four miles wide, by about two to three deep. I was of the opinion that any of our aircraft flying along our side of the border must have seen and reported such a large area of cultivation. They must also have seen the large populated area we were now looking across. Yet there was no sign of it marked on any of our maps, another bell jangled in the back of my mind, but I left it there.

Let me explain, there were six villages in the area, quite evenly spread over it. There were also a few corrugated tin shacks which passed for houses spread around the cultivated plain. The most worrying thing of all was there was also what looked to be a large military camp on the far side of the plain. The longer I examined it through my binoculars the more my fears grew as I realized it was going to be really hard to get into it and have a look around. It was a well sited position on top of a rise which enabled the sentries to observe the whole of the open plain. All the villages were in complete view and it looked as if the jungle was about five hundred yards behind it. The jungle looked to be primary jungle, but I believed that there had to be some access through the jungle to the camp. There was no sign of a road to the front or the left and right of the camp, but a camp that size couldn't be maintained from the local area to any great extent. There had to be a road leading to it from somewhere.

Having looked the camp over for a while I came to the conclusion that I needed to take a closer look at it. From my position I could not see too clearly just what the land was like behind it. It was then that I knew I would have to cross the plain at some time in the not too distant future and examine the camp close up. As the Brigadier had said, it was a camp of about battalion size. Crossing the plain to get a better look at it, well that was one task I was not looking forward to at all.

After another hour or so of looking at every detail we could see, both Nobby and I settled down to draw maps of the area. Every once in a while we would compare notes to see if we had got the details right, then settle down to do some more map drawing. It is surprising just how engrossed you can get when doing this kind of work. We had become so engrossed in fact we had not seen the Indonesian patrol heading our way. The fright which we both got when we heard Indonesian voices just a few feet away doesn't bear repeating. At least both of us had the presence of mind to freeze instantly.

The voices seemed to separate, most of them moving away, but one was still muttering just in front of our position. I motioned Nobby to stay exactly as he was, and I raised myself up inch by inch on my knee to have a look to see who our visitors were. You could have knocked me over with a feather; there was my little headhunter friend grinning at me from amongst the maze. I looked to the right to see a patrol of about ten Indonesians moving along the edge of the jungle, with one a little way behind. When I looked back into the maze my friend had disappeared from view.

That's one more I owe you my little black friend, I thought. Nobby now raised his head, and I pointed to the backs of the Indonesian patrol; we then both looked at one another and just shrugged.

We kept at our tasks for a little while longer, and about mid afternoon I suggested to Nobby, "You should go back to see if our signal friend is all right. I will come back in a little while."

Nobby said, "You're sure you will be okay? We should go back together."

"No," I said, "I want to plan a route to the other side of the plain. What I have to do, is to get a look at that camp over the other side."

"Okay, but why?" he said. As I didn't reply, he left.

Well, I thought, as he quietly moved away from our position, it is going to be hard getting past those villages with their blasted dogs. Even though we stank to high heaven, the dogs would still smell us as we approached the villages. While I was deep in thought the hairs on my neck started to stand on end. Gently, I eased myself a little to my right and close into the side of a tree, eyes like organ stops and nerves like razors.

I saw him before he saw me; I waited as long as I could. Then, just as he was about to turn I touched him, I would not have done so, had I not known he knew I was there. Anybody who has seen an Eban strike with a panga will know what I mean.

"You lucky today, big shit."

"Let's hope I stay lucky."

We then sat side by side and looked out over the plain together for a little while as it got dark. He did not say anything and nor did I. I think we were both back in the Malay Jungle some years earlier. Times were better then, there was none of the double dealing that went on these days, things were black and white as they say.

When the sun had finally set and I was starting to get ready to go back to the others, he then spoke.

"Your two friends in shit!"

"What shit?"

"Men in black!"

"Oh shit," I said, "Let us go then."

"Okay big shit, you follow me."

With that he motioned me to follow him, something which I did without any question. (You must remember this man had saved my life more than once in the past.) We moved back to where I had left the signaller earlier in the day. We did not go by the route I would have taken, but by an easier and quicker one. When we got to the edge of the area where Nobby and I had left the signaller, I could just make out three people who were hidden around the position. Had I approached from the direction which I would have done had I been alone, I'd have walked right into them.

The old man and I sat and watched them for a little while. Really we wanted to see if there were anymore we had not yet sighted. At least, that was why I had sat. I found out later my old friend had thought I had gone soft in the head, or lost my balls. Still I was not to find that out for some while yet.

When I was satisfied there were only the three of them there, I motioned him to move in. I took out the one nearest me and he took out the other two; we worked as we had in Malaya, as if no time had passed. It was uncanny really.

All For A King's Shilling

Not one of the three knew what had happened to him. They all died without making a sound. We then moved in closer to the place where Nobby and the signaller were. I could see Nobby sitting with his hands on his head, a bamboo pole tied through his legs, and another one through his arms. His hands were tied to his head with what looked like wet leather thongs around his head and then down his face and around his throat.

He looked as if they had already given him a hell of a beating in the short time they had held him. Our intrepid signaller, well, he was tied up in much the same way Nobby was. Except he was leaning over on the poles at a rakish angle and he was completely out to the world, or worse still, dead. There were two more of the black shirt bastards, just sitting there looking at Nobby and poking him every once in a while with the points of sharpened bamboo sticks.

I wanted to rush in and kill the bastards there and then, but my training held me at bay. It was some time before we did move; it may have only been a minute or so but to me it seemed like ages. What I had decided was which one of the bastards was mine, and then we moved in; inch by bloody inch we went; it was nerve-wracking to say the least. It was my intention that the bastard was going to see my face when I killed him. In all my service I had never had a feeling like that before, but by hell I had one now.

I would have to pass the idiot signaller to get to the bastard I was going to kill. Of course the signaller would have to regain consciousness just as I got to him. As he muttered something to me the man in the black shirt turned and saw me, he raised his gun to shoot as I rushed him. It was when I was about two feet from the muzzle of his gun that I saw the flash from it. The flash was so bright it blinded me, and something hit my head, and down I went, dead. Just as I was falling I felt a flush of wind as something passed over my head and I saw the head of the sod that had fired at me as it was split from the top of his skull to his neck.

At the same time I felt somebody galloping over the length of my body. The next second I was face down in the mud of the jungle floor and I remember thinking this will do my wound the world of fucking good. As I was waiting for the pain to start I just lay there for a minute or two thinking, if this is what it's like when you die, it's not too bad.

Well I was not dead, I am glad to say; I was blinded for a few minutes and in that time I had hit my head on a bloody branch of a tree. Then, as I started to fall, my little black friend's son climbed over my back to get at the bastard who had fired at me. Something was bothering me for a while and it was not until I had had a good look at the half head I realised what it was. I had hesitated for a second or two because when he turned to fire at me, I had been put off by the fact he was not what or whom I had expected him to be.

I do not know who he was, but he was not from the east, he was from the west, he was as the Americans say, to whit, a Caucasian. Just what the hell he was doing in that part of the world, in those clothes with the others we would never know.

Nobby was to say the least not too pleased with the way they had roughed him up. Nor was he happy about what had happened, but one thing we were both sure of, they would have killed us all had we not killed them first. Another thing, we were all for moving out just as soon as we could and so was my little friend. He told me they had been watching me ever since we crossed the border, both he and his son had been watching all of us.

Then he said, "They killed my brother last night. They had already got your friends when I joined up with you."

I was about to ask him why he hadn't told me at the time, when I realised Nobby would not take kindly to that at all.

We managed to get our signaller back to some sort of normality after a while and my Eban friend's son took off after a few words from the old man. The rest of us remained where we were for the remainder of the night. The old man, Nobby and I took turns to keep watch. After the ordeal the signaller had been through I thought it best he got as much sleep as he could. The poor bastard had had a hard time of it since he met up with us. It was obvious once we set off that he was not suited for this kind of work. Also he was I suspect not suited to service life of any kind. I think he felt utterly miserable at the time. If we could get him out of here alive he would have a tale to tell his mates.

It was nearly dawn when the old man's son returned with the rest of his family. To my surprise they had a bloody army stretcher with them. After some haggling between themselves they agreed with the old man that they would take our signaller to their village and hide him till he was fit to travel again. In the meantime the old man and his son would come with Nobby and me till we had done what we came to do; we would then pick up the signaller on the way back across the border.

So we packed up and the old man's family left in one direction, and we took off in another. We moved further to the left from the position and keeping undercover we made our way along the edge of the plain until we were more or less directly opposite the Indonesian camp. At least we would not now have to pass too close to any of the villages. Also I felt that for once things would go right. We now had a guide who knew the area, someone who did not like the Indonesians or what they were doing to his beloved jungle. It was going to be alright.

When we got to a good position we settled for the rest of the day, first to eat some of the food the old man's family had provided. I was bloody starving. We also needed rest as both Nobby and I were out on our feet. While we were having our cold food, Nobby asked me, "How did you come to be with the old man and his son last night?"

"First, I didn't know it was his son who was with me. It was not until he was climbing over my back to get at the guy who fired at me that I even knew he was there. You know I'd seen the old man in the market outside Brigade HQ before we left and had a talk with him then. That was when I had arranged to meet him when we crossed over this side and I met him that first morning. He had been keeping tabs on us ever since and the lot that got you and the signaller had already killed the old man's brother who was watching the signaller!

"The old man was a lead scout with me in Malaya in fifty and fifty-one. I spent two years living in the jungle with him. You never forget something like that or what it does to you. His son is his double, mind you; not all of them look alike you know, but he could pass for his father when he was the same age. They are not too different from us; they were just born to a different way of life. We soon get to be like them when we live out here for any length of time."

All For A King's Shilling

Nobby said nothing, he just sat and looked out over the plain towards the enemy camp, he seemed to be in deep thought and then he asked me "Is there anywhere in the world where you don't know anybody or have anybody watching your back?"

"No!"

We settled down to sleep for the rest of the day, the old man's son had returned with two other members of the family. If they had not and we'd not been able to get any sleep I don't believe we would have lasted much longer. Not after the traumatic situation which Nobby and Corporal West had suffered. We were both losing track of time and God alone knew what Corporal West was losing track of, but from past experience I knew that losing track of time was a very dangerous thing to happen to you.

We slept right through the day, and I for one had a good rest; what was more to the point when I woke it was just getting dark. There was no rush to do anything, we were I think the safest we had been since the chopper had lifted off at Brigade Headquarters. I hadn't felt right while we were at the border post at all. Still, I think my nerves were acting me up before we left there. Now I was ready to carry on with what I had been sent to do, I felt refreshed and ready, if not rearing to go. I was still trying to reconcile the dilemma as to whether I should tell Nobby what I had really been sent to do on that side of the border. So many men's lives would depend on me getting it right and the Brigadier had warned me not to trust anybody; not even Nobby, so I put it off once more!

When it was fully dark, the time between last light and the moon coming up we moved out. We had split into two parties, I was with the old man and Nobby was off with his son. The others cleared up the place we had been in, removing all trace of us having been there, and then returned to their village. The four of us travelled half way across the plain in a group before we split up. At that point the old man and I went to look over what he had told me was the main army camp in the area, while his son and Nobby took off to skirt the camp and see what was beyond it. The old man said there was another camp, but as we hadn't seen it Nobby was going to scout it out for me. The old man also told me that the group we'd seen on the first day were from the camp which he and I were going to look at. They went up every morning to join the ones who were manning a border post and the ones who were already there, then came back at night. So from what he had told me I reasoned that they had two companies on the border during the day, but only one at night. A rather odd arrangement I thought and they just could be in for a shock one dark night in the not too distant future.

The old man and I arrived close to the camp just as the moon was coming out. At first it was not too bright, so we used what light there was to move in closer. My old Eban guide said not to worry as they did not have too many guards. I found it hard to restrain him; I told him he could move around here without too much trouble, but they would not take too kindly to a six-foot tall Englishman doing the same. He at last saw my point and slowed down a bit, not a lot, but a bit, perhaps a concession because he still looked on me as an old pal, ha! We arrived at the camp at the right-hand corner as we had looked at it the day before. It seemed to be a lot bigger than I had imagined when I had first seen it; it also seemed to have quite substantial defences. I told the old man I was going to get close to the wire, to have a better look at the place. He pointed to a sandbag emplacement and said it contained a big 'bang-bang' gun, much bigger than the one I had. Well, I just had to see that 'bang-bang' gun now didn't I!

With that I left him in the ditch we were in at the time, and off I went to have a look at his big 'bang-bang'. As I approached the emplacement I did so with great care. It was a well- built place, double sandbags, and about two feet of soil on the outside. The soil had been well wetted with rains and gave the impression of a small natural mound. I got very close to it and just listened; after some little time had elapsed I assumed that it was not occupied, or they were all asleep. Well, I thought, no bloody good sitting here, so up you get and have a bloody look.

So, I popped my head over the parapet and back down again rather like a dipper in a waterfall. There was nobody in the place, of that I was sure. So I vaulted over the top of the sandbags and as I landed my heart nearly stopped beating. I'd felt a body under my feet. My knife was out and I had the body by the hair ready to cut his or her bloody throat. Before I could a voice said, "You take long time get here, big shit." I just looked at him in the dark and knew the little bastard was laughing at me. This bastard wanted my head on his bloody pole, I was sure he did. The little shit kept trying to give me a bloody heart attack.

While I tried to recover my composure I just sat and looked at him, the grinning little bastard I thought. I'll bloody do you next time you brown faced little shit. Mind you he was correct about his bloody big' bang-bang' it was a Russian 12.75 heavy machine gun and it looked to be okay. Once I'd recovered from my shock I then took particular note of where it was pointing. Then I looked around to see what else was there; much to my surprise I found a very well laid out range card for the position, which I copied. That done I decided we had been in the position too long and turned to tell the old man we were going to leave; he wasn't there. Before I had time to even curse the little sod I heard two men talking, what was more they were getting nearer to the place I was in! I remember thinking I was certain that little shit was out to get me, he'd buggered off and left me without so much as a by your leave, or 'lookout there are a couple of Indonesians coming'.

With the barest margin I managed to get out of the place and slither down the bank as they entered the Sangar itself. There, they stopped dead in their tracks and there was no noise at all and then much to my relief they started to jabber for a while and then settled themselves. They had obviously heard me; the old man told me later they had thought it was an animal of some kind. That bastard had heard them coming and just left without telling me. I was beginning to have doubts about him because he kept leaving me in the shit, as it were. Mind he always called me big shit, all those years ago in Malaya. Well, we stayed where we were for about half an hour to let the two sentries settle down to their task of dozing off to sleep which they eventually did. After that we moved off to have a look at the rest of the camp.

We moved very carefully round the perimeter stopping every few yards to look at the wire and also any more gun positions. I must admit it was pretty well defended, if all we saw from the outside was manned and armed the same as the post I had been in. The old man told me, "They are the same all round the camp, two men and big 'bang-bang' in each. No need to go and look – all same, same, big 'bang-bang' ha! ha!"

All For A King's Shilling

"The way you have been acting since we came out here tonight I have only one word for you mate, 'bollocks'. I'm going all the way round this place. I want to see everything."

So I had another go at getting into the camp. I think that I was really glad I did. After studying the place for a while, in fact I got up and walked in through a blind spot. Or what I thought was a blind spot and I was proved right, I got right into the bloody place. It was a different ball game inside the camp. I had been looking at it from lower ground and I could only see the tops of buildings, or nothing at all, the reason became obvious once inside the place.

The camp was built in the shape of a U; the main living quarters of the barracks were across the base part of the 'U'. Down one side looked to be the officers and senior rates. Opposite was the cook house and wash places, also what looked like stores and armouries. Right in the corner between the officers and the men was the entrance and what looked like the ammunition dump. I remember thinking at the time that they did not trust their men.

For something like an hour I had been wandering around the camp, and looking into different huts, the cook house area stank to the high heavens. The food must not have been up to much, because there were no dogs hanging around. I was a little surprised to find that out. When I first got into the camp, I had anticipated having to leg it out followed by a pack of dogs; perhaps they had eaten them all. After an hour I thought I had pushed my luck far enough and decided to leave the camp. So I went round to the back of the officers' quarters and made my way to the wire. It was all quiet and I just walked up to the wire, where to my amazement I found a gate. I just opened this gate and walked out. It must have been an exit for the officers to visit the local girls, or an escape route should their men turn against them.

Once out I went to the last place where I had seen my old friend and found him asleep; got the little shit, I thought. Just as I was going to grab his bloody little neck I felt a sharp piece of steel against my throat. The sod had been playing the possum with me. "No chance big shit," he said.

We moved off together to complete the circuit of the camp; as we went past the main gate into the camp we crossed a well made-up dirt road. I looked at the road and asked the old man, "Where does this road go?"

"To the other camp, the one hidden in the edge of the jungle; they have big guns in that camp."

For the first time I started to worry about Nobby; although he had been acting like a fool of late, he was still the only pal I had left since Mick had been killed that is. I was in a bit of a quandary; should I go and look for him and risk a shoot-out between us? He would not be expecting me to be in that area and it is likely he would shoot first and ask later should he be confronted by a couple of armed men. Then I thought well nothing untoward has happened yet and he has been out there some time now. So it was I decided to make my way back to the other side of the valley and hopefully get some sleep before dawn.

This we did, but the old man and I only arrived back just before dawn. People were stirring in the small kampongs as we were nearing the edge of the jungle. Because of this we entered the jungle along the same track the Indonesians used. It meant a hard trek along the edge of the jungle to get to the camp we had left the night before. It was a necessary ploy to try and let the locals think I was just an Indonesian soldier out with a local guide. There was no way of knowing if our guise worked or not. Perhaps more to the point the people in the villages were just not interested in the coming and going of the soldiers. Perhaps they just wanted to get on with trying to make a living from the situation they were in. I don't think they greeted the Indonesian troops when they were around, so I was hoping they would just not register what they saw.

We made it back to the little base we had made the night before and we had been there but ten minutes when Nobby and the old man's son arrived from the opposite direction. "Time we had some breakfast, Nobby, then we can go into what we came across last night."

We were just going to start preparing our breakfasts when the old man and his son started looking around and listening. My first thought was, here we bloody go again, and I had seen him do this so often in the old days in Malaya. So, I immediately grabbed my gun and was just about to take cover when the old sod waved at me and grinned. I thought you old sod, you are putting my nerves on edge. Just as I was putting my gun down the old man's other sons and I presumed one of his daughters came into the small clearing loaded down with palm leaves wrapped as baskets round food.

Without so much as a word from anybody the women laid out an array of local food, rice, fruit, meat, and what looked like daffodil plants, also a handful of leaves.

"What is all this?" Nobby asked.

"Well I think it is breakfast. Mind I have a strong feeling if we ask what the meat is, or what those daffodils are, we will not eat them; that would offend the old man's daughters but I do know what the handful of leaves are; they are quinine and you need to chew at least one a day from now on okay."

When we had eaten and the food had tasted quite nice surprisingly, the four of us, Nobby the old man, his son and I went to sleep. While we slept the old man's other sons, and it turned out his latest wife, kept watch over us. Normally it is not easy to sleep during the day in the jungle; because of the oppressive heat and the noise most newcomers are kept awake at night. We would have to work at night from now on and we'd not had any sleep since yesterday before we left on patrol. The night's patrolling had taken a lot out of us and in no time at all we were fast asleep after we'd eaten the food the old man's family had provided.

I awoke at about four that afternoon with a stinking little hand over my mouth. At first I was in a bit of a panic then I saw that grinning little face looking at me from about two inches away. He held my mouth closed with one hand and handed me my weapon with the other and I could see from the look on his face he was not kidding about it. As he eased his hand off my mouth I could hear the noise and then the voices of some Indonesian soldiers who I assumed were coming through the jungle towards us. The old man pointed to some thick undergrowth on the inner side of our little clearing. Nobby and I were in it like two scalded bloody cats. The old man's two sons planted themselves on the ground in front of us. I could see between them into the clearing, but Nobby could not. He was to tell me afterwards it had been the most frustrating time he had ever known. Not being able to see what was going on, and not understanding the tensions in the voices of the visitors or the old man.

All For A King's Shilling

Anyway, three Indonesian soldiers entered the little circle within seconds of us settling in the undergrowth. They did not have full equipment; only two of them had weapons, one had a pistol, the other had a rifle, an Armalite which was more modern than ours, so thank you once again, Mr America. As I said, the third had nothing. They jabbered away to the old man in Indonesian, he jabbered back in some old dialect, which even his sons told me later they did not understand. The Indonesians looked at the old man for a while and their mood went from friendliness to hostility and then to downright hatred. Because of the venom in their voices it was at this point I eased off my safety catch and waited. I felt, more than heard, Nobby doing the same. One of the sons signalled with his hand not to do anything and the other started to talk to the Indonesians in their language.

This seemed to settle them down a bit. They told the Indonesians that the old man was one of the old tribal elders and he wanted to go out into the jungle once more; to follow the trails and to hunt as they used to in the old days. It seemed to satisfy them and they left wishing the young men the best of luck with the old fool. As they left I thought the old man's young sons have just saved your lives, at least for the present. Nobby and I waited till they were well out of earshot before we emerged from the undergrowth.

Once things had settled a bit and the tensions had subsided, I asked the old man, "How is my signaller doing, is he all right? If everything goes as I'm now hoping it will I'm going to need him very soon."

"He's okay." Then touching the side of his head and making his eyes roll he gave the impression the lad was silly.

"What's he on about Bill?"

"It looks as if they have been pumping him full of their jungle juice."

I could have kicked myself; he had all the code books and the bloody radio. To make matters worse he would probably be out of his tiny mind with the booze these sods made. There would be no telling what he was up to. So I asked the old man, "Can you send your youngest son back to get all the radio gear, books and everything and get it up to me as fast as he can? We are going to need that bloody radio and it won't be to talk to the Signals Officer at Brigade Headquarters."

With that under way I then asked Nobby, "Right, tell me what you found out last night and how you got on?"

"Well, Bill, we had no problems getting to the other side of the plain; we made it to the edge of the jungle, without any problems at all. We had just got into the undergrowth when a group of Indonesian soldiers came along and set up an ambush position right in front of us. We were then stuck there for the rest of the night, taking turns to watch the Indonesians."

"Was there any activity in the camp on the edge of the jungle?"

I received the fascinating reply, "Well, Bill, that is the point; we didn't make it to the camp because the Indonesians were so close we couldn't move."

"That's bloody great, isn't it? I find a camp, I have a walk around inside it then I find out there is a well-made road leading out of it. The old man tells me there is a camp further back in the edge of the jungle, which has big guns in it; the one you are supposed to look at. You aren't a bloody stone's throw from it and you spend the bloody night taking turns to watch an enemy ambush position. God man what has happened to you, I've seen the day you would not have let such a small thing as an enemy ambush position stop you having a look around. You know it means we will have to go out again to have a look at this camp. When you consider the sloppiness in the camp the old man and I were in and this lot behind them laying ambushes and the like, we could be in for some trouble. Perhaps the Political Officer's bunch was right after all."

It was important now, I had to get my bloody mind into gear or the Brigadier would be in the 'shit' as they say. How many days had the three of us been here, for god's sake? There was no doubt I would have to go and take a look at the damned place myself. So I started to formulate a plan, but first I needed to know where the ambush position had been. With that I took Nobby and the old man to the edge of the jungle and I got Nobby to point out on the ground the place where he had seen the enemy ambush the night before. When he had done this I asked him to get everything ready to move out at last light.

When he had gone I asked the old man, "Do you know anything about this ambush?"

"Yes, they lay two ambushes on the forward edge of the jungle every night and two more in the jungle behind the camp every night."

His reply was a little disconcerting to say the least. For one thing, I did not think the Brigadier thought they would have ambushes out in such strength, if at all. Then I asked the old man, "How long has this camp been there?"

"About ten weeks," was his reply.

His reply shook me somewhat and I looked at him for a while, then I said, "They seem to have achieved a lot in those few weeks, haven't they?"

To Nobby, who had rejoined us with our bits of kit, I said, "I'm really going to have to have a close look at this camp. I don't like it, but it is now a must." I thought if I didn't sort it out we could face a bloodbath.

We left our position at last light; the radio and code books had arrived from the old man's village. They also told me they had started to sober up the signaller. When they told me that I asked the old man, "Can you see to it that the lad gets back to our side after all this is over?"

"No problem big shit, you no come back?"

"Yes, I am coming back; you will not get rid of me that easily, just I may not be coming back through your village."

Out of the corner of my eye I saw Nobby's face looking puzzled as he earwagged our conversation, and I wondered if I really could trust him after all these years?

Chapter Eight
God, Will I Never Get Out Of This Bloody Jungle?
Borneo, The Far East 1964

These Dragons are real and can kill you.

We set off that night to cross the plain and I hoped to set up camp on the far side in amongst our friends, the enemy. I had been making plans with the idea that all the Indonesians in this area were low quality troops, not all of them were following the rules or good military practice. For instance being alert at all times and not presenting easy targets for an enemy, but judging by what I had heard from Nobby and later from the old man I reasoned that some of them might be that little bit special.

Nobby had told me that the reason he had stayed put the night before was because the Indonesians who had laid the ambush were far too alert for him and the old man's son to move. "They are not sloppy, as the soldiers in the other camp are. No mate these Indonesians know what they are up to."

Keeping this in mind, I had to place my trust in the old man and his son. I asked them if they knew of a place we could move to, on the other side of the valley, from which we would be able to have a look at the other camp in relative safety.

"Okay," was all he said. I was not quite sure just what that answer meant, or why he was now legging it over the rice paddies in that carefree jog of his. Now I was starting to formulate the idea that perhaps he meant to get us captured so that we could have a good look at the camp from the inside. By now I was getting really bloody paranoid about everything; something that wasn't doing anything for my equilibrium.

He was a strange little sod; thinking about it, what loyalty did the man owe me? After all I was an intruder in his homeland; he had seen at first hand our exploits in other parts of the Commonwealth. He could just turn us in any time he wanted and I was kidding myself if I thought he owed me any loyalty from the old Malay days when he and I were lead scouts for a few months. Just a few months of mucking in together in the jungles of Malaya, and here I was expecting his undying loyalty. Strange as it might seem I was later to regret those thoughts!

What shit we servicemen put on old associations, expecting the ultimate sacrifice from our old combat mates years after the event. When perhaps we have both changed and changed to the extent that we cannot stand the sight of each other. Still, all that aside, I was committed to a course of action. What is it they tell you on your promotion courses? Select your aim, and do not deviate from it. Well, I'd selected my aim and we were on our way. To possible oblivion and god alone knows what?

At about two in the morning we arrived at the edge of the jungle. We had seen nobody during our crossing of the plain and because of the noise we were making in our efforts to keep up with the old man, there was no way we could have heard anybody else moving about. It had been one of the most unnerving experiences I had ever undertaken, and I had undertaken a few in my day. It frightened me more than any of my trips into the USSR ever did.

Nobby then came close and whispered into my ear, "After that my nerves are shot to hell. If you have any more stupid ideas, then keep them to yourself. You are getting bloody madder as you get older."

"Don't blame me. I'm a jabbering bloody heap myself after that little episode. The old man is fast becoming a bloody idiot. I have had visions of Indonesian troops popping up all over the bloody place all the time we were out there. Just where he is intending to take us now I shudder to think."

"You mean to stand there and tell me you don't know where this little long lost-friend of yours is taking us. Good God man, are you completely insane?"

Before I could answer, "Probably" the old man came up to us and said, "We go now."

Then without a second glance, off he went into the jungle.

I looked at Nobby, shrugged my shoulders and said, "He's got us this far without any problems, let us follow him now. After all he is all we have got."

So I turned and went crashing into the jungle at one hell of a pace behind the old man and his son.

It was about an hour later we came out on to the hard track the old man and I had crossed the night before. Only this time we were some way into the jungle behind the camp and I asked the old man about the two ambushes.

"Are we near the ambushes you told me about last night?" I asked.

You could have floored me with a feather when he pointed to them a few yards down the track and I was for strangling the little sod, there and then. It was his son who saw the way both Nobby and I were. He pulled us into the undergrowth over the other side of the track and explained what that old sod should have already done!

"We are on a track used by dragons and the Indonesian soldiers would think we were perhaps just a dragon crashing through the undergrowth; they move around quite a bit this time of the year. The Indonesian soldiers will not come anywhere near them."

At first I thought Nobby was going to have an attack of apoplexy. With great difficulty I steadied myself, leaned forward and told the lad. "It is my considered opinion that I am going to have to kill your father one of these days. If not today, then perhaps I may have to do it tomorrow!"

All For A King's Shilling

"You know you won't do that because you two are too close for that, and you also know that I can't let you do that! Anyway you will be okay in a little while, he scares me as well, but please don't tell him I told you that."

With that we were off again in a mad dash down a well-worn track, too bloody worn for my liking and I had visions of coming face to face with one of the bloody things they call dragons.

Memories of my days in Aden a little earlier started to flood back as I half trotted and half stumbled behind the old sod. We had a local guide that time too, a bloody National Federal Guard. Commonly called 'N F Gees'. We were out on a 'hearts and minds patrol' in the Radfan Mountains, when this guide spotted a snake in some bushes. He made a big song and dance as he pointed it out to the Company Commander; it looked to be a very big snake. It was about three inches in diameter and he got so excited about it he asked the Company Commander if he could shoot it.

The Company Commander was about to say yes, when the Company Sergeant Major suggested it might not be such a good idea. At which the Company Commander said, "Look, Sergeant Major, it's his bloody land and it is his bloody snake, so let him shoot the bloody thing." The guide then raised his rifle and shot it.

First of all there was a noise which definitely didn't come from any bloody snake! This was followed by a thrashing around in the bush and at this point all the Marines in the patrol were picking up what bits of their kit they had laid down and were slowly and very, very quietly backing away from the bushes.

The next thing to happen was so quick and funny it still brings tears to my eyes as I recall it. Out of the bushes came an Iguana which stood three feet at the shoulders if it stood an inch. He, or she, had the biggest mouth full of the biggest bloody teeth I have ever seen in my life. I can assure you that nobody stayed to count them, as one hundred plus of Her Majesty's finest and bravest disappeared in all directions, over the rocks and sand of a plateau high in the Radfan Mountains. It took the best part of half an hour to get everybody back together as the place rang out with shouts of 'has the fucking thing gone'?

But that is long gone now and everything has changed.

I'd also seen a training film once showing what these Indonesian dragons could do to another animal, let alone a human being. So yes, I was scared, not shitless but not too far removed from shitless, as I stumbled along the track behind the old man.

It took us three quarters of an hour to reach the place the old man was making for and then we stopped to catch our breath as well. We were in a clearing about twenty feet wide. There were two large trees on each side. The old man pointed to one and said, "We go up now."

I thought he has definitely gone do-lally, but I climbed my first large jungle tree in total darkness. Something I was glad of, for when the light came, we were some hundred and seventy-five bloody feet in the air. I've always believed to get that high in the air you need an aeroplane, a balloon or wings or even a helicopter. I'm not frightened of heights, I will climb any mountain you wish to name and I'll look down on trees from helicopters, aeroplanes and mountains, but climbing trees just isn't my idea of fun especially not in total darkness.

As it got light the old man pointed out all the surrounding points of interest, especially the camp, which was our main reason for being there. The two ambush positions were quite close really, in my mind too sodding close, but they paid no attention to us in the tree, just two hundred yards in front of them. We had only been in the top of this tree for about ten minutes when they packed up and left in twos and threes to make their way back to the camp. The only thing of interest to me was they had two radios, and also the number of them. There were a little too many of them for our own good. I would also think they had the capability to call artillery support, or even air strike support. I was starting to feel good about being here already. We were well up in the top of the canopy now, the oppressive heat was off us, it was hot, but not that terrible heat on the jungle floor. Some time in the past a platform had been built in this tree for some reason or other. I was not too keen to find out why. Down below us was the track which was used by these supposed dragons; a platform above that track would not be there if there were no dragons. So I hoped we didn't have to go down there too often. From the back of my mind I kept remembering that those bloody things could outrun a man. It was a certainty I was not about to test in any way.

We got ourselves organized into two observation parties. I needed to know certain things about this camp. The old man and his son told me that the ambush positions were in the same place every night, with the same number of men.

Nobby then confirmed, "There looked to be the same number of men in the first ambush position as I saw the night before."

Next I asked him, "How was it you had been unable to move that time, during the night that is, but two of you had still been able to leave long before first light to make your way back before the ambush was lifted, when the Indonesians were still there?"

He told me, "By the time we had realized that the enemy in the position had gone to sleep it was too late to have a look around so we just made our way back."

I was starting to wonder just what had happened to my good old pal 'Nobby'. Still I had more important things on my mind at the moment. I was starting to worry about the Brigadier, was he being set up? I would have to get more information than I had at that moment.

So, I settled down to spend the rest of the morning observing the camp laid out on a small rise just clear of the jungle's edge. Two things stood out right away; first it was a better built camp and secondly, the men seemed to be better disciplined than the others in the first camp we had come across. They held a parade on a rather large parade ground, at about eight thirty. Interestingly, they were not carrying side arms or personal weapons when they paraded. Also the sentries at the gate only had side arms, nothing larger. But I needed to know for certain about that. There was one worrying thing though, they had six what looked like one-o-five pack howitzers dug in facing towards the border. Later during the day I was to observe them doing gun drill on those guns and they seemed to know what they were up to. I was interested to see that they only used three guns at a time; the other three it seemed were always laid on their DFSOs tasks and I needed to find out what the task was!

Something in my mind was starting to tell me the Brigadier might have taken on too much; still that was up to him. I was just to have the information ready for him when next we met. After a while I took the old man to the back of the platform and asked him.

"Tell me my old friend, where does this hard track we are sitting over lead to?"

What he told me made me think the Brigadier, or the whole British force, was being set up by somebody. I did not like it one bit. A couple of things now started to clock in my mind. The first day there had been a rather large party of Indonesians near us when we first came over. Then some Indonesians had been right in front of the place from which we had been observing. After that, we then ran into trouble with the men in black. Now we came across this well laid out camp, a very good road, along which I think reinforcements could travel with great speed. To say I was beginning to dislike this setup very much could be said to be the understatement of the day!

One thing more, the old man mentioned some white men in the area; he had not mentioned them since and I was really getting strange vibes now. So I had to make some sense of it all very soon or a lot of good men were going to come a cropper. I had to believe the old man about what was at the end of this road. Also I had to believe what I had seen myself. I was forming the opinion that the men in the camp out on the plain, were not as untrained as they looked. Now I was on the train of thought as to whether they knew Nobby and I were here and why we were here?

What if some nation other than the Indonesians were in control here, what would they expect to gain from it? What would they gain from our suffering a large defeat when we happened to be over the border?

Well oil does spring to mind!

So what?

Well we were now doing exactly what they expected of us. They kept clumsily bumbling into us, checking on our progress.

So what?

They knew how we operated and what our next move would be. If it had not been for Nobby running into that ambush the night before last we would not have come to the rear of this place.

So what?

The Indonesians or some other outfit wanted us to find out something here. We were where they wanted us to be, they wanted us to lay an ambush here.

So what?

It was obvious they needed a big propaganda victory and they meant to catch us over the border in strength.

So what?

They wanted to turn the tables on us as the invaders, instead of their being the aggressors because at the moment the whole world saw them as the aggressors. That was why they were showing us the things the Brigadier needed to know, so that he would commit a large force to attack this lot, and that would be their trap.

All right, so how could we turn the tables on them? That was what needed to be done. It was not up to me to make those decisions; all I had to do was to report the facts, that is what all my training had been for, to tell the man the facts. "It's time we made our way back to the border area," I told the others. "That we will do tonight when it gets dark, but first I need to get into that camp."

Before Nobby could say anything I told him, "We'll talk about it tonight." If I'd made a correct appreciation of the situation, then I didn't think that would be too much trouble. Just so long as I didn't make it too obvious. Next I must have a look at this road, I needed to know where it went and if there were any more surprises in store for us. Then I would have to make an effort to pull the plug on them somehow. So I then sat down at the back of the platform to make some plans.

Some time later when my plans were made, and just before last light, we got together in a huddle. I then told them what I had in mind. I said. "The old man and I are going to make our way down and if possible into the camp with the guns. We, or should I say I just need to check it out. It is important we get the type and calibre of their guns then we will know their range which is very important."

Nobby said, "Those guns cannot reach our camps on the other side of the border."

"Right , Nobby and why not? Why have them here at all if they cannot reach the enemy? Something I think the Brigadier should know about, don't you, Nobby?"

I asked the old man's son, "Do you think you can guide Nobby to the other camp – the one out on the plain?"

"Yes, no problem there, but why?"

I had not told Nobby what to do yet, but I said. "We should be able to make better time tomorrow; our load will be a lot lighter by then."

The old man's son gave me a funny look. "Don't worry," I said as I looked at him. "We will just ditch all our unused food and batteries when we head back. No point in carrying extra weight."

"Oh," he said and seemed satisfied with the answer.

"My old friend here and I would like to take a look at this camp, then I will have a last look around this side of the plain. While I am doing this my old friend will go and get the radio from his village and bring it to the place we left the other night. Once he has it we would then all meet up there. Then I would report to the Brigadier. Once I had done that we would smash the radio, and leg it back to the other side of the border. It would then be up to the Brigadier what precautions he took. We would have done our bit and would be out of it."

Just before last light we left the tree top and once on the ground we split up, I told Nobby I would see him on the other side of the plain. Once my report had been sent we would then go to the old man's village to pick up the signaller if he was still there, that is. I made sure the old man's son heard me. I did not want him to miss a thing before we parted. Somehow at that moment I felt that Nobby's life depended on the old man's son knowing I would be joining up with them both later. So it was we started on the most frightening part of the whole bloody thing.

As we parted I thought we needed something to distract these sods in a few days' time, to maximize on our efforts; the guns were out and I had to assume that they did gun drill every day. It had to be something else. Just what, I did not at the time know. One thing I did know was that I was going to have to talk to the Brigadier very, very soon indeed. I did not relish the idea of him and his merry men doing an Errol Flynn over the border in the next few days.

I thought our fate really rested in this camp, and the mass of men the old man had suggested were to the rear and down that hard road. Why had they let us go on so far if not to let us see the things that we had? Perhaps they didn't think we would know or find out about the mass of men to the rear, or even about this artillery camp. At one time I had been starting to think more strongly that the old man was all part of their plan too. Now I was not so sure but I had placed a bloody large question mark over his son.

He had told me things, but his son was not very forthcoming, and he only stated the obvious. Well, so be it, let us play them at their own game. When the old man and I were just outside the camp I said we should stop as there were too many people moving about inside it for us to go in. I told him I also wanted to get my equipment ready. He took a great interest in what I was doing. After some time he asked, "What are those things you are fiddling with?"

I said, "Things have certainly changed since the old Malay days, my friend. Now we don't need to overrun a camp to make sure we kill the enemy, no sir! We just plant a couple of these little things around the outside and so long as they are looking at each other, any shells we fire, any bombs we drop, or any rockets we fire, even from Malaya, will land dead in the middle of where the lines of these little things cross one another. So all I have to do is line up these things, with two of them pointing at the guns. Two at the ammunition dump, two at the accommodation block. Then within the first few minutes of an attack this camp will be no more, or the poor bastards in it. Even if they find them, they will have to get rid of them and wherever they put them that's where the big bangs will be. So don't you bloody pinch any of them, will you?" With that I settled down to rest with one eye open from now on.

The old man and I just lay there for the next three hours till all in the camp was quiet. Then I said to him. "Here we go then for the last time. This time, stay with me and do not take off as you normally do and please do not touch any of these things; it could cost your family their lives if you do?"

Much to my surprise he stuck to me like glue. As we made our way around the camp I could see he was watching me very closely, but I made sure he was not close enough to see what I was up to. As we moved very slowly around the camp, every few yards I would make my way to the wire. Then crouch down and look around and make a fuss of aligning the guns, the ammo dump, and the accommodation, I made a great fuss of the accommodation. So it went on all night. I do think I had confused him enough. I know I confused myself. The main thing was he thought I had sown hundreds of the things that bring the big bangs in. Mind only time will tell, if he saw the ones I really did lay and if he then removed them, or left them to do what they were there to do.

Just before it started to get light I made my way back into the jungle at the rear of this camp. We had just got ourselves nicely into cover when a group of Indonesian soldiers came along the edge of it making their way back to the camp from their ambush position. So this must have been the lot that Nobby had seen the first night we had come over this side of the plain. When they had passed I said as much to the old man and he agreed with me. At this point I was starting to have doubts again about my ideas of him and his sons, but I forced them out of my mind. The thing was that if I kept on thinking that way I'd be indecisive when the chips were down and I was going to have to do some very unpalatable things before this lot was over!

Both the old man and his son had saved my life now, the old man in Malaya, and the son here the other night. Mind it would have been in their interest to save us from those black-clothed men, if they were working for the Indonesians; after all they themselves were Indonesians whether they liked it or not. So I still thought I was right. Also, I did not like the look of three of those men in the ambush party; they were white and had a very pronounced way of speaking English. I had hoped it was not so, but there was no mistaking which side of the Atlantic they came from. No wonder the Indonesians had the latest M16 rifles.

When we had moved further into the jungle, I dispatched the old man to get the radio. He was then to meet up with Nobby and his son and I would join them all tomorrow night when I could cross the plain. With that the old man took off, and I started to make my way back to the area, towards the place where the old man had told me the Indonesians were camping in force.

It only took a short time to reach the place and I heard them moving about and talking long before I saw any of them. Quite noisy bastards really. I was very surprised to see their setup; they had set up three camp areas, which were just on the edge of the jungle, on the far side of a gorge; they had a sentry position on each side of the 'Bailey' type of bridge they had built over the gap. The sentries were lax; they obviously did not think anybody would be looking at them.

'Here I go again, thinking they are sloppy when they are not'. So I had better get a grip of things. Well I thought I cannot stay here thinking too bloody long, I had better get on with the next part of the plan, oh yes, I had a plan. As I did not have any explosives with me to blow this bridge, that was out of the question. What I did have though, were two of my homing beacons left. So I picked a point in the centre of the bridge and lined one of them up on it, it was a good clear view of the bridge with no overhanging branches to deflect the beam. Now I had to get over the road, it would probably be the hairiest bit to date. So I made my way back into the jungle, and to the edge of the road.

It took me the best part of an hour and I was wringing wet by the time I got there. From there, I now faced another hour on this side, plus the trip back to the other side of the plain. By now the rigours of all this exertion, and going without proper food and rest, were starting to exact a very heavy toll on me. Still I had a job to do and many lives depended on me doing it, so I had no option in the matter.

Maybe, I thought, I might just get lucky and the going would be easier over the other side of the road. It certainly looked it from the side I was on. Then I stood in the edge of the jungle for about half an hour getting my breath and my composure back. All the time waiting and watching the bridge to see what, if any, routine the sentries carried out. By the end of that time I came to the conclusion they really were very slack. They just lounged around smoking and talking to one another. The problem was you could never work out just when they would glance up the road. In the end I just set off and walked across it, to my surprise I got away with it.

Then I made my way through the jungle which was pretty thin for the first couple of hundred yards. After that, I hit bloody bamboo again which put another two hours on my trip, but I at last made it to the edge. Made it, I bloody well nearly walked over the edge of it. When I had once more regained my balance, hanging on to a willowy

All For A King's Shilling

type of branch which seemed to be made of elastic, I finally planted my last homing beacon, pointing it at the same spot I had pointed the first one.

Once I had rechecked everything, I slowly, ever so slowly, turned to face the sound which I'd just heard behind me. As I turned I thought if this is a bloody dragon, I'm going to shoot and I don't give a shit if I do get caught. I'd rather be a prisoner than provide a bloody dragon with his dinner. It was when I was just about three quarters of the way round that that old voice said, "You all right, big shit?"

Once more, that old sod had me nearly filling my trousers with the warm brown stuff. "I am going to kill you one day mister. How bloody long have you been here with me?"

"I saw you cross the road, and so did one of the soldiers."

"They did not."

"Yes, one man, back up the road, he saw you. So I kill him, you all right now. Now I show you quick way back, we had better go before they miss him."

"Why is it every time you sneak up on me, some poor mother's son has to be killed? You are a bloody danger to the human race mate."

"You alright now," he said and flashed his toothy grin at me.

We then set off back the way we had come, and I said, "I thought you were going to show me a quick way back."

"Yes, you cut bloody fine trail, big shit."

"I will bloody kill you yet, you bloody aggravating little sod, you're a little shit you."

As we went I decided it was no good talking to him, far better just make my way back and get on the air. There were lots of things I had to report to the Brigadier. The things I had seen, and the things I had done. It was no good me mucking around out here putting homing beacons in the ground if there was nothing to home them in on, was it?

Again the old man was right; he did know a quicker way back to the edge of the jungle. It seemed no time at all before we were back to a point overlooking the plain, the one with the two camps on it; one of the camps on the edge of the jungle and the other one out on the raised ground out in the plain, and off to our right. This meant we would have a clear run to the other side once it got dark; we would also see any ambush position laid by the Indonesians on the forward edge of the jungle if they took up position before we left.

After I had been there for about half an hour it was about 4.00 p.m. and I realized I was bloody starving. We had not had anything to eat all day in fact, and I could only just remember when I had last eaten. The last proper hot meal I'd had was in "A" Company's camp some time in the last century, I think it was. Another thing that worried me was I didn't know if Nobby was still alive or what if anything, had happened to him. The whole bloody lot was getting on top of me and I was starting to feel very tired and old. Hell it felt as if I had been at this game for at least a couple of centuries or more. There was one thing of which I was certain, this would be my last trip. I had to find myself a square number somewhere before I became too old or too dead to enjoy a good square number somewhere.

How long I'd been thinking I didn't know, but I came back to reality pretty quickly when the old man's sweaty hand suddenly clamped over my mouth. He was also pointing to the track behind us. My first thought was, what is the old sod up to now? I could hear nothing at all. He could hear something though for he pointed to a place some way back. Sure enough the leaves moved, and quite violently. I thought here we go. What a bloody time to come face to face with a bloody dragon, right on the edge of the jungle, not a kick up the arse from both of the enemies' camps. Any shooting now and we're goners.

I'd hardly had time to come to that world-shattering conclusion when the old man let go of me and drew his carbine up to his shoulder. I thought that it might be just prudent for me to do the same. He sank down to the floor of the jungle till there was hardly anything to be seen of him. Although a lot bigger than him, I did the same and hugged mother earth till I felt I was under it instead of on top of it. We lay there for some time and watched the place where we had seen the movement; it seemed hours. It probably was only a few seconds or minutes but it seemed a hell of a long time, then at last when this figure emerged, it wasn't a bloody dragon. No, it was a Caucasian, dressed in black, those black bloody pyjamas again.

He came creeping towards us; it seemed to me he was looking right at me. I distinctly felt we had eyeball to eyeball contact. He was coming right at me, and I was bloody mesmerized by him, I remember thinking 'he's a fit looking bastard'. It was at this point I saw the second one; he emerged some five to ten yards behind the first. This one was also a Caucasian, not as tall as the first and he looked the heavier of the two. It was then a third bastard came into view. Shit I thought at this point, we have had it.

That was when I looked to the old man, but he had gone, I thought the bastard, he's buggered off and left me, and all the time these sods are getting nearer. So it would really be 'shit street' this time. Well, I thought, if this is it, they are going with me and that old bloody man as well, when I catch up with the bastard.

They were now only a few feet from me. I dared not move a finger yet it felt as if my whole body was shaking with fear. For the first time in my life I felt like a lump of wobbly jelly. I thought I was just about to wet myself. Christ, I thought, I am losing control. Also I remember thinking I must be a coward, shaking like this. Then I started making excuses, such as, I am so exhausted I am losing control of my body, again I was finding out just how weak the flesh becomes when exhaustion does set in. All the time these three men were getting closer to me. All this was happening in milliseconds, but it felt as if it was in ultra slow motion.

It was at this point I managed to get control of myself. I realized that the first one was not even looking at me. He was no more than six feet away and he was looking above me and to my left. I also remember thinking at the time, they are not that good. Why, you ask? Well because they were too close together. None of our men would be that close together. Because of that, I knew there were only three, because the fourth, had there been one, would have been in the open by now.

Well, I thought, you have given me the biggest fright I have ever had in my life, so now you must pay. I edged the safety catch off my gun and slowly, ever so slowly, raised the muzzle, ready to start the killing. It was at that point the first guy turned to his left and started to move off in that direction. As he did I felt a slight relaxation go through my body, and I relaxed my grip on my weapon. Then I watched with bated breath as the three of them then moved off to my right and their left.

All For A King's Shilling

As I looked after them, it was at this point I saw the old man; he was hardly discernible among the trees but he was there. He had his panga out and he looked as if he meant business this time. I remember seeing him with that look on his face years ago in Malaya. So I laid my rifle down, and ever so gently got hold of my machete. There was no way I could draw it, but I did ready myself to get up, and get up bloody fast. The old man was going to kill, and I had to be ready to help him. Even he could not manage the three of them at once. Judging by the way they were holding their guns they would shoot at the first sign of movement. Well all was set now; the die was cast and the dice as they say rolled.

Then I suddenly knew when the old man would strike. So as the last man was just past my position, I moved, I came off the ground with a yell and struck the last man down. When I turned to the next one, the old man was standing grinning at me. The two were lying dead on the ground poor bastards, they didn't have time to utter a cry. Suddenly, I was no longer hungry. We hid the bodies in the undergrowth and I checked them to see what identification they were carrying; they had none, there wasn't a damned thing on them at all, not even dog tags. After it was all over we settled down to await the darkness which I hoped would soon engulf me in its protective comforting jacket.

While I was lying there a deep thought about my old friend beside me crossed my mind. I looked at him and thought you could never tell if he even had the powers of thought, but then he must have. The things he did although they looked like animal cunning, were always natural well planned acts of violence. Once more I changed my mind about him. I wished to hell he would let me know if he was playing with me, or not. What I did not like, was being on the side of the mouse, the cat's role in all this was more to my liking. My mind then turned to my partner Nobby and I wondered how he was getting on with this old man's son and if he, like me, suspected him of treachery.

Still I could not spend too much time contemplating that. There was too much on my mind to think too deeply about it. The main thing was I had to get a message to the Brigadier before he committed himself to the plan he had outlined to me before we left because I was of the firm opinion that he was being led into a trap – a trap which could kill off his career as well as perhaps that of half of our Government. Not to mention a Commando or two.

It was all these thoughts running around in my head that must have overtaxed my brain because I dozed off to sleep. The next thing I knew it was dark, and the old man had his hand over my mouth again, and I was starting to get just a little pissed off with it. His placing of his hand over my mouth set me off once more. I was just starting to get into panic when my mind jumped back into gear. The old boy was pointing to the forward edge of the jungle where an Indonesian patrol was passing. I could not help the awful feeling I had, that they knew we were there; some of them kept looking in the direction where we were lying.

Again I had that awful feeling we were being used. With all the bodies we were leaving around, then surely if they knew where we were they would hunt us down and kill us off. I'd do so if I were in their situation and knew the agents responsible for it.

To the old man I said, "They must be off to lay that ambush again."

He just nodded. After that we were silent for a while, getting our gear ready for the move over to the other side of the plain. When I thought enough time had elapsed I moved to the edge of the jungle to have a final look at the place where they had laid the ambush.

It seemed to be in the same spot Nobby had said, the night the old man's son and he had first come across it. So it looked to be a standing ambush. I marked it on my map and settled for that final darkness before the moon came out. Although it would be harder going, I thought it would be better to start off in complete darkness than to risk being seen in the moonlight by the ambush party.

So, about an hour later the old man and I set off to cross the plain. He always put the shits up me at night. He seemed to forget that although he was at home so to speak to me this was a hell of a dangerous place to be. I could not just get up and walk along one of the many tracks leading across the plain amongst the fields, as he could. If he was stopped he had a reason for being out, he was a native, but me, I was a six foot bloody Caucasian. I'd no chance. Still, either I made the trip with the old man or was left to make my own way over. Let me tell you, it was one of the most hairy bloody trips I have ever made anywhere in the world up to then, even worse than the trip when we crossed over the other night. This time I had some very important information to deliver and I was terrified I would be caught.

Needless to say it passed without any incident at all; the old sod even led me through a village at one point. He did say afterwards, "Not good, dogs no like you."

"Thanks a million, I have been trying to tell you that all bloody week."

Eventually we entered the jungle on the other side of the plain, at about two thirty in the morning; he then said I should follow him to a good place to hide. This I agreed to and off we went again, only this time we were travelling through the jungle down what looked to be a well-worn track. It was nearly dawn when we arrived at his village. He stopped me just outside and went in himself.

A few minutes later one of his daughters came to lead me in. I was taken to a hut near the far edge of the village, the side nearest to the border. In it I found Nobby who looked as if he had just woken up, and our intrepid signaller, still sound asleep. Again the three of us were together, Nobby and I having had a bit of a rough trip, and Mr Bloody Wonderful here, Corporal West, was still sound asleep, happy as a pig in shit.

It perturbed me so much I was about to kick his arse as hard as I could, when Nobby saw my intention and stopped me. He said, "He is not very well Bill."

"Nor am I," I replied.

Nobby settled to cook me a breakfast and I sat down to contemplate what had transpired these last few days; it seemed a lifetime since we had left Brigade Headquarters on this crazy bloody mission. Still I did not like the way things had been put together so hastily, or the way the signaller had been foisted on to us. Nothing in the thing rang true, apart that is from the talk I had had with the Brigadier before I left. Something I hadn't told anybody about, not even Nobby. I don't know why I did not tell Nobby but I hadn't, and I felt it was too late now to let him know. He would only throw a 'wobbly' anyway. Best left unsaid.

I asked him, as he gave me my first cup of tea for some days, "Has the signaller been on the radio to anybody at all, Nobby?"

"No, he hasn't that I know of. It seems he has been practically unconscious since he got here."

Then I thought things might be all right after all, and settled back to put my report together When I had completed it, I had to encode it and burned the notes I'd used. When I had finished all I had was the encoded copy of my report. Next I got the radio and set it up ready to transmit the report. When that was done I sat on the floor to eat one of Nobby's more spectacular breakfasts, curried beef and rice, at six o'clock in the morning. I must admit I ate the lot; I was starving and as they say, I could have eaten a scabby horse between two scabby mattresses.

It was about eight o'clock when I made my first transmission. This was to alert the Brigadier that I was still around, and from this he would know I had a message for him. Now when I made my report I would just join in the normal early morning log requests, which the companies would be sending through to base for their re-supply drops later in the day. Then I just waited, and had another cup of Nobby's tea; when I say cup, of course I really mean a mug.

It was not long before I heard the familiar "DAH DEE DAH" coming over the air. Now I challenged the sender and received the correct reply. No chance of it being wrong, only two of us knew the answer to that. Then, once I knew who I was sending to, I set off and sent part of my coded message, and 'Roger so fared' it. Only to have to repeat most of it again, so the Brigadier was on the air himself. This was going to be a long job, and a long job we could not afford to have. No way was I going to stay on the air long enough to be traced. So I then coded another quite short message, and transmitted that. When I had sent it I asked for an acknowledgement, which I got. With that I closed the set down for half an hour. The signaller had by this time wakened up, and was looking at me with what I could only describe as hatred.

I asked him, "What the hell is eating you up so bad?"

He just replied, "You; when we left I was supposed to be your signaller on this trip and all I have done is sit in this bloody hut since those men attacked me. Thanks to you I have been a prisoner here ever since; they won't even allow me out of it."

"Good, I'm glad to hear that, the reason you have been held here first and foremost was for your own and the old man's family's protection. Secondly you were in no fit state to carry on the mission with Nobby and me. Also there are plenty of people in this area who would sell you to the authorities if they had known you were here. What's more important though, the old man's family would have been killed if you had been caught in their hut. They had to keep you out of sight of the other villagers for the same reasons. Not all the villagers here think as much of the old man as the Brigadier and I do; it was all for your own safety. You know, I told you that you were a nauseating bastard when I first met you. I don't like you one little bit; you nearly got us all killed the other night. So why don't you just sit yourself down and shit in it and against my better judgement I will look after you! "

It was at this point I turned the radio on again, and within no time I heard them calling me again. When I did not answer them the first couple of times they called, the signaller was about to say something and Nobby said it was best he did not. After the third time they called, then I replied, waited a few seconds and then launched into my message in Morse code. Even though I say it myself, my Morse key work is very fast, a lot faster than any service requires it to be. When I had finished sending I was only asked to repeat three small bits of the message and that was it. I then packed up the radio and settled down to get some sleep.

The signaller then asked, "Can I have my radio back please?"

"No, I'm afraid you can't have it back. I will look after it for a while; it will make a good pillow while I catch up on a little sleep."

"You don't trust me do you?"

"You have never got anything so right before in your life lad."

With that I went off to sleep and for the first time for days I felt safe. No matter what happened to us now the Brigadier knew how the situation was over this side of the border.

I had been asleep for some time when I was awakened by Nobby, "There's a load of Indonesian soldiers approaching the village. What are you going to do, are we to make a fight of it, or just get to hell out of here?"

"The latter I think Nobby; you get the signaller and his kit, then get back here and let's thin out pronto mate."

We then busied ourselves getting our kit together and putting it on, which takes longer to tell about than it took to do I might add. Once we were ready, I looked at the two of them, and I thought, what a sorry looking bloody pair you two are.

I told the signaller, "From this moment on if you want to live you do exactly what Nobby or I tell you to do, no question, just instant action from now on!"

Next I told Nobby, "Make your way to the edge of the village and see if they have surrounded the place. I'll join you there in a minute or so."

Our intrepid signaller was still putting his gear on and carrying on as if he was getting ready to go for a Sunday stroll. Then I did something I had never done to any junior rank before and have never done since. I stuck the muzzle of my gun against his guts and said. "If you don't get a bloody move on Corporal I am going to ventilate your bloody guts, if you have got any that is. For Christ's sake man, do you want to die here because I will leave you if you do not get bloody moving?"

With that he took off after Nobby, leaving me to carry most of his bloody kit. If the Indonesians found any trace of us the whole village would die and I didn't want that on my conscience. When I got to the edge of the village Nobby had the signaller on the ground holding him down.

As I arrived beside him he said, "What the hell is going on? This bloody fool was just going to barge out there into the jungle. I think there are a couple of Indonesians out there but I am not sure."

Time was running out, the main body of their patrol was about to enter the other end and we were pissing about thinking there might be somebody out there. Our signaller was acting like a bloody great OD and Nobby was playing nursemaid to the bastard. The thought did cross my mind that we might just as well surrender now, or better still, I'd blow my bloody head off and let them stew. Then I thought 'fuck that for a game of cards'.

Instead I said, "Get up, get your bloody loads on and get moving into those bloody trees over there. If there are any bloody Indonesians over there, then bloody kill the sods, right. Now fucking move and act like the bloody soldiers you are supposed to be."

All For A King's Shilling

With that we made a dash to the trees and we were lucky. There were two Indonesians in the trees and lucky for us, they were not acting very professionally at all. In fact I don't even think they were looking our way as we made our dash into the trees. If they did see us they never let on. So we took off into the jungle making for the thickest bits of undergrowth we could see. After thrashing around in the jungle for about three hundred yards or so we stopped and waited to see if anybody was after us. It did not sound as if anybody was following us and after about ten minutes, we relaxed a little.

The sweat was running off us, I wasn't sure if it was fear or exhaustion, yesterday I would not have sweated like this. The main reason was probably because I'd taken on a lot of fluid since I'd arrived at the village and I was now losing it. Mind you, the other two were in a worse state than I was. The smell the signaller was emitting was terrible. He stank to high heaven of the local booze, shit and rotten food they had fed him. As I looked at him, I just shook my head as I noticed his neck for the first time. "Oh, bloody shit!" I said to myself, as I noticed they had tattooed him, but I motioned for them to remain silent for the moment, and to rest their gear as much as they could. Then I gave the signaller his radio and other equipment which he had so readily left.

I told him, "If you ever do that again I will kill you." As I looked at him I also pointed out, "If the old man or his family is harmed in any way this day I will kill you anyway. There is something about you Mr which arouses my killing instinct; God I'm sick of the sight of you. All I've done since I met you is to threaten to kill you and that is wrong; I should not have to keep doing that, but you act so stupidly and do such stupid things that you fuel my killing instinct. So if you do what I tell you to do from now on I will stop threatening to kill you."

He looked at me, his face ashen and said, "You can't do that!"

"If it is loyalty to your officer I'd forget it if I were you; he was flown out of Brigade back to the UK the day we arrived on this side of the border. You are on your own now, Corporal, nobody back in Brigade to help you!"

At this point Nobby interjected, "Look, Bill, I will take care of him from now on. I will see he is no trouble."

All I said was, "Okay then, but you had better hope the old man is all right."

I then decided to have a look around and see what could be salvaged from our situation. As I left I heard Nobby say to the lad, "He will do what he says, you know. So for god's sake don't antagonize him any more. Just about everything which could go wrong out here has gone wrong, so for god's sake do as you are told and keep your bloody mouth shut. If I didn't know any better I would believe you are deliberately trying to ruin the whole operation."

As they talked I took off into the jungle towards the area in which I had seen something moving in the trees just as we'd stopped. It was important and I had to know for certain how many, if any, of these Indonesians were on this side of the village. I'd been going, albeit very slowly, for about ten minutes when I heard a noise off to my right. Standing as silently as I could I slipped my gear off and hid it under some bushes, then very slowly and as quietly as I could carry only my rifle and my hunting knife, I made my way towards the noise I had heard.

It sounded like something or somebody, I could not make out which, stamping its foot or feet, and rubbing itself against a tree or something. For one horrible moment

I thought I might just be creeping up on a bloody dragon. Discretion being the better part of valour, I decided to stop and listen for a little bit, and see what more if anything I could hear, or perhaps even see through the undergrowth. Well I have never thought of myself as a bloody coward, but I never thought of myself as a fucking hero either, so slowly does it.

It was to be softly, softly, ever so bloody softly now. We were nearly ready to go back across the border and I didn't want to take any more chances than were necessary. No more than you need to my old friend I thought. As I settled, I felt my confidence rise, and looking back over the last couple of days I knew nothing could happen to me now. I was all alight, all my nerves were screaming, the adrenalin was coursing through my veins. I believed I could have walked on air right at that moment in time, but I didn't, I just edged myself forward on my belly. Like some hovercraft, only I could have crawled under a snake's belly I was that low.

Eventually I got to a position where had I reached out my right hand I could have touched the man who was standing not one foot from me. He had leather calf-length boots. They were funny, those boots, highly polished brown boots, very strange those boots, highly polished brown boots, here in the jungle and not a road for miles. Highly polished brown boots, the only dirt was on the welts caused as he had been stamping his feet. As I looked at them, then I started to shake a little, brown highly polished boots here in Borneo; the shaking got a little worse and I was having difficulty in controlling it. How could it be those brown polished boots here, when I knew the wearer had gone into the water in Murmansk all those years ago? My shaking was now becoming a rage and slowly I put my rifle down and inch by sodding inch I withdrew my hunting knife from its scabbard. I lay there watching the feet stamp up and down; after a minute or two I was just about to make my presence known to him before I killed him, when I heard something or someone approaching him. So I thought it best I easy myself back into the undergrowth and see just who his visitor was.

As I did, I heard the man who approached, and not unsurprisingly it was a voice that spoke to the great man in the brown boots most reverently. He spoke in broken English and I couldn't place the voice. Brown Boots then asked the man, "Have they got the Englishman yet?"

"No they have missed him," the broken English voice said.

It did not take too much to figure out that I was the one they were talking about and the one who had to be got. It was Brown Boots' voice that threw me into a blind panic, because I knew that the brown-booted bastard who I thought had died in those dark cold waters off Murmansk was a bloody Russian agent. By shit I knew that voice and I had believed its owner to have been dead for some years now, dead and frozen under the ice of Northern Russia. My heart was pounding in the back of my throat. I think I nearly gave myself away there and then. With great difficulty I managed to stifle a cry that was in my throat; Mick, I thought, that's what happened; and Nobby had indicated that he had seen him in the market!

This sod has been operating out here for some time plugging away organizing his little revolutions. Then the three of us arrive out here. The only three men who were supposed to have seen his death, then report his death to the authorities? That's why Mick died, how were these bastards who killed him to know he was like an increasing number of young Marines these days – teetotal, never touched a drink of alcohol in his life?

Drunken driving my arse; all my feelings said I had to leap out and kill that bastard right there and then. With a lot of control I managed to stop those feelings turning into acts, and it was just as well they had moved a little way off. There was no way I could get off my belly and into action quickly enough to get them both; there would be another day, believe me there would be another day.

Right now I needed to talk to big 'Sunray', I had to talk to call sign nine. Now I was in a quandary about how to extricate myself from this little shindig. Just then a third person joined the other two, treachery abounds today, I thought. It was the old man's son, so that was why the old man kept a watch over us. He was not spying on us, he was getting between the Indonesians and us, those times when he kept showing up from nowhere. He must have known his son was working for them, yet he still went along with us and still allowed his son to accompany us. Now I had my doubts the old man was still alive as he had remained in the village when we had beat our hasty retreat.

I'm sure that our signaller wouldn't have had anything to do with his death. Things were getting confused, I could no longer hear what was being said and I doubted if we could last for much longer. They had obviously been keeping tabs on us all along, ever since we crossed the border. It was now imperative I had to get a message to the Brigadier and it was more important than trying to even up the score for Mick, or the old man. No it was more important the Brigadier knew what was afoot in this neck of the woods; he had to be told about this person.

Again I moved with great caution as I slowly, ever so slowly, edged my way back the way I had come. It took me a damned sight longer to get back to the place where I had left my gear than it had taken me to get to where I had come across those bloody brown boots, I might add. I'm certain that I did so without them knowing I had overheard their conversation. It was just as well the son didn't have the old man's skills, for he would have killed me before he even spoke.

When I did get to my equipment I made it as fast as I dared to the place where I had left the other two. You can well imagine my surprise at seeing the old man, who was grinning at me from the bushes behind Nobby. I must admit I felt relieved to see that wizened old face looking at me. Then I asked him if he knew what his eldest son was up to. He just grinned and nodded yes. When I saw that look on his face I really felt very sorry for him. It was then I think he knew that either he or I would probably have to kill his son now if we ever came into contact with him again.

Next I explained to Nobby and the signaller what I had just come across and what I had heard. As I did so I didn't mention to them my thoughts about Mick, but I could see Nobby's mind working overtime as I suppose mine must have done earlier. I would let Nobby sort it out himself; because now, I was really getting fed up with the whole goddamned organization. So I explained my plan of action, I was going to open up the set and contact the Brigadier and inform him of the discovery which I had just made. The signaller suggested he do that and I was at first on the point of letting him do so, then I thought he had suddenly become helpful, why? He was no longer the clumsy idiot that he had been since we set off on this operation, now he was helpful and I didn't like that; so I didn't let him near the radio!

Then with the old man in tow I moved a little way further into the jungle, and set up the radio. When ready I encoded my message and turned on to the channel the Brigadier had reserved for us. You can imagine my horror to find it full of traffic. Just about everybody in the British Army in Borneo was on the air.

As I listened, I just sat and looked at the old man and said, "Shit, we could be in trouble now, my old friend." I then started to look for the spare channel which we had decided on before I'd left, to cover just such a blocking incident. For some reason I had pushed it to the back of my mind, thinking I would never need it. It took me a good ten minutes to remember it and even then I was not too sure. It was only after my third call that I got the right reply to my code. When I had passed the message and received new instructions from the Brigadier, I could hardly believe my ears. He was still going ahead, and he wanted me to make my way back into the area of the Indonesian camps. There to await his arrival on the scene, which would be in the next couple of days or sooner. If he couldn't make it himself, he would send somebody whom I would know.

As I had sent him full details of the situation as I had seen it, I had also planted all the homing beacons he had asked for. This he knew, since I had reported this latest bit of information, he was now as wise as me; well probably a hell of a lot wiser than me. The only thing I could think of was perhaps he had already committed the troops to his plan. If he had, then it may be the whole thing was too far advanced to stop. Now I had a deep foreboding that a disaster was about to hit our imperial forces in this godforsaken jungle. I looked long and hard at the old man as I mulled the whole thing over in my mind.

I had done the old man an injustice. I had thought he was playing a double game and getting ready to set us up for the Indonesians. Yet all the time he had been playing one of the most dangerous games of his life, he must have known it was his son who was fitting us all up. Looking back, he must have been trying to warn me when I first met up with him I remember he was reluctant to involve his family in this whole game. Now I felt sorry for him. I knew he would kill his son when the time came. It crossed my mind that I should do it for him, but I had a feeling he would rather do the deed himself. The old affinity we had all those years ago seemed to be back. It was as if I could feel him telling me to get on with what I had to do, and he would do his part, as he always had, with that inscrutable grin on his face.

Now I told the other two what was afoot. I also told them I needed time to make my plans, and that we had better get our arses into a better position than we were in at the moment. When I told the old man what was needed, he nodded. With that we loaded up our kit and followed the old man into what looked like an impenetrable piece of jungle; he parted the branches and pointed for us to step through. When through, we discovered we were on a well-worn track; the old man then rearranged the branches behind us and led us off up the track at quite a cracking pace. In all my years I do not believe I have ever travelled through jungle so easily. We made no noise either because the going was so easy. It had often crossed my mind how it was that the natives could move through the jungle so easily, now I knew. Also I noticed at this time that our signaller was very quiet, but he was going well, very well; he seemed to have changed his attitude this last hour or so from an uncontrollable idiot to a fit, organised Marine. He had his full load and seemed to have come into the world of the living again. I felt a little remorse at putting him through the torment I had these last few days, but I could still not trust him, He seemed to have recovered too fast, it was as simple as that!

I could only assume Nobby had given him the lowdown that I just might shoot him, or leave him for the Indonesians after all. Whatever had transpired while I was away he had changed, I even caught a smile on his face at one point. Put me back on my guard again did that little sight. We made very good progress with the old man in front. Now and then, he would stop and call me forward and point out some Indonesian position, some of them manned, some of them not; I marked all these positions on my map. The old man told me the numbers of men manning each one and just as important, the type of weapons. My only wish was that I had had some homing devices left.

While all this was going on I came to the firm conclusion that the Indonesians must have been laughing at us all the time. I also reasoned that if they were, then why hadn't they lifted us when we started killing some of their men? Or was that a pleasure that was yet to come? Now the old man was leading us on his jungle tracks I did have the feeling we could move without the Indonesians knowing too much about it. The old man's son was the one joker who was causing me the greatest concern at this point. It followed he knew as much about these tracks as the old man.

It was well before night when we arrived back in the area of the jungle overlooking the plain. What I wanted was to have another look at the place; I needed to know if there were any changes since last we looked at it. Was I in for a surprise? The camp out in the plain was a hive of activity; they had what looked to be armour in it. I thought Christ, I have got to check this lot out before the Brigadier or his representative arrives the day after tomorrow or whenever. Now I was starting to have grave doubts about us being able to pull this thing off at all. First I had banked on the reinforcements, if any, being trapped on the other side of that ravine where I had planted the markers the other day. As I could now see, some of the armour was in the camp on the plain. I had to confirm that it was armour and not some mock-up stuff and I would have to inform the Brigadier as soon as I could. I hoped this would be before he had committed himself too far and was unable to stop the whole thing going ahead.

I formulated a simple plan. It's time that signaller earned his keep, I thought. So I gathered them around me and briefed them on what I had in mind. "I am going to take the signaller with me tonight, and we are going to have a closer look at the camp." Then I asked the old man, "Will you take a walk while it is still daylight? I want you to check the activity in the other camp. When you have done that, meet the signaller and me in the place where we stopped the first night we were out there."

Next I told Nobby. "You get some sleep now. I need you to go to a position which I will tell you later, to meet with an agent. You are to bring him to a rendezvous early tomorrow morning at a place I will tell you just before you leave. Have you any questions?"

"No," was his reply.

"Once he gets here I will brief him on all that we have found out and done. He will then make whatever recommendation he sees fit to the Brigadier. The Brigadier will then decide as to any attack taking place."

"What the hell do you mean?" Nobby asked. "If any attack is going to take place? When we left, I thought we were only here to find out if the Indonesians were here in strength enough to attack us; nothing was said about us attacking them."

"Is that so? Well, you might be interested to know, Nobby my old mate, just about the whole Brigade has, over these last two nights, been crossing the border. They are now lying in position not too far from us, waiting for the final situation report which I shall soon be passing to whomsoever you meet. You do not think for one stinking minute the Brigadier did not know who, or how many troops were facing him, do you?

"The whole reason for us being over here was to find out three things. First, how much heavy stuff they have here and how it is deployed. Two, the exact defensive positions and strengths, and thirdly and last, who was the spy?"

Eyeballing Nobby for a minute, I finally said, "It has been known for some time by the hierarchy that there was a spy in the system. So they decided to send a reconnaissance party over this side of the border to scout things out. The idea was to make the plan secret but not too secret. Only certain people were to be told a part of the plan, but others wouldn't; thus whetting some appetites, but only enough to arouse interest. They thought it was possible that once the reconnaissance party was over the border, the spy would show his hand. Which he has; I spotted him earlier today when we left the old man's village.

"The Brigadier has been getting three lots of information for some time now. One set through political channels, the second one from his own network of old Eban trackers. Eban trackers were the men we used in the fifties in Malaya and they are fiercely loyal to the British Forces." Turning to the signaller I told him that was something he had better remember. "The third source of information was from me, when you lot were otherwise engaged. One of the reasons I had to get you out of the way," I said, pointing at the signaller. "Firstly, because we could not trust you, with all those stupid orders you kept spouting that you had got from your Signals Officer!

"You see, Mick Smith was supposed to be with me and he was killed under mysterious circumstances in Malaya. Then you turned up from nowhere to come along with us.

"Well, as you can see there was no way I was going to trust you, when I sometimes have problems trusting good old Nobby here. What was more you would have been able to read any signals I sent in Morse, so I had to get you out of my way."

"You can think yourself lucky he didn't kill you then if that was what he thought of you!" piped up Nobby. "That's the way he normally gets people out of his way." He looked at the old man and continued, "He was even talking about killing you at one stage the other day. What do you think of your friend 'big shit' now then?"

"He knows better than that Nobby. The Brigadier and I both worked with the Eban trackers, and that is the reason why the old man is with us now. Remember, Nobby, I had a long talk with the Brigadier before we left; well I got some extra instructions then and the latest update on the spy, and anybody who was working with him. When I went to the marketplace I went to contact someone. That someone was the old man; I made arrangements to meet him over here at the place I hoped to be the next morning after we crossed the border. He waited all night for us and then gave me an update on all the Indonesian activity in this area.

All For A King's Shilling

"We met while I was out scouting around that first morning after we had crossed the border and you two were resting. The old man has been keeping a watch on us ever since. Now I have discovered who the spy is and I intend to inform the Brigadier. Then I'm going to do something about it, but first we have to do something about the situation in these camps. We are all involved in a very dangerous game now, so let's make sure we get it right."

"What we have been doing these last few days, that has not been dangerous then, Bill?" Nobby asked.

"Well, you know what I mean, Nobby, this is the last part of the deal, so let's make sure we all come out of this little shindig alive, okay."

"You know Bill; everything I have ever done with you has been bloody dangerous, you can't even cross a road without you leave chaos and mayhem behind you. How many bloody people have died since we crossed over here. Christ man, you are a bloody one man disaster area, looking for somewhere to happen."

"How long have you felt like that, Nobby?" I asked.

"Oh, quite some time now, I don't know, Bill, maybe I'm getting too old for all this 'Queen and Country shit', I'm just so bloody tired."

"Perhaps I had better change my plans, Nobby, then again perhaps not. Maybe, just maybe, you will become a good soldier again, and pull yourself up by your arsehole and do the job they pay you for. Just maybe, we can all again be more professional about the whole bloody thing. Then, maybe we will all get out of here in one piece; the last bloody thing I need now, Nobby, is for you to go all wobbly on me. You normally only go like this when you have had booze."

I turned to the old man and asked him, "Have any of your people been filling this 'shit' with booze, because if they have I'll shoot the bloody lot of them?"

"Go shit, big shit," he said and this I took to mean no.

I looked at the signaller and said, "Don't you dare go bloody wobbly on me again as well."

"Why shouldn't I the way you have treated me out here?"

My god, I thought, this is all I need now; we are in the middle of the Indonesian Army and my team are acting like a bloody bunch of kindergarten pupils fighting over the milk.

"Look, you pair of bastards, I've spent most of my time trying to make sure we all survive this bloody fiasco. For Christ's sake, get your bloody acts together or I'll leave the pair of you out here. Now, let's get about our work, we are not here on a bloody safari holiday, do you understand?"

We all sat looking at each other for a moment and nobody spoke, then the spell was broken as Nobby said, "I'm getting my head down for a bit, if you don't mind that is, Mein Fuehrer?"

"Nobby you are turning into a right arsehole, now let us get some rest."

The old man went off and returned a little later with two of the women from the village. He said they could look out for us while we got some rest. I agreed and he went off to have a look at the camps as I had asked him to.

I awoke later with a hand over my mouth, and when I opened my eyes I was looking into the yellow, filed teeth of the old man's eldest daughter. When she saw I was awake she took her hand away from my mouth and stepped back. As I looked around the place I could see the others getting up, and that it was starting to get dark.

When I'd packed up my things, I made my way to where Nobby was sitting and settled down beside him and took out my map. "This is the place you are to go to," I said pointing to a place I had already marked on the map.

"How in hell's name can you expect me to find that place in the dark, Bill?" he asked.

"One of the girls will take you. She will also bring you back here along with whomsoever you meet up with. I only hope to god that it is the right person you bring back, Nobby."

"What the hell does that remark mean, Bill, 'the right person'? Whoever I meet there has got to be the right person."

"Has he?" I asked.

With that I nodded to one of the girls and she motioned Nobby to follow her. I stood and looked for quite a while at the place where they disappeared into the undergrowth.

When at last I turned around, I saw the signaller standing watching me. As I moved towards him he said, "Old mates you two, Colours?"

"None of your fucking business, Corporal, just get your bloody gear on; you are going to earn your pay for the first time since you joined the bloody Royal Corps, so move your arse."

I didn't feel any better for that outburst and I was just going to turn around and tell him I was sorry, when I thought, shit why should I, Nobby was a man whom I had trusted with my life many, many times over the years, what the hell had it got to do with a young bloody whipper snapper of a signal corporal?

We were ready to move out when the old man entered the little clearing. "All big trucks with big guns gone," he said.

"Are you sure about that?" I asked.

"You no trust me, big shit?"

"You know better than that, you bloody little shit."

Well I hoped the news he had given me meant they had just been having a practice of some sort. I turned to the signaller and said, "Let's go, we are going out to mark out a couple of FUPs. Because, arsehole, by first light the camps over there are going to be in for the biggest bloody surprise of their lives. They are going to come under a full-scale Brigade attack."

"You said that the Brigadier wouldn't get the full briefing before tomorrow."

"Ah yes, I did, but I lied about that, my friend. You should have listened to Nobby when he told you to watch me. Something he has forgotten in his double dealing. I lie like hell, just give me half a chance and my lies will have you all running around in circles until you all disappear up your own arseholes. Now, move your arse."

Without another word, we set off into the open plain towards a place I had already decided upon earlier to lay out the FUPs. It took us a little while to reach, but once there I gathered the others around me in a little huddle. Then I told them what I wanted doing.

First I told the old man, "I want one of your daughters to stay with me to help me mark out the first FUP. I want you and this corporal to lay out the next one. I will show you where. Then I need you to go back and meet the Brigadier and Nobby, and bring them out here to us. The Brigadier's party are placing guides out to bring in the troops as they arrive."

"Okay," said the old man and then he told his daughters what I had just told him.

"I thought you said that Nobby was to meet the Brigadier's representative, now you are talking about guides and all sorts of people coming in here."

"Shit Corporal, how the bloody hell do you think that a Brigade attack takes place? It's not bloody section attacks at Holmingbeam for Christ's sake. This is the next thing to total war. These bastards have been attacking us with impunity for too bloody long. That lot are going to get one hell of a bloody licking in a couple of hours' time. So just get on with what you have been told to do and thank your bloody lucky stars you are not serving in one of those camps over there."

He looked at me for a moment and just as I was about to really lose my blob, he walked over to the old man, who was waiting for him. Then they disappeared into the night. The old man's daughter and I then set about marking out the place for the unit which was to come into here. Marking out a battalion size FUP takes a little time and we had just finished when the old man and the signaller returned.

I had a word with the old man and asked him, "Can you explain to your daughter that I'm going to need her to lead one of the unit guides into the FUP which she has just helped me to mark out?" This he did and I then told him, "It is time you took off to meet your old friend, the Brigadier." At this he grinned and disappeared into the night.

I then left with the other two for the place I had selected for the third and reserve battalion. It took a little while longer to lay out this FUP and once we had finished I told the signaller, "This will be your job; when the guides arrive you will bring the ones from the reserve battalion to this place, and make sure you get it right. Any cock-up and we could lose a hell of a lot of men over here tonight and tomorrow. Right!"

"You can count on me, Colours," he said.

I looked at him in the dark, but kept my mouth tightly shut and just led them away from the position. When we got back to the main track leading across the plain and we had just got ourselves strung out into a single file a hand touched my arm. As I turned to face the threat I saw that bloody little grinning man looking at me and crouched behind him, also grinning, was the Brigadier. There lying on the bank of the track was the whole Brigade "O Group".

Well, I thought, it is all bloody go now and I stepped down off the track to join the Brigadier. "Everything is done," I said. "My little group will show your guides where they are to go. Then if you and I and the COs go back a little way, out of the line of march, I will show you the lie of the land, sir."

"Good, Colours, let's just do that, you lead the way and we will follow."

With that I motioned the others to get on with the tasks I had given them and the rest of us made our way to a small knoll I had selected for the purpose a few days earlier. I made sure Nobby was with us when we left the rest.

Once we had got established on the knoll I motioned Nobby to stand watch and to make sure nobody joined us.

"Right, sirs," I whispered, "if you look in that direction," and I pointed out the camp, "that is the main objective; from the right edge of the camp as we see it, about three degrees and in the forward edge of the jungle is an enemy ambush cum guardpost. It has about platoon strength in it."

After they were all satisfied with that I went on to describe the other enemy positions of interest to them. Once they were all familiar with the ground and they had no more questions for me, the Brigadier went through his orders. As he was doing this I went to where Nobby was sitting keeping watch.

"All right, mate?" I asked.

"No. I'm not all right, I have been with you for bloody years and suddenly I no longer get to know what the hell is going on. You give me some cock and bull story about just having a look over the border; when all the time you are looking for a bloody spy, and at the same time laying the groundwork for a bloody Brigade attack. What has happened to us?"

"Something serious has happened to us, Nobby. Did you know that of all the men who started out in Scotland, you and I are the only two left alive? Are you into something else besides the work we do, Nobby? Are you being conned into reporting to some other organization?"

"You bloody shit, Bill, do you think I would compromise you and Mick, that I would spy on my own mates? Bloody hell, man, what do you think I have become?"

"That's the point, Nobby, what have you become, you tell me?"

He just sat there, his shoulders hunched and he looked completely dejected.

Neither of us spoke for the next fifteen minutes and the Brigadier's sniper came up to us and said they were moving off.

I put my hand on Nobby's shoulder and said, "It's all right, mate, but you have got yourself in one hell of a mess. You are the only one who can sort it out. I have some other work to do right now. I would ask you to come with me, but can I trust you as I used to in the old days?"

"Yes, Bill, you can trust me with your life."

"If you come with me Nobby I shall be doing just that."

"I mean it, Bill. I will be alright."

Just then the Brigadier joined us, "The Commanding Officers are off to join their units, Colours, I think it is time you were off on your next phase."

"Yes sir, I am taking the old man and Corporal Clark with me, if that is okay sir."

"Yes, shouldn't you take the signaller with you as well?"

"No, sir, I think I shall manage with just these two reprobates, sir."

"I'm sorry, Colours, but I insist the signaller goes with you."

I looked at the Brigadier in the darkness and thought he knows something he is not telling me. To Nobby I said, "Go and get the team together then we shall be off; I shall meet you at the first Battalion's FUP."

"Right," he said as he disappeared into the night.

The Brigadier then said, "You know who you are after then Colours; is it the one we thought?"

"Yes, sir, it's him. I saw him earlier today, but unfortunately the old man's son is mixed in with him; he's his top agent. The old man knows, but I'm not sure he will kill his son. If not then I'll have to do it."

"Well that is between him and you; I'd rather you didn't get involved, but you will have to see to the other one, though."

"Right, sir, I think I had better go now; they will be waiting for me."

"Fine, now here's a little something for you. Once things get going here and you should have completed your job, then you are to set this going. You will be picked up by chopper and taken out to one of the ships offshore; from there, you will be returned to Malaya. Once there, you will be returned to your main base in England, so best of luck Colours, you are going to need it!"

That said he shook my hand and I turned and went to find the others. They were waiting for me on the track by the FUP of the first unit. Then with the old man leading and the girls bringing up the rear we set off for our own Armageddon.

We were about halfway between the camp and the ambush position which Nobby had found that first night when we left the track and made our way into the jungle. The going got very tough, we had a fair distance to cover and it was very hot in there. Thanks to the old man and his daughters we made good time and arrived at our destination with time to spare.

The old man had led us with uncanny accuracy to within a few yards of the position I had told him I wanted. Once there, we took our loads off and I took the old man and Nobby with me leaving the girls and the signaller in what had become our base.

The three of us made our way a little further down the road; there we laid the explosives we had brought with us. Once everything was ready I took Nobby to a position on the opposite side of the road and said, "Look, Nobby, before long all hell is going to break loose. It is important that you set these charges off at exactly the right moment. I expect that when it all starts, a vehicle will come hurtling down this road heading for the camp out on the plain. In that vehicle will be a person we have been ordered to eliminate. All I ask is that you set these charges off at the right moment, and then use your rifle to encourage the occupants to take cover over there." I then pointed to a position on the other side of the road.

"Once they enter the jungle you are to leg it and make your way back to the Brigade. From there, you must join up with Brigade Headquarters and get back over the border with them. I'll see you when I get back, okay?"

"Don't worry Bill, I'll be all right, I'll see you back in Singers."

I looked at him for a second or two; how did he know I was going to Singapore, but I nudged his shoulder and left him.

Next I took the signaller and positioned him along with one of the old man's daughters. When he was happy with his position I told them where Nobby was and that if anybody came along the road instead of Nobby and into the jungle he was to kill them. Then I asked the old man if he would ask his daughter to make sure the signaller got back over the border.

Next the old man, his other daughter and I made our way to the point where we intended to intercept the people as they ran into the jungle. When we were all in position we settled down to get a little rest before the devil arrived.

The trap was now set and the devil would soon be coming to breakfast. Soon the area on the plain would become a cauldron of death as the camp out there would be wiped out. As I leaned back against a tree I looked skyward and could just see the first signs of the new dawn.

I looked down again and the old man was watching me. Just then we heard the first faint thump of the heavy artillery being fired. The old man held his thumb up as he grinned at me, then we heard the plop, plop of the brigade mortars joining in the fusillade. By now the old man, his daughter and I were fully alert with nerves tingling. Just before the artillery shells and the mortar bombs landed we heard the first pulsing of the rotor blades as the first gun ships throbbed into the area. We were all looking at each other as we held our breath, then we heard the crescendo of noise as the artillery shells, mortar bombs and rockets landed on the camp in unison. Then suddenly the jets were screaming overhead, as they launched their attacks on the other two camps.

The distant thump of the guns could no longer be heard, as the explosions in the area of the camp were blotting out all other noise. Then I heard the sound of something else; the old man had heard it too as he pointed to the road. Sure enough there was a vehicle coming down the road from the camp. It seemed as if time stood still as we listened to it getting nearer. The explosives we had laid started to go off and the next moment I heard Nobby firing his rifle on automatic.

Then I could hear them coming through the undergrowth and I came up into a kneeling position. As the first of them burst into the clearing I shot him with a single shot. Everything then seemed to be a dream,

Next I remember being pushed sideways, and as I turned to deal with it I saw the old man's daughter looking at me with a large hole in her chest where her bust had been a few seconds before. She had a look of terror on her face as she slowly sank to the ground.

Standing behind her with his mouth open and a look of utter amazement on his face was her brother. He still had that look on his face as the old man removed his head from his shoulders. Then I looked in horror as the old man turned his panga, placed the hilt of the handle on the ground and fell on to the blade.

I tried as I was watching him to get forward and stop him but he was as he had always been – too bloody quick for me. When I got to his side I picked him up and held him in my arms; he was already on the verge of death. I thought God, what have I done to this man and his family? Three of them have died here in the space of a few seconds. He just lay in my arms grinning up at me, then the life slowly ebbed from those small dark eyes of his.

As I held the old man I felt a sob rising in my throat, but it died before it could be uttered, for it was at that moment I felt the presence beside me. I looked down and there were those bloody brown boots, highly polished, bloody brown boots. Then I felt the cold steel of the muzzle of a gun, poking into the side of my temple. I squinted round and there he was; it had been years since I had seen that face as it had disappeared through the ice, all those years ago in Murmansk Bay.

Before I could speak the hatred which was now rising up inside me, I heard a shot. At first I waited for the pain, but there was none, I looked and there on the ground were those brown boots, still highly polished but twitching a little now. Then I turned

All For A King's Shilling

my head just in time to see a figure disappearing into the undergrowth. Well done, Nobby. With that I laid the old man down and walked to the road. It was daylight now and I switched the thing on which the Brigadier had given me and I sat on the side of the road, my head in my hands.

The Brigadier was true to his word; in no time at all I was in a helicopter and on my way to the rusty "B". From there, I was flown to Kuching and then on to Singapore. Six hours later I was on an Air India 707 on my way to Heathrow.

We landed at Heathrow after three stops. As I was leaving the plane, I overheard one of the stewardesses telling the pilot, "That man has never left his seat since we took off from Singapore; he hasn't eaten anything and he hasn't said a single word; he has just sat and looked at the rear of the seat in front of him. It's really weird."

"Perhaps he's deaf and dumb," proffered the pilot.

Before she could say anything else I looked at her and said, "Thank you for a nice trip." With that I walked off the plane. I went to the Union Jack Club in London and got pissed out of my mind.

Two days later I arrived in Plymouth.

Chapter Nine
Here I Go Jumping In The Bloody Freezer Again
United Kingdom 1964

Can I have A Single from Plymouth, to Norway Please?

To think! I could have been a Red Coat.

I'd been back in England for about three weeks, and while I was enjoying a spell of well-earned leave in my home port of Plymouth, I received a visit from a young Royal Marine Officer and he ordered me, yes he ordered me, to report to the nearest Royal Marine Barracks. That just happened to be 'The Royal Marine Barracks, Stonehouse', the very Barracks from which he had just come. Before I could get ready to go back with him, he pissed off and I ended having to catch a bus into town.

Once I was ready to go I told my wife that I should be home about four that afternoon, then off I went. Had I known what the future held for me, I would have been out when the Land Rover with the young officer in it had called at my house that morning.

When I did at last arrive in the Barracks, I was asked by the Regimental Sergeant Major, "Just where the hell have you been, Johnston?"

"Colour Sergeant Johnston, sir," I replied before I could explain that the young officer who had called at my house had pissed off and left me.

He, the RSM that is, said. "Go and report to the Guardroom right now."

"Yes, sir," I said and immediately left his office, having seen enough of him.

When I arrived in the Guardroom under the gateway arch I was told by a young corporal, "You are to report to the Movements' SNCO as soon as possible."

"Colour Sergeant Johnston," I said.

"Yes, Colour Sergeant Johnston," the Corporal said.

"Yes, Corporal, that's right, I am a Colour Sergeant; you wouldn't like it if I or anybody else didn't call you Corporal, now would you?"

"No, Colour Sergeant, I would not like it; I worked hard to become a Corporal."

All For A King's Shilling

"Not half as bloody hard as I'm having to work in these Barracks to be addressed by my correct rank, Corporal. You should hope and pray that we never serve in the same unit in the future, as I'm a real vindictive bastard when I get riled." With that I walked out of the Guardroom.

One thing I failed to understand, when the RSM knew I was to report to the Movements' SNCO, why didn't he tell me to do so in the first place?

The movements' SNCO then went into his little part in this pantomime and he told me, "You are to report to be in the MoD in London by nine o'clock tomorrow morning."

"Colour Sergeant to you, Sergeant, I've already been through all this performance in the Guardroom. What is it about this place that makes none of you have any respect for rank at all? Now do you mind if I ring my wife to tell her what is happening?"

"That's okay, you can use the phone in the other office," he said, pointing to an office at the rear.

"Colour Sergeant," I reiterated for the second time that day.

When my wife answered the telephone I told her, "I'm afraid I have to catch a train to London tonight. I've no idea what it is all about but I shall let you know as soon as I do know myself."

Then I went on to say, "I'll be home soon, as I would need to pick up some things, and then I would be off."

To repeat what she said in reply to that would make even an old sea dog blush. She was not a very happy woman, but I told her, "I assume any break in my leave will be made up to me when I get back when all this is over."

What an understatement that turned out to be.

Again she interrupted me, telling me in unrepeatable words of two or more syllables what she thought of the Royal Corps; but more so what she thought of me!

When she paused I told her, "I'm going to try and find out what I can from this end before I leave. This I can do more cheaply by ringing from the Barracks than using our telephone to do their dirty work for them."

Again I received an ear-bashing down the phone, and I thought I don't need this shit. So, I hung up.

Then I made three or four calls to people whom I knew in London, asking them all, "Any idea of a flap or the like going on?"

All my calls drew a blank so in the end I thought I am wasting my bloody time, I'd be better off spending what time I had at home with my wife and children. So I collected my travel documents from Movements, and headed off home to my family. Had I had any sense, that is were I should have stayed. Still, we all grow wise with time and hindsight, don't we?

As it was I caught the late train to London; I'd hoped to get some sleep on the journey so I'd be fresh when I arrived next morning. The last thing I needed the next day was to be tired. If the meeting was really important, then I had to be fully with it, fully alert, as they say, but unfortunately that was not to be. When I boarded the train I'd picked an empty compartment and settled down for the journey.

I'd made myself comfortable in the compartment and the station staff were walking up and down the platform as they always seem to do just as the train is about to depart. There was a noise further down the corridor and about half a dozen drunken sailors were piling into the corridor of the coach I was in. I was to find out later as everybody else in the coach did that they were on their way to join a stone frigate (Naval name for a shore establishment) somewhere near Thetford in Norfolk. They'd gone on a good binge in Plymouth before joining the train, and had arrived just before it was about to leave. They just managed to scramble aboard with their kit bags as it started to pull out of North Road Station from platform seven. All this hilarity of them scrambling aboard while the train was moving caused much amusement among some of the other passengers in the compartments of the coach. My god, I thought, please do not encourage them, none of us will get any sleep if you do. Then guess what, they decided my compartment was for them.

To say I hate sailors is a little bit of an understatement. I make no bones about it; I have hated them for bloody years. They have big mouths and are living on the glory of their day during the war. At sea they are okay but ashore they are nothing but trouble. So I decided to just sit in the corner for the rest of the trip, and hoped they would not involve me in their carrying on. Most of them are just twenty mile snipers anyway. You know they have not won a decisive victory since Nelson was killed.

Of course it was too much to ask, wasn't it? They laughed and jabbered on for most of the time, played cards, chain-smoked and generally made arseholes of themselves. Somehow they think it is being big and manly. It took some time before I realized that because I had a civilian hair style, they thought me a civvy. Made me chuckle a bit that did!

It has always been at times like this, when I meet people like these, I think of my father. I make up comments, comments that I think he would make about them, as I study them, one by one, and then have a little laugh at what I imagine he would say about them. I was sitting smiling about one of these, when one of the young men decided I should not be smiling, at least not at him, which I wasn't.

"What do you think you are laughing at?" he asked me in an aggressive manner.

I gave the impression I was thinking very hard then I said, "It cannot be very much at all, as I am looking at you."

He was on his feet in a flash, and threw a punch at me. As I said, they had been drinking and although he was quick to his feet I'd a feeling his brain was not as fast as his body and was only half way to the standing position when he had reached the upright stance with fists raised. All I had to do was deflect the blow with my hand and he was on the floor of the carriage; in the words of Kilroy, I never touched him, your honour.

This, of course, brought his pals to the rescue and it was at this point I thought it best to stop it all there and then. So I said in a very loud parade ground voice, "Who is in charge of this party?"

The one who had thrown the first punch and was still trying to regain his feet said, "I am."

Producing my identity card I said, "I'm Colour Sergeant Johnston of Her Majesty's Royal Marines. You, young man, you're setting a fine example as a leader. It's time we all settled down, then I'll need all your names and numbers and details of your movement orders."

When I had taken down all their details including their destination, I then informed them, "I will be submitting a report to your commanding officer. I will also

All For A King's Shilling

be charging all of you with striking a superior officer, offering violence to a superior officer and bringing the service into disrepute."

This at least had the effect of settling them down and sobering them up rather quickly. Of course I then had to spend the rest of the journey to London trying to explain to them that after what had happened, as a Royal Marine Colour Sergeant I could not do anything else but charge them. It would be up to their commanding officer to decide if they were guilty or not.

Much to my disgust, I arrived in London tired, fed up and irritable.

Once the train had halted alongside the platform in Paddington Station I alighted and made my way to the washroom. When the train was arriving I had told my travelling companions they would be hearing from me. As it happened I never did get round to submitting any charges to their new commanding officer in Norfolk.

When I'd completed my ablutions and I felt like a human being once more, I made my way to Admiralty Arch. There, I turned down the street behind the Whitehall Theatre, next I turned right into the road running parallel to Horse Guards, but behind the Ministry's buildings. About fifty yards along the road, I turned into a door on the right-hand side, leading to what looked like an ordinary block of flats. When I opened the door, I was immediately asked by a voice in a small cubicle, "Who are you and what do you want?"

Before I could even manage to enter the rather heavy door a large gentleman who looked to be ex Guards stepped out from the rear of the cubicle. So, without saying a word, I produced my movement order and handed it over. This he read line by line in a slow laborious way. I stood fascinated watching his lips as he formed them round every word on the sheet of paper I'd handed him. Eventually he arrived at the bottom and, satisfied that all was in order, he then gave the paper to another man inside the cubicle, who then commenced to read it from top to bottom also. I was absolutely fascinated by all this but said nothing as I watched them.

When at last this man had also satisfied himself that all was in order he wrote out a pass which he then handed to me. At first I was going to stand there and read the pass line by line and word by word. Instead I looked at it and I could see at a glance it allowed me to go to a room on the 4th floor. Still I played their game a little and I took my time reading the pass. It was then another large gentleman who had appeared as if from nowhere escorted me to one of those cage-type lifts. Installed in the middle of the old-fashioned stairwell, he sent me on my way upwards to God alone knew what as if he was dispatching goods from a store basement up to the sales floor. Looking back, I suppose that is exactly what he was doing, sending me to be sold a load of crap.

As the lift rose I did notice that this large bloke who had shown me to the lift remained standing where he was, watching me all the time as the lift rose through the open trellis work of the lift shaft until it reached the 4th floor. It was only after I had disembarked from the lift that I heard him going back to his little room just inside the entrance, which I presumed he shared with the ex Guards type and the one with the voice. They obviously didn't want me getting out anywhere but the 4th floor.

I stepped out on to the landing and there, waiting for me, was a very young smart and good-looking man in a brand new suit, looked like a Gieves and Hawke's. He could have been a civil servant, or a young serviceman fresh from Dartmouth, or some other military academy, but I took him to be a serviceman and not a civil servant.

"Colour Sergeant Johnston?" he asked.

"Are you expecting anybody else?"

"Well, no."

"Then I must be he." I replied.

I'm certain he was not amused by my reply. "You are Colour Sergeant Johnston?" he asked again.

"Yes, I am," I said.

He then asked to see my papers and my pass. At least he read them more quickly than the man downstairs. They all seemed to satisfy him, and he showed me to a room that looked to be the rear of the building. He told me somebody would collect me soon and then he left.

There was already one occupant seated in the room when I got there so I picked out what looked to be the best of the empty seats, the one between him and the wall. Even though there were at least ten other chairs I chose the one between him and the wall, purely to upset him and put him ill at ease. Then I did what we all do in this situation, I looked the place over, noting the poor decoration of the room. Then after staring at the small table containing some prehistoric magazines I stood up and picked up one of them. It turned out to be the *Navy News*, which was the last thing I needed right then. As I did so, the other occupant of the room asked me, "Are you here for the interview board, or have you already got an appointment?"

Appointment, I thought, as I seated myself between him and the wall again, I suppose I should play their little game. "Well, yes, I suppose I have come to take up my new appointment. First Sea Lord, would you believe."

He gave me a rather funny look, then asked me, "Where have you come from?"

"Newcastle, Newcastle upon Tyne that is, not the other one."

He then asked me, "What do you do there?"

"As little as bloody possible; why, is this part of the interview?"

"Oh, no," he replied, "just passing the time of day."

"Well," I said, "I spend most of my time playing with my bloody self, behind a very large desk and an even bigger locked door, okay."

I would have to say he was not amused at all by that remark. They must think I came up the Clyde on the last bloody banana boat. Because he was a plant, if ever I saw one. The Civil Service mentality never fails to amaze me.

After that he shut up and within three minutes smarty pants, who brought me to the room, was back. He asked the other smart arse if he would go with him. Both smart arses then went off, just about holding hands as smart arses seem to do these days.

It was some ten or more minutes before I was called forward; this time I was collected by what looked like a third smart arse. As I looked at him, I thought the place is swarming with them. This person showed me to a small office, which was still further in the rear of the building. Any further in this direction, I thought, and I will end in the middle of the Mall. I also remember thinking, the people I'm to see mustn't be very important if they are this far to the rear of the building. Any further and we would be nearly in the tradesmen's entrance of Buck House.

All For A King's Shilling

The office contained a desk, on which there were some empty filing trays. There were two chairs behind the desk, and one in the front. There was a window behind the desk, which meant the two people sitting behind the desk were more or less silhouetted against the morning light. They would have been more silhouetted, had there not been a rather large man standing behind them. Even so their faces were hard to make out; it was an old dodge, but the way they had done it, it showed their inexperience. In time you get so accustomed to the light that you can see them quite clearly. Something they never seem to realize, also the change in the light as time passes has the same effect. I thought, please God will nobody save me from these ex college boys and James Bond addicts. When will they grow up, everything is still jolly old hockey sticks and rugger to these people, if they had brains they would be bloody dangerous.

As soon as I'd entered I was told by the man standing behind the desk, "Sit, Colour Sergeant Johnston."

The voice gave the speaker away immediately.

"So you have eventually made it to the great and wonderful MoFWD, sir. Ministry of Faceless Wonders?"

"Yes, I have, Colours, but I don't see that it is any of your business."

"You're right; it has nothing to do with me, but if I'd known you were involved with 'this' whatever 'this' is I would have pulled the emergency cord on the train last night and disappeared. Now we have got these stupid charades over with, perhaps you can tell me what is so important that my leave has been curtailed and why I have been brought here? I must tell you, I am not very impressed with your young men's play-acting. As you know I am not an actor, I like to think I'm a bloody professional serviceman but even that is in doubt these days since you got mixed up in my life! What is more important, I am still very good at my job and I don't like jumped up, pimply faced ex grammar school boys, or university students for that matter, playing silly buggers with me. So your story should be a good one, sir, or I shall be on the next train out of Paddington bound for the West Country and all stations west to Plymouth. You have got one shot at this, sir, so you had better make sure that it is a good one."

There was a quick intake of breath from the young men seated behind the desk as I made my spiel. By now I could see their faces clearly and one of them was about to say something, but before he could the voice behind him went on.

"It's really quite simple, there's a job which needs doing and it's been decided you are the person to do it. (A reference to an old rag game that was popular with silly bloody public school boys.) Even I think you are the man for the job," he concluded.

"Is that so? Am I supposed to feel better for all that? And just who are these people who have decided I'm it? You see, over the years it has been my experience that people who use the expression, 'It has been decided' are only keen for some other poor sod to either clear up their mess or to take the rap for their cock-up. They are normally covering their own backs when things have gone wrong. So, just who are these faceless bastards who dare not face me with their bright and stupid ideas? I have just had a very bad experience with the 'you are it' brigade, which you probably already know about. An experience which I must say I'm not too keen to repeat. So, why not cut the bullshit and get to the point. Why is it that you lot have to pussyfoot around so much, especially when you are up to no bloody good? For Christ's sake just come out with it. Then I can say no and get back to my family."

Then I heard that dreaded voice behind me say, "Well I told you young men he was a bolshie bastard, didn't I? Always argumentative and insubordinate, yes this is my man." Then to me he said, "I think this time, my friend, you will have to put your money where your mouth is. This time it will be the worst job you will have ever done or have to do for me. Yes, this will be the last one. I know the last job you did was the worst I have heard, but this could be even worse. I do know that your old Eban friend killed his son and that you couldn't stop him taking his own life as is the custom when he did what I understand he had to do."

"Excuse me but how did you know all that and how it all happened; have you been talking to Corporal Clark?"

He did what he normally does with me nowadays, he ignored me.

Oh shit, I thought, here we bloody go again. "I thought they would have put you out to grass by now and what's all this, 'the worst job' or 'the last job'; I don't like the sound of that 'last job' bit. It was always 'jolly hockey sticks' and all that crap before. So why now the 'worst' and the 'last' job crap? If this is going to be until death do us part soldiering you can bloody count me out right here and now, I'm off to Plymouth."

"So they have, my dear boy, so they have," he replied. "So they have. Well, they sent for me last week though, so not to be outdone, I sent for you this week. I agree with you, we need not pussyfoot around anymore, need we? I can imagine by now you have an idea what it is all about, don't you?"

The bastard hadn't listened to a single bloody word I had said. "No, sir, I don't know what it's all about and I don't want to know. As I said, I'm off to Plymouth; nice seeing you again, sir. See you some time if you are ever in Plymouth, Trooping the Colour or some such activity."

"Yes quite, now as I see it you are the only one who can get in and out without even our knowing how you do it. That is why it has to be you, old boy, you do see that, don't you?"

It then dawned on me the only map on the side wall of the room was of the north west corner of good old Mother Russia. "No way, sir, the last time I was there you said I'd done my bit and that was it."

"I said that, did I? Well if you say so you are probably right. There is just one thing though, we seem to be having some trouble with the setup at the moment. Let me tell you what the situation is, and you can then take it from there."

"No point sir, I am not interested in the least, and I would like to go back and finish my leave. I keep telling you I'm off to Plymouth to finish my leave and then join my new unit if you don't mind, sir! Some day I may just make Sergeant Major; worse things have happened to the Corps, then I will be out of your clutches for good, sir."

"Well, be that as it may, I do think you should hear what I have to say before you decide to leave, Colours. In fact I'm going to bloody insist that you do."

The silence in the room was unbearable then at last he spoke again.

"Now there's a good chap. Let's not get unpleasant about it, you know I don't work that way. Keep the lads happy is the way I work."

All For A King's Shilling

"Look, sir, I have worked with you lots of times on and off these last few years, and it may come as a shock to you, but I have never, never been bloody happy about any of it. Nor to my knowledge has anybody else I know been happy working with you. In fact, sir, I would go so far as to say the opposite has always been the normal when working with you. Like everybody else who has ever worked with you, I hate your bloody guts."

"Now, now, Colours, let us not give these young men here the wrong idea. I was only telling them yesterday what a great chap you are to work with."

I just sat there with my mouth open; I was speechless.

"Close your mouth Colours and follow me."

Like the bloody fool I am, I did just that.

We then took the lift down to the basement and made our way through a maze of corridors. Eventually we came to an operations room, in the bowels of the MoD. There was not much activity in the place at all. It did contain some rather powerful radios in the room and they were all manned. Nothing was happening though, which gave the first impression it was all for show. Nobody took the slightest notice as the five of us entered the room. The two men who were sitting with their backs to the window looked as though they had just come from university, the same two who had played silly buggers in the waiting room. I'd my doubts if either of them had much experience in anything at all, let alone the type of work the old bear and I were into. They gave the impression they were hanging on his every word. The Commander, well Commander Fitzsimmonds, he just trailed along in the rear not saying a word.

The two young ones went round the different operators and had a chat with each one. Then they reported to the old bear, "Nothing has changed since last night, sir."

As I stood and listened, I thought, I suppose they feel important doing that. I doubt if they knew they were just doing lackeys' work. Still I didn't care if they knew or if they didn't, I just wanted out of the place. What I'd seen was enough for me to put two and two together and come up with a crazy feeling I knew that I'd been right from the start what it was all about. The setup looked all too familiar to me. I had seen that operation room elsewhere; that somewhere else being the north coast of jolly old Scotland.

To say I was not happy at all would be a very correct assessment of my situation. So I was immediately looking for a bolt-hole and damned quickly at that. Then the old bear asked me, "Do you remember the old control room? Of course you do, you have seen two such rooms as this haven't you, Colour Sergeant?"

It is a few months since I last saw a room with the same gear in, but I had to say, "Yes, I've seen one like that. You must remember that I left the place in Scotland before it was finished. So it is only the other one that I have seen."

"Well, Colours, we transposed the Scottish one down here to London not long after you had departed for Russia. In fact we were operational before you had finished setting up that place in Russia, and you never guessed, did you? Of course we did not bring the men, or equipment, which they had just set up. No, we used a duplicate set of equipment here, then all we had to do was to tap into the cable. Then Bob's your uncle, we had all the news but none of the discomfort of the other place. The Russians were none the wiser, you and the others hadn't a clue. Not even the men in the north of Scotland knew for that matter."

"So, I have been right all these years, what a shit you really are; can't do without your London life, clubs, messes, and the good life. After seeing this little lot, I hate you more than ever now and the two young pimps you have working for you, you old shit. God, but I could kill you right now when I think of all the lads who have died for a completely unnecessary operation. I doubt it even fooled the Russians. If I ever get the chance, your bloody days are numbered, sir; and while I'm on the go, one of you two had better tell me what happened to Corporal Mick Smith in Singapore after I'd left for Borneo; because that ranks as one of your biggest cock-ups ever. You never even checked his documents, did you! You see he was TT teetotal, never touched drink in his life; didn't know that, did you? You think all of us are like you lot, just a bunch of piss-heads. Well, we aren't, and there was no way Corporal Smith would be drunk."

When I glanced towards the place where Commander Fitzsimmonds was standing he looked at me, his face completely emotionless. So I went on and told him, "You have changed from the role of the blundering idiot that you acted out in Singapore haven't you, well I don't like you either, so come the revolution you'll be one of the first up the dreaded thirteen steps, I can promise you that."

Brown didn't take offence at what I had said, he just carried on as if I hadn't been insubordinate at all. "Come, now, Colours, let's not get too upset about it all. You had an idea what was going on, you said as much the last time we talked. We have seen all we needed to see in this room."

With that he made for a door at the far end of the room and motioned for me to follow him. As I started to move towards him one of his pimps ran to open the door for us. Just as I was about to walk through the door behind the old sod, this pimp stepped in behind him and let the bloody door go. It closed fast and bumped on to my right shoulder before I could do anything about it.

I looked at his back as he walked in front of me and said, "You ignorant young sod, that was my bloody shoulder you just bashed with that door."

"Don't you ever talk like that to me in that way again or …" That was as far as he got because as he turned to face me the point of my twelve inch bowie knife nicked his throat.

That was when, much to my surprise, Commander Fitzsimmonds stepped in and said, "You were at fault letting the door close and bump the Colour Sergeant's shoulder; it will be your fault if he is unable to go on this mission because of any injury he may have received by your action."

Then further to my surprise the young man said, "Sorry, Colours."

To which I replied, "Colour Sergeant, and I'm sick and tired these last few days of having to keep reminding people that I am a Colour Sergeant!"

Then as I pulled myself together the other young sod went to push past me and into the room. That was when he saw my knife at his pal's throat and it stopped him dead in his tracks. My shoulder was aching like hell, I'd got a bigger bump than I had at first thought, so I pushed my knife against the young man's neck until a spot of blood appeared.

"Please put that bloody knife away, Colours, and how did you get the bloody thing in here?"

All For A King's Shilling

"Well, sir, that is for me to know about and you and your security to think really hard and long about, isn't it, sir?"

That was when the penny dropped and I realized why the door had closed so hard on my shoulder. The air spring on the rear of the door obviously had too much pressure on it and you really had to push it hard to open it. I'd had a lucky escape, but I had convinced myself the incident was not an accident.

When I did at last get into the room the two young pimps were smirking although one was wiping blood from his neck. It occurred to me it was because they were a bit jealous of the familiarity between their boss and me. At this point I was of a mind to just say sod it and walk away. Looking back, I should have, it would have saved me a lot of grief, but I would also have missed out on a lot of happiness.

The old man started his story of why he had recommended to the 'powers that be' I was the man for the job. "You see, Colours, something has gone very, very wrong with our operation in the north. We have been getting very strange messages every day or so for weeks now. Things were going all right until about three months ago. We had just put a new team in for one of the usual six-month stints, the handover had gone well. There had been nothing untoward with that part of the operation, everything went as normal."

At this point one of the young men said, "Perhaps, sir, the Colour Sergeant is not aware of what you are talking about."

With that the old man rounded on him like the wild bull he used to be, "Doesn't know, doesn't know, you bloody insignificant little pups? He built the bloody place. If it had not been for him and a few more just like him, the greatest deep penetration post ever established in another country would never have been established."

I interjected at this point, "Sir, you were never ever to have told anybody that little gem of information. It means you have put these young men's lives at risk, they now know too much about me and it could cost them their lives, as it has with all the other men who were with me up north. At the last count I believe there were only two of us left after Corporal Smith's accident; but now I'm not so sure, I'm not sure what has happened to Corporal Clark after he saved my life a few days ago?"

"Don't you start," he said as he rounded on me. "I have enough trouble with the likes of these two, without you starting that shit with me."

He stopped in midstream, then he looked at me as it sunk into his head what I had said.

Looking at him I said. "I don't know what you have in mind, sir, but if it concerns me then I would rather these two young 'friends' of yours are not told any more about my part in whatever it is you have in mind. Providing that is all right with you, sir?"

This he agreed to, but for my money he was too ready to agree to it. Then he made a big show of sending them both back to the operations room. I didn't think for one minute he would keep that confidence and not tell them just whatever it was we eventually did decide to do. I knew he would tell them everything later when I was not around to challenge him; and no, I didn't trust any of the bastards. They did not seem to take any offence at the way he spoke to them, but if looks could kill I'd have died on the spot as the two of them left the room.

When the Commander, Brown and I were alone he then launched into the biggest lie of his life to date when he gave an account of what had really happened to the setup. "Everything had gone according to plan without any problems at all; reports of submarines leaving the northern waters of the Soviet Naval Base in Murmansk. Every damned submarine and for the last few years every Naval vessel has also been logged. Every one tallying with our logs here two to five days after they leave Murmansk. Right on the button we would pick them up crossing our buoys and into the Atlantic."

Brown went on. "Just as I have said, things have now started to go wrong. It first manifested itself just over three months ago when we got a bit of a garbled message. When it reached the desk of the duty officer, he immediately sent a signal requesting verification of the message and its contents. This was done, the message was corrected and the whole thing checked out with no problems. In the end it was all put down to problems with the ether; they say there had been a lot of solar disruptions at about that time."

I thought typical signal jargon, when they have a problem it is always the sun and its eruptions, but I said, "I would like to see the signal which was sent and the one asking to have the original verified. Also what did you mean about that time, what time are you talking about, sir?"

Ignoring my question Brown went on. "The problem was first picked up by the duty officer of the day. Two days later as it happens they returned him to his regiment as unsuitable for this kind of work. It seems that he had trouble fitting in with the rest of the crew manning the operations room. The young officer, the one who let go of the door so that it bumped you, well he was sent here to replace him. There was as I see it no handover between them."

Realising that they had no idea that I had worked out just what they had been up to for years, I played along with their little game of charades. "Sir, surely it is against all the rules for that to happen. For one person to relieve another without a handover of some sort, that is criminal."

"Not with things the way they are at this moment in time. Everything is very sloppy you know, not like the old days."

Looking at the Commander I said to Brown. "Well, no, sir, I didn't know everything was, 'very sloppy', as you put it. If you end where I think you will, sir, and I end where I think you would have me end, then things had better not be 'sloppy', as you say, in any way, shape or form. I admit that the pair of you were very sloppy out in Singapore but then that seems to be you two all over. It was also another fiasco in Borneo, even worse there because the replacement for Corporal Smith was very amateurish!"

The Commander started to say something, but one look from Brown and he didn't. The more I looked at this new man, Fitzsimmonds, the more my flesh began to crawl. As to Brown, I had the feeling that he was a very tired and very old man now. I had the feeling the fire had gone or something was wrong. He had been at this game for far too long. I was starting to wonder just what he was up to and it was starting to worry me quite a bit. If as I was now pretty certain would happen, I did not want to be over there with a tired old man, a suspect Commander and a couple of stupid, young green men to watch me. If things were as bad as they looked I needed somebody to cover me who was as good as the old sod used to be, but then in the early days he was good; then again I ask myself now if he really was any good even then. Another thing was I had this feeling I was being sucked into whatever game was afoot and control was not in my hands. Despite this, in my heart of hearts I knew he would talk me into doing the job. I knew, regardless of my doubts, suspicions and premonitions about the setup, that I was hooked. I needed to see for myself without anybody knowing I was there. I had to find out if I was right. If I was then they could kiss their little scam goodbye for ever. If I had had a hand in doing wrong then I would certainly have a hand in righting that wrong!

So it was I attended the briefing of a lifetime some hour or so later. It was a fiasco from start to finish, there was none of the normal situation, enemy and friendly forces, mission, execution and the rest of the standard orders system we followed these days. No, this briefing consisted of the old man just saying to one of the young men, "Tell him what has happened." When he had finished it was the other one's turn. I arrived at the conclusion that not one of them knew what was going on in the north. The only details they were insistent about were the list of names and addresses they gave me. Miles of them, some completely off any route I was ever likely to take and, even if things did go wrong, then I'd be too busy dragging my arse out of there to worry about bloody Russian dissidents who might or might not help me. God, they even gave me names and addresses in Moscow; why the hell should I go to Moscow? Six hundred yards over the border is my idea of deep penetration; as for Moscow, forget it. A place there was no chance I would ever go near, not of my own volition anyway, but they were insistent I keep all these names and addresses no matter what happened, pages and bloody pages of the bloody things. They said I should memorise them all; one of the cheeky bastards remarked that I was the expert and it should be a doddle for me as I was supposed to be able to do anything. He did change his attitude a little when he saw me reaching for my knife again.

When they had finished telling me all they had been told to tell me, I said, "It's all very well giving me all these names, but just what the hell do you want me to do with them all? You expect me to go in and sort the other end out, when you do not know if you have another end? You do not know if it is under Russian control, or if the Russians have closed the thing down completely? None of the built-in checks to discover these things without risking any more men were ever carried out. You have acted like a bunch of bloody boy scouts out for a weekend camping and now you try to load me down with miles of bloody names and addresses. Not to mention the bloody reams of bloody passwords, each one different for each area. Has either of you two ever been on an operation or not because you know what you can do; you can stick all these lists up your well greased little public schoolboys' arses?"

To all of this, they just looked sheepish and they didn't say a word. So changing the subject I then asked them, "What arrangements have you two made to get me in and out of the place? I suppose you need answers about the situation like yesterday?"

"Well, yes, we do," one of them muttered.

To which I replied, "That rules out a submarine then, doesn't it?"

"Yes it does, but we had planned for you to go in by air."

"Have you, and just how, and when, is this flight to take place?"

They then dropped the bombshell, "Well we had intended for you to go north on one of the RAF's normal reconnaissance flights tonight. You are to be flown to

Lossiemouth in Scotland. Then you will be dropped over the edge of the Russian border nearest to Murmansk."

Well, I just sat and looked at them. "Over the edge of the Russian border," I asked. "Do either of you have any comprehension of what you have just said?"

"Of course we have," they said in unison.

I looked at the old bear, he just shrugged his shoulders and grinned. Then I looked back at the two young men and they could see nothing wrong with the idea and one of them said, "The RAF can drop you to within fifty yards of your drop zone."

"Oh, yes, you should tell that to all the Allied troops in the last world war, and quite a few since; tell those who have had the shit bombed out of them by their own air forces over those years. Not least of all, tell the Canadians who survived Caen, in France."

Then I said, "Do you have any idea of what that fifty yards you are talking about means? Let me tell you before you all get on your high horses. First, has either of you ever seen the border between Russia and Norway in that area? It is a swathe cut through the forest, with a rather large electrified wire fence running down the middle of the swathe. If I were to land ten yards inside of Norway I would be still inside your fifty-yard accuracy, but on the completely wrong side of the border fence. Now I cannot see how the Russian Frontier guards couldn't fail to see me, it being full daylight, twenty-four hours a day just now and oh, there is no way I will be jumping out of an RAF plane in that area. Not at this time of the year anyway. In the winter well, maybe, just maybe with a directional parachute I might go along with it, but not at this time of the year. If the RAF go and get it wrong, like they often do, by just a few yards, I'd be in what is known as Shit Street. Then if I were to land in Finland a bit further south the Russians wouldn't have to look for me at all because the Finns have an agreement with old Ivan that any Englishmen they catch in Finland will be handed over to Ivan and that way he will not invade them this year."

"Well," I was asked at last after the pregnant pause which occurred. "Just how do you propose to get in?" There was another long, pregnant pause.

"There seems to be one small point you have all overlooked! I haven't said yet I'd go. If I do go, and it's a bloody big if, then there is no way I am going to tell you how, where and when. What I will tell you is, all you have to do for your part is to get me into Norway without anybody knowing. A small plane will do, forget the RAF or any other 'F' you have in mind. All you have to do is get me to Norway. Leave me alone, and I will do the rest."

There was silence in the room for about two minutes then the old bear asked, "I take it you are on, Colours?"

"Well, yes, sir, I think I can do this chore for you, but it is the last. There will be no more after this. I do not want either of these two mixed up in it in any way at all?"

"Okay, done."

He then told the other two to leave while he and I talked over how I would do the job. He then proceeded to give me a whole spiel about his contacts in Norway and also some in Russia. I must admit that these names and locations I immediately file in my permanent memory banks, the Kim's game banks! I would need to contact Carl to do some checking of this little lot for me.

"I take it you want me to forget that load of names and addresses your young men gave me?"

"No, you still need them; they may come in handy later."

At that I looked across to where the Commander was sitting and still not taking any part in the discussions. He just raised his shoulders a little and gave a shrug; but he did have a self-satisfied look on his face and that worried me somewhat.

That was the point when I smelled the biggest rat. The young lads were just pawns in the game. No, the Commander and the old bear were the problem. My better judgment told me I should just make my way back to Plymouth or to my sister's house in another part of the UK and sit this one out. My curiosity was aroused though and I had to know if they had been using the base in the north to infiltrate the West and flood it with agents every six months. I had to know what I had helped to set up all those years ago. Not that I would worry myself sick and top myself, no I would just rectify my earlier mistake by closing the place down and if anybody were to be topped then these two looked prime suspects to me.

So I was committed. "Now, sir, if you don't mind I'd like to call my wife and tell her I may be away for a couple of weeks. Also I need to get some kit together. I'd like to be left alone to do that, so if I may, I'll leave you now and I shall be back in a little while."

I walked out of the building telling the men at the door that I was going for a meal and I'd be back in about half an hour or so. Then I made my way to Trafalgar Square and the public call boxes there. First I rang a number in London and told them I needed assistance to contact home. Then I rang off; next I called my wife in Plymouth and told her I might be a week or two then we could continue with my leave and our current fight. Her reply was unrepeatable so I again hung up on her. Next I went and got something to eat at one of the small cafes in the area.

On my way back to the MoD I again called the number I'd called first. They told me, "If it is the MoD who is flying you to Norway in a light aircraft, they usually refuel in the north of England near to Newcastle prior to crossing the North Sea. If you think that you need to change transport, then a boat should be able to get into the Tyne in the next couple of hours, just in case you need it."

"That would be well with me and if I do take up your offer, it would be best if I were not observed arriving by air." I received some further information and then I hung up.

Happy with the news I'd been given, I made my way back to the MoD. As I did I stopped behind one of the young men who had annoyed me so much earlier and told him, "My wife would love to talk to you, young man. I'm going back to get some kit together now. You can walk with me or you can carry on with this charade, it's up to you?"

He coughed and spluttered a bit but said nothing and he then followed me back to the office about ten yards behind me.

When I got back Brown asked me, "Who have you been telephoning, Colours?"

Well, sir, I had to call a neighbour to ask my wife to go to the call box at the end of our road as we don't possess a telephone. Then I called back after I'd eaten and spoke to her."

He looked at me for at least a minute and then just grunted and left the room saying over his shoulder, "You know where the stores are, don't you?"

"Yes, I do," I replied.

Later that afternoon I took off in a light aircraft from Black Bush Airfield in London to fly as I was told to Norway. My contact was right because after we were airborne the pilot told me. "We will be refuelling at a small airfield in the north of England. Then we will fly on to Norway during the night; we'll refuel again in the south and fly north the next day, stopping for more fuel as and when we need it and depending how far north you are going."

"Thirsty bloody plane, isn't it, still, you are the pilot. Haven't they told you how far I'm going?"

"No, they haven't, they just said Norway."

"Do you really expect me to believe that they have chartered you to fly me and not told you where other than Norway?"

"That's right."

Bloody hell, I thought, who do they think they are dealing with, but I only said. "I intended to get some sleep so you can wake me as we land."

With that I lay back against the side window much as you do in a bus or train, but with about half the space. I do not know how long I slept, but it seemed to be only a few minutes; the side of my face was freezing and we were landing in the north of England. The pilot taxied up to what looked like an over-large garage. The pilot got out and went into the place and I followed him in. It was just like a large garage, except instead of cars there were a couple of light aircraft.

My illustrious pilot was talking to a couple of blokes at the rear of the place. He then came over to me and said, "I've another person to take to Norway as well as you, it seems. It will be a bit cramped but we will be okay."

His change of plan peeved me just a little, so I asked him, "Have you got clearance from London on this extra passenger?"

"Nothing to do with them, I own this aircraft and I'll take whatever passengers I want and if you don't like it you know what you can do?"

So I said, "Okay by me, I will do just that, I'll get my gear out of your little plane. First, though, tell me where and what is the nearest town to this little hole?"

"Newcastle upon Tyne, it's about fifteen miles away."

"Right, as I don't intend to travel any further with you, and you have already been paid to take me to Norway, you can pay my taxi fare to Newcastle, and I will make my own way back to London."

"Please yourself," he said.

While I was waiting for the taxi the pilot and his new passenger were drinking tea or coffee from a couple of dirty mugs and smoking. I went outside to stretch my legs. The mechanic or whatever he was had refuelled the plane and was on his way back to the garage cum hangar when I saw a figure in the dark make his way to the plane, open the hatch at the back of the cabin where the luggage was, and place a small package inside the plane and then shut the hatch again. As he turned to leave he saw me watching him, hesitated for a moment and then gave me a sort of salute and left.

I stood and looked first at the place to which he had disappeared and then at the plane. To say I was in a dilemma was an understatement. I reasoned the only people who knew I wasn't getting on the plane again were the pilot and me. Now I knew he hadn't called anybody to say I was leaving the plane; so I had to assume that if it was a bomb it was meant to kill me whilst flying over water to Norway. So, I did and said nothing to anybody, I just made my way to the car that had arrived at the gate by the garage cum hangar.

Shortly after that I left the field by taxi; the owner of the airfield had got the driver out of the local pub. We arrived in Newcastle upon Tyne about half an hour later and the taxi dropped me in Clayton Street. From there, I made my way to the Haymarket and rang the Harbour Master's office and asked if there were any ferries sailing to Norway that night. The lady on the other end told me that a ferry had sailed about two hours earlier and there would be nothing now until the next one in three days' time. With that little bit of information I then made my way to North Shields and towards the fish quay. When I got there, I visited a couple of bars, checking to see if I were being watched at all. It was about an hour and a couple of pints of Newcastle Breweries Blue Star beer before I heard what I was listening for. I'd finished the drink I'd ordered and I was just about to walk out when I heard that unmistakable Norwegian accent. When I looked around the place I saw this rather large man with a ginger beard. He was half standing, half leaning on the bar ordering drinks. So, with an empty glass in my hand I half staggered over to the part of the bar he was propping up. I bumped his elbow as he was about to take a drink and split some of his beer. After much apologizing and finally buying him another beer, I started to have a conversation with him.

It was some five pints of Newcastle Blue Star later when we left the bar. We then staggered along the docks bouncing off one another as drunks do until we were alongside his fishing boat. Then with much noise and laughing he invited me aboard his boat for a drink. Once below, we looked at each other and hugged each other like the long lost pals we were.

"Carl, you old so and so," I said. "Am I pleased to see you."

"How are you keeping, my friend, it's about two years since I last saw you. What have you been doing, and how is your family?"

"Oh, I'm all right, and the family is okay, but I need two things, Carl, I need a good lawyer to handle my divorce and I need to get to Norway. I need your help now, Carl, I think I'm in deep trouble. Let's have some black coffee first then I'll tell you all about it."

Once we had settled with our coffee I started to tell him what I feared.

"Carl, you remember the time you found me and the other two on the coast that day?"

"I remember it as if it was yesterday, Bill."

"Well, I hate to tell you this, but the other two are dead; well I know one is dead and I'm pretty certain the other one is too!"

"How did that happen, they looked to be switched-on guys?"

"They were, and that is what worries me. Mick was killed in a setup if ever there was one. He was supposed to be a drunk and driving a car in Singapore. This car was supposed to have been involved in an accident on the Thompson Road. Well that was bad planning on the part of the people who did it. They must have thought that all

Royal Marines were piss heads, you see not only would Mick not drink he couldn't drive either. So killing him that way was a bad mistake on their part."

"I see, but who killed him, was it the Russians out for revenge?"

"No, Carl, I think it was our lot. You see Mick and I had just done a job in Singapore, which it turned out was our silly bloody boss doing a favour for the Americans. Anyway I went off to Borneo to do some good old fashioned Commando work and left Mick in Singapore. That's another thing, the hostility I met in the unit was bloody terrible, from the CO down. I got over that and I had just settled into a good company when I got called to Brigade HQ. A helicopter picked me up from the jungle while I was out on a hearts and minds patrol. You've heard of them, hand out a few codeines and give them some water purifying tablets and a few sticky plasters. Anyway, Nobby was already in the helicopter when it picked me up to take me to Brigade, I didn't even know he was in the same unit, but he was and he was the one who told me that Mick was dead."

"So what has happened to Nobby, I thought you said they were both dead?"

"That's the problem Carl, I don't know. Remember I told you that I never trusted that bastard who wore the brown boots, the one who never did any work, in the place up north. You know the one the three of us saw fall through the ice and we presumed he had died. Well, Nobby and I were working over the border in Borneo and we came across him. He was working as a Political Officer in Sarawak, but the bastard was also working for the Indonesians. It pains me to say this but the bastard had the barrel of a gun against my forehead and I know he was going to kill me when somebody who I thought was Nobby shot him."

"So Nobby could be alive for all you know, Bill?"

"That's the rub, Carl, he was listed among the dead when the operation was completed. True to the Brigadier's promise, I was picked up by helicopter and flown out of the battle area and then back to the UK. Before I left Singapore I checked the casualty lists with the Rear Party Sergeant Major and Nobby was listed as 'missing presumed dead'. Obviously I was never able to see Nobby's body or Mick's for that matter because I was in different locations when each was supposed to have died, so I have to accept the word of the authorities, haven't I?"

"You want me to check it all out for you, Bill?"

"In a word, Carl, yes."

It was half an hour later, when the smartest and cleanest fishing boat the Tyne had ever seen, sailed and it was next stop Norway for me now. So it was on a wet dirty night I sailed from the Tyne River and headed for the North Cape of Norway. They were supposedly sailing for the Arctic cod, but it was the steel, Russian, nuclear powered type of cod they were after.

Some time later I realized that I was the fox which the Commander had set running that day. The operation as he had called it was now under way and smart as I thought I was, he was at that moment just that little bit smarter. He knew that I would disregard all the orders I'd been given to carry out the job; he knew that I would go my own sweet way and that I'd do the job as I saw fit!

We had been at sea for some six or seven hours when Carl said I could go on deck and help them if I liked. "We have had a call from your coast guard and they have asked all shipping in the North Sea to keep a look out for the wreckage of a small plane. It looks as if a plane has gone down somewhere between Newcastle and Norway early this morning. The Mayday call was received from an unidentified small aircraft just before first light, a couple of minutes before it ditched in the North Sea."

Listening to the radio that morning, I couldn't help wondering if the aircraft that had ditched was the same one on which I'd travelled from London to Newcastle the day before? When I went up on deck, I got one or two strange looks from a couple of the crew. Still I decided I could live with that. Perhaps I would end up over the side if I caused too much of a stir among them. So I spent most of my time when I was on deck pretending to look for any aircraft wreckage.

It was getting lighter each day now as we sailed north, until on the third day after leaving North Shields it stayed light for the full twenty-four hours. It was then as we rounded the North Cape, that Roald, the skipper of the boat, decided to do a trawl for some four hours. After all, that is what fishing boats are supposed to do, isn't it. I think he only did it because he probably knew he was being watched from the depths by some submarine belonging to either the East or the West. Anyway, I just went below out of the way. I was no fisherman, although I think I was starting to smell like one, but I wasn't alone. Mind you I didn't believe very many of the crew members were fishermen either. Radar operators, sonar operators and wireless operators yes, but fishermen, no way.

It was some six days after we had sailed out of the Tyne and the boat was 'pretend fishing' off the Varanger Fjord. The boat had been there for a few hours when it developed trouble with the engine. Immediately this happened I got my kit together and had a chat with Roald and Carl. It would be best if I were not observed by too many of the people in Kirkenes when I went ashore. Kirkenes was the small port in which they were going to try to repair the engine, which had developed this sudden and unexpected trouble. Kirkenes was also the best stepping-off point for me to make my way into Russia.

As soon as the boat arrived in Kirkenes the skipper tied up alongside two other boats which were already in the port. When I say port, it was more like just a jetty with a small right angle bit at the end. This was nestled in between the headland which was to the north of the bay and the mainland to the south. We had only just finished tying up when what looked like the local mayor, lawman, customs officer or whatever, came trotting along the jetty to the boat. He spoke to Roald, who invited him aboard.

As he waddled over the two boats already tied up I made my way below decks trying to act as naturally as possible, as if I were an old hand on the boat. As I'd already prepared my gear earlier, I collected the two bags and made my way aft. I came back on deck near the stern. When I did Carl was there; he took one of my bags and I had the other and we made our way across the other two boats and climbed on to the jetty.

We had just picked up the gear and were about to walk away, when the official looking person came out of the bridge with Roald and seeing us he asked, "What are you two doing?"

Carl told him, "We are going to get some bits of pipe mended and we will be back as quickly as we can," adding as an afterthought. "Time spent ashore in this

Godforsaken place is wasted money to us. We need to be back out at sea as fast as we can get."

With that the man climbed down the ladder behind the bridge and made his way below decks talking to Roald as he went.

Carl and I then hurried as if we were on an urgent mission. We reached the end of the jetty and went into what looked like a workshop of sorts. More like a home workshop than anything else. There was a bloke in the place whom Carl knew and when he was satisfied there were only the three of us there he pulled two lengths of copper piping from under his coat, each of which had a split in it. He asked the bloke, "Can you braze these two lengths of copper piping for us?"

Grinning, the man said he could, but it would take at least half an hour. "Fine, we'll stretch our legs whilst we are ashore, then once the pipes are mended we will be off to sea again. Don't want to miss the cod," he said.

Then we walked around the equipment in the workshop and out of the rear door. We walked the half mile or so up the slope to the rear and into the woods. The climb was steep but it wasn't long before I got my landlubber's legs back and started to feel good as we climbed the hill. We went into the woods for perhaps twenty yards or so and I said to Carl, "We should wait here a moment."

Carl looked at me as we sat against a couple of tree trunks and watched the town. "Did you know, Bill, we are thinking of moving our operation up here? We shall be getting rid of that pompous official if we do. Roald says we should be established here by next summer."

"Fine, Carl, and who's going to replace Mr Pomp and Circumstance, then?"

"I will probably get my sister Helga!"

I looked at him for a while and then said, "I don't seem to remember you having a sister?" For the next forty minutes or so we just chatted about things in the past. Carl again asked me, "Give it all up, Bill; come and join us. You know you belong with us, your father's job in the UK ended when he died. All debts have been paid, so come back home to Scandinavia, Bill; you will be better off with us."

We were both silent for a while and neither of us made any move to speak. Instead we just sat there with our backs against the trees; everything seemed just quiet and peaceful. There was no sign of anybody following us and I was now satisfied that all was as right as it would ever be.

So after a few more minutes I told Carl, "You should be on your way back friend." As we shook hands I looked him straight in the eye and said, "Carl, this trip is bad, it has stunk from the word go. This time I may need your help to get out. The whole bloody setup gives me bad vibes. I'm certain I am being set up and I could lose it all this time."

"You'll make it my friend, you always have in the past, and you will also make it this time, so don't worry!"

As he turned to go back to the workshop to collect the pipes we had left I said, "If, and this is important Carl, anybody ever asks you if you have seen me, for your own safety you must say no. You must deny you have ever met me or even know me; your life may depend on it. Thank Roald for me and tell him the same. Those bastards in London must never know I came this way. It could jeopardize your work here and that is the last thing I want to happen as I may need you to help me one day."

All For A King's Shilling

Without saying a word, Carl nodded and made his way down the hillside and back to his boat in the port.

While he made his way back I stayed there for another three hours until long after the boat had sailed. I watched it with Carl standing on the stern looking at the place where I was sitting among the trees until the boat rounded the point and disappeared. As I watched the small port for the next hour or so nothing happened to make me suspect the people in the village thought I was still ashore. The whole place seemed to go about its business as though nothing extraordinary had happened.

Satisfied all was well, I then set to and reorganized my kit into the order I would need it in my forthcoming adventure. Did I say adventure? I must be going soft in the head. Where I was going was no adventure, anything but. I took out the radio and turned it on. It seemed to be working, but without making a call I would not know. There was no chance of my doing that just yet. Not after the way things had gone so far. Anyway that was the least of my problems at the moment. According to my timetable I should have been into good old Mother Russia and be on my way out by now. For a moment I wondered what those young fools back in London were making of the old bear's 'top spy' right now, lost without trace.

Then when I was satisfied all was in order, I hoisted my gear on to my back and taking one last look at the Norwegian port of Kirkenes, I turned and headed off towards the Russian Frontier. Little did I know at the time just what I was letting myself in for or how long it would be before I ever set a foot in Norway again or in the West for that matter.

Chapter Ten
Just A Short Walk To Murmansk And Our Hole In The Ground
Russia, The Arctic 1965

Once I was shipwrecked on the Mary Loo
In the land of the Eskimo!

As I moved off, I kept the inlet on my right. The border in this part of Norway pushes out into Russia from the inlet to the coast shaped rather like a buxom woman's tit. I could cross over from the side of the inlet I was on, or I could cross over at the point where the nipple would have been. To be honest I had no idea where I was going to cross. It had been my intention to make a crossing from Norway into Finland and then from Finland into Russia. Now, having arrived so far north, I had no need to cross Finland at all.

I'd always hated crossing through Finland, I never felt safe. There was no guarantee if they caught you coming in from Norway they would not hand you over to the Russians anyway. In fact you could arrive in Russia a damned sight quicker than you had planned and under very unfavourable conditions. So when I'd decided to leave the fishing boat at Kirkenes once I knew we were putting in there, I'd told Carl I would leave the boat there and I needed his help in getting off without drawing any attention to myself. It had been my belief at the time that Carl didn't know exactly what I was up to at first, but he would have to have been the thickest agent in the world not to have guessed I was on my way into Russia, knowing the people I worked for. In the end I'd told him everything as I believed I would need his help soon, but I hoped no ill would befall him over his association with me, or on any trip he would have to make into Russia on my behalf.

After I had been going for a couple of hours, I heard some voices out in the forest to my right front. As I believed I was now close to the border, I would have to take it easy from then on. The most likely source of the voices would be the Norwegian border guards, or they could be foresters. So from this moment on I decided I should move very carefully forward and with caution. My aim was to get over the border as soon as I possibly could. As I saw it, the sooner I was out of the border area the better.

All For A King's Shilling

With this in mind I kept the voices to my right front and just kept moving carefully and surreptitiously past the voices. If I kept on the track I was on I figured that our paths would eventually meet.

After about half an hour of this I realised that the voices were if anything moving away from me! They were moving away at about the same speed I was trying to close with them. I stopped for a moment and listened and sure enough the voices were getting fainter. They were also still moving to my right front, in a south easterly direction. Well, I thought, they could be Norwegian border guards, or they could be bloody Russians. Whoever they were, they were steadily making their way towards the border.

I decided to follow them for a little longer and if they were Russians, then perhaps I could slip over the border behind them. Better than trying to cross not knowing where they were. Having made my decision I hoisted my rucksack on to my back and took off after them. This time I increased my pace, and after about ten minutes of steady walking I suddenly realized that the voices were getting louder, but more to the point, closer. As I moved forward I slowed down dramatically, even so I had difficulty and I just managed to stop myself from walking into them, another few steps and I would have been in the circle with them.

They had stopped and two of them were lighting a fire. They were in a group just on the other side of the trees I was standing behind. If one of them decided to go behind a tree to have a pee, it was very likely he would walk right into me, or worse still, pee on me. Realizing the danger I was in, I spent the next ten minutes trying to back off to a more safe position without making the slightest noise. A very difficult task under the circumstances, I might add. The other thing which struck me, now I was this close, they were talking in Russian, yet they were all dressed as Norwegian border guards.

Not that I could make out what they were talking about. At that precise moment in time, I was too bloody interested in getting further back before they spotted me. It crossed my mind that I might just be over the border. Then I thought, it can't be, I had always had it drummed into me in so many briefings that the fence ran all the way from the Gulf of Finland to the eastern side of the Veranger Fjord. Since leaving Kirkenes, I had not come across any bloody wire fence, or any other signs of an international border.

After a great deal of sweat and adrenalin I managed to get myself into a clump of broken branches and settled into a heap of pine needles under them. Once I had eased my rucksack off my back I gently rummaged around the top pocket for something to eat. All I had in there to eat were a couple of bars of Dutch chocolate which Carl had given me on the fishing boat. As I settled down to munch them I looked at my watch and it said 10.30. Well, I thought, is it 10.30 a.m. or 10.30 p.m.? I just did not know that I had forgotten to set the outer bezel of the dial. Cursing myself for being so stupid, I settled down to go over the recent events since I'd reluctantly left Plymouth. My marriage was falling to bits; but I knew if I started to dwell on that I'd lose it altogether and I put it completely out of my mind right there and then.

It seemed as if the whole episode was unreal. Ever since I had words with the pilot of the light aircraft back in England things had left the rails a little bit. Nevertheless, if it had not been for my past connections with Carl and his organization then I'd probably have still been wandering around the north of England. Still, I thought, I've got this far with no great hardship. If those fools back in London have lost my trail then things may just keep going smoothly and I will be home in no time at all. What a bloody understatement that turned out to be.

Tiredness and the fresh air up here in the Arctic Circle must have overtaken me because I fell asleep for a while, but I was brought back to reality with a start. As I woke up I could hear some voices and they were very close; this I deduced in my sleepiness because the voices were so damned loud. First I located the direction of the voices, which was to my right rear. Next I very carefully eased my head round to see who it was that was talking. The voices were Russian, which I knew from past experience meant nothing in this part of the world. Then I saw them, sitting not ten feet away from me were two border guards both wearing Norwegian uniforms; one was an NCO and the other an ordinary guard, whatever rank they were.

I thought, oh shit! I'm snookered now; I don't think I can make a run for it from here. If I so much as move any part of my body the chances are they will hear it and be upon me before I could even get to my feet, so I just froze. How long I lay there I have no idea but it must have been for some considerable time as I tried to listen to their conversation. Then at last it dawned on me what they were talking about and my ears pricked up and the excitement of what they were saying sent my mind into a whirl.

I heard the NCO say, "The English agent we were told to look out for this last week has still not appeared. The KGB had expected him to try and get in through Finland, but so far the Finns have not seen anybody resembling him crossing any part of Finland."

"Rumour has it the agent was killed in an aeroplane crash some time last week. It seems his plane went down in the North Sea, sir."

"I cannot understand why we are still out looking for this spy if the KGB now believes he is dead!" concluded the officer.

As I sat there trying to take in what these two were saying my first thought was that perhaps all this would now work to my benefit. Then after thinking it out I concluded that perhaps they had spotted me while I was asleep. I had probably been snoring again and given myself away and now they were baiting me. There was no doubt I was the English agent they were talking about and I didn't know what to make of it. So again I did the only thing I could do, I just lay there completely still with my pistol ready to shoot as many as I could before they got me, but I'd rather not do that as it would only complicate things. I was still in Norway. All the time my mind was working overtime; how could two Russian border guards know all about me and my mission, not only to Russia, but more important, how I'd intended to enter their bloody country.

While all this garbage was going through my mind one of them said, "Thank Lenin this is the last night we will spend out here wandering around on the Norwegian side of the border; this is just asking for trouble. It was okay when we were in Finland, but Norway is a different kettle of fish altogether."

So, I thought, I was right, I'm still in Norway. They must want me badly if they are prepared to cross over into Norway. As I lay there I started to put a plan together; perhaps, just perhaps they would lead me through the border. I reasoned that they

All For A King's Shilling

must have places to get through the wire without arousing suspicion just the same as we have in our defensive positions. It would be wise, I thought, if I were to stick with these lads. They could just save me a lot of time and a lot of problems, because crossing this stretch of the border was always going to be the worst part of the whole operation.

Because of what I'd heard I stayed awake from that moment on. I was too frightened to go to sleep again anyway. As long as they were near me I knew that if I so much as moved a muscle I would be dead, of that I was certain. So being the coward I am I just lay there as rigid as I could get myself to be; there then followed one of the longest four hours I have ever spent in my life, longer even than the middle watch on the main gate in Stonehouse Barracks.

It was four o'clock when an officer who seemed to be in charge came to collect them. He said, "It's time we left, lads, the local KGB has informed us that it is unlikely the man we were looking for will be coming this way now."

"So they have at last come to their senses?" the NCO said.

The officer who had just arrived then said. "I think the KGB has at last realized that the agent we have been looking for must have been the one who was killed in the plane crash over the North Sea. There were two people in it and they think he must have been one of them, they were both killed. I do not want any of our men to be caught on this side of the border when the Norwegians come along the fence again, so let's get a move on."

With that the two men picked up their gear and followed him back to the area they had been in when I nearly walked into them.

Once they had gone I breathed a sigh of relief but it was then I discovered my damned legs had gone to sleep on me. Just as well I didn't have to make a run for it, I thought; I would have fallen flat on my face in more ways than one. As it was I spent the time they took to pack everything up and remove all traces of the fire they had made, by rubbing my legs to get the circulation back into them. They were up and moving very quickly and I let them get out of sight and I watched all this, making sure they had not left anybody behind as an ambush party for me, that is. After a respectable time had elapsed I got to my feet and followed them.

As I did, I could still hear them about a hundred yards in front of me. They were not moving in a tactical manner any more, they were more like a group of Squaddies out for a stroll in a country lane. Chatting away and having general discussions. Something which had me thinking, that perhaps they were not too worried about the Norwegian border guards. As before, I was too far behind them to make out any of the things they were talking about. We carried on like this for some two hours. they were not making fast progress, but it was a steady progress in a south easterly direction, with me tagging along behind them, rather like a frightened deer who knew he was making the mistake of his life. I was beginning to understand what the remark 'death wish' meant. The sun was still high in the sky and I'd now completely lost track of whether it was night or day.

Later they stopped and had a meal. I do not think they cooked anything, they just stopped and as I got closer I could tell they were eating. Their conversation was stilted as it can only be when members of the group are eating. I decided on the same; I pulled some digestive-type, high-protein biscuits from one of the side pockets of my rucksack and just sat there munching them. As I ate, I kept my ears and eyes peeled just in case they tried to creep up on me as I sat there with my back against the thickest tree I could find. Nothing happened and after about an hour they started off again. This time they struck out due east. This was it, I thought, we were off to the border and over into good old Mother Russia.

The going was faster now as if they were in a hurry to get home. Some half an hour later, we arrived at the border. The reason that I keep saying 'we' is, I suppose, because I had latched on to this group and I was now considering myself one of them, but now I started to move with caution. From the increase in noise and chattering I believed they had met up with some other Russian border guards. The voices which I could hear now sounded as if there were two groups talking, exchanging experiences and swapping stories as all servicemen the world over do when they meet up with comrades. So, I just kept moving along behind them all nerves working, picking up all vibrations, sounds and also lack of them every now and again. By this time I was tuned into them and I knew the instant they stopped.

Slowly this time I moved forward very, very carefully indeed remembering my last near encounter with them. Now I needed to get a better look at what was going on, how many there were and what they were doing. Eventually I came to the edge of the trees and there before me was a gap in the trees reaching to the left and the right, as far as I could see. There was a rather fearsome wire fence which ran the full length of the gap as far each way as you could see. The group I had followed had stopped near the fence and was talking to another group on the other side of it.

The two groups were asking one another what had happened. The ones on the Russian side wanted to know if the hunt was still on, or had the KGB given up at last? Then the group over this side of the wire seemed to think it was all a wild goose chase.

It was then I heard one of the leaders say, "I think we are wasting our time, Comrades. This Englishman was killed in a plane crash over the North Sea some days ago according to the latest KGB information. It was obvious he would not be coming to invade Good Old Mother Russia after all."

At this they all started laughing. They also said some rather uncomplimentary things about their bosses in Moscow. All the time I was only about fifteen to twenty feet from the ones I had been following. The men on the Russian side of the fence were the ones who interested me; I thought they are the ones who will open the fence if anybody does. The two groups stood chatting through the wire for about fifteen minutes, with the usual type of service banter flying between the two groups.

Then the commander on the Russian side asked, "Well, my fine men, are you ready to come through the wire yet?"

The reply from this side was, "Yes we have clearance to return now."

The officer, the one whom I had seen earlier, then told the group I'd been following to load their kit on to their backs and follow him. He then strode off in a southerly direction along the wire. His pace was faster this time and I had a hard job keeping up with them as I had to move through the trees while they were in the open and didn't have the obstructions which I did. Before long I was starting to get a bit desperate trying to keep up with them, when again they stopped.

All For A King's Shilling

While I stood there trying to catch my breath I noticed that the ones on the Norwegian side of the fence were passing through a gap in the wire. To enable me to get a better look at the gap I took my glasses out and when I looked at the fence I was just in time to see the men from the other side refastening the wire. For the next few minutes I looked at the post they were working on; I looked long and hard. Hadn't I just seen it open? One would never have believed there was an opening there, I could hardly take my eyes off the post. Now I was starting to wonder how I would find the place once they had gone. It was then I saw that the ground had been disturbed at the foot of the post. There was just enough to mark the place where they had gone through the fence. So all I had to do now was to wait until they went so I then settled down into a more comfortable position.

For a while I sat and watched them; they spent the next half hour trying to contact somebody on their radios. Both patrols had a go, first the one that had been waiting by the wire, then the one I had been following. They were having no joy whatsoever. Well, I thought, the Yanks and our lot are not the only ones with duff radios. It pleased me to see them having the same problems with their radios as we have. They eventually gave it all up as I would have done and moved off down their side of the fence in a southerly direction. As they moved off, I slowly got my gear together and studied the ground by the wire and also the direction in which they had gone. I knew that once I came out of cover I would be fully committed to this mission. There would be no turning back then.

Right at that moment in time I could still turn around and make my way back to England. I might have some explaining to do, but I could walk away from it right now. With that thought flashing through my head I made my decision, I took one look back the way I had come, shrugged my shoulders, hoisted my rucksack on to my back and stepped out into the open. When I was fully in the open, I stood still for a full minute or so listening to the sounds of the forest and then I walked deliberately up to the place where I had seen them go through. There I stopped at the wire and thought you will look a right 'pratt' to anybody watching if you cannot open this little lot.

I looked at the pole on the side of the gap. I had seen the guard fasten the wire to this; sure enough, the pole had a split right down it from top to bottom. From this I deduced the half to my right would come away from the other half; so I undid the three fastening wires I could see and gave it a tug. Up it came and the gap in the wire was open, but the half of the pole I was holding was bloody heavy. Then without a second look and mainly because I thought I was going to drop the bloody thing, I stepped through. Once through it was a hell of a struggle, but in the end I managed to close the fence behind me. As I turned away from the fence I stood still; now that I was in Russia I half expected to be arrested there and then. Nothing happened, so I walked straight into the trees on the Russian side of the border and turned to look back at the fence. As I stood looking I was just about to turn away from the fence when a bird settled on the top wire and was instantly fried. The shock of what I had just witnessed was so great that I nearly dropped dead in my boots.

Immediately I turned from the fence and made my way further into the trees, where I stopped and threw my rucksack on the ground. The sweat was rolling down my face and then it dawned on me just why the patrols had been calling so insistently on their radios to say they were through the wire and to turn the power on again.

If they had been able to get through on their radios the first time while I'd been watching them, then I would be dead now. Those bastards back in London had not said the wire was live; I'd a bone to pick with them when I got back. More important now, I thought, was the quicker I got away from here the better. So the order was, head down and go, go, go, or you may just not see another day, even though days don't dawn up here, at this time of the year.

So I did just that; up went my rucksack high on to my back, then with my head down away I went. I didn't care too much if I were careful or not now. My feelings were that I just wanted to be away from that fence. There was also a lot of anger to be worked off, anger I was feeling toward those sons of bitches in London. Some of my best thinking is done while I am working off the energy which anger gives me. After about half an hour of crashing through the trees I stopped. The realization had hit me right between the eyes; it was just possible those guards had intended me to get through the wire in the first place.

With the realization of that scenario, my thoughts were then off on a tangent, thinking was it the old bear who had set me up or his young bum boys. The ones he told to brief me on the border crossing. Or had they genuinely not known the wire was live? One thing was certain, I should have known the wire was live, but I could not remember at that moment anybody mentioning it. It would all come back to me as time passed; have no fear of that, my young whipper snappers. I'll sort you bastards out when I get back and then Brown and his friend the Commander are in for it.

At this point I steadied my walking down to a more realistic pace; I thought it is no good going off like that. You will only get yourself killed, or even worse, get yourself arrested. It's a funny situation when getting arrested is worse than getting yourself killed. Still, I'd never be able to go back and face them if I was killed now, would I? With that, I adopted a more realistic approach to my situation. First, I decided to stop and make some plans and I needed to take a long hard look at what had happened to date. Something I'd tried earlier but it had all gone squidgy in my mind. Also I needed some rest and something to eat so while I was trekking through the trees I was on the lookout for some place to lie up for a day or so, while I tried to sort everything out and put it all into perspective. I wondered if everything that had happened to me so far was in fact all by accident. Or was it planned? But I was not convinced and I was starting to get a little paranoid about it all. For some reason I believed that Nobby's and Mick's deaths would be resolved by this little jaunt, but now, well I don't know, perhaps I was too tired and just dreaming it all.

For some reason which I could never explain, I had taken an immense dislike to the pilot and I left the light plane bringing me to Norway at Newcastle and walked away. It seemed that the plane had since crashed as it was on its second leg from Newcastle to Norway over the North Sea. Or so I was led to believe from the news on the fishing boat's radio as I crossed in the fishing boat and now listening to the Russians, if I were to understand them correctly. The person who had placed the package on the plane at Newcastle had given me a salute when he saw me and I'd wondered if the package had been equipment for me or not. Now, of course, it could possibly have been an explosive device and they had not counted on my leaving it. So my leaving the plane and then its subsequent crash, could that have been an act of God, or an act of deliberate sabotage? The answer to that question seemed to be

All For A King's Shilling

that the events elsewhere must have led them to believe that I was somewhere in the bottom of the North Sea. I bet I knew one man who didn't believe that for one minute; and he would move heaven and earth to get my body up from my supposedly watery grave. So, now the game was really afoot as he used to say.

Interestingly after all that I had found it easy to get to Norway, too bloody easy. I had arrived in Norway via the fishing boat which just happened to be able to reach the Tyne in time to help me and also just happened to have Carl aboard. After my telephone call I had expected that I would be able to make a contact in Newcastle, but I was a little surprised to see it was Carl. Was that luck, or was it string-pulling, covering all eventualities? Were Carl and his organization involved or was it pure luck that he was there? Now who was it who made Carl's luck?

Next I'd come across a Russian patrol on the 'Norwegian side' of the border who had just happened to lead me to an opening in the wire. The same patrol then had trouble calling their HQ to say they had come back through the wire. Then after I managed to get through the wire and refasten it, the next living thing to touch it was fried. So, what the hell was going on; and how did the Russians know that I had left London on that silly little plane anyway? Did the person only put the package on the plane at Newcastle after he knew I'd decided to leave it? Was it to help me or was I the target?

So what? I ask myself, is it all luck, good or bad; or am I being manipulated? Was I watched when I came through the wire, and then the call to 'electrify' the wire put through once I was clear? If so it looked as if I had some big, big problems, perhaps it was time I disappeared for a while. Then we'd see just what came out of the woodwork, as they tried locating me again. With that in mind I jostled my rucksack higher on to my back and headed off in an easterly direction, this time with caution. Eyes wide open and ears like bloody radars.

After I'd been going for some time, my nerves all on edge and I might add a very worried little agent, I heard Russian voices again in the trees off to my right. Once more I stopped for a while to find out in which direction they were moving, or even if they were moving. It took about two minutes to realize they were not moving at all. So I scraped a small hole near the base of a pine and put my rucksack into it and recovered it with pine needles. Then I moved off in the direction of the voices. It took a little while to reach them and I had to cover the last two hundred yards on my belly.

When I reached the area I believed the voices were coming from I edged my way to the foot of a pine tree which was on the edge of a clearing. There in the middle of the clearing was a wooden hut, the type that the Americans call log cabins; the Russians call them dachas, to the rich in England they are just known as garden sheds. Some of the voices were coming from the inside of the hut. How many people were inside I did not dare to hazard a guess, but outside there were two men.

Now these two men were dressed as people in this part of the world always dress, more for warmth and comfort than style. All their clothes were what I call homespun, homemade to be exact. Most of the stuff was elk or deerskin joined by those big stitches one sees in clothes of the American Frontier. Their boots looked to be good though, much too good quality for my liking, they looked out of place. While I lay there just watching this homely situation, I felt something was wrong. I did not know what it was that was wrong. The boots were part of it though, but also their voices and their conversation. Lying there, looking at them and listening to their chatter I had the feeling that it was all false; everything that I was watching seemed to be forced. It just seemed to me that they were chatting too much. Forcing the conversation along and trying too hard to be natural, as it were. Their voices were not steady as they would be in a normal conversation between two friends. It was more like watching a play where the actors are not yet comfortable with their lines or their timing.

Because of my unease with the situation I thought I'd better have a look around this place and slowly I made my way back to where I had left my rucksack. Having got my gear back together and once more hoisted it on to my back, I then took a last look around. Satisfied, I moved back from the place I was in and headed to the east and north of the hut and clearing. Once on the move I went very quietly and very steadily round the hut in an extended circle. All my past stealth training was called upon as I moved through the trees. Stopping, observing all the ground, then when satisfied, moving to a new position to have another look around, then moving on again. Each time I stopped, I paid particular attention to the ground between me and the hut, using my glasses each time to check every bush, tree trunk and fold in the ground, before I moved on.

The whole thing was getting through to me, and I was starting to think I was being paranoid about it, when suddenly I saw a slight movement off to my left front. The excitement of that movement sent the adrenaline racing through my body, all nerves tingling, eyes and ears on full alert. Again with great difficulty because of the excitement, I settled down behind the tree I was standing beside. Gently, so as not to do anything at all which would give my position away, I raised my glasses and slowly searched the area in which I thought I had seen the movement. Nothing; I thought you are getting too bloody jumpy mate. Then I caught a glimpse of movement again and then it happened once more. This time I was on to it with my glasses right away.

It took a little time, but at last I could just see the heels and two soles of a pair of Russian army boots. So, I thought. He, whoever he was, was keeping watch on the hut. I lay there, it must have been for the best part of half an hour, just watching him. The man never moved a muscle again. He's good, I thought, but I wonder what made him move before. Then he moved again; fascinated I watched as inch by inch he moved his right arm slowly under his shoulder and then down along his side. Eventually he reached back along his right thigh and ever so slowly put his hand into the pocket on his right trouser leg.

I was absolutely fascinated watching him, wondering what he was going to do. Then he slowly pulled out his hand and it had a packet of cigarettes in it. He repeated the slow and tortuous return of his hand to his chest. There, he took out a cigarette and then just as carefully lit it. Then a small cloud of blue smoke arose from the undergrowth in which he was positioned. It took him the best part of ten minuets to do this. So I must have seen him lighting a cigarette earlier, or perhaps it was the cloud of smoke coming from the undergrowth which had drawn my attention to him.

Now I really was disappointed, all that patience, lying so still all that time, only to ruin it by smoking. After watching him light his cigarette, I concluded he really was not very good at all. So with that I started to look first to his right and then his left; I was certain there would be more of them positioned around that hut. First I saw the guy on his left, and then I spotted one on his right. There was about thirty yards between each of them. Next I kept the one on his left in view, and I slowly travelled to my left. When I was behind this one I looked to his left and sure enough, there was another one. Again about thirty yards to his left.

I had seen enough; it was an ambush. I did not know if it was for me or not. The only thing I did think was who else could it be for. Then I slowly made my way off to the east, leaving them to keep their ambush in place. They seemed quite happy just to lie there smoking; why should I disturb their peace? There was no way I was going to approach any Russian habitat from now on, not without a thorough check of the area first.

How long I travelled that day I don't know, but there came a time when I had to rest because now I was really hungry and tired. What was more, it had started to rain about an hour after I had left the ambush position.

My clothes were wet and I was now very miserable; the rain was not all that heavy but the water from my hat had now started to drip down the inside of my collar. Of all the things I hate when out in the open it is the rain trickling down the inside of my collar. Rain I can stand, but when it trickles down the inside of my collar, and the rest of my body is dry, then I get irritated to hell!

Time I started to look for somewhere to get some rest and sleep now, I thought, I've had enough excitement for one day. Yet it wasn't long before luck popped up again and I found what I was looking for. A rather large fir tree, that had fallen down probably in a storm and struck against another smaller tree as it fell, had thus created a rather large type of shelter very much like a wigwam laid on its side. I had a good look round trying not to disturb too much of the ground covering of pine needles. Once I had satisfied myself I had not left any tracks, I moved in under the tree and had a look. It was quite dark inside and it looked rather like the inside of a large animal's rib cage. Inside I made myself a bed of soft dry undergrowth, and I used my rucksack as a pillow, rolled my oilskin over me like a blanket and within no time at all I was sound asleep.

For years I have always been able to dictate to my body how long it should sleep. Over my service career, I have always been able to say to myself, as I go to sleep, that I'll wake up at, say five o'clock, and sure enough I am awake at five o'clock. This time I said nothing to myself and because of that omission I think I slept the clock round. It must have been a long time for when I awoke I felt fully refreshed, but I was bloody starving. With only one bar of chocolate left my next priority would be to get some food. I ate the chocolate and packed my oilskins away in my rucksack, then I sat for a while studying the surrounding woods for any sign of movement, noise or anything which might warn me of troubles.

Then after about half an hour of this I was satisfied I was alone apart from the animals which I'd heard or seen scurrying around. As I watched them I realized that there was not a lot of game around here and I thought food might just be a little scarce. Again I picked up my rucksack, hoisted it on to my back and set off to find a substantial breakfast, supper, or whatever meal was due at that time of day. It was no longer raining, so that was better, the sun was in the sky and things were looking good except that it was bloody cold; even so I had a good feeling, and I was keeping an eye out for something to eat. The way I felt at the time, I would settle for some berries;

meat would be better, but anything with protein would be better, but that could come later, not much later, but later.

After I had been going for about an hour, I saw a slight movement to my right and I stopped dead in my tracks. There in the grass not ten feet from me was a baby elk-like creature. Perhaps baby elk was not the right description, as it was about two months old at best. There was perhaps enough meat on him or her to keep me going for the next few days at least. I was getting ready to belt it over the head when I heard some noises off to my left. For a second I hesitated and the baby elk took off like a bloody jack rabbit. It ran right through my legs and I went down, arse over tit. Just like a raw recruit on his first venture into the field. As I fell, I heard a shot ring out and at the same second a bullet struck the tree behind me, then a voice shouted, "I got him." I thought shit, that bastard was firing at me.

I lay there for a second, wondering what to do, and then I said to myself, 'Time you weren't here, old pal,' so I then crawled off as fast as my bloody arms and legs would let me. Next, I heard another voice shout, "You are a stupid bastard, that was a baby elk that you shot at." As I crawled away, I could still hear the argument going on. When I thought I was far enough from them, I was up, and I was off like a bloody jack rabbit myself; at that moment I felt empathy for the young elk; I even decided that I would only eat young elk as a final resort. Caution then went out of the window in the hope that whoever they were or if anybody was in charge of them, they would think I was a deer, elk or whatever it was they called them up here, running away. Now I knew how a hunted animal really felt, I certainly felt like one right then. What was more, there was no way I would ever hurt a deer again in my life. That little thing, that baby elk, had saved my life.

For the rest of the day I just kept going, stopping for nothing. It had been a narrow escape I'd had. All thoughts of food had long since left me, when some hours later I stumbled across a small hut. It looked to be overgrown and I was certain there had been nobody there for quite some time, years I would have said. Because I had stumbled into the open before I saw the damned thing I just stood there and had a good look around, but I could see no trace of anything or anybody. No sign of any ambush as at the last hut, so after standing outside the hut like a spare prick at a wedding I eventually picked up enough courage and went straight up to the door. The door was locked, but not with a very substantial lock. So as they say, 'A lock only keeps an honest man out', in I went.

The place was about twelve feet square on the inside and I had a good look around. It had a small cot-type of bed in one corner and a small pot-bellied stove in the middle of the place. Three of the walls had some cupboards on them, the fourth wall had a door in the middle of it. I had a look at the cupboards and to my surprise they had some tinned things in them. One of them had some flour and oats along with some resident crawling things. There was some coffee of doubtful origin. Next I had a look at the bed which had a straw mattress on it, and a couple of blankets laid on the top of it. Somehow I got the feeling the hut was a bolt-hole for some Russian. Perhaps it was a summer hunting cabin but not a winter one. There was no way you could spend the winter in this cabin, unless you were very desperate, or nuts; two categories that fitted me perfectly.

All For A King's Shilling

I do not know why I did it, but I pulled the bed away from the wall. There was a small flat package against the wall, behind which there was a small door. Once I had pulled the door open and peered inside I saw there was a small overgrown trench leading out toward the trees. So, I lay down and crawled along it. After about twenty-five yards or so I reached the end of the trench; it just led out into the trees. It was a straightforward bolt-hole. I turned round and made my way back along the trench and into the inside of the cabin. Once I was in, I closed the door and pushed the bed back against the wall. Then I had a look at the food in the tins and jars. I had no intention of lighting a fire here, as I was not keen to attract any visitors. I'm afraid it would have to be a cold meal for now. Hot meals would have to wait until I'd reached safer surroundings.

Next I selected some cans which I took to hold food that would be edible when cold. Tinned fruit, cooked meats and the like. When I was ready I had a meal of the Russian equivalent of good old bully beef, and tinned peaches. There was nothing to drink other than water, so I washed the lot down with a mug of cold water. Then I sorted myself four days' meals out of the remaining tins. Two cold meals and one hot meal for the four days; these I packed into my rucksack, which was now bursting at the seams. It was also getting to be a little on the heavy side. Still I was prepared to put up with the weight if it saved me having to become a hunter gatherer each day.

After I'd eaten and packed everything I had selected into my rucksack, I took the empty cans and a couple of empty bottles I had found outside, and set up a small warning system. I knew the whole thing could be set off by an animal, or just as easily by a man. It would make no difference if it was man or beast, I would be on my way out of the back trench just as quickly. When I had completed this I sat in the hut to see what was in the package I had found behind the bed. When I opened it, I got a bit of a surprise. It contained a lot of sheets of paper. They were all filled with writing in a hand which I did not know. Best of all, though, was a map of the Murmansk area of Russia, south of any area I had ever worked in before.

After I had studied the map for some time, I traced the coast as far to the west as it went. Unless I was badly mistaken, it ended on the Norwegian border. Next I traced the border south. As I did, I noticed that every mile or so there was a mark on the border fence. Perhaps I had found a map marking all the gates in the fence, like the one I had come through. Now I tried to estimate the distance I had travelled since leaving the fence. In the end I realised that I had no idea whatsoever of where I was. The gap in the fence I had come through, and the position of the first hut and also the position of this hut I was in, were all Double Dutch of course. There was no way I could be sure, but I had an idea that I was at one of three pencil marks on the map; which one I was at was, of course, a toss-up. Satisfied, I finished studying the map and lay down on the bed to try and get some sleep. As I did, I wondered who would want or use a map so marked.

When I awoke the sun was high in the sky and the weather looked to be fine again. I debated with myself about lighting the fire, but decided against it. Instead, I had another tin of fruit, and then hoisted my load, which was considerably heavier now, on to my back and left the hut. After studying the map, I walked off in a southerly direction. Once I was in the trees I stopped and turned to watch the hut for some thirty minutes. At the end of this time nobody had appeared, but most important, nobody had set off to follow me, so I turned and headed off towards the south trying to reach a point south of Murmansk.

Now I timed myself very carefully in my pace and movement and also the direction in which I was travelling. It was time I got a hold of myself and stopped wandering around like a bloody headless chicken as I now felt I'd been doing these last few days. My intention had been to go south for about eight hours, then I would stop and try to make a meal of sorts and once I had eaten, I would walk south for a further four hours. It was then my intention to turn due east and walk until I reached the north/south road from Murmansk. I knew that if I were south of Murmansk I couldn't miss it. Oh, yes, and who said that?

To my surprise it took me three days to reach a road and at first I was not sure if the road I was standing beside was in fact the Murmansk road. The trees on the western side where I was standing were thick and gave me good cover, but I had to get across the road to see what was over the other side of the trees opposite. At last I moved in closer to the edge of the trees to see the standard of the road. I was a little perturbed to see it was not to the standard I would have expected the main road south of Murmansk to have been. As I waited in the trees to check there was no movement on the ether side of the road, it looked as if everything was clear and I was about to get up and make a dash for it, when I heard a train alarm sounding, the sort of hooting noise all diesel engines the world over seem to make. So I decided I would stay where I was for a little while longer or until I knew just where the railway was.

It was not long before I heard the train moving slowly along some railway tracks further on through the trees on the other side of this dirt track. I decided I had hesitated long enough so once more I had a good look to the left and right of the dirt track as in no stretch of the imagination could it be called a road. When I was satisfied all was clear again I made a dash across it and into the trees on the other side. As soon as I made the trees, I moved through them to the other side where I stopped; as I'd started to do now every time that I moved, stop and see if I was being followed, stop and have a good look behind me. It meant I didn't make such good progress, but I felt a lot safer. As it was, this time nothing happened to make me think I was being followed. So I turned again to give the view to my front all my attention. I needed to know what this railway was all about.

When I had come to the edge of the woods which were about two hundred yards or so wide, there before me was a single track railway and a rather large estuary. As I looked, my heart sank; although I thought I knew this place, I also knew I was miles off course. The place I was at was north of Murmansk and I needed to be miles further south. It was going to take me at least two or even maybe four days, to go far enough south from here to a point where I could safely pass Murmansk, always providing they had not built any more installations to the south of the port.

To say I felt a little despondent at the time would have been an understatement. Coming all this way, virtually blind, only to find that I was now too far to the north, was only to be expected, I suppose. Of course, I had hoped I was way south of the port; instead I think I was even north of their base at Polyarnyy. My spirits were not the best as I moved a little way back into the woods and found a clump of trees to hide in. Once in, I settled down to have a rest, a little food, and I hoped, to think things out. For the first time since leaving Kirkenes, I decided to light a small fire. By using dry pine needles to get it going and some larger dry twigs once it was on the go, I hoped to keep any smoke to a minimum.

Once I had the fire going and there was no smoke, I opened two tins of meat and set them on the fire. All the time I kept my ears peeled for any noises while I cooked the tins of meat. Once the meat was cooked, I ate it straight from the tins. After I had finished, I filled the tins with water and heated them. I made a drink of coffee with one and had a wash and shave with the other. I must say I felt a lot better after that, even if I was bleeding like a stuck pig after I had finished shaving. At least the mosquitoes would no longer have to bite me to get my blood, they could just land and lick it all up.

While I had been doing my ablutions and feeding I had done some thinking. After considering all the angles, I came to the conclusion it would be just as easy to go on now as to go home. I could save myself a lot of time if I could cross the estuary instead of having to go to the south to pass Murmansk, because, once past Murmansk, I would only have to track all the way back north, which could be a very dangerous trip indeed. So, I decided now that I was fed and watered, so to say, I might as well get some rest and sleep on the whole thing. With all this going round in my head I settled down to get some sleep. Sleep was what I really needed right then, the food was lying heavy on my stomach and making me feel sleepy and in no time at all I was fast asleep. It amazed me that even though my nerves were shot to hell I still fell asleep so easily

Again I think I slept the clock round. Nothing had happened to change my plan in any way when I awoke. I was more refreshed, but that was all. I was in the same predicament, except it was about twelve hours later. The sleep must have been deep as I had not heard any more trains or been awakened by anything out of the ordinary. All seemed well, and I just sat for a while, and then decided to make myself a hot drink. My body told me I needed something hot inside me. Again I lit a small fire with very dead wood. There was no smoke to give my position away, so I felt pretty confident. The coffee I drank tasted great; it was the last of the coffee I had taken from the hut. Mosquitoes were still eating me, but I had more pressing needs on my mind right now than to worry about them.

I finally realised that my most important task now was somehow to get over this estuary. What was more, I must admit I did not fancy the long trip to the south just to find a place where I would be able to ford the river; I'd have to go bloody miles off course. Nor was I was keen to become involved with all the Naval, Army and Air Force camps to the south of Murmansk. Let alone those further north of my present position. I must have sat and pondered this for at least an hour when I heard a train coming along the railway track. With that I sparked into action, I picked up my gear and edged to the front edge of the trees. I felt that it was important I got a better look at what was passing, and in which direction it was going. It turned out to be an empty goods train moving south along the track; and the line was too straight and open for me to attempt to get aboard it, so I dropped all hope of getting a lift to the south that way.

Once the train had passed and it was just a dot in the distance I set off down the track, still heading south. I had resigned myself to the fact I would have to head south and make my way round Murmansk. The estuary was too wide for me to try and swim it; and without survival gear the coldness of the water would kill me in about thirty to forty seconds. Even if by some miracle I did make it across then I would still have to head north again in a pretty bad state of health to get to the area I needed to reach. It was the only way I could find out what had happened here. My only hope now was that the hunt for me was either still in the border area, or had been called off altogether. The latter would suit me right down to the ground. As I walked along the track, I kept my eyes and ears open as I made my way south.

A couple of times I had to deviate into the woods across the road to bypass small settlements which consisted of the odd cabin and the like and after I had travelled about three miles or so I did notice a couple of motor launches in the estuary. I presumed them to be private launches, then I remembered that not too many people in Russia were likely to have private motor launches. Not on this estuary anyway with all its secret military establishments. I decided to have a good look at them and I settled down with my binoculars to study them. While I was watching them a skiff cast off from a complex of buildings and headed out to them. As I looked on fascinated what looked to be a Naval Officer boarded one of the launches. It slipped its moorings and headed up the estuary to the north. After a second or two the penny dropped that there was a crew of some sort on the launch because the officer type guy wasn't driving the bloody thing. Hell, I thought, I'm going do-lally, surely you don't drive launches, do you?

A little while later another launch came from the south and tied up to one of the buoys; the skiff came out and another Naval Officer stepped off the launch and was taken ashore. It was then that another penny dropped; it was the harbour master's pilot station and I thanked my lucky stars I'd not gone too bloody close to it, but watching the launches heading north did set me thinking that I might just nick one if they left them unattended.

Then as I moved on I was thinking of a plan and it was forming in my mind, very slowly I must admit, but it was coming along. Subconsciously I started to look for any sign of a boat on the side of the estuary. As I walked, I thought if I could get out there and make it look as if I was fishing, then I might just have found an easy way of getting across the estuary, but there was nothing. I'd gone another couple of miles, which was just as well considering where the pilot station was, when at last I noticed what might just fit the bill. A small skiff was tied to a pole in the estuary about ten yards out. The estuary looked to be about two to three miles wide at this point and I moved from the track into the trees to see if there were any buildings around or if anybody was about. There were none which I could see. The only thing was a track leading from the road to the railway track. I had a good look past the place where the boat was tied up and there was nothing to be seen on the other side either. So, I made my way back to the boat. Still nothing as I looked out into the estuary; I saw there were no people fishing that part of the estuary. Now I had the problem of getting to the boat without getting wet; getting myself soaked at this point in the proceedings might cost me my life if things went wrong when I got out into the estuary.

I went into the trees and found myself a couple of branches about ten feet in length and about three inches in diameter. I peeled the bark off these and then I took the branches and the stripped bark to the water's edge. Once there, I set about my task and hoped to God a train would not come by. Next I used the strips of bark to tie the poles together, thus making one pole of about sixteen feet in length. When satisfied with my handiwork I waded out into the water until it was up to my knees and it was bloody cold, I can tell you.

Then the pantomime started as I tried to hook the rope tying the boat with the poles. It took me about twenty-five attempts before I finally managed, but I made it in the end. Once I had hooked it I then pulled the boat in and I was just going to let the poles go when I noticed that there were no oars or other means of propulsion on the boat, so I waded ashore to the water's edge, pulling the boat. Then I loaded my rucksack into the boat. Next I undid the bark strips I had used as bindings and put the poles into the boat, I then hoisted myself aboard. When ready, I took one of the poles and pushed the boat back out into the estuary until I felt the current take hold and the boat started to drift to the north and away from the shore. I remember thinking thank God, we were drifting north and not south. I'd hate to end up in the middle of Murmansk Harbour in this thing; I'd be the laughing stock of the Corps.

I was disturbed when I saw the boat didn't have any oars; shows how sea soldier orientated I'd become, pushing off in a boat with no oars; but I'd have given anything if there had been an outboard motor on it. What I did have was a means of crossing the estuary. Now I would not have to walk all the way round, with all the dangers that exercise would hold. With string I had in my rucksack, and one of the straps from the rucksack, I managed to tie one of the poles to the rear of the boat. Then by pushing the pole from side to side I propelled myself into the deeper waters of the estuary. After about twenty minutes of this I was some way from the shore, and I was starting to drift faster as the stronger current further out in the estuary got hold of the skiff. The current which seemed to be going out was very strong so I assumed it had just turned and I thought it could very easily turn into a potentially dangerous situation, but I was also, so knackered. I thought I would let it drift for a while and see where it took me. I thought I was wise enough not to let the ebb tide drag me out into the Arctic Ocean. What was more, I could see the bank on the other side of the estuary now; also I was approaching the Harbour Master's pilot station now.

As I let the boat drift for the next half an hour or so, I rested and I kept a good watch on the boat's position. I had no intention of ending in the bay, among the patrol boats, but I was worried about any traffic in the estuary as I had very little means of getting out of the way of any ships which might happen along. When I felt a little refreshed I started to propel the boat by use of the pole again, at an angle this time using the tide and the pole to guide me towards the other side. As I reached a point about three quarters of the way across I looked round and saw one of the fishermen I had seen earlier. He was doing the same as me but in the other direction. He gave a wave and a shout, so I returned his wave and shouted to him. With that he just kept on going, and I did the same.

It took me the best part of four hours to get over to the other side of the estuary, but I reckoned it had saved me up to six days' travelling. When I was close to the shore on the other side I travelled along it in a northerly direction as far as I dared. What I was looking for was an inlet of some sort. I had decided on the way over I was not going to relinquish the boat unless I was forced to. A sixth sense told me I had gone just about as far as I dared, and I was about to head for the eastern side of the estuary anyway because I was in dangerous waters just opposite the Polyarnyy submarine base, when I found what I was looking for about a mile past the Island of Bol.Oleniy, a small inlet that was marked on my map as Guba Bol Volokovaya, the sides of which seemed to be overgrown with young silver birch saplings and reeds.

Once I had manoeuvred the boat into the inlet I had to work hard with the pole to get it to go against the current, but I eventually got it about a mile and a half into it. Next, when I'd spotted a suitable site, I dragged the boat in using the branches of the saplings to pull myself and the boat in until it was hard against the shore and completely covered by the over hanging foliage. When I was satisfied the boat couldn't be seen from the main channel of the inlet, I undid the pole from the stern and used the strap and bark to secure the boat to one of the young saplings on the shore.

Now that I had the boat secured I sat in it and prepared myself a meal of cold food and water. After looking at it for a few moments I thought, no way, I cannot eat that. I must get some hot food inside me or I would not survive the day. I was just going to go ashore and find a place to cook the food, when I heard the engine of a small launch chugging by in the estuary. Against my better judgement I sneaked a look out from the rear of the boat I was in and I was just in time to see a small Russian Naval patrol boat slowly pass the stern of my boat, which thank God was well into the saplings and they couldn't have seen it or me.

As I couldn't see anybody on the deck of the craft I presumed that they must all have been below decks, or crammed into the cabin. From my past experience I knew that they patrolled the coastal areas of the bay, but I didn't know they would come this far up the estuary and into the inlets like this one. It did worry me for a little while, but I watched the boat disappear out of the end of the inlet and made my way over the front of the boat on to the rocks to see if it was heading up the estuary or if it headed back into the bay. When I did get to a point where I could see it at the edge of the trees, I looked out only to see the boat was still chugging along at the same speed, having turned up the estuary, heading for Murmansk itself.

It was then that I noticed that the palms of my hands were sweating and I thought your nerves are starting to get to you mate. You had better start to take it easy or you will make a big mistake and go off at half cock altogether. With that thought I went back to the boat and I ate the meal cold, but I did manage a hot drink which helped me. When I had finished eating I packed everything I needed into my rucksack, the few things I had left I tied around a piece of rock with the last of the bark I had and lowered it into the muddy water under the boat. Then I hoisted my rucksack on to my back once more and set off on my relentless task to reach the place where I had spent so much time in those earlier years.

As I stepped out of the trees and into open country I noticed the weather was getting decidedly worse. I'd not noticed whilst I was in the trees and shrubs just how much it had deteriorated. The wind had started to blow a little and I knew that in itself was a bad sign up here at this time of the year. The temperature can fluctuate so much in these parts. One day it is warm and the next you can be freezing your bollocks off, the next it is boiling hot again. This time I didn't like the way the wind was picking up. My trousers were still a little wet and I thought I would be in for a rough trip; I was bloody glad I was off the estuary now. As the weather changed I could see I really wouldn't have done well out there with my two poles in this wind. My luck must still be holding, I thought, as I just put my head down and headed into the wind, my compass in my right hand and always heading in a nor nor east direction. No point in worrying about ifs and ands at this stage, just get on with the job in hand.

While I stepped out on the last leg of my journey, unknown to me at the time, the old man who had shouted at me whilst fishing in the estuary stepped ashore on the western side of the estuary. After securing his skiff he walked off with his catch of the day – a couple of Arctic cod that he had taken from his refrigerator earlier that day – hanging from his right arm. He made his way slowly across the railway line and into the cabin in which he lived in and which was further back in the woods. When he entered the cabin he first put the kettle on and then he marked the fish before he put them back in the refrigerator. Next, he made himself a cup of tea and then, lighting his pipe, he settled down to encode his message. After he'd finished his tea and his pipe had gone out he stood for at least half an hour studying the ground to the front of his cabin. When at last he was satisfied that nobody was out there he moved over to the cupboard on the back wall and took out the old-fashioned radio stored there. From a hiding place in the wall of the cabin he took a Morse key; he then went back to the window and had another look over the ground, but all looked well so he went back to the table. Then with a dexterity which would have put many younger men to shame, he transmitted his message. Without waiting for an answer he first burnt his message and then replaced the Morse key in its hiding place. He then turned the radio to the main Russian station and sat listening to the classical music which was being played.

The old man then poured himself another cup of tea from the pot which was simmering on the side of his stove. Next he proceeded to fill his pipe once more. He took a drink of the tea and took a taper from the side of the stove and lit it. He put it to his pipe, but before he could take a puff his forehead burst from the front of his head and some of it splattered against the stove, sizzling on the heat. Still with his left hand holding his pipe and his right hand holding the burning taper, he rolled slowly forward from his chair and crashed into the stove. The burns he received from the stove as he crashed into it would have caused him excruciating pain had he not already been dead. They would also probably have killed him. As it was the stove toppled over and the hot ashes and burning wood spilled out on to the wooden floor of the cabin. Within minutes the whole cabin was ablaze and was like a beacon on the side of the estuary.

About five minutes later Roald and Carl were on the bridge of the fishing boat in the Norwegian Sea; they looked at the signal which the duty operator had just brought them. "Well, Carl, it looks as if your man is in deep trouble if this signal intercept from Murmansk to London is to be believed."

"Looks that way, Roald; short of going in and snatching him from under their noses he just could end up in front of a firing squad. The thing is, Roald, if the Russians know where he is they are keeping very quiet about it. I have a feeling he might just make it yet, Roald."

"Well, Carl, all we can do is listen and wait. If he does head out to sea when he has finished whatever it is they have sent him in to do then it's best we position ourselves so we can pick him up without their guessing what is going on. So let's give it a few more days."

"Right, Roald, but this time when he comes out I'm going to insist he stays with us from now on. Those fools in London don't deserve a man of his calibre."

Carl then left the bridge and Roald took over the watch as they pretended to be fishing, as did the Russian fishing boat sailing just over the horizon.

Despite the wind I made good progress, my trousers were starting to dry out and I was feeling warmer. After I had been going for some four hours I started to see parts of the coast ahead, which I could clearly recognize and associate with memories and incidents. So I was at last near to my destination; I had not had the encounters with the Russians that I had expected. Perhaps I had been wrong to tear up and burn the list of Russian contacts and addresses I had been given and which those young officers had insisted I must carry. I had subsequently burnt them all as we left Newcastle on Tyne; all of which seemed so long ago now. Still, that was in the past. Something else I've learnt over the years; never dwell on the past, it does you no good.

From now on I started to take more care in the way I travelled after the troubles I had undergone to get this far. There was no way I intended to walk into a Russian patrol, Police, Army or the KGB for that matter. Now that I was getting very close to the place I had come so far to check out, I decided to sit for a while and have a meal of sorts, as I was by now again rather hungry. I would not have much time for food once I started to do what I had come to do. I felt as if I were now about to enter the lions' den.

Finally I found myself a place which overlooked the position for which I was heading. It was a place I had marked many years before, when we had been setting up this position. A lot of water had passed under the bridge since then, I thought. It was possible I was the only Royal Marine left alive out of the twelve who first entered this bay all those years before. This was not the time, though, to reminisce about old times, old pals, and old ships, but I could not help but think of them a little. As I lay by the roots of the tree and watched the position through my glasses – which I had come so far to check out – lots of memories of mates and friends passed through my mind. I do believe I was starting to get sentimental while I was lying there. Now there was a turn-up for the books, me getting sentimental.

Before I could get carried away too much, I saw something I had dreaded ever since I left London; I saw a soldier of the Russian People's Red Army step out of the concealed entrance to the OP. As I saw him I felt myself suck my breath in and curse, so it was under Russian control. Just as well I had not walked right up and asked for a hot meal, wasn't it. Well, it was now for plan 'B'. If I had any sense I would turn round and leave right now. But then what was it that sod Brown had once written on my report, 'Good man even if a little Stolid'. So it was obvious my superiors didn't think I had much sense; not 'stupid', but 'stolid'. It was obvious now even to me, stolid as I was, that the Russians had the place under their control. The thing I needed to know was whether there was any hope for the men who had manned the place before it had come under Russian control, or what had happened to them. So you see I could not just turn round now, could I? I had to know if it was twenty- four men a year who had been sent to the post each year of its operation only to be killed and replaced by Russians who then were taken to the UK in place of the men we had taken in.

All For A King's Shilling

So I spent the next half of the day getting into the proximity of the place without allowing myself to be seen, let alone caught. It was not easy and it was a case of 'standing room only from now on'!

I had to assume they were expecting me, but the amount of activity here was a little over the top even for me. My only hope now was that the position of our spare gear had not been compromised and that it was still serviceable. The landward side was out of the question, so I therefore had to work my way round to the water's edge. That in itself would take some doing, it was wide open. Then I had somehow to get past the place to the dump, which only two of us ever knew about, Mick, who was now dead, and myself. Well it never crossed my mind for one minute that he might have been turned.

To reach there I could try to get between the post and the sea, or I could go the long way round via the land. I didn't even want to consider that because I was sure the rear area would be well defended. It would depend how far from the position they had any observation posts as to just how long it would take me. The sea would be by far the quicker route but the chances of getting past them without being detected would be small. So I sat and pondered the problem for some time. Then, after much gnashing of teeth and biting of fingernails, I opted for the seaward side, I did not think I had the time to spend making my way around the place. If I was seen then the sea offered a better option than the KGB or the GRU.

Once I'd made up my mind I immediately set off to move down to the water's edge, which took me most of the day. When I was about five hundred yards from the rear of the post I got myself into some sort of bush and watched the beach and the small cliff that abutted the trees. For a while nothing happened and it was as I was about to step out and make my way along the foot of the cliff that I saw something I had dreaded. So I took my glasses out and had another good look at the place. There was nothing at all to see. Christ, man, I thought, you are starting to see things; for god's sake get a grip on yourself. Still, just to be sure and on the safe side get up the cliff and into the trees. Then just settle down and do as you have been trained to do. Do your bloody job properly.

So with a greater urgency I moved into the trees and with painstaking care made my way along the coast, keeping in the trees on the top of the cliff. After I had been going for about ten to fifteen minutes I was about to say stuff it and stride out when I felt a hand on my shoulder. As I turned, I had my knife out and it was into the man before he knew. He was still smiling at me as he hit the ground as if poleaxed. His mouth opened in a look of surprise as he lay on the ground. I think he was dead even before the surprise reached his brain; he just lay there with that stupid half grin on his face. Quickly I covered his face. I could not stand to look at that grin; hatred I could handle, but grins were out as far as I was concerned.

It seemed to me that I stood in the half-turned position for what was only minutes, but it felt like hours, and it was far too long. My ears and my eyes were straining to hear and see if there had been another man with him. It was then that it dawned on me that I was in the place where I thought I had seen some movement earlier. My mind was praying that he had just come to this place when I first saw the movement and it would be a couple of hours before anybody else turned up. While all this was going through my head I pulled his body into some birch saplings. There, I covered him as best I could and continued my journey. I reasoned that if they had sentries out here, then they would be likely to have them nearer in. They would also have them on the northern side in a similar position. It therefore followed that I had one hell of a problem.

When I realized that, I went back to the man I had just killed and took his top clothes, his coat, hat, belt and equipment off. These I put on myself over the top of my clothing then, having donned his helmet, I took his gun and moved off through the trees, acting as best I could to look as if I was a Russian soldier on a wandering patrol. The only thing, I thought, was that it would look odd being on patrol by myself. They normally wandered around in twos and threes. Still it was the best I could do at the time and I had to take the chance. It was very nerve-wracking moving through the edge of the trees and trying to look and act naturally. I remember thinking, what does a Russian wandering patrol look like? From what I had seen of them in a group, I had not been impressed, so I took a rather slovenly slow walk through the trees. It took some time to reach the place I was making for, but in the end I made it still in one piece.

As I walked, I had noticed other static guards, but none of them challenged me, so I assumed all was well. The main thing was I had at last arrived at the place I was seeking. At first I walked past it, then I stopped and edged back towards the place as if I were having a second look, just in case I was being watched. As I had no intention of going round the circuit again, I stopped near the place and leaned against a tree for about half an hour. When I had convinced myself I was not being followed or watched and I couldn't see or hear any movement anywhere near me, I slipped down the small cliff which led into another small inlet. This inlet I knew quite well.

Once there, I spent ten minutes looking for the place where I had buried the gear when last I had been here. The equipment took some digging out and I was a little surprised how deeply I had to dig. It was all the harder because all I had to dig with were my hands and the bayonet from the Russian's rifle. Eventually, though, I made it to the waterproofed box in which I had buried the gear. Once I had got hold of one end of the box it came out very easily and in no time at all I had all the gear out. Then I removed the bits and pieces I thought I was going to need from my rucksack; when I was happy that I had what I needed, I put my rucksack and the clothes I'd taken from the Russian guard into the waterproof bag. Next, I put the box back in the hole and I buried it once more and left everything much as I had found it.

Then I set to and inspected the equipment I'd just recovered. It seemed to have survived pretty well. Then I tested the cylinders; they seemed to be working all right, but only time would tell. When this was done I started to put the wet suit on; I noticed that it was a little perished in places, to say the least, but I would have to risk it. I had thought of putting it on over all my clothes then I thought better of it. If it did fail all my clothing would get soaked and that would mean certain death in this climate. So I stripped to my short pants and vest, the rest of my clothes I stashed with my rucksack and the water proof bag. Again, when I was satisfied with my handiwork I made my way to the water's edge and after wading in up to my armpits I slipped under the water and looked around to get my bearings.

Much to my disgust I have to admit I floundered around for about ten minutes, completely lost. So I came to the surface to see if I could get my bearings. When I did reach the surface, I nearly died of fright, there standing on the rocks not twenty yards away, throwing what I at first took to be a hand grenade into the water, was a Russian soldier. My immediate reaction was simply to upend my arse and dive, when I thought you silly fool, if it is a grenade it will blow your bloody ears out even if it does not kill you. So with great difficulty I managed to stay where I was just rising with the swell. I felt like a seal waiting for a harpoon to strike it. As I looked at him I realised he was engrossed in just bouncing pebbles off the surface of the water, the way we all do when we are kids. With that settled in my mind, I looked around and picked out my bearings. Then slowly I sank back into the water, hoping that if he did see anything he would take the movement and noise to be a seal. Now I had my directions, I swam towards the place I had been looking for.

It took me five minutes to pinpoint the place exactly, but once I had it then it only took me a couple of minutes to get the rubble shifted and the entrance to the passage open. Once I had cleared enough of the rubble for me to get through, I swam along the passage until I reached the end. Once there, I looked up, but I could not see any lights; everything about me was total blackness. Slowly I let myself drift up until my head was clear of the water. I stayed exactly as I was, trying to discover if there was a welcoming committee waiting for me in that blackness. When I had convinced myself there was not, I turned my torch on and slowly looked around. The place seemed the same as it had been years before when Mick and I had built it. As I looked around I thought about Mick and I renewed my promise, I would one day get the bastard who had killed him. All the reports from the Singapore Police and the armies' SIB would never convince me his death was an accident.

When I was completely satisfied all was well, I hauled myself out of the water and once I had taken off the tank from my back and the flippers from my feet then came the important bit. I tried to undo the wing bolts that held the door in place. To my surprise and relief they turned without any trouble and when I had completed undoing them all I edged the door open. Again to my surprise it also opened very easily. After all these years I'd expected a little bit of trouble with it. That submarine engineer did know what he was doing after all. As I opened it fully it made no noise whatsoever. I waited a second or so and then I crawled through the gap into the space between the rear wall of the base and the cave wall, into which the door was built.

Once I was in, I turned and closed the door behind me. I didn't want to effect a change of air and atmosphere in the place. Then I decided to just sit down and rest myself for a few minutes. I felt I was now safe for a while anyway. Safer than I'd been since I had left the fishing boat; after a while, when I had got my thoughts together again, I felt around the back wall of the base until I'd found the thing I was looking for. It was a cover over a knot in the wooden wall of the base. When I found it, I took a firm grip on it and gently started to turn it first one way then the other. I was very careful and it took some time before it moved.

When it did I eased the pressure of my hand as the last thing I needed now was for this plug to turn quickly and squeak. So it had to be a very slow and gentle action. At last I got it to move and then I spent a good ten minutes removing it from the hole. Once it was out I put my eye to the hole and I had a good view of the working part of the base, the control room. There was another underwater entrance to the place, but it was too small for a man to enter. It was round an outcrop of rock, about fifty metres to the south of the one I had come in through. It led to another part of the base. It was also the place into which all the cables from the sonar buoys went.

Only two people had known about this entrance and those had been Mick and me. We had built it together when we were left alone here in the early days of the base erection. We had only had time to do one dummy run at the place to see if it had worked or not. It had and now, after all those years, it had not let me down. It had worked again. I was in and as I looked through the hole, I thanked the submarine's chief engineer and Mick.

The room itself was much as it was the last time I had seen it but I was a little taken aback at first. The place was manned by Russians and I wondered just how long they had been in control. Still, I was not here to find that out, was I? The situation did make me wonder though if the Russians had completely replaced the men I had escorted into the place some years earlier. Perhaps the ones I'd brought out later had been Russian agents, the ones who had looked so anxious when we put them on the freighter. Not the actions of men wanting to get the hell out of a dangerous situation, more the actions of men just about to go into one. A couple of us had always thought it odd that when these handovers took place, we never brought out the ones we had taken in. When you think about it, we could have been bringing anybody out for all we knew; we never picked them up from this place, we always had to meet them in Murmansk.

I looked at the men in the control room and sure enough they were Russians and they didn't even look right. There was one thing that was a certainty, no way was I going to risk my life finding out though. Somehow I just knew in my heart of hearts they were not British Servicemen. They did not act like British Servicemen, their mannerisms were all wrong. So I made my decision there and then, I would destroy the place.

After reaching my decision I then I sat for a while considering what it was I was about to do, because once I'd set the charges, I knew the place would go up with a massive explosion. Then again, if the charges were too old, they might just go off like a giant damp squib. Whatever the case, I believed I had no choice in the matter; I had to set the timer up, connect all the wires and get myself a few miles away before it went.

It was going to be down to work soon and the whole place was in full swing right now. I figured it would be unwise to wait a while until they relaxed their activities, when they would be more likely to hear me scrambling about the outside of the place. Then there would be less chance of me being heard moving around them, under them, or on top of them while they were busy going about whatever work it was they were doing in the place. So I settled down to sort things out. Then I could get started scurrying around, connecting all the charges we had built into the place all those years ago. I was now glad I had heeded the advice of the Royal Engineer Captain who had advised me of the safeguards I would need to install into a building of this kind. He said that one day we might just need to get in this place again and do just what I was contemplating right now. With that thought I settled down to the task at hand, priming and wiring up the explosives. A right messy job it was, too, removing the protective greases with which we had covered the equipment so liberally when we had stored it.

All For A King's Shilling

Later, I was aware of the smell of food being cooked, which only served to make me realize I had not had anything to eat myself for some considerable time. I'd not had anything to eat of late which smelt as good as the food which they were cooking in this place. The desire for cooked food was so great I decided I would be better off working than letting my taste buds run amok while smelling the stuff. The cold was also starting to make my limbs ache quite a bit. Getting the cramps worried me even though I was still in my wet suit which had leaked a little and now I was starting to feel the cold. With the sort of distances I was going to have to travel when I left here the cramps were the last thing I needed.

Using my torch I located the tunnel that went under this part of the base. I got down on to my belly and made my way to the other end. Here I got to my feet and made my way along the narrow gap between the actual operations room and the commander's office. At the end of this I climbed up the ladder we had fastened to the end of the first accommodation hut. Next I moved over the top of the hut and into the area behind the generators which provided the power.

When I got there, I looked around for the wire which we had left all those years ago, next I located the charges and detonators; the charges looked a bit sweaty, but that was all. The detonators looked to be okay but I handled them with kid gloves just in case they had degenerated during the time they had been sitting here. They looked quite good for their age so, provided I took care while setting up the charges, they should do the job. Having collected enough for my first couple of charges I took a couple of the rolls of masking tape I had brought with me to tape the explosives together when I set the charges up. Then I retraced my steps to the accommodation blocks.

At this point I recalled that when we had set up this place we had debated long and hard about blowing the place up. Eventually we all came to the conclusion that if we were the ones who were in the place when it was destroyed and we were left under all the rubble to die, it would be better if we were killed in the main blast rather than taking days to die, trapped under all the rubble. So when I started to prepare the charges for the demolition of the place I doubled the amount of explosive which we had calculated would be needed. As I worked I thought it was funny that I had spent all that time putting the bloody place up and now I was the one to demolish it.

Once I'd completed one of the charges I wired it up and moved further back along the way I had come, preparing other charges as I went. The explosive seemed to be in good condition considering the time it had been there, but only time would tell if the wire was also in good condition. As I moved along I checked the wire as best I could and to my surprise I only had to cut out about a foot of it in the first fifty feet or so.

It was bloody hard work trying to get it all done, under the conditions in which I was working. It was very delicate work and I had to be extremely careful not to make a noise. Because of the confinement whilst working behind the huts, I got one hell of a sweat on; the space was very limited in most places. At one stage I was perspiring so much I was worried they might smell me, let alone hear me. It took a lot longer than I had expected and I was wringing wet, sweating like a pig, when at last I reached the rear of the complex and placed the last charge. At last I'd finished them all and I was most relieved to get out of there and into the area at the back of the operations room. There I sat and settled myself before I attempted to replace the bung which I'd removed when I first arrived. Before I replaced it I had one last look to see if all was well and they looked to be working as normal, or so it seemed, and it didn't look as if I had disturbed them at all. Slowly I replaced the bung, then I laid the wires through the hatch into the area just above the water where my diving gear was.

Next I closed the hatch and settled down to try out the timer which I had brought with me. After some quick calculations I worked out that even if all went well I would need at least two, or better three hours to get clear of this place before it blew just to give myself a chance of survival, as my escape would be restricted to travelling the way I had arrived, on foot. This lot, or should I say their companions, would be chasing me with vehicles, helicopters and all that entailed. Vehicle check points with helicopters flying around all over the bloody place. I'd a plan in mind, but only God knew if it would work, so I set the alarm for three hours and then made myself as comfortable as I could and I tried to sleep. All things being equal, the thing should wake me in two hours' time; if it did not, then I would have to adopt Plan 'B' whatever Plan 'B' was or perhaps even Plan 'Z'.

As I lay there trying to sleep, I thought they believe they are bloody good kids, back in London, until I remembered that perhaps they had not intended me even to get this far. With that little puzzle and all it entails going through my mind I eventually dozed off to sleep.

Much to my surprise, the alarm worked, so at least had survived the rigours of the journey. Let me just hope I survived the journey out. For a while I sat and thought about my plan. If I were to stay as close to this place as possible (and I did not think they would expect me to do that) I could lie low for a couple more days. Then when things were more relaxed I might just stand a chance. The more I thought about it the more I liked it. Then I reasoned that with this cave complex located here, there might, just might be other caves in the area and those others might not be too far away, caves in which I could hide for a few days.

It was then I thought that if I were to stay here at all I was going to need something to eat while I was waiting to make my run for home. So with the determination of a starving hamster I made my way back into the complex which I had just wired with explosives, the complex I had planned and built all those years before. Even then I had had the foresight to build in escape doors and escape provisions just in case. Well, this was 'a just in case' time. If ever the time had come when I needed them, it was now.

Once I was back inside the cave I put all my kit together so that it would all be together when I was ready to leave. The last thing I would have to do would be to set the timer. Now, when all was as I wanted it, I went back into the listening post complex and retraced my steps until I came to the rear of the galley. When I was about halfway along the galley wall I used my knife to locate a small door which we had built into the wooden wall. Just above that door was a small spy hole which had also been built into the wall. What I wanted was to see if it was the same as when I had last visited the place. As I uncovered this hole and looked in I saw it had all changed but then I thought it would have, wouldn't it? No need for them to disperse the cooking smells the way we had. They were not worried if the Russians found them. Simply because they were the bloody Russians, I muttered to myself.

All For A King's Shilling

The change was to my disadvantage, the food store was now obviously in another place. Just where that place was I did not know, although I did intend to find out. As I withdrew my eye from the small hole through which I had been looking, the light emitting from the other side of the hole went out. "Shit, they have had a power failure," flashed through my mind and then I realised it was not a power failure at all. As I felt a piece of stick or something pushing against my cheek, then it dawned on me that one of the men inside had seen something in the hole, and the only something he could have seen was my eye.

Just as I was about to pull back my face from the area of the hole, the stick itself was withdrawn. For some reason which I have never been able to explain I lay flat on the floor and that was no mean task in such a small space. Then I heard him telling somebody else there was something behind the wall. At this moment in time I decided it was time I left. So, crawling flatter than a snake with a top hat on I made my way to my right and still moving like a snake I hauled myself up on to the roof of the place as silently as I possibly could.

I was not a second too soon. The next thing I heard was a burst of automatic rifle fire and bullets ripped through the wood. When it had stopped I heard a voice telling all around, "That will frighten the bloody rats or whatever it is that lives behind these walls." Suddenly I had the feeling I was not alone behind these walls. Better I try and get what I came for and get my arse out of here. Wracked with the fear, firstly, that something nasty was prowling around behind the huts with me; and secondly, if that stupid bastard with the rifle had hit one of the charges then I wouldn't be writing this now, would I? So I slithered down the other side of the hut. I was hoping to reach an area to which I thought they may have moved the food store. As I edged my way along to the end of the hut I felt to see if any of the boards were loose. There were none and I began to feel a little despondent, when at last I found a hole. There was no light shining through it, so I thought it safe to assume the maniac with the automatic rifle was not in there, at least not yet.

Expecting to be blown to kingdom come at any moment I eventually raised enough courage to switch on my torch and have a look. He was right, that man with the gun, there was something behind here other than me. He had a right to be frightened. The hole was quite big, bigger than anything a mouse would have made. When I looked in through the hole, I saw the boxes of rations had been eaten from this side of the pile by something. Whatever it was, it could not open cans, that was not to say it did not have big teeth. Without any desire to stay any longer, I grabbed a couple of what looked like boxes of rations and took off.

One maniac had taken a shot at me already today. I'd no desire for a repeat episode, or for that matter to meet whoever or whatever it was who was eating things around here. Although I did not know what kind of food it was which I had grabbed at the time, I did not intend to stay there and find out. So I just made my way to the rear of the complex, crossed over the roof of the operations centre and dropped back to the ground by the hatch through which I had entered. I must admit I was glad to be away from them and whatever 'it' was; that was when I realised I had to go back and see if that maniac arsehole had shot out any of my wires.

If my reactions hadn't been good back there I would have been shot. Perhaps I'd have been eaten or god knows what might have happened to me. This whole thing was getting too bloody dangerous by half, I thought. Better I make a check of the wires and then be on my bloody way.

When at last I got back to where I'd put my things together, having done my checks of the wires, I had a look at what I had managed to grab from the food store. Two boxes of bloody oatmeal biscuits, I thought, oh! God, I hate the bloody things; but I won't have to worry about cooking now, will I. I'll be eating on the hoof as they say. Still, they have plenty of goodness in them. With that I packed everything up, connected the timer to the wires and set it for three hours. My main worry was that I would have to come back if it didn't blow. Next I passed everything through the hatch, eased myself through and when satisfied all was okay, I reached back in and switched the timer on. After a last glance around I pulled the hatch to and secured it with the latches. Then in total darkness once more I lowered myself into the water and made my way back to the entrance of the tunnel through which I had entered.

Once I was clear of the mouth of the tunnel, I let myself rise slowly to the surface. I stayed as close to the rocks as I could. When I reached the surface I had my back to the rocks and I was looking out into the bay. What was most disturbing though was that I was also looking at the hull of a Russian patrol boat. It was not moving so I took it to be anchored. Again I felt the sweat of fear rise to the surface of my skin. In a matter of seconds I'd regained my composure and I let myself sink down below the surface once more. Then when I was below the bottom of the hull I slowly swam away to my right. I wished I'd had a limpet mine with me, but I didn't, so I was just thankful they did not see me. It was with great care I made it back to the place where I had left my kit. Before I actually went to it, I inspected the place from the water's edge and as far as I could see none of the little things I had deliberately left around had been disturbed; but I was becoming more and more of the opinion that these bastards knew I was here and every fucking move I made.

If anybody had seen me earlier, they had not seen fit to make any attempt to inspect my kit. It was with a feeling of relief I changed into my clothes again, because I had become cold going into the place. Then getting very hot and sweaty whilst there, I was a little worried. The last thing I needed was to catch a dose of 'flu or even pneumonia. Now that I was dressing again, at least I felt I had a chance, albeit a small one, but if I did have to make a dash for it then there was hope. Having made the journey to Norway in a wet suit from here once before it was not an experience I wished to repeat. It would have to be overland this time; there was no chance of my making it by sea this trip with that wet suit.

When I'd sorted out my gear again, I buried all the stuff I felt I had no need of and then I set off inland. My mind was set now; it was important I find a place in which I could hole up for a few days until the hornets' nest I was about to stir up had settled down. At last I dressed and I was ready to depart the area. I'd worked out that I had about two hours thirty minutes to get clear before all hell broke out. Mindful of this, I made my way under the cover of what few trees there were further inland, away from the coast. It was after I'd been legging it for about an hour that I thought I was acting in a bloody stupid manner. There was no way I could find a place in which to hole up while I was making a headlong dash through the countryside. It stood to reason that any troops searching the same area at a more leisurely pace would also find every bloody hole in the area.

All For A King's Shilling

Whilst I was in full flight I had another change of plan. This plan was the simplest yet, I decided to just keep going. To make things easier I started to drift in a south easterly direction and then more southerly but other than that I just kept the pace up. I was frightened I might be seen by any foresters working in the region so I kept searching left and right, but mainly I just kept going, head down and arse up. If anything I could have done with another couple of pairs of eyes, but still I had now committed myself and there was no turning back. It was then that I thought it didn't matter how many of their people were killed, I would be in deep shit anyway if they caught me.

Just before the two and a half hours had elapsed and I should soon hear a big bang, I stopped and had a look around. To see the results of my handiwork I needed to be on some higher ground. I had to confirm with my own eyes if the place did go up and if I had done the job properly. It was no good where I was because I couldn't see the place which I'd just left and I certainly could not see very much. So I picked out the largest and what looked to be the strongest tree I could see and climbed up. When I had got myself as high as I could without swaying about too much, I was perched in a position where I could see the coast and the place which I had just left quite well. It did cross my mind that perhaps I was a little too close to the place for comfort, but the clock had been set and events were up and running as they say.

In my haste to get to the top of the tree, I had forgotten to take my rucksack off, something I was to be glad of, but once I'd got myself settled in the tree I decided to take my rucksack off and lower it to the ground. Just then, as I was loosening the shoulder straps, I heard voices quite close by and I thought Oh! Shit, the last thing I need right now is unfriendly visitors. I froze as close as I could to the bark of the tree and hoped the knocking of my knees would not alarm them. When eventually I glanced down, I could just make out three foresters, woodsmen, I don't know, they could have been bloody generals for all I knew or cared; but they were passing under the tree to the top of which I was clinging. In fact had I not stopped to climb the tree I'd have walked slap bang into them.

They were no more than twenty feet past the tree I was in, or up, depending how you look at it, when there was one god almighty bang. After a few moments, I felt the tree I was in begin to shake, or it might have been the tree felt me begin to shake. As I looked across to the place I had recently left, all I could see was what looked like a rolling wave of thick sea mist rushing towards where I was and I could hardly believe my eyes. Then this mist which was like rolling clouds hit the tree a few seconds later. The bloody part of the tree I was in then bent over with such a force that it nearly reached the ground as it swayed away from the force of whatever this rolling wave consisted of. It immediately crossed my mind that I had better get a bloody good hold of this tree trunk because when it swung back again I could find myself being launched back towards the place I had left, by air and without a bloody parachute. Possibly like a bloody air to ground missile or one of those bloody Roman war engines!

With great difficulty and after sapping nearly all my strength, I did manage to hang on to the tree as it was dragged by a sucking of air in a whiplash effect towards the direction of the explosion. Stuff this for a game of cards, I thought, and as the tip of the tree touched the ground, just in that second when it was stationary before it swung violently back again, I let loose. It was only a matter of two feet to the ground as the tree started to swing back the way it had come. A lot of the trees were down and I climbed on top of them to see what was happening and I could now see that there was a cloud like a small atomic cloud. This was rising from the place which I had left and which had now exploded. It crossed my mind that the explosives I had planted could in no way have caused the type of explosion I'd just witnessed; there had to be some other reason for that cloud.

While I stood there on the fallen trees with my mouth wide open like a cod on some fishmonger's slab, I realised there was no doubt that I was in a state of shock. There was no way I felt any pride in that little lot and no way in creation could the amount of explosive I had used cause an explosion of that magnitude and size. It was then I heard the men in front of me asking, "What the hell was that?" I was in such a state at the time that I just managed to stop myself telling them what I had just seen. Then I looked again at the place which had just exploded; the cloud had detached itself from the ground and was climbing higher in the sky like some gigantic weather balloon. When I looked at the men again I could just make out that they were heading through the damaged woodland in the direction from which I had just come. Mind, I did find time to wonder what the 'boys' in London would make of the abrupt end to their signals arriving from there that day?

After the size of the explosion had eventually sunk in, it dawned on me that I should be on my way again and the sooner I was away from there the better it would be for my health. The further from here I could get the better. For the next hour I half climbed and half fell from tree to tree as I made my way further and further away from what I believed could only have been a nuclear explosion. When I got to clear ground where the trees were still standing I set off as fast as my legs would take me; this time I was heading due south. The sooner I was out of here the better, I thought.

For the next four or five hours nothing much happened. I heard choppers flying around; most seemed to be heading in the direction of the explosion. So I just kept 'legging it' southwards. It was important to me now that I placed as much distance as possible between me and the place of the explosion. During the rest of the day I kept mulling over and over in my mind the cloud that had risen from the explosion. It looked so much as if it had been an atomic shell or an atomic bomb. The tree I had been in had shaken to its roots, the ground had trembled. That could not have happened at that distance with the explosives I had used. Still, the job I had been sent to do was now, as they say, done and I was on my way home. That was all that I could think of then; I was on my way home and I made my mind up that this was the last time I would ever set foot in this horrible land they call Russia; yet strange as it may seem I felt quite proud of myself.

Chapter Eleven
Russia Is A Big Place And They Have Given Me The Wrong Maps Again!
Russia, Hell hath truly frozen over

"Did I tell you I met this gorgeous bird? Long legs, Long hair, big tits and a gauche moustache."

Five days had passed since I had blown up the listening post and I had been on the go ever since. Now I was in a state of exhaustion in which I could in the end make some very stupid mistakes. The time had come when I needed to sleep before I collapsed on my feet or, worse still, walked into some Russian patrol. The first day after the explosion there had been much helicopter activity in the area, but there had been very little helicopter activity over the woods in which I was still trying to make my escape. Since that first day, things had changed and there was constant activity in the area.

I didn't know what was happening in the area of the post, but over the woods the activity had become intense and had now reached the point where I could only move in short bursts. It was important therefore that I now find somewhere to hole up for a day or more if possible. My biggest problem would arise if they were putting stops out in front of me with other troops following up behind me. Which meant I was in a bit of a quandary. Although I did have a contact within a few miles of this area, I was not sure of his loyalty and in his shoes I would not be sure of my own loyalty. If I turned up on his door he might just hand me over to the KGB, especially if there had been much loss of life in the explosion, which I am certain there was.

Maybe I should take that chance though if I did not find a place soon, most of the time I was in a stop and go situation. When I heard a helicopter coming I hid then, when it had passed, I continued on my way. If I heard or thought I heard voices, I stopped and went into hiding again. To be honest I didn't think I was making very much progress at all. I'd only covered a couple of miles in the last six hours.

William Atlay

Three things were worrying me now, one of which was my tiredness and the second was the increased activity in the area. The third and last was the hunger I was suffering, the hunger I felt was so bad and I could hardly remember when I last tried to swallow some of the biscuits that I took from the post. I'd reached a time a couple of days ago when I couldn't face eating another of the damned things. Now it looked as if I was going to have to contact one of the agents the boys in London had told me about. There were several in this area and I was going to have to make contact as quickly as I could or it just might be curtains for me. At least I had an idea where I was now, but it was only a rough idea, give or take a few miles. In my infinite wisdom I had calculated that with the way in which I was travelling it would take me at least two days to reach my contact. Considering the condition I was now in and the conditions under which I had to travel, even with rest and food I thought I couldn't make it in less than one and a half days. My problem was that I was getting weaker by the hour and I had to decide soon what course of action I was going to take. The question was? Did I go on and risk all, or did I stop and try to eat some more of the dry biscuits I had and then try to get sleep. Or did I keep going as I was, thus risking all and collapsing with exhaustion later on?

After tossing the situation around in my head, I decided that no matter what I did, either way I'd be risking all anyway. It made no difference what I did, that was the catch twenty-two situation I'd found myself in. In the end I decided why not go out fed and rested. At least I would feel better if nothing else and that was how I made my decision. That was how I decided to stop, make myself a much-needed hot drink, try and eat some of the biscuits and maybe rest for an hour or so. Because I was going to do just that, which showed how tired, worn-out and really exhausted I was.

After about ten minutes looking around I came across what I was looking for; it was a small hollow in the ground. The hollow was about eight feet long by six feet wide. It was no higher at its deepest then eighteen inches, and it was beside a fallen pine tree. It would have been perfect if the tree had fallen across it, still I could not grumble; at least I had found some cover. I walked some distance from it until I found some loose branches from another, more recently felled pine. Of these I collected enough to build myself a good hide over the hollow that I had found. When I had covered it to my satisfaction, I put all my kit inside the hollow, all that is except the food I intended to eat. This I took with me and went to the place from where I had collected the branches.

Here I built another hide, this time not as well, but a good one just the same. It was here that I cooked myself a meal of a porridge-type mixture from the biscuits. I had lit the fire of dead wood which gave off very little, or practically no smoke. Then I settled into the hide and ate my meal, making sure I left plenty of evidence of my presence there. It tasted better than anything I had ever had in a restaurant or mess for that matter. When I had finished, I then skirted my way back to my first hide. Just short of it, I stopped and watched the place for a good half hour. All looked well, so I made my move and quicker than a jack rabbit could move, I was in and settled. Within minutes I was sound asleep.

Some hours later I awoke and to my surprise I felt quite refreshed, but instantly scared shitless out of my life. I could hear Russian voices all around me. As I lay there, still as a church mouse, I thought they were waiting to see if I was awake. Then

All For A King's Shilling

I thought, like hell they were, they didn't know I was here. So I lay dead still, playing possum I think the Americans call it. Anyway, I tried to pick up as much information as I could from what they were saying.

They were talking about the place they had found where the English agent had spent the night. "He had the cheek to light a fire and cook himself a meal – a meal of Russian army rations," the sergeant said.

"The cheek of the bastard; I'd like to know where the capitalist pig had got them," said a young lad who was no older than eighteen at the most!

Oh, bloody big deal, you young bloody fool, I thought as I listened to him. The bloody biscuits I'd eaten were from the stock of food we'd shipped in, so up yours, you bloody peasant.

"Perhaps these capitalists are not as well off as they would have us think," said, another one of them!

I must admit in the end that to hear them was enlightenment. We didn't have all the answers in the West, that much I did know, but to be so proud of a system that killed its own people as readily as theirs does, beggars belief.

Well, I did not believe we could ever beat people like that and I could see how it was the Germans were on a hiding to nothing the minute they crossed the Polish border.

By now I was getting quite engrossed with their conversations and I was starting to forget the predicament I was in. Mind, I came back to reality with a thump when one of their KGB officers arrived; he stopped their philosophizing about me in no uncertain terms. They all jumped up when he arrived, for a start; he then laid into them for sitting talking when they should be scouring the woods for this imperialist pig.

"This man who has caused the explosions at the underground factory on the coast to the north where so many of your comrades have died, this pig is to be shot on sight. You are to give him no quarter. Some of our men have found his camp so the animal cannot have gone very far." He was shouting at them by now and his voice was starting to quaver. "In fact," he went on, "the pig could be within earshot of you all right now."

I thought, you do not know how bloody true your statement is, mate.

The result was they all took off in a southerly direction in hot pursuit of me, I presumed, but the KGB officer didn't. No, the bastard just stood transfixed to the spot, looking in the general direction which they had taken.

After they had all disappeared into the woods, he lit up a cigarette and paced backwards and forwards about ten feet from where I lay. When all was quiet and there was no more noise of soldiers crashing through the woods, he threw his cigarette on the ground and stamped it out by twisting his foot on it.

Then he gave me one hell of a fright; without any warning he turned and faced the place where I was hiding. As he did, he spread his feet and placed his hands on his hips. The look on his face then took on a violent, twisted expression of hatred.

"You can come out now, you English pig, you are going to make me a Colonel, "he said.

I didn't answer him, but lay dead still and just looked at him. When I fired the gun which I was holding I think he half twisted his head towards me and that was the first and last he knew that I was even there. He may have seen the flash from the muzzle of the silencer or he may not, but I shall never know, will I?

The bullet took half his head away; you see, he had not been looking at me when I fired, but towards something a little off to my left. I don't know what it was he was looking at, or if he was just practising his lines for when he was going to arrest me. Perhaps he was just acting out a fantasy, but whatever it was, it had cost him his life and for that I felt sorry. I was extremely glad he had not captured me after that look of hatred on his face. That look of hatred was the only reason I'd fired, it had worried me so much. He had hardly landed on the ground and I was by his side; in no time at all I had his coat off him, before too much of his blood spilled on to it. Also, I took his belt, pistol, and hat. Then I was off like a jack rabbit in the direction he had just sent the others. After a while I could hear them as they crashed through the trees in front of me. Strangely I felt a little better then.

It was some time later that I was moving to the rear of the soldiers, the ones who had been talking when I woke up. I listened to their banter as they moved through the trees, not really looking for anybody, more like a stroll in the country. The more I listened to them the more hopeful I became. The men gave me the impression they were not at all interested in being out and about in these woods. Also, they thought they were wasting their time out here in the woods looking for someone, who to put it in their words, was 'The Invisible Man'. It seemed they all believed that the man for whom they were hunting was a figment of the imagination of the party bosses, a scapegoat whom the bosses said had set off an explosion on the southern coast of the bay, the explosion which they all knew, as anybody with any common sense would know, was the result of scientists working in the underground bunker up there on the northern shore and making a cock-up.

That little lot gave me something to think about as I followed them through the trees. I had also noticed it was starting to get darker than I had expected. Perhaps the summer of the famous midnight sun was ending a little earlier this year, or we were in for one hell of a storm. I would have preferred some darkness but it looked as if I were going to have to be content with a storm. While I was thinking about all this I did notice it had also got a damn sight colder in the last half hour or so.

The men up ahead had come to the same conclusion as me. Another of their officers was calling them together, and he was telling them they were calling it a day for now. They would resume the hunt from here tomorrow. As they were heading off to where they knew there was a road, or track of some sort, the last man in the line looked round and saw me. He called to say they were leaving; I waved to him and said I would be along shortly. I think it satisfied him, because he turned, without another word, and left with the rest.

Once they were out of sight I moved off, but I kept looking back to see if there was anybody following me. Occasionally I stopped and listened for the noise of anybody, but also to slow me down. My intention was to take it a little easier now; I had a Russian KGB officer's coat on and I had no intention of bursting upon any Russians that might or might not be ahead of me. The weather had taken a turn for the worse and it was nearly as dark now as the half light just before the full Arctic winter hits. Now I had to keep looking at my compass to make sure I was still heading in the right direction. The wind dropped after about an hour or so and there was a very quiet period of about fifteen minutes. During this period all the birds around the area started to chirp and sing.

After about ten minutes of this, the whole place became silent again; it was like being in a dream. Every movement appeared as if in slow motion and with no noise at all, as an eerie and complete stillness crept over the place. It was at that point the alarm bells started to ring and I stopped dead in my tracks. Immediately I started looking for a place to take shelter. I felt like an animal must when he knows there is danger. Like me he stops dead in his tracks looking this way and that, knowing that devastation and destruction is about to strike, but also knowing there is nothing at all he can do about it. The air was charged with electricity; my hair was standing on end. It was as I stood there, glancing this way and that, that at last I saw what I was looking for. Two pine trees which had fallen in opposite directions, and had come together to form what one could only describe as a barbed wire obstacle type of shape, the type of thing which one sees in all the old war movies blocking roads and with armed men standing behind them.

Their branches had locked together very tightly and it took me some minutes to get inside them. Once in, I could hardly see out as their branches were so closely locked together. Kneeling down I cleared what bits of wood I could from the ground inside to make myself a small place to lie down. The bits of wood I'd collected I used to block the entrance which I had made when getting inside. Then I scraped all the loose cones, pine needles and what other stuff I could together to make a kind of bed. When satisfied with my work, I settled down to sit out whatever it was that was coming my way and believe me something big was coming my way. I could tell by the way the animals and birds had all gone to ground. Nothing was stirring out there and they didn't do that for nothing.

As I lay in my new little home and waited for the storm to strike, I mulled over the events which had happened to me these last few weeks. Was it weeks, or was it only days? I had forgotten. As I went over the events I thought more and more about the conversations which I had overheard earlier. The talk about the scientists, and their underground research establishment which had just exploded, made me wonder just what had been going on in the place. I knew the explosion was far greater than the explosives I'd used could have caused.

It was a very clever move by the Russians, I thought. Not too bad, really; the surest way nowadays to keep people away from establishments is simply to say they are atomic testing establishments, or even that they make nerve gas, statements guaranteed to keep everybody who had a vestige of common sense at bay, except the eccentric English nutcases, that is. Tell that Ban the Bomb Brigade in England that a place is an atomic testing station, or it makes nerve gas, and they couldn't get there bloody fast enough.

I should think the only thing which would have that kind of effect on the Russians would be to tell them it was a secret vodka factory. To tell the ordinary Russians the place was a secret atomic or poison gas plant would be enough to keep them at arm's length. It was at this point of my thoughts that I noticed a slight wind had started to blow. This lasted for about twenty minutes, and then it stopped again. I was just about to come to the conclusion that all the Russians who lived up here and all their wildlife were chicken when it struck. It came so suddenly. The roar was the loudest I think I have ever heard. Then the cold hit, it was like walking naked into a large commercial freezer plant. It chilled to the marrow of your bone, and I had two lots of coats on. Even though I'd spent some considerable time up here in the past few years I'd never experienced anything on this scale.

The tree structure in which I was had seemed so strong, yet it waved around like a leaf in an autumn wind in England. To say I was scared and frightened was an understatement; to say I was shit scared or terrified, would not have been too strong a description of my feelings. As I lay there in the not too strong shelter, I thought I don't know how long this will last, but I pray and hope it is not long. It was while I was praying that it happened, a tall pine tree came crashing down on to the top of the place I was sheltering under. When I heard the ripping noise above me, I looked up and instinctively I knew I was in the worst situation I'd ever experienced in my life. It was the sight of a large branch from the tree coming down right on top of me which absolutely terrified me.

All I can remember is that I watched in fascination as the smaller branches on it were stripped away like feathers as it came through the shelter in which I was cowering. Then I watched in horror, as I muttered to myself, "Oh shit, you are about to be stabbed by the biggest bloody spear in the world; even the bloody Zulus haven't anything to match this." At last, my fascination and fixation with the branch broke and to this day I still don't know how I managed it, but I did manage to drag myself away from the point where I knew it would strike. Somehow, I just managed to turn out of the path of the bloody branch and I rolled as far as I could on to my right side pressing myself into the branches of the fallen trees which I was already under. All the time this loud terrible roaring of the wind was now howling all around me like a wild banshee. It completely blanked out the noise of the tree falling and my screaming which had eventually reached my mouth.

Then as I felt the branch pass my back, at first I thought I'd got away with it, but that was not to be. The next thing I felt was the flesh on my back being ripped from my bones as the thicker part of the branch arrived and it was at this point that without a sound I passed out. There is no way I have of knowing how long I lay there. I was unconscious and all I knew when at last I came round was that I had been out for a long time. To my surprise I could not feel any pain in my back at all. So I just lay there for some minutes trying to work out what had happened to me. As it all came back to me, I wondered why my back was not hurting me. It was at this point that I had this horrible thought – which was more a panic really – that perhaps the branch had broken my back. To be honest, I just lay there quietly for some time without moving. To be honest and truthful about it, I was too bloody frightened to try to move my feet in case I discovered I was paralyzed from my waist down.

While I lay there in the cold and in complete panic, it dawned on me that I could still feel my feet. Although they felt very cold, it didn't help to reduce my fright or fear. As it was I must have lain there for ages trying to build up enough courage to make the effort to move into a better position. Then I took the bullet in my teeth and I got ready to move away from the branch, which was still hard against my back. With much concentration, sweat and pain at last I managed to move and as I did, I let out a scream, a scream which they must have heard in Norway. The pain was the most excruciating I had ever felt; never before or since in my life had I felt pain like it, and

All For A King's Shilling

I didn't think I had done my back one little bit of good. The movement I made must have wakened every sleeping and numb nerve in my body. As my pulse throbbed, so the pain beat in time to the rhythm of my pulse. The pain was so excruciating, I even got toothache, and it was so intense throughout my body that I just lay there and screamed and screamed for at least twenty minutes. It was probably a damned sight longer and I no longer gave a mouse's tit who heard me, I needed bloody help and I needed it fast.

It goes without saying that help didn't come fast. How long I lay there, and screamed, I never knew, I had completely lost all trace of time. What I do know is some time later I thought, what the hell is it you are screaming about, you stupid sod, nobody is going to hear you in this storm. It was only then I realized the storm was still raging all around me. That I could reason that bit out made me think perhaps I was not really as badly hurt as I had at first thought. So I shut up and listened to the wind, sleet and snow. It seemed to be a mixture of all three. I then settled down and accepted the fact that nobody would be out in this, only perhaps the KGB. So I should conserve whatever energy I had left, until I could again get up and be on my way, ever the optimist.

To this day, I believe I fell asleep again. The next recollection I have of anything tangible is hearing the storm abate, then some time later hearing voices. I did not know at the time if they were soldiers, police or whatever. What I do know is I shouted out for help. After that all was hazy. I seem to remember there were people looking at me, then a spell when I was all alone again. Then the people were back and I remember the pain as they none too gently pulled me from under the trees. Also, I have a distinct memory of somebody saying in Old Lapp, "Shut the bastard up, or we will all get hung."

It was then I thought that it was odd really, they do not hang people in Russia, they just shoot them. Well, either they shoot them, or work them to death in their labour camps. At the time I didn't give a shit what they did, all I wanted was to be out of that hell-hole I'd been in for God knows how long. The last I do remember about it all was that they loaded me on to something or other and covered me with blankets of some sort and the tree tops were going round and round above my head. It was then I believe I passed out again.

When next I came to, I was not in a clean hospital, or even a dirty one for that matter, but in a small, damp, dark room. I was to learn later it was not a cell, as I had at first thought, but an outbuilding of a local forest worker's hut or house. I was all alone and the first thing I did was to try to move. As I did, I felt a searing pain through my back. It felt like a small atom bomb going off in the middle of my back, and again I cried out with the pain. Just then the door, which I hadn't seen, was flung open and this large, scruffy looking Russian came in and said, "Any more of that whimpering, and I will hand you over to the KGB right away."

He then punched me on the right shoulder, just as if to emphasize he meant it. As his fist contacted with my shoulder, I felt a stab of pain in my back from this, but I did manage against all odds to keep my mouth shut. The thoughts I had about him then would bring him no good, in the future. Had I not been injured, then big as he was I would have taken him. Taken him, I'd have killed the big bastard. He then stormed out as quickly as he'd come in.

I lay there for ten minutes trying to see as much as I could. I still had my clothes on, the ones which I'd been wearing when the tree came down on top of me. They must have seen I was not a genuine KGB man as I only had a coat and a hat. As I looked at the belt, I noticed the pistol had gone from its holster. Slowly, I turned my head looking around the room as best I could. The pain in my back was practically unbearable, but I had to do it. It was most important, as I was trying to locate my rucksack because without it I knew I'd be in serious trouble. Unfortunately, I couldn't see it anywhere in the place. If the KGB, or the others, like the man who had just been in, had my rucksack, then I could be in deep trouble. Again with great difficulty, I felt under the things which covered me, to see if he had done anything to my back. To my surprise I found I had a bandage round me. Which felt like a tight girdle, but it was just a bandage. The way it looked to me, there was very little I could do right then, so I let myself drift off to sleep again.

I woke later to the sound of a woman and a man whispering in the corner of the room. They obviously saw I was awake, because the woman then asked me, "How are you feeling now, comrade?"

I was a little slow to answer; I was wracking my brains to see if I could recall the silly phrases which those stupid goons back in London had tried to drum into me. The phrases which I was to use to identify myself on just such an occasion as this to contact our so-called friends in this Godforsaken country.

Then at last it hit me; just as she was going to say something else, I managed to blurt out, "I am always at my best in Kiev in the spring."

"Ah! So you have been in Kiev this last spring?" she replied.

Christ, I thought, is that the right answer? I can't bloody remember; I wracked my brains but I couldn't think of anything to say.

It was nearly dark in there and I could not see her face in what little light there was. Therefore as I could not see her facial expressions and I couldn't tell if I were making a fool of myself or not, I felt I had to go on with it and not knowing any of the correct answers, I just said, "No, it is now six years since I was last there."

As I said it I thought, what shit is this I am talking. I can't believe I am doing this. What a right arsehole I must sound. It must have been the accident which had befuddled my brain, but I went on to add, "And you, my good comrade, how long since you were there?"

She replied, "Oh no, comrade, I do not like Kiev, but then I have never been there."

It was at this point the old man came in again. "Well," he asked, "what are you going to do with him?"

"We will take him and hand him over to the Police. It is better they deal with a KGB impostor," she replied.

Hearing that my heart sank; I would not last ten seconds with the famous fingernail pullers of the KGB, not in the condition I was in at the time. As these thoughts were going through my mind, and a thousand and one other thoughts of how to escape, the old man hoisted me unceremoniously on to his shoulder and carried me out of the hut. The pain in my back was so severe I had trouble stifling an urge to scream as he carried me out of the place and dumped me down on the back seat of a large car.

He looked me straight in the eye and said, "You will scream well enough when the local boys get hold of you, my fine friend."

Whether it was the look on his face or just the excruciating pain in my body I don't know, but at that point I just looked at him and passed out.

When next I came round I was in a clean bed, with clean sheets; I smelled of carbolic and I felt warm. I remember thinking it was the first time in my life I had ever felt warm in this part of the world. As I looked around my new room, prison or whatever, I must admit I did feel comfortable in there. It was a large room, about sixteen feet by thirty; it had one of those old Victorian ceiling centre pieces, which to my mind look stupid, without a chandelier hanging from it.

There were two windows on one side of the room and none at all on the other three. Not a corner room, I thought. To the left of the bed, and opposite from the windows was a large wood-burning fire. Facing me was a door in the centre of the wall and to my right rear in the wall behind the bed was another door which was about one foot from the corner of the wall which had the windows in it. Then I spent the next ten minutes thinking of ways to get out of the place. My thoughts came to an abrupt end when an attractive young woman came into the room. She entered through the door opposite the foot of the bed and as I looked at her I realised that I was starting to feel a little better, due mainly to my reaction when I looked at her.

When she spoke, I knew it was the woman who had been talking to me in the old man's house. "Well," she said, "and how are you feeling now, my fine young Ukrainian?"

"I feel a lot better than I did the last time we met."

"So you should, you have had some very good medical treatment since then. It's not every country which treats captured young enemy agents so well."

There was what could only be described as a pregnant pause in the room when she said that and as we looked at each other, eyeball to eyeball. The longer I stared at her, the more certain I was that I would spend the rest of whatever life I had left with her. Without question I knew there and then that we had been born to be together. Also I knew nothing in the world would ever keep us apart for long, other than death, imprisonment and the usual vagaries of life in the USSR. It was with a slight tremble in my voice that I said, "Talk like that will not help my recovery; as you know I am a KGB man, surely you have looked at the documents in my coat?"

"Ha! KGB man, is it?"

I was sure I could sense a slight tremble in her voice the same as mine. Then with sternness in her voice, which I thought she fought hard to impose in it, she said, "They brought the body of a young dead KGB man into the KGB Headquarters the day before we found you. The man was killed out in the woods and to our surprise his coat, hat and gun were missing. So don't you think it odd that we found these missing items of his just happen to be on you? All except the gun, that is."

By now I was a very troubled man; here I was in a bed, unable to move the upper part of my body, and in a place I knew not where. When they found me I was wearing a dead KGB officer's coat and hat and also in my possession was his gun. Now I hoped I had not completely misread this beautiful young woman's recent body language?

When at first we met in that dark room I'd gone through all that shit, which those bastards in London had given me, all to the wrong person it seemed. That was the main reason I had made a point of not making any contacts with any of the people on their list since leaving London. Firstly, I didn't know the background of any of them; secondly, I had decided I would be better off not to get in touch with any of their contacts. If I were going to have to seek help, I had decided only to contact Carl's agents or my own when it became obvious all was not as it should be. For some stupid reason I had also assumed, obviously wrongly, that this beautiful young woman was among the contacts they had given me before I'd left London. Some bloody old man in the woods finds me injured and contacts this beautiful young woman and I assume she is one of London's agents. I must have been running a brain in for an idiot. Talk about 'His dick takes charge of him'; what an arsehole I'd turned into. It made no difference to my feelings for her though. Of that discovery I was most surprised, so now I knew what it felt like when a person became besotted by someone else.

This beautiful young woman then looked at me and said, "When we were talking in the old man's house, you were about to say something to me as he came in. What was it? Or can't you remember?"

"I was about to tell you that they say, Kiev is to Russians what Rome is to the decadent West, all roads lead there."

"Ah! So you were trying to tell me you are not the person I at first thought you were. You are not a KGB man after all, but one of those radicals about whom we hear so much these days. Well, whoever you are, you will not be moving for some time my fine comrade. You see, you have had a very serious injury to your back. You are lucky not to have damaged any bones in your back. Mind, you do have some nasty muscle damage."

She then swept out of the room, saying, "We will talk again soon."

I do not know for how long I stared at the closed door. It was as if I could still see the back of her framed in it. With that, 'we will talk again soon' remark, she had gone. Yet I could still see her in the closed door.

As I eventually settled back into the pillows, and looked at the door which she had closed behind her, I felt I had some deep thinking to do. It did me no good at all; I just got more and more depressed. Here I was, acting like a young OD who has just met his first love, and I was just digging myself deeper and deeper in. If she was who I really thought she was, then my being here was going to put her life at risk. Her death was the one thing which I did not want laid at my door, not only because of my feelings for her, but also because it would be such a waste of a lovely young life.

Who the bloody hell was I kidding, my mind had been in turmoil ever since I first laid eyes on her; I had never had feelings about any woman before of the kind which I had for this woman. To put it mildly, I was head over heels in love with the woman and I don't mean lust, puppy love, or anything else like that. No, I was besotted by her. Her presence filled not only my mind and my thoughts, but my every feeling; even the pains had gone because my feelings for her had taken precedence over them. I did not hold with harming women, but that was nothing to do with my feelings right now.

I was in bad shape, this I knew, and I had to get out of this place and this country. I'd one hell of a long walk in front of me and it was going to take God alone knows how long before I could move again. For a start I had to get fit before I could even attempt that trip and I was not going to get very fit in this place. What was more to the point, winter was coming soon and we all know what winter means in this part of the world.

Then, I thought, you big stupid fool. There is nothing in the world which you can do about your situation right at this moment in time. So why not get some sleep and see how you feel next time you wake up. With that I eventually went back to sleep. She even filled my thoughts while I was asleep and I dreamt we were together in the sunshine, just loving each other and living a life of bliss.

Later another young woman awakened me; this one was wearing a nurse's uniform and I was disappointed she wasn't my other female benefactor. I'd expected to be in the arms of the woman I had fallen so deeply in love with when I woke. Mind, the uniform had a most sobering effect on me; it set me off thinking that perhaps I was really a prisoner in a Russian hospital. This nurse did not talk at all, although I smiled at her a couple of times; she showed me no emotion of any kind. With a sort of hiss she just took the bedclothes off me, none too gently I might add, and changed my bandages, and then she rearranged the bed and left the room.

While I lay there I thought something was wrong and I could not put my finger on it. The atmosphere in the place was electric. It was the same as standing under those electric pylons which cross the English countryside in all directions. She was back again in no time at all with some hot food. She then commenced to spoon feed me what turned out to be a goodly tasting soup. Next she spoon fed me a very good dinner of meat and vegetables, which were quite tasty. The meat I think was bear, but I would not swear to it, but it did have that bear taste which we had experienced when we first landed here those years earlier. It was at this point I realised what was wrong. The place was too clean for a Russian hospital and the nurse was too slim. Also, she had a petite hat on, not one of those tall cooks' type of hat that you see them all wearing on the few pictures which come out of Russia.

So what was going on? I concluded that I must be in the hands of a group of people whom I'd had instructions to contact, instructions which those goons back in London issued to me in Whitehall before I left. Those idiots thought they were in charge of events, while all the time they were just sitting in their cosy little rooms back in London watching coloured pins which their subordinates moved around on wall maps. If my assumptions were right, then all these people could be in great danger. Simply having been in contact with me could cost them their pretty little necks. To have me in their home would mean certain death.

When the nurse came to see me the next time, I started to ask her some questions. She simply ignored me and I thought to hell with it. I did not wish to let them know I had more names and more stupid bloody conversations to hold with other Russians. Russians who, like them, thought that by helping me they might just end by getting a better way of life than the one they had at the moment. If I said too much then I would give myself away; I was really trying to think of some way of warning them that my presence among them would bring them nothing but harm. If they insisted on keeping me here then there was nothing I could do to help them. I wanted to say something to her which would sound gibberish to anybody who might be listening to our conversations, but it would warn them. As it was I could think of nothing and

I came to the conclusion that no matter what I said I would in the end give myself away.

So the next time the nurse came in I said, "I am thankful for all the help; I don't think those capitalist pigs in the West have anything as good as this." I then said, "Mind the last time I was in Kiev, they told me the rats in London hospitals were bigger than the rats in the old warehouses in Leningrad."

The nurse never even batted an eyelid, she just finished changing my dressings and again she fed me, then left. As she closed the door, I thought, shit, you have done it this time, mate.

She had hardly been out of the room ten minutes when the young beautiful Katrine returned; I knew she was called Katrine because I'd heard her name mentioned in the dark room in the woods. She closed the door and then just stood with her back to it looking at me. The silence of that period was deafening. At last as she was just about to move away from the door, she stopped. Then she turned and walked to the hand basin in the corner of the room; there she turned both the hot and cold water taps on. So, I thought to myself, she must think or perhaps know this room is bugged and our conversations were recorded. Well, it is obvious she doesn't want anybody to hear what it is she is going to say to me. Mind, I too need to talk to her to get things sorted out between us, things, my beautiful young comrade, which I'm not too keen for others to hear.

With all this going on in my mind, when she arrived at the side of the bed I reached out and took hold of her hand. She made no move at first, then after a couple of seconds elapsed she returned my grasp by squeezing my hand. We looked at each other and I knew that I'd move heaven and earth always to be with her. It was at this point I smiled at her and said in English this time, "The last time I was in Kiev, they told me that some rats there were as big as cats and just as crafty."

"They are kittens compared with the ones in London. Now in London they have rats as big as cart horses, most of whom wear bowler hats and carry rolled-up umbrellas," she replied; she then just stood and looked at me for a couple of minutes. Then flashing the most wonderful smile I've ever seen she said, "I must know who you really are."

Watching every movement of her face, drinking in all her beauty, at last I said, "Do you know how I feel about you, Katrine? May I call you Katrine?"

"Yes, I would like that and yes I think I know how you feel about me. After all, you haven't tried to hide it, have you; it is so obvious when you look at me I'd be a fool not to know," she replied.

My delight at hearing her say that sent me off into a flight of ecstasy as my heartbeat increased and it felt as if my heart was rising up into my mouth. I thought I was about to choke with happiness, but at last I managed to say, "Well, Katrine, I've made this trip to Russia several times before. The only reason I have always been so successful in the past is because I have never sought the help of any of you. You must believe I had no intention of doing so this time, if I had not had this small problem with my back." Pausing a moment, I then went on. "If it hadn't been for that old man in the wood who found me I still wouldn't have come anywhere near you. The old woodsman was wrong to get you. You know, of course, Katrine, all your lives are in danger. You will all find yourselves in deep trouble if anybody were to find out I was here."

She squeezed my hand a little tighter and just looked at me.

"We are both in a catch twenty two-situation, Katrine. You are not sure really who I am. There is no way for you to know for certain if I am a KGB man who is trying to uncover any people who are disloyal to the Mother Land. Similarly, I don't know if you are who you say, not for certain, that is; you could be the KGB. If not the KGB, then you could be working with them in a setup to trap dissidents or just dissatisfied people, or even enemy agents. Then again you could be who you say you are, only controlled against your will by the KGB. To me the whole setup could be a double KGB sting, which I have now got myself entangled in. Yet again, we could all be really whom we say we are. What with me an enemy agent and you, well, you are a Russian dissident, aren't you, working if not for the West, at least prepared to help a lost Westerner."

Katrine looked a little hurt. I thought she was going to say something but it was not to be. She just looked at me for what seemed a long two minutes. Then she gave my hand another deliberate squeeze and withdrew her hand from mine. Next, she leaned forward over the bed and kissed me on the lips. Before I could say anything she put the index finger of her right hand over my lips to stop me saying anything. Without a word she walked around the bed, turned the taps off and left the room.

When she had closed the door, I just lay and looked at the back of the door after she had gone. For at least ten minutes I just lay and thought about our predicament. It would be such a shame if a beautiful young woman like Katrine should have to end being shot or, probably worse for her, put in a labour camp for years on end. What a waste, I thought. It was at this point I realized just what my real feelings towards Katrine were. With that I closed my eyes and tried to go back to sleep.

Some four hours later my trend of thought was interrupted by the nurse; she came in, and again changed my bandages. She then went out, only to return a few minutes later with some food. I told her I could probably feed myself now if she would let me try. This she did, much to my surprise. I was very careful and tried hard not to spill any, but I didn't succeed. The first three spoonfuls I did very well, but I spilt the fourth. She did not scold me; she just took the spoon and finished feeding the remainder of the soup to me. When she had completed this she left the room and returned within a couple of minutes, this time with Katrine. Together they set about changing the sheets on my bed. It became apparent to me right there and then that neither of them were nurses in any sense of the word.

As Katrine leaned over me to adjust my pillows, she came the closest to me she had been since she had kissed me in those fleeting seconds earlier. She had that pure smell which only certain women have, like peaches and cream. As I looked at her face I saw her complexion was perfect, like a peach. I was so glad I was in the bed at that point, because I fear I would have collapsed at the knees had I been on my feet. It was then I knew what I would be doing the rest of my life, God willing. Nothing in this world would keep me from her if I could help it.

When they had finished they started to leave. At the door Katrine turned and closed the door behind the one dressed as a nurse. She stood for some minutes before she slowly walked back to the side of the bed. It was as I was about to burst out and tell her of my undying devotion for her that she again put her hand to my mouth as a way of telling me to be quiet. It stopped me dead in my tracks, and the moment passed.

She looked at me for a moment or two, then she said, "Alright, if you are who we think you are, what do you intend doing?"

I picked up on the "we" bit, but said, "Well, I need to get out of this country as soon as possible. You must believe me when I tell you I have never been keen to meet you, or people like you, for one reason. You see, I believe, in fact I am certain, that I'm being very, very closely observed by the GRU. To tell you the truth, Katrine, it seems to me that this whole bloody escapade is just a ploy to unmask the people in Russia like you and your father. Don't get me wrong, I am glad I met you; I am delirious with happiness that I have met you, because, Katrine, I have fallen deeply in love with you, but I do fear I may have put your life in terrible danger. All of you are a real pain in their necks, you know.

"Because of this I have stayed clear of all of you, I came to Russia to do something, and I have now done it. What is more, Katrine, I fail to see why I should have had to make contact with any of you on my way in, or on my way out. I've never needed to do so in the past and I have been here plenty of times before. The only reason as far as I can see is to uncover you. As the Americans say, to finger you and others like you."

She looked at me and then she said, "If you are a double agent and are working for the KGB and if you are here to trap us, you know the others in our group will kill you, don't you?" She then looked at me a little puzzled as she went on to say, "Why would the people in the West send you here to unmask us, when we helped them so much in the past?"

Looking at her I said, "All I can tell you, Katrine, is what I believe. I think you must all have become a threat to whomsoever it is who wants you all dead. Perhaps you unwittingly know some person who, unknown to you, is working for both sides, East and West. All I can tell you is that I now believe your lives are in danger, as is mine. I've been a constant danger to you ever since you came to the old man's house. What is more important, I do have a distinct feeling, Katrine, that your life and the life of anybody who comes near me, is also in danger, very grave danger."

Pausing, I looked into her eyes and I saw a sadness creeping into them. I said. "Something is not right, Katrine; I don't know what it is, but I can feel it, I can sense things are not right. This sixth sense I have has kept me alive in the past more than once, I only hope it works for both of us now. You must have realised just what my feelings towards you are, Katrine. I shall do whatever is in my power to see you are safe as I could not bear to think that I was the reason for your being locked up by the KGB. That is something I know I could not live with. No, Katrine, I would prefer to die than live with that; you see, I have really fallen hopelessly in love with you."

Before I could say anymore, she put her hand to my mouth and said, "Hush! I know how you feel, I would be a fool not to have realised that. What is more I have the same feelings towards you. Unfortunately, we have things far more important than our feelings involved here. Let us leave that until better times."

"I'm sure it will help us to survive and we do have better times to look forward to, Katrine, I can promise you that."

All For A King's Shilling

I sat and looked at her for a moment, then said, "God, if only we could say to hell with it all, we aren't going to take part in your silly games anymore. We are leaving to set up home together and do not want to know anymore about this entire spy, agent, our side/your side nonsense."

It was at that point Katrine said, "You are hurting my hand."

I looked down and sure enough I was not just holding her hand, but squeezing it against my chest, having taken it away from my mouth as she had talked. So I released the pressure of my grip on her hand, but there was no way I was going to let it go. We sat like that for ages, just looking at each other.

Then she grinned and laughed, her eyes sparkling again in her beautiful face as she just said, "Yes, I do."

My mind went into overdrive of delirious emotions as I took in the full meaning of what she had just said. Eventually I managed to get my brain back into gear and said, "Katrine, I can't think properly, my mind is off on a trip round the stars I'm so much in love with you."

"Please, for your own sakes, take me out into the woods to where you found me and just leave me to make my own way out of Russia. It would be healthier for both of us if you were to do that. The sooner I am away from here the better for all our sakes. Then the sooner I can arrange to get you out of here to live with me in the West."

"That is out of the question; firstly you would not last ten minutes out there in your condition, and secondly, it is too late now. No, you will stay here for a little while longer, until you are at least a little bit fitter. Oh I know it is a risk, but it is a risk which I'm willing to take for you. Now I know how you feel about me and you know how I feel about you, please don't spoil it all for us. If you were fitter, then there is nothing I could do to keep you here. In fact, I would even go with you if you'd have me."

I looked at her and I think I was filling with joy right then. Here was the most beautiful person I'd ever met, the most wonderful thing which had ever happened to me, and here I was finding it very hard even to move, the pain in my back being so bad. If I could, I'd have left there and then, and taken her with me, if I'd been able to travel. "Take you with me," I said, "I would carry you to the border if I had to, and I love you so much. There, I have said it, now I want to shout it to the world."

Katrine just laughed and said, "Winter will soon be upon us and you will not be going anywhere, not until we think you have a chance of getting away."

Again she used the expression we, and I wondered who the 'we people' were? "How can you talk like that right at this time?" I asked.

She just smiled then and said, "Because somebody has to keep a level head at times like these." With that final remark she withdrew her hand from mine, leaned forward and kissed me on the forehead. She then turned and swept out of the room.

Conversation over for today, I thought, enough excitement today. One thing is certain, I shall never wash my forehead again, ever. She is right about one thing, though, I wouldn't stand a snowball's chance in hell in my present condition. With that I closed my eyes and went to sleep, only to dream of better times to come with this beautiful woman with whom I was deeply and madly in love.

The next time I saw Katrine was four weeks later. The so-called nurse would not tell me where she was during that four weeks. I was nearly out of my head with worry. Then I thought, I've been had, the bloody woman was using me to get what information she could from me. I formed the opinion that perhaps she had gone to Moscow to report our talks. Then I thought, you arsehole, if she had to report on our conversations she would have just gone to the nearest KGB office.

When I saw her, I cleared all thoughts like that from my mind. A beautiful-looking young woman like her would not be a KGB officer who was trying to trap me and send me to my death. When she came into the room I was standing by the fireplace; I had dressed in Russian peasant's clothes which the young nurse had brought me some days earlier.

I heard the door open and I turned towards it; she was standing in the doorway, framed like a picture. She seemed to fill the doorway with radiant sunshine and I could not see anything outside the room. For all I knew, it might have been an outside door with a busy thoroughfare out there. Mind, I was not looking too closely at the outside of the room, or its surrounds, for that matter. Katrine was now the centre of my attention and my mind, my body, all of me, I had become enthralled by her. She stood there, she fascinated me and she was to say the least radiant. I just looked at her. The thought crossed my mind, I think I am getting better.

When she spoke her voice was like music to my ears, "I see you have improved since the last time I saw you, and you will soon continue your journey, now won't you?" With that she stepped into the room and closed the door behind her.

In a brusque voice I said to her, "I am looking forward to that, where have you been?"

Without waiting for an answer, I continued, "I have asked for my old clothes and some extra clothes to help stop me freezing to death when I am out there in the wasteland."

Again I asked her, "Where have you been?"

Ignoring my questions, she said, "You'll have good clothing when you do go, but first before you leave we need to talk. But not yet, perhaps maybe tomorrow will be better. I shall come to see you and we will talk over your plans and see how we can best help you to get out. You may be in a better frame of mind by then."

Without another word, she left.

After she left the room seemed to be so empty and cold that a shiver ran the length of my body. It was a room without life anymore. I felt a little depressed about it all after she left. I know I shouldn't have let her affect me in this way. Still, I'd a job to do and the sooner I dropped all the thoughts running round in my head about this woman, thoughts of love and caring for one another, the better. It was obvious to me she was working for the KGB; there was no other explanation for it. I sat in the chair by the fire and settled into deep thought about my predicament. As I sat and looked into the flames I felt a tear roll down my cheek. Who the bloody hell was I kidding? All my thoughts were about Katrine, I thought of her first and last, all I did was think about Katrine. That was the only explanation for my outburst, about where she had been these last days. Shit, man, just who in hell's name do you think you are? You haven't any hold or rights over this beautiful woman, have you, you arsehole?

All For A King's Shilling

Six weeks had now passed since my problem with the tree in the forest. I don't think any of the people in the house, except Katrine and the old man who had been with her the first night, had any idea where the old woodsman had found me. As to me, I did not even know just where the hell I was in Russia right now. This house could be anywhere in Russia, I could even be in bloody Moscow for all I knew. Mind, I hoped to God I wasn't. It would be one hell of a walk if I were, I thought.

My next thoughts were, what had happened to my rucksack? I needed it if I were to have any chance of getting out of here alive. I'd searched all my belongings when I'd got them back. None of the important items I had been carrying at the time of my mishap were among them. So I now had no compass, no map and I'd no weapons at all, not even a bloody pen knife. The way items I'd had hidden had been removed from my clothes did give me a little anxiety. Not to put too fine a point on it, an expert had inspected the bits and pieces of kit I'd had with me. This did frighten me somewhat.

No matter what, I had to get my rucksack back, but I didn't even know where it was. For that matter, as I've said, I didn't know where the hell I was. What I did know, though, was that I'd lain here far too long as winter was now upon the place with the enthusiasm one only ever sees in this part of the world. My plan had been to be back in Norway a long time ago, but the main thing was I was still alive and that was a bonus in itself. Even if I were in the hands of the KGB, which I was now of the opinion I was, it looked as if for some reason best known to them they were going to let me make a run for the border. Perhaps they wanted to see how many more of their dissidents I would uncover for them in my attempt to get out and in my belief of this, I was already making plans for just such an event.

It was early the next day and I had just had my breakfast when Katrine came in to see me. "We have been thinking about you," she said.

"Yes," I replied, "You keep saying 'we', Katrine; tell me just who might 'we' be? Just what gem of a solution have the two of you, or are there more than two, decided upon? What is my great escape plan? How am I to escape from here?"

"Do I sense a feeling of bitterness towards the people who are risking their lives to help you?" she asked.

"Look, I've been here too long already and I should have been back over the border some months ago. I have not got any of the things I need to enable me to do that, they've all gone from my equipment. By what I can see of it my equipment has had an expert search it, Katrine, or maybe you are the expert. Did I make a fool of myself with you, Katrine?

"How many laughs have you all had at my expense when you listened to the tapes of our conversations? You must know that without my bits and pieces I don't stand a chance, Katrine, but maybe that is what you want."

Before she could protest, I went on, "Now you and this 'we' person or persons, Katrine. You have made your plans, laid your traps; perhaps you might be a good sport and give me just a small chance of winning this game you have fixed against me. Just give me all my equipment, ten hours' start and I will give you all the greatest run of your lives."

She looked very hurt when I'd finished and with much difficulty she said, "Don't be such a silly man, do you think I'd let them send you on your way without the proper equipment for you to survive our hard winter? I thought you knew how I felt about you, why have you changed the way you have? Why this hostile reception? Don't you know I love you, do you not realize I am risking my life for you?"

I stood looking at her for a moment; she came over and took hold of me by my shoulders. Her eyes were full of tears; I could not help myself, I put my arms around her and just held her close. The touch of her body, the smell of her, which I'd enjoyed the first time she had come close to me, it all sent me into orbit trying to make some sense of my feelings for her. I was really besotted by this woman; I felt I was going crazy.

When I eventually came back to reality, I felt her putting something into the rear waist band of my trousers. As I held her closer for a time I could feel her heart beating next to my chest; I looked at her and said, "I am so sorry, Katrine, it's just that you left without a word. What was I to think?"

"You know we believe you are who you say you are and we are going to help you get over the border. Have no fear; things will go well for you."

God, I thought, I wish she had not come as close to me as she did; all my bloody sense, caution and training went out of the window, up the chimney, or some such place, whenever I touched this woman. At this moment our bodies were only separated by the clothes we were wearing; I was getting to be putty in her hands. It seemed that all she had to do was to smile and I was like a dog with two tails, and I really mean two tails. Holding her in my arms was more than I could stand. I turned her head towards mine, and then looking deep into her eyes I kissed her fully on the lips. When we broke the embrace I knew I would never be anything without her. From now on I'd be like a zombie, or worse still, a bloody green OD.

Katrine brought me back to earth with a jolt as she whispered into my ear, "You will be on your way tonight, my fine young English lover."

She looked me in the eyes then and she must have read my thoughts for she said, "We have believed your story all the time, but we had to make certain, just in case. We also had things to organize. Now I must go and get the rest of your things, then we will plan your trip."

Katrine then told me she would spend the rest of the day briefing me on how to get out and where to go for help and such. With that she said she would be back in a little while and left the room. I sat there and thought so, I shall be on my way tonight. Then I felt the back of my waist and pulled out the thing she had put there while we embraced. It was a piece of folded paper. Holding it in the palm of my hand I crossed to the bed and lay face down on it. Why, I don't know, but I was glad I had. With my hand close to my body, I opened the piece of paper under my chest and slowly edged it forward so I could read it.

It started with Katrine apologizing about why she had been away. Then she went on to tell me that the nurse who was looking after me was a member of the KGB. Katrine then went on to say that the nurse had infiltrated the local group and of course they had not known when they called for somebody with nursing training to look after me that it was the nurse who was the KGB informer. She had informed the KGB when she had confirmed I was an Englishman. That was how the KGB had found out about her and her father. Katrine went on to write that the KGB had been running things in the house since the third day.

All For A King's Shilling

They had taken Katrine's father away and told her that if she did not cooperate with them, they would execute him. She said she could not do otherwise. They had said they would accept her father's story as a true account, mainly that it had just been by chance and a silly old woodsman, who had once been their gardener, had involved them. They told her that once they had me working for them, her father would be out of prison and they could go on plotting their stupid little revolutions as much as they wanted.

The KGB had then taken her to Moscow; once there, they questioned her for two weeks and in the end she had agreed to do as they wished. She was sorry, but she had to save her father. The KGB had a plan to let me go that night; they would have all sorts of interior ministry troops out looking for me. If they killed me, it would be too bad. If they didn't kill me, then the KGB believed that I would lead them to more of these silly groups, groups like her father's who plotted all the time against the State and didn't know what was good for them.

She ended her letter by saying, "I'm sorry, but I could not do anything else once they took my father; although I truly love you and long to be with you, I still have to try to save my father. Please forgive me, Bill, I love you so much and I will miss you forever once you have gone."

So I thought, I wonder what plans they have for me? I can do nothing about it anyhow, not until I am out there and on my own. Then we shall see just what little game the KGB are playing. Thank you my sweet, beautiful young lady of Russia. Katrine, I thank you for the information you have given me in this bit of paper. You may just have saved my life, but I fear for your own and your father's lives. Once I leave your house, my dearest Katrine, I'm afraid the KGB will have no need to keep you alive anymore. For this reason I'm afraid I may have cost you your life.

When I had finished reading it, I pushed the paper back into my shirt front and as nonchalantly as possible I stepped over to the fireplace. Then I sat on the floor and picked up the poker. With my back to the rest of the room, I wrapped the paper around the poker and pushed it into the fire. When it had burnt completely I poked the fire a bit more and replaced the poker by the side of the fireplace. Nobody came dashing in so I assumed all was well.

I didn't have long to wait after that, within ten minutes Katrine was back. She and a man I had never seen before came into the room bearing all my gear. Not only did he bring the Russian KGB man's holster, but my rucksack also. They laid them down and she told the man to leave. He smiled at me and left, I didn't like that smile one little bit. I had the distinct feeling he had been watching me all the time I had been there. He was about thirty-five, six feet tall and about fifteen stones and he looked like the real Russian brown bear, or should I say KGB bear.

The thought that he might be Katrine's husband never entered my head. They just did not seem to fit together at all. So I must have automatically dismissed the idea. The thing was I now had all my gear back, even my rucksack. I was looking through the stuff trying to seem nonchalant as I did so; I was also trying to see if it was all there. At the same time I was trying to see if the KGB had placed some of their famous bugs in it. When I satisfied myself all was well on this first cursory look, I then settled down to find out what plans they had told Katrine to brief me about, plans which would, supposedly, get me on my way home.

She looked at me and I could see she wanted to know if I had read her note. "It looks as if all my things are here. I see somebody has burnt the scrap of old notepaper which I had in here."

I was holding the waist of my trousers as I spoke. "Now tell me, Katrine, just what wonderful route you have picked for me. Is it the short one, or the longer, more scenic one?" I asked.

She looked at me a little puzzled for a moment then as the penny dropped and she realized what I'd said she flashed that smile which had me going weak at the knees.

The plan, it seemed, was to take me as far as they could without endangering their own lives. Then Katrine told me, "Movement around the area is very much restricted. Much more than it is usually. This is because the search is still going on for the terrorist, the one who blew up the atomic storage plant on the other side of the bay. I must admit I don't believe it for one minute, security isn't any more or less than it is normally."

"You know, they taught in training that if you cause a problem for the Russians, their security sparks into operation very quickly. You know, Katrine, I saw the explosion and I heard some men talking in the woods the next day. The men said that the explosion was the work of the scientists, who made a serious mistake in their calculations. Then the KGB reacted in a very predictable way," I said.

Of course, I had refrained from telling her I had once spent quite a long time in the area of the explosion and that I had revisited the place more than once. What was more, I did not mention the fact that it was I who had blown the place up. It was not my fault if they had thought it right to store atomic weapons there. It would be best, I thought, for her welfare and for mine that she did not know too much about that side of my mission. I still wasn't certain that everything was okay; I had an idea I might just be the fox which they were letting run to see who and what came out of the woodwork.

The plan which they devised for me was to take me back to the place where Katrine and I had first met. Surprise, surprise, it was their intention to take me to the old woodsman's hut. Once at the woodsman's hut, they would then decide whether it would be safe to take me any further towards the border. They said it would all depend on how active the police and the KGB were. This lot I took with the large pinch of salt it required. To my way of thinking and training the whole plot smelt just a bit, to say the least. For instance, how was it they could get me to the place where I was first picked up without any trouble, but they couldn't take me to the border? What crap, the KGB could take me to the nearest airport, put me on a plane and fly me out of the country to Heathrow if it wanted to. It was obvious that Katrine had no choice in the matter; she had to tell me what the KGB had told her to. Still I would have thought even the KGB could have come up with a more plausible plan for them than this.

Still I was their guest so to say and I was the ball they were going to play with, to bounce and kick about just as they wanted to, but thanks to Katrine I knew the score. In the beginning I would have to go along with it. It was obvious I was getting better as even with these odds stacked against me, I was getting impatient. Now I was eager to be on my way, to me it didn't matter if I were a fox, hound or ball, the sooner the game was afoot the better. Since I was again on the run, at least I would have a chance and that was the important bit, I'd have a chance. As long as I remained in a static place, like this house, I was easy picking for any of them, goodies or baddies. I asked her what information she could give me on any of the patrols in the area. She said she couldn't give me any. I was trying to play my part in the charade for Katrine's sake, but the bastards had told her nothing.

Then I thought it was time to get my things ready so I set to and checked out all my kit thoroughly. It was at this point I found out I had a problem with my pistol, which had now been returned to me. First, the firing had been tampered with, at least the end that mattered had. It had been filed down and I doubted if it would strike the base of any of the rounds when they were in the chamber. Secondly, they had doctored the silencer in some way or other. There was no sign of the KGB officer's pistol in the kit.

That was not all, either. The map they had given me was not the one I'd had when I was found out in the woods; it was of another area. I do not know where or what part of Russia it covered, but it definitely wasn't the map I'd had when the accident with the tree occurred. There were some marks which I had made on my old map and they were not on this one.

It was at this point I realized I was in real trouble. I felt they would give me a load of cock and bull when they got me to the old woodsman's hut later tonight. Another thing, why set me off at night? I would be off, trudging along in the wrong direction completely, with no clue where I was by daylight. So I was not in a very happy mood at all with this little lot. Okay, they had done a good job on my recovery, but I would now be completely under the control of the KGB. As for Katrine, well I could not believe she had anything to do with the KGB and in my book she was in the clear, but then I would, wouldn't I? One thing was for certain, my brain, what little of it I had left, was working overtime formulating a new plan as fast as I could. Now I knew the KGB plan then I had something to alter.

It was at this point of my deliberations that Katrine asked, "Is everything all right? I will half kill that woodsman, if any of your things are missing."

"They are all here, Katrine, and there is nothing to worry about. I shall get by with what I've got here."

"Well, it will not be long before we part company for the time being. Will we ever meet again?"

"Don't worry, Katrine, we will meet again soon."

"I was thinking I could come with you and help you until you reach the border."

As I looked into her beautiful face, I said, "Katrine, there is nothing in the world I'd rather do; I would like to take you with me away from this life you have. I'd like to take you out to the West with me so that we could live together and forget all about this place and these people. If you came with me as far as the border there's no way I'd cross it with you coming with me. You must know that, but you must also know that I'm involved in a deadly game. I know the KGB are using me, just as they are using you. There is no way they are going to let me cross the border. I'm just an end to a means for them and the bottom line for me is that they will kill me when I've outlived my usefulness. I'm afraid, Katrine, that when I step out into the snow later tonight I am as good as dead."

We were both silent for a time, then Katrine asked, or rather pleaded with me, "You must take me with you; if you are to die then I don't want to live, not now. We must go together and face whatever comes together."

"No, Katrine. That is out of the question. You know they would never allow that to happen. Now it won't be long before I must leave you, so let's not discuss it anymore. I must thank you for looking after me so well, I would never have survived without your help. Katrine, I owe you my life and I will repay you, you can count on that. When things look the blackest for you then one of my friends or I will come for you and we will take you away from all this; don't worry, it will be fine, I'll make it, you will see."

"Perhaps one day you will come for me, but I'd rather go with you now and take my chance. What I've done for you is the least I could have done."

She paused there and looked around in a nervous way. "There is one thing more you could do for me, though."

"Oh, and what might that be?"

"You must promise me you will not take unnecessary risks. You can still have a great influence in this game you are playing. I've never liked rats," she added.

At that we both burst out laughing and the ice of tension which had been building up between us broke.

She came into my arms and we looked at each other with our foreheads touching and our arms locked around our waists for what seemed a good five minutes without saying a word.

Then at last I broke the spell, "I love you more than you could ever imagine, Katrine, but now is neither the time nor the place to bring our love to any sort of fruition. That is beyond our wildest dreams for the moment. You must know that, Katrine; we are but two pawns in a far bigger game than we can handle. Perhaps we are just in a time slip, if you know what I mean."

She just nodded. I felt she was okay and had in her way tried to warn me that all was not what it seemed to be, something which I'd already arrived at not long after I got there. She stayed for another hour; we held hands and chatted about life in the Soviet Union and its difference from life in the West. It seemed to me the contact of our bodies as we held each other was far more important than anything we said. It was a more positive gesture, but as I told her of the life in the West, the brighter her eyes shone as she listened to me. When it was getting close to the time for me to leave, I turned the water on in the hand basin and left it running.

Then I said, "Katrine, listen very carefully, there is a small fishing village in Norway, which is not the most beautiful place in the West, but it is a place where a friend of mine is soon to be based. Now, if I'm captured later and I come to trial in open court here in Russia this friend of mine in the village will probably attend the trial. I'll get a message to him somehow and one day soon after that he will come and collect you. He will know something about us which only we know, so when he comes for you, you are to go with him, don't ask questions, just do as he asks. No matter where you are at the time he will find you. He will take you away from all this to a place where if I'm alive I will one day join you. If I am not, he will still get you out of this godforsaken country. He and his sister will take care of you; it is the least I can do for you, Katrine, to repay you for your help."

As I looked into her eyes, I could not tell if she understood the gravity of what I'd just said. I think I had got my message across to her, but I wasn't certain. It was then the nurse came in with my evening meal.

With the arrival of the meal, Katrine said, "I will leave you to eat in peace."

She then left the room and I ate my meal alone as if it was to be my last. As I ate, I felt a cold shiver down my spine which gave me a feeling of doom. I just wanted to be on my way.

So it was that about an hour later the man whom I'd only seen once bundled both my kit and I unceremoniously into the rear seat of a large black car, a Zil I think. It was very dark and it took me a couple of minutes before I realized the person sitting on my left was a woman. She put her arm through mine; I looked up and was about to pull away when I caught a whiff of her scent. It was Katrine who was sitting next to me looking at me out of the fur hood of her coat.

I looked to my right and there was this man who had brought me all my gear. He did not look right. I felt the hairs on the back of my neck rise as I looked at him. I had a distinct feeling there was no love-lost here.

As I looked at Katrine, I said, "Here we are, about to part company for ever and I do not even know who I am to send a Christmas card to this coming year."

She looked at me a little strangely at first, then she flashed that smile, and all my troubles were over whenever she did that.

"Just Katrine," was all she said.

She then withdrew her arm, took out a handkerchief and blew her nose. This guy sitting on my right was watching her every move and as she replaced her handkerchief in her coat pocket he settled back into the seat. Next Katrine replaced her arm in mine, but she did not interlock with mine right away. Instead I felt her searching for my pocket and once she had found it she placed something inside it. She did it so well our companion sitting on the back seat did not know what had happened, of that I'm sure. Katrine then gave my arm a slight squeeze, then she edged her hand down my arm until our hands touched and then we grasped each others' hands tightly as the car sped through the greyness of the late afternoon. I let her know I knew what she had done by giving her hand a distinct squeeze.

We then settled down for a long drive, far longer than I had thought we would have. It took the best part of five hours; for some reason I'd had the feeling that the house I had stayed in these last few weeks was only an hour's drive at most from the place where I had had the accident. That couldn't have been the case considering the time this trip was taking. At last we turned off the road on to a track leading into some wood. I thought at the time how funny it was that we hadn't in all the time we had been travelling, seen any of the extra security on the roads. Still, we might just have been lucky. I doubted it, though.

We then went down the track for about an hour or more and at last we came to a hut. The car stopped and we all got out; the guy who had been in the back with us went into the hut. An older man, who got out of the front passenger seat of the car, came round to the back of the car to help me get my gear out of the boot. As I lifted it out of the boot of the car I felt a stab of pain in my back and flinched. This guy then took the rucksack from me and carried it into the hut for me. As he took it from me, he said in a hushed voice, "I'm so sorry, my young friend." He then walked into the hut, his shoulders hunched in the way of a man who already knows his fate. I was next, followed by Katrine, and the driver brought up the rear. He had left the engine running in the car and I thought of making a dash for it, but I knew I'd never be able to get the bloody thing turned round before they killed me.

When I got into the hut it took about a minute or so for my eyes to grow accustomed to the light. When they did, I looked around at our sorry looking group and said, "We are a happy bunch of pilgrims, are we not?"

There then came a grunt from the side of the fireplace, which drew my attention to it. Sitting in an upright position was a heap of rags in a corner by the side of the fire. As I watched, the heap moved and I saw a man's face. At first glance in that light he looked similar to the man I had first remembered picking me up from under the tree in which I had been hiding. He was also similar to the man who had picked me up when they had taken me from the hut those weeks before. Now it seemed like ages ago, not weeks.

Then I looked again at the face; only this time I had a better look at it in the light from the fire and I was certain this time that he was not the man who had found me. This man's face well, it didn't have the ravages caused by the time and hardship spent in these woods winter after winter, as was the case with the man I remembered. So I thought the game is well and truly afoot now. This man was similar to the old woodsman, but he wasn't the same man at all. Then I looked at the rest of them and I realized that the only two who were with me that night were the man who had carried my gear into this hut, and of course Katrine. Everybody else in there, well, they were strangers and I now really had alarm bells ringing in my head. Not only was I in trouble, but also Katrine and the other older man who had helped me with my gear were as good as dead. It was then the penny dropped; the old man was Katrine's father. As I looked at them both, I just shook my head; there was nothing I could do for them now and nothing they could do for me.

For the first time in my life I understood about the selection procedures the Gestapo made in the camps. Only now had I finally understood how they got away with it and why the people never rioted. There was no point; it was completely pointless to do so. You were going to die anyway. What difference would a few minutes make, better spend a little longer with your loved ones.

By now I'd had enough of this bloody charade and I said to all of them in the room, "Well, I think I will be on my way now. I am glad for all the help you have given me. We don't need to drag our goodbyes out too long or it will be daylight and we don't want you all to get arrested by the security police on your way home now, do we? So it's best if I get on my way."

Then I walked round the small table to Katrine and I took her in my arms. As I hugged her close to me I whispered in her ear, "I love you, Katrine, and I shall never forget you. Some day my friend or I will come for you to take you from this place, then we will be together for always."

When I released her from my hug, I looked her in the eye and said, "Thank you for everything you have done for me. Without your help I might already be dead." I then leaned forward again and whispered in her ear, "I know what is going on, Katrine; I'm not so much of a fool as these bums think I am."

Then I looked at the rest and said, "I haven't met any of you, except the old woodsman, before today so I can only say thank you for getting me back on course. When I get home I shall drink a glass of vodka in London, in memory of you all."

With that I picked up my kit and put it on, trying not to show the pain which that little action caused me, and then I turned and walked out of the door.

The driver and the other guy who had been on the back seat with me came outside behind me. One of them said, "Better you than me, Mister. Just how do think you are going to get out of Russia?"

With that I turned and looked at both of them and then I said, "Oh! Don't lose too much sleep over that. You see, that is for me to know and you, well that's for you to think a lot about, but I shall do it as I have done it every time I have visited your lovely country in the past. There is always a way, somehow there is always a way out." As they looked at me with their mouths open, I turned and made my way along the track and into the woods. Where I was going, I hadn't the faintest bloody idea. At that precise moment in time I didn't know if I was going north, east, south, west or bloody vertical, but I was on my own and I felt free.

I made my way up the track and after a short time I heard a car rev up and it sounded as if it had left the area. I kept going for a little while longer taking it very slowly and easily, searching the woods on each side of the track for the thing I needed to get me off the track. At last I found what I was looking for and stopped. Standing on one foot at first, I balanced myself then, satisfied it was just right, I placed my other foot one stride in front of me. In that stance I surveyed the tree with the large branch which was hanging over the track about seven feet above it. Now the hard bit started, I set off again up the track and after about fifty yards I turned to my right and walked into the cover of the trees. There wasn't too much snow here so I decided I didn't need to go any further into the woods.

Here in amongst the trees I rested for a moment or two listening to hear if I was being followed. When I was satisfied I was alone, I made my way back to where the snow started. There I turned and with much hard work and sweat I began to retrace my steps the way I'd come, only this time I was walking backwards. Taking great care not to disturb any other snow, I slowly and painfully made my way back to the overhanging branch. Once I was under it, I hoisted myself up on to the branch and slowly pulled myself along it to where it joined the trunk of the tree. I sat for a few minutes getting my breath back and then I lowered myself down on to the floor of the woods and the safety of the blackness beneath the trees. Next I made my way into the forest for about half a mile and sat against the trunk of a tree to wait and recover. I now realized that the whole episode had taken more out of me than I cared to admit.

It wasn't long before I started to feel the cold and it was then I realized I was not in any shape or form to make it over the border. Somehow or other I had to find somewhere to stay over winter, or to stay until I was at least a bit fitter. Also, I desperately needed to know where the hell I was.

Because of the cold and my poor health I must have dozed off, because I came to with a start. By now it was cold, bloody cold, but it was daylight. A layer of white frost covered me, so the air must have been very cold while I was asleep. As I looked around I could not see any sign of disturbance other than I'd made. To say I was freezing my parts off was, as the saying goes, putting it bloody mildly and I sat a while rubbing my arms and legs before I got up. Last time that happened, old pal, the situation was bad; you will die if you start letting yourself adopt that attitude.

Then I picked up my kit and made my way back to the track. At the edge of the track I stopped and studied the situation for a moment or two and all seemed clear. Then I headed back the way I'd come, only this time I stayed in the woods, travelling about twenty yards or so in from the track. It took me less time to reach the hut which I had left the night before than it had taken me to reach the place where I had spent what remained of the night. Now I stopped just short of the hut and spent the next hour watching and listening. The birds were singing as I approached and they had stopped when I got near the hut. Now after I had been there about ten minutes they had started to sing again. I still waited though; if I was going to die today I had no intentions of rushing the job.

As I stood against the trunk of a tree I watched the area of the hut. It was then I remembered what Katrine had done in the car, so I felt in my left-hand pocket and there was a small packet there. After I took the package out, I settled into a sitting position behind the tree to see what I had. I could hardly believe my eyes when I saw inside. First, there was a firing pin for my pistol; there was also a note written on some coarse cream-coloured paper. The note I put away in my pocket again, then I took my rucksack off and got my gun out. Next I proceeded to repair the gun; first things first was always my motto, anything to do with saving my life was always top of any lists I have ever had. Once I had the gun back together again, I tried it out, not firing it, but by pressing against the rear of the pin. This way I checked that it protruded sufficiently to strike the round in the chamber when it was hit by the hammer on firing. Satisfied it was working okay, I repacked all my kit and put everything ready so I could move instantly.

Whoever had worked on my gun had done a first class job of work. The one thing I didn't understand was why they had fitted a new shorter pin, instead of just filing down the one in my gun. Funny really, still not to worry, I now felt I might just have a chance of getting away. Mind, I would not know until I had to use it for real, then we would see if it would work or it wouldn't. It would be too late to worry about it, anyway.

Again I took out the packag which contained the letter from Katrine. In this she said some stupid things, things about how in trying to help me, they had probably in the end caused my death. She was sure the KGB were going to kill me once they had let me go. I thought Katrine, you silly girl. She had not grasped the idea yet, had the KGB wanted me dead, then dead I would be right now. No, they intended to use me, I was to be the bait to flush out more people in the area, people like her and her father who were prepared to help some poor traveller such as me. People prepared to help me, instead of turning me over to the KGB in the first place, people who dared to resist the all-encompassing state monolith which they had over the years created in this place. Neither Katrine nor her friends knew in just what danger they had been these last few weeks.

The poor sods would probably know by now. They would by now all have gone straight to a KGB interrogation house. Katrine and her father would have gone there after they left here last night. I think her father knew the score, though; having survived under Stalin he would know the routine they used. She then went on to say how good it would have been for us had we met under different circumstances. I thought about that for some time and then I put it to the back of my mind. It was a good dream, but nothing more than a dream now.

There wasn't anything I could do for them now. I was still in a hell of a mess myself. It would take all my skill and all my expertise to get my backside out of this mess. There was no time to think about them now; there was just a chance I could probably help if ever I managed to get out of this Godforsaken land.

It was at this point that the hair on the back of my neck first started to tingle a little, then I heard the noise, or should I say the lack of it. The birds had stopped their chatter and all had gone quiet. The hair on the back of my neck now stood up and I came alive immediately, not as fast as I should have, but not too slowly. Provided I lived the next couple of days out, I felt I would get my edge back, at least I kept telling myself I would, but God, I was cold.

By this time my ears were up like a deer's. As I strained my every nerve I could just make out a slight noise; it was of men coming down the track up which I had gone last night. As the noise got louder, I could hear a faint swish of fabric brushing together and then the first of them came into sight. They were very tactical in their movements, they were not mugs in any way, shape or form, no rush to get down the track. No, they were good, they had white camouflage over-uniforms on and they were well spaced out. Had I come across them on the move, there was no way I would have got them all, for the simple reason that they never presented themselves as one body of men, they were dispersed too well for that.

No, had I met them on the move I would have died. The fourteen of them filed past me in a very professional way and they really did impress me. It was at this point I also realized I had a real problem if this lot were after me. I would be very lucky to make it out of Russia, very lucky indeed. These were not your average soldiers, this lot, these men were specialists, if I ever saw any. No, these men were much too good to be border guards or police, or even the KGB for that matter. In a way I am glad I had seen them so early in the game; now I had a good idea what I was up against. A few weeks ago when I was my normal cocky self, I would have run rings round them. In my present condition that would be impossible. Then I remembered I'd had a run-in with this lot before, or some of their mates up on the western coast of Russia, but I hadn't been alone that time. I had had Nobby and Mick with me.

As I watched, they made their way to the hut and then took up a defensive half-circle around it. When he was satisfied with their performance, their leader went inside. From my position I could hear nothing of what was going on inside the hut. Shortly the leader came out with another man dressed in civilian clothes. I had not seen this man before. I must admit he did worry me. The commander of the troops I respected, but this guy sent shivers up and down my spine. The two of them stood chatting for a couple of minutes. The only thing I did hear of any significance for me was, "Not to worry, we probably can pick him up later. I'm just sorry he did not walk into your ambush back there. It would all have been over now. Instead, we will all have to go chasing around the bloody country looking for him and playing the KGB's silly games. I've already told my boss this man will not contact anyone and he agrees with me. Still had it not been for his misfortune and bad luck getting himself injured, they would not have got the nest of vipers who are at this moment on their way to

Archangel, from where the KGB will ship them to Moscow. Still, now we will have to play their silly games and go through with the original plan."

So I now had an idea what this man's first plan was. As to the KGB, I now had the proof as I'd suspected that they wanted me to contact as many people as I could on that stupid list they had tried to give me in London. Obviously, looking at the troops I had just seen, I was now glad I also knew that the first plan was finalised. Mind, I would have liked to know if there were any more plans and, if so, I'd dearly have loved to know what they were. Then I thought it was about time I found out where the hell I was, but I could hardly step out and ask them, now could I?

Next thing I knew, the men were getting up and forming into three ranks, turning right and moving off down the track. All was deathly quiet after they had gone. I was not sure, but I did have the feeling the man who had come out of the hut with the commander of this little lot had gone back inside it. I was not sure but I thought he had. As I did not see him going down the track with the men in the snow suits, I reasoned he must have gone back inside the hut. So I just sat tight for a little while longer and I am glad I did. For within the hour two trucks arrived, coming up the track and stopping outside the hut. When they had stopped, the guy who had travelled in the back of the car with Katrine and I came out of the hut and spoke to a driver. Then the trucks turned round, in what little space there was, and parked outside the hut. They were not large trucks, but the kind we would call fifteen hundred weights, or even one tonne trucks. The next thing did surprise me; I had believed the only Russians around were the ones in the white snow-suits and the one or two in the hut. I now knew there were at least two in the hut.

When one of them came out and blew on a whistle, I got one hell of a fright. About fifteen men in snow-suits arose and stepped out of the trees. My knees shook as I watched them. I could not believe that none of them had seen me come down the track and into my present position. It was then I realized that they knew exactly where I was. It was the most frightening thing of the whole operation. They had intended to kill me the night before, claim it was an accident, then that would have been it. Because I had stopped short of the ambush, they had called it in. They knew I was near the hut, they must know. Also they were confident they could pick me up any time they damned well pleased. That meant only one thing, they had bugged me, the way people do with birds and animals in the West when they are studying them. Thinking about it, I had visions of KGB men all over the place with aerials trying to tune into me. Well, I thought we shall see about that, you KGB men.

As I watched they packed all their gear into the trucks and then all climbed aboard. As they drove off I thought, now to see what they have left behind in the hut. I was just about to get up and go and see when the guy who had been in the car with Katrine and me came back up the track. That was a hell of a close shave. He shouted something I could not quite make out. The next thing, one of them came out of the hut to talk to him. They chatted for a little while and then he turned and set off down the track again and the other one returned to the hut.

Perhaps it was shock, but I sat for a few minutes, my legs shaking. I had nearly walked into that bloody hut. Christ, man, I said to myself, for God's sake get a bloody hold of your self. You are acting like a recruit on his first field exercise. For heaven's sake, man, pull your self together or it will be the end of you. After the trucks had left, I waited for another half hour or so and then I retreated into the woods.

Once in the trees, I made my way into the thickest part I could see, which was about a mile or more from the hut. Once I was sure I was not in view, I started with my rucksack, then the KGB overcoat that I still had. What I was looking for was something which remotely resembled a transmitting bug. I just about stripped down to my birthday suit, but still I found nothing.

When I had put my gear back together I sat on a log to have a little think. I started with the premise, now where would I put a bug on a person if I had the job to do?

Well, I thought, there are places but I would know if it was there. Could they have implanted it when I was unconscious, during the first couple of days I was ill? I discounted that idea, because I did not think the KGB had become involved in the game until after that period. So it had to be in my equipment, or in my clothes. Now my clothes were Western, I doubt if they had any bugs designed like Western clothes.

From that I therefore reasoned it must be in the KGB coat, so I could leave the coat behind and all would be well. No, sir, I thought, if I left the coat behind I would have no way of knowing if I were right and if they were still tracking me or not. So off came the coat again. This time I examined not only the cloth, but every thread. It was while doing this I came upon one of those threads one finds now and again in material. It is very hard and sharp like a needle. I got hold of it between my teeth and as I pulled, it came out without puckering up the cloth. Well, I thought, what have we got here, could this be an aerial, or not? It was not a cotton thread. Then I traced the thread to a button inside the coat. This was it, I thought, a bug and I do not mean the type that crawls all over you.

So that was it, get rid of this and they would never know where I was. Don't you believe it, I thought, if they have planted one, they most certainly will have planted another backup one. So, start the bloody search all over again. This time it had got to be the rucksack, it had to be in the rucksack if there was a second one. So it was I ripped the rucksack to shreds and yes, I did find another one. They had used the frame as an aerial and planted the bug in the corner of the bag, in the thick leather part which was as stiff as a board. God, I wish I could have caught a fox or a deer to attach these bugs to; I'd give them bloody bugs. It was not to be though; I must get rid of them, but not on the move. Let them think I had not found them; keep going and the next time I stopped for a rest leave them behind when I moved on.

The best time to do that would be at night. Let them think I had stopped for the night, leave the bugs hanging from a tree, then just keep on going, but I'd have to change direction though. No sense heading the way I intended to go, it would only be pointing to a place ahead of me where they could then pick me up whenever they felt like it. So the plan was starting to formulate in my head, first to set off slightly off the course I wanted to follow, then after some miles to stop for the night, leave the bugs and carry on. As it would be morning, or with any luck late morning, before they thought something was wrong, hopefully it would be late afternoon before they got anybody out to check. They would take it very cautiously in their approach, which should be one day to me. Maybe it would take them till the next morning before they got anybody out after me so with any luck I might get one or even two days' start on them.

Well, it sounded good to me. The only thing was, which way did I go from here. I needed to know where I was before I could decide on that. I knew I was nowhere near the place where Katrine and her father had picked me up. The biggest problem I had to figure out was where I was. It would be dark soon and I probably could get some sort of fix when the stars came out, always providing I could see them. They would not have let me loose without knowing the weather would be overcast. So far, since they turned me loose, all I had seen were clouds and flurries of snow, not a very conducive atmosphere for the deadly escape and evasion game in which I was deeply involved, with my life as the first prize.

Now, as I'd ruined my rucksack and I had nothing to carry my gear in, I looked at the mess at my feet. Then I remembered the blanket rolls the Americans used to carry during their Civil War. So I set to with what bits and pieces I had and constructed a similar type of roll with the remains of my rucksack. I then hoisted this over my back and across my shoulder and set off in what I hoped would be a westerly direction. I made steady progress for what remained of the day, but there was no way of telling how many miles I had covered when it started to get dark. Once I got into my stride I did not stop before darkness fell.

Just before it got completely dark I found a small hollow in the ground in which I set to. First, I made myself a small hide and I made it as windproof as I could in the circumstances. Then I prepared myself a meal from the scraps of food they had let Katrine give me while they were still play-acting back at her house.

When it was nearly dark my prayers were answered and the skies cleared; it was not for long though. I would have preferred a longer look at the heavens, but that was not to be. By chance or fluke I did manage to get a glimpse of the Pole Star, though. It was enough; I marked its position by a tree-top and the place in which I was standing in the snow. Next I hid the bugs, one in the snow and the other in a tree. When I was happy with my handiwork, I loaded my kit up again and went and stood at the point I had marked. First, I took a fix on the top of the tree and looked long and hard; I knew I was clutching at straws, but straws were all I had. Slowly I turned until I was looking what I believed to be north by west.

Here I hesitated for about a minute and then I looked again at the top of the tree, which I believed was due north, and I shook my head. Looking in the direction I believed to be north by west, I stepped out and said aloud, "This is it; the game is now really well and truly under way. Let us now see who are the smartest pants around here." With that I was away. It might just be that the hide I'd built would help to delay and maybe confuse them. They might think I had spent the whole night there. I may have gained some time, but then again I may not.

Dawn broke with a slight wind blowing in my face; the trees had thinned and I thought it looked as if it was going to be a good day after all. I felt good, I think I had made good progress during the night and I thought things seemed to have changed for the better. I even raised my pace and opened my stride I was so confident. Yes, things were at last looking good. The next few hours were completely free of rain, snow or sleet; the clouds kept clearing for maybe half an hour at a time. In my reckoning they were all heading in a south easterly direction. Mind you, I could have been completely off the mark, I was travelling blind. Russia is a big place and I could be anywhere in the Soviet Union for all I knew.

Chapter Twelve
The Evil Sods Have Finally Got Their Dirty Hands On Me!
Russia, Arctic Circle 1965

You needn't stand upon the seat,
The crabs in here can
Jump six feet

    I was going to say that it at was at least three, possibly four days, after I'd set off on the little stroll I took through the forests of Northern Russia when I had my first real fright; but to be honest with you I didn't have a clue how many days it had been. The forest in that area seemed to be never-ending. Unfortunately for me, I think it was during the third or fourth day that I stumbled out from the trees and into open countryside. Since I'd started the walk I had suffered the indignity of being frozen to the bone and soaked to the skin. My body, from the top of my head to the soles of my feet, was scratched, cut, and badly bruised by the branches of the trees as I had stumbled through the forest.
    By the time I realised I had stumbled into open countryside, which I might add was one of my worst fears, I felt so naked with nowhere to hide. My body at the time was being blasted by the icy wind that hardly ever rests and it was as if I were in a sandblasting tunnel. To make matters worse, most of the clothes I was wearing were by then frozen to my body. Also, I was suffering the most gigantic loss of energy I had ever suffered. This was because I was nearly dead from starvation and lack of water. I had not eaten for quite some time and didn't even have the strength or inclination to try and catch a small rodent to eat, but worse still I had stopped sucking on any ice or snow to provide liquid for my body. It was just to cold and I was frightened it would chill my internal organs too much. More to the point, what little bit of my brain that was still functioning had decided that it would be unwise to stay in one place long enough to set traps and the like.
    It was after questioning that decision for the umpteenth time that some sense of reality started to return through the cold numbness of my mind, because at last I realized that sooner or later I was going to have to stop and find food from

somewhere or I was going to die. I remember thinking, well at least when I died I'd stop this automatic plodding on and on. Or maybe my ghost would just keep trudging around this part of Russia until eternity.

Before I had set off I had no idea just how bad my earlier back injury had been or how much it had sapped my strength. Oh, I'd suspected that I would be moving at least a third to half the speed I was used to travelling at but never at the snail's crawl I was doing then. While I was starving and stumbling along, trying to make my way to what I hoped was freedom, I was doing a lot of thinking, most of which was pure drivel. The one thing I did believe I'd worked out, though, was when the KGB became involved with the local people who had been looking after me.

Not that it made any difference to my situation when the bastards got involved as I was already in good old shit street and I knew it. 'Land of Hope and Glory', 'Life on the Ocean Wave'. Ye gods what an arsehole those bastards in London had turned me into. Good for King and Country, or is it now Queen and Country? So if everything on the 'overseas front' had been as 'tickety-boo' as those bastards in London had claimed it was, then why hadn't they, instead of sitting in their snug warm offices back in London, come out here into the real world to check out the situation for themselves? To find out just how painful 'tickety-boo' could really be.

When I was first in Katrine's house, I was forever going on to her that I should be back on the move, and the sooner the better for all of us. Must get moving, I kept telling her, I must make a start to make my way out of Russia. The longer I stayed there, I kept telling her, then the worse it would be for her father and she if I were found in their house. "It's for your own good," I had pleaded with her, but she would have none of it. She insisted that I would not be allowed to leave their house until I was fit. "You will never make it out of Russia in your present state. With the weather the way it is at this time of the year, you would not stand a chance," she had insisted.

She was correct in her assessment of my health and my situation, of course, but I still kept on insisting that I had to leave. I told her over and over that it would be safer for all of us, but by the third day after I'd left the old woodsman's hut I began to believe she had been right all along. What I do remember most is that she was so adamant I should wait the winter out with them. The discussion I remember did get a little heated at one stage. I knew I had fallen in love with her and for some reason she stopped coming to see me for a few days. At first I was a little worried, but then I thought she is just like a typical Western woman. She can't get her own way, so she goes off in the huff. Oh boy, just how wrong can you be?

When next she came to see me I was too self-centered in my own predicament to notice she had completely changed her attitude to my leaving. It was she who now kept suggesting that the time to go was now, right now, I should be on my way now. More to the point she insisted that I should leave that night; and that is exactly what happened, I left that very night. I think it was some three to six nights before I had stumbled out into the open country.

The night I left I knew from the first moment I saw the car that something was badly amiss. For one thing, the move from her house back to the woodsman's hut was too well organized for the dissident group with which Katrine and her father were loosely associated to have organized. So much so that the members of their group couldn't have arranged the type of car that carried Katrine, her father and me. There was no way that group of nonconformists with whom both Katrine and her father were involved could have had access to such a car. Her complete and sudden change from being adamant that I should stay, to her persistence that I should go, and go that night, should have told me the KGB had arrived early for Christmas dinner, with me being the turkey, a part I seemed to be playing more often than I would like. I should have realised that neither she nor her father was in control of the situation anymore. Although everything had seemed normal, thinking about it now, I noticed the change of atmosphere after Katrine had stopped coming to see me each day. Then the day she returned it was suddenly all systems go!

"You must get ready to be on your way, you will be better off leaving tonight," she had blurted out as she entered the room. Not a word about how are you feeling, William, or Bill? Nothing at all, just this blunt Russian interpretation of the old Royal Marine Commando expression of 'Time we thinned out of here mate'!

I remember the way she made the statement that I should get ready to leave that night had confirmed all my suspicions but I was too besotted at seeing her again to make anything of it. Looking back, I must have been running a brain in for an idiot. Mind you, coming to the conclusion and realising the situation I was then in did nothing for my state of mind or my well-being right then because I was and still am completely besotted by the most beautiful woman that I have ever laid eyes on, and I'd seen a few in my time.

There was one very large practical and just about insurmountable problem indeed at that moment and that problem had to be sorted very quickly. As I'd been told umpteen times on innumerable courses I'd attended, "Once you know what the problem is then you can do something about it." So, I knew what the problem was, I needed food and I needed water, and I needed them as they had become a matter of life or death. According to my past training, I should have been able to deal with the problem. Like shit I could! Oh, I could get water from the snow and ice, there was plenty of that around, but food, well, that presented another problem altogether. I couldn't seem able to spot any food around the area. There were no coffee houses or transport cafes around that part of the world, mate. Not even a bloody farm house in sight that might provide bed and breakfast or maybe just breakfast! There was nowhere that I might obtain succour. Mind, I knew that if I didn't manage to get something by nightfall, then I'd be a goner.

It must have been while I was stumbling along and rambling on to myself trying to think about all of this, considering first this plan and then that plan, wracking my half-frozen brain as I tried to come up with some answers; trying to work it all out as I stumbled around like a drunken man in my fatigue-induced stupor, that I first realised I was no longer walking amongst the trees of the forest.

At some time in my delirium I must have walked out from amongst the trees and on to flat open ground. When the enormity of this discovery dawned on me I stopped dead in my tracks. I stood for a little while thinking about it all. Gone was the quick reaction commando bit. Now I was a man in a stupor unable to relate to the events in which I was fast becoming the star turn in a death scene.

When the grey cells did work the first thing I did was to turn and look back the way I was certain I had come; and sure enough there were the trees; so that bit was right. I judged them to be about a mile behind me. As the situation dawned on me that I was totally exposed to just about any Russian in the area who happened to be watching, I just stood there frozen to the spot. I was rooted there unable to move, looking back at the way I had come; transfixed with the kind of terror a rabbit must feel when confronted by a car's headlights in the middle of a road. After a moment or two, for some reason that I will never ever be able to explain, I slowly shuffled around in a complete circle, studying all the ground around me as I turned. Well studying may be a bit of an exaggeration!

The ground was flat for as far as the eye could see; if there were any dips I didn't see them. Even the trees that I had just left were, or seemed to be, on flat ground because all I could see was the front edge of them. At that moment I began to think that I was wandering in my mind, as well as in Russia. When I had completed the circle I stopped, and I remained looking in the direction I'd been travelling when I had first realised that I was no longer in the forest. Then very slowly my half-frozen brain began to realise something else. There was something my eyes had seen but hadn't registered at all. Something my eyes had seen when I'd turned the circle, but my brain had failed to record. But it should have because something in my head was flashing a red warning light.

Having stood there a while, willing my brain to recheck its memory, there was nothing and my brain seemed to be saying, "Bollocks, sort it out yourself." In the back of my mind I did have a vague recollection that I had seen something that wasn't right, but obviously that something had not registered fully in my feeble mind. Well, I stood there, and I couldn't for the life of me think what it was I had seen. That was when the first attack of shaking started!

So, being the well-trained fool that I was, I realised that action was the only remedy that would stop the shaking, and I did the best thing I could think of at the time. I turned another full circle. This time I studied the view more thoroughly and gave it my full, feeble attention. Slowly, very slowly, as I again turned in a complete circle, I tried to concentrate more than I had the first time. This time if there was anything out there, then I wanted to see what it was. I had to know if I had seen anything or not, or if it was just the first sign of the madness that I had heard could come upon people in this wilderness.

By the time I had turned most of the circle I was starting to think that I must have gone mad. That was when I was about three quarters of the way round the circle and I was starting to relax again when it hit me.

There it was again, this time it did register and I realised that there was somebody standing out there watching me, so, hurray, I wasn't after all mad; you must be bloody joking mate! Even though it had registered after the slightest hesitation I still continued to turn the full circle. Why? I don't know, perhaps I thought the person might go away, but I knew all was not well. My hands had started to shake again and my knees were not holding up too well either. So once I had completed my second circle I started to turn around again, but this time in the opposite direction, only this time I stopped when I was facing this person who was still just standing watching me. He (and I presumed it was a he) was just standing there, his hands tucked into his coat pockets. He was standing perhaps about a hundred yards away from me but the way my brain was working it could have been a mile; and he was not moving at all, just standing there watching me.

I had by now stopped all movement. My fit of the shakes had stopped, having been replaced by a cold sweat of terror or fear. Call it what you like, but I was scared. There I stood, rooted to the spot just looking at this person, who was also just standing there and looking back at me. We were full face to face and staring at each other, not moving or saying a damned word. For the life of me I could not work out exactly how far away from me he was and that seemed to me to be an important thing I should know. Also, I hadn't a bloody clue what, if anything, I was supposed to do or if I should do anything at all.

Finally, after a couple of minutes of this, my brain, god bless it, suddenly sprang into action and suggested that I should introduce myself to this person watching me. Before I realised that was the last thing I should do, I started to walk towards him. As I did so I was trying hard to bring him into clear focus, but I couldn't. His blurred appearance did not change even as I got nearer to him or at least I thought I was getting nearer to him.

For all I knew I could have been walking towards a KGB man, a local policeman, a local peasant, or just a mirage; and it was with great difficulty that I managed to keep my eyes on the person towards whom I thought I was then walking. For some inexplicable reason I seemed to be taking a long time to reach him, or perhaps her. Then just at the moment I thought I was starting to make progress, I fell to the ground. Maybe I was close to the person then maybe I wasn't, but I couldn't be sure. At first I just lay there looking at the cold dirty ice-covered snow for a moment. Then I remember thinking how dirty the snow and ice in that place was. To my surprise I could see some insects rather like fruit flies hopping about on the ice. Then with a superhuman effort I managed to get to my feet, only to flop down flat on my face again. The shock of my flopping down must have frightened the fruit flies because there were none this time. What I do remember after that was thinking that this was it, mate, you have now come to the end of the line. Goodbye cruel world, you've got me at last!

The next recollection that I can bring to mind, but couldn't make too much sense of at the time, was that I was in a warm and dark place. I remember that I was being fed some kind of warm and utterly vile-tasting food. After having the food pushed into my mouth I must have passed out because I still couldn't remember anything else until some time later. I do recall that I was in a small sort of room that was possibly about twelve feet square, but it was hard to tell. The place was stuffed and cluttered inside with every type of rubbish one could think of and it was filthy.

When I next surfaced from the oblivion I think I had been in, I saw that my body was completely covered with some heavy furs, or maybe they where just rags, I wasn't too sure. What I was sure about, though, was that I was crawling with lice. Not your ordinary body lice though, these little bastards were like the pictures you'd see in police stations in England in the forties and fifties, the ones you used to see on the posters warning about the Colorado Beetles that were causing a problem by killing the potato crop off at the time. They were not unlike ladybirds in shape and had black and yellow markings on their backs; more to the point those little bastards couldn't half bite. These little bastards didn't suck blood they used knives and forks!

All For A King's Shilling

At first I thought they were country cousins of the famous Texas cattle ticks the way they went after me. The feeling that I got was that if I didn't get out of there soon I would be eaten alive, literally eaten alive! The people would then be able to hang my skeleton up, in a similar way to those you saw in the doctor movies of a few years ago. The other thing uppermost in my mind was, could I still walk. Also, into whose hands or into what den of thieves and cutthroats had I fallen?

Needless to say the worry about the lice and who was holding me did help to pull me back to the reality of my situation and concentrate my mind on the problems at hand. It took a big effort, but I managed to get myself up off the heap of rags that passed for a mattress to have a look at my new surroundings. I set about cracking the skulls of as many of the little bastard ticks or lice, call them what you like, as I could, having a good look around the place as I did.

It didn't take me too long to realise that this place was far, far removed from the type of Russian home I'd been in while I was the guest of Katrine and her father. Their house was a palace compared with this hovel. This looked like the inner sanctum of a prehistoric caveman's dwelling. It consisted of a room about twelve feet by twelve, as I've already said. You would never have believed it was possible to have such a large assortment of trash in such a small place. I'd never seen anything like it before. It was as if a day's collection at Charleston Meadow, Plymouth City's dump, had been tipped inside the place. There were bits of what looked like old farm equipment, bits of animal harness, old tattered and torn blankets, boots, shoes, and clothes. There was even a pile of ash on the floor, which I was certain contained excrement in it. Standing in the midst of all this trash was a large pot-bellied stove. It was at one end and near to what looked like a door covered with an old blanket. It gave me a distinct feeling that I was in a dugout of some sort, because there were no signs of any windows. I lay back on the heap of garbage and rags that was my bed and even though the bugs were biting like hell, surprisingly I still managed to fall asleep again.

When next I awakened, it was just before an old man came into the room. He saw I was awake as soon as he entered because I hadn't been quick enough in closing my eyes, and he asked me, in what I thought was a reasonable manner. "How do you feel now, my fine KGB man?"

As I looked at him his reference to the KGB puzzled me a little, but for some reason I seemed to be able to reason that he must have been the man I'd been walking towards when I fell down. So the old grey matter looked to be playing the game again and taking an active part in my life once more and I told the man, "To tell you the truth, I feel bloody awful."

He then told me something that caused me some consternation when he said, "You have been asleep for three days now. My wife was able to get you to eat some food when we found you and then you passed out completely. We have just kept you warm since then; and we both thought you were going to die in here. Mind, we are so glad you didn't. The one thing we can do without is a dead Russian KGB man on our hands."

I thought, not half as bloody glad as I am, friend, if that is what you are, but I somehow doubt it and I kept my mouth tight-shut feigning drifting off to sleep again. I did however think his remark about a 'Russian KGB man' was a little odd; all KGB men are Russian, so who and what were these two if not Russian?

William Atlay

A little later I was to learn that neither he nor his wife considered themselves to be Russians at all. When he told me that my first reaction was that I foolishly thought I would be on good ground with them if that was the case, I was about to tell the old man that I did not consider myself a Russian either. Then, for some reason, why I don't know, but I didn't. If I had, I do believe he would have killed me there and then, but it was only at the last second I changed my mind. I don't think I shall ever know why I didn't blurt out who I was; I had realised by his attitude that I was the closest to death that I had ever been in my life. It was that something in his manner I suppose that stopped me just in time.

There was also something in the way he had talked about having a dead Russian on their hands, well, that set me to thinking. Why would that upset them, or even why would it cause any problems for them? I had a frightening thought that dead bodies wouldn't have worried this man and his partner whom he kept referring to as his wife; they just looked too well-fed living as they did in what can only be described as a wilderness.

Then he asked me, "What were you doing out there?"

My brain must have started to thaw out because I was quick and pleased not only with the speed of my brain but also with the lying answer that came out as I told him, "I was with a party of our men looking for some dissident who had escaped from a Gulag." I then went into a rigmarole about how I became parted from the others, much to my disgust. I told him that about four days ago I got lost from the main party and I was completely alone out there in the woods, totally lost, without a map, or anything else to help me.

At this he just grunted, and it was at this point his wife came into the place. Looking at her I now had my doubts about which one of them I'd seen out there the other day.

The old man broke the silence that had descended as she entered and he said to me, "I expect that we will get a reward for helping you to get back to your unit."

"That is no problem; once I am back with my unit I shall see to it that you are both compensated immediately. Just whereabouts are we, by the way?"

"Don't you know?" he asked, a little surprise in his voice. "You are on the eastern bank of Lake Onega. It is a deserted and lonely place even in the summer, let alone at this time of the year. The dissident you were following must have been mad for coming this way. There is no place to hide out here. There is nothing here at all, the man must have been mad."

I tried to hide my surprise at the disclosure of where we were, but I was not sure I had succeeded. Lake Onega was about five to six hundred miles from the Kola Peninsula. That is where I was when Katrine and her father had found me after I'd injured my back. While I sat looking at them they suddenly started talking in a dialect or language that I'd never heard before. Also, there was something in their voices that worried me. They kept lapsing into this strange dialect and that had me scared shitless and I believed at that moment that I was in really big trouble. I'd made a very bad mistake by being unable to hide my surprise at where we were. As long as I was with these two I had no doubt they would kill me if the urge took them. Looking at them I also knew that if I showed any sign of weakness at that point I would be finished. I knew that the biggest mistake I'd made was to pose as a KGB man. They knew as I did that a true KGB man would only have shown arrogance towards these two. He would have ordered them about and treated them like shit, and I hadn't!

So, attack being the best defence, I went over to where my bedding roll was hanging from a pole that was propped up against the wall. As soon as I saw it, I went cold. They had rifled my bedding roll, it was hanging open and not only was my gun missing, but all the other bits and pieces I had had in it were also gone. The things they had found in it were not the kind of things a KGB man would carry, anyway. It hadn't taken much reasoning to arrive at the conclusion that the pair already knew that I wasn't a KGB man.

Realising I was in really serious trouble, I turned around to face the two of them. That was when I found myself looking straight down the barrel of the gun that I had been looking for in my bedding roll. I just stood looking at his old grinning face; I thought, surely this is not the end. Surely this cannot be the final part of it all. My eyes focused on his finger, which was round the trigger. As I looked I could see his finger tightening on the trigger. Suddenly there was a flash which nearly blinded me. It was followed by a crack of thunder, from which my ears have never recovered, as the gun went off; I knew I should have been dead, but for some strange bloody reason I wasn't.

When the blinding flash disappeared my vision was just a blur and I had trouble bringing things into focus. It must have lasted only seconds because I just caught a fleeting glimpse of the firing pin from the pistol as it buried itself backwards into the place where the old man's right eye should have been. The next moment there was a massive spurt of blood arching its way towards me from the old man's face. It was coming from the hole in his face where his right eye should have been. To me it looked as if his eye had burst and where his eyeball should have been there was a thin, pointed piece of steel in the centre of the fountain of blood, as it splashed over my face. A sickly, salty, warm, smelly mess of red that was quickly spreading all over my face.

The woman had started screaming her head off by then and shouting in the same indistinguishable tongue I had heard before. It looked too as if the silencer on the gun had something wrong with it; anyway whatever it was, the old man was staggering around half blind and obviously dying. The firing pin from the pistol was embedded in his head where his right eye should have been. From where I stood it looked as if the gun had backfired on him, or perhaps the gun had been doctored, I don't know. For a start I did not have time to work out what, if anything, had gone wrong, just then I felt I had more important work on my hands.

I finally sprang into action and I was on the man more quickly than I thought I could move in my half-dead state. All this happened more quickly than I can tell and I had already launched myself at him. With a twist of my wrist I had the gun off him; just why I grabbed the gun from him I still don't understand. It wasn't going to harm me now, but I suppose old habits die hard. Mind you, I did belt him over the head with the butt of the damned thing. What I mean to say was, that I hit what was left of his head with the butt of the pistol, but it made no difference, he was nearly dead anyway. He fell forward and struck what little of his head remained on the bed on which I had been lying just a little while earlier.

As I straightened up I caught a glimpse out of the corner of my eye of the man's wife. She was screaming and shouting at me in that gibberish tongue of hers. More to the point, she was coming for me with a stick of some sort that she had raised above her shoulder as if ready to hit me over the head. So I lashed out with my right leg and kicked her as hard as I could in the crotch. She fell forward across my leg and slightly to my right. Because of the speed with which she was coming at me, she carried on past me and in her fall she head-butted the pot-bellied stove with her forehead. There was a horrible sound of flesh melting – the kind of noise one hears when a slice of bacon is dropped into a red-hot frying pan, but a rather different smell. The pot-bellied stove in its turn toppled over, cracking from its top to its ashpan and spilling its contents all over the place.

I glanced towards the old man to make sure he was out of it, and he was. So I turned my attention back to his wife, who was trying to disentangle herself from what remained of the stove. Surprisingly, she was managing to get to her feet and was again coming at me; she was a tough old bugger because her fall would have finished most women, but not her. As she made it to her feet I saw that this time she had a knife in her hand. It looked as big as a bloody machete from where I stood. Then after a short fox-trot around the place, which was getting hotter by the minute as more and more of the garbage in there caught light, I finally managed to get her by the wrist and upper arm as she stabbed at my lower stomach. With difficulty I managed to deflect the blow she launched at me. Because of her weight, as she came at me we both fell to the floor, which was by this time well ablaze. She fell on to the knife with such force that not only the blade entered her, but the handle entered her abdomen also. I think she died there and then; at least I believed she was dead because as I let her wrist go I couldn't feel anything. Not that I was feeling for anything anyway. As for the man, I did not know if he was dead, or not for certain, but it looked to be a good bet that he was, or soon would be!

What was more important just then was that I didn't intend to hang around the place to find out. It was starting to get too bloody hot in there. By now the whole place was ablaze. With great difficulty I managed to grab what I could, not only of my kit, but I also grabbed a handful of bread as I made my way to the exit. The blanket covering the door was by now well alight, yet I couldn't understand why I didn't feel the heat, or why I didn't think that the fire was a danger to me.

Why, I don't know, but I stopped at the entrance and took one look around to see if there was anything else that I could take with me. By now I couldn't see either of the two occupants of the place because of the intensity of the flames. To my amazement there was no smoke at all, just flames! Then, once outside, I made my way to the edge of the frozen lake. There I hid in some small but thick bushes. It was important now that I pull myself together before I went off any farther into this wilderness. Especially then, because the only food I had in my possession was the small handful of rotten bread that I had grabbed as I left the burning hut.

If what the old man had said was true, then I had one hell of a walk on my hands. After what had just happened to the old man I was extremely glad that I hadn't needed to defend myself against anybody with that damned gun. They must have known Katrine would give me the firing pin, so the bastards had fixed the gun somehow. It looked as if they had more than likely doctored the silencer as well. It was obvious that they had made sure that if I tried to shoot any more of their men then I would die.

Well, I thought, as I sat as close to the bush as I could, what a fine kettle of fish you've got yourself into now. There I was, a soldier without a musket, and I was beginning to think without much hope. What a hell of a mess I had landed myself into again. I thought of that day in Poole when I should have just walked out of the bloody gate and buggered off all those years ago now. Still, you pay your money and take your bloody chance, as they say. My biggest worry, though, was just what part of bloody Russia was I in? Not for the first time in my life I believed I'd become a fully paid-up member of the 'Where the Fuckarewe Tribe.' God alone knew how I got where I was, but to add to my troubles right then, the bloody dugout behind had started to explode like a bloody huge firework on bonfire night.

This meant that I was standing too near to a well-lit beacon for my own damn good. So, decision time had arrived once again and I hastily dressed and took off along the bank of the lake in what I hoped was a northerly direction. I also hoped that I was on my own and that no bloody Russian KGB or GRU man was tagging along for the ride.

The weather, well it was cold and bloody miserable. It was foggy and damp. The surface of the snow and ice was now wet, and very slippery. I had difficulty trying to keep my feet on it, let alone walk on the bloody stuff. I believed that this trouble was caused by the short thaw that they get up there after the first snows, just before the big freeze sets in up here, just to fool them it starts to thaw a little. It is far worse than the worst winters we get in England, but is just a starter for the poor sods who try to make a living up there.

It was as if the weather was giving them a warning and getting them ready for the big one, the big freeze. It was this change in the weather which really meant I had to get my bloody arse in gear and get a bloody move on if I was ever going to haul my arse out of that Godforsaken wilderness. I knew that come what may I couldn't give in now!

After about six hours of plodding in what I hoped was a northerly direction, I stopped and looked around. Convinced as I was that I was alone in the area, it felt as if I were the only person left alive in the vastness of the wilderness. Even so I took no chances and I lowered myself to the ground. Then after watching and listening to make sure I wasn't being followed for about five or so minutes, I crawled on my belly towards some bushes a little way off. Once I got to them I selected what looked like a strong looking bush and I sat with my back towards it. Then I slowly pushed and wriggled my body backwards until I was half in and half out of the bush. This way the bush provided me with a rest for my back; moreover, my pushing had compacted the branches and provided me with a windbreak. Once I had settled myself I ate some of the bread that I had taken from the dugout and I tried to put my situation into some sort of context, but I couldn't.

After a little while longer I realised that my position in this game was a hopeless one and in my dismay I looked back towards the way I had just come. The fire must have gone out because I could no longer see it or any smoke from it so I deduced the fire had gone out. Or just maybe I'd travelled farther than I had thought, too far for me to see it anymore. I hoped the latter was the reason I couldn't see the fire, but in my heart I knew it had just burnt itself out.

It must have been the KGB coat I had on, which I then noticed was all torn and dirty, that had stopped them from killing me right at the start. Then, when they had realised I was not even a member of the KGB, they had obviously decided to kill me anyway. They would then claim whatever reward they could for my dead body by telling the KGB that they believed me to be the dissident I'd mentioned. It was to be a lot later that I first realised that my premonition earlier might just have been right; they might not have been going to kill me to hand my body over to the KGB. The reality of it all came home to me when a person I was to meet reminded me that a human body can provide a hell of a lot of protein for starving people. The old custom of the sea came to mind.

Anyway whatever it was that they had decided to do, they had turned decidedly hostile towards me. So all in all I was lucky to be alive. Funny that looking back, there I was stuck in the vast and hostile wilderness of the Arctic, at the onset of winter; I had no food, I had no clothes to speak about and I didn't really know where the hell I was. I'd just had one of the nearest brushes with death I'll ever have and I thought that I was lucky; and it was all due to the backroom boys of the KGB being too smart for their own good. The mind boggles!

If it had not been for the KGB experts outsmarting themselves, it would have been me who was lying dead right now in that filthy place, with part of me being prepared for the pot. So the fact that I was still alive was in no little way thanks to the guy who had doctored my gun. I bet he never thought he would be saving my life when he did his handiwork. They obviously did not want me running around killing any more of their men. To them I must have been a walking disaster area waiting to happen. It looked to me at the time as if everything I tried turned to shit. I reckoned that it wouldn't be too long before the whole might of the USSR descended upon my head.

Mind you, in all this despair the thought that the KGB had unintentionally saved my life gave me a bit of a lift and I now looked at the bits and pieces of the gun that I had left. After a little thought I kept the small amount of food that I had. It was the black and rotting bread that I had managed to grab as I had hastily fled the burning dugout. Next I looked over the garments that I had grabbed in my flight and decided to keep them all. I put them on there and then, over the top of the KGB overcoat that I was already wearing; for now I was really beginning to feel the cold. For the second time since I had arrived in Russia I was really very, very worried now. Oh, I had thought I was going to die a couple of times, but this time I knew it would happen soon. So with that sorted out in my mind I knew what I had to do!

The gun which the KGB had so graciously given me was itself completely and utterly useless, but then again I could possibly use it, if only to bluff my way out of trouble. Perhaps I would be able to hold people at bay with it, at least long enough to be enable me to escape or better still pinch his or her gun. It would now be a case of, "Ha! Ha! You're dead," as I legged it into the sunset; or more likely into the snow clouds, darkness and oblivion. Hell! I thought, it might just help get me out of trouble in the future so I'd hang on to it. With the decision made I removed the broken silencer and had another look at it. Looking from the muzzle end it didn't look to be damaged at all, so it might fool people long enough for me to disarm them and get myself a serviceable weapon. The rest of the stuff I hid under the bush and hoped nobody would ever find it.

My worst problem, of course, was that by now I was so bloody cold but I had the sense to see that it was also making me very tired. That meant I needed some sleep, but I also knew that if I did sleep in this condition then it would be my last sleep. Also, I had to get farther away from the place I was at. With a strength that only comes at death's door, I somehow managed to haul myself off my arse and started to walk; so one foot at a time I set off for god alone knew what.

Well, I thought it was walking, but I was so tired my walking was nothing more than a shuffle. I was constantly having to tell my brain that if I did rest, then I would die. My brain's answer to all that was the good standard one, "So what?" which is the favourite reply of the "Appreciate the situation merchants back in the leadership training centres of the British Forces".

"The enemy are over there," someone would say.

"So what?" some smart-arsed instructor would say, expecting a tactical answer to his "so what?"

"So I'm fucking off. That's what," some student would reply under his breath, of course! Speaking it aloud would have been a suicidal answer!

So it was with all these stupid thoughts going through my feeble brain that I again started my trek to the Kola Peninsula and hopefully home. With this in mind I got up what I thought was a head of steam and off I went along the banks of the lake looking for the northern end and a good left turn.

Some time later I had been going at what I thought was a reasonable pace and it looked as if I was nowhere near the northern shore. It had started to get very dark and I had the most awful thought. How the bloody hell was I supposed to know when I'd reached the northern shore of the lake? The lake didn't have corners, you stupid fool, I told myself. You could end your bloody life just walking around the bloody lake forever. Like a bloody fish in a bowl, round and round and bloody round. In ever-decreasing circles; like the proverbial ouslam bird until I disappeared up my own arsehole. My next terrifying thought had me almost having a damned heart attack. How in god's name do you know which side of the sodding lake you are on? My feeble frozen brain had suddenly realised that I'd been walking for days before I saw the old man and I hadn't seen any bloody lake. At first I thought about stopping for a while just to try and resolve the problem. Then I thought I could be anywhere in the world for all I knew.

As I kept on walking I was slowly convincing myself, with some little success, that in this place and in the condition that I was in at the time, any bloody thing was possible. Then I made a momentous decision that stopping was out of the question. If I stopped walking I'd die. In the back of my mind I kept remembering a point that one of my instructors kept labouring during training, "The ones who lie down, die"! Now for the first time in my life I knew exactly what he had been talking about. So I just kept plodding blindly on all night long. I'd worry about it all tomorrow, I told myself, as I concentrated on putting one foot in front of the other. I remember repeating over and over in my mind, one two three four, swing those arms in line with your shoulders, come on that man in the front, pick up the step; left, right, left, right, stick those chests out, straighten your backs. Come on, show these bastards just what Royal Marines are made of! During that night I think my mind, body or whatever part of your brain it is that drives you on, was on auto pilot. My memory of most of the night is still a complete blank.

My next recollection of reality was when it started to get light. I remember stopping and looking at my surroundings as I stumbled along; finally after an hour or so of this I stopped to eat the last of the bread, the mouldy bread that I had grabbed as I exited the dugout with the blanket over the door covered with flames, as I made my hot and hasty retreat. This in itself was a completely automatic reaction as I cannot remember making a conscious decision to do so.

When it was fully daylight I took a more detailed look at my surroundings. I was now desperate to find some way of finding out just where in the hell I was. I had spotted a group of bushes and saplings on a small hump that looked for all the world like a Salisbury Plain barrow. So I made my way towards it. For some reason, I know not why, I thought that I might be able to see more of my surroundings from there. It was a useless waste of energy, of course, climbing the hill, that is. The view from there was much the same as from lower down except that I could see about a couple of miles further on. It was just a vast array of small trees. There was no sign of life whatsoever.

Disappointed at my failure to see anything that might have helped me in my quest to put some sense of order and direction into my wanderings, I decided to get some rest. My old instructor's teachings of 'do not lie down when you are completely cold and exhausted or you will die' which I had been so engrossed with the night before had completely gone from my mind by then. Again I found a small group of bushes that I considered suitable for my purpose and I settled down and pushed my back against a small bush in the centre of the group. The bushes were on the leeward side of the hill and therefore I hoped would give me some shelter from the cold wind that was blowing constantly. Then in the misbelief that I was the only human being in the area, I settled back against the bush to try and get some sleep.

I knew in my mind though that it was very unlikely. My memory drifted back to the time when along with seventy-five men I had travelled due south from Tripoli for about two hundred miles. We had stopped at about five that evening to make camp and we had been there no more than twenty minutes when a bloody Arab came over the top of a sand dune shouting, "Eggs, Johnny, oranges, Johnny!" Several of us ran to the top of the sand dune and there wasn't a thing to be seen except sand. So you see from past experience I knew I wasn't the only person around there. It seems there are always people somewhere. No place in the world is now sacrosanct.

Anyway, I'd already encountered one pair of destitute people who had passed themselves off as human. So it was only logical that there were others living off the land out here. For all I knew some of them could be watching me right now. My only hope was that the bastard sold eggs and oranges. It was then – as I half sat and half lay against the bush I had pushed myself into – that an amazing thought crossed my mind. In all the time I'd spent wandering around this godforsaken land I had never heard a dawn chorus in the area. There was a dawn chorus over the border in Norway and I presumed there was one in Finland, but I'd not heard one in Russia. Just goes

All For A King's Shilling

to show how dominant the control of the Supreme Soviet is I thought as I tried to go to sleep.

While I was doing so, trying to sleep that is, my mind was mulling over the two big problems that I had. They were that I had nothing to defend myself with now other than my bare hands, that is, and I had nothing at all to eat. Perhaps the time had arrived when, provided I could find some food, I would have to put all that unarmed combat training to the test; but I hoped not, as I had forgotten most, if not all of it.

It was at this point in my mind's debate with itself that I interrupted it. You are wasting energy and time mate, you should be on your way; and then with an energy that surprised even me I dragged myself back to the reality of my position and up on to my feet. With one last look around the place, I staggered on, hopefully heading in a northerly direction, at least I prayed it was northerly. So I started once more. If I was ready to sit and die my brain wasn't and it had overruled my mind and stopped me from sleeping.

Forever the optimist, I prayed that I wasn't going east or bloody south. Some short while after that everything went into that red haze one goes into at about the seven-mile marker on a fifteen-mile speed march, that unknown world, the world of wakeful unconsciousness as I always call it; when the body is still trying to function and the brain is continually trying to shut it down.

Just how long this confusion lasted I shall never know, but some noise of some sort finally penetrated the red haze that engulfed my brain. The noise first came to me in what I now know was the middle of the afternoon. In my tired, befuddled state it was only natural that I took no notice whatsoever of it; I just assumed it was a noise of nature. That just goes to show how far out of my tree I really was at that moment in time. Not to put too fine a point on it, I was not taking too much notice of anything going on about me at all.

For all I knew I could have walked through some small town; right down its main street and out the other end. I would not have noticed and it wasn't until the sound in my ears was like thunder that I eventually stopped and listened, trying to sort it out.

That was when I realised for the first time that I had entered some trees; pine trees, spruce trees, fir trees, I didn't know what kind of bloody trees they were. I do remember that the fact that I was in among trees seemed to surprise me somewhat. Why that was so I don't know but I realised that I was no longer on the side of 'the lake' or even 'a lake' and I began to wonder just where the hell I was. There was no lake, and I just kept thinking that there was no lake! For some unknown reason that made me very unhappy. There had to be a lake, but there wasn't one.

The track I had been following had led me into some sort of woods, or forests, or whatever, but there was no bloody lake to be seen anywhere.

I pondered this for a little while until I suddenly realised what the noises that I had been hearing for some time were. They were the sounds of woodsmen cutting down the trees. Pleased with myself, I leaned against a tree trunk and listened to the noises. Whoever they were, they were using chain saws and axes, but what was more frightening was that I suddenly realised that I was only a few feet from one of the crews. Call it luck, call it what you like, but I didn't think they had seen me. If they had, they were totally ignoring me, possibly hoping I would go away. I slowly backed off until I was far enough away from them to be able to make my way off to my left, from where I was hoping I would come across the shores of the lake because by now I was convinced that I'd wandered away from its shore. Once I was back on the lake shore I would then make my way past these men, by travelling on the ice if necessary, if there was any ice that is.

I was trying hard to use what skills I could still remember when I nearly burst out on to a vehicle track that ran at right angles from the path through the trees along which I was walking. It was an effort, but I did manage to stop myself from bursting out of cover by hanging on to a small tree. I looked around to see if I'd been heard and I then hid myself behind a larger tree, a tree that I was so tightly up against that at first glance to anyone passing it would have looked as if I were part of the tree.

Of course I hoped this would happen because shortly after that some people who were in what could only be described as the Russian equivalent of the American jeep passed by the tree that I felt I was glued to. I watched them pass and I looked to see if they were soldiers, police or the KGB. There was no way I could tell. As I looked at them they could have been civilians for all I could see of their clothes. They were all dressed like a bunch of tramps. They could have been Martians for all I knew, but I thought that would be unlikely. I couldn't see what Martians would want in these desolate woods.

After the jeep type truck had passed the place I was hiding at I waited and strained my ears to see if I could see or hear anything else coming along the track. There were no sounds so I edged to the side of the track and crawled under a bush and had a look from the under growth up and down the track. What I saw was that I was actually on a slight bend in the track. It was just over a truck's width and it was a well-used stretch of track. I waited no longer, I just got up and walked across. Much to my own surprise I did not run, as I did not want to slip on the compacted snow and ice that covered the track, so I just walked across. Even so, and not for the only time that day, I broke into a cold sweat.

When I was safely over the other side I hurried as best I could into the trees. When I believed that I was well clear of the track I stopped, but I could still see no sign of the lake. Then, as I looked around and tried to listen to all the noise and activity going on all around me I decided I had definitely walked into a rather large logging operation. What was more I was right in the middle of it, so I decided to settle down against a tree and try to work it all out.

When night came the activity stopped and the men seemed, from what I could hear, to be making their way to a central point. This point was some way off to my right front. So, gingerly I got to my feet and started to follow them. At first I toyed with the idea of joining the supper queue that I could see forming by a wooden hut.

As I got nearer to the queue I realised that as they joined the queue a guard was checking something that they carried and he was also counting them. The sound and sight of the guard stopped me dead in my tracks. No, sir, I thought, you can keep your supper queue. It was then as I watched it all that I realised I had stumbled upon one of their labour camps. These workers were the inmates. They were out cutting the wood to earn their crust of bread and hoping to stay alive long enough to complete their term of imprisonment. When the realisation of what the place was first hit me, my self-preservation took over and I felt myself moving backwards; farther and farther away from the noise as if by instinct I moved. When I considered it was safe enough,

I settled myself down to try and work out how best I was going to get away from the place.

Some ten minutes later I was still sitting against the tree, absolutely motionless and just trying to think of some way of getting away from the place, trying to make some sense of my situation. Then the hair on the back of my neck slowly started to stand on end. My whole body started to shake and twitch a little, but somehow I managed to steady myself and finally to remain dead still. Then and with great difficulty I at last got my breathing under control. It was then that I felt the presence, more than heard it. Although I was looking the other way I could see the danger behind me as if I were looking at the man. In my mind's eye I saw him raise his rifle to the on-guard position and line it up on the middle of my back. It was as if I were watching it all being played out in front of me. Then my senses told me that he had lurched forward to place his bayonet in the middle of my back. To this day I've not the slightest idea how I did it, but at the last possible second I moved suddenly to my left and away from the point at which I knew he was aiming. As I did, at first I thought I'd left it too late as I felt the bayonet pass through the layers of clothes I was wearing. Next I panicked and got mad as hell, because at that moment I felt the cold steel of his bayonet as it touched the skin of my right side. The steel then passed along the flesh of my side and its touch sent a shiver of death through the whole of my body.

I remember thinking if I'd been a couple of pounds heavier he would have taken my side out. As it was, it just missed penetrating my side. He must have slipped, tripped or something because the bayonet came out of the front of my coat and it plunged between my legs missing my right upper thigh by the merest fraction of an inch. The force with which he lunged at me, and perhaps his weight as he fell, buried the rifle and bayonet up to the foresight in the snow and ice between my feet. The rest of the rifle, from the foresight to the magazine, had now become entangled in the clothes I was wearing. It was only the magazine that stopped it going any farther in.

It was at this point that he lost his balance completely and fell to the ground at my right. I was on him with a speed I did not know my tired and half-starved body could muster. Somehow, I know not how, I managed to get hold of the front of his helmet and still in a crouching position I managed to get my left foot pressed hard against a protruding rock. Then I got the knee of my right leg, with his rifle still entangled in my coat, into the middle of his back between his shoulder blades. Then using what strength I did have I pulled him half round with his back towards me and pulled on the front of his helmet with all the strength I could muster.

I pulled and pulled until my arms started to shake with the exhaustion that was beginning to take over. My leg was trembling as I tried to force it harder into his back; I thought his neck was never going to give. Then at last, just as I was sure I'd have to let go because my strength was ebbing fast, I heard the crack as his neck finally broke.

I don't know why, but I still hung on to that helmet for at least a further five minutes or so. As I did I was sucking great gasps of air into my lungs because the effort had sapped all my strength and my blood lacked oxygen. Ever since that day I have kidded myself that I had no intention of killing him and that I only intended to knock him out and take his rifle. All I could think of at the time was that once again my luck had held and I had a weapon, and this time it was a semi automatic rifle. I spent about ten minutes hauling air into my tired lungs!

All I needed now was some food and I'd be in with a chance, but I had my doubts if that was the real reason why I had killed him. Perhaps I was starting to regain my touch and I'd been bloody lucky in my condition to have killed him. I was sure that he hadn't meant to take me alive. Then again it was perhaps true that I was completely mad after all. Maybe my brain was starting to get the upper hand over my body; mind over matter and all that shit is all right as long as you're not a mad man.

One thing was certain, I felt completely exhausted now and I needed rest and sleep and I needed it badly, but what I needed more was food. I also had to be miles away from there by morning. It was then I thought of stealing one of their jeeps, and I needed to work out how I could do that. The main problem was that I'd never driven one of their vehicles before. Oh, I could drive all right, but I had never seen one of these vehicles before. To get clean away I would need to walk right up to it and just drive as if it was something that I did every day. If I hesitated by looking at the gears, brake and clutch pedals and the like it would give me away if I were being watched.

That was when I finally released my hold on the man's helmet and looked at him. From the way he was dressed I realised that I had just killed one of their guards. With my mind again in the survival mode I thought, well I needed to get rid of him for a start. His boots looked okay and he had a well-worn but thick quilted type of greatcoat on. So I thought I'd have that off him for a start, but I needed some food badly. So I set to and searched his pockets. They were empty, but in a small pack he had there were four small bars of what looked like chocolate so I scoffed the lot. Within a few minutes I was as sick as a pig!

When I'd settled my stomach I took from him what I needed to stay warm, well, warmer than I had been for some time now. When I was satisfied that I'd taken everything that I could make use of from him, I pushed his body as far under the scrub and bushes as I could. It was my vain hope that they would not find him for at least a day or so.

Just as I was about to leave him after hiding him under the scrub, I remembered his rifle. Hell, I thought, you nearly forgot the most important bit of equipment that he had with him. I grabbed it and checked to see if he had any more ammunition than was in the magazine on the gun. To my surprise he had two more magazines, both of which were full, so I took them as well. Next I cleared the barrel of the snow and ice that had gone into it when it had plunged between my legs.

Satisfied that I'd seen to everything and that his body was as well-hidden as possible, I set off through the trees towards the noise that I could hear ahead of me. Dressed in his coat, I felt a little safer than I had before and I moved more openly than I had earlier. I figured that a guard wouldn't crouch and bob and weave from tree to tree. So I made a great effort and kind of strolled through the trees towards the sound. I was trying to look like any prison camp guard who was pissed off, cold and bad tempered at being posted into this wilderness!

I'd not gone more than two hundred yards when I came across a clearing in which there was a lot of activity going on. Not sure about it all and unsure of myself I lay down, adopting a firing position, behind the trunk of a tree. From there I could observe the clearing and for a time I just lay there behind the tree watching. There seemed to me to be an awful lot of activity in the place considering it was now dark. There were people queuing up for food and others were being chased around the place by guards. More sinister though there were men who looked like prisoners without any change in their dress to mark them out as guards, gangers or foremen. These men were beating the shit out of other prisoners with sticks and what looked, god forbid, like bull whips. At that point I realised that it was important I missed nothing of what was going on in that clearing. This time I knew that I had to get it right. My life was really on the line now and I knew any one of those bastards would cheerfully beat me to death without any hesitation. For the first time in my service career I felt that this time I really could lose my life. It meant that this could be my last shot at getting away from the God forsaken land.

While I lay there, my mind started to wander a little and I thought about Katrine, I wondered if she was all right. My hope was that she had had the sense to make a deal with them, a deal that would put all the blame on me, like telling them that I had forced her and her father to help me, on pain of death! A story along those lines might enable her to make a deal that would let she and her father go free. It might seem strange to people, but I now knew that I loved her so much and that I would do anything in my power to save her. In my mind I knew also that I'd rather suffer more pain just to see her go free than to have her go through the Russians' prison system, a sample of which I was still observing. I prayed that she knew she had to think only of herself and her father because I was not important to her. There was no chance we would ever see one another again; let alone ever live together as man and wife, not now, not the way things were going. I was a lost cause and I now knew that I'd been living on borrowed time ever since I'd crossed the Russian/Norwegian border. The bright part in all the problems was that I had met Katrine and no matter what happened from now on that made it worthwhile.

That just went to show how much my mind was wandering at that time. It was a little while later that my thoughts returned to reality and I realised what was going on around the clearing. Everybody, it seemed, was engaged in loading the small trucks that were moving around from place to place. They were similar to the four-ton type of trucks the American services use. The people were loading these small trucks with rather large loads of the timber, the timber which they had obviously cut and cleaned of its side branches and which had obviously been dragged from the woods by hand during daylight. It seemed to me that every thing was done by hand – the chopping of the trees and the dragging of the trees from the woods to the loading area, then the loading of the trucks was done using ropes, pulleys and manpower. There were no animals or machinery around that could have done the job other than the couple of jeep-type vehicles that kept buzzing around. It looked to me with the way they worked that it was a very dangerous place to be indeed. What with the darkness and only a few hurricane type lamps to provide any light I found that moving around would now be easier than before.

The whole process there was being done entirely by hand and under the very poor lighting conditions and I was sure that there must be some people who got killed or injured in the process. I think the Americans call that type of operation an exercise in the economy of scale. It was then that a very disturbing thought crossed my mind. If I were caught, then I could find myself working in these conditions soon. That was when I made a resolve that I would die before they ever caught me. I was always making plans of how I intended to proceed these days, but so long as there was a pulse in my heart and a cell still sparking in my brain I would just plod on towards Norway!

With that, I stood up and moved out from the trees to a point on the edge of the clearing, from where I could watch the activity going on. Nobody took any notice of me, let alone looked at me. If anybody had seen me they didn't give it a second thought. So gaining courage by the second I stood out there in the open for about ten minutes taking in every detail of what was going on.

I watched and noticed that after a truck had been loaded with trunks about twelve to fifteen inches thick on the first two rows, it then moved to another area where it was loaded with a large number of trunks that were about six inches thick. When that was completed an armed guard climbed into the cab beside the driver and it went off down the only track leading out of the clearing. Looking at the setup I did toy with the idea of just walking over and getting into a cab and riding out of here as a guard. So I decided to watch a couple of them as they went down the track by following their headlights as they moved through the trees, and after I'd checked them more closely I was glad that I hadn't. My heart sank as I noticed that they stopped for a time farther on down the track, and then just before the next loaded truck arrived, the first one moved on. My brain was now functioning very well as it reasoned that there must be a checkpoint there.

I supposed it was about a mile or so farther down the track where they stopped, but in the dark it was difficult to tell. After a little consideration I decided it would be best if I went to see what was happening there. So, I turned abruptly and moved back into the trees around the clearing. Once I was sure nobody had taken any notice of me, I skirted the place where the loading was taking place and headed off through the trees towards the track. It did not take me long to locate the track and I followed it. I stayed in the edge of the trees until I came to a place where I could see what was going on where the trucks were stopping.

It turned out I was right, it was a check point and the trucks were given a really good search by the guards from the hut. Once the guards had completed their search the driver, who looked to be a prisoner, and the guard went into the little hut. I presumed the truck and its load, driver and guard were logged or booked out, or some such thing. So I then decided I needed to be closer in to get a better look at the whole operation. So I stepped right up and crossed the track to the edge of the trees beside the hut. At last I managed to get myself half in and half out of a bush against the side of the hut. It was on the opposite side of the hut from the camp, the outside so to speak.

The guard and driver came out of the hut just as I'd got into cover. They climbed into the cab and the truck took off at breakneck speed as if it was on the Monte Carlo Rally. Just then the next truck arrived and it was about a quarter of an hour after the one that had just left had arrived. My heart sank as I saw sitting in the cab alongside the driver were two guards. Well, so be it, I thought. When the truck stopped outside the hut the three of them got out of it and another guard came out of the hut to join them, making four people in all standing around it. The three guards then searched the truck, not that there was much to search, still they did it. When they had completed

All For A King's Shilling

their search the four of them went into the hut and I could hear them laughing and talking in there. This is it, mate, I thought, it is now or never time.

With my body screaming with pain and a turn of speed that would match any tomcat escaping from a vet with a scalpel in his hand, I came out of the trees and I was up and on the back of the truck in a flash and I was lying down on top of the timber. I surprised myself with the speed and ease with which I had got on to the load. The timber had that smell of sap which only newly-cut wood has. It took me only a moment and I had managed to get a hold of the canvas type of straps holding the timber. Having just got myself settled, the driver with one of the guards came out of the hut. They climbed into the cab, then with a crunch of the gears we were off. All I can say is the driver was a bloody maniac. It was now the middle of the night and the snow and ice on the track cum road was frozen solid like a skating rink. This stupid sod of a driver was going flat out through the trees, and I reckoned flat out was about thirty-five or so miles an hour. The thought did cross my mind that I might just have committed suicide.

As we went hurtling along, I did notice that we were passing along a stretch of the road that had a cliff along one side of it. My mind was trying to work out when I should jump off when something frightened me more than going over the cliff could ever do. That was when I noticed that the tree trunks were not fastened securely at all. As we went hurtling down the track, the bouncing and vibration of the truck were combining to cause the trees to roll about, only a small amount at first, but moving they were and with each bump the movement got worse. The only thing stopping them falling off was the upright timbers down the side of the truck. It was then that I knew how those Canadian lumberjacks who ride the great log jams in Canada must feel, the first time they ever get on to them. God, but it scared me just about out of my wits; I knew I was getting away from the place, but at this rate I might never make it. For the first time in my life I now really knew what the saying, 'Holding a tiger by the tail' really meant.

A little while later and after we had cleared the part cliff area I had the idea of how best to hang on to the load. That was when I started to notice the obvious as we hurtled down that track. To call it a road was an insult to McAlpine, but on each side of the road I could just make out the shapes of many timber trucks. They were piled up and wrecked among the trees on each side of the road. As we flashed past them I wondered just how long it would be with a suicidal maniac driving before we joined them. Then the thought hit me, what if the crazy bastard driving this thing was a suicidal maniac just looking for a place to kill himself and take a guard with him? I cast that thought out of my mind and made a new plan as to when I'd jump clear of the damned thing.

There was no way of knowing how far we had travelled. I had been too busy trying to hang on and not get crushed by the timber to try to work out silly things like speed, time and distance. Remember your training lad, I thought. What was it the man said, to estimate your speed time the telegraph poles, they are all set the same distance apart all over the world. Time them for a minute and count how many you pass. From the number you pass you can work out the distance and therefore figure out the speed at which you are travelling.

"Great, Sergeant, but there are no fucking telegraph poles here, what does one do in this situation, then?"

"Don't be a silly lad, everybody knows all countries have telegraph poles."

"Well, Sergeant, you are a bloody liar because there are no bloody telegraph poles here or we may just be going too bloody fast to see them!"

Enough of my reminiscing, tiredness was overtaking me now and holding on was sapping what little strength I still had left; and it seemed that the effects of the bloody chocolate were wearing off. The time had come when I thought I would have to let go and fall off. I would prefer to do it under some sort of control, otherwise I would be certain to die, but I had to get off somehow; and all the way through my service I've been told you have to die some day, so perhaps today was my day.

When at last I could see it was starting to get light over to my right I could have wept with joy. Facing the front of the truck and with the dawn on my right, I took this to mean we were still heading north. That was when I decided I could put it off no longer. I was going to have to get off this 'Tiger' and pretty damned quickly. There was no doubt the driver or the guard would spot me or anyone else who was about; and believe me this bloody part of the world was turning into Piccadilly Circus. But once it got light I would have to be off this bloody 'tiger'. It didn't look as if we would be slowing down because I could not make out any hills ahead; so the truck would be slowing down soon, 'stupid' and I came to the conclusion that I would definitely have to abandon the thing while it was going flat out and on the flat or preferably when and if it slowed down on the hills; always assuming of course that we were 'heading for the hills' as the old saying goes.

When I looked over the side it looked a hell of a long way from me to the ground. Now that the sky was getting lighter I could see better, and it terrified me to bloody death. That was when the thought came to me that it would be better to go off the back. It was my opinion that the guard or the driver would not be likely to see me if I dropped off the back of the load. Dangerous though that might be, I very much doubted if this driver or his guard used a rear-view mirror, or if they even had one.

As the motion of the truck was throwing me about on top of the load I was hanging on for all I was worth. I was also trying to edge my way to the rear of the truck. At the rear of the load there were one or two pieces of timber that were longer than the rest. They were, need I say, the thinnest of them all. So I decided, smart-arse that I am, to edge as far out on these as I possibly could. Now that is easier said than done, I had much trouble making this brilliant move; I'd already cut and bruised my hands and legs somewhat during the process of trying to stay on the top of the load as it travelled through the early dawn. The move to the rear only exacerbated the pain I was already suffering; it was at this point I realised that I must be a masochist! Finally I did get far enough out from the rear of the truck to cause these two pieces of timber to bend downwards. As they did, I gingerly lowered my feet to the road. I felt the ice and ruts on the road buffeting against them. The thought then crossed my mind. "You must be absolutely bloody mad, completely out of your tree, mate. This ice, when you land on it, will cut your legs, your arse and any other part of you which touches it, to bloody shreds." The problem was I'd reached the point of no return as I was too far out over the end of the truck to get back on to the load. There was no way I would ever get back up the length of the two pieces of timber that by now I was now hanging on to for grim death! So once again I had started something without thinking the thing through and now I really did have the bloody tiger by its sodding tail!

There was nothing for it, I thought; I really needed locking up! I was hurtling along over an icy track, hanging on to these thin tree trunks for all I was worth and expecting to die any minute so I started to count, one, two, three, and at three I let go. I fell to the road and I remember saying to myself, keep your bloody head up, which fortunately I did manage to do. The next moment I was sliding along the road heading after the truck, lying on my back feet and with my head stuck up in the air like one of those bloody maniacs in the Winter Olympics. After a few seconds of this I had a very distinct feeling that I was catching the truck up and before I could do anything I shot under it and it was one of those 'oh shit' moments as I had visions of shooting out from under the cab of the truck and disappearing down the track with the guard shooting at me! But fortunately that was not to be as at last I managed to stop myself by digging the butt of the rifle I had acquired earlier hard on to the ice. I also managed to burn both cheeks of my arse and my right elbow, and also the heel of my right hand in the process.

The bloody truck had stopped, and at first I thought they must have seen me. My next thought was to try to get the rifle, that I think was slightly bent, off my chest and into a position to shoot the pair of bastards who had caused me all this grief, to whit, 'the driver and the fucking guard'. By this time I was in one hell of a foul mood; it seemed every bone in my body was aching and on fire, to say nothing about my forearm and hand, my elbow and the cheeks of my arse, all of which were raging like a bloody volcano exploding, and felt as if they had thousands of red-hot lumps of molten rock wedged in them. I was so bloody mad I was about to come out from under the truck and ask the driver, "Just what the fucking hell do you think you are playing at?" Regardless of his answer, I was then going to blow both him and his bloody guard's heads off! Then I stopped dead in my tracks as I heard through the haze of my temper a voice which just asked the most dreaded words in the USSR, "Papers, driver?"

When I looked to the left-hand side of the truck I saw a pair of Russian army boots standing by the cab. Next I then looked to the other side and saw nothing but trees. Discretion being always the better part of valour, I slowly edged my way to the side of the truck. From there I looked out from behind the right-hand rear wheel and there was nobody there. So I took a gamble, I got up into a crouch position and in that half-stooped walk that only trained soldiers can do without looking stupid, I made my way into the trees.

Once there, I found the thickest tree I could see and got myself well and truly behind it and I checked my rifle and I waited for the chase to start; but nothing happened! As I stood behind that tree and nothing happened I started to shake and within no time at all I was shaking from my head to my toes, I think the bullets in the rifle were even rattling, I shook that much. My body was shaking in the same way as a child who thinks he has just seen a ghost shakes. My mouth was dry and I don't think I could have shouted even if I had tried. If any Russian had come up to me there and then I believe I would have given in. I thought, I've had enough of this bloody Cowboys and Indians game to last me the rest of my life, however long or short that might be.

Then after what could only have been a few minutes, I heard the truck drive on. It was about five minutes after that I heard people at the roadblock talking, so there must have been more than the one checking the papers, but I'd not seen any. As I strained my ears I tried to hear what they were saying. That was when I realised that the noise of the wind while I'd been on the truck was blocking out my hearing and there was no way I could make out what they were saying, so I stayed where I was and I just stood there behind the tree.

Standing there, I realised that I was in no fit state to have a go at any more Russians. Not just yet, anyway, there were too many of them for me and they just never stopped coming at me. Slowly I slid down the trunk of the tree I was behind and a voice in the back of my mind told me, "This is it, you cannot go on like this anymore, you need sleep."

"Yes, I agree with you, after that bloody ride, and you are going to have to have some sleep," a voice said and I was certain for some time that I was talking to myself, but now I'm no longer so sure!

An interesting thing was that after that, I noticed that I didn't feel the cold any more. At last I had relaxed enough and I just sat there and closed my eyes. There followed what I can only describe as the strangest feeling I have ever had; I had the distinct feeling that somebody was looking into my face. I remember wondering why he was telling me to keep quiet, I was not making a sound, and with that I went to sleep.

Some time later I remembered having a hot steam bath, then I was smothered in white powder and then I went back to sleep again and I was really enjoying my dream. The next thing I remember about the dream was that I was having one hell of a meal. First I had a large steak with a side salad and all the trimmings. Then I had a large helping of a fruit pie and hot sweet custard. The waiter tried to force a cigar on me but I refused. I did not refuse the large, Three Star Brandy which he brought me, though. It was all so weird, but one hell of a comfortable dream and I remember sleeping in a good soft bed with clean white sheets. There was a lovely warm fire glowing in the darkness of that room. Every now and again, I can't remember how often, but somebody would come in and talk to me and I do remember talking to them. Most of it was all a very hazy dream and at first I thought that perhaps I had died and I was on the entrance course for joining heaven. What I do remember thinking is, it's not too bad so far, this being dead, that is. Everything was in a lovely warm haze, I could not recognise any of the people. I did have a lovely feeling of security, comfort and warmth. It felt unreal, but it also felt absolutely bloody great.

When I eventually woke up and came to, I was leaning against the tree, but I was not too cold, it was cold but not too bad. Really, I felt okay; I was no longer hungry and I felt cleaner. Also I noticed that I had no stubble on my face. It seemed that I had shaved my beard off while I was asleep and I'd also changed my clothes and fed myself somehow. You know, much to my surprise I never questioned my change of circumstances. It just seemed so right I should be like that, clean, well-fed and with a change of very good quality clothes. At the time I just thought, it's time I was on the move again.

For a while I listened to see if the roadblock was still there and as I could not hear anything at first I waited for a little while longer just to make sure, but nothing. Then

All For A King's Shilling

I heard a truck coming and I thought well, we shall see in a couple of minutes if they are still there. While I waited for it to arrive, I thought I should be itching by now with those bloody lice. The truck passed, but it did not stop, or even slow. With that I gingerly got to my feet. I was unsteady and felt a little dizzy. I though hell, man, you are worse than you think.

So, I just stood leaning against the tree until my equilibrium returned, which took about ten minutes before I felt well enough to move, in a competent manner, that is. When I did I started to make my way to the track; I felt a sudden pain in my right arm. My first thought was that I must have hurt it when I got off that bloody roll-a-coaster of a truck. Then I reached the trees on the edge of the road and there was no roadblock or any sign of there having been one. For some stupid reason which I could not work out the track was different, it was a well-laid road, tarmacadam and white lines, the bloody lot.

The pain in my right arm was now killing me and I looked at the heel of my right hand, thinking that it might be the cause of my pain. I wanted to see how badly infected the heel was after my fracas getting off the timber truck. Much to my surprise the hand was clean and the heel only had a small purple scar on it. There was no open skin at all. I realised then that the cheeks of my arse didn't hurt when I walked either. Again I didn't question anything, I just shook my head and like the famous chicken, I crossed to the other side of the road. Once across it I quickly moved into the trees on the other side, but it did not look right. Oh, I know I did not get a really good look at the place when I came off the truck, but I was certain this was not it.

Standing trying to get my brain in gear and not succeeding, I found myself a place in the undergrowth and settled down to try and make sense of it all. It seemed I was forever going to ground when things didn't look right to me; and it seemed that things were not looking right this trip. Anyway, I then opened my coat, the Russian soldier's coat, that is. My mouth dropped open like a fish out of water, I just looked in amazement because to my surprise I was wearing the complete uniform of a captain in the KGB. Next, I felt in the pockets of the uniform, only to discover I had papers and an identity card with my photograph on it. The complete works! Putting my hand to my face, I got a further shock, not only had I shaved and the stubble of my beard was gone, but my lips which had been badly chapped and sore, were healed. My arm still hurt, so I took off the tunic and rolled up the sleeve of the shirt. The upper part of my forearm had a clean bandage on it and the inner bend of my elbow had a large area covered in bruises and hypodermic needle marks. Then I felt my waist; again a shock, as my back wound, which Katrine had last bandaged, had now been rebandaged with an Elastoplast type of bandage. The injuries I had sustained on my hand, elbow and arse as I dropped off the truck, as I'd already discovered, were now nearly completely healed. My name now was Captain Ivan Ordripov of the KGB. It was then I started to shiver uncontrollably and it was not anything to do with the cold. For the first time in my life I was suffering from the effects of real fear, the only thing I didn't do was to defecate. I could not control my shaking and then I started to sob, taking in great gasps of air. Who were these people who were manipulating me, who could pick me up as and when they wanted without my knowing anything at all about it? Then drop me down again with a completely new identity. Then after about five minutes the cold started to get to me and I realised that I still had my arm bare. Quickly I started to replace the uniform in which they, whoever they were, had dressed me. It was important that I kept warm if I was going to get the better of these bastards.

Hastily I put the rest of my clothes on and I was in a hell of a turmoil, about what had happened. Who had done all this, and why? One thing I did know, the sooner I got the hell out of this uniform the better. The last thing I needed now was for the KGB to arrest me with this bloody lot on me. Then I thought it prudent I go through the pockets and see what other goodies I had inherited. So I emptied everything on to the ice in front of me. My face must have been a picture for I had now become the proud owner of a compass, a map, a pencil, a notepad and some food. All the food consisted of was some dried strips of meat. Much to my surprise I had acquired, besides the 7.62mm semi-automatic rifle, a .38 automatic revolver and a holster. I had just discovered the true meaning of another English saying, the criminal expression of, 'being fitted up.' For now I was in a hell of a predicament, which was the worst I had experienced since I started out on this fiasco. For the first time since I had entered this Godforsaken place, I was, in my mind, in a death sentence situation. If they ever caught me dressed like this, I'd be dead inside a couple of hours. At least if they caught me and I wasn't wearing this uniform I'd stand trial before being shot out of hand. Dressed the way I was I'd just be shot out of hand.

It really did concentrate my mind, and I thought it better I find out just where I was before I made any movement in any direction at all. First I started to take some bearings with the compass and to do this I had to climb a tree. Once up there, I took a good long look at the landscape around me. At last I plotted a couple of features I could identify on the map and took the bearings. Then I oriented the map as best I could, and tried to back-plot the bearings I had taken. I came back to the ground and spent the rest of the daylight, which was very little, poring over the map. Eventually I came to the conclusion I must be about three to four miles farther north, and about one hundred to two hundred miles farther west than I was when I fell asleep by the tree trunk. I had come to the conclusion and there was no doubt about it now, I knew they were manipulating me.

Alright, mate, but by whom and why is all this going on?

As you can imagine I didn't get much sleep that night, now that I was really scared shitless, as they say. The realisation came to me as a shock when it dawned on me that these bastards could pick me up, dress me up, and drop me off, as and when they bloody liked, and I could do absolutely nothing at all about it. The question was why? I had not led them to anybody and I had kept away from all the places where I could have got help. If it was the people themselves who were picking me up and perhaps were trying to help me, I wish to God they would not. First Katrine and her father had helped me and now somebody else was doing so, but surely that was only a dream. Each time I woke up from one of these events, I found I was hundreds of miles away from the point where I last remembered being. God, I wished I knew what was going on. It was possible that they had dressed me as a KGB officer because they had put a wanted poster out on me and wanted me shot on sight. Some soldier or peasant kills me and they have got rid of me as easily as that. All the time I wondered if I had talked about contacts at all when I was under the influence of their drugs because I knew they had drugged me. What drugs they had used on me I didn't know, but I had all the symptoms of drug abuse. The insecurity and fear I had when I first came

All For A King's Shilling

round were classic symptoms of being drugged. What I did though was to come to the conclusion that I had to get out of this uniform if I was to have any sort of chance at all. That was when I at last dozed off to sleep.

I awakened to hear birds singing in the trees just above me, and I lay there for a time just taking in the sounds. It was as light as it gets up here at this time of the year. The decision I had made last night was the only one I could make and when I awakened I knew I had to get rid of the clothes I was wearing first and foremost. It was then I realised that they were the first and only birds I'd heard singing! I stopped and thought for a moment and came to the conclusion that the sooner I was over that bloody big fence and back into Norway the better; I was too bloody thick to understand their bloody mental games, so the sooner my little hairy legs could get my arse back over the border into Norway the better; the James Bond types could then take over and play their mind games with them! Consequently I took the compass and put it on the map where I thought I was. Then after a little time spent studying the map and ground, I set a bearing that I hoped would take me to the nearest place on the map that showed any habitation. When I had satisfied myself the bearing was accurate, I picked up my rifle and off I went to find myself some new clothes, preferably peasant ones, and as I went I chewed at a piece of dried meat for my breakfast. I was surprised at just how good it tasted so maybe there's something in this James Bond shit; at least they give you better food.

It took two days and one night to reach the place I was aiming for. Mind, I would have gone straight past it by two miles if I had not seen the lights of the village during the night off to my right front. Just before dawn I took a bearing on them and then spent the remainder of the night and the next day walking towards the place. When I eventually arrived on the outskirts of the village it was getting dark again and there was quite a bit of activity going on so I hid behind a small kind of hut. Looking at the situation I thought I had two options here. First, I could walk in and ask for a bed for the night. Or secondly, I could sneak in, plant some poor sod on the head, then take his clothes and leg it. By now I was starting to wonder if they had tagged me, if I had a homing bug aboard me somewhere. If I'd been in their shoes, then I would have done so, and they had tagged me before. Not to worry, from where they had dropped me they must have known this was the place I would make for and they might already have some sod here ready to report on my progress. So it was that I reasoned it had to be the latter option, plant some poor sod and leg it with his clothes.

While I was on the outskirts of the village I had noted there was still a lot of activity going on around one of the huts, houses, call them what you will. So I decided to give it a pretty wide berth and I looked around until I found what I was looking for. A hut, or house where they all seemed to have settled down for the night. Then I carefully moved up to it and tried to see inside. At first I thought I could hear something in there, but I could not tell what it was. After a little hesitation I decided to get inside so I went to the rear of it and found the back door. The door was closed, but not locked, and it crossed my mind that this was too easy. Anyway, I was in and from what I could see it consisted of four rooms. I was in a room with a stove in it and I could hear snoring coming from another room. There was a smell of cattle and I could hear the clucking of hens coming from another room. Hell, I thought, all I need now is to set the bloody hens off. As I was committed to this house I had to get what

I needed from here. So I waited and listened for at least ten minutes and then, when I was certain that nothing stirred and the hens had stopped their clucking, I presumed all was okay.

My eyes had become accustomed to the dark by now and I could see quite well inside the place. First I saw a wardrobe type piece of furniture over in the corner of the room next to the room from where the snoring was coming. I looked around the room I was in and saw a large knife laid on the table. This I picked up and then I edged my way to the cupboard. I used the knife to ease the door open and, bingo, it was full of clothes. Quickly I picked out a jacket, a fur coat, and some trousers. It was then that I thought, you have pushed your luck about as far as you can, mate, time you were out of here. So I edged my way back to the door through which I had entered. Once there, I opened it and stepped outside. Within a few minutes I was back out of the village and on my way. I felt great, and glad that I had not had to use the knife on anything other than the wardrobe type of cupboard, that is.

I set the compass to due west, and set off with a lighter step than I had taken for some days now, since the day before the tree had ripped my back open. When it got light I stopped and changed my top clothes for the ones I had stolen. Then I burnt the KGB papers that I had on me. I dug a hole in the snow and ice and I buried the KGB uniform, after which I checked everything I had for tagging devices, but found none; I still did not feel right though. Had I been able, I would have burnt the lot, but there was always the possibility the fire would give my position away. So after having done all I could, I then did one final check looking for transmitting devices, but found nothing.

Satisfied, I set my compass to travel due north and set off again. I made good progress as the country was more open, but still covered in scrub, and the snow wasn't too bad either. Mind, I had the dense forests of the border regions to tackle yet. It was now my intention to stay on the course due north for two days. By the time I turned west again I had eaten all the dried meat they had put in my pocket. Also, I had got rid of the rifle and pistol they had given me and I was now travelling light, as they say. Again I was sucking pieces of ice to keep my body fluids up and I had tried eating lichen from the trees at one stage, after which I was as sick as a pig, so I stopped that little game. After the second day I turned due west again. This time I increased my pace. I was still feeling very hungry, but I felt heartened with the belief that I didn't have very far to go now.

It was after the fourth day of heading due west that I had the first sign of trouble. A Russian Army helicopter landed about half a mile in front of me. It could have been just a normal thing, but I decided I would skirt the place. So I turned due north again and I spent the rest of the day heading north. Then again I turned due west and headed off in the direction of what I hoped was Finland. Just before last light that night another Russian helicopter landed, this time off to my right. Now I believed I had Russian patrols to my right and to my left. It was my opinion that I was now very near to the border otherwise there would not be all this activity. So I decided that instead of resting I would keep going. About two more miles farther on I came across the border fence. Well, I had all but made it, my elation was unbelievable; no words could describe the feeling I had as I looked at the fence.

All For A King's Shilling

All I had to do now was cross that flaming big fence that they called the border, but I had one big problem, though, the fence was electrified for its whole length. What should I do? I looked at it for some time. Getting closer before I was ready to cross could be risky and I was beginning to wish I had had a better look at it when I'd last seen the damned thing. Too late now, though; so I started to look around for something, timber or anything else that was non-conductive which I might use to scale this side. Then perhaps I could just leap off the top of it in the hope I was not going to hurt myself landing. It did not take long to find what I was looking for. It took time and hard work getting the piece into place. In the end I had it propped against the fence like a ladder up against the side of a house.

Then very slowly, watching the wire all the time, I climbed the tree trunk. As I reached the top I got the shakes, rather like a tight-rope walker does when he is trying to make his act look more difficult, only I wasn't trying, it was real. Then I straightened up and launched myself into the space beyond. So it was I arrived in Finland as a twisted heap. Unfortunately, I had bumped and bruised my head; also I had twisted my leg, but I was free, I was out of Russia. For a second or two I just lay there and then I picked myself up, dusted the snow off and stepped out into Finland. I was hobbling a little because of my twisted leg, but I was free.

Of course I knew they would intern me for a while, but once they had checked me out, when old Brown was told I was out well, he would bail me out of Finland in no time. Now, for the first time since I had left Plymouth, god knows how long ago, I was feeling good, not just good, I was feeling bloody good. I was feeling over the bloody moon with myself and I turned towards the fence and gave Russia a big 'V' sign. Then off I went into the safety of the West, free at last.

I do not know how far I had walked when I saw them, but they had obviously seen me before I saw them. I was walking very openly and I was not trying to hide at all. They had me covered from about half-a-dozen places and it was all very tactical, but then I'd always been told the Finns were very good soldiers, although this little lot's appearance did surprise me somewhat! They were Finnish border guards, not your regular army this lot; another thing was they had on all the modern gear, good parkas, muck lacks, and SLR rifles. Even so they acted more like Russian Spatzi, but I just grinned at them and announced that I was glad to see them. Then I told them I was English and I had just escaped from Russia. This brought chuckles from a few of them, but they seemed to relax and started chatting amongst themselves. Then one of them asked me, "What were you doing in Russia then, I presume you had a reason to be there?"

My ears did prick up a little as I detected some venom in his voice that I didn't think Finnish guards would feel towards me, but I just told him, "I went there on a merchant ship and I got drunk the night the ship sailed and I ended in gaol." He seemed happy with this and did not question me about it anymore.

They then took me to a border hut that they said they always used when they were on patrol. Once there, they gave me a hot drink of strong tea, and a sandwich of bacon. I'm afraid I was so hungry I just wolfed it all down like the starving animal that I was. Once I had finished the mug of tea, I just sat back and I felt quite pleased with myself. Their officer meanwhile had switched on the radio in the cabin to call his HQ, he said. He told me that he had to report the fact they had found me so everything seemed normal to me.

When he had finished, he told me, "They are sending a helicopter to take you out of here. It will take about an hour to get here, it would be best if you try to get some rest. You must be tired after your long journey?"

"Yes," I said to him. "That is a good idea; to tell the truth I think I could sleep for days."

Within no time at all I was sound asleep in the chair I was sitting in.

Some time later I was rudely awakened by one of the guards. "Steady on there," I said, "I'm not a prisoner, am I?" Then I heard it for the first time; the noise I heard had a disturbing effect on me. It was that of a helicopter approaching. My first reaction was dead panic! I thought, shit, that is odd, it sounds like a bloody Russian machine, must be my nerves playing tricks on me. Then as I heard it land about forty yards from the hut I was certain it was Russian. Next thing the door of the hut was flung open and as I turned towards it I was face to face with a Russian dressed as a KGB Major. He was standing silhouetted in the door of the hut just looking at me. Then as he stepped into the hut, the remainder of the Finnish border guards dashed out through the door. It was then that I noticed that they had all changed. The ones who had brought me in were no longer dressed as Finnish border guards. They were all dressed in KGB uniforms and the officer who had just arrived, when he saw the look on my face, well, he looked at me and said, "Oh yes, English, you are still inside Mother Russia. You kept evading our patrols at every turn, we had to let you think you had made it. That was the only way you would ever give up. Now I think the game is ended for good. By the way, tell me why you didn't contact the people who could have helped you?" he added as an after thought, but I knew he already knew the answer to that question.

"Strange as it may seem to you, mainly because I never had any contacts to contact."

He just laughed and said. "We shall see, English, we shall see."

Then with that I was forcibly removed from the hut. I emerged through the door and I groaned, for standing there in two rows between me and the helicopter door were all the men who had been in the hut and some more who must have come in the helicopter. Obviously I was going to have to run the gauntlet to the helicopter. In my own mind I was determined to walk to that helicopter and not run. Also I was determined that I would stay on my feet because if I didn't it would mean death there and then. So it was that I was put aboard the helicopter in a not very gentle way, having had to walk the gauntlet of rifle butts to get there. I was in pain when I reached it, real pain, the kind of pain more often called bloody agony, but as they closed the door I could not resist holding up to them the famous English archers' salute to the French – the two erect fingers, because I knew, in my heart of hearts, that I'd beaten the bastards. I'd probably not done my chances of surviving any good, but the only way they had caught me was to move the goalposts. Typical Communistic way of winning, the only way they know how to win is by lies and cheating. How I would beat them in the next phase of my war with them I'd no idea, but by shit, I'd give it my best shot!

Chapter Thirteen
Torture, Trial And I Became A Gladiator
Russia summer 1978, The Devil has come to tea.

Sing, sing, or show your ring
We don't want to see your ring
So sing you bastard sing

It was years after my trial, conviction and sentence that my mind eventually turned to the consideration of the position that I was in. Conviction and sentence for what, you may ask? Well, that is another story; oh I deserved being locked up for what I'd done; but not to be put through the deprivation that I had suffered those last few years. At least by then, I thought, I would have been exchanged for some Russian illegal rotting in an English prison; it never did happen though so at first I thought that they had forgotten me. Of course, I was soon to realise that it was not so; they never had any intention of exchanging me. Or maybe the Russians didn't want anybody that we held to be sent back; that would be on a par with my fucking luck, wouldn't it! So I was destined to live a sort of 'up the creek without a paddle' existence, perhaps right up 'Shit Creek without a shovel' may have been a better description of it all.

I do remember that for the first six weeks my captors, whom I believed to be that stalwart organisation of the Red Army – the 'GRU' and not the dreaded 'KGB', kept me in solitary confinement. Well, they weren't likely to stick me in a cell with a load of bloody Russians, were they? They captured me in what I thought at the time was Finland, but the bastards had moved the goalposts, a most common practice amongst the Russian intelligence society. Occasionally I caught glimpses in the dark basement corridors where I was of other prisoners. At least I believed them to be prisoners, but one can never tell with the Russians. They dress their own men up to look like dissidents, so one must always beware. Everything in Russian prisons is not what it looks. That was something I was to find out over the years the hard way.

In those first few days I tried hard to keep track of time, as I'd been taught. "You must try and keep track of all the questions they ask and the number of days they interrogate you. It is most important you can recall all the questions asked by them so that when we debrief you, we will know just what they know and what they don't know," my tutor had said but I soon gave up all that shit as a complete waste of time and brainpower. I soon decided that was a most unnecessary worry considering the position I was in at the time. Perhaps I missed the lesson in my training when they taught us to ask for a transcript of the questioning and the proceedings in connection with the Geneva Convention. All of the remembering part only seemed to help the Russians to stress me out all the more; along with the constant waking me up and feeding me a breakfast or supper of a type of pigswill that they passed off as food when even I knew without having to do too much thinking that I had eaten some of their garbage only a little while earlier, and that didn't help my disposition at all. If anything it got my back up even more; but I didn't refuse the food at all, every little helped, as the woman said when she peed in the sea, and that was the attitude I adopted. It was better than starving to death as I'd been doing since I'd left Katrine's house, except for the time when I'd got off the timber lorry; but I still didn't know if that was real or not.

I was never affected in the first few days of the cat and mouse game; me being the mouse, of course. I knew that I hadn't had much time to sleep before they came and got me for another blast of questioning, mainly because of the way they made a big thing of asking me, "Did you get a good night's sleep?" Or some other stupid remark like, "You are always asleep, have you caught sleeping sickness?" They didn't give a shit if I had slept or not! But I played along with their little game; even so, after a little while I couldn't be bothered even to play their silly little game any longer. After all I'd been wandering all over the north of Russia not getting any sleep, anyway, so I could possibly say that I was already acclimatised to all that shit. However, I eventually passed their first interrogation test; I lost all track of time. Still, I suppose it was all I could expect in the situation considering that I'd lost it long before they got their grubby bloody hands on me; time, so what, mister? To me time itself had become irrelevant anyway. One thing I must remember to do is to compliment our trainers on being hooded and made to stand against a wall for hours on end until my body was numb with pain as the 'experts' back in Britain had insisted would happen. I'd no complaints about them getting that bit totally wrong! From what I saw I don't think the Russian economy ran to that much experience. Mind, I don't think any of my trainers got anywhere near any Russian who might just capture them, so how would they know? If it's from debriefing, then I've a surprise for them, we all tell lies!

The Russians who held me at that time did most, if not all, the other things my instructors had said that they would do to me if and when they caught me. It did cross my mind occasionally how it was that my instructors knew exactly what was going to happen to me when the Russians caught me. Did these monsters swap training pamphlets because I'd never met anybody who had gone though this system and come out the other end to talk about it?

Funny that, isn't it, how all your instructors seem to know you will be captured, but more to the point they know without ever leaving the UK exactly what is going to happen to you. Rather like the chicken and the egg, wouldn't you say?

I do recall now thinking at the end of the first day just how everything had happened exactly as the weedy looking little man back in England had said it would.

He had told us during one of his lectures entitled "What to expect should we ever be caught by the Russians"! The man had spent the best part of a week telling us blow by bloody blow what would happen and he got it word perfect. Perhaps he was moonlighting from the KGB or the GRU whilst on holiday in London, or perhaps he was an exchange instructor from them. Not as strange as it may seem, I do recall that when the Borneo confrontation started there were two Indonesian Marine Officers serving in Four Three Commando Royal Marines, in Stonehouse Barracks, Plymouth. Enough of that, I've my own problems to sort out.

So, as I was half marched and half dragged to my cell that first night after I'd arrived and been seen by the chiropodist, at wherever it was that I'd arrived, I distinctly remember thinking that if the rest of what the man in London had said was as accurate as his prophecy had been so far then I was in for one hell of a rough time from here on in.

The Russians had seen to it, of course, that I was not going to have too much time to consider my plight during the first three months, that is. They intended, I think, that what they had in mind for me would come as a shock each day. Each day would be a new and frightening experience for me. There was the first period of questioning, where everything was brutality. The time when I was being constantly beaten; well these times I called the 'Gestapo time'. That was followed by the psychiatric period, when everything was question and answer. Now this period, I called that the 'Chinese time'. Then came the 'American time'. That was the time when, as the song says, 'Everything Goes'. That was the worst, drugs, beatings, electric shock and insane questioning all rolled into one! I got electric shocks and kicks or punches even when I got the fucking answers right. So I gave up in the end and just said whatever came into my mind at the time. It is a little surprising really that after it was all over I was still in one piece, albeit battered and done in. That I didn't know too much about those first three months, anyway, was I think very understandable.

Apart, that is, from the first forty-eight hours, and oh boy, as the little man had said, I would always remember those first forty-eight hours, and he was right about that. I shall never forget those first forty-eight hours. My recollections of what happened to me after those first forty-eight hours really are very, very vague, but not those first forty-eight hours. Perhaps it would be fair to say that a lot of the time since those first forty-eight hours have been, and still are, non existent. I do know that I had the pleasure of the Russian interrogators' hospitality for a further three months before I even knew I was back in the land of the living. Of what happened during that time I have no real memories. Oh, vague memories of those three months do occasionally keep popping up every now and again, but they are mostly unexpected and it is probably better if they all stay that way forever. The least I know the better, because what I can't remember I can't dream about, can I? Well, unfortunately that is really not true. The flashbacks do occasionally demand to be seen and heard. However I do remember that first day after the border guards had handed me over to the GRU only too well.

The helicopter in which I was travelling landed in the centre of what looked to be a barracks' complex. I'd received a rather severe kicking during the trip as I lay on the cold floor of the machine. When it landed and the door was slid open I was unceremoniously dragged out by the scruff of the neck and punched to the icy ground. The big hero of the Soviet Union who did that is another son of a bitch I shall never forget. It has always been my desire to meet him on a one to one basis some day. He's the type of man who normally, unless of course his victim is handcuffed, or held by others, would run or scuttle away like the rat he is. No, I shall not forget that little bastard easily.

From the ground I was helped to my feet by being kicked several times until I was upright. Then I was punched and hit by anybody who could get near me whilst I was made to walk; in that half walk and half crawl of submission between two lines of these brave Russian 'heroes of the Republic'. "Come on," I was shouting, "get your Red Star Hero of the Republic cub badges here, two roubles a punch, roll up, roll up!" It probably wasn't the cleverest move I've ever made; but I had to do something to stop myself from falling unconscious. I knew if I did, and consequently went down again, that it would be the end. Of course, I did eventually flounder, but before I fell to the ground I was caught by two guards and unceremoniously dragged up on to my feet. They were 'the angels of the devil' who helped me the rest of the way into one of the dirtiest looking buildings I had ever seen. Dirtier than most of the ones I had noticed in my wanderings around Russia. Then again, everything in that part of Russia was dirty, the buildings, the countryside, the snow and most of all the people.

Just inside the door of this building I acquired two new guards, the previous ones it seemed were to return to their public who were cheering them as the heroes who had captured 'the English pig'.

My two new guards, well they looked as if they didn't know if they should beat me or kiss me. In the end they dragged me down some steps and into a cellar of some sort. There they put me into a room, cell, or as I found out, the butcher's shop, call it what you may, but it smelled like an abattoir. Which one it was, was anyone's guess; it smelt of stale rotten blood and flesh, so perhaps butcher's shop would be best. What I do know is that the smell of rotten blood did somewhat frighten the shit out of me. Well, not to put it too mildly, I believe that I'd be right in saying that I've been frightened before; but for the first time in my life I was really scared shitless!

The room was small, dark, and as I said, stank of stale blood and rotting flesh. These two gallant heroes of the Republic then pushed me into a chair that was situated in the middle of this terrifying place. The room was only about ten or twelve, maybe fourteen foot square at best and the chair in which they had plonked me down, well it was rather large for the size of room it was in. The chair not only dominated the room but it looked completely out of place. At first it reminded me of the type of chair that one would normally see at the head of a company's boardroom table. Then, on second thoughts, it was more in keeping with the image one is led to believe of the 'fat cat local council chairman, or the fat cat union chief at the annual general meeting' than the chairman of a private company. Shows how frightened I was making stupid observations like that, at a time like that, when it was possible I could be dead before the day was out.

I'd sat there for about ten minutes and the pain from my beating was starting to subside a little, when the door was dramatically thrown open and this large gorilla of a man who completely filled the space where the door had been, appeared. He stood there a moment or so and then, obviously pleased with his entrance, he walked into the room. The two guards who were in the room with me watched the following proceedings with an air of uninterested detachment. Whereas I, on the other hand, eyed this gorilla of a man with a great deal of apprehension and trepidation, because I had the distinct feeling that the bastard was here to do me harm and from the look on his face I just knew he was going to enjoy every bloody minute of it. He was definitely not one of those "This will hurt me as much as it is going to hurt you merchants"! He looked as though he was well versed in the art of pain, other people's pain!

In his huge left hand he had an equally large kidney-shaped tray. This he put on the floor beside the chair in which I was sitting. By now I was transfixed with the contents of this tray. But my gaze was interrupted as he removed with his right hand two strong looking leather straps which were tucked into his waistbelt. These straps he proceeded to use to tie my wrists to the arms of the chair in which I was still reposing. I watched all this with interest and to tell the truth I must have looked like a bloody jack rabbit caught in the headlights of a car late at night. Too late I realised that this was the point in the proceedings when I should have insisted in standing up against any type of interrogation, quoting the Geneva Convention and stating my name, rank, and service number; but for some reason I didn't. As I was soon to find out it wouldn't have made the slightest change in what was going to happen to me!

Next, from the kidney-shaped tray he took what can only be described as a pair of rusty old pliers cum wire cutters or strippers. The type of things one sees in the old electrician's kits of years gone by, the type of kit one can only see in the museums of the early engineering age nowadays in the West.

At this point in the proceedings this gorilla of a man had my undivided attention, boy did he! I just knew now that he meant me real harm and that he was up to no good. I was watching him so intently that it hurt the back of my eyes, but I didn't have much time to think too much about that or to wonder what he was about to do.

He just put the flat heel of the palm of his hot, sweaty left hand over the back of my right hand and with the great strength I just knew the bastard would possess, he pressed my right hand flat against the arm of the chair to which it was now strapped.

Then this sadistic bastard started to remove my fingernails, first from my right hand, one nail at a time. He carried out this task so deftly that I was at first too fascinated at how he did it to scream! Well, that was a lie because I screamed and boy, did I scream, but at the same time I was fascinated at what the bastard was up to. First he pushed this rusty tool under a fingernail and then without looking down, but grinning in my face, with a deft flick of his wrist he cut first to the right edge of the nail then back across to the left edge of the nailbed. This left the nail still secured to my finger by the bottom and both sides then, as his grin widened, looking me full in the face so close I could not only smell his stinking breath but just about taste it, with a little flick the nail was hooked out by its roots. The first time he did this my mouth opened wide, as wide as it ever had in all my life, but by now I was determined that I wouldn't scream so I just sat there with my mouth wide open and screaming my fucking head off. The noise coming out of it was the highest note in the universe. At last he was finished with my right hand, and he then went on in a similar fashion to remove the nails from my left hand.

The worst part of the whole episode was that the bastard didn't even ask me any questions; so I couldn't even tell the ugly pig any lies! That really pissed me off! Not the fact that I couldn't tell him any lies, but that I went through all that sodding pain for nothing. But looking back I very much doubt if he had the intelligence to ask me any questions. I had always been led to believe that asking me questions was a part of the interrogation procedure which, when I lied to him, would have given him a legitimate excuse to remove my finger nails, if that was what turned the evil bastard on. As each nail was flicked from my fingers I became so enraged with the man that the hatred building up inside me made me swear that one day "I will kill you for this, you big ugly swine, I'll cut you into burger-sized little lumps of rotting flesh!" The big bastard infuriated me more because when I'd finished my outburst he just grinned and even had the audacity to wink and nod his bloody head at me!

At one stage during the procedure I noticed the guards had their fingers stuck in their ears, obviously to cut out the screams of agony that they knew I was emitting as this gorilla of a man continued with his extremely painful operations on my hands. So I think I was the first to hear the noise at the door, and looking up I noticed, in between the opening and closing of my mouth, that an older man had entered the room. This newcomer was dressed in a white coat and what always looked to me like a master chef's hat. My mouth remained wide open while I watched him as he walked up to the two guards and tugged one of them by the sleeve. I saw his mouth open and close in the rapid way one sees on parade grounds all over the world. Judging by the two men's reaction, I think he ordered them to take their fingers out of their ears pronto, because that is what they did! They also gave away any subterfuge of a disguise that the man in the white coat and hat was trying to use, because they clicked their heels to attention in his honour. So I reasoned that the man must at the very least be a field marshal chef, or even a pastry chef.

By now the gorilla operating on my fingers had finally got the last of my fingernails in his kidney tray. The pain, which I wish I'd been able to suffer in silence, had not lost its first intensity at all. Although I'd managed at last to stifle my screams, which had been, against all my orders, escaping from my mouth, I had not however been able to stop the tears as they rolled down my cheeks or the sweat pouring off my forehead. I've always tried to convince myself that the tears were tears of anger, but they were not; I was crying my bloody eyes out like a bloody baby with the pain.

When the last nail had flopped into his tray I thought that it had been a complete waste of pain. I'd not been asked a single question. I soon realised in the next few days that it wasn't a complete waste of pain at all. It was a demonstration to me, that they could and would do just whatever they wanted to my body and there wasn't a damned thing I could do about it.

Satisfied with his work the gorilla picked up his kidney dish and left the room. As I watched him go I thought that at least the worst was over, but I was completely and totally mistaken in that assumption

Firstly, I should have realised that when the field marshal chef didn't leave that little butcher's shop the game was not yet over. The two guards and the field marshal chef stood expressionless against the wall watching me while I sat in the ridiculous chair and watched them. It was a game I was getting a little bored with and I was about to open my big mouth when the door opened and the gorilla returned. This time he was carrying another couple of straps, only these two were a lot thicker and larger than the ones he had already used on my arms. Also he had under his left arm a contraption that looked like one of those stools which one sees in shoe shops in England. The kind which the large-arsed assistant sits on while she forces your foot into shoes she is making you try on, and they are the ones you don't want, anyway, at the same time flashing her great big nutcracker thighs in your face and the ugly monster you know is hiding in the darkness of the upper reaches poised ready to spring out and bite you!

It wasn't the stool that frightened me so much as the second set of straps. They struck fear into my heart, and when he started to attach the stool-type object to the front legs of the chair that I was still strapped into by the wrists. Then, without any more ado he strapped my ankles to the chair legs and then my feet to the stool contraption; satisfied with his handiwork he first looked at the field marshal chef, who just gave an ever so slight nod of the head, and the bastard gorilla commenced to remove all my toenails. First, he inserted the same rusty pliers type of tool under one of my nails and with the same swift and deft movement he had used on my hands, he removed my toenail. His action when inserting the tool under the nail was designed to cause the maximum of pain. Then when this pain had started to subside, just a fraction, with a little swift twist first to the right and then to the left, he reactivated the pain to its maximum intensity. It was at this point, when I felt I couldn't stand any more pain, that he gave a swift jerk with his hand, and that was when the pain reached a new height of agony and the grin widened across his ape-like face. In the next second another of my toenails was removed from my foot. This heathen of a gorilla then grinned in my face as he slowly raised the nail up to my eyelevel and dropped the blood-splattered toenail into the kidney dish that was on the floor. The bastard then had the audacity once more to wink at me; then making some flourishing movements with his rusty instrument, flicking the bloody thing in front of my face, he approached my foot again to remove yet another nail. He had the look of someone who really enjoyed his work and he had my undivided attention!

This time, though, the animal had achieved his aim because I began to really scream totally and uncontrollably! It was then I saw a grin of satisfaction come over the face of the field marshal chef and with a slight nod to me, he left the room. I realised as he went that he wasn't the field marshal chef after all, but the field marshal torturer and much to my disgust the nod was the start of a bond between us, in the age old torturer's cat and mouse game of who wins. He had hardly closed the door behind him when the guards had their fingers stuck in their ears again.

After the evil-looking gorilla of a man had completed his task, I still could not understand why they hadn't asked any questions in between my bouts of uncontrollable screaming. I knew that I would have my nails removed in the first few days, that much I'd been told on every course I'd attended, but I'd always understood that I'd be asked questions. They had not even asked my rank, name, or regimental number. Something that I was fully prepared to tell them, but they'd never taught us in training that when the time came the bastards wouldn't even ask us that. But then these bastards already knew all that shit about me, my history in the Corps, places I'd been and things I'd done, oh, they knew all there was to know about me. More than I'd ever imagined they could know about me, a fact I was to find out later.

Once the task of removing my finger and toenails was completed, a kind of numbness came over me and although I was still screaming, the intensity of the pain had started to diminish; until, that is, the guards, having regained their bravery, started to drag me by the scruff of my neck with my arms stretched across their chests. While they were hauling me along the corridor they gave the ends of my fingers the occasional rub against the walls as they took me to what I presumed was a cell. I was to learn in time, though, never to presume anything at all where these Russians were concerned. A cell in the UK is at least habitable, the Russians don't have anything that I have seen so far that could compare to a British cell; nor did I ever see one in all the time they held me.

The most painful part of the journey to my cell, though, was my poor bloody feet, or the parts of my feet where my toenails used to reside. They were being dragged across the rough concrete floor. Worse still, I was being dragged so fast by this pair of goons that I didn't have a chance to walk, therefore the dead weight of the lower part of my body was resting on the ends of my toes. More painful yet was the part where they dragged me down some dirty steps leading to a basement of sorts. My feet flopped from step to step, sending shock waves of pain up my legs. That was when the pain in my feet became excruciating and it even reached the roots of my teeth at the back of my mouth.

I was at that time in such pain that I made a vow to myself that in no circumstances would I ever answer any bloody questions when they eventually decided to ask me. Regardless of what they did to me, from there on in answering questions was a definite taboo. You see in my foolish state of mind I still believed they knew nothing at all about why I was in Russia in the first place.

It was much, much later that I realised that as the sole surviving member of the original team sent into Murmansk, I had been sent to Russia to be 'eliminated', as they say.

The cell, when we finally arrived there, was very small. It was about seven foot long and four foot wide, the walls were black with damp and the floor was covered with wet, uneven flagstones. There was no trace of a bed in it at all. I did notice that there was a hole in one of the corners at the rear. The smell emitting from the hole brought my attention to it as soon as I landed face down on the floor of the place. I was soon to discover that the hole wasn't only my toilet, but was the main highway for the rats that were constantly coming and going as they passed through the cell, probably on their way to visit other parts of the barrack complex in which I was being held.

Some of the rats were really tame; they would stop and look me over when they were halfway between the hole through which they had entered and the one they would depart through. The hole they exited through was obviously a rat-made one as it was too neat for a Russian to have made it. They, the rats that is, would sit and look at me and make that squeaking noise that rats make. I watched them watching me, and I often wondered if they were offering me advice or maybe they were just laughing at my predicament; or were they perhaps eyeing me up with a view to a good meal at a later date? The more I looked at them the more I came to wonder if it was true that as a human being I was really a higher life form than they were. They were the lowest type of life form, according to the things I was taught as a child. Yet here I was, in a dirty, wet, cold cell soon to be eating scraps of food and drinking a soup mixture that could only be described hopefully as 'dish water'. I was unable to leave the cell and I was unable to keep myself warm, but the rats never looked cold and the little bastards could come and go as they pleased.

I knew that once I was through the initial interrogation I was going to be perpetually hungry. Yet here were a group of low life rats who were free to come and go as they pleased and as fat as bloody pork pigs. They probably had the first choice of any of the food my dish water soup was made from; they most likely ate what they wanted and got their leg over occasionally. Watching their activity I had to ask myself if Darwin's theory of evolution was right after all, it was just a question of who was evolving here and who wasn't. It seemed to me that the rats had the better part of the deal than I did and I was supposed to be the brainier one of the two species, and that, my friends, 'pissed me off' somewhat.

For the first time in my life I realised that everything around and about me had become relevant. From that day onwards I knew that staying alive meant that I had to take notice of everything that occurred or happened to me; and it was during the next day that the real truth of my situation was brought home to me. That was when I realised I was not very well, physically, that is. Of course I'd been mentally ill for years as everybody who knew me was only too well aware, but this day I found out about 'relativity'. To me relativity is anything that happens or is planned, that has anything to do with my – and I repeat my – well-being. Einstein's theory of relativity is all to do with space, time and all that shit. Well, that doesn't affect me so I don't worry about it; but my well-being is a different kettle of fish altogether, as they say.

The previous night I had wolfed down the dirty stinking food my guards had brought me. For all I knew they could have pissed in it, masturbated in it or, god forbid, shit in it! All of which are common practices carried out by twisted guards of special prisoners the world over. As a matter of fact you don't have to be a prisoner for some twisted chef to pee in your soup! I can tell you. The fact that I was starving made my wolfing down the food a necessity in order to stay alive, but I knew later that perhaps I should have died instead.

Later that night as I lay on the floor and tried to sleep the first twinges of pain started to ripple in my abdomen. If I slept at all, I can't remember, but I realised that I was, to say the least, a little under the weather. At first I presumed it was caused by the treatment that had been meted out to me on my first day as a prisoner. The pain came in spasms, each spasm a little worse than the previous one. I'd move a little and there would be a little twinge in my left side just about where my waistbelt would normally sit. Then it would subside as quickly as it came. The first time it happened, when it subsided I thought good, it was a false alarm, but I was wrong. Without any warning whatsoever the next second there was a stab of excruciating pain in my side about an inch lower down on the opposite side as if something was taking a bite out of my insides.

My first reaction was one of 'abject bloody terror'. Hell, I thought, I've got a bloody live carnivorous worm or snake inside me. Then the pain subsided and I came back to reality; and the fear left me for the time being. Some twenty minutes later it happened again. First the little spasm, which after a second or two subsided, and then the violent bite this time just a little lower down and a little more to the centre of my body. By now I was climbing the wall with fear, screaming my bloody head off. I firmly believed that I was being eaten alive from the inside out.

William Atlay

My heart was racing far more than it ever did when I stepped outside an aircraft at twenty thousand feet. I had for the first time in my life cracked in my head and I was definitely 'off my skull, do-lally' as they say. I'd never in my life known such fear and to make matters worse nobody came to see what I was screaming about. All that happened was that the little light in the grill on the ceiling of the cell was turned off. This had the effect of turning me into a jabbering, slobbering heap huddled up into the corner of the cell in total darkness, and led to the terrifying thought that I was dying alone in total darkness; what a fucking way to go!

I was sitting there terrified at my fate, the thing, whatever it was, was now biting me lower and lower in my bowels and with a frequency that made the pain now constant. I was convinced I had but minutes left to live. I stood up and removed my trousers, with the intention of crouching over the hole in the cell floor, and then it happened. Two things happened at once as if they were timed to coincide. The light came back on and my bowels emptied all over the cell floor. A ginger-coloured fluid with lumps of dark clotted blood and red streaks of new blood spread out on the floor before me.

My reaction surprised even me as I crouched down and started looking to see if the snake or thing that was eating my insides had been flushed out with the rest. When I couldn't see any snake-type animal on the floor I was worried in case it had disappeared down the hole before I'd had a chance to see it. Then I spotted something lying on the floor that seemed to be moving a bit. It was a whitish, small bladder-type of thing. It sent the fear of god through me as I looked transfixed at it. Then I saw little worm-like things coming from it and at that moment I nearly passed out. "Oh my god," I said aloud, "it's had bloody young."

Just then the door opened and the man in the chef's hat came to the door of the cell. He looked at me and then at the mess on the floor and he was not best pleased with what he saw. He shouted something that I didn't catch and the next moment two men in white coats came into the cell, picked me up and dragged me out and back along the way I'd been brought earlier that night. Again my toes were bounced off the lip of the stairs as they dragged me screaming up them this time.

These two men entered a room that looked like a third-world doctors' consulting room, and I was thrown on to a cot-type thing and strapped to the head of it in a half lying, half sitting position. Before I knew what was happening, these two bastards started ramming a bloody garden-type hosepipe up my rectum. Then I was given (not too gently I might add) what I think passes in Russia as an enema. My first thoughts were that they were going to drown the snake inside me, but when I saw my belly start to swell and swell to alarming and painful proportions I thought they had devised a new type of water torture. "I'll tell you anything you want to know for Christ's sake, just fucking well ask me!" I yelled at the top of my voice.

The pain was now at a pitch that in my wildest dreams of withstanding torture I could never have imagined, my lungs and other organs in my chest were being forced up into the back of my throat, or so I thought. The 'chief torturer' with the big chef's hat on came in and told them in no uncertain terms to stop. Which thank god they did. Then one of them took hold of the hosepipe between my legs and laughed in my face as he jerked it out in one excruciatingly painful pull.

All For A King's Shilling

If I hadn't been in such excruciating pain the next second would have had me roaring with laughter. It was obvious to me that he had no idea how much water he had pumped into me, or how much pressure had built up because as the end of the hosepipe came away from my rectum so did a jet of water containing what little had been left in my body and all the bugs that had ever resided in me. Because of the position they had strapped me to on the bed, he took the full blast of this just about where his necktie would have been had he worn one.

Before he could assault me, he and his mate were ordered from the room by the chief torturer. Then the chief torturer, when they had gone, just stood and looked at me for a minute or so and with a shake of the head he also walked out of the room; and believe it or not, within half an hour of being left alone and with the pain having subsided to an acceptable level, I fell fast asleep! When I awoke some time later it was dusk and I looked myself over. The blood caused by the violent attack on my rectum had stopped running and my belly was so flat I thought I could see my backbone; as it was my navel stood out from my skin like a ping pong ball. Then I looked at my feet and, by twisting my head, at my hands. I realised that my finger ends and toe ends had become a little infected and were starting to throb somewhat. They seemed to be throbbing in unison with the frequency of the pains, although slight now, that were still in my stomach.

So, stupid arsehole that I am, I thought the infection in my nails and toes and my stomach could be connected. I knew why my rectum was so painful and it had nothing to do with the rest of my problems. Next I tried to rest my head on the back of the bed to which I was still strapped, but it was difficult. I was still sitting in the dampness of the bed, where the gunge that had shot out of me so violently some little time earlier had soaked away. Even so, against all the odds, I managed to doze off again for a little while. At the time I thought sleep was probably the best thing I could have at that precise moment.

I'm not quite sure what time it was when a presence next to me brought me awake. Standing by the bed looking at me as if I was something the cat had just dragged in was a buxom, well buxom was a kind word, but I think it was a woman. She had a small trolley like thing, on which there was an enamel plate of some sort; on the plate was a meal of what looked like porridge. With a perfect Birmingham accent she said. "They have told me to feed you the same food we get, until you are better; then it's back to the shit for you, my fine English pig. I don't know why they just don't take you out and shoot you, you killer and rapist of women and children."

I just sat there with my mouth hanging open. "Now just a sodding minute there. I have killed men, I agree, but I draw the line at women and children. I've never harmed a woman or child in my life."

With that she punched me straight in the mouth and I swallowed a broken tooth. You cow, I thought, you I'd make an exception for; I'd shoot you, strangle you, even stab you, you fat bitch, but rape, well that's out of the question. I did have the presence of mind to keep silent though. Too many broken teeth in an empty stomach could be bloody dangerous.

Without another word she fed me the garbage that she had said was the same food that they ate. I felt sorry for them, it was bloody atrocious. To make matters worse she kept putting large amounts of salt on it and she also rattled the spoon around my mouth; by the time she was finished I was going crazy with thirst and my mouth ached like hell, then I'm not sure about the hell bit, but I now knew I was on my way!

It turned out that unbeknown to her in her attempt to torture me she actually did me some good as the salt, although very painful at the time, helped heal the ulcers that were forming in my mouth.

When she put the last spoonful of the stuff in my mouth she rattled the spoon around just one more time and then started to push it down my throat. I really thought I was a goner that time as I started to choke on the thing. My guardian angel came in just in time to save me. I was starting to get a little worried about him, like Batman he was always there to save me. That f-ing bastard was up to something, I remember thinking.

They left me there all night then and they didn't lock the door. I spent the worst night of my life. The salt was driving me crazy with thirst and the food was rumbling around inside my stomach. To make matters worse the wet mattress they had left me strapped on was starting to freeze, or it felt as if it was. I prayed for my Batman chief torturer to come and rescue me, but he didn't, the bastard!

I don't know what time it was when they finally came to get me, but it was still dark and I think it was well into the early hours. The two guards were new and to my surprise they were not too violent with me. They untied me from the bed and helped me to the floor. The problem came with my legs when I tried to walk. At first it felt the way one does when one has had a little too much vodka to drink; and although you think you are okay, you wobble a little when you move a little too quickly. That was how I felt, drunk.

The guards must have noticed because they both held me and guided me towards another room at the end of the corridor. This room was much the same as many rooms I was to enter and which I came to hate. I hated them far worse than the cells they kept throwing me into when they had finished practising their butchery on my now badly-beaten and broken body. I was never sure how long I was in that place, but it seemed like years.

The guards took me into the first one of these interrogation rooms that I came to know quite well. There was a desk at the rear of the room with a chair behind it. There was a three legged stool standing in front of the desk. It was obvious to anybody with even a little bit of sense that the chair was for the torturer and the stool for the likes of me. The chair, which was a large captain's type of chair, was situated behind the desk. It was overpowering and it looked completely out of place behind the desk. I soon learnt that every pair of guards I ever had would plonk me down in the chair and not on the stool. They would then step back to stand one on either side of the door. There we would stay until my tormentor, whoever he was, came in.

Well, this time we stayed like that for a good five to ten minutes; not a word, sound or gesture passed between us. I was sitting in this big chair, which incidentally I knew I shouldn't be in; but I sat there with only a shirt on as I'd lost my trousers somewhere between my cell, where I'd had them in my hand, and the room where I'd been strapped to the bed.

They stood looking at me with complete indifference and I must admit I sat in that chair and I wasn't in the least little bit interested in and didn't give a shit about them either. If I'd had my trousers on then I might have taunted the hell out of them,

All For A King's Shilling

but bare-arsed didn't seem to be the best-dressed position to be in to start a fight, so I just looked at the pair of bastards and gave them my hard man look, probably looked more wimpish than hard by then.

Suddenly the door between the guards was flung open nearly hitting one of them; now that would have raised a laugh in me, but that would have to wait a few years yet. The man who had dressed as a master chef, my Batman, the last time I'd seen him, had now burst into the room. He marched across the short distance from the door to the table and he kicked the three legged stool across the room. Next he leaned across the desk and with his face not more than two inches from mine with the foulest breath I'd ever smelt, even worse than the gorilla, yelled at the top of his guttural Russian voice, "Get up you stupid English pig."

I stared back into those ice-cold black eyes without flinching a nerve, in what I thought was my tough, really hard-case look, and replied in pidgin English. "I'm so sorry, Russian wanker, but you will have to speaky, speaky a lot quieter and speaky, speaky a lot slower, or better still speaky, speaky in English if you want me to understand anything that you want to say to me!"

Before I knew what he was up to, he had reached forward with his right hand and I felt a searing, burning pain which shot up my left arm and into the area of my head just behind my eyes. Before I could stop myself I let out an involuntary scream. "I see you speaky, speaky that language, my fine cocky English pig," he growled at me.

"You bastard," I shouted, "just you wait for the revolution; your bloody days are fucking numbered." Then, looking down at my left hand, I saw two of my fingers were bleeding profusely now. Then I saw that this Russian bastard had what looked like a small suede brush in his hand. It was the type one sees on sale in the shops in the UK which sell Hush Puppy type suede shoes. The handle was wood and the bristles of the brush looked to be copper or brass wire.

At this point he held the brush up in front of my face and said, "Looky, seey, the little bits of your fingers that are stuck on my brush. Before I'm finished, English pig, I'll have all of you stuck to my little brush. Now get round here," he screamed at me as he pointed to where he was standing.

Realising that the bastard had me by the short and curlies, as they say, I did the next best thing I could think of. I moved round the desk and as I did so I looked at the guards and said, "I'll kill all three of you bastards before I escape from here." They just looked at me as everybody else had looked at me since my capture, as if I were already dead, which by their past experience they probably knew I was, dead! that is.

Once I was on the other side of the desk the chief torturer walked across the room and picked up the stool which he had so violently kicked earlier. He placed it in front of me and told me to sit on it and place my hands on the desk.

I for my part was a little reluctant to put my hands on the desk, but he was very insistent in his manner; and after a swift kick on my knee I knew I had no option but to comply. "Sit!" he screamed in my ear, so I began to sit very carefully by placing my hands about the seat of the stool. In the back of my mind I knew I'd seen one of these fucking stools before. He then tapped the desk with the handle of the brush and bawled at me to place my hands on the desk.

So, I placed my hands on the desk and lowered myself on to the stool. Immediately I placed my weight on the stool I lost my balance and my left hand slipped from the desk. With a great effort I managed to stop myself falling on to the floor by holding on to the lip of the desk with my right hand until, that is, I had the most excruciating pain shoot up the back of my right hand then along the underside of my forearm. This pain then continued on its way over my upper arm and across my shoulder and into the base of my neck. It then travelled up over my head and burst out behind my forehead like one of those large coloured fireworks one normally sees on November the fifth.

In the background I could hear this swine screaming at me, "What is the matter with you, you English pig, can't you even sit still when you have the chance? Now pick up that stool and sit on it."

It was then that I finally understood why my nails had been removed the first day I arrived there. It was like a joining routine.

When I managed to pick up the stool with my hands that were by now on fire with pain I tried once more to sit on it, but exactly the same thing happened again. Again I suffered a brushing of my fingers and again I screamed in agony, with him screaming in my face, "Sit, you English pig. Sit, what is the matter with you?"

Again I fell from the stool and this time I ignored the swine completely, because in my aching painful brain a spark was starting. I asked myself why I couldn't sit on a normal three- legged stool without falling off. So instead of getting up, I sat on the floor examining the stool. I heard him stop shouting for a moment and I felt, rather than saw, him looking at me. He then suddenly screamed at the guards to get me up.

By now I'd had enough. I now realised where I had seen that type of stool before in my life. I had seen it on an escape and evasion exercise in Britain. Not even Superman could sit on one of those bloody stools. The time had come when I didn't give a shit anymore and I reasoned that it was time to fight back. I came off the floor in an action that my old instructor would have been proud of. It was such a shock to the guards and I floored the nearest one before he could stop approaching me. The second one started to bob and weave a bit, but he didn't stand a bloody chance as I floored him also. By now I only had one leg of the stool left and I turned on my tormentor. As I turned all I could see was the sides of an automatic pistol as it rested on the bridge of my nose. I knew I should have knocked it aside with the leg of the stool, but to my eternal shame, I didn't! Oh, I'd have died, but I'd have taken that bastard with me; but some years later I was glad that I hadn't killed him!

I looked at the hand that was grasping the butt of the pistol and I saw a slight tremble as he tried to hold his hand steady and his gaze firm; and to my surprise I saw bubbles of sweat forming on his knuckles as he tightened his grip around the trigger. Then suddenly the gun was gone, the tension drained from me and the pain returned to my head and arms with a vengeance. I went weak at the knees and sank to the floor just as the door was flung open and the place filled with other guards. Within seconds I was dragged to my feet and half carried, half dragged back to my cell. There I was thrown into the cell and the door was slammed behind me.

At first I just lay on the floor and tried to get my thoughts into gear; I was going to need a clear head from now on. Then it hit me, by felling the two guards, I'd probably just committed suicide. In a panic I started searching the cell for anything I could find to protect myself with, but the bloody place was bare as a baby's arse except that is, for my soaking trousers. While I was panicking and trying to put them on – have you ever tried to put soaking wet trousers on – I could hear the guards gathering outside my cell and a lot of shouting was going on. Words like 'kill' and 'make the bastard suffer before we kill him' were being bandied around in the corridor. For the first time in a long, long time I thought of praying, but then I thought, don't be a bloody hypocrite, mate; it's too bloody late for that.

It really was too late for that sort of stuff anyway, because my cell door was thrown open at that second and the two guards whom I'd downed came into the cell. They were followed by about a division or so of their mates. There were that many of them that I was more likely to be crushed to death than beaten to death.

What happened next I don't know, but one thing I'm certain about was that those guards had the same survival instincts as I had, mate, because we all tried to lie down on the floor at the same time. Some arsehole had fired his gun in there and a bullet was hurtling around ricocheting from wall to wall around the cell.

When all the panic had stopped a very authoritative voice was bawling and shouting orders and the place remarkably emptied. Another opportunity I missed, I should have just walked out with the crowd; but I didn't and I saw my torturer standing in the doorway of the cell nodding his head. After a moment or two he slammed the door and I propped myself up against the rear wall of the cell. Reflecting over the day's events, I thought that they were a right bunch of nasty bastards; and they had really fucked up my day, good and proper. I was glad for them that it wasn't a Wednesday, 'make and mend day', otherwise I'd have got really mad at the bastards. Shortly after that performance I fell asleep, I'd done my resisting bit for one day and, god was I tired. Fall asleep wasn't what I did really, I just passed out.

When I came round some time later, how much later I never knew, I was surprised to see two rats curled up asleep on my legs. They looked like a couple of cats at first, then when they felt me move they scurried off my legs and sat watching me for ages. Suddenly they looked at the door and then they scurried off down the hole in the corner of the cell. Just as they disappeared the cell door was flung open and three bloody great big Russian women wearing white coats came in. One of them was the bitch who had smashed me in the mouth. Before I could move to get up or even make any derogatory remarks they pinned me to the floor and stuck a bloody great big needle in my arm. Attached to the needle was what looked like a bucket, the syringe was that bloody big.

In no time at all I just lay there on the floor and I couldn't move a muscle; I couldn't speak, but I could hear and see everything that was going on around me. Not long after the women had left the cell four guards came into the cell and picked me up by my limbs and carried me out to a waiting truck. They threw me in the back and cuffed my wrists and ankles to some cargo fastening rings on the floor of the truck. I do remember one of them saying, "Well that's the end of that bastard, I wish they'd let us kill him." The truck then drove off and suddenly a large piece of rock came hurtling in over the tail gate and landed in the back of the truck between my legs, another mile an hour slower and it would have crushed my knackers. Those men really were a bunch of nasty bastards! I was obviously going to be better off out of their hands.

Now they were really nasty bastards, but after that I was to meet the nasty bastards from the KGB's first division which made my first stay look like a kindergarten because for the next three months I was too busy trying to stay alive to worry about all that name, rank and number shit. Which was something my bloody interrogators weren't interested in the slightest bit about, they had their own way of knowing who the fuck I was anyway, as one so politely put it! The bastard already knew all of that shit about me as it was he was more interested in who it was who had organised my trip, how had I got into Russia? Why hadn't I followed the instructions I was given in London? How had I escaped the aircraft crash in the North Sea? I was minded to ask him how he knew I was on a plane that crashed into the North Sea but I didn't because I never caught him in a good enough state of mind. But my negative answers to all these things seemed to upset him somewhat and he would clench his teeth. That was the sign that meant my fingers or my toes, or even both were going to get a grooming with the wire brush that he always had in his hand. Then when my screaming subsided a little it would all start again.

Who was helping me, and why hadn't I followed orders? Orders which I think he knew more about than I did, these were the questions he kept asking me. When he was unhappy with my answers he would again stroke either the ends of my fingers or my toes with his wire brush, just to encourage me to tell him what it was he wanted to know. I was beginning to believe that these Russians must all have Hush Puppy shoes in their homes because they all seemed to have those bloody little wire brushes.

It was during this time the penny finally started to drop and a couple of frightening revelations came to me during all this questioning and torture that I was being subjected to. The first revelation came to me when my speech started to become a little slurred one day. The next day it was a little worse and that was when I realised that I was being systematically drugged each day, which I presumed was with truth drugs and the like that my superiors kept talking about back in the good old UK. The second, when I realised it, was the most frightening of all. It finally dawned on me that the pain my interrogator was inflicting on me by aggravating the sores where my nails used to be was much to my surprise helping me to keep my mind clear. My speech was slurred somewhat and I could no longer tell the bastard to 'fuck off' properly; even though my mind was as clear as a bell I couldn't talk properly. It would come out as 'uck foff' or even 'koff uck' or similar words. By helping to keep my mind clear he knew I would resist him all the more, thus prolonging my interrogation, but he also knew that when I finally cracked and the speech-wrecking drugs were stopped, then the floodgates would open. I would then reveal all there was to know about my entire life from the cradle until the last thing I could remember just before my capture. The next and most important realisation was the fact that the Russians had known everything there was to know about the place we had built outside Murmansk. They had known since the first day we had arrived off Murmansk. He even mentioned the time the defence launch had followed the first freighter in, checking to see that we had arrived okay and there was nothing to impede us in our, or should I say, their operation. Nice of them to keep an eye on us, I wondered what they made of the two frogmen we anchored in the bay, but I wasn't minded to ask them anything about that at all.

There was one particular snotty little bastard who started to attend the interrogation sessions with the interrogator, and who used to dress like the chef at the last place I'd been. He was probably brand new and just out of the box, but he was a little bastard. Well, this little snotty bastard kept telling me, "If you, or the fools in London and Washington, thought that you could do anything in Russia which we didn't know about, then you must all be mad."

"Yeah, yeah, and what pile of crap have you just crawled out of, mate?" I was going to say, but it came out in as good an Irish accent as I could muster as, "I'm terribly sorry, sir, but I don't know, sir, but then again it could be Murphy the spy." In his exasperation and frustration at my insistence that I hadn't a clue what he was talking about, he once remarked, "Even if a starling farts in Russia, some fool looking for advancement like a better job or a better flat, will report it to us. You are all mad, no wonder it's called the decadent West. All of you have had your brains scrambled."

Looking at him I said, "We may have had our brains scrambled mate, but if it wasn't for the stupid left wing loonies, who by the way only want your money, you bloody idiots wouldn't even know there was a Western world and a capitalist one at that." It was of course not only bullshit, but it was a very stupid thing to have said to him, because he was as I have said, an evil little sod; and the next day the heavy beatings started again in earnest. I knew something was going to happen when later that night the guard told me, "Wrap up well tomorrow, Englishman, they are going to beat the shit out of you!" You can't get a clearer warning than that now, can you!

After the beatings and the torture stuff were over the pains in my hands and feet started to subside. The drugs which I believed they were now putting in my food began to have a rather nasty effect on me and my dining partners the rats, who all seemed to be bloody junkies! Slowly I started to drift into a state that could only be described as 'oblivion'. From that point on I spent a lot of the time drugged up to the eyeballs, and it was a relief not to feel the beatings as I had in the beginning. At first I thought I was getting used to the pain, but then I reached a stage where I wasn't quite sure what was happening to me anymore. It came to a stage when I didn't quite know even who I was anymore, it must have been the drugs, but I have to admit that at that stage I no longer gave a shit anyway.

Some time later while I was conversing with one of the old rats; the one who used to come and sit near me, in the bemused and brain dead state I was in, I decided that I needed to do two things. First I had to find out what, if anything, they intended to do with me once they had finished playing silly buggers with my body. Now that proved a little harder than I expected; the guards who fed me and led me around the place wouldn't tell me anything, probably something to do with sparrow farts, I think the man said. Anyway, if they did tell me I've never been able to remember it. The plan the interrogators had in mind was, I believe, that I should lose all sense of time and location. Well, if they did but know it, I didn't know 'who the fuck I was' or even 'where the fuck I was' or when I was where I was.

Then the thought hit me, they didn't give a shit if I knew what day, week or month it was or even where I was being held, the matter was irrelevant. There wasn't a bloody thing I could do about it anyway. Even so they still kept me well and truly drugged up to the eyeballs with some hallucinatory drug. It was certainly a hell of a mind-bender drug that they were pumping into me. The flower power people in the West would have loved it. In my drugged state I eventually realised that they had also started to move me around quite a lot from prison to prison. I only found out because I once walked out of my cell and turned in the direction I was used to and walked into a wall, not only that, but I also missed my rats.

At first I thought my rats had given up on me. Then I finally realised that the cells were different every now and again so when taken out of my cell I used to hesitate and see which way the guards went before I made a fool of myself by walking into a wall again or going the wrong way. These little points were very important to me; they helped me keep a sort of grip on my mind. I thought at first that I was being moved around the prison because I was never in the same cell for more than a couple of weeks at a time; at least I think it was a couple of weeks. But for all I knew it could have been months. Then the penny finally dropped I was forever changing hotels, yes I'd started to rate my accommodation by the RAC star method. I knew I was no longer in prison; I was in Russia's first class hotel system. Perhaps they had heard the old grey rat and me planning my escape, so they had moved me into this government hotel system. Easier to keep tabs on me and keep me away from my mate, King Rat! Not as silly as you think, for who else knew his way around a prison better than a rat.

The thing was, I was now getting a little more than worried; in fact I was starting to panic more and more as the days went by. The further they took me from the Norwegian or Finnish border then the harder it would be for me to get home, and I was also getting to be a little panicky about my health. In the beginning I had believed that they had thought I would lose all hope of escape, rescue, or even exchange. Exchange for one of their men held by the West.

I should bloody cocoa! I'm not that sodding important to them, or those non feeling bastards in London whom I refer to loosely as 'our side'. Mind, now, when I refer to 'our side' I say it with 'tongue in cheek' as I am no longer quite sure what the expression 'our side' means. I'm certain of one thing though, I could not see Brown and company even admitting that I existed, let alone exchanging me for some other poor soul they were torturing and abusing, as the Russians were me. Oh! Sorry, silly me! They don't do anything like that in the West, do they? You should ask some of the people in the American secret organisations if you think not; even their government doesn't know half of the things they get up to.

For a long time now I have held the opinion that there are people on both sides of this damned Iron Curtain who are, not to put too fine a point on it, very good friends. It is also my belief that these people on both sides of this Iron Curtain keep the whole bloody spying thing going just to suit themselves. To them, it is a career and a cosy way of making a living; they get well paid and they all accept money and other things from the other side as a kind of perk. To them it is just one big game of chess or a game of bridge or, dare I say it, cricket. The problem is, of course, that there are people under their control who do not see the 'game' part of it in quite the same light as they do. To these people it is not a game, it is a chance to vent their evil desire to inflict torture and the pain associated with torture upon their fellow human beings in the excuse that it is for the good of the nation. These people carry out their duties in a real and brutal way, and they enjoy every minute of it! I do get a little worried when I get the 'nation's good' pushed in my face as a kind of order. "Whose bloody nation?" is what we should all be asking.

When some poor unfortunate persons, such as me, fall into these underlings' hands then we are very lucky indeed if we get out with our lives. For people like me from outside their cosy little world, well, events can become very scary indeed. It is for this reason alone that I viewed my future with a great deal of trepidation, not for what I had done to any of them. The KGB is known to kill more Russians at a drop of a hat than I could ever do harm to, so my rampaging around wouldn't bother them too much. There have always been some very, very dangerous men working in the lower echelons of the secret organisations, men who are answerable to nobody, or so it seems. These are the people who carry out their masters' thoughts, let alone their masters' instructions, to the letter. Even if those thoughts are just idle ones, it makes no difference to them, but it makes one hell of a difference to me and others like me.

It is also my belief that they have an 'esprit de corps' with their opposite numbers on the other side of these so-called Iron or Bamboo Curtains, call them what you will. They seem to have an unofficial contest going on to see who can inflict the most pain. So I think the ones working on our side are no better or worse than the ones over the other side. They are not beyond doing favours for each other over the divide either.

Now I hated them all, and what was more, if the Russians had but known it, any hope which I may have harboured of exchange left me completely at my trial. Surprisingly, it all came to me during my trial, that was when it all fell into place. As my senses were coming back to me, the last piece of the jigsaw puzzle finally fell into place. It was as I sat in the dock and glanced around the room that I first saw him; he was sitting as large as life in the middle of the front row of the public courtroom. He was one of the men who had attended my last briefing in London. Even though I was still under the influence of the drugs, I could still just make him out through the haze of the distorted vision from which I was suffering at the time.

Perhaps it was due to the reduction in the strength of the drugs that they had been pumping into me; I'm not sure, but I believed when I saw him that they hadn't forgotten me. It was when I saw him that my morale was lifted so much that I made the decision that I had to get away from the prison or whatever the place was that they were keeping me in.

Meanwhile, as I sat in the dock, I watched my compatriot sitting there, large as life, and chatting to those around him and having a good old chinwag; as one does when standing around waiting for a meeting or a briefing among fellow officers. At first I believed that he was here at my trial representing not only my Embassy, but my Government, perhaps with a view to negotiating my release. For some reason my mind went into top gear and I had the crazy idea he had probably already negotiated my release; and regardless of what sentence the court passed on me I would, in no time at all, be quietly shipped back to the UK. The man was after all sitting beside a rather large, rotund, thick-necked Russian general; or someone who had enough medals and brass to look like a general. Both their caps were dripping with the 'scrambled egg' that officers are so prone to wearing on the peaks of their caps.

As the proceedings went on, I was looking down at my hands and at the scabs that had formed on the ends of all my fingers where my nails used to be. While I looked at the scabs my mind slipped back to the time when they had caused me so much pain as the bastards rubbed them with the wire brush. That was when I remembered that my mind had been a lot clearer and less confused then due, I think, to the pain I had suffered. It was just an impulse at first, but I put my hands under the iron bar that went round the dock in which I was sitting. As I sat and looked at my finger ends my body began to shake as my brain suddenly anticipated what I was about to do. My hands started to shake and I tried hard to stop them shaking as I pressed them hard against the iron bar; at first the pain was slight and then I pressed my fingers harder against the bar and slowly, deliberately I dragged my fingers against the bar and then pulled them out from underneath the bar with a sharp dragging movement. I looked down at my handiwork and saw that I had dragged all the scabs off my finger ends, only the ones on my thumbnails remained.

The nailbeds on my fingers were now oozing blood and the pain was horrific but as I raised my head, as if by magic my vision started to become clearer, and for the first time I could bring more of the people in the room within my field of focus. Now that my hands were clear of the iron bar and the finger ends had started to bleed I started to shake a little. It was all I could do to stop myself crying out with the pain, but I finally managed to control myself. Slowly I turned my head until I had the two men, the general and my officer, in full focus.

That was when I just kept looking at the two of them. There they sat, and they were chatting away ignoring the procedures going on around them. Sitting in the dock looking at them, I knew there was something wrong with the vision before my eyes. Then it dawned on me, even in the condition I was in, why I had started to shake when my vision had got better; it was nothing to do with the pain I was in. That was when I realised the bastard was not representing my Government or my bloody Embassy for that matter. Oh no! Although he had attended the briefing I'd had in London to come on this bloody fiasco, there was no way he had anything to do with our Embassy, here or anywhere else for that matter.

The horror and sickness I now felt in the pit of my stomach was far from the feeling of hope I'd had when I first saw him. Now as I looked at him sitting in this courtroom attending my trial it nearly had me vomiting in the dock. The bastard was sitting there and proudly wearing the uniform of a Major, but not a Major in the British Army. No, the bastard was a Major in the Russian Army. More to the point he was a Major in the bloody GRU, that was what that bastard was. Well, that was just about the last straw, and I remember I heard a rumble of chatter go round the courtroom as I let myself drift back into the warmth and comfort of the drugs, resigned to my fate. The last thing I remember was the floor coming up to hit me in the face as I fell off the wooden bench that I was sitting on and just before I head-butted the floor I started to fall into a deep black chasm, that was just before I passed out completely.

When I came to, I was back in a cell, which my two stalwart guards informed me was under the courtroom and that as soon as I could stand I would be returned to the courtroom for sentencing. Both of them took a delight in telling me that sentencing would take place once I was fit enough to return to the courtroom, fit enough to die; and the younger of the two added that this fool and one of his collaborators would get the chop together. The other traitor, the old man whom I'd corrupted, had unfortunately died during interrogation, thereby defeating the firing squad, but he

All For A King's Shilling

was to be shot anyway they told me, the sentence of the court must be carried out even though the collaborator was already dead.

The younger of the guards then took much delight in telling me, "You are both to die before the day is out." When he had finished mouthing off, I asked the second guard, the older of the two, who looked as if he was a more reasonable man, "Well, just who is this collaborator, the one who is going to be sentenced to death along with me? Not another figment of the KGB's imagination is he?"

He made fun of me then, and made some sexual gestures with his hands but only said, "The court in its infinite wisdom found both you and your so-called 'collaborator', a slut from Murmansk (although slut is too good a title for her) guilty! Just as you, hero that you are, collapsed on the floor of the court. Ha!" he went on, "they don't even produce good spies in the West any more, and you are all homosexuals these days. You should see some of the babies they send into Russia nowadays, no wonder the West is dying."

As he was speaking I lost all interest in his gibbering and my mind drifted back to the courtroom. I was thinking about the Russian Army Major, the one wearing the insignia of the GRU, who I knew was also serving as a completely different officer in the MoD in London, and the guard's words, well, I'd given up on him because I had more important things on my mind than the utterings of an old Russian guard. I suppose I was still in shock at seeing him at my trial dressed in the uniform of a Major, a Major in the Russian GRU. My mind was in turmoil and I didn't know if I was coming or going. Then in my semi-drugged state the realisation of it all finally penetrated my thick skull and the penny finally dropped. At last I realised how I and all the others had been set up; the bastard really had worked for the Russians from the start. That explained how, as one of my interrogators had said, they knew all about our operation from the start.

Well, that was it, now I really knew just how much I was on my own. While I was sitting in the cell with the old guard rabbiting on about spies and the like, the reality of what I'd been mixed up in all these years finally hit me. My feelings at that moment flooded over me, engulfing me completely and believe it or not, it really was quite a relief, a relief to know now what it had all been about. It explained all sorts of things, it explained what had happened to me in both Russia and the Far East and why men had died or had to die. At first I was a little surprised by my feelings. Slowly as the fog of the last few years lifted everything became clear. Then, suddenly, what the guard had been saying earlier breached my defences and it was starting to give me just a little trouble. It was something he had said about a collaborator and I wondered who they had rounded up and stuck in the dock beside me now; because I could not remember anybody else sitting beside me in the dock of the courtroom. There had been nobody near me or with me. So, I thought, they must have been having me on and very foolishly I brushed it from my mind.

My mind moved on to other problems that I perceived I now had; I thought provided I survived the rest of the day then perhaps made it through the next few days, then maybe, just maybe I might stand a chance of getting alive out of the bucket of shit I was in. The quality of whatever life I had didn't at that time bother me. Where there's life there's hope, as the old saying goes. So I relaxed a little and immediately I could feel the drugs taking hold again. They seemed to come over me in waves now, sometimes my mind was as clear as a bell; then I would start in my bemused and drugged state to try and put some sort of plan together, plan for what? I didn't know and I invariably wouldn't be able to remember them later anyway

In my few moments of clarity parts of my training would come wafting back and forth, coming back to me in fits and starts. During these moments I was fighting like hell trying to get my brain into gear again. One of the things I'd been told over and over again was, "Your greatest chance of escape is when you are first arrested, after the first few hours your hopes will diminish by the day." I believed I had missed my chance under the first criterion but I had some stupid idea that I might still be able to easily outwit them, after all they were just Russian peasants, weren't they? When I believed that one I was definitely running a brain in for an idiot, or officer, depending on how you look at it. There was no way that I could not remember how long it was since they had arrested me, so I believed I was still in with a chance. The state I was in at that point in time was pitiful, to say the least. I had no idea how long I'd been in the stupor I was in, but I reasoned that it could not have been more than three months. So in my semi-drugged stupid state I reckoned I was okay, and still had time to make my 'getaway'. It just goes to show what kind of fool I was, brainwashed from the bloody first day I joined the Royal Corps. No wonder the nudge, nudge, wink, wink brigade preferred the old school tie boys for this kind of work. It seems that people such as me only cock the whole game up by getting caught in the first place. Even when they catch us we are of no exchange value anyway; well, I mean, who'd want to swap me for a top flight Russian spy? Mind, I'd rather it was some old Etonian who was standing here in this place instead of me, I can tell you that much.

You know, ever since I left Plymouth and let them talk me into coming to this Godforsaken land I had been in trouble. Right from the start I knew this whole bloody plan was a fiasco, a fiasco from start to finish; and did I do anything about it, did I shit! I'm now fully convinced that I have not been in control of my destiny since the day I left London en route to Singapore. Those evil bastards in London and their equally evil bastards here in Russia have consistently manipulated me from the word go. It wouldn't surprise me one iota to be told that Aeroflot had flown me home from Singapore on my last posting. It looked to me as if the bloody Russians had been involved in everything I'd done for years now.

"Oh," you may say, "you are just looking for people to blame for the situation you now find yourself in."

Well that maybe so, but to be honest I have laid the blame for my predicament at everybody's door; from the Chief of the General Staff right down to my dead comrades. In the end though, I have at last come to the conclusion that, although they have had a hand in manipulating everything I have done from the start, I have now realised that because of the restrictions they placed on me I never had the freedom of deciding my own actions to enable me to react more positively to the situations I'd found myself in. With hindsight it's as if the GRU knew where I would be at any given time. There is no doubt that I had complete freedom after the plane crash in the North Sea but the moment the listening post exploded, well, they knew I was back on the job, so to speak. Even though I had outwitted them at the start by doing the job they had sent me to do, I then went on and played right into their hands.

All For A King's Shilling

To be honest I should have holed up for a couple of months until they had stood all their patrols and such down. That is when I should have blown up the listening post, but I was too keen to get on with it and get the hell out of Russia. That was when I'd thrown it all away; I'd blown any chance I had of getting back alive because of my haste. My freedom of action, which is a necessity on a task of this kind if one is to make any sort of a success of it, that is, went out the window; and by so doing I had forfeited my life. No, I had nobody else to blame, nobody at all; no I'd snookered myself there, I'm afraid.

What was more annoying, of course, was that I sensed it all from the very start of this last trip. Right from the damned start I knew it, but some crazy idea of being the great hero drove me on, and I was soon getting deeper and deeper into trouble. The proof of the pudding of course is in the eating. My standing there in a Russian courtroom awaiting the death sentence well, just how much pudding does one need to know one has 'cocked it up', as they say? The problem as I saw it then, though, was that I'd let myself be manoeuvred into this situation so it would now be up to me to get my arse and brain into gear and haul myself out of the shit, not to put too fine a point on it.

Having come to that conclusion I sat and pondered on 'what next'? That was when I detected stirrings amongst my guards and their bosses, so there was very little I could do right then. Plus of course I was far to unfit what with the drugs they had pumped into me and the beatings and lack of good victuals, as they say, to face a long trek across Russia; even if I did manage to get away from my guards. So, my only hope was that they didn't march me out to the back of the court and shoot me! That was the latest trick that the damned Russians, like the Chinese, had taken a great delight in doing a lot of these days. "Now that would really fuck my day up, wouldn't it?"

Enough said. There was no point dwelling on that; I would only have got more morose about it all and started to feel sorry for myself. The deed was done and there were more important things to be sorted out just then; I had to pull myself up by the crack in my arse and get the hell out of their Godforsaken land, and the sooner I did that the bloody better. So let's get back into the court and see just what little surprise they had waiting for me.

As I waited in the cell I was all keyed up, just the way you are when the light goes on over the door of an aircraft that you are foolishly about to leave without a safety rope, a safety net, or any other kind of bloody safety protection; that was how I felt as I waited for them to come and collect me and take me back into the courtroom and pronounce my fate to all and sundry. Suddenly all the noise, shouting and carrying on stopped and the commotion outside the cell died away. Once more I was left to sit and twiddle my fingers deep in my own thoughts, in silence.

After a little while, which was probably only a couple of minutes, but felt like hours as the energy of the past moments left me, my mind wandered back to the time when I was first captured by the GRU. For years I had had a fear in the back of my mind that if I were ever captured by an enemy of the crown I would not be able to hold up under interrogation. Oh, yes, they train you well enough in England with their escape and evasion exercises, exercising you in what to expect when caught and what to do and what not to do.

William Atlay

The problem is, no matter how good the training they can never train you for the stress of a real interrogation in a foreign country, that is. A country where they don't give a toss about Queen's Rules and Regulations, the Army Act, the Manual of Military Law or any other law! I have also always found it funny that the men who conduct this type of training have never themselves been in a situation anywhere remotely like the one that I found myself in then. You see, in training you are interrogated for just twenty-four hours, and give them their due they do a good job in that twenty-four hours. The twenty-four hours' training course bears no relation whatsoever to what really happens to you when the Russians get their grubby bloody hands on you. I can vouch for that, but I can't speak for the other enemies of the Crown. What shit am I talking, who the hell decides who the enemies of the Crown are, anyway. All I knew was that some countries' interrogators didn't even bother asking you anything, they just tortured you. There are a few of the Crown's enemies who just get on and behead you in the first few minutes, but the men back in England, that green and promised land, well they cannot put you through that now, can they? They also cannot put you through the mill for twenty-four hours a day seven days a week, week after week, and month after month for God alone knows how long, by the end of which you'd be a walking wreck like me.

No, in this situation the strain of trying to keep everything from them is far worse than any physical torture the boys back home could dish up. The worst ordeal is when you find out that they may, as happened in my case, have known all about you from the day you enlisted. The courses you have attended, your grades and passes, but the biggest shock of all is the revelation of the knowledge that they have of your family. If that wasn't enough to send you schizoid there were the drugs! These bastards used drugs the Western world hadn't even heard of yet. Very frightening, I may add, but my worst shock, even worse than all the other stuff, was when they produced a drawing of a barrack room I was once billeted in, in RM Barracks Stonehouse, Plymouth. It was a sketch of me standing by my locker in the corner of the room overlooking the parade ground. They also showed me a very good pencil sketch of the main gate and archway of the Barracks' entrance, with Neptune and his daughter sitting over the bloody gates in Durnford Street. I tried to tell myself that they had sketched me into a drawing they already had of the Barrack Room, but I'm still not sure that I believe that.

As I said, I was to discover that the swine had a file on me with details of every course I'd attended and copies of my reports and results. Units I'd served in and ships I had travelled on as part of an embarked force. It was the most unnerving situation that it had ever been my misfortune to encounter. Worse, I was in no fit state to reason out how they had got all the information on me. The bastards even knew when I got married, how many children I had, so when it came to the crunch there was no way I was going to suffer too much of their roughness just for those shits in London. "Remember, dear boy, mum's the word," they would say at the briefings. "Mum's the word lads," my arse it is! With the Russians knowing everything there was to know about me. Well I think I told them everything I knew, but it still didn't stop the bastards knocking the shit out of me just for the hell of it.

No, it didn't stop the bastards making me suffer and putting me through the almost ritualistic barbarity of their interrogation and methods of torture in the dubious search for information. Information that one or more of my bloody superiors had more than likely already given them over a couple of pink gins at some bloody office party somewhere in London, Moscow or bloody New York , for all I knew. It seemed as if it was almost mandatory that I had to complete their entrance exam of being drugged by them and physically abused before they would even think of bringing me to trial for something they alleged I'd done, or maybe not done. I got the distinct impression that truth didn't even enter into the equation. It seemed to me to depend on how they saw it, or more to the point what message they wanted to send to their opposite numbers in other countries, on the other side of the wall, curtain, barbed wire, iron, bamboo or any other bloody kind of curtain. It was that which the truth in their eyes became.

It was while I was waiting to be taken back into the court that I came back to earth with a hell of a bump. I'd realised that these intrigues and games that they all played didn't matter to me any more; from now on my life wasn't worth the paper the death sentence would be written on. My mind was at that moment a complete blank; I'd no idea whatsoever, what if anything, I'd told them. Well, that's not strictly true, because I think I told them everything I knew and a few things that I made up along the way. The thing was that was the point when I realised that I really just didn't care anymore about their silly bloody games, I'd been too far out of my tree with the effect of the drugs they were pumping into me and in too much bloody pain from their torturous methods to know what I might or might not have told them. At that precise moment in time I didn't give a shit either. For now I knew and believed that if I were ever going to see my family or Katrine again, then the only loyalty I had right then was to myself.

While I pondered these thoughts I felt as if a huge weight had been lifted from my shoulders. A feeling similar to that one has when taking off one's equipment, equipment which you had worn continually for days on end. The feeling of relief was so great because now I understood that really I was just a prisoner, albeit a prisoner of the Russians. That in itself is a daunting enough prospect, but all the questioning shit was now behind me. They had now dragged me into court, okay I was in a drugged and bewildered state of mind, but I wouldn't be here at all if the worst of it all wasn't over. They had tortured me, of that there was no doubt, and I now felt as though I had just come round after some kind of major surgery, or perhaps a full fifteen-round bout against the heavyweight champion of the world. The only difference was that I'd had my hands tied behind my back and he'd had brass knuckle-dusters on instead of boxing gloves. I also knew from what the older guard had said that the court would, in the end, sentence me to death and even so I still had a feeling of relief. To tell the truth I was beginning to feel good. It was a feeling that perturbed me somewhat as I could not understand it. Oh shit! But was I out of my tree! I was thinking things out and I hadn't a fucking clue what was going on around me, I was in a complete dream world; my brain could no longer handle the information it was getting, simply because none of it made any bloody sense any more. I heard the old guard say to somebody, I know not who, "He'll die happy; they always do in his condition. They don't have a clue what is happening, or going to happen to them."

Perhaps this feeling of euphoria had come about because I had regained some feeling of normality, but what normality was by then, I'd no idea. Whatever it was it didn't last very long, because shortly thereafter I slid back into the zombie-like state in which they had kept me for so long. My brief moment of sanity and reality, as I thought it was, slipped away from me and the trance that I had been in, which was no doubt caused by all the drugs I'd had pumped into me for so long; it would take years, not months, if I were going to overcome it, more than rubbing the scabs off the ends of my fingers would be needed. The unreal world of drugs in which I had been since the second or third day after they picked me up was a terrifying nightmare that I knew I was slipping back into, and I could do absolutely nothing about it. At that time as my mind slipped into the drug-induced oblivion I didn't think I would ever overcome or for that matter forget what had happened to me, no matter how long I lived.

Of course survival could maybe only last until later that day, if the GRU and the KGB ran true to form. The one thing I was certain about was that I would never forget the face of that ugly looking bastard, the evil gorilla who had stuck that bloody instrument under the nails of my fingers and toes. Nor would I ever forget the evil sods who had kept on stroking the ends of my fingers and toes with their bloody wire brushes, keeping my finger ends and toe ends red, raw and infected so that even then it looked as if my nails would never grow again. Because they had kept me in such a heavily drugged state for so long, I still even now couldn't remember the faces of any of the others. Whoever else asked me all those stupid questions and kept stroking the ends of my fingers and toes to keep the pain in my hands and feet alive were to me by now just a bunch of blank, cartoon-like faces. I was certain I wouldn't recognise them if I fell over them.

When the Russians picked me up? Well, I can remember that bit only too well, and boy, was I in full flight then. I had a full head of steam and was going like the Flying Scotsman as it headed north. I was huffing and puffing like a great big steam engine, I had ceased taking any precautions whatsoever. In fact I was walking quite openly, albeit quickly and with a spring in my step for the first time since I'd left Carl. After all, I was in what I thought was Finland, but then I had not been very good at taking any precautions and thinking was something else I'd not done too much of either. It was true that at the time they caught me I'd convinced myself that I had crossed over the large electrified fence that is the Iron Curtain in the area of the Russian/Finnish border. So in my mind, therefore, I was sure that I was well and truly into that wonderful country, Finland; otherwise, I would certainly not have gone anywhere near those men in uniform.

Mistakes, hell, I'd made plenty of them this time, far too many to mention, but like the fool I had been right from the start, I did believe that my famous luck was still holding fast and it would see me through. To say I was running a brain in for a monkey well, I'd say that would have been an insult to the bloody monkey. I've seen baboons around the world wiser than I've been of late. Much more to the point, I was vain enough to think the reason they hadn't arrested me earlier was due to my cleverness at outwitting these thick Russians. Just how stupid can one be, a regime that has controlled a nation the size of Russia for so long and I thought that I, 'wonder boy' could outwit them? I might add I had been brainwashed to think of them as thick by the same bastards who'd sold me out to them. As I said, suckers didn't come much blinder than a good old patriot. Looking from where I was standing I must have been greener than those silly bloody American servicemen one meets, who believe their president is God. Shit man! Just how bloody stupid can anyone get. Well, it seemed a lot more, a bloody lot more.

Now of course with much hindsight, I could see that every operation 'we' had ever carried out in the north of Russia was controlled from start to finish by the KGB or the GRU; my money was on the GRU, and once they had achieved all they could from it, they pulled the bloody plug and some arsehole had to pay the piper and that arsehole was me; I was the one who had ended up in the proverbial shit.

It terrified me when I thought of all the men that I and others like me had escorted into the most secret place in our plans. We had put men in there believing them to be as safe as houses because nothing untoward had happened, or so we thought. The truth was far worse, only now I knew that most, if not all, of them were up to their poor bloody necks and were either dead or suffering in a Russian labour camp somewhere; their places in the post having been taken by Russian agents, agents whom arseholes like me then escorted back to jolly old England. No wonder the teams who took the men in were never the teams who brought out the ones they had escorted in. No, because if we had been we would have spotted the change and the game would have been up. To think the British taxpayer has financed the movement and absorption of all sorts of Russian spies into the West. All of this done in the name of the British people who believed that their taxes were paying to keep all our shipping lanes open, for commerce and trade to the greater betterment of the people of the Western World. Except of course that we were not at war and our shipping lanes were not in any danger at all. Much to my everlasting shame I was one of the bloody fools who took part in this scam and I unwittingly helped the bastards, but there was nothing I could do about it then and now it is far too late.

There is another precedent for this anomaly and that is Northern Ireland. All the members of the IRA are currently classed as unemployed in the British Isles. They all draw every type of social security benefit that is available. We therefore have a situation where the British Government is paying the enemy of the Crown their wages each week to enable them to carry out their 'military activities' against the very taxpayers who are funding the war for them. This is all due to the weakness of the civil servants entrusted with the task of weeding out the false claims. I would put money on a bet that if the IRA were a bunch of unmarried mothers in England they would soon have had their funding cut.

So you can hardly blame me being in the big-headed state I was in, still fully convinced that all was well. You see, I hadn't fathomed all that shit out and I didn't know that the 'stupid Russians' knew everything there was to know about our actions. Therefore in my big-headed way, I didn't have an inkling that I was walking, as I was at the time, right into captivity. Well, when I saw those men whom I took to be Finnish border guards (and they were after all dressed in Finnish border guards' uniforms) I knew that I was home and dry. Oh, I knew that I might have to spend some time in their custody before my Government got me out, but I knew that my ordeal was over; I was out and I was on my way home to England. Mind, I hadn't made any plans for anything like this. So, being the fool I was, I approached them like the proverbial lamb to the slaughter. What a right shit I must have looked to them; I just walked up and started talking to them. It was no wonder that they laughed at me, the walking 'tornado' had gone out like a damp squid.

They, 'God bless their little souls' had just spent days chasing me halfway over Mother Russia and like a silly bloody recruit on his first exercise in the field, well, what did I do, I just walked up to them? It never crossed my mind that once I'd managed to cross that sodding great big wire fence I might not be in Finland. The fence looked identical to the one that I had crossed behind the Russian patrol, the one that I'd followed into this Godforsaken land in the first place. Still time and tiredness are the only excuses I can offer, besides the truth, which was plain and simple 'stupidity'.

When I think about it, I still shake my head in wonderment. It was something I should never live down, if I ever did manage to get my arse out of the hole I was in.

As I said, none of my plans when I started out had included any thoughts of a six-month stay in a Russian type of Hilton (Lubyanka) or the rest of the chain of hotels owned and administered by the KGB and scattered all over the Soviet Union by courtesy of 'the GRU', being drugged, tortured and generally ill-treated. Then to cap it all, according to my guards I was to be shot dead before sunset that very night. Hell, you could have laid me out with a feather when the ugly-looking guard had come out with that one, and it had finally sunk into this thick lump above my neck which I mistakenly call a brain, that I was finished, kaput!

One word of advice I have for all spies and their masters around the world, if your spy is always 100 per cent successful, I would take a very close look at him. For I have reached the opinion, if anybody is interested in it, that 'there isn't a spy living who is that good'. He or she has got to be getting assistance from the people whom he or she is supposedly spying on. So take heed, you men in grey suits in the corridors of the Western intelligence services, it is just possible you are all being promoted by the opposition you think you are bettering.

I believe they had deliberately let me come out of the drugged state that they had kept me in for the last however many months to let me hear the judge as he passed the death sentence on me. Gory bastards, aren't they.

The old guard brought me back to the real world when he jabbed me with the butt of his rifle and told me to stand up. "Now you are going to be told when you are to die," remarked the younger man with a grin like 'Joe Brown behind the eight ball'. Painfully I hauled myself up to my feet and in between the two guards I was bundled unceremoniously back into the court. When I was back in the dock of the courtroom I looked around at the people seated in the place. As my gaze wandered around the room I thought to myself, they really are an ugly looking lot of bastards. Then I saw that face again; the bastard had even come back to be in at the kill. Looking at him I knew that no matter how long I lived, be it a few hours, a few days, or a few years, I would never ever forget the face of that bastard GRU Officer, and a right bastard he was. There he was, sitting there as large as life, and he really looked pleased with himself. Had I been fit I would have been over the front of the dock and I'd have strangled the bastard there and then.

I have no complaints about anybody who spies on his enemies; that is what I do. Keeping tabs on one's potential military enemies is the only way to survive in this modern world. Contrary to the way things looked at that point in my career, I really was quite good at my job, but to spy on your own people for the enemy though, which then puts the life of your ordinary citizens and not just servicemen at risk, well, that to me is one crime which should and still does, carry the death penalty. The bastards like the one who attended both my briefing for this god-awful mission and now my trial, only this time wearing his true colours. There he was sitting in that Russian courtroom after I'd managed to get myself caught on the wrong side of the fence, and he had the audacity to wear the uniform of an enemy officer. Well, to my mind, hanging was too good for the bastard. I felt like ripping his heart out and making him swear on it that he was sorry for what he had done to me. Then I'd kill him!

The Russians must have been really confident that I was going to die or they were confident that I was too far out in cuckoo land with the drugs to be able to recognise him, otherwise they wouldn't have dared to let him attend my trial, would they? It never once crossed my mind that perhaps they were so confident I would never get away, because they really were going to shoot me. Well, that thought just never once entered my head at all; even though the guards had told me that I was to be shot, I just could not comprehend that I was going to die, and in a very short time at that.

The only thought in my mind then was anger because the bastard traitor was there, in for the kill as they say. Their overconfidence I believed was all to my benefit, it would mean I would be able to make my plans to escape and I believed I would be able to do all this without arousing suspicion. Even as I looked at the pig in the courtroom I was again making plans to get out, and what was more I was certain that before long I would be back in good old 'Blighty', even though I knew they might be going to take me out and shoot me against the nearest wall or tree stump that didn't matter, I was going to escape.

How bloody stupid could you get? I now know that anybody who believed all was well as I did at the time, must be completely off his trolley. My reasoning at the time, of course, was that I would not only be able to escape, but that they would help me escape. Because of their lax and negligent ways, caused by overconfidence I would escape and it would be in a couple of days at the most. They would also present me with the opportunity to get away. That was the full measure of my degradation and the stupidity to which my mind had now sunk. I'd not been able to escape since they caught me and here was I, a complete arsehole, thinking I would be away in a day or so on my way home! How big a wanker can one become?

The wanderings of the damned I think they call the emotions that my mind was going through at the time. 'Gibbering idiot' is another expression that comes easily to mind that would fit my condition very well.

Looking at it in a rational way it just shows what shit fills your mind when you are in the most hopeless of situations. Still, 'if ifs and ands were pots and pans' there would be no work for tinkers, would there. Well, pots and pans had nothing whatsoever to do with my situation, but a more appropriate description of the situation I was now well and truly in could be 'Shit Street'! Shit Street was the one I was well and truly in. So I made a resolution there and then in the court that should I not be executed that day I would never forget, nor could I ever forgive, any bastard involved in my present situation. What was more, their names would be forever tattooed on the inside of my head, just above my eyes, within easy recall.

All that I needed was for my captors just to give me half a chance. Then we would soon see whose 'shit hit the bloody fan'. Of course, I knew deep down that I didn't stand a snowball's chance in hell of seeing the night out alive, but to admit that would have been the worst sin of all.

If I did admit it then I would just about be at the stage where one starts to blabber and whimper as one reaches the point of imminent death, but that was not to be. No, I was defiant to the end, I knew I'd be plotting my escape as they tied me to the pole against which they would shoot me, and I knew I'd refuse the bloody blindfold. I'm that sort of a fool.

It was at this point in my wanderings that the guards made me move my seat in the dock. The old boy told me that my collaborator was joining me for the passing of the death sentence, as he drew his hand across his throat in a cutting motion. Looking at him I growled that if he didn't stop tormenting me, I'd flatten him. At which he just grinned. He knew that the main problem holding me back was the restriction placed upon me by the chains; it is a little hard to flatten anybody when one's chained the way I was. So I was in a rather edgy frame of mind as I settled again on another part of the bench seat in the dock. I had been in there, sitting with my head in my hands for a little while, when I felt the movement of somebody else joining me on the part of the bench I had just vacated. So, I thought here comes my collaborator and I turned to have a look at him; it was then that I nearly collapsed again. At first I was steady, then I started to shake from head to foot for there starting to sit down beside me was Katrine. Finally I managed to stop shaking and turned fully round and looked at her; as our eyes met I could feel mine filling with tears. Then as we looked at each other she must have seen my tears because she tried to give me a comforting smile. It was very difficult for her, with her lips still swollen from some beating she had suffered, and they looked to be new bruises, so she must have suffered the beating in the last day or so. At least I hadn't suffered any beatings as recently as yesterday that I knew of, that is.

My first reaction was to try and take her in my arms and comfort her, and tell her how sorry I was for causing her all this trouble, trouble that I had brought upon her and her father's shoulders; it looked as though, if the guards were to be believed, we were both going to lose our lives long before the day was out. Yet before I could say anything to Katrine, one of the guards grabbed me from behind and pushed me, not too gently, to the other side of the dock. So when I managed to sit with some sort of dignity again, I half turned my body and sat looking towards her thinking to myself, stuff the bastards and stuff the judge and all the other traitorous bastards in this court. Seeing my movement, she managed to swivel herself on the seat also until we were facing each other. From that moment we both forgot the silly bloody fiasco of the court and just sat looking at one another as the voices of the court officials faded into the background. Without saying a word we spoke volumes to each other simply with our eyes. We sat there communicating our love for one another.

A little later our concentration was finally disturbed as we were both unceremoniously and not too gently hauled to our feet and made to face the judge. It was then, as I glanced around the room that I saw another person whom I knew in the courtroom. He was standing among the press and he was looking intently at me. When I saw him it took all my power to stop myself showing any outward sign of recognising him. I knew there would be people in that room watching me, looking to see if I recognised anybody when I looked around the room but there, true to his nature, standing at the back and looking directly at me and standing head and shoulders above all the sorry looking people in the room, was my old boyhood friend and mentor Carl!

As I looked around the room my gaze halted for the merest of split seconds and with a slight shake of the head I informed him that I had said nothing about my involvement with his organisation. That was probably because I was never asked. Satisfied he'd understood me I then continued my gaze around the courtroom. What I did know then was that whatever I tried to convey from that moment on, the pleading with my eyes or my making what small gestures I could, in my fantasy world I just knew that Carl would know I was sending him messages and that all of my messages would be for him. I was, in what I thought at the time was a really intelligent way, pleading with him to get Katrine out of the situation that she was in. God alone knew if he could understand what the hell I was trying to tell him, but the faith I had in the man meant that I had no doubt that he was receiving my messages. It was at this point of the proceedings everybody in the court except Katrine and I sat down. When we tried to follow them and sit down ourselves we were both grabbed and I might add roughly handled and forced to remain standing.

The judge then started a long boring story of our guilt, of the crimes we had committed against the Union of the Soviet Socialist Republics. He made not one mention of the poor English souls who had been removed from the listening post and probably executed, as I now feared Katrine and I were about to be. I was about to tell him that I had only been doing in Russia, what his people were doing on Plymouth Hoe and along the parade at Southsea, watching the boats go by and telling our superiors about it. The only difference was that we didn't torture them or execute them when we caught them. No, we just stuck them on the next boat or plane home. Then I thought it was probably immaterial to him what happened to me or them, he'd say he was just carrying out orders, the cop out for all weak and insignificant people. So I kept my mouth shut as he went droning on and on. God, did he have a dose of the verbose! He listed all the crimes we had committed against the Motherland and how I had led this young, upstanding Russian woman astray. If it had not been for me, she would still be a happy member of her family in the north. He added a few crimes I didn't even know I'd committed.

Some joy there, mate, I thought, but I did notice that he did not name Katrine's whereabouts in the north. It was at this point that I sensed in his rhetoric, rough though it was, that he was going to give Katrine a chance, but I felt it would mean that I would be for the long drop, the chop, or the big bang just as the bullet strikes. After all, in this system somebody had to pay the piper and it looked as though I had drawn the short straw. Not only was I going to collect the bill, but it looked as if I were going to have to pay the bloody pipe major as well. There was something about the way he kept harping on and on about it all being my evil influence over her. From all this rhetoric I concluded that perhaps Katrine might have to suffer some token imprisonment, but not the death penalty which I was certain was heading my way. Even so, no matter how low you get, or how much you expect the worst, I wasn't ready for it when it did eventually come. I don't believe you can ever ready yourself for the death sentence, that is.

As he was chattering on and on, I remember muttering to myself, "For God's sake, get on with it, you silly old sod." Then without pausing to take a breath, he did just what I had asked of him. In the same monotone voice he said, "As for you, Englishman" (no name was used, which made me think a bit) "the guards will remove you from this courtroom to a place of execution behind this building and there you are to be executed by firing squad." I nearly fell over. Then I looked at Carl and he just shook his head and shrugged his shoulders and then nodded towards Katrine. As he did so, she let out a sob, and then started to cry. When I tried to move closer towards her, the younger of the two guards took hold of me by the scruff of my neck and dragged me unceremoniously from the court. While I was being dragged out of the courtroom by the neck I tried to look at Katrine, but I was unable to see her; and it was then that I decided that I would have to forget Katrine because there was nothing I could do for her now. This was only because I had one very serious problem staring me right in the face at that precise moment; they were, as far as I knew because I couldn't see any reason why they would not, going to take me outside and shoot me, as the old guard had said they would and I couldn't for the life of me think of anything I could say or for that matter do that would change their fucking minds.

Within seconds I was ashamed of the thought that I could even think of forgetting Katrine and her very existence. The thought itself was like being shot, I was so very ashamed of myself and with that shame came a terrible feeling of guilt for even thinking that way. I was so distraught with myself that if it had been possible I think I'd have done away with myself and saved them the bullets. Even though I could be of no help to her whatsoever from now on, I still had very strong protective feelings towards her. I knew in my heart of hearts that I had met the only woman in my life who would ever mean anything to me. To me she was the only reason for my being on earth but as soon as I'd found her I was about to be shot. Even though nothing of any consequence had happened between us, physically that is, I knew her name would probably be on my lips as I died. So for the first time since I was small I prayed, I prayed as they took me out to the courtyard at the back of the building and I prayed that perhaps she had received a short prison sentence because I could not see her surviving long in a camp in the wastes of Siberia, or in a camp in any other place in any of the Soviet Republics for that matter.

By now my mind was in turmoil as the two guards took me, pushing and kicking me as they forced me into a small, high-walled section of the rear of the courtyard. There I was marched up to a seven feet tall by ten inch diameter wooden pole which was situated about two feet from the wall. I noticed that the wall was full of bullet holes and I knew as they turned me and placed my back against the wooden pole that the end was near. The old guard seemed a little reluctant as, without removing the handcuffs and chains, he tied me to the pole. When I looked to the front, standing about five yards away were six riflemen. "My firing squad I think," I said to the old guard, but he said nothing. "The bastards don't intend to bloody miss, do they? If they were any closer they'd be in danger of shooting themselves with any ricochets."

The old man just grunted and before I could protest he put over my head the blackest bloody hood I had ever had placed over my head. I then heard him shuffle away from me; very wise move, old man, I thought; if I were you I'd get out of this little yard completely. It was then I heard the familiar orders countless thousands of poor souls before me must have heard.

"Present, Aim, Fire!"

There was a roar of noise as the six rifles discharged all at once and then in the next millisecond the most searing pain in the back of my head. Then the lights flashed and whirled around in my head and I could feel my legs giving way underneath me; at that precise moment I could smell my own blood as it welled up in my throat and filled my mouth and nostrils. Then a complete blackness descended over me as I died!

Some time later, god knows how long it was, I didn't know, I was certain that I saw a light shining in my eyes. To say I was a little confused would have been a gross understatement. As I looked into this opaque light I tried to see what was there. Bloody hell, I thought, if this is the afterlife and everything is this colour then it is going to be worse than the red of hell that I'd been expecting; I'll go crackers in no time at all in this light. Of course it never entered my head that perhaps I'd already been crackers for years; but I raised my hand in front of my face to see if I could block out the light. Not only could I not block the light out but I couldn't see my bloody hand either! So I thought it is true only one's soul goes to wherever it is we go after we die; but I was certain I could feel my arms, my legs and the rest of my body. At that point I decided to sit up and that was when everything went jet black again.

Some time later the jet black bit passed and I came to again, only this time it looked as if I had failed the entrance exam for heaven because this time everything was a red haze, not the bright red of the good old English pillar box, the horrible dirty red of a worn out Russian flag. So I had to presume I had lost another trial and I had been drafted back to Hell. Again I raised my hand and much to my surprise I could see it this time. My mind reasoned then that I was definitely in Hell; I'd been unable to see my hand in the white light because I'd not need it in Heaven, people didn't work there. But here in Hell I would need my hands and arms as I would be expected to work for eternity. The redness of the place must be from the torment of Hell, the inferno as Dante put it, wasn't it him who said that? I missed so many lessons at school so I am probably wrong again. At this point I think it was all getting too much for me and I passed out again, but not before I felt a sharp stinging in my right arm.

I do think I drifted in and out of Hell several times before things seemed to settle down. The first couple of times the red haze of the place got redder and redder, then I noticed that the colour began to get a lighter shade of pink. As it did I thought I might still end up in that white place one day soon; perhaps my case was under review or maybe the sentence was waiting for confirmation, one could but hope!

Then one time I opened my eyes and I could see a whitewashed ceiling above me. It was very disturbing and I was very confused at first, then I raised my right hand to see if I could see it. The first thing I noticed when it came into focus was that my nails had grown again. They were nearly at the end of my fingers. Slowly I looked around the place I was in and I came to the conclusion I was in a cell of some sort. Shit, I thought, they have bloody gaols in Heaven and I'm in one. Overcome with the idea that I was even locked up in Heaven, I passed out again.

I do believe that some weeks then passed, with me drifting in and out of consciousness, and then much to my surprise I came to one day and a bloody Russian was standing by the cot-type of bed I was in. "Oh, bloody Hell, don't tell me you bastards are in charge up here as well?" I said.

"Yes, we are in charge all over the place, but I'm pleased to tell you that you are after all still alive, my not so fine English Capitalist Pig."

"Don't bullshit me you ugly sod, I'm dead, your pals shot me if you remember; and what's with this capitalist shit anyway, I am the poorest peasant in the Western Hemisphere so you can forget the capitalist shit."

"I'm not bullshitting you, you were never shot. We fired a few blank cartridges at you and one of our men bobbed you on the back of the head with a tent peg mallet, but that was all that happened. No, pig, you are alive, you have also developed a craving for what is in this needle. You are no better than the rest of your types in the West. Your one redeeming factor is even after all these weeks you have just told us a load of gibberish. You haven't revealed one secret. We have wasted a lot of drugs on you and for that you will be made to pay."

"You lot are the stupidest bastards in the world. Where did you get the idea that anybody in his right mind would tell me any secrets they bloody knew I'd tell you all at the first sign of pain and trouble? Anyway, it's not my fault you silly sods wasted all your good drugs on me!"

With that he slapped my arm so hard I nearly fainted and then he stuck the needle in my arm and within a moment I had fainted and drifted back into oblivion again.

One day I opened my eyes and I knew I was no longer in Heaven because I was sitting in the corner of a small room. There was a small light in the ceiling of the room and it was about four inches in diameter. It was situated inside a wire grill and it kept flickering as if the bulb was on the blink, or the power wasn't connected properly. The lower half of the walls was painted with a tar-like substance and the top half of the walls was painted with a filthy white powdery paint. To add to the decor nearly all the previous occupants of the cell had left their names and dates of birth, also the names of their home towns on the walls. To this day I don't know how I happened to be in that cell, but I was there. One other problem was that I had this terrible feeling and craving, my guts felt as though there were about two hundred maggots crawling around inside them. At this point in my observations I noticed that I was shaking somewhat. To be honest I was shaking uncontrollably. I lay in the corner of the cell and I looked around the place, then before I could stop myself I broke into uncontrollable sobbing, my shoulders heaving and my head lolling from side to side. My shoulders heaved and heaved, and then I rolled over on to my right side. As I did so I jumped off the wooden bench that was my bed and away from the wall. Now I was screaming with agony; my upper arm had touched the wall and caused a pain of such excruciating intensity that it must have reached at least fifty on the Richter scale. This pain went shooting up over the outer part of my shoulder and into my neck; it then shot up the back of my head and to a point in my head just behind my right eye. The pain disappeared as fast as it had come and my sobbing stopped. I stood in the middle of the cell and felt my arm. It was swollen and when I rolled the sleeve up I caught sight of a large black lump. Before I could see anymore the light in the ceiling went out. Now I was in turmoil, the upper part of my right arm was swollen and black and I was in a stinking rat hole in complete darkness. I was hungry and I had no idea if I was in Heaven, Hell or a Russian bloody gaol. To be honest, I didn't know if I was alive or dead. I had a vague recollection of a Russian telling me at some stage that I hadn't been shot; so by now I really was one confused frogman, frogman I thought, what the hell is a frogman? I must have finally flipped over the edge!

At some stage I probably fell asleep, but for how long I will never know. I know that when I woke the light in the ceiling was on and a plate of what looked like water with a lump of bread in it was on the floor just inside the door. My guts felt as if there was a tiger loose inside them. I reached to the door and picked up the dish with the bread and coloured water in it. I took a bite of the bread and drank some of the water. Within seconds I was lying on the floor retching and writhing as my stomach emptied on to the floor. By now, the sweat was running from my forehead down my face and dripping on to the floor from the end of my chin. I brought my hands up to my face and looked at them. It was then that I noticed my nails; they were about a quarter of an inch beyond the ends of my fingers. As I watched the sweat start to run back along my fingers to the back of my hand a thought passed through my head. How quickly do nails grow?

Unlike the time when I was first in the care of the Russians and the food wasn't too bad, now I wasn't sure who was looking after me, but they couldn't cook. I did seem to be having a problem keeping the food they were giving me in my stomach. My health suffered somewhat, all part of their strategy I suppose, but I did not think so at the time. Of course, I now know that it was, as I have seen so many follow the same route since. The food was not very much better, if anything it was still a damned sight worse than anything I had ever experienced before, but then nothing here was very good and there was nothing else. To be honest, I don't think that it is intended to be any good for you; the longer you live the longer they have to keep you and feed you. That is not the aim of the system, there are plenty of replacements to fill the camps and prisons in this land. It is therefore, a state of simple logistics, the quicker you die, the quicker your place is taken by some other poor soul. There's no problem with overcrowding in these goals, they operate a 'more the merrier and the sooner you die regime'. When a prisoner dies shooting is still the quickest way for them to exterminate him. Then the quicker his place can be filled by some other poor sod who has upset them, a poor soul who may or may not have upset the KGB; it is possible he or she was arrested just to meet the quota, a quota that some planner had written down. So if the system manages to get some free labour out of you before you die in the process of imprisonment, then so much the better for them, they would rather work you to death than pay you.

They have a way of speeding the process up somewhat, first by beatings. During these they pay particular attention to your kidneys and liver, then if you do not show signs of deteriorating quickly enough they start into your chest with their heavy jackboots. One of my former guards gave me that advice, he was fascinated by the West, and he was eager to hear all I could tell him about life in the decadent West, as they call it. In return he gave me tips on how to survive in the camps if I ever ended up in the Gulag system, tips such as wrapping your body in as many clothes as you could get hold of; wrapping them round your chest and your lower back in particular. You must pad yourself up as much as you could because you would not only have to survive attacks by guards, but the guards would also set other prisoners on to you, sometimes for sport and sometimes because they would have had a telling-off for slackness themselves. If you couldn't fight and you were not prepared to kill, then if you wanted to survive you had better learn to fight, and I don't mean prancing around like boxers; you would have to learn to fight to the death and if you didn't you would not last a month. Don't wait for them to start, strike first whatever you do, don't give your opponent any sort of a chance! "You will have to kill, or you will be killed, that's the situation out there in the camps, you know, but no matter how well you do, you will all die out there in the end you know," he told me the last time I saw him.

Yet people do survive in the system; I have met people here who have been in the system for years. The art is to just become accepted as part of the furniture and keep your head down, especially when the going is hard and tough and the guards go on the rampage. Survival is the name of the game; you should only do enough work to be sure of your survival by earning your daily food. You just never know, you might be released some time in the future, it has happened before.

You know, I have never understood these idiots who find themselves in a place like those camps where life is not only extremely hard, but downright uncomfortable, and to stay alive you need every scrap of nutrition you can. These idiots then go on a hunger strike of all things and expect to live; moreover they expect to gain some concession from the system by their actions. Or worse still some go on a hunger strike over something as stupid as a principle. They then upset the guards, get a beating, which damages their vital organs, then wonder why they suffer so much before they eventually die, normally being forced to fight some other criminal type of prisoner like a Christian against the lions in Rome!

It was hard enough to survive with all your organs intact, without having them damaged. So I had carried out the first lesson I learnt from the guard, I managed to get some extra clothing. This I wrapped around my body as a kind of armour and it had helped to absorb most of the kicks I had received so far. These were the kicks that cannot always be avoided; but I had padded my kidney area as best I could. That way, if I did get a good kicking in the back for any reason at least I now had a chance of not having my liver or kidneys damaged, or not too badly that is. If they stripped me and beat me, well then I think it would be a case of kissing everything goodbye because I had no idea just how much I was damaged during my interrogations.

If the chance to escape ever did present itself, unlike some of these people who wouldn't stand a snowball's chance in hell of making it, I would be off like a bloody jack rabbit. Some of these poor sods wouldn't make it to the end of the cell corridor, let alone over the huge walls of stone or the barbed wire which the bastards have put up around the outside of all the prisons I have been in so far. To the guards this was all a big, sarcastic, cruel game; to me it was a matter of life or death.

I was certain I was going to make it out; you see I had a new reason for living, I had become what the Americans in the religious profession call a 'Born again Christian'. Now I had a mission in life, a mission to convert a traitor; to convert him into dust. As some good man had once said, 'earth to earth, ashes to ashes, and dust to dust'. Well, that would be the Major because either way the Major would be a dead Major when I got out of here. It was no longer a case of if I got out, but when I got out. Then our Major's days would be numbered. He would only have the time it took me to get back to Blighty to attend as many Embassy parties and as many night clubs as he could, because he was going to die.

All For A King's Shilling

He might have had a successful life to date as a 'double agent or single agent' but that part of his life was now going to come to a very sticky end; the clock was ticking; Major. The final chapter was going to be written, and written by me. The biggest mistake he had made in his life was to double-cross me. It would not be a very pretty sight to look at, believe me. He had caused me much sorrow to date and I had a debt to settle with him. Not only did I have to exact revenge for myself, but for Katrine also. I'd no idea what miseries or depravity Katrine had had to suffer during this time, but whatever had happened, she would be avenged. When we met I was going to exact it all from him, I might have a lot more time to go yet, but I would get him, by god I'd get him. His face was etched on my brain; what was more, I could superimpose his face on to anybody I saw or anything I looked at.

To achieve this man's death I had not wasted these last few months, indeed not. For I had spent them doing the one thing that I should have done before I even left England on this ill-fated mission and that, my friend was 'planning and preparation', planning every part of the operation properly. Of late I had never ceased my planning, I'd made plans to escape and each time the big 'E' day had drawn near the Russians had moved me. It was as if they knew what I was thinking and planning. The nearer the day came to execute my plans, they moved me from the prison a day or so before I had planned to leave. Firstly, to another prison, and then to on to a second prison; and then before I could get settled into another, it was always a double move. I had made plans to escape in every prison in which they had held me, but now I was full of plans. I was certain though, plan or no plan, given half a chance and I would be off like the proverbial jack rabbit.

Now that the torture and all the nasty part of my incarceration was over and it was only a matter of time before they up and shot me for real I was no longer being pumped full of drugs. Well, that was the time when I started taking stock of how I came to be in this situation in the first place.

The whole operation was basic really, but like the fool I am I got myself caught up in the rush of the emergency and what a well-planned emergency it was, too. Of course, I fell for it hook line and bloody sinker; but now I look back it was more curiosity than anything else that drove me on; one could say I was a willing idiot really. With that I started to overlook points, many important points. To say I was exhausted after my trip to Borneo, although true, was after all really only an excuse. I had made a complete arsehole of myself by thinking I might be able to resolve all the queries about what was happening with the place, that was the real reason why I was in this situation! The only positive item to come out of the whole episode so far was that I now knew for certain that I was really on my own, well and truly on my own. I also now knew that I always had been; I was on my own for the rest of what life I had left. Carl was perhaps the only exception and Katrine also, but I might never see either of them again so the rest was at the moment all negative.

I know I was egged along the way with the tide of events, briefings that did not ring true, details that I would normally have questioned, pushed, nagged, and I persisted until I got some satisfactory answer. Well, like the fool they took me for I was true to form, and I let them gloss over everything; I didn't question details or anything. Even though the major details that I needed to know were left out they were all there all the time niggling in the back of my head and the questions were there all the time. I just kept pushing, putting them to the bottom of my list of my priorities and I went along with it all; even so I did think that if I ignored all that they had insisted I should do I could pull it off. Well , I nearly did. If it had not been for the storm and my injuries I would have done so and those bastards in London wouldn't have had a clue where I would be holed up now instead of in this prison system!

So I could make all the excuses in the world as to why I let it happen, it would always come back to the point that it was I who had let it happen. So I 'cocked it up', I was the one who ran around in circles in the London centre like a headless bloody chicken. Even when I was on the ground and in Russia and the game was 'afoot', as they say, I still did not stop long enough to study the field and think the problem through. If I had gone to ground for a couple of weeks, or better still a month, I had always found that when you disappear for a week or two it frightens the shit out of them. If I had done so, I know I would have made it; instead I went along with their cock-eyed plan, but only just. In all of my reasoning it always came back to the same point, I had no other person to blame but myself.

As you see, I let myself get carried along with the tide. The truth is I couldn't let it go, I felt that if what I had suspected was true then I had to be the one to put things right. I could have holed up in Northern Norway with Carl and his friends for the coming winter, again I didn't. So when it all boiled down to it, the accident I suffered in the woods was just unfortunate and how I had kicked myself for losing such a wonderful opportunity to stuff those bastards in London and now, as I said before, I was completely on my own, up to my armpits in shit, as they say. There is one thing though, the 'powers that be' in London hopefully would now have written me off. No doubt the GRU Major would have seen to that and reported my death! So for the first time I now had a small, a very small chance, providing that I could stay alive in this bloody system and if whoever it was who had helped me so far could still help me when things got really bad as I was certain that they would. The rest now was up to me, it was shit or bust time now!

At last, through one of the old guards I had eventually managed to make contact with some people on the outside, people who would give me a helping hand as and when I did make a run for it. The getting out was entirely up to me and they did not want to know any of my plans for getting out. That way if I didn't make it, then they certainly would not make the slightest effort to help me! If there was any trouble they would not be implicated in any fracas during my escape attempt; what is more they would hand me over to the authorities as soon as I met them, anyway. Getting out was my problem as I had said. Mind you, I was not too certain that I would use their help even when I did get out. I was not too keen to trust too many people at the moment, but I would try to get whatever information I could from whatever source I could, all of which might come in handy one day for my own purposes once I got out of whichever place I happened to be in when I made my dash for freedom.

Something that really surprised me was they used the same code in these prisons as was used in England when tapping out messages. From the messages tapped on the pipes and walls of this place, I do believe that I was then in Lubyanka prison, the one in Moscow that is. I kept getting asked about England by one prisoner to my right, but I wasn't sure if he was a prisoner or a Russian interrogator. This had been my sixth or seventh move in as many months and they always took me in the back of a small

All For A King's Shilling

Land Rover type of vehicle. First my feet and hands were cuffed, and then a chain was passed from my feet cuffs up to and around my waist. From there, the chain went up my back, then once around my neck. From my neck, the chain was first brought down the front of my chest and there it was padlocked to my handcuffs. I had studied the way they did this and I thought if I flexed my muscles when they were fitting them, well, when I relaxed I should be able to get them off. The problem is they then handcuffed the chain to a roof bar in the vehicle as it passed around my neck and they never left me alone once they had me chained up. Most of the time they blindfolded me and they used some horrible Russian version of our masking tape which, when removed from my eyes, had removed most of my eyebrows.

From the number of previous moves I had been through my eyebrows had by now nearly all gone. You can well imagine that I spent most of the time during the journey praying that they didn't have an accident. It was not worth thinking what would happen to me if they did, it would probably save them a bullet some day. All this fear shown by me was to the amusement of my guards. For my part during this, well, I sang songs, songs like, 'The Lobster Song', 'The Red Flag' and the old favourite of the Second World War:

"This is my story this is my song,
I've been in this Unit too fucking long,
Roll on the Nelson, the Rodney, Renown,
This fucking Commando is getting me down."

They didn't understand a word I was singing, still what the hell, it didn't seem to upset them, but it did my morale the world of good and that to me was important. They normally started by telling me to shut up. Or more accurately they told me in Russian to 'shit in it'. Then after a while they just ignored me, I occasionally got a slap round the side of my head, but they never marked me. You see, in each prison they stripped me and I was examined by the prison doctor, or should I say, veterinary surgeon, when I arrived. These doctors for some reason known only to themselves paid particular attention to any marks I might have acquired during my journey.

It began to look as if I would be at Lubyanka for some time. I had been there for about three months and it was getting on for a good few years since my arrest. It was my hope that I would be able to make my escape from there. For the first time since my capture I thought they were not going to hang, shoot, or even exchange me for some Russian held by the West. The longer my stay went on though, the more I felt the hanging or shooting bit had passed. I had also come to the conclusion that Moscow was not the best of places for me to make my escape, but to be honest I would make my escape for freedom wheresoever an opportunity arose. Oh, yes, I would go in a trice.

There was no doubt I would stand out like a sore thumb in my prison clothes. So after much haggling, a change of clothes was the only help the contact I had made would give me. Other than that, pointing me in the right direction towards the outskirts of Moscow to get me out of the city as quickly as he could was the most he was prepared to do for me. It was not the best of plans, but then it was the only plan which I had been able to come up with in the time and considering how tight a control they had on this place.

Considering the situation of the regime under which I was a prisoner I was quite proud of my little self really. Some of these people had been here since the Second World War and had not managed as much. Mind you, I must ask myself why I had managed to achieve so much in such a short time. For my sanity's sake I tried to forget that question because I didn't like the answer that I kept coming up with. I was not fully convinced yet that they were not still playing games with me. I had started to have interviews with a very charming Russian of late. He had hinted that I might be exchanged quite soon if I was prepared to help him in his analysis of certain ways of life and political setups in the West. Judging from his remarks of late I think they had a lot of trouble trying to understand why we in the West did not welcome their ideology with open arms. He told me he had many plans for me when I got back to England. Not as many as I had for myself when I got back. Still, I played along with his little game because, ever the optimist, I might be able to arrange for one of their plans to backfire on them.

I knew I did not reveal any of my escape contingency plans when I was under this interrogation and that is what it was, interrogation. This man was the silky smooth bastard who was only looking after my interests, like shit he was. I was certain I told him nothing of my plans to escape, because he never asked me about them. This led me to think that perhaps he would let me make my escape. They could then pick me up at their leisure, any or all the people in the places where I stopped and asked for help. So in my efforts to get out I might uncover a network of spies, but then whatever surprises they had for me didn't worry me too much.

Some weeks later events took a turn for the worse; during this time I lost most of my enthusiasm for the escape plans. It seemed as if they all turned to shit and I had no chance of getting away. All the hard work cultivating prison staff had gone for nothing. The people who had become friendly with me had been moved to other parts of the prison. That is what the new guards told me and these new guards were not only hostile, they were downright brutal.

I had taken to worrying all the time now about Katrine and what had happened to her. I often wondered if she was following me around this prison system. My only hope was that Carl had somehow been able to get her out and away from all this. The prisoners in the system I was now in since I left Lubyanka were like animals. Mind, I didn't hold that against them. It was the only way they could survive because weak people did not live long in this system. Katrine's face at my trial still haunted me; I sat in the black dingy box-type structure they called a cell and I worried about her. My morale at that moment was at its lowest. I knew that once I got out of their hands and I was up and running there would always be the chance I could make it. Now I felt it might be better to just end it all by trying to escape. It would be better than rotting to death in one of their bloody labour camps, which I'm sure would be my next stop now they had weakened me sufficiently.

So it was some time later my premonition came true; they shackled me up again and off I went; this time they didn't blindfold me. Once they had settled me in the truck I started my singing in the normal way, but to my surprise they took no notice, no backhands, nothing. They just looked at me, grinned and drew their fingers across their throats in a cutting motion. I could tell from their gestures alone and their delight in making them that my very existence was going to hang day by day, on the merest whim of some insignificant guard and my singing died in the back of my throat.

Within no time at all the truck carrying me stopped and I could hear the sound of a steam locomotive. At this point I must admit I felt a little relieved to hear that sound because I had thought I was on my way to die against some unmarked wall in the grubby outskirts of whatever city it was that I was then in. The guards removed me from the back of the truck and they threw me into a railway goods van, where they then pulled the chains from me.

I looked and blinked at the sight as my eyes became accustomed to the darkness of the interior of the rail truck that I was in along with about another fifty or so people. It was only when the smell started to hit me that I realised they must have been in there for quite some time. As I looked them over I thought what a sorry looking lot you are, you look as though you have been to hell and back. I learnt later that they had looked at me thinking much the same thoughts as I had of them. It took me only a few seconds to spot the leader of the van; the one of whom the others were afraid!

So I made my way to him; he had the only place where fresh air came into the van. When I at last reached him, I took him by what remained of the lapels of his coat, pulled him forward and head butted him. Then I started to beat him unconscious; when I had finished my vicious, unprovoked attack on the man I turned and looked at the rest of the people; they all just turned their heads away. My fists hurt like hell and I thought I might regret what I had just done if I got frostbite in them. With that I settled down in the place where the other man had been; I needed time to study my present situation.

Just then the train started to move and I hoped and prayed that I was on to the right wave length of thought. The GRU bosses knew I would be looking for the first chance I could find to escape. This was the first time they had moved me anywhere without any chains from head to toe or blindfolded. So perhaps it would not be long before the fox would be up and running. By hell, wouldn't he just? Only this time he wouldn't be as daft as the last time. No, sir, I had some foolish ideas they would let me run. This I reasoned by the fact that this was the first time since my capture that I had not been under their constant guard and observation. So I now formed the opinion that they wanted me to run, but to run only under their control. They would give me just enough rope to be able to flush out any of their people who where prepared to help me. Yes, they would use me that way, so I should have to be on my guard if it did unravel in that way.

The second morning I awoke with the side of my face that was against the airvent feeling very numb. At first I thought that the cold night air had caused it until I felt my cheek. Then it did not take me long to realise that the left side of my face was frozen. Immediately, I started to rub it with my bare hand. For a good twenty minutes I could not feel anything and my hand was starting to get cold. It was at this point I started to panic as I looked around the truck and saw that nearly everybody was either asleep or dead. Some of the bodies had a covering of ice all over them and some were shivering quite violently.

As I surveyed the miserable mess in the truck I saw a bundle of rags get up from the floor and make its way towards me, over the other heaps of rags that lay on the floor of the truck. I braced myself for the fight I knew I must face if I were to keep my place at the airvent. When the bundle of rags got within striking distance I raised myself up and adopted a defensive stance. As I was about to throw my first punch, the bundle of rags pulled off the blanket it had covering its head. There, standing before me, was a woman who looked about sixty. She grinned at me and I could see she had very few of her teeth left in her head.

She then grinned at me and said, "The side of your face is frozen and you need to take care of it and I can help you, but it will cost you."

I looked at her and said, "Cost me, cost me what, you old hag?"

"Talking like that, wont get you any favours from me young man; anyway, I'm not an old hag, I'm not thirty yet."

"Well I'm sorry about that, but you look like an old hag to me, so once more what is it going to cost me?"

"Look, frozen face, how long do you think you will last where we are going with a frozen face like that? It is your death sentence, you won't last the week out, but I can help."

"Bloody hell, woman, I've already asked you three times, what do I have to do, to get you to help me?"

"Well, first of all you have to give me your place by the airvent. Then when you have to unload the bodies from this truck the next time we stop you are to take me off with them, as a dead body. Do you agree?"

"Of course I agree, now what can you do for me?"

"I have some cream here which will help your skin to heal now that it is thawing out and I have an extra blanket. I'll give you the cream and the blanket to put over your head to keep it warm and also to hide the frozen part of your face."

"Right, let us get on with it then."

Later that day, I had to help unload the bodies as she had said I would. By the time we had finished I was just about out. I did manage to get her off the train and behind a wall the other side of the one against which we had piled the bodies. The last I saw of her she was walking away from the place in what I hoped for her sake was a southerly direction.

I applied the cream she had given me to my face and it stung like hell; I thought at first she had given me an acid mixture. Whatever it was it did the trick, because in a couple of days my face had healed. That old hag, or young woman as she insisted she was, had saved my life that time and I owed her a debt, which perhaps one day I could repay.

Three days later I disappeared in through the gates of hell. There are no other words to describe what happened to me over the next eighteen months after my train journey. That was how long it was before I could give any thought again to escaping; I had spent the time just trying to stay alive. They had during this time been putting me in with some of their worst types of criminals. Each time they moved me, I had to fight to stay alive. Each time I arrived in a new camp or prison, the guards always pointed me out to these strange subhuman people. They were men who had transcended the barrier between animal and human, they were pitted against me in a never-ending stream. People died in those places daily; I shudder to think how many I either had to kill or had damaged so badly that their death was but a matter of time. Not all who died in those camps died from ill treatment by the guards, although there was quite a bit of that going on, but most of the men died at the hands of other prisoners, killed by people like myself just trying to live long enough to escape from the living hell in which we had found ourselves.

Life in these camps and prisons had truly descended into the 'dog eat dog society'. More so, I think, in the gaol I was last in. I kept hoping that I had not descended as far as them down the slide to hell, but I had to kill or I too would die in that place. As I was still alive among them I thought that perhaps I too had transcended the barrier between man and animal, and that I had also, like them, become an animal. Even if I had to kill the whole bloody campful of prisoners I would and I thought I would go on so doing, for as long as it took for me to get out of there. I was lucky, because each fight I had, I managed to win and I saw each success as one step nearer to getting that bastard in London, if I did not end on the wrong end of one of those fights in there, that was. I strongly believe that my hatred for that bastard who put me in this situation was the one belief that kept me alive in those dark evil days.

He was probably swigging his pink gins back in the UK during that period of my troubles, but if he only knew it, I would be calling on him. I had much anger in me and it was all building up for him. Oh, I would be coming to visit him, of that he could be sure. I would be coming for him.

Eventually, they moved me to another camp. Conditions there were very bad also, but not, thank God, the same as at the last prison. Killing and fighting amongst prisoners was strictly forbidden in the camps and prisons of the Russian labour system. Only the guards had that privilege in this camp and that was a bad omen altogether. Amongst yourselves, you had a chance, but against the well-fed guards there was no hope. Survival here was dependent upon pure luck and just how many rags you had been able to secrete around your body under your outer garments. At least most of the people here were not out and out criminals, as they had been in the last few places I'd been in. Nowadays I looked on all those places as my apprenticeship in the Russian prison system and I did hope I had passed my test.

Since I got here I had been able to make a friend, the first since I arrived in this system. He has been in the system of Russian gaols and camps nearly all his life and knew it well. My friend was an old man whom the KGB, or the NKVD as it was in those days, had arrested in the streets of Moscow long before the Second World War, would you believe. Since his arrest he had gone from camp to camp and from gaol to gaol for nearly all his adult life, a pattern I was starting to recognise in my own situation. To this day he did not know why they put him in prison in the first place. He kept asking me what I had done to have arrived at this camp in the condition I was in. I just told him much the same as him, nothing. This kept him quiet for a while, but then he started again. When he described the condition of my health as he saw it, it worried me somewhat because I had been certain that I was fit. In my foolish way I had thought I was in quite a good condition considering what I had just gone through.

I had started again to make plans to escape. There was nothing outside this place except just snow, ice and more snow. Everybody here knew this was the place where they sent you to die. If you had made it through all the hell-holes they had and you seemed to be lasting the pace, then it was off to this camp. They were so confident about this place they did not even have any fence around it. So I said to this friend one night, "Why don't we go for a walk one dark night?"

To which my friend replied, "You have no idea of the distance it is from here to the nearest inhabited place do you? We are in the Arctic Circle; if the wolves don't get you the bears will. If we were to walk into any village we might reach, they would turn us over to the KGB. If they didn't, then they would end here as prisoners, just the same as we are. No, we have no chance, we are doomed, we are here to die. Nobody cares, you know."

"Well," I said, "for what it is worth, I think you are wrong there, my friend. Thanks to you I've just seen the light of day for the first time since they put me in this bloody prison system."

I didn't tell him what I had in mind, but I had just realised that in their attempts to make this place impregnable, they obviously thought anybody who was not only fit, but also stupid enough to try and escape would head back into good old Mother Russia. In 99 per cent of cases they would probably be correct and in every case except one they were correct, that one exception was me! The last place on earth I would head for would be the centre of 'Good old Mother Russia'. No, sir, I'd be off in a different direction completely, northwards for me, mister KGB.

So now at last I had the necessary drive to start all my planning again. It was as if I had got a new lease of life and now that I had at last learnt to conceal all of my feelings I knew this time I would succeed. Once before I had given myself away. When I was within two days of making my escape, the anticipation of it had shown on my face. No, sir, this time I would die here, before I left on my way home, because the guards here only looked for live escapees, they never wasted time looking for dead men.

The plan was simplicity itself; first I was going to build myself up by eating whatever food I could lay my hands on, rats and anything else I could lay my hands on. Also I would try and store what bits of food I could and storage of food in these circumstances was easy just as long as no other prisoner found your catch. Then when the time was right and the days were at their shortest, I would simply walk out and head south. The south would be just in case some other prisoner saw me as I left. He might or might not raise the alarm but would certainly inform on me some time soon after, if extra food was offered as an inducement. Once clear, I would swing wide of the camp, and head out north over the Arctic ice. Straight over the North Pole and on to Canada, Norway or more than likely into oblivion – that would be my way out. Still, no matter whatever it was to be, I would be free when the end came. God damn them, I would be free. At least I would be trying to get away from them and by trying I would be fighting back at the bastards in the only way I could and that to me was the most important bit, fighting back.

A few weeks after I had made my escape plan and I'd been eating well, I had made a big indent on the rat population by the number that I had managed to catch, having remembered from my survival training days there are parts of a rat that is poisonous. Not your sick stomach type poison, more your dead type poison, but I couldn't, for the life of me, remember just what part of the rat it was. I tried so hard with the first rat I ate to remember what bit it was, but could not and by the time I caught my second I just gave it all up and ate the bloody lot. Mind you, I was awake

All For A King's Shilling

most of that night waiting to die, but I didn't, but I nearly did die the next day, and as I was too bloody tired through lack of sleep to do my quota of work, it would be unlikely I'd get any food that night and if it had not been for my old pal, I would not have, or got any rest that night either!

I believe I would have died the next day if it had not been for him. So I decided that I would eat the bloody rats and go to sleep. If I were to die, at least I hoped I would be asleep when it happened. Suffice it to say, I didn't die of eating the rats, so I set about in earnest catching rats and eating them. Six weeks later I was really starting to feel the benefit of all this extra protein I was getting. I managed to hide the small lumps of bread we got, and soon I had a fair supply of them as emergency rations, ready for the time when I would make my escape. I was fully confident that this time next year I would have been back in the UK for at least eleven months, that's how cocky I had got.

The weather then took a turn for the worse; we had a white-out for about three days and it never occurred to me in the past that so much bloody snow could fall in three days. It must have been ten feet or more by the time it stopped. They still insisted that we went out each day to meet our quota of timber felling. They roped us together and then tied the ends of the rope with us on it, to the nearest trees that we were to fell. We could hardly see each other and you were as likely to get killed by a falling tree as anything else. These days I had decided it would be wiser if I took my hoard of food with me, just in case I got a chance to escape during all the confusion as they tried to rope us all together and it was causing them some terrible problems.

The snow was intermittent for days after the white-out, but they insisted on sending us out and as we didn't reach our quotas each day during this time, we didn't get fed. We couldn't tell night from day anymore and one old lag told us, "The last time this happened they lost two-thirds of the prisoners, who died because of the storm and hunger from not reaching their quotas." He then went on to say, "They pray for one of these storms every year as it helps them meet their quota of prisoner vacancies each year."

We all just looked at him as the reality of what he was saying sank into our numbed brains. So it was with what the old man had said ringing in my mind that I decided that, come what may, I would go the next day. With the situation likely to get very difficult here there was no way I could run the risk of the others finding my food. I could not allow myself the luxury of sharing my hoard of food with anybody, even the old boy. No matter how good a pal he had been, this was now a life or death situation I was in. If I was to get any weaker than I was then it would spell curtains for me, so it was over the hill for me tomorrow.

Next morning I could hardly conceal my elation when we lined up for work. I was sure my pal knew what I planned because he gave me a look that said farewell. My elation was very short-lived though because the guard called my number out along with four others. Instant panic settled in as he detailed me to go with the four others to a new place of work; I didn't even have time to wave farewell to my new found pal. This interfered with my plans and at first I thought that some bastard had split on me and then I thought that couldn't be, because no one knew my plans.

Even though we asked, the three guards would not tell us what the new work was or where it was. The five of us lined up at the back of a small one-ton vehicle, ropes were then tied around our wrists and the other ends were secured to a bar across the back of the trucks. In the back was a shelter in which we found one of the guards was to sit. It was the type of shelter that one sees on the back of council trucks used by road repair gangs in England. The three guards chattered for a little while, then one climbed into the back of the truck and the others got in the front. The third guard went into the back and sat in the shelter and he covered himself with what looked like a thick quilted blanket and then he put a bearskin over the top of it. Next he thumped the floor of the truck with the butt of his rifle and with that the truck took off at a hell of a pace, which pulled all five of us off our feet. It was in this way that we left the camp, flat on our faces, as the truck dragged us along at about twenty miles an hour. Well, I thought, you are never going to see this place again, or any other place if you do not do something fast. It didn't look as if you would see anything ever again, not after this. Then when the truck was about half a mile outside the camp it stopped.

I remember thinking well, at least you are still alive, if only just. The guard told us all in no uncertain terms to "Get to your bloody feet and when we set off again," and here came the most obvious statement I'd ever heard in my life, "anybody who falls down will die!" This time the truck started at a more steady speed and we were able to trot along behind it. At first I stumbled along and it was some time before I got into a rhythm. It had been a long time since I had done any doubling, trotting or even running. Because of this, I was very stiff, and my legs were not loosening up at all. After a while, I realised that we were heading in a northerly direction. This, if I was right, would suit me all the more provided I could keep it up. The farther north we went the better for my plans; which just went to show how far into madness I'd sunk. It was not long, though, before I realised I had to make my escape soon. I was too unfit to play this silly game of running behind the truck for very much longer, another mile or two and I would be dead anyway.

Now I knew for certain in my heart that I was never going to make it out of here at all other than by death, that is. Today was going to be that day and for the first time in my life I now understood the Jewish saying, 'Next year in Jerusalem'. All my thoughts and plans that had kept me going all these long years were really for nothing. So, who had I been kidding, I was never going to make it and they had known that all the time. It was then I decided that I would at least go out fighting and I finally succumbed and prayed for the first time since I was a young choir boy. When we arrived at the new camp I knew I wouldn't have time for that, I'd be too busy making my escape as soon as they unhooked me from this bloody truck, if I ever reached the new camp, that was?

I must have been dreaming, or in a stupor or something, for now I could see two ropes hanging loose over the back of the truck. It was then I noticed there were only three of us still doubling behind the truck. I wondered what had happened to the other two, but that was something I didn't have to wonder about for very long. We were all stumbling about now rolling from side to side as we gasped for breath in the thin Arctic air, yet still we managed to trot along behind that bloody truck. All three of us were sucking in huge gasps of air as we concentrated on putting one foot in front of the other without falling over on to the hard ice that we were now traversing. The pains in my chest were by now excruciating! Then it happened, one of the other two still with me fell, and the truck dragged him along on the ice. He had no chance of getting on to his feet again, nor could we help him in any way. There was no chance of him getting up, they didn't even slow down, let alone stop, and they just kept on at the same pace. The guard in the back of the truck just looked on impassively at the man as the truck dragged him along.

After some time, God alone knows how long, he had stopped struggling; he was making no effort whatsoever to get up. At that moment the guard in the back of the truck leaned forward and cut the rope which dragged the man along. As I watched all this, it was then that it hit me; we were all out here to die. If ever I needed one of my plans, then now was the time, so I started to formulate one as fast as my half-frozen brain would let me. It had to be now or never, this I knew. Some sort of plan was forming in my mind and I waited for what I thought was a reasonable time. As I was coming to a good solid idea and was trying to find a way of carrying it out, fate took a hand in the events.

Firstly, I stumbled into the other guy and then I fell to the ground, or snow, for God knows how far the ground was below us. We were completely out of the trees by now, and we must have been out on the Arctic ice at least. As soon as I landed on the ice I thought, I have once more just committed suicide, as sure as if I had jumped off Tower Bridge in London. By shit, but did I panic as I struggled to get back to my feet, but to no avail. Then I saw a large lump of ice coming up under the truck. To this day I still remember the pain and flashing lights in my head, then there was what I can only describe as a thick blackness! The blackness was a complete all round blackness in which I felt warm for the first time in months or even years. What was more I could feel no sense of movement and to my surprise no pain at all.

I never knew how long that state of euphoria lasted but it was heaven while it did. Next, I remember thinking so this is it, this is death and there's just nothing, a void, no Hell and no Heaven, shit, what a bloody let down; it seemed worse than the last time I had died when the bastards carried out their mock execution. Well, I thought this could not be right, but it must be. I tried to open my eyes and nothing happened; I thought you are a silly sod, your eyes are open, it's just that everything is a dense blackness. After that I didn't remember very much for a while, except that the blackness seemed to last quite some time before it cleared and daylight returned again. Then I felt a blinding pain in my head again and I thought the dead bit was too bloody good to last. So I tried to open my eyes again. This time it worked. I could see two feet stumbling alongside me, so I was still tied to the bloody truck and I was not in Heaven, but I could be in Hell. Just at that point the stumbling feet shot past me and I slithered to a halt on the ice.

Much to my own surprise, I did have the sense of mind not to look up because if I had done so I'm sure I'd have got a seven point six two calibre bullet in my head. As I lay there, I waited again for what I believed to be ages, but could only have been a few minutes. When at last I opened my eyes and lifted my head I could just make out the truck heading off over the Arctic ice, with its last prisoner still trotting behind it. I did not think he had long to go either. So if I was to make good my escape, I was going to have to make a move. If I stayed on this ice for much longer I would stick to it and never get away. Then with what I have always considered to be my most superhuman effort, I forced my aching body to its feet and headed off into the growing darkness, at right angles to the track that I had been on.

William Atlay

Don't ask me which direction I was heading in, I didn't know if I was heading right, left, north, south, east or west. What was more important, I didn't care either, because I was free. For the first time since I had thought I was in Finland I was free, for the first time for only God knows how long. Here I was, alone with only some scraps of brown bread to my name, on the ice floating on the top of the Arctic Ocean, and I felt like dancing. Half dead, covered in rags and vermin, a lump on my head like a bloody football, and I felt like dancing. Okay, I said to myself, you will not make it, I knew that, and soon I would die, but I would die a bloody free man; I felt great no, I felt fucking great, and I shouted as loud as I could. "You can all stick your fucking RED FLAG with its Hammer and Sickle right up your fat Russian arses, but I'll stick it up your bloody stinking Major's arse!!"

It was some time later that the reality of it all landed on me, and I stopped dead in my tracks and thought for a while. I had no chance, this I knew, but I meant to give it my best shot. Clothes, I thought, I needed more clothes, I needed food, and most of all I needed rest and time to get myself into some sort of shape, at least a little bit better than I was now. It was then I decided to return to the track, and then make my way back towards the tree line. What was more, I also intended to take the clothes from the man who had fallen and was cut free from the truck before me.

To my surprise I came across him a little sooner than I had expected. At this point I started to realise that in my condition I was having trouble co-ordinating time and distance. Also I was hoping they would now list me as dead in the camp records. It is strange how your mind works when you are frozen and tired. My real hope was that they would not look for me, which meant I could take all the time I needed to get myself sorted out. I needed somewhere to lie up and do just that, and of course to eat, hell, I needed to eat.

With all of this in my mind I stripped the body of the old man who had died and was cut loose by the guard before me. I took all his clothes and the rags he had wrapped over his boots. Much to my surprise he was wearing a rather good pair of Russian jackboots. So I took the lot and I then rolled his body away from the track and into a cleft in the ice. As I used my boot to push him in deeper, I saw the two headlights of a truck coming back along the track. I had the presence of mind to get behind some cover as it went by, and I could see the back of it clearly, and there they were, only four lengths of rope hanging from the back. So, we hadn't all died and I wondered what had happened to the last bloke, but I knew if I stayed where I was much longer I would be a goner and I gave up wondering what had happened to him.

Just standing there, I was already feeling colder, so I put the old man's clothes on top of mine; then I made my way slowly back to the tree line keeping at what I hoped was an angle of forty-five degrees to the track. I just plodded on all night. There must have been a thousand thoughts going through my mind that night. My first elation was at being free, yes, free! Then reality set in and I thought who in God's name did I think I was kidding, free! I was no more free now than when they were dragging me along behind that bloody truck, but I was going to make it was the only thought that kept coming back to me; over and over again I kept saying to myself, "You are going to make it, lad." Every time I had a negative thought it was always ended with the phrase, "But I am still going to make it."

All For A King's Shilling

How long this went on I shall never know; I just knew that sometimes it was light, sometimes it was dark, sometimes I was in the trees and sometimes I was in the open. I came to very suddenly when I heard a noise, a noise I had not heard for a long time. It was the barking of a dog. I thought it was a wolf at first, then I realised wolves don't bark. It had to be a dog. My confusion was because all dogs that enter the camps get eaten and they never get the chance to bark. My next thought was that there was a lot of meat on a good-sized dog or a wolf for that matter. So I got behind a tree and waited to find out from what direction the barking was coming. I listened for a while, wondering how the hell I would kill the damned dog or wolf once I found it. Then I heard it again, over in the thicker trees. I must get this half crazed mind of mine into gear. The last thing I wanted now was to walk into another bloody Russian prison or more likely an army camp.

Next I got myself a hefty branch from the trees and started to edge my way towards the noise, or where I thought the noise was coming from. It took quite some time to get anywhere near it, but at last I could smell smoke and I could just make out a hut of sorts. Outside the hut was a large, half-starved dog, tied to a tree stump. The stump was about four feet high and the dog was well and truly tied to it. By now he was making one hell of a fuss about me. He really had got my scent. I looked at the situation for some time and I honestly did not know what to do. I was just numb with cold and I just didn't know what the hell to do. My brain must have turned to solid ice on me; here I was the great all-thinking, all-singing and dancing bloody Commando, and I just didn't know what to do.

It was as I was about to get up and just walk in and give myself up that I felt this prod in my back. Then a gruff Russian voice asked me, "What does a scum bag like you want with my camp?" As I turned to look at him, I could only seem to focus my eyes on his cocking of the rifle that he was prodding me with. I do not know exactly what happened next, nor do I think I ever want to know. All I remember of the incident was that I was sitting on his chest, looking at what had once been a human face, albeit an ugly bastard. Now it was nothing but a mess of flesh, blood and bone and horrible black and brown teeth. Oh, he was dead alright and I was glad I had not seen his real face. Then I thought shit, I wonder if there are anymore in the hut and it was at that point I suddenly remembered the dog. By now it had stopped barking and was just lying by the tree stump watching me.

The next bit must have looked comical had anybody been watching. I had the rifle in my hand and I was doing this Commando bit, creeping up on the hut. The dog, meanwhile, was sitting on his haunches, head cocked on one side, watching me with much interest. The thought crossed my mind that he was probably saying to himself, "Who's this arsehole? Looks like I've just swapped one fool for a bigger bugger!"

The door to the hut was closed and as there were no windows to see in or out through I thought 'what the hell', got up from the ice and just walked in. It was total darkness inside because the place had no windows and the light from the door didn't penetrate it at all. However there was a large fire burning in the centre of the room, from which there was a pipe going out through the roof. I could only assume this was the chimney. The first thought to strike me about the place was the warmth in there. It was years since I had felt warmth like that. Secondly and most important to my mind was the smell of hot food. I burnt my hands getting at it, and then I burnt my mouth, throat and stomach eating it. What it was I did not know, I also didn't care, but it was the most beautiful food I had ever eaten in my life. When I had finished it all, I just lay down and went to sleep, too full to move.

Just how long I slept, I never knew, but when I came to, the fire was nearly out and it was starting to get cold in the hut. I looked around for something to burn and saw some wood in a corner and with the old rags I had taken from the old man I managed to get it going again. At this point I realised I was hungry again. So I looked around for something to eat, but it was so dark. Eventually I found a lamp and managed to light it. After having a good look around the place, and seeing nothing, I heard a whimpering sound outside, and I remembered the dog.

If I let him go he might go home or somewhere and that would raise the alarm; I would then have to leave the place. That I was not ready to do; having just taken possession of this delightful residence I intended to try and recuperate somewhat before I left it. So I decided to have a look outside and see if the dog was alright. He was, much to my surprise, quite friendly and I brought him into the hut. He immediately lay down by the fire. The poor old thing looked as cold as I had felt and I felt sorry for the poor sod.

Now I settled down to take stock of the situation. I think I was in a fur trapper's hut, or a trapper of some sort. First I searched among his belongings, a task that gave me a strange feeling, and then I reasoned it had been either him or me. I knew that if I had given him half a chance the roles would have been reversed and he would have done me in, as I had him. You see you can justify all your actions if you so wish and want to get rid of any guilt feelings you may have. I didn't think I had any guilt feelings, but I did justify killing him, to myself anyway. One item I found among his belongings was a map. Once I had unfolded it I studied it for a long time. I had to concentrate very hard to make out what part of Russia the map was of. After a while I decided it could wait for another day or two, I was tired just now.

Then I checked the rifle I had been carrying around since I had taken it from the corpse out there on the edge of the clearing. It was then I suddenly thought of the corpse. I had to hide it; if anybody did come before I moved on I would have one hell of a job explaining the body away! As I thought about that I looked at the dog. He looked quite happy just sitting by the stove and I thought I'd leave him in there. Then I had second thoughts about that; the sod might not let me back in again, so I decided to take him with me. He was no trouble, I just put the rope round his neck and off we went.

When I got back to where I had left the body, I had a distinct feeling that the body was not as I had left it. Still, I had been in such a daze when it all happened perhaps it was just my imagination playing tricks on me. The body was now frozen solid and it was also frozen to the ice. It was now part of the ice and I couldn't move it. No matter how hard I tried it was stuck there. There was nothing for it, I decided to just cover it with what snow and ice I could move and leave it at that. The dog sniffed around his old master for a minute or so and then just sat by my feet. You are a lucky bastard, I thought, life just goes on for you, mate, you have just accepted me as your new master. How do you know I don't eat dogs for my dinner?

By now I had the body covered and if there was any more snow it would remain covered until the first thaw; it never thaws completely here, but he would eventually come to the surface again. I had no intention of being here when that happened. I would by then be long gone. Back in the hut I started my search again. This time I unearthed some large rifle bullets. It was then I looked at the rifle. To my surprise I saw it was an old bolt action French Martini Henry, of pre-World War One vintage. The weapon was covered in rust; even so it did look as if it would function alright, but to be honest it looked quite a lethal bloody weapon not only to the person firing it, but to the target as well. The condition of the gun and the ammunition caused me to wonder if it would be the person who fired it or the target he was aiming at who would die. My only hope was that I would never have to use it for real. With that in mind I put the ammunition back in its box and placed it and the rifle by the door. Ready for action; I suppose old habits die hard.

Next I looked at the food supply and I decided there was enough food for some months, provided I did not go mad and make a pig of myself as I had done last night. It could have been the night before for all I knew. Anyway, I sorted it out and felt quite pleased with myself. It looked as if I had more food here than the total they had for the camp I had just left. Next I decided to make a full search of the inside of the hut. The hut was about ten feet by fifteen on the inside, but about twenty by thirty-five on the outside. So it was quite thick. The inside was constructed of six to eight inch diameter logs and there was a sleeping bench on the back wall. I was relieved to note it was the only sleeping bench in the place. Had there been two, I think I would have fled. The stove was a pot-bellied one in the middle of the room and it gave out a hell of a lot of heat.

I was starting to feel at home in here, but I thought I'd better not get too comfortable as I might have to leave at the rush. I decided the man whom I had killed must be a trapper of some sort. This presented me with some problems. If he was a trapper, and he had set some traps, he could after his death still possibly get the better of me. If I went wandering off too far from the hut, I might just end in one of his bloody traps. He must have put bear traps out in this part of the world and I had no intention of becoming one of his trapped bears. Again I searched the place, but I didn't find a trap anywhere in sight.

Watching me, the dog must have thought I was schizoid or something, as I had done nothing but search the bloody place over and over. As there were no traps in the hut, I concluded he must have set them all over the bloody place. I must have been very lucky when I came in here that first night not to have stood on or in one. I thought well, my luck has held for me so far, this time I am going to make it. Mind, I had better keep my eyes open for traps from now on.

Still life must go on, so I got some snow from outside the hut and melted it down to make a drink and to cook some food. What I cooked I don't know, but it was bloody vile. Still I ate it anyway, but the dog would not touch it; he did chew on some raw stuff I threw him, though. All the time as I worked I was formulating a plan to move on from here. The dog was going to help me in more ways than he would think. First, he would help me carry the food and stuff I would pack with me and when that ran out, he would become my next food supply, if I hadn't made it out by then. So I thought I had better feed him, as well as myself, from now on; he was going to keep me alive when the time came.

William Atlay

After about four days, it may have been longer, I began to feel a lot better. The searing pains in my head were not so bad; I was feeling fitter now I had eaten my fill each day since I had arrived. I was also feeling better in myself. I noticed for the first time I smelt to high heaven; even the dog was not too keen to come near me. It was being in a heated place for the first time for years now. So I decided it was time to take a bath. With that I collected snow and ice in every container I could find. It took hours to melt it all down on the stove but by the middle of the night I had what I considered enough.

Then I very slowly, and I mean very slowly, peeled my clothes off. Well, I had not removed them for so long the innermost bits were like sticky, tacky sheets of dirt stuck to my skin. They were also alive with lice. Strange, really, I had never noticed the damned lice for ages and I had almost forgotten I had any. Some of them reminded me of the posters warning about Colorado Beetles some years ago in most English police stations. Still, I was now naked in the hut. If dogs think, I would dearly like to have known what that dog was thinking about then.

I shall never forget the feeling which swept over me as I splashed that first hot water on to my body. The first hot water I had felt for God knows how long since I had been in Katrine's house. I washed myself from head to toe. As I did it came as quite a shock to realise that I had not taken all my clothes off when I got into the tub. As I washed and rubbed myself I could feel my skin coming away in lumps. It was a very frightening experience until at last I realised that I still had another layer of clothes on. At that point I nearly collapsed completely. When I had got over that shock and I had finished scrubbing my body I lay back in the tub and I felt really great, on top of the world, which literally I really was, on top of the world that is.

Then I sat in the water for a little while longer before I started to look around for something to dry myself with. Nothing, I just stood and looked, and there was nothing. I picked up one of the furs that made up the bed and rubbed myself with it. As I did I could feel the lice crawling back on to my body and it was then I realised I had made my first big mistake.

For years I had been able to ignore the lice I carried because I could do nothing about them. Now I had been free of them for perhaps an hour and a half and here they were, coming back, and I knew they were coming back. As they did I started to kill them, but there were too many. I spent the rest of the night on a louse hunt that nearly drove me round the bend. I scratched and rubbed myself red raw with the bloody little bastards. It was well into the next night before I fell asleep exhausted and red raw with scratching. As I dozed off I thought, all right you little bastards, eat me and get it over with.

Chapter Fourteen
Walk With Dog After Escape To Village
Still in Russia, but now free 1978

The singing has died here, I doubt it ever started.

It is some weeks since I arrived in this place. The weather if anything is getting worse. I think the winter is getting deeper, the snow no longer falls but what has fallen has now turned to ice. My lice and I have settled down again and they only bother me occasionally now. The dog has taken to me and I can let him off the lead and he does not stray at all. Probably he is like me and is reluctant to leave the hut, and when he does, he stays very close to it. Both the dog and I have now been able to take better stock of our situation and I am afraid we are going to have to start looking for the traps his master laid. Not for the furs or such, but for the food from any animals his traps managed to catch. The thing is I do not know where to start.

When I first arrived here I thought I had a lot of food. I think most of what there was has gone rotten, so I must find some more, and find it fast. First I thought of starting to work round the hut in circles, increasing the distance from the hut each day. What I did not want to do was to stray too far, only to get lost in the dark.

The dog and I at last took the bull by the horns and went out to look for traps and any food which might be in them. He found a couple of traps, and they had both been sprung. Whatever they had caught had been eaten by something else, or they had eaten their own feet off to get away; whatever the case, all there was left were bloodstains on the snow. The traps only contained some bits of feet and bits of frozen fur. There was nothing worth keeping; I did however come across some rather large animal tracks while I was out there and heard some weird noises. I had not taken the rifle with me so I went back to the hut at the rush. That night was the first time since I had been there that I heard wolves howling. So it seemed the animal life of the area was still pretty active and life was carrying on as normal out there.

I was starting to get a bit worried and I thought both the dog and I had stayed here too long for our own good. When I was in the camps I had heard animals wailing and the like, but I took no notice of them, mainly because I could do nothing about them.

In the camps I had developed that fatalistic attitude which is required to stay alive in the circumstances which existed. Don't worry about things you cannot control or influence.

That was a lesson which had always stood me in good stead in the past but since I had been in the hut I had got too warm and I had got too damned comfortable. I had got to the point where I was reluctant to go out; I was reluctant even to check the hunter's traps for my next meal, or to check and see if anybody was out and about out there. The thought that I too would die, as had my predecessor, if I ventured forth was uppermost in my mind now. I was not going out there in case somebody hit me over the head, as I had done to whomsoever it was who had been the previous occupant of this hut.

I gave this a great deal of thought, and then came to the conclusion that if I were to get away from here, then I must either make my move now or at the least start to get myself ready. Perhaps I thought the best way to achieve this was by leaving the hut and living out there on the ice. Somehow I had to get back my survival attitude, or I would be a goner. It was also important I make my move now in the depth of winter; if not now, then before the thaw started. God knows how many people would be up here in this area once the thaw had set in. The place could be like Piccadilly Circus, there would be that many people around.

So with all this in mind, I got the map out again and laid it on the floor by the stove. Then I started to look for names of places I could relate to. As I looked, I turned it this way, then that way, and I could not make anything of it at all. I looked and looked, but nothing seemed right. It might just as well be a map of the moon as far as I was concerned. I was getting that 'tomorrow is another day' feeling and thinking I might just as well sleep on it. I suddenly stopped and thought, what if the map was of the area as it looked covered in ice. Now suppose it was made from aerial photographs, and what if the people who read those photographs had got their hills and valleys mixed up. Then what would it look like? I was full of what and if, I thought, still let's turn it round and see what we have.

Let's read this hill as a valley, those two valleys as two hills, and then what have we got? Well, I thought, if that mark there is this hut, it is in a valley, which is correct, but the valley is pretty steep and this place, although in a valley, was not steep. The camp I was in was also in a valley and it was reasonably steep. Hey, I wonder if the mark was the camp. Well, let us see. When we left the camp that day we left in a northerly direction but how far did we travel before I fell, I dare not hazard a guess? How far did I travel after I left the old man on the track? I didn't know, or what is more, in which direction.

So, I thought, let us see what I did know. The truck I was behind took us out on to the Arctic ice, or so I thought; I was then cut loose. When I got up from the ice, I made my way back down the track to the old man. It could have only been a few hundred yards before I reached him. From there, I then took off at an angle to the left side of the road, I think in an easterly direction. I am right-handed, so I would tend to drift to my right as I walked. This would take me back towards the track. I remember going through some small stands of trees, about seven to eight feet tall. So what? They were either young trees or they were stunted, growing on the edge of the tree line. If I had crossed the track I would have been heading in a westerly direction, and

All For A King's Shilling

if I went far enough, I would be heading east again. So if I left the track heading in a south easterly direction, and drifted right all the time, I could have ended going due west at some time.

Now if that mark was the camp and this was the direction that we travelled behind the truck, then we would have left the area of the trees there, or thereabouts. Which was not the Arctic ice at all, but it was a lake. The next thing was, to work out how far out we went on to the lake. First, let's draw a line in a roughly northern direction from the camp, or what we thought might be the camp, out across the lake. Now let us pick two places. Say we went this far, and also let us say we went this far. So now here comes the clever bit. Let us say I left the track here and walked, stumbled off in this direction. I then started to drift to the right in a line like this, till I came back to the area where I started. Now if I did the same for the other place, I should end with two lines on the map.

All I had to do now was to search between these lines and I would then find this hut marked there somewhere, or so the theory went, and a merry Christmas to you too mate. Well, it's good stuff in theory, so God knew if it would work in practice. It had at least given me hope and was also something to fix my mind on to, something to stop me going off my head. So I then spent what I thought was some five or six hours looking for a place I could recognize, but I had to give up in the end. Even though I was not ready to admit it, I was completely lost; it was a dead certainty that I was. Tomorrow I would start again. What I needed most at this moment was sleep and some good food.

I was full of hope three days before I started looking for the hut on the map. For some reason, I had believed the person who had the hut and the map before me, the one whom I had killed, would at least have marked the hut on it. What was the sense of having a map if you did not mark your own position on it?

After a while I had marked out that many start points, I doubt if I could have found the bloody thing under all the lines I had drawn, anyway. Mind, I did have a perfect picture in my mind's eye of the area the map covered. I would know it the minute I laid my eyes on it, wherever it might be. The only thing I was convinced of was that the camp I had been in was some way off to the south east. With that information, I decided I should therefore be better heading off to the west. Then I hoped I would be in Norway in the not too distant future. I could be getting ready to make the biggest mistake of my life. I could be taking off in the wrong direction completely. If I had been held in the eastern side of Russia, then I would have one hell of a walk in front of me. If it turned out that was the case, then I would be better off making for Bear Island, or even Canada. I had decided to go straight over the Polar ice; not east or west along its edge, but straight north, then south until I reached perhaps Canada. For all my planning I kept getting the feeling I would end just wandering around out there until I reached oblivion. What was I talking about? Oblivion was not a place, was it? God, I must be going mad out here, my moods changed so very quickly these days.

Somehow, I don't know how, but I had got the hang of trapping, all my old survival training was starting to come back. I had started to eat fairly well, if a constant diet of meat can be called eating well. I did not know if I should have been eating these things or not, they did not seem to be doing me any harm. They were small things; I think we call them stoats in England. I could be completely wrong of course. When I had caught my first one I thought it was a large rat. In the camps I had eaten rats, so I thought why not? I am starving, and I need to eat something.

It did not take long before I began to feel fit enough to start the long walk, the longest walk I shall ever have undertaken in my life, or am ever likely to take, the walk out, that is. I was in better shape than I had been for a hell of a long time. So I made my mind up, I should be on my way in two days' time. Once I had made my mind up, I only hoped I was nearer to the west side of Russia than the east. The thought of taking the longest road home did not bear thinking about. It was important I put those thoughts completely out of my mind, right there and then.

So this was it, the day I was to start my walk had dawned fresh and clear, no storms and the sky was blue. That was a very good sign, blue sky. What better omen could I have wished for?

Packing did not take long, and I had packed what I believed to be a reasonable load, consisting of the food I had managed to save and some furs. At first I thought I could carry it all without being too much of a burden. After a little thought on the matter, I decided this was not so. I had made a small sledge from a cupboard which was in the hut. I had also rigged two sets of harness from bits of rope and leather straps. One was for the dog, and the other one for me. The dog was watching me all the time, so I told him if he wanted to eat, then he had to work. I think he understood me. We stood on the edge of the little clearing around the hut; I think the dog was as unsure about leaving as I was; he kept looking at me with his big eyes which seemed to say, "Are you sure you know what you are doing, pal?" For the last time I told him, 'yes' I did know what I was doing. As he looked at me, I hoped I sounded confident to him, more than I felt myself; I am not so sure I did.

I had built the fire up in the hut and it should burn for quite a long time, long enough for it still to be on should we decide to make it back. We had both decided to do this should the going get too tough. The dog seemed quite happy to pull the sledge. He hadn't been told yet, but if it had not been for him I would not have been able to take enough food for us to eat, or furs to keep us warm when we stopped to rest. For some reason I couldn't explain I was convinced I was to the west of the prison camp and also to the westernmost side of Russia. It was my belief I would not get any trouble from the camp. I felt so confident now that I was on my way home and I seemed to have found a new lease of life. What would I do when I got home was the question which kept coming to the fore these days? Oh, what thoughts, "Mush, mush, you silly Russian hound. No good just standing there looking at me; we are on our way home, so, mush."

Both the dog and I had now been going for about sixteen hours or so. What I was saying was, "I haven't got a bloody clue how long we have been going." It felt like two-thirds of the day, therefore the sixteen hours bit. There was clear sky and a little sun earlier in the day when we started and it cheered us up. Well, it cheered me up, so I told the dog, and it must have cheered him up as well. I think he agreed with me, he did not say he didn't, so I assumed all was well with him. I would have plotted my course by the sun using a watch as a compass, as they taught you in all the survival courses we all attended. The only problem was I did not have a watch. Some stinking Russian prison guard got it a long time ago. I pretended to read it anyway, I didn't want to upset the dog too much, I didn't want him to know I didn't have a watch. He would have twigged then that I didn't know really if I were in Russia or on the planet Mars, both of which are red, you know. You know what these Russians are like for Western watches and such. Then I had no reason to think their dogs were any different from them. Mind, I didn't think the dog noticed what I was up to; if he did, he didn't let on. Perhaps he was trying not to upset me too much. All the time I kept telling the dog we were just ahead of schedule and he seemed pleased with that. Once I told him if things went as well as this over the next week or so I would more than likely not have to eat him. That seemed to please him. Mind I did not like the grin he gave me after I told him that. I think he had thought of it the other way round. It was not long after this we decided to stop for the night. It was getting really cold now so we put up the little shelter of furs I had invented back at the hut. Well, I put the shelter up. That sod of a dog, well he just flopped in it and went to sleep. I then crawled in beside him and it was not long before we were both asleep. My lice were now feeding on him, and I think his had taken a liking for me. Still what are friends for if they can't share their lice?

When I awoke some time later I felt quite warm. The first thing I saw was the dog lying next to me, looking at me. He had that bloody grin on his face again and I thought, yes mate, I would have to keep an eye on you. I didn't like that bloody grin of yours. I tried not to let him know I was on to him though so I patted his head and stroked his side just to see how fat he really was. Not bad, I thought, you should keep me going for some time when the time did come.

With that, I took the shelter down and packed everything on to the sledge. Then I took a bit of frozen meat from the bag and put it in my pocket, as close to my body as I dared. Next I hooked the dog and myself to the sledge and away we went. It was quite dark but there were no clouds and I could make out some stars, one of which I took to be the Pole Star. So I set a course keeping it on my right shoulder. I told the dog what I was up to, so he could keep me right if I started to wander at all. During the course of the next few hours I would take the meat out. With great care I would break it into half and then hold them together to show my mate I was not robbing him of any of his share. I would give him his, which he would gulp down in one go, but I would chew mine as we walked, making it last a lot longer.

I have no idea of the distances we travelled those first few nights. But I had a feeling we were doing okay. We always followed the same system, walked for what we thought was about sixteen hours, then rested and slept until I awoke. Packed all the bits and pieces up, then put a piece of meat into my pocket and off we would go. When the piece of meat had softened enough, I would hand over his half to him and we would eat. He would gulp his half down in one then we would be off again. I would try and make my bit of meat last as long as possible. We would go for what we thought was another sixteen hours or so. Then I would try and suck a piece of snow or ice each night, once we had put the shelter up. I had to try and keep the liquid in my body. The idea came from the dog, who I noticed just licked the ice each night, which seemed to be plenty for him.

So it went on like this for perhaps fifteen to twenty days, by which time we were both becoming too tired to do much of anything. I did not think we were doing anything like five miles a day now. It looked as if the dog was too tired to eat me; I was certainly too far gone to have skinned the dog, had I taken it in my head to shoot him. We no longer put the shelter up when we stopped; we did not know if it was night or day. We just flopped down at the end of what we thought was a day and I just pulled the furs from the shelter over us wherever we lay, still tied to the little sledge we had pulled all this time. I had no idea how much longer we could go on and I thought as I went to sleep one night, after a particularly rough piece of ground we had crossed, really, I didn't care if I didn't wake in the morning. All the plans and thoughts of what I would do when I got back to Blighty had now left me. If I did not wake, I knew I would have given it my best shot; I knew the dog felt the same, and he was already asleep.

How long the dog slept I did not know, what I did know was when I came round the dog was not there. That I think was the lowest point for me; I really had become attached to the beast. Now he had seen fit to leave me and to make it on his own; I didn't blame him really. He had helped me, and now I was near to death he had left. He probably knew where the nearest village was and he could go there. I certainly could not go anywhere near a Russian village. So I pulled myself together and loaded up the furs on to the sledge and set off again.

As I walked, I took the last bit of meat I had in my clothes, and started to eat it. I think I was competing with the lice for the meat now. I did not know how long I stumbled along in a daze, trance or whatever. What I did know was the ground and countryside I was now passing through seemed familiar once it had got light. Exactly what set me off I did not know, but I was sure I had been in this place before. The more that I thought about it, as I stumbled on, the more I marvelled on how wonderful the human mind was. Here I was in the frozen wastes of Russia and I convinced myself I had been here before. Just to prove the point, I was stupid enough to close my eyes and slowly turn my head to the left.

I said to myself, "When you open your eyes there will be smoke rising from a small settlement over there about a mile away."

As I opened my eyes, I nearly shit myself, for the first time in days. There, about a mile away was a small settlement of four or five huts with smoke coming from them. As I looked, I thought, well it looks as if you have passed the first test to get into Heaven. Everything was clear, crystal white. Got to be heaven I thought, all white and such. I was still feeling a lot of pain though; I thought, when you get to Heaven there is no pain. Then it hit me, you stupid arsehole, it was a Russian settlement.

I fell to the ice and just lay there thinking. I thought I must have died. Then I knew I hadn't died. Perhaps I had shit myself, though. Slowly I raised my head and looked again in the direction of the huts. There was nothing there, I could not see them. Dreaming, my son, I said, it was all a mirage. As I lay there, shaking, I decided I had fooled around long enough, time I was on my feet and moving again. Slowly I raised myself from the ice and took another look just to put my mind at rest, and there I could see the smoke again. Once more I fell to the ice and just lay there, trembling with fear. Very slowly it started to dawn on me that the place was real, the reason I could not see it on the ice was because I was too low. You silly great shit, I thought, you are forgetting everything you have ever been taught. Line of sight is shorter when you are lying down than when you are standing up. I slowly rose to one knee, and sure enough there were the tops of the huts. Rise a little further and there were the huts in full view. As I looked towards the huts I slowly realised why I thought I knew

All For A King's Shilling

the place. It's the bloody map, I thought, the bloody map, it's the bloody map. With that I went to the sledge to get the map and another thought hit me, and it hit me right between the eyes.

No wonder the bloody dog had done a bunk; I had brought the damned thing home. Well, I had done one good deed for once in my life. One good deed, you stupid fool, if you have brought the dog home, then the wife, mother, father and all the other relations of the trapper I had killed would be looking for him. They would assume the dog had run ahead of him and they would be out looking for him. One thing for sure, I had better get to hell out of here, and at the bloody rush. I immediately moved off to the north, or what I thought would be the north. My idea was to put as much distance as possible between the settlement and me by the time it got dark. I thought I would stand a better chance in the dark of fighting my way out of whatever trouble I had now landed myself in. As I made my break I was moving at what I believed to be a good pace, the light was dimming and I thought I had made it. That I was making good progress I put down to the stupid idea of how well I knew the land, and it was because I had studied the map often enough, back at the hut. Just as I was starting to feel all right, and to think I had a chance, the bloody dog was there, trotting alongside me.

At first I did not get the real meaning of his presence, and then a voice asked me, "Are you lost, Comrade?"

In all the panic of trying to get away, I had lost the rifle. You know I did not even miss it until then; I didn't even make a move to defend myself. I was to learn later it saved my life. As I turned, standing by the sledge was the biggest bloody Russian I had ever seen. He held in his right hand a rifle, it was a new semi-automatic. I was pleased to see it was not pointed at me, he was holding it loosely in his right hand. What was more worrying, he looked as if he knew how to use it. It was at this point I collapsed, all I remembered was falling to the ice and the dog licking my face. I remember thinking, "What a wimp, at the crucial moment, you just faint," after that, I remember nothing.

Over the next few days some rather unexpected things happened to me. For one, I seem to remember eating hot food; I also remember being scrubbed by somebody, or perhaps two some bodies. At one point in the proceedings I had a steam bath and later on I had all my hair shaved off from head to foot by a young Russian woman. Being rolled in the snow a couple of times was another memory I have. What else they did to me I still do not know, other than the fact that they saved my life. They told me afterwards I was the nearest to death of anybody they had ever seen who had not died. They showed me a hole they had dug to bury me in. I had a funny feeling they were also giving me a message when they showed it to me. How long it took to get me round from death's door I would never know; what I did know was that they looked after me, they fed me, they gave me a good warm bed, they deloused me, and they gave me good Russian clothes to wear. The thing I remember most about the place was the warmth, the soft bed, and for the first time in years, a full belly.

I do believe the food was a problem in the beginning. It seemed I could not hold any of it down. I had vague memories of throwing all the food I tried to eat, back out again. As time passed I did start to keep some of it down, and my body no longer rejected the food. I ate like a horse. Everything they put in front of me was gulped down as if there would be no more.

They told me afterwards the way I ate gave me away. They soon realized I was from the camps. When they told me that, I started to think they were fattening me up for the kill. They would send for the GRU, KGB, or the Militia as soon as the weather improved. I thought they were no different from any other Russians I had met to date. Most of them, if not all, were just as afraid of their own authorities as any outsiders were.

The main thing as far as I was concerned now was they were feeding me, feeding me as I could not have fed myself. More to the point, the fitter I got, the better my chance of getting away. So I decided to go along with them at this moment in time. Just so long as nobody had left the village, I felt I was okay. It never entered my head for one minute that they might have already sent a message out by radio or some other means. For all I knew a Russian helicopter could be on its way to pick me up. The other thing was, not one of them had asked me how I had come by the dog, or what had happened to his previous owner.

Time was presenting me with problems. I was having great trouble with it; once more I must admit, I had lost all track of it. I was starting to put some weight on; and now I had stopped pigging my food when I ate. From that alone I deduced I had been there a while. Most of the people had started to look at me in a better light. Spring was near as the weather was improving and it was getting warmer. The days were getting a little longer, and the snow and ice was starting to melt. It was still damned cold, but nothing like the cold I had suffered in the camps these last few years. The weather was no warmer than any other year at this time. It was just that I was fitter and better fed, so I was able to stand the cold better. Mind you, I had always suffered from the cold ever since my first visit to Murmansk Bay all those years ago.

I was sitting one day on the step of the hut they had me living in, just resting and soaking in the lovely fresh air of the place, when I heard a sound, a sound I had listened for ever since I had first returned to reality. A sound I had been certain would one day come and now it had. At first, I must admit it gave me an attack of instant fear. I started to look for a place to run and hide; I must admit I was terrified.

I was just going to say thank you very much, my friends, when the man who had found me on the ice came running across from his hut. I thought this was it. "Come with me, keep quiet, don't speak, just do as you are told, if you want to live, that is," he said.

For the life of me, I did not know what made me do as he said, but like the lamb I had become, I did. I got up and followed him to one of the other huts. We went round the back of the hut and he pulled the logs away from against the wall. He was now shouting in perfect English. "For God's sake, give me a bloody hand."

He was also calling me some very rude names in the process; I just looked at him in amazement. I thought it looked as if he had found out something, so you had better just go with it mate, you might as well, you had no other choice really.

Together we managed to get all of the logs cleared and he opened a door in the wall of the hut, a door which I did not see until he opened it, it was so well disguised. I was pushed through the door by the big fellow, and then with no further ado he slammed the door closed behind me.

All For A King's Shilling

Then, he shouted to me through the door as it closed, "You are not to make any noise at all, because if you were to do so, you could be the cause of every person in this community being shot!"

Then he was gone; I was alone in the dark, under the hut, not knowing what the hell was going on. He also said he would come for me later. As the door had closed, I thought you bloody fool, he has locked you up and you bloody let him. What sort of a stupid shit are you turning into? That English was probably just a shot in the dark and you fell for it. God alone knew what sort of a bargain he was conducting now for your hide, you fool. What had you done, you had trusted strangers, and Russian strangers at that. I was on the point of shouting out and cussing him, the way he had cussed me. For some reason I shall never know, I didn't, I just sat in a corner and thought and here we bloody go again. At that moment I think I could have cried, I thought of Katrine for the first time in days and the tears fell from my face.

How long I sat in that frame of mind I will never know, but it could have only been seconds. When I came back to reality I heard a very loud sound to the left side of the hut. The sound turned out to be what I thought, a helicopter. It was now landing not fifty yards from where I was hiding. My only hope was that at least I was hiding, and not a prisoner again.

The only kind of helicopter landing in this place would be a Russian military one, and a GRU one at that. Now the GRU knew all about me, so my mind automatically knew they could only have come for me. The only reason these people had fed me and looked after me was because I would be easier to look after if I were fed, watered and kept warm. None of them had asked me anything, who I was, where I came from, or anything like that. They didn't need to, did they? Somehow, they knew I was English, otherwise why had the big man spoken to me in English? I still may have saved the day; at least I had not answered him at all. Oh, no, you hadn't answered him, no, you just stood there with your great stupid mouth open. What a stupid shit I had turned into, I thought. God, if I had a box of matches I would burn the bloody lot down. I moved to the side of the door and just sat saying over and over again, "Shit! shit! shit! shit!"

I sat there for a while and tried to think of what to do; I was in the underneath part of the big man's hut. It was dark in here; it was divided up into three rooms. After a while I felt my way around the place. It was also bloody cold. It looked as if he kept his supplies in here, there seemed to be some foodstuffs and some old clothing. Among the old clothing I found an old fur coat and wrapped myself in it. Then I settled down to await them coming to collect me and take me away in the helicopter. I was convinced that was what would happen, but at least I felt warmer in the old coat. Well, I thought, this coat would serve me well when they put me back in the camps.

Some time later, I am not sure when, as I had fallen asleep, I heard the wood outside the door being moved as if somebody was going to open the door. This was my last chance, I thought, whoever it is coming in would not be able to see me at first in the dark. That's when I make my bid to get away, so I took up a position just inside the door and slightly to the right as I looked at it. When I saw the figure silhouetted in the doorway, I made a grab for it. As I got hold of the figure, I got one hell of a shock. It was a woman whom I had pulled in; I had her by the neck and I was applying pressure to it. I was going to strangle her. With great difficulty I just managed to stop myself at the last moment. It just was not worth it. If I killed her, I would have become an animal pure and simple, just an animal at that moment. Really, I had just about sunk to the bottom of the pit. I felt I had lost the last traces of any dignity I had ever had. For some reason, I know not why, I held her close to me in a massive bear hug and I think I regained some of my humanity if I ever had such a thing. As I let her go she reached past me and pulled the door shut. Then she sat and gasped for air. I do not think she was amused at all; I had nearly killed her after all the help she and the others had given me when they had found me lost and three quarters dead on the ice, that I should repay them by killing one of them; then to my surprise she came and sat next to me and snuggled in close to me and put her arm through mine. We sat like that for some little while; I suppose we were both deep in thought.

Some short time later she whispered to me, "Keep very quiet. The Russian pilot and his crew are up in the hut above your head. There are ten of them and they will be leaving in the morning, as soon as it gets light. So keep as still as you can and don't make any noise. Uri is giving them vodka, but the pilot won't drink. So, please keep quiet, or we will all die. I've brought you some food, but all there is, is cold leftovers."

It was at this news I remembered I was hungry and with that she opened the door and slipped out into the darkness which had fallen. I could not get over the lack of any animosity to- wards me. She carried on as if I had not done her, or meant her, any harm at all. Yet I had nearly killed her, and as I munched the cold scraps of food I mulled over and over her attitude towards me. I just couldn't believe it.

The next morning things were as she had said; the helicopter took off and she, not the big fellow, came to collect me. As she took me up into the house above, I tried to apologise for what I had done the night before. She would hear none of it, said I was not to worry and it was only natural I should feel that way towards them. After all, I did not know the full situation in the village.

As I walked into the hut, I realised it was showdown time. The whole settlement was sitting behind a large table made from a single log of wood. As I looked at them, I remember thinking they didn't get that log from here; I had never seen a tree this far north from which a log that size could have come. I was right about one thing, it was showdown time. The big fellow pointed to a chair in the middle of the room and I sat in it. So, I thought, he was the leader or a political commissar, or whatever they called them here.

"Okay," I said, "It's question time, I realise that, but first before we get too political about it all, please tell me where I am?"

Before anybody could answer, "I think I am not too far from Naryan Mar. I am probably wrong, but that's what I think."

The big fellow grinned, the first time I had seen him grin since we met that day out on the ice. "Yes," he said, "not too far; in fact had you kept on walking, or more to the point, had you been able to keep on walking, you would have eventually walked right down the main street and you would have been in big trouble then my friend. Now perhaps you will tell us who you really are and why you came our way and with Valdansk's dog?"

"He seems to like you better than he ever liked Valdansk," said a kindly-looking old man sitting in the corner.

All For A King's Shilling

"Enough now, talk," said the big fellow, "and no bullshit."

I had to think hard and fast. I had been toying with the idea when the big man was talking as to what cock and bull story I could tell them. Or should I tell them everything! Then when I looked at them sitting there, I thought you are going to hear just what you want to hear. For some reason you had not turned me in. If I told you everything about myself, that might change. I believed the reason you had not turned me in must be that you were at odds with the Government of Russia yourselves, or you had something to hide. It might be that you were playing a bigger game than I had ever been involved in. Whatever the reason, you had not turned me in, but you had been told something by your visitors that had set you on the question trail. Well, as one of my instructors once told me, "If you have to explain your presence or anything like that tell the truth and just embellish it a little and you will get away with it. If you make a story up always remember facts can be checked out, so tell the truth, and just leave little bits out here and there."

So here goes, let us see if you could buy this tale.

"Well, it all started some six years ago, when I lived in Moscow. A very good friend of mine got himself arrested. All he was doing was crossing the middle of Red Square, and for some reason they jumped on him as if he was a common criminal. It resulted in his being sentenced to a ten-year prison term, for something which he had not done."

There was not a flicker of recognition of that situation on any of the faces behind the table which gave me encouragement that I might be on the right trail, so I went on.

"It was all on the word of a no-good layabout who, although he had a job, wouldn't work. I could not understand how in our Great Motherland this type of thing could happen. I was incensed, so I decided to put things right. More to the point, I intended to get my friend released." As I looked around the room, there still was no sign of life from them, but on one or two faces a slight look of understanding.

"Well, that was when my troubles really started. You could not believe the things that have happened to me. Things I did not believe could have happened in our Great Motherland. Of course I did not know the layabout who had testified against my friend was in fact a party member."

This brought a little murmur of understanding.

"It so happened that he was a well-liked, and much respected man. He was a member of the party which it seemed entitled him to be a professional layabout and informant – you name it. This man had friends in high places, so it was only a matter of time before I was denounced myself.

"So that was how I ended in the hands of the KGB, and for the last six or seven years I have been moved from prison to prison without so much as a trial in a court of law or anywhere else, or ever having been charged with any offence. I have been beaten and abused by any guard who had a grudge to bear and in all this time I was never put on trial, yet here I was in prison. Then one day at muster a prison guard read out my sentence, ten years' hard labour. I protested my innocence, only to be frogmarched to see a more senior guard, who doubled my sentence. So I decided to fight back. That was when my troubles really started. Before long I was in the labour camps.

"At first it was not too bad. The camp I was in was in the south of the country and although it got cold in the winter, it was nothing like you get up here. As I was to find out, it was not as cold in the winter there as it is in the summer up here. Yes, Comrades, the people in the south (both prisoners and non prisoners) have it very easy. I did okay, though, I met my work quotas and I managed to get by, even with the shortage of food in the camps. We used to say in the camps we got short rations, so god help those patriots outside the camps."

I hesitated here and glanced round the room. I could see no hostility in their faces so I went on. "The day came when they told me I was going to be released and I was going to another place to be rehabilitated before being sent back to Moscow. So it was with this in my mind and believing that justice would prevail in the end that I willingly boarded the train. We were all to be rehabilitated, so we were all happy, we were talking about what we intended to do once we got back to Moscow. Some were even singing. I had completely forgotten about the friend to whom I owed my predicament; I was too happy to be going back to my wife and family."

There was a nod or two among them and the old sigh of recognition of my situation.

"It wasn't until the weather started to get very cold on the sixth day of the journey that eventually the realization hit me that there were a hell of a lot of people who needed to be rehabilitated – an unrealistic number to be sure. We started to get a little worried, more than a little worried really. When the train stopped that night so that we could be fed, we asked the people feeding us if they knew where we were headed. Not one of us believed what they told us; it could not be possible. We just could not believe what they told us."

"Don't you know? You have lasted too long in the south, you are going to the Arctic, you won't last much longer up there."

"What hurt most was they laughed as they told us. They were laughing at our misfortune and at the fact that most if not all of us were going to certain death. I remember thinking that not only had the people in the camps been brutalized but the whole damned nation had. There was no sorrow from them; it was all a joke to them. A train full of their fellow Russians being sent to their deaths and they thought it a joke. Mostly for non-existent crimes and they thought it was funny. I just let my plate fall to the ground and somehow I managed to get back on to the train. I found a place in the corner and just sat on the wooden floor."

I stopped there and looked around the room. Some of them showed sympathy towards me, but the rest were non-committal or they were bloody good poker players.

"So it was I arrived in the camps in the Arctic, the camps with no wire. It was not long before I learned why there was no wire round these Arctic camps and I also learned why the guards were there. You see, the guards were there to be punished themselves. You had no chance. They were not happy at being there, and they took it out on the prisoners. I was moved from camp to camp, I learnt to eat rats or anything else that lay down and died near me."

`At this point I stopped talking for a while; I just sat and looked at them.

All For A King's Shilling

Nobody spoke for what must have been half an hour or more. Then one of the older men asked me how I had come by the dog. I thought this was it; they seemed to have bought the first bit, now for the rest.

"Well," I said. "That was something else. Some time ago, not long after the first heavy snows, another four inmates and I were tied behind a truck. We then set off on what we all thought at first was a journey to another camp. We set off at a walk at first, but once out of the camp the truck speeded up and we had to trot to stay on our feet.

"The further we went, the more the truck seemed to speed up and we had to go faster. When one of us fell he was dragged for a while. The guard made no attempt to stop the truck to help us get back on our feet. Then when the prisoner no longer showed signs of life, the guard sitting in the back of the truck just cut the rope. I did not see who was the first one of us who fell, I was too busy getting my breath back after the initial run. I did see the second one go, though; he was an old man who had been in the camps for years. It looked to me as if he must have given in at last. The poor man had spent the best part of his life in these camps, now the poor bastard was being dragged along on the ice behind a prison truck. So I was stumbling along, trying to miss him as he swung from side to side. It was not to protect him, but to stop myself tripping over him and ending up on the ice along with him. There was no way he would ever get up again. It was then the idea for my escape came to me. I thought this could be a way out, one way or the other it was my way out.

"So I decided to take the chance. I let myself fall to the ice; I had to make it look good. So I tried to fight against it just long enough to make it look good. The problem was that I got myself knocked out on a lump of ice and it nearly was the end for me. When I came to I made my way back down the vehicle track until I found the old man who had fallen before I did. He was stone dead and I managed to get him off the road and stripped off his clothing. I had just finished putting this on top of my old rags when the truck came back. It had four lumps of rope hanging over the tailboard. When it had passed me, I then wandered off into the dark clothed in two lots of clothing and wearing, for the first time in years, a good pair of boots that I had taken off the old man.

"Just how long I wandered I do not know but eventually I arrived at a hut, a hut with a starving dog tied up outside it. I went into the hut and fell asleep. It must have been two days later, or even more, when at last I came to. The dog was nearly dead, and so was I. After a little while I decided I had better pull myself together and try and get something to eat. As I rummaged about the hut I found some oil, and some matches, things I had not seen for years. Then at last I managed to get the lamp going, and then the fire. It took a little longer to find the food, mostly frozen meat, what kind I did not know. The main thing was it was food. Both the dog and I were sick after having eaten some of it, but by the fourth or fifth meal we were able to keep it down, and we both started to recover.

"We heard wolves baying in the area quite a lot and decided they had probably got who ever it was who lived here. It was some time later. I had managed to trap some animals, and both the dog and I started to get better. We were no longer sick when we had a meal and both of us put on weight. It was at this point, when I decided we had a goodly supply of meat, that both the dog and I decided to move on and perhaps find some other human beings who could help us get back to civilization. So we packed what we could and set off to walk out of the hell-hole in which we had both found ourselves. How long we walked before the dog took off I do not know.

"I know I was down to my last bit of frozen meat and I was wandering around completely lost when I heard a man talking to me. Even now I could not tell you what he said, but I felt relieved to hear another human voice, so much so that I did not care if it was the police, army or KGB who was talking to me, and I must assume it was one of you who found me. What happened after that, you all know better than I do?"

The silence in the hut was deafening in the extreme. They just sat and looked at me; I had to force myself to stop squirming on my seat. I knew that should I show any form of worry they would not believe me. At last, after what seemed like an hour, but could have only been minutes, I was asked, "Did you see any sign of the trapper Valdansk, surely he was there at the hut?"

I just replied, "I saw nobody at the hut. It was empty, it was cold, there was no fire on, or lamps lit. It looked as if it had been left for quite some time. The dog, as you can see, is not the fattest of dogs, but he was just skin and bone when I found him and the hut. In fact, the dog could not even bark when I came round after first collapsing in the hut. As to this Valdansk guy well, I have never laid eyes on him at all."

One of the older men said at this point, "You are very lucky not to have met him, he killed people for pleasure. If he had been there, he would have killed you with no thought, just like swatting a fly."

"If you have spent the time in the camps as you claim you have and you were as weak as you say, then there is no way you met Valdansk," an old man said.

"You would have been dead within seconds of him seeing you," said another of the older men.

"It must be that Valdansk had gone out to set traps, or to tend his traps in a drunken state; he was nearly always drunk, and he must have had an accident and perhaps frozen to death," another of the older men said.

I thought I was lucky when I met this guy Valdansk, if it was Valdansk, which I was beginning to doubt. He had not put up much of a fight for a man with such a reputation, so he must have been drunk out of his mind when I killed him, or it wasn't Valdansk I had killed. I wondered if some other person had killed Valdansk before I got there. That might explain the ease with which I disposed of the man at the hut, whosoever he had been.

Even so, I was not going to tell them what had really happened at the hut. It could have been one of the members of this village who had gone out there and killed him for all I knew. No, I made my mind up; I was not going to say any more about it. I then noticed the big fellow was staring at me; he had a rather cynical look on his face. It was then I realised that perhaps he had killed Valdansk. I do not know how, or when, but I just had an idea he had done it.

They did not seem to hold any animosity towards me, for which I was glad. I felt I could ask them, "Why have you chosen now to ask me where I was from and who I was? Was it because of the people in the helicopter?" I asked.

They then told me, "The helicopter was on its way to Naryan Mar and had called here because they had come to collect Valdansk. The authorities ordered them to pick him up and take him there. He was to be questioned about something he had done there before he took off into the wilderness when the winter started. What he had done the crew didn't know, but it was the first chance they had of getting out here, because of the weather."

One of the old men said, "He has probably killed somebody, that is what he seems to do most of the time; if it's not animals he is killing, it's humans."

At that point I was glad I didn't adopt the name Valdansk, or I could end in a worse situation than I was in already. It also began to dawn on me that as far as the authorities were concerned I no longer existed. I'd died out on the ice. They would no longer even be looking for me. What was more, I now had an idea just what part of Russia I was in. So I was about six hundred miles east of the border between Russia and Norway. Six hundred miles. I just thought, only six hundred miles to go. Not even the length of the British Isles. I really felt elated now, and I just hoped I did not show it too much. Then I was brought back to reality by the big man. He was telling me, "Go with 'Sharon', she will look after you while the committee decide what to do with you."

So that was it, I left the hut with the girl who had brought me the food last night, the girl I had nearly strangled. She took me to her hut, which I'd been staying in since I had come round the other week. At least I thought it was a week or more ago. As I said, I had lost all track of time. I had not realised that the hut was hers.

When we arrived in the hut, I asked her if there was any chance of something to eat and drink, as I had not eaten so far today. She told me that if my story had not been good enough, I would not have had anything else to eat ever. With that she made me a bowl of porridge-like stuff, and some hot sweet tea, for which I had developed quite a taste. As I was eating, she sat at the table and asked, "How long have you been in Russia?"

"That is a funny question, after I have just told you how my friend was falsely accused and how I got into all this trouble over him. I have been in Russia all my life."

"Well," she said, "If that is so why, when you dream and have nightmares and you curse and swear revenge when you are asleep, do you do it in English?"

With this, I stopped dead in my tracks, and just looked at her. I had my mouth half full of her porridge, the spoon halfway between my mouth and the plate, and I just looked at her.

After a while she laughed and said, "It's all right, Uri doesn't know, I haven't told anybody here, I've kept it to myself."

You could have knocked me off the chair with a feather; I was completely taken aback. Just what could I say. I had hesitated too long in giving an answer to the girl and so I'd given myself away in the end. Within a couple of weeks, living among real Russians, I had given myself away completely. As I looked at this girl I thought it was all over now, they were probably making arrangements to hand me over to the regional committee right now. They would be certain to get more Brownie points from the local committee than the KGB, GRU or the Police. That was why they had hidden me from the helicopter and its crew.

She must have seen the resignation on my face, for it must have been a picture. She said, "Don't worry; I haven't told anybody; you will be safe with us for a while.

They believe you and they will help to get you out of Russia. That, though, I am afraid, is easier said than done. If it was easy, we would all have gone years ago."

I was about to speak to her when she put her fingers to my mouth. At that contact, we both trembled, just a little, and I think our reactions to the touch shook both of us a little. Then at last she broke the moment as she gently stroked the beard on my cheek. "No, it is better I know little or nothing about you. If they question me, the less I know of you the better," she concluded.

Then she said, "You know you only gave yourself away for a couple of seconds. If I'd not been an ex English teacher I would not have known what language you were talking. Do not blame yourself; you were near to death when we got you in here."

"What about the big fellow?" I said. "He knows something. I can tell by the way he let me ramble on like that. He was staring at me all the time I was telling that story."

"Never mind him, stop talking and eat your food before it gets cold. It is better the rest of the people think your story is true. That way will keep it safe. After all they are nothing more than old gossips."

With that I tucked into the best food I had tasted since I arrived at the place. One thing did worry me about the whole situation. If they were as anti Russian as they tried to make out, how come the Russians did not know about it. They had spies everywhere, that was the main reason we could never put any successful spies into this Godforsaken place. The local spy is on to you like a shot. They would do anything for a little praise in the commune's eyes no matter what happened to those they denounced. Mind, I was still free, or thought I was, only time would tell when I tried to leave the place. Then the bitter truth would out, if it was to be bitter, that is. In the meantime I enjoyed my meal and for the first time for years I fancied a woman. Not any of the women they have here, mind you. I could not face these women, except perhaps the one who just aroused my desire for the first time in years, Katrine, the woman who had helped me all those years before. She was perhaps still languishing in a filthy camp in this Godforsaken land.

Chapter Fifteen
The Desk Jockey Dismounts And World War IV Nearly Starts
Whitehall

If Old Soldiers never die.
Then they just "Get in the bloody way".

It was early the next day before Graham had at last completed reading the bundle of assorted scraps of paper which Mr Cogan had given him. Graham now believed he understood as best he could the contents of the papers that he had just read. Finally he put the last of the sheets on which the story was scribbled face down on top of the pile. Then he diligently shuffled them into a neat pack, as one would a pack of cards, and turned them over. He looked at them for quite some time while all manner of thoughts passed through his mind. Eventually he leaned back in his chair and he felt that he was now as conversant with the story which he had just read as he was ever going to be.

There was one rather perplexing and somewhat worrying part of the story that he found frightening, to say the least. Could it be that this Colour Sergeant of Marines who it was said had written these notes, had unwittingly stumbled across one of the biggest stings the intelligence world had ever seen? Was it possible that the Russian security services, both the GRU and the KGB, had been sending groups of agents into Britain at six month intervals? Sending them under the guise of British servicemen who were returning home from some overseas posting. God, he thought suddenly, what had happened to all the men we had been sending out there every six or seven months as regularly as clockwork?

After a while he collected the scraps of notepaper and the notes that he had made together and locked them away in his briefcase. This in turn he secured in his safe, having first had the presence of mind to change the combination. Then, satisfied with what he had done, he made his way to the washroom and started to have a wash and shave. Time I had a talk with my superior, he mused as he looked at the haggard face staring back at him from the mirror. A wry smile crossed his face as he realised his boss was not going to like this story one little bit. This was going to be a meeting which he knew he was really going to enjoy, he mused as he put his razor to his face. He was looking forward to this meeting more than any he'd had these last few years.

Having eventually completed his ablutions he realized as he straightened his tie that for the first time in years he hadn't cut himself whilst shaving. As he left the washroom he had a spring in his step, for the first time in years.

When he returned to his office he made a list of all the people his superior would have to arrange for him to see. Protocol would have to be followed if he was to get anywhere with this little lot, he mused. He'd have to see somebody in the Royal Marine Office and the Naval Intelligence Office for a start. Also he would have to see somebody from the Foreign and Commonwealth Office and MI6. Oh, he thought, and somebody in our own organisation. Lord, but he was going to enjoy this day's work. His superior would not, but by hell he knew he would. He was going to enjoy watching him try and squirm his way out of this one.

Standing up, he crossed to the table by his window and made himself another cup of coffee. Then he went back to his desk and made a note that he would have to visit Norway. He made another note for one of his staff to check Somerset House for all traces of this Colour Sergeant Johnston's birth certificate. He would also need Colour Sergeant Johnston's father's and mother's birth certificates and wedding certificate if they existed. He needed to know everything there was to know about this Johnston family. He very much doubted that Johnston was indeed their correct name.

Satisfied with his planning, he then rang his superior's secretary and arranged a meeting for ten o'clock that morning. Then he left his office and went out to have his breakfast at one of the many cafes situated in this central area of London.

Graham arrived for his meeting with his superior one minute early and the meeting was something else! In his usual brusque way, Graham pulled no punches as he presented his conclusions and summarised what he believed had being going on for years. He pointed out that it would still be ongoing to this day if this supposed Colour Sergeant Johnston had not put an abrupt end to it all by blowing up the place in Russia. As he made his report he could see his superior was in a state of utter panic. He watched the man's face first go that sickly white faces go just before fainting. Then slowly he developed a twitch under his right eye. The more the enormity of what he was being told started to sink in, the more rapid became the twitch. While he talked Graham was fascinated by the effect his report was having on the man. He also knew by instinct that his superior's brain was now locked into thinking only of his promotion and his subsequent knighthood. Something which Graham, too, could see disappearing over the horizon if his superior didn't handle this problem carefully. Another high-flyer without a knighthood, the idea was beginning to please Graham, but unfortunately he knew that in the end he would have to help the man. He did intend to see the man squirm somewhat before he helped him, though.

His superior was beginning to think he had made a bad move by accepting responsibility for this department, a department that he knew so little about, but he had seen so many of his older colleagues gain their knighthoods this way that he had followed their lead. He had the audacity at one point during the meeting weakly to suggest to Graham that he shred everything and get rid of Boris to the Americans on the next plane out of Heathrow; a suggestion which Graham completely ignored.

All For A King's Shilling

The whole of the meeting was a bit of a laugh and Graham enjoyed it all the more because of the reaction he had elicited from his superior. Well, enjoyment was a little bit of an understatement, ecstatic was a better description of his feelings. He liked nothing more than to see one of the civil service high-flyers in trouble.

Graham had an inherent dislike of people who rode the elevator of success on the backs of hardworking, loyal civil servants. There were still some staff in the Civil Service who diligently did their jobs, day in and day out, regardless of the abuse they had to put up with from these nerds who considered themselves superior in all respects to the staff they controlled. To bring down one of these pariahs would be worth all the unpopularity which it would bring down on to his head. Unfortunately, to Graham's mind the more frightening scenario was that the rest of the department and he might just be stuck with the man until time immemorial. If this investigation was to turn into a fiasco the department would be stuck with the fool for ever. This thought was too much even for Graham, so he resolved to get it all sorted. He would sort it in a way that would make his boss look reasonable, but it would leave a slight trace of the brown stuff, which is always guaranteed to ruin a civil service career. Well, just enough of the brown stuff to make the man suspect and to stop the jolly old knighthood from ever landing on the fool's shoulders. Maybe just enough of the brown stuff to elicit an early retirement from his boss!

So, as Graham placed his list on to his superior's desk, he told him he needed him to arrange meetings with MI6, the Army, the Navy's intelligence department and everybody else on the list. His first priority was to clear up conclusively if the operations in Northern Russia and the actions in Borneo and in Singapore that were mentioned in the scribbling did really take place. He needed to know if the people mentioned in the scribbled notes really did exist and were not all fiction. Graham had to make certain it was not all fiction tumbling around in the imagination of some Russian nutcase who was locked away deep in the bowels of the KGB or the GRU.

It was then that he dropped the bombshell he had purposely kept until the end. At the door he turned and told his boss that he believed the answer to the killings in London and the Home Counties lay with the Carl character, the man it seemed was a member of the Norwegian Secret Service. As the Norwegian Service had been having troubles with double agents of their own of late he felt that they would be only too pleased to help the department. So he concluded that as he would need their clearance to visit Northern Norway, Oslo would be unlikely to raise any objections. What's more, he believed now that Boris would have to remain where he was until this entire thing was resolved.

Reluctantly Graham's superior agreed to all of his requests. While he walked back to his own office he had a distinct feeling that his superior would be going home on sick leave before the day was out. He had been back at his desk for only a few minutes when he received a call from MI6 asking him to go round that very afternoon.

Shortly after that he had a call from his colleague who was at Somerset House. It turned out that Colour Sergeant Johnston was not the man's original name. It had been changed when he was four years old. His father had changed his name by deed poll in 1934. His father's name was Johansson. This Johansson had been born in Norway of a Scottish mother and a Norwegian father. The family had returned to Scotland after the First World War and had become farmers in the north of England. This Colour

Sergeant Johnston was born at Fourstones, a small village in Northumberland on the North Tyne.

Next, Graham told his colleague to dig out all he could about the family and then come back to the office. Over the next half hour he received appointments with all the other departments with which he had requested meetings. He found it strange that all these departments who normally wouldn't give him the time of day were suddenly so helpful. Making himself another cup of coffee, he settled back in his chair. As he raised the cup to his lips the phone rang. This time it was MI6 again. They were not very subtle in their approach as they suggested they should take over the case from his department.

It was at this suggestion Graham thought it was time he had a word in an ear or two further up the pecking order than his own boss. Shortly after he made these calls, MI6 rang back to confirm their afternoon appointment with him. In passing the caller remarked that on second thoughts he might be the best person to get to the bottom of the affair. Replacing the receiver, Graham smiled as he thought this old fool still had some pull around the old city.

Within two days he had not only all the details on the missing Royal Marine Colour Sergeant, but also on his family. MI6 had allowed him to read a file on the man's father and mother. It contained a report of their activities working for the allies during the First World War. Also, details of his father having travelled Nazi-occupied Europe as he continued his activities during the Second World War. His wife had also worked with her husband during this time. In 1939 William Johnston and his sister were sent to Sweden to spend the war years with their mother's mother and returned to the UK in the autumn of 1945. Then the MI6 official had shown him the files they held on the two characters whom the Colour Sergeant had reportedly killed. He was surprised to note that MI6 had not known that the two who were killed were in truth Russian agents, something they had only discovered when examining the effects of the two deceased. One of the men had died in London and the other had been shot in a farmhouse in the Home Counties along with a group of ex-servicemen whom he had been employing in some kind of security firm he was trying to set up.

It was when he returned to his office the next day after his meeting with MI6 that he was told the Norwegians were only too pleased for him to visit Norway. Graham could hardly believe his luck. It was like Christmas again. He had one last interview with Boris to tell him his trip to the States was off for at least a fortnight, something which didn't seem to upset Boris very much! Another thing that seemed odd to Graham, but he let it pass.

Graham's colleague had already been out and about getting him some suitable clothing for his visit to the Arctic Circle. That night he had one last meeting with his staff, when he told them what had been going on. He then told them that they were to continue trying to trace any of the men who had served in the OP in Russia. He needed to know what they had done since returning, how many had left the service and how many were still in the service and what jobs they were all doing now, in or out of the service. Graham felt there was a pattern, a key or something to be found in that information. Then with all his new Arctic clothing from Harrods he left for Heathrow and a flight to Norway.

All For A King's Shilling

When he stepped off the plane in Norway he was met by a middle-aged man from the Norwegian secret service. Graham was whisked away by this man to an office in the centre of Oslo. There he was to meet a man to whom he took an instant dislike. Graham had this feeling that there was something wrong with the setup. He was asked about the reason for his visit, a question which surprised him a little. Graham had been given a cover story for his visit by the Norwegian secret service – that he was in Norway to arrange Arctic holiday trips to the northern coast and trips to Bear Island.

Well, if these two were Norwegian secret service members they should already know that. Graham kept to his story and after a little while he was taken to a hotel in Oslo and left with his bags on the steps of the place. As the car disappeared into the night, Graham looked at the back of it. Well, he thought, if this was the life the operatives led in the field then he was glad he was just an office wallah.

Picking up his bags, he entered the hotel to be greeted by a tall blond young man in his late twenties. The man asked him, "Why are you late, your flight landed three hours ago?"

"I've just had an interview with some of your secret service men, that's why I'm late, and just who might you be, young man?"

"Me? Mr. Watkins, I'm your secret service contact and whoever it was who interviewed you they were not from our secret service. I'll get you settled in and then you will have to give me descriptions of these two men."

Graham looked at the young man for a moment and thought what in hell's name have I let myself in for and at my age? He said to the young man, though, "Tell me how long it will be before I can make my way to Kirkenes? The sooner I get this sorted, the sooner I can get back to the comfort of my desk."

"The ferry leaves Bergen for Tromso in the North tomorrow night. You will have to spend one night in Tromso, and then you catch a small coastal freighter for Kirkenes."

"Good!" Graham said. "Now perhaps I can get some sleep and if you can call me in time to catch the train to Bergen in the morning, I would be grateful."

The young man nodded and left the room. Outside he looked at his colleague and just shook his head. He was a little perturbed that this man from England who had been abducted by two people posing as Norwegian security men didn't realise the danger he was in. No wonder the British had trouble catching spies he thought as he made his way to the room his boss was using further along the corridor.

When he entered the room he saw by the grin on his boss's face that he had been listening to the conversation he had just had. "Don't worry, Jan, we will send this fool on his way north tomorrow. Carl and his sister can deal with him. Remember we mustn't let him take our friend Johansson. Don't worry, everything will be all right, you will see."

Early next morning the young man helped Graham on to the train bound for Bergen. Another member of the security service was already installed in the compartment when the two arrived. Glad to be rid of his charge, the young man watched the train leave and then headed back to the car waiting outside the station.

Later that evening Graham was asleep in his cabin on the ferry as it headed relentlessly northwards up the Norwegian coast. The Norwegian Secret Service had withdrawn all their men from covering his movements. They had decided to just let the game be played out to its natural end

---

Four days later
Kirkenes, Northern Norway!
The Cabin of Mr and Mrs Johansson, Mink Farmers

This last winter had been very severe and both Katrine and I had hardly been out of the house at all. The only trips we did make were to visit Carl and one or two other friends we had made since our arrival here. Oh, and of course we had to feed our livestock.

Carl first told us when the winter had started to lift that he had been asked to go back on the fishing boats for a while. The authorities told him that they were a member short on Roald's boat and he had accepted. Both Katrine and I knew what that meant, he would be trawling the seas off Northern Russia again looking for any human flotsam which turned up occasionally. They would also be logging Russian shipping movements. Keeping an eye on Red Navinski! they called it, but it was a bloody dangerous pastime.

Katrine and I were both surprised when he said he was going, especially after what we had just been through in England. "Are you sure this is what you want to do, Carl? After all, we do have enough money for all our needs. You don't have to go to sea again."

"Yes, I know that, but they say they need me and I can't let them down, can I?"

"Of course you can let them down, Carl, they should leave you alone. You are soon to be Uncle Carl, so we can't have you running off all over the place on a fishing boat, can we?" Katrine said.

As I looked at Carl, he grinned and said, "You are an old rascal, this calls for a drink."

"I am not drinking any of that bloody homemade stuff you have Carl, I don't want to go blind just yet, thank you."

At this we both fell around laughing our heads off. I tried to talk him out of going back to sea, but it was obvious his mind was made up. It would only be a matter of a couple of days before the bay was open, and as soon as it was Carl would be off. I thought there was no point in arguing with him anyway.

So the next day a brand new fishing boat that was very well equipped with all the latest electronic equipment slowly edged its way into the bay. Even though the bay was not completely free of ice it eventually managed to break the ice by the jetty and tie up. Well, Katrine, Helga and I knew it had just called to collect him.

Everybody in the village went down to have a look at this new boat including Katrine and me. The boat had brought some supplies and mail, but for Katrine and me the most frightening thing was that it also brought a visitor. Now we do get the occasional visitor in the middle of what little summers we get up here, but this early in the year is a little disturbing to say the least.

All For A King's Shilling

Who the visitor was what worried me. He was dressed in full Arctic clothing. The problem was all the clothes he was wearing were new, brand spanking new. In fact, he looked as if he had stepped straight out of the Harrods' North Pole expedition window. I could just see the situation in Whitehall. "Go and get yourself kitted out in Harrods and see what you can find in the North." Alarm bells as loud as 'Big Ben' were ringing in my head as I looked at him standing in the waist of the boat.

When Roald came ashore Carl, he and I made our way to Carl's cabin. It was Roald who had brought me out of Russia and although he stayed quite aloof we had become friends. Once we had drunk our first glass of whiskey, he told me that the visitor he had brought had spun some yarn about looking for somewhere to bring people on adventure holidays.

Then Roald looked at me and said, "I for one don't believe a bloody word he says. Bill, I think you should take great care, my friend, or better still sail with Carl and me until he tires and goes home."

For a moment I looked at him, "Thank you for your offer of help Roald, I know you are thinking of my health. The problem is, unlike you two I have spent time in the hands of the Russian KGB and worse still, their prison guards. You see I could never go through that again. Oh I know the work you both do is right, and I owe both of you for giving me my life back, what's more to the point, I owe you both for Katrine's life."

"We both know what you mean." Carl said, "But we do not think it will be safe for you here, not now this man has arrived."

"Well, if it isn't this man, it will be somebody else. I will have to face them some day, if not this year, then next. So I may as well get it over with this time, as any other. I'm not getting any younger, you know."

"Okay, you have a point, but take care while we are gone. Would you like Carl to stay with you until he goes, or whatever happens to him? I can always come back and pick Carl up later."

"No, but thank you for your offer. It will be best, I think, if Carl goes with you. I don't want to get him mixed up in any of this, not in his own backyard that is. It will be better if he is not here, I think."

With that we said good night to each other, Roald went back to his boat, and I made my way to Katrine's and my cabin.

Next day the visitor came ashore while the boat was getting ready to leave. He asked around for some place to stay and said he was looking for somewhere to bring people who wanted adventure holidays.

"I have a funny feeling about him, I don't like him, and I think he means trouble," Katrine told me as we watched him.

"You are getting too much like your husband. He doesn't trust anybody either." Carl said.

"That's right, Carl, the only people I trust now are you and the two reprobates, Roald and Helga, of course."

"Alright, I will get one of my friends to keep an eye on him, and he'll also watch your back while I am away on the boat."

"That's alright, Carl, I can take care of myself, but I do appreciate your man's help."

It was later that day when Carl sailed on the new fishing boat but the visitor it had brought stayed.

It was another day before he made his move on me. Katrine and I had just sat down at the table to have some fresh coffee, about mid morning. Coffee that had arrived on the fishing boat, the first since the winter had set in. There was a knock at the door and when Katrine opened it he was standing there.

He said in English, "Hello, my name is Graham Watkins. I have come here to look the place over with the idea of bringing tourists here for adventure holidays. I've called to see if it is possible your husband is interested in perhaps working for me?"

Katrine just looked at him and then in her Old Lapp tongue said, "I do not understand a bloody word you are saying." Then, she shut the door in his face.

I looked at her and started to laugh. "It is no laughing matter," she said. "That man is trouble for us."

"Alright, Katrine I shall take care but he will persist and I will have to see him some time or other. Otherwise he will think there is something wrong and that perhaps such a beautiful woman as you has no man to keep her warm at night."

The next day he was back again. He walked up to the door and just as he was going to knock, I opened it. I tried to make it look as if I were just going out. We stood there and eyed each other up for a few minutes.

Then I broke the ice by saying. "Do you want to see me? If not, would you mind letting me past? You see, I have to go up into the hills to look for a bear that has been round our hut this last couple of days."

"Perhaps I can come with you and we can chat as we go. By the way do I know you?"

"Yes, you can come with me and no, you don't know me," I grunted in answer to his stupid question.

With that we set off towards the hills behind the village, the very same hills I had travelled all those years before. That time, although I didn't know it, I was on my way for a glimpse of hell.

After we had gone about a half mile I could hear him panting quite a lot. Eventually I stopped and said, "If you are that unfit, then the bear is likely to get us and not the other way round. You sound like a bloody steam engine, man."

"Well, I'm not used to activity of this sort, I am sorry; perhaps we had better talk another time when you haven't got to go out after bears and the like."

As I looked at him I said, "The bear can wait, another day won't harm him. What is it you want from me?"

"You know I think you are an Englishman, and you are living here illegally. What is more, I am certain you are a Royal Marine deserter who went missing some years ago in Russia."

At this I just stood and looked at him, "You must be making some kind of sick English joke mister, I'm a partner in the mink farm you see behind my house. I have farmed it along with my partner Carl for years now. Good God, man, how did you come up with the idea that I'm English, I should be so bloody unlucky?"

"Well, I think you are who I say you are, and I aim to prove it."

As I looked at him, I thought Oh! shit, who is this guy, but I said, "You are not only unfit, mister, but you are bloody, how is it you English say, 'off your trolley';

you must be mad. You can check with anybody you want. What is more, I don't think the people in Oslo will take kindly to your coming here, probably illegally, and saying such things to a loyal Norwegian citizen at that."

For the first time I saw a flicker of doubt in his mind. Before he could say anything I went on, "I shall call Oslo tonight when I get back, and I shall ask them just what you are doing up here. I heard it was to organise holidays, well I wonder what Oslo will think when I tell them that you have come here and are accusing me of being some – what was it – English deserter? I am sure your visit here hasn't anything to do with holidays, has it, Mr Watkins?"

"Well, yes, that is the official reason why I am here, but you know, I am positive I know you."

"Well, I can assure you that you don't know me. Now perhaps if you let me get on and look for my bear, we will all sleep a lot easier in our beds tonight, once I have killed him."

"How can you kill this bear you are after, when you don't even have a gun with you?"

"Oh, I don't need a gun to kill a little old bear these days, or any other vermin, which I may come across in my travels for that matter."

With that he gave me a strange look and left. I watched him as he started to make his way back to the village. Then I followed on about a hundred yards behind him. I kept to the trees and stayed out of his sight. I just had the feeling he would go to my cabin and try to talk to Katrine, and I was right. He did not even look around, he just walked right up to the door. He knocked at the door and I was just going to run down to the cabin when I saw Helga. She stepped out from the side of our cabin and spoke to him.

What she said to him I don't know, but she must have said something that worried him, because he half ran down into the centre of the village. After looking around for a minute or two, he then walked to the house in which he was staying. He was lodging with an old man in the village whom nobody liked very much. Some thought he was a Russian spy. Others, just that he was a silly old man in his dotage who drank too much wood alcohol. Although I knew this was not so, I was still not too sure who the old man was, but I must admit he had done me no harm yet that I knew of.

To say that I was a little worried that he might in his drunken stupor let it slip just how long Katrine and I had been in the village or how the two of us came to be here in the first place, was to say the least, an understatement. To be quite honest, I must admit I was more than a little worried what the old man might tell his guest about Carl, Helga, Katrine and me. Also, I just hoped he did not say anything about our little trip last year away from the village. There was no way he could have known where we went, but you could never tell what the old drunk knew or didn't know.

So, I waited a while in the trees, until he was back in the house where he was staying. As I waited and watched him go to the house I mulled everything over in my mind, but in the end having not come to any conclusions, I made my way back to my cabin. It was by this time starting to get dark so I made a last check to see all was in order with the minks, and then I went into the cabin.

"Well, what did he want?" asked Katrine.

"Oh, he just thinks he knows me, and that I am English."

"The minute I saw him, I just knew he would be trouble. You will have to kill him, you know."

"No! I am sure it will not come to that, I told you after we returned from England, that I am sick of all the killing, I have no desire to kill anybody else."

"But what are we to do, darling?"

"Trust me, I shall find a way out of it, Katrine. By the way, what did Helga say to him?"

"I don't know; when did she talk to him?"

"She spoke to him just before I got back from the woods, where I was looking for an invisible Russian bear."

"Oh, I didn't know she was here."

With that, we let the subject drop. It was about half an hour later we had our supper, after which we went to bed. As we lay there awake I think we were both contemplating the change the arrival of this man was going to cause us. I knew I had never seen Katrine so frightened by anybody as she was of this man. Not even when I was an invalid in her father's house was she as frightened as she was now. She needed reassuring, so I reached out and pulled her close to me. I held her so close I could feel the beat of her heart as she pressed herself close to me and shortly after that we both fell asleep.

The next morning we arose and ate our breakfast in silence. I could see Katrine was still worried sick about our situation, and I must admit so was I. When we had finished eating our breakfast that morning I reached out and took hold of Katrine's hand. "It is no good, Katrine, we must carry on as if there was nothing wrong. I shall deal with this man as and when the time comes. There is no way he is going to destroy the life we have. I promise you I shall not let that happen."

As she looked at me, I could see relief spread over her face. "Bill when you said last night that you would not kill him, I thought you had given up and you would let him take you away from me."

"There is no way that will happen, Katrine. Roald said he would bring his fishing boat in at night and take us away if I wanted, there is no way I will ever leave you again my darling."

We looked at each other for a while, holding hands across the table. I then said, "Katrine I must go to the minks, they will be eating each other for breakfast if I don't feed them soon."

"Yes, Bill, you must go."

"Don't forget, from now on talk to him only in Old Lapp if he comes to the cabin when I am not here. You don't need to swear at him, though," I added.

With that we both laughed for the first time since the visitor had knocked on our door.

When I reached the mink pens, Helga was already there and she had started feeding them.

"Hi, I saw you talk to the visitor last evening. Did he have much to say?"

"No," she said, "But I did, I told him we did not need any officials from Oslo here, we can look after ourselves."

"Tell me, just what did this visitor say to that."

"He said he was not from Oslo."

"So! Where did he say he was from then?"

"He said he was from London, and he was looking for a place to bring English people on adventure holidays."

"Did you believe him?"

"No. I think he is after you and Carl."

I looked at her, and thought you are a very astute young woman indeed. "So, if he is after Carl and me, what are you going to do to help me deal with him? If I have to deal with him that is. You know Carl has other important pressing business to attend to."

"Yes, Bill, I know. Katrine, Carl and you can count on me for that matter. I will do all I can to help."

"Good. Now let's get the mink fed before they eat us, never mind each other."

It took us a further two hours before we had fed and then sorted the breeding pairs and cleaned the cages and tidied the place up. When we had finished it all, I suggested that she should come and have some coffee with Katrine and me. As we walked to my cabin I asked her, "What did you really say to our visitor last night? You know, Helga, I was watching the cabin from the trees, and after talking to you he ran all the way to the jetty."

At first she was silent then she said. "You know when you and Carl were away in England, well, I was recently in Oslo and I was told a couple of days before I left that they had received an inquiry from London about Carl and another man. It was about some people who had left a trail of dead bodies around England. I asked my friend in Oslo what this man making the inquiries was like and he told me the man was a Mr Watkins. This visitor fits the description he gave me of this Mr Watkins who, incidentally, works for MI5 counter intelligence."

"So, what did you say to him?" I repeated trying not to let my surprise that the man was MI5 show. It also set me thinking of my time with the Home Office. Perhaps that is where he thought he knew me from.

"Well, I told him that if he touched any of the people in this village I would have him killed by my contacts in the Secret Service. Now are you satisfied?"

"So, both you and Carl are in the Service?"

"Well, it would only follow, wouldn't it?"

"Okay, but not a word to Katrine about it."

"Of course not, Bill, but you realise the people in Oslo will want to talk to you at some time. The men you and Carl were involved with may have done a lot of harm to Norway as well you know. So don't leave town, as they say in America."

"You mean that, don't you?"

"You had better believe it," she said as we climbed the steps to my cabin.

"Believe what?" asked Katrine as we reached the top step.

"Oh nothing, by the way Helga is staying for coffee."

With that all three of us went inside. I told Katrine that Helga was going to help me keep an eye on the Englishman who had arrived. I then lapsed into silence as Katrine and Helga started talking about baby clothes and the like. Carl must have opened his big mouth and told Helga, if not the whole village.

I was trying to fathom out what to do about this man from London. He seemed to be after me in a very earnest way; I do not think it entered his head that I might just kill him if he got too serious about it all. The point was what to do about him? Carl, Katrine and I didn't know how he had got on to us, for that matter, but he had and one of us would have to do something about it soon. How was I to get rid of him without spilling any more blood, well that was the big problem? Oh, I could go and kill him today, and feed him to the mink, but there would just be another one arriving here before the ice returned. He would arrive with another cock and bull story, but in reality he would be looking for me.

While I had been trying to sort things out in my mind, Helga had left, and Katrine had prepared our evening meal. She had just put the meal on the table when there was a knock on the cabin door. I told Katrine to sit still, I would go.

When I opened the door it was our visitor from London. Katrine looked past me at him and said, "So, it is you! Have you no place to stay?"

"Yes, I have found a place to stay until the next boat arrives to take me back." He paused and then added, "south that is."

Well, I said. "There is not much point in going north from here now, is there? Not unless you want to visit Bear Island that is."

He looked for a minute, and then he said, "You could always go east from here."

"Not if you have any sense you won't," Katrine said.

I looked at the two of them and said. "It is my opinion that you do not care for each other."

To our visitor I said, "Would you care to share our meagre supper with us, or not?"

He looked and said, "No, thank you very much, I have already eaten, but I would like to continue our chat while you eat."

I looked at Katrine; she just shrugged, then in Old Lapp she said to me, "He has less sense than the wild reindeer, let alone your silly mink."

"You are probably right Katrine, but he is also a very dangerous man. Can you now set an extra cup and saucer, and give our guest some coffee while we eat?"

He just chatted about the place while we ate. I was not sure if he was testing me, or if he was trying to learn about it. One thing I was certain of at the end was that he was here unofficially. It also crossed my mind, if I played my cards right, I just might be able to turn the tables on him. I might even be able to turn it into a diplomatic incident. So, when Katrine and I had finished our meal I told her to go and get Helga. Once Katrine had left, I settled down with our man from London to have a little chat.

As we finished our coffee I asked him, "What is it you are really after my friend?"

He looked for a moment and said, "You."

"Why me?" I asked.

"Well," he said, "I think you are the man who killed a couple of British intelligence agents in England, last autumn."

"I think you are one hell of a, what is it? Mixed up civil servant, secret policeman, a counter intelligence agent, or perhaps you are just an ordinary policeman? Whatever it is you are way out of line, mister. If I call Oslo about these accusations you are making, well, you will find yourself in a Norwegian funny farm before you know it."

All For A King's Shilling

"I do not think so," he said, "I don't think you could stand too close an inquiry by the Norwegian authorities. So, I do not think it would be I who 'ends up' in a funny farm. It is more than likely to be you who 'end your days' in an English prison."

As we faced each other eyeball to eyeball for a minute or so, you could have heard a pin drop in the cabin. So intense was our posturing that we did not hear Katrine and Helga as they came into the cabin.

It was I who broke the silence, but not the stare, as I hissed at him through my teeth, "No, mister, you have got it entirely wrong. It is more likely a certainty you will find a resting place under my mink hutches forever, than there is any chance of me ever putting one foot inside any of your English prisons."

Helga was the next to speak and she said. "Now, gentlemen, there is no need for these threats. There are two things that have to be sorted out right now. First, Mr Watkins, you will not be taking our Mr Johansson anywhere. That means there will be no point in your finding Mr Watkins a permanent place of residence under your mink hutches will there?"

With that we both still sat looking at each other, sizing one another up. Katrine came and sat by me and looked this Mr Watkins in the face and said, "If you try to take my husband from me, I will kill you. Some people who were cleverer than you tried it once before, but as you see, here we are, still together. So do not think of it, not if you want to live."

"Now, Katrine," Helga said. "Nobody is going to separate you two. We all worked so hard in Norway to help you both to get together. We are not likely to let some fool out of an office in London do anything to spoil that now, are we?"

I could see a change come over Watkins' face at that. Then I said, "You don't know the half of it do you? You have no idea just what you are now involved in, do you? Well, what I will tell you is that if you persist in this foolishness, not only will I plant you under my mink hutches but I will let you live just long enough to see that you may not only have created a worldwide diplomatic incident, you could possibly also have started a bloodbath. You could be causing havoc in the world of intelligence amongst agents and counter agents."

Before he could say anything Helga interrupted to say, "I think things have gone far enough tonight. It will be better if all of us sleep on it; I will contact Oslo later tonight, for further instructions. Then I can perhaps get my boss up here tomorrow or the day after."

At first light the next morning we were awakened by the sound of a helicopter as it landed just outside the village. This machine had brought Helga's boss, as she had promised. The man was called Larvidson, a very common name in Norway. He had breakfast with Helga and then came to see Katrine and me. He then explained, "Helga has told me what has happened and you shouldn't worry too much about this man, Mr Watkins. It would be nice to get him to commit himself into revealing what evidence if any he has. After all, the man must have some evidence which he and his superiors consider to be well founded. Otherwise they would not have let him come this distance to look for you. So my recommendation is, let us hear what he has to say."

I looked at Helga and said, "What sort of fool is this? The British Government would send a man to the moon if they thought a spy was hiding from them there. Come this far, to look for me, what sort of madman is this they have sent, Helga?"

Before she could say anything he turned to her and said, "If you can go and get him, Helga, and bring him to your house, we will meet you there."

I looked at him in disbelief, but Helga left and Katrine and I made our way to Helga's house with Larvidson. Helga went off to collect Mr Watkins from his lodgings.

About ten minutes later we were all assembled in Helga's house and seated around her table.

Mr Larvidson introduced himself and then asked Mr Watkins, "Now what exactly is it you wanted from Mr Johansson and his wife?"

Mr Watkins then launched into a long story about a Russian defector who had turned up in London. This defector was an ex KGB man, and he had a story about an Englishman who had been held in the KGB Gulags. This Englishman it seemed had been sentenced to death, and then just left in the camps to rot. It turned out this man had not died after all, but some years later had escaped and made it to a village in Northern Russia. Whilst there, for some reason he had written his story down on scraps of paper. Paper which was given to him by a woman who looked after him in the village!

At this point I could see Katrine was looking at me with a worried look on her face. I smiled at her and shook my head and this seemed to settle her.

Meanwhile, Mr Watkins continued his story. He went on to say, "These pieces of paper had been obtained by this KGB man, who then passed them on to a clerk he knew in the British Embassy in Moscow."

While I was listening to all this, for the first time since I left her village I thought of Sharon. I wondered if she ever did make it out of Russia, or if Uri took his revenge out on her because I had successfully escaped from his clutches. Then I was distracted back to the present as this bloody man was ranting on.

Mr Watkins was going on about how this KGB man had told him during his debriefing in London the name of the person in the British Embassy to whom he had handed these pieces of paper. He now had them and had brought copies of them with him.

"Alright," Mr Larvidson said, "but I fail to see what this has got to do with our Mr Johansson. He cannot be your prisoner as he has lived here for years. He may have done a little smuggling in and out of Russia, but then that is a pastime of the people up here. They are all bloody related anyway."

"Well," Watkins said. "The man I am looking for came to England recently and killed some of our agents. Two men in particular, both of whom were officers – a Major and a retired Lieutenant Colonel, who both worked in our secret service. He also killed their body guards, but the two senior officers are the ones in whom I am interested. It is my considered opinion that your Mr Johansson, as you insist on calling him, is really Colour Sergeant Johnston of the Royal Marines who was reported as executed by the Russians some four or five years ago. Now it is my opinion that this Colour Sergeant Johnston came to London recently. I believe he came to exact his revenge on the man who he thinks betrayed him and that while he was in England, he did in fact kill the two officers I have just mentioned."

Katrine had that worried look on her face again. So I said to Mr Larvidson, "Look, my wife is pregnant and I don't think any of this claptrap is good for her in her condition. Perhaps it would be better if Helga were to take Katrine back to our cabin. If anything was to happen to Katrine because of this English idiot, I'll not be held responsible for my actions."

This Larvidson agreed to. Mr Watkins wasn't very happy about it, but I thought, stuff you mister. Katrine has been interrogated by better interrogators than you and survived.

When they had gone, Mr Larvidson said, "Look, Mr Watkins, it seems to me you have come here to hound Mr Johansson and his wife on the say-so of a Russian defector. A defector who may be giving you a load of disinformation and you are prepared to hang our Mr Johansson on his say-so. Well, I must say, Mr Watkins, I am very disappointed with your judgment. My superiors and I thought you would have some concrete evidence to support your accusations, but I do not think you have. Not the disinformation you have told us about. Perhaps it would be best if we ended our discussions now and we will meet again tonight when I have had time to digest fully what you have in these notes that you have with you. I assume you are going to let me read them?"

"Oh, yes," said Watkins, "I had intended that you read them." With that he handed copies of his notes to Larvidson. He then said, "I'll see you again soon," and left!

Just as he was leaving, Helga returned saying Katrine was now more settled, but could I go to see her.

When I arrived in our cabin Katrine flew into my arms and said, "We are going to be alright aren't we?"

"Of course we are," I said as I hugged her. We then had some coffee and I said. "This is no good, I must get on with looking after our stock. The last thing we need now is those little blighters eating one another."

I returned to the cabin later to find Larvidson there. He had the papers with him, which he showed to me. "I think you should read these papers, Bill."

"Why should I?" I asked. "You know I wrote them in the first place and it seems so does our fine Mr Watkins. The thing is how do we get this man off Katrine's and my backs without having to kill him, that is. Because I will if I have to, I have told Katrine I wouldn't, but believe me, I will if I have to."

"Well," he said, "what I require from you is confirmation that the men whom he said were killed in England were the two Russian agents we thought they were?"

"Oh, you can count on that," I said. "I know Carl wrote a report on the whole thing when we got back. No, the thing that worries me is that the KGB man this Mr Watkins keeps talking about – well, Mr Larvidson, he has to be Uri. Now if Uri is in London acting as a defector since these two agents were killed, then to my mind it only confirms that the two who died were after all top KGB men. What is more, it points to the KGB seeking revenge. That leads us to the subject of Uri. He was on the fishing boat on which I left Russia when I met up with Roald and Carl. So he knows the system of getting people out. It's also how he got hold of the papers in the first place. They were in the bundle of stuff I had with me when I left Russia, but he wouldn't hand me the bundle as I crossed from their fishing boat to ours. By the way, he also took a shot at me as I stood on the deck of our boat."

Larvidson looked at me long and hard and his stare was so hard it made me feel uncomfortable. It was Katrine who broke the ice when she asked, "Do either of you want any more coffee?"

At last Larvidson said, "I do think we have a problem, and it is not this Mr Watkins. We need to eliminate this Uri agent. The question is how do we do that? Mr Watkins told me that this Uri is still being held in London, or the Home Counties."

I thought, so you have been talking to Watkins, well, well what next?

He must have seen some reaction to his remark in my face because he went on to say, "I had a talk with Mr Watkins after I'd finished reading the papers. I needed to clarify some points in the story. I must also say I am sorry that you had to suffer so much. Carl had reported to us what had transpired at your trial, and I must admit the only person who thought you would still be alive was Katrine. When we got her out, she tried always to convince us you would still be alive, even though your death had been confirmed by the British Embassy in Moscow."

"First, Mr Larvidson, if you needed any clarification on the notes, why didn't you come to me? After all, I wrote them. What the hell could that so and so from London clarify about my experiences in bloody Russia? Secondly, you are telling me that these notes and bits of paper are the only proof the British have that I'm still alive. You then go sucking up to this man and ask him to clarify what is written in the notes. Shit, man, I don't believe you."

"Well, yes, I suppose it was silly of me to talk to Watkins about the notes," he said.

"Silly, silly, it was down right bloody stupid. Mr Watkins will now think that he has you convinced. What you have to do is convince Mr bleeding Watkins that this agent they have is lying; that gets me off the hook. Watkins will have to look elsewhere for the killer of his agents. By the way one of them fell over as he stepped off the pavement and got killed. I had nothing whatever to do with it. For that matter Carl, Katrine and I never touched him. Still, you already know that, don't you?"

"Well, yes," he said, "also we already know that the other agent was killed as he was about to kill Katrine."

"So," I said, "what's the problem? Send Watkins packing. Then all we have to worry about is Uri once the British release him, as release him they will if they think he will flush me out into the open."

Larvidson looked at me and said. "You have this way of seeing things so clearly and cut and dried, haven't you?"

"Look, Mr Larvidson, after what I have been through, and what Katrine has had to suffer, there is no other way we can look at these problems. We have managed not only to survive the terror of KGB interrogation, but we have both made it out of the camps to talk about it. The situation we found ourselves in was caused by two-timing double-dealing secret agents. Bastards I call them. Now for all we know, this Watkins and you, for that matter, may just be getting your orders from the same place as Uri and the two dead officers. You see our experiences have taught us not to trust anybody. We survive by trusting only one another. Do I make sense to you, Mr Larvidson? You must understand, Mr Larvidson, if for one minute I thought that I couldn't trust you, well, you could just as easily end up being eaten by our minks for breakfast as Mr Bloody Watkins could."

Larvidson looked at Katrine, then at me, and then back at Katrine. He then gave a sort of shiver, a small throaty cough, and asked for some more coffee. When he had his coffee he looked at us again and said, "I suppose nobody who hasn't been through an experience like that is really qualified to pass judgment on the morals of those who have."

I had a distinct feeling that for the first time since he had arrived here he had finally understood exactly what the situation was, and his position in it. When he finished his cup of coffee he said, "I shall leave you now, and I'll be back shortly with Watkins. You should not worry anymore, I shall soon have everything sorted out and all will be well, you can take my word for it."

"Mr Larvidson, it isn't your word we shall be taking if you don't get it sorted, it will be your life."

After he had left, Helga came in from the room at the back of the cabin and sat down at the table opposite me. She looked at me and her shoulders seemed to droop just a little bit.

I said to her, "Well, Helga, what do you think of your boss now?"

"Seems to me he is a little worried, don't you think? I think it is the first time he has come across a real field agent and a really bad situation, don't you?"

"He was a little taken aback with the way I talked to him. If he had read all those bits of paper he had in his hands, then he should have expected the reaction that he got from me."

"He told me he had spent all his life dealing with field agents, perhaps now I think he lied a little about that. I'd thought he was the right man for this job, but maybe I was wrong."

"Oh, shit," I said, "you should have told me he was just an office wallah. All this advice he keeps coming out with is just so much shit, isn't it? It could be we are going to be in real trouble. Is there any way we can get hold of Carl? We need him here badly and we need him like last night. They cannot have got too far yet. Perhaps we can get them back?"

"I doubt it," Helga said, "they will be keeping radio silence right now; they wouldn't answer even if they heard us. No, Bill, we will have to handle this one ourselves. We need time to think."

Katrine interrupted just then to say, "You don't have any time at all, both of them, Watkins and Larvidson, are on their way here right now."

"Okay, Katrine, you and Helga go out the back and go to Helga's house, and I will wait here for the two of them."

A couple of minutes later I let them both in, while Katrine and Helga left by the rear door of our cabin. "Back so soon?" I asked as I opened the door for them. "Better come in and sit down."

Once the three of us were seated at the table I asked them what it was they wanted to know now.

Watkins was the first one to answer. "Look, I am convinced you are the agent who killed those two agents in London. Mr Larvidson here is convinced you are not. He says you are who you say you are. He has produced copies of birth certificates, copies of school reports and records, driving licence application and all the sorts of things one would expect a good cover organisation to have produced. What is more, his bosses have given him a marriage certificate to prove just who both of you and your wife really are. I still don't believe him; look, I could produce the same papers in England for a person if I had to."

I interrupted him there. "Just a minute, Mr Watkins, what you are saying is that you could produce papers in England to cover such an event, as you claim the Norwegian Government has done in my case. Before you answer I would ask you to think long and hard. First, how do we know you are not a Russian agent for whom what you have just outlined has also been done? How do we know you are a true blue Brit, a born and bred Britisher, Mr Watkins? Why should we believe you? You could be some Bladovichski or some other Russian person for all we know? After all you came here telling anybody who would listen that you were a tourist guide, didn't you, and that was a lie. How do we know that you aren't a Russian agent who has killed the real Mr Watkins on his way here?

"Secondly, although by your own admission you can produce false documents in England, you seem not to have studied our laws. To do what you have said is not possible in this. Because, you see, there is no need to. You only have to say you are a politically persecuted person and you can stay in this country for as long as you like under Government protection. There would be no need for me, if I were who you say I am, to go through the elaborate deception you talk of. All I need to do is tell them 'I am being persecuted by the Russians or the British' and then I would be home and dry.

"What is more you would not be able to take me out of the country. So, Mr Watkins, think long and hard before you answer, or Mr Larvidson here may just be able to have you deported. I think Mr Larvidson can confirm what I say is right. Now if you will excuse me I have to see to my mink. I have to make a living somehow, you know. I don't have the privilege of a Government income as you two do. I have to earn my living somehow or other."

With that I rose and went to the front door of the cabin. When there, I turned and said, "Please close the door fully when you leave because I would hate to find a Russian bear in here when I return. It would be a shame to have to kill him! I don't believe in killing, not even bears, Russian or any other for that matter."

As I stood outside the cabin I listened at the door, but everything inside was quiet, they were obviously thinking about something or other.

After a minute or two I made my way to the mink sheds and sat inside the door of the first hut. From there I could see the entire village in the half-light of the moon. It was about ten minutes later that the two of them came out of my cabin and made their way to Helga's cabin. They both went in, but Larvidson came out a few minutes later and made his way into the village, leaving Katrine and Helga alone in the cabin with Watkins. As I watched the cabin, I fought the urge to go there in case I got myself carried away and started killing people again. Something I had no wish to start, as I did not want to sour my relationship with the villagers here. After all they had been very good to both Katrine and me ever since we had come here.

I was quite surprised therefore to see Watkins leave Helga's cabin shortly after Larvidson and make his way slowly to the place where he was staying. So I had one last look at the mink and then made my way down to Helga's cabin to see what had happened, if anything.

When I entered the cabin Katrine was sitting by the fireplace with Helga and they were in a huddled conference by the table. I went and sat by Katrine and they both stopped whatever it was they were talking about, I could see Katrine wasn't well, so I put my arm around her and said, "Come, Katrine, I think we should go home."

She just nodded and we began to leave. I looked across at Helga and I was about to say something and then thought better of it.

As we left Helga said, "I'll see you both tomorrow."

Once I got Katrine home I put her to bed and I sat by the bed talking to her for about two hours. It was the first real heart-to-heart we had ever had. When we finished she was in no doubt whatsoever that this Watkins guy would never split us up. Never again in our lives, no matter how long or how short, we would never ever be parted again.

About an hour later when Katrine was asleep I sat by the window in the front of the cabin overlooking the village for another half hour. Then after I made sure she was still asleep, I left the cabin and made my way to the house where Watkins was staying. Having made my mind up about him, I stood outside for about a minute and then I stepped up and knocked at the door.

After a while I heard somebody shuffling up to the door inside the house. Then I heard something I had not heard in this place before, I heard bolts being withdrawn, next I heard two locks being unlocked. It took quite a while, but at last the old man was standing in the light coming from the doorway.

He then shone a torch he had in his hand into my face. It surprised me when he spoke to hear he had a guttural accent, as he said, "Come in, I have been expecting you." With that he turned and disappeared into the darkness of his cabin, the torch bobbing a light in front of him as he shuffled down the passage.

I followed him into the cabin and closed the door behind me. Then I followed him down the passage and into the room at the back. The room was a lot larger than I had expected and Mr Watkins was sitting at a table at the far end of the room. The room was about twenty foot square and along the right-hand wall was some of the most up-to-date radio equipment I had ever seen. Watkins looked up from the table and seemed to be surprised to see me standing there.

"Come to admit your guilt, have you?"

"No, I've come to kill you. I don't know what you have said to my wife, but she has broken her heart since you left Helga's cabin. I have had enough of your meddling in my business, making stupid accusations about who I am and who I am not. Well, mister, you have said all that you are going to say!"

With that I took a hunting knife from my waist and moved towards him.

The next moment, I felt an iron grip round my wrist, and when I turned to look, it was the old man who had hold of my wrist. Before I could react to his grip I felt myself being twisted round and my arm going up my back. It was the first time my arm and back had hurt me so much since I made that jump when I escaped from the Russians.

Just then the old man's voice hissed in my ear, "We have not gone to all this trouble with you to have you end up on a charge of murder in Norway. Now, sit your bloody self down."

"You are a bloody strong bastard for an old man, aren't you?"

"Too bloody strong for you, so just sit and shut up."

As he had relieved me of my only weapon I did what he said, I sat down. I looked across at Watkins and he was not grinning, as I had half expected him to be. He had a frightened look on his face; I didn't know what had happened to frighten him so much. Next I turned and looked at the old man, and he just looked at me with a completely blank expression.

"I have somebody who wants to see you," he then said to me. To Watkins he said, "You and your petty little government departments with their mandarins and ponces. Well, Mr Watkins, you will be very lucky to get out of your next appointment with your life."

For the next five minutes or so we just sat and looked at one another. For the first time for years I didn't know what the hell was going on. Something must have happened to Watkins because he looked really frightened.

The old man put some glasses on the table and produced a bottle of pure wood alcohol. He then poured three good shots of it and handed Watkins and me a glass each. Once we had drunk this I got my tongue back and said. "Just what the hell is going on here anyway?"

The old man just said, "Shut up."

So, I stood up and went to leave. It was then I found myself looking down the barrel of a rather large revolver. So, I sat down again.

I looked across at Watkins. "I think we could take this old man, Mr Watkins. He may kill one of us but one of us would survive. Fancy your chance?"

He just nodded his head in a negative way.

"You seem to have lost your voice, haven't you?"

Again he just nodded.

"Seems to me you have lost all your Whitehall courage today, Mr Watkins. Well, if you are not going to do anything, I am. No way am I going to get myself interned by anybody, Russian, American or bloody British for that matter."

Having mouthed off I then watched the old man for a while, and started to make a plan to get at him before he could do anything to me. I think he must have sensed what I was at, because he looked over towards me and said. "Don't even think of it. I will put a hole in your head as soon as look at you."

For a moment I thought about that remark. It did not take me long to realise he was bluffing. If the man thought that way, he would already have killed me. From his remarks to Watkins I deduced he was holding him for some people or persons at the moment unknown to the two of us. Now it could be he was keeping me for the Russians, who I think would dearly love to get their hands on me again, or keeping me for the Americans. Now, that thought worried me somewhat. To me, they were crazier than the bloody Russians. So, there was no way that I was going to end up in their hands. At least the Russians had set procedures when torturing you, but the Americans, well, they had free enterprise on their side. It turned my skin just thinking about what those crazy bastards would do once they had me handcuffed to something or other.

What I could not understand was why the fight had left this Watkins guy. He had been full of his own piss and importance only an hour or so ago and now he was like a wet dream gone wrong. I wondered what the old man had said to him earlier. Whatever it was he was now scared shitless. As I looked at him I saw he was starting to shake a little, he also kept glancing at his watch. Each time he looked at it, he shook a little more. His nervousness was starting to get to me now and I thought, I'm going to have to do something very quickly before I crack up also.

It was as I was thinking about all this and my mind was starting to go into negative overdrive that I first heard the noise. I was looking at the old man at the time and he did not even flicker an eyelid, so I reasoned he had not heard it. As I sat there trying to get my mind into gear I heard it again. This time I knew I had to do something fast.

As I looked across at Watkins I said, "Well, Mr Watkins, it looks as if we are both headed for something very nasty. Just in case we don't get a chance to talk again, you know you have been right all along. I am who you think I am. Mind you, I didn't kill that bloody Major; you must know he was a bloody Russian, though. I didn't kill the silly sod. Now Brown? Well, he was a different kettle of fish. With him it really was a case as they say of him or me. It just so happened I was too quick for him."

"So I was right all along, but it will not do either of us any good now, will it? This old man has sold you to the Americans and me to the Russians. So what is the use?"

"Oh, we still have a chance because I bet he hasn't got his money yet. There's always a chance if he hasn't been paid, believe me"

The old man grunted and just laughed.

I turned to Watkins again, "Don't listen to him," I said. "We do have a chance. All is not lost yet, my fine English knight."

The look on Watkins' face was a picture. If anybody was ever out of his depth this man was. So I stood up; the old man pointed his bloody gun at me and told me very pointedly to "sit!" This I did, but this time I sat down next to Watkins and the old man took no notice of this.

When the old man had settled himself again, I turned to Watkins and said, "Look, the shit is going to hit the fan shortly. Don't ask me how I know, I just know. Now when things are about to start I shall push you to the floor and for god's sake stay there until it is all over. Not only will you hamper things, but you will end up dead if you don't stay put once I push you down. Do as I tell you and maybe, just maybe we will both get out of this alive."

I was not sure if he understood what I was talking about, but I would genuinely try and help him. I had no interest in seeing even him killed this way. Pushing him under cover was about all I was prepared to do for him though. Taking the old man out was the least of my troubles. I could do it now if I wanted or later. It would not alter the fact that the Russians and the Americans were due here shortly, and if it wasn't sorted out now they would only be back later. Make the whole project too public for them, that was a plan I had in mind. What an arsehole of a plan it was as well.

With that decided, I then settled down to wait for their arrival. Mind, I did think it odd, two submarines here at the same time, one Russian, one American, and them not trying to sink one another. Still, I suppose it was not such a surprise to some as one might think.

We did not have too long to wait because soon after that the old man started to get a little bit fidgety. That was when I came alert and fully alive, just like old times. The blood was flowing and the adrenaline was pumping throughout my body. Here we go again, I thought, will this bloody pantomime never end? It was then I heard the noise outside the front door, then a few seconds later the old man and Watkins heard it also. Watkins looked at me and he had a look of complete panic on his face. I put my hand on his arm and held him steady for a second or so. He was trembling and shaking very badly. A few seconds later the door at the front of the house opened and a group of figures dressed in black came into the room from the passage.

It was at this point I heard the slightest noise of a safety catch being released on a weapon behind me. As the first of the newcomers reached the centre of the room the rest of them were crowded just inside. My moving earlier from the chair I'd been in when I first entered the room meant the person behind me had a clear view of all the visitors.

These men were dressed in the usual dark blue trousers favoured by the Navies of the Northern Hemisphere and the equally dark blue woollen pullovers. They also wore full face balaclavas used by all seamen who operate in these Arctic waters these days. Most frightening of all, though, was that they were all, including their leader, carrying Kalashnikov assault rifles. In the few seconds while I looked at them I just hoped to God that whoever the person was who had just released his safety catch as they arrived, was on my side. Because it was at that moment I dived for the floor half under the table in front of me, dragging Mr bloody Watkins reluctantly with me. As we went forward in a falling motion I felt, more than heard, the first bullets pass over the back of my head. I remember thinking while I was in mid-fall; you have cut that bloody fine my old friend, whoever you are.

When I looked up at the turmoil going on in front of me, I saw the old man was turning to face us. He had escaped the first burst of gunfire because he had not been in line with the passage door. It was then I grabbed my knife from the floor where it had fallen from the table, where the old sod had left it. I took hold of it by the handle and launched it at him with all my might from a half lying, half kneeling position on the floor. Just as my knife left my hand I felt myself being pulled to the floor by Watkins. He reached up to my chest, and I thought he was trying to get his hands around my neck. You bastard, I thought, and hit him with my clenched fist on the top of his head with all the strength I could muster.

It was as my fist connected with his head I felt an excruciating pain shoot up my arm, along my shoulder and into my head. It felt like a bloody electric shock and I remember thinking the bastard's wired full of electricity. The pain made me cry out for the first time since the time in the forest when the tree fell on me. At first I thought I was going to pass out, but I didn't. Once the pain had subsided I managed to look around the room. The old man was sitting looking at me with both his hands clasping my knife, the handle of which was protruding from his chest.

"You are an evil bastard, Johansson."

"You are not too sweet yourself, you drunken old sod."

"I did not mean you any harm; it was just that they offered me a lot of money for you."

"No, you didn't mean me any harm, it was just that the money you were offered was too good to miss, eh?" I grunted in his ear. Then I reached forward and pulled the knife from his chest, "Mine, I think," I said, and he screamed with pain. It was to be the last scream he would make as he then slumped back against the wall, dead.

Next I turned and grabbed Watkins by the scruff of the neck and headed for the passage leading to the front door. It was as we reached the passage I heard movement in the front doorway. Without waiting to see who it was I turned and headed for the window at the back of the room. Still holding Watkins by the scruff of his neck, I launched us both like a pair of unguided missiles through it.

We landed together in a heap outside, having knocked over the person who had been firing the machine gun through the window. I could hear a woman's voice saying, "Carl said you were a mad bastard, and he was bloody right. Now let us get to hell out of here before they come round the back."

"You call me mad, Helga; where the hell did you get that bloody cannon from? The one you nearly took the back of my sodding bloody head off with in that bloody room. You did wait until I ducked, didn't you?"

"Of course I did, you fool, now let's get to hell out of here."

With that we took off to the west end of the village, dodging in and out of the doorways until we at last reached the trees. "Were the men who landed Americans or bloody Russians?" I asked her as we made our way there.

"I don't know who the hell they were."

At that remark Watkins tried to stop, but I was having none of it. I was still pulling him by the scruff of his neck as we continued on our way.

"Oh my God, I hope they are not young Americans lying dead back there," he muttered.

"Oh, shut your bloody mouth, you stupid arsehole. I don't give a shit at the moment, Mr bloody Watkins. I don't really give a shit if the dead are American, Russian, Chinese or bloody Aliens just so long as I am not one of them."

When we had reached a point about a hundred yards into the trees we stopped to get our breath. It was then I looked at Helga and said, "Perhaps I should have that gun now. Then we can make our way round the village to our mink sheds."

"No, I will hang on to this gun for the moment, but you are right, I think the mink sheds are probably the best place for us at the moment."

"You are all mad," Watkins muttered, more to himself than to us.

"Yes, I agree, but if Helga had not killed those Russians back there you would be heading for Russia right now in a Russian bloody submarine. So I would suggest you keep your bloody mouth shut, okay?"

We then set off for the mink sheds. We moved very cautiously now, taking our time and checking every few yards to see if we were being followed.

We arrived at the mink sheds and the three of us sat still on the steps of the sheds trying to get our breath back and watched the village. About half an hour later we saw some shadowy figures moving in the docks' area and we readied ourselves in case of an attack. In the end it turned out to be some of the locals who had come out after hearing the gunfire. It was obvious that they were very reluctant to get involved and soon everything was quiet again. It must have been about an hour after we had arrived at the mink sheds when we saw the last of the remaining Russians leave in their rubber boat.

That was when we decided it would be alright to go to my cabin and at least have a warm drink, as it was bloody cold outside.

"By the way, Helga, where is your Mr Larvidson right now?" I asked.

"He is busy summoning help from the Norwegian Navy right now, if you must know."

"Thank God for that," added Watkins.

Just then I noticed another bunch of men on the end of the jetty, "Where the bloody hell did they come from?" I asked Helga.

"I don't know, but I think we had better get Katrine before things get any more involved."

"Involved? Helga, what in hell's name do you think tonight has been so far, if not involved?"

Then I made a half run, half trot to my cabin in a crouched position. Watkins was behind me, with Helga bringing up the rear. She was still clutching that bloody cannon that she seemed to be so fond of across her chest.

Once inside I went to the bedroom to see if Katrine was alright.

"Oh, Bill, where have you been? I heard the shooting and I have been in here not knowing what to do. I've been so frightened. What has happened?"

"It is all right, Katrine, it is Helga who has been doing all the shooting; I just hope to hell she has finished. We must take care, though, a group of strangers has arrived on the jetty and we don't know who they are."

"You are not going to go and try to find out, are you?"

"No, Katrine, I am not; perhaps we can send Watkins. He is here with us. You know that old sod he was staying with, well he had sold Watkins to the Russians, and me, would you believe it, me mind you, me to the Americans? He will not see his profit now, unless they can pay the old sod in Hell."

"So he is dead?"

"Yes, Katrine, he is dead. It wasn't Helga who killed him, though, I did it."

Just then there was a sound outside the hut. Before Helga could get ready to start shooting, Carl called out, "Is everything alright?"

I think the three of us sighed with relief. It must have been him and his men whom we had seen on the jetty. I opened the door and Carl stepped into the cabin. "Are you three all right?" he asked.

"Just how the hell did you manage to get here so quickly anyway?" I asked.

"Well, we were only a few miles out from the coast when we detected a submarine. Roald decided to follow it for a little and lowered a sonar buoy. While we were checking its fingerprint we detected a second submarine. Both submarines seemed to be heading for the fjord so we stayed with them, following the two of them, that is. The problem we had was when we had identified them, because one was Russian and the other was American. Roald believed that they knew of each other's presence but neither of them took any evasive action, they seemed to be sailing in convoy. Just outside the fjord the Russian submarine surfaced and moved in past the headland into quieter waters. He has now submerged again and we think he has moved back out of the fjord, but the American has moved into the fjord and is lying on the bottom close in to the shore. Roald thought it would be best if we came ashore in force."

He then went on, "Larvidson has now managed to get through to the Navy, and with any luck we should have some support in here within the next ten hours."

"The next ten hours! Hell, Carl, the next ten hours is no good. Do you know that old sod whom Watkins was staying with had sold him to the Russians, and me, can you believe it, me to the bloody Americans? If I had not gone to the house earlier tonight Watkins would by now be on his way to Russia, and I would be getting an early call from the US secret service. Shit, what a mess we are in."

"We have suspected the old man for years, Bill, but we could never get any proof of what he was up to. Now we know we can have him arrested."

"No need for that now, Carl, I'm afraid you are too late. Bill killed him during the fracas while I was trying to save Mr Watkins and stop him being handed over to the Russians," Helga told him.

"I am not so sure that we made a good move there, Helga. Perhaps we should have let the Russians take Watkins with them and then killed the old man before the Yanks come ashore."

"Still too late to think about that eh, Carl, got to find out what the bloody Americans want me for?"

"We shall no doubt find out soon enough, Bill. For the moment let us get ourselves into a better position, just in case they are mad enough to come ashore in any kind of force. The Americans are, after all, a little mad; they think they have a god given right to do just what they want, where and when they want."

"Yes, Carl, you are right of course. We had better make sure Katrine and Helga are safe. Mind you, as long as Helga has that bloody cannon in her possession, then nobody around here is safe at all. Did you know she nearly blew the back of my head off?"

"God, you don't half exaggerate, Bill, I missed you by an inch, and an inch is as good as a mile they say," she sniggered.

"Yes, but you don't get your bloody hair singed at a mile, Helga; anyway we have to decide what to do with this smart-arse from London. How long do you think we have got, Carl?"

"Well, I cannot see the Americans coming ashore before daylight, so we have a few hours. Everything must look as normal as we can make it when they do arrive."

"What about the old man's house? Surely they will be expecting to meet him there and me also, for that matter. I wonder if they knew what the old man looked like. Perhaps we could have somebody imitate him, and then we could perhaps sell Watkins here to them instead of me."

"You don't change, do you, my old friend?"

"Not when it is my freedom and my arse that is on the chopping block. No, my friend, I don't bloody change."

Just then Katrine came into the room with some large jugs of coffee laced with Schnapps and some cold-meat sandwiches. It was a welcome break and in silence both Carl and I ate our fill and drank our coffee. I was thinking of all the things I'd been through, by myself and with Katrine. I came to the conclusion that no way was I going to surrender what I had now. There was no way I was going to die under torture, by the Americans or the bloody Russians for that matter. Oh, no, this time I would end either dead or as free as a bird where I stood. Whichever it was going to be, then Katrine would be with me to the end.

There was one decision I had made, and that was that we would never ever be parted again. On that I had made up my mind when I came out of the old man's house alive earlier tonight. No, this time either we walked away from this free, or we would die and we would do it together. No more parting. I could have died earlier and left her alone, but from now on we would always be together.

It was Carl who broke my trend of thought. He seemed to know that I had come to a decision about it all. He just looked at me for a while and then said, "Come on, Bill, we have things to do, plans to make and hatch, we have plenty to get on with."

I nodded to him, and turned to Katrine, "Katrine, I want you to change into your travelling clothes and then get the small case from the back room. Carl and I will be outside waiting for you." As I was talking to Katrine, Carl was telling Helga and his men that we had some work to do outside and that they should detain any Americans who came ashore. They should detain them until Larvidson and the Navy arrived. Then Helga and the men left and made their way to the jetty.

A little while later the three of us, Carl, Katrine and I, were also on the jetty. One of Carl's men joined us and we then boarded their rubber boat. It was bitterly cold on the jetty, but strangely it seemed warmer once we were down in the boat. We paddled the boat out until it was just round the edge of the harbour, and then Carl's man started the outboard motor. It seemed no time at all before we arrived at the trawler and we all clambered aboard.

Once we were aboard Katrine and I settled into a cabin just behind the wheelhouse. Roald came to see us. He seemed genuinely pleased to see the two of us and sat at the map table, which filled the largest part of the cabin.

When we were all settled he said. "We have a right fine mess here now, don't we? By the way, Carl, it was a Russian submarine that was in the fjord earlier. He has now settled on the bottom, just about here." With that he pointed out a position on the chart. "Better still, Carl, there is another submarine now on the surface just round the headland here." He pointed out another place on the chart.

"If that one is the American he has moved," said Carl.

"Well, yes Carl, that one is the American, but we also have another submarine lying on the bottom about three miles from the Russian and about two miles from the American over her," Roald concluded.

I looked first at Carl, and then at Roald and said, "You two are the experts; you tell me what is going on."

"Well, it is not that easy. You see there is also a Russian trawler steaming backwards and forwards across the mouth of the fjord. He is just outside the old three-mile limit. Not that limits have ever worried them in the past."

"So you see it is a case of who is after whom, and what if anything are they all after. Again, just how far are they prepared to go to obtain their objectives? That is the sixty-four-thousand-dollar question we need to find the answer to."

"Okay. How about I make a suggestion then."

"Go ahead," they said in unison.

All For A King's Shilling

"Suppose you dock this boat of yours in the harbour, I presume you can still keep an eye on all these ships while tied up alongside?"

"Of course I can, Bill."

"Well, as I see it all or any action that is going to take place, will be on land. Now, it just may be that the Russians only want their dead men back! It is obvious the Americans still want me; otherwise they would have gone by now. It is certain they don't know what has happened ashore. That leaves the third boat. Well, if it is British it could be it has just stumbled across the Russian and the American in this area. It is probably just hanging round to see how cosy these two are. After all, Roald, the British don't trust either the Americans or the Russians. It may be, just may be, they are here in support of our gallant Mr Watkins. Boy, what an arsehole that man is."

"Yes, Bill!" said Carl. "Helga told me you gave him a bit of a dressing-down."

"You could be right about the other submarine, Bill," said Roald. "Yes, I think we should dock. Mind you under no circumstances are either Katrine or you to appear on deck. You should be able to watch all that is happening ashore from the bridge, okay? I mean it, Bill, you stay on board."

"Okay, Roald, we will not show ourselves at all."

Half an hour later the boat was alongside the small jetty. Katrine and I were both in the wheelhouse. We must have looked odd as we swivelled our heads around like 'tuppeny budgies' trying to see what was happening or going to happen.

For the next couple of hours nothing at all happened. Then Roald came to tell us that the Russian submarine had surfaced again. They had launched a small boat of some kind, which had now left it and was heading into the harbour.

"I wonder what they are after now? If they want Mr Watkins, then perhaps we might oblige them and hand him over, but I suppose that would be morally wrong, wouldn't it?"

"Yes, it would," Katrine piped up. "I wouldn't hand my worst enemy over to them. We both know what they are like, Bill; I'm ashamed of you for suggesting it in the first place."

"Katrine, if it comes to you and me, or him, ending up in their hands, then I'm afraid he is the one who has drawn the short straw."

With that we just sat and looked at one another until the Russians' small boat entered the harbour. It was a 'Gemini' type of boat and it had an officer and three ratings in it, none of whom were armed. Larvidson and Helga went to the end of the jetty to talk to them.

It transpired that the Russians had decided to cut their losses and just wanted their dead back. I learned later that Helga had insisted that they remove the old man at the same time.

So it transpired that the Russian threat to our lives had ended. Now we only had the Americans and, of course, the Englishman to deal with.

Next it was decided that Katrine and I, plus all the men who could be spared, would go to our farm and set up a small defensive perimeter around the cabin. This task took a little over an hour to complete to our satisfaction, some of the men seemed to think that it was no big deal and that the Americans would not come ashore to fight. Carl, Roald and I thought differently though. We all had experience of working with the Americans. They seemed to have the idea that they could go anywhere they pleased, do anything they wanted to and nobody had a right to oppose them in any way. If the Americans did come ashore armed and ready for a fight, then they would certainly get a bloody nose for their troubles, as they say.

We all waited and we were on edge for some time. Then at last one of Roald's men came running up to tell us the American submarine had surfaced and that the skipper had asked to dock in the harbour. Larvidson, god bless him, refused them permission to do so. So again we had to wait while an American 'Gemini' craft made its way to the jetty. This time it contained the submarine captain and six of his crew, all armed. I would have loved to hear his comments when he stepped on to the ladder of the jetty to be told by a buxom Norwegian woman who was standing on the jetty holding a submachine gun in her hands and wearing a bloody big cannon of a handgun on her waist, "Take one step further, Captain, and you will be a dead Captain. This is Norwegian territory and we have already repulsed one invasion today. It will not take long for us to do it again. What's more, we have some anti-submarine planes due here in the next ten minutes, so if you don't want your submarine sunk as well you had better state your business and leave as quickly as you can."

Helga told me later that he asked Larvidson (and he knew Larvidson's name) for Mr Johnston to be handed over to him as agreed by his government and the Norwegian agent for this area.

Before Larvidson was able to answer it seems Helga told him, "I'm the government agent for this area of Norway, and we don't have anybody in this area called Johnston. So perhaps you would be well-advised to just step back into that little rubber boat of yours and head back to your little submarine. Then you can get out of our waters before you get blown out of them."

"Oh, and by the way did you know that you are being shadowed by two other submarines out there?"

That it seemed was the end of what could have become a very dangerous confrontation. I don't think anybody wanted to escalate the situation any further. The American left and then about four hours later the English submarine departed. We would never know why he was there, if he had a mission or if he was just in the area and took a very quiet look at what was going on. The main thing was the threat was over for the moment; all we had to do now was to have a chat with our man from Whitehall, Mr Watkins.

Before that, though, we all needed some rest and perhaps a few glasses of Schnapps to drink; anyway I for one had had enough excitement for one day. So we all trooped off to Carl's house and had a few drinks.

After we had been there about half an hour I went with Katrine to our own cabin. Some time later Watkins arrived to see us and he and I began to have a discussion about the previous night's activity. I started the conversation.

"I hope you did not take too much notice of what I said to you last night, Mr Watkins. As you know, I was at the time under a little stress, as they say."

"I didn't take any notice of that."

"Why not?" I asked.

"Well, if I did say I'd taken any notice of you, you would kill me right here and now, wouldn't you? I've seen you in action now and I must say you live up to the reports I've read on you. I didn't believe them before, but now I have seen what you are capable of I see they were not exaggerating in what they said." he answered.

"The man has a point," Katrine piped in.

"Alright, he has a point, but I need to know what the man is going to do, then perhaps I might just be able to let him go. Oh, by the way, Mister Watkins, did you know that a British submarine was here earlier today? They didn't see fit to come and rescue you from those nasty bloody Russians now, did they? Maybe the men back in London want rid of you."

Just then Carl and Larvidson came into the cabin followed by Helga. It was Helga who spoke and said, "Well, Bill, it looks as if we have a deal with Mister Watkins' boss. We send him home fit and well, and they will stop looking for this Royal Marine who has been missing for so long. It beggars thinking about. The man has probably been dead for years if the truth was known. I think this is all a story put about by the KGB, a plot to stir up relations between the Western allies. They nearly had the American and British submarines attacking one another today, let alone our aircraft ready to join in. The main thing is, Mister Watkins is to be taken south to Bardufoss and they will fly him out from there. Back to his desk, I think."

The look on Watkins' face was one of disbelief as Helga finished her spiel. "When will I leave for Bardufoss?" he asked, hardly able to conceal the nervousness in his voice.

Larvidson then spoke. "You will be leaving with me in a Government snow track that should be here in about five hours or so. You and I will go to the old man's cabin and collect your kit then you will be ready to be on your way. As for our Mr Johansson, well, you must forget you have ever seen him. I do hope you understand that point, Mr Watkins? You see, it is so important to your health for if Mr Johansson was to die from anything other than natural causes, then I'm afraid it would only start off a wave of killing, and we don't want that, do we?"

After a little thought, which took about ten seconds, Mr Watkins said, "No."

"Do you mind if I have a chat to Mr Watkins while you wait for the snow track to arrive, Mr Larvidson?" I asked.

"No, be my guest. I have some business to attend to anyway." With that he left the cabin.

"Be careful, Bill, in what you say to this man." Both Carl and Helga said as I saw them from the cabin.

When they had all gone and Katrine was comfortable by the fire I asked Watkins, "What do you know so far about this whole affair?"

"Only what was in the papers that a KGB defector told us he had given to an Embassy Clerk in Moscow. I managed to retrieve those papers and the story ended in a Russian village in the Arctic Circle."

"What was this fellow like, this Russian KGB man?"

"Well, his name was Boris Trovalov; he was the biggest man I have ever known. At least he seemed to be the biggest man I have ever met."

"It sounds as if you have met Uri, the only con-man who is operating in Russia these days! I'll bet he has certainly given you lot the run-around?"

"What do you mean the run-around?"

"Well, he is no more a KGB man than I am; he is what you might call a roving policeman, but if you can afford to pay him you go free. If you have read the papers you say you have then you should have known that your Boris was Uri. He is a bloody big coward when it comes down to it, otherwise he would have got out of Russia with me. That is why I have always believed he never intended to defect at any time. He's got bloody millions stashed away all over Russia and I don't mean paper money. The Uri I knew wouldn't ever leave his gold behind.

"Now, Mr Watkins, I think I'm going to have to tell you the rest of the story. If you ever breathe a word of this to anybody you will be dead within a week. Now I really hope you understand that threat, Mr Watkins. If you breathe one word of what I'm about to tell you there is no doubt you will die. So when Katrine has our coffee ready, I'll start."

I then recounted the events that had taken place after I'd left the village with Sharon watching Uri and me heading away from the village.

It had taken my writing the story of what had happened to me down on paper for me to realise who it was. Who had manipulated me and also how some of my fellow Marines, the ones it seemed had not joined the cause when asked to, had over these last few years been eliminated. Once the penny dropped, as they say, and things fell into place I knew that I had a task. It was not a nice task but it had to be done. I had realised when I first went into the camps what was required of me and why I had at all costs to survive and escape from the system. A task which overshadowed the problems of staying alive and it had tempered my thinking. Now it had all come back to Brown, Fitzsimmonds and Nobby. They had already got rid of Mick and most of the others. Now that I had at last got it together I knew what it was I had to do, and I would this time do it.

One thing was for certain, big as he was, Uri was not going to stop me getting away and finishing the job, a job I should have done in Borneo all those years ago; I would have saved myself a lot of grief. So look out, sir, I am on my way. Perhaps now I had the extra incentive to be successful, now I had Katrine, who had probably saved my life at the cost of possibly losing hers. That was my frame of mind that last afternoon in the cabin with Sharon, another woman who had helped me at the risk of her own life.

There was something else, Mr Watkins, I could not prove this, but even though I went through hell in those camps, as did Katrine, there was somebody in the hierarchy of the KGB who every once in a while reached out and helped me. As I say I could not prove it, but I did have an idea who it was. That is all you would ever get from me on that subject, so don't try to find out who I think that person is.

It was getting dark, and it was also starting to get cold, not that it was anything else really. Sharon and I had a good meal. She had not been with me as much these last few weeks. I think she had been hurt by what happened between us; I had stopped her from coming into my bed after the first time. She took offence when I told her it was not good for either of us as nothing could ever come of it. Still, I think it was inevitable we would sleep together. We both knew from the start I could not stay with them for too long. My presence would only bring misfortune upon them, if I were arrested anywhere near their village. It would be obvious even to the ordinary Russians that because of my fitness somebody had been looking after me. When I had finished my meal she had come to the table and stood by my side. She stood quite still for a few moments and she then thanked me for what I had done for her.

She then said, "We will meet again, you know. Maybe in London next time, you can show me Piccadilly Circus and Trafalgar Square one day."

I just looked at her and said, "I would love to do that, and you must keep that date."

"What's a date?" she asked.

I said, "I will tell you that when I meet you in Piccadilly Circus."

With that I picked up my little bag of possessions and stepped outside the hut. Uri was waiting on the steps. He told me, "I will take you to the edge of the trees, and see you on to the right path. Also, I have something for you, which I shall give you when we part."

With that I looked back at Sharon standing in the doorway, and said, "Don't forget our date, will you?"

She shouted. "I will not forget. I will be there."

I turned and walked off to heaven knew what.

As we walked away from the village, Uri asked me, "What is this date thing you told Sharon not to forget?"

"Oh," I said, "It was just my birthday. Sharon is going to get drunk on my birthday each year from now on; I will be doing the same and we will remember each other that way."

Uri laughed, but it was not a sincere laugh, it was a forced laugh. Because of his actions and manner I was starting to change my mind about this big man. I was getting very wary of him and his grandiose plans for my escape from Russia. He had in these last few weeks changed. I did not know what game he was up to, but I had this dreadful feeling that it involved me and would be detrimental to my health.

Within no time at all we had cleared the ridge of the basin in which the settlement was. We came to a place which was quite close to the settlement. Uri stopped and turned to look back and he asked me, "Do you remember this place?"

"No, should I?"

To which he replied, "It was here that we first saw you. Sharon was the first, and she called me. We thought it was Valdansk returning, and she was terrified. She called me to come out with her and shoot you, as it was you had passed out and when we got near to you we could see you were not Valdansk. Had you not passed out, my friend, I would have shot you."

I looked back at the settlement for a few minutes. I could still see Sharon standing on the steps of the hut I had been sharing with her these past months. I think I sighed, and then I turned, looked at Uri and said, "Which way, big man?"

With that we passed over the ridge and out of sight of the settlement, heading in a northwesterly direction.

We walked for most of the night, and well into the next day. I think it must have been around two-thirty we stopped at last to have something to eat. First, we set up a small wind break in which to light a fire. It was under some trees and behind some large boulders. We lit the fire and boiled some water to make some tea with. Uri then heated up some of the porridge-type stuff which he produced from his bag. Uri and I had not talked much during the night's and morning's walk, and we did not break the habit, now we had stopped and were eating.

When we had finished our meal Uri said, "We should sleep now until it gets dark. Then we can set off again, once we have rested." As we settled down to sleep, I realised just how tired I was. All I remember thinking, as I was falling asleep, was that I could hear a helicopter in the distance. At first I thought I must be dreaming, but I could hear that famous sound which all helicopters make as their blades grab for air to keep them up. I am not sure if the helicopter left the area, or I just fell asleep. I know I stopped thinking about it as I went to sleep.

How long I was asleep I shall never know, what I do know is I came awake fast, as I saw this big figure leaning over me putting his hand over my mouth. It seemed we were in a storm. The trees we were under were thrashing about in the gale that was blowing. Dead pine needles and cones were being blasted around all over the place. As I remember it, I felt as if we were both in a giant sandblasting machine.

It was then I came to realise, as I became more wide awake, that a helicopter was hovering right above us, and it was Uri who was holding me down. His actions, I think, were to stop me bolting like a bloody jack rabbit. I remember thinking we had had it. Then, to my surprise, the helicopter started to move away to our left and the storm stopped. Uri slowly released his hold over my mouth, I then looked at him and we both just sat there without moving for the next ten minutes. As the helicopter slowly edged its way to our left, I could not understand why its crew had not seen us, or had they? I was starting to get really bad vibes about this Uri. Still, you come across some strange things when you are out like this.

After the helicopter had cleared our position it seemed to dip down into a valley, but it still took a long time to move away out of earshot. We sat and ate some cold food that Uri had brought with him. It tasted vile and I just hoped I would not get the runs from it. The last thing I needed now was a touch of Delhi belly.

We gave it another hour after the helicopter was out of earshot before we made a move. I said to Uri, "I think it would be best if we take our time for a while and move very carefully from now on. The helicopter may just have dropped some men off in ambush positions before it got to us or since it passed out of our sight."

He said, "Yes, you are right, we must take it easy."

"Just how long was the helicopter hovering over the top of us last night, Uri?"

"It didn't hover over us and it did not stop at all," he said.

It was just that it seemed to me that it had been hovering above us, waking up as I did, while according to Uri it was passing over the top of us.

"Are you sure it didn't hover over us, Uri?"

He did not even bother answering me. With that we left the place where we had rested and started on what was to turn into one hell of a journey.

As we went I was still of the opinion that the helicopter had dropped men off to search for us. The feeling I was like a beacon glowing in the dark was very strong. It was dark now, and I could not get rid of the feeling I was in the light and I was surrounded by Russians who were grinning at me. Grinning at me for thinking I could have the audacity to travel around their homeland without them knowing my every move. It had always been my opinion each time I had entered Russia that they were always watching me; it seemed that I could not move anywhere in this bloody land without they knew my every move.

I think it came from the knowledge of the kind of society they are. They inform on each other to seek favours from the state and its officials, even if most of what they say, or the tales they tell on their neighbours, are pure lies. It makes no difference to them, just so long as they are left alone.

Never had I felt I was such an impostor in other countries, as I did when I was in Russia. For some reason I had always felt I was an outsider, and under the microscope all the time. I believed every move I made in this godforsaken land was being plotted on some general's map.

Although I must admit I felt a lot better now we were on the move again, even though I believed the whole of the bloody Russian Army, the KGB and every bloody Russian's aunt were watching every move I made. Still, we did make steady progress even though it was dark. Uri seemed to know the track we were following and he was striding out at a good pace. I realised how unfit I had become. My time in the camps had not been an inducement to fitness, and I was having a hard time keeping up with him. I thought, now we were on the move, his idea of walking to Austria was not such a bad idea, if he could keep this pace up for a few weeks. Still, I was more in favour of heading for Norway. I knew that once I made it to Norway I would at least have some help, and more to the point I'd be safe. At least I thought I would. It was of course familiar country for me as well.

We did not encounter any Russian ambush during the rest of the night, but we did make good progress. It was not long before I was so knackered I lost all thought of looking for any ambush. It was not long before I threw caution to the wind, and just fell in behind Uri, putting my head down, and trying to keep up with him. I do admit to feeling a little pleased with myself when it got light. I was still in behind him and plodding on. He did not let up when it got light but just kept on going with the confidence of a man who was entitled to be there.

Now I knew enough to realise that your average Russian, who was as far away from home as Uri was now, would be starting to get scared, probably as scared as I was, or even more so. From my experience of Russians I had met, when the majority of them were as far away from their homes as Uri was well, they would be terrified. Frightened in case some bloody Russian official jumped out into the track in front of them to ask them what they were doing so far away from home. Also asking them for papers, which had to be signed by the right authority, permitting them to travel away from home. I would have loved to hear Uri's reason for being where he was, and that in itself would normally have meant a visit to a camp for a while.

It was at this point I decided to keep an eye on the direction we were heading and on Uri himself. The last thing I wanted now was for him to lead me into a trap, not now, when I had come this far.

You can imagine then how pleased I was when he said, "We should stop for a rest and to have a meal now."

It was mid afternoon again, and I had the feeling we would do as we had done the day before, eat, sleep, and then when it was dark, take off on the road again. Also, if Uri was working with them, and I think he was, they must know where we were. They could know by two means. First, he could be carrying a transmitter in his gear, or more likely I could be carrying the damned thing in my bundle. So I thought I would have to make some excuse to re-pack my bundle, to have a chance to search it. If there was nothing, then I would have to assume he had one, and then I would have to part company with him. Killing him was out of the question, I did not for one second think I could, for no other reason than I was not fit enough to do it. He was too big for me, and he would be able to swat me like a fly if I were stupid enough to try anything.

He just looked at me and grinned. So I set to to re-pack it, taking the chance to, as I said to him, "lighten my load". This I used as a pretext for deciding if I should keep the piece or not, checking everything for any suspicious lumps or shapes. When I had finished the only things I had left were the bits of dried food Sharon had given me. Also, bits of clothing I deemed I might need, should I get a chance to change any of the rags I wore that passed as underwear.

The rest I put to one side, and using a rather strong stick which I had found, I dug a scrape and put them in, and covered them up. It was then I came out with the bright idea that this was not the best of places to stop for a rest. "Would it not be better if we moved a bit further away to have our rest, and to look for a bit more cover?" Uri said he agreed and that he was about to suggest the same. With that we picked up our bits and pieces and moved off. After about half an hour we came to a place that suited us better. It was a small outcrop of rocks that had a small crevice in the middle of them. Both Uri and I managed to get into the place, then in as comfortable a position as we could find for ourselves, we fell asleep.

Just how long we were asleep, or more to the point I was asleep, before the call of nature came upon me I do not know. The need was very great, so I got up and started to edge my way out of the position I was in. It was then I suddenly realised that Uri was not there; I had a little panic at first, then I thought perhaps he had been called by nature the same as myself. Very carefully I eased myself out of the crevice and stood still, listening to see if I could hear Uri, which I could not; I now had my second panic.

My condition was such I could wait no longer, so I stepped into the undergrowth a little way off the crevice. It was just as I was about to answer the call of nature, when I heard it. At first I was not sure what it was, then I realised it was somebody talking a little way off. My nerves were immediately on edge. The adrenaline was really pumping around my body now and I had not felt like this for years. With great care and trepidation I made my way to the area in which I had first heard the voice. By this time I was down on my belly, making like a snake, something else I had not done for years. I edged nearer and nearer to the sound, until at last I could hear the voice. It was not Uri who was talking; it was some other Russian who had a touch of the verbals. My mind was all agog with ideas, the bastard had sold me out, I was right about him, right from the start.

As I was just about to burst in on him and whoever he was with, I nearly died as a hand landed on my shoulder. It was Uri; he was looking at me and motioning me to stay quiet. For a second or two I just looked at him. I was dumbfounded, my mind was all mixed up by now. His action had completely confused me. I had just lost all track of all the intrigue which was going on around me. This big goon Uri, well I just did not know what to make of him any more. He gave me the impression he would sell his grandmother if the price was right. As I was not his grandmother why would he watch over me this way? I did not know and I just gave up. Uri in the meantime gave me a knife, a vicious-looking thing and he then pointed to the left side of the bush and dramatically held up two fingers. Looking at him I thought, shit, he is giving me the best part of the deal, he is giving me two of them.

Well, I thought, stuff you, Uri, you take the two and I will take the one. He shook his head and with that he launched himself through the undergrowth. I realised that I could do no more now than join him. When I broke cover I could see what he meant, there were five of them and he was at the three on his side. The two he had left for me were getting to their feet to attack him from the side as I crashed through behind them. The first one I got as he half turned towards me. As I laid him down, bleeding from his neck, I hardly had time to see what was happening to Uri. The second one turned fully round to face me, he had an assault rifle, but the bayonet was folded. He was trying desperately to cock the weapon as I opened his chest. When I turned, I could see two of the others were doing a dance with Uri.

Then I heard one of them cocking his rifle. I decided he was the one I was to take out. As I landed on his back he pulled the trigger. Then he fell forward with me still on his back. He had just shot his friend in the back. The first one Uri had taken on was wounded, but not too badly, and was getting to his feet to make a run for it. When he was halfway to his feet, I managed to take him in the middle of the back with the knife Uri had given me. As he fell I sat astride him for God knows how long, sat there just looking at Uri; I could not make it out. The big bastard had not got one of them. He had taken on the three, had only slightly wounded the first, I had taken the second, who had shot the third, who was getting the better of Uri. All this after I had managed to dispose of the two he had said I was to get.

As I looked at him, I said, "You have never done this before have you, Uri?"

It seemed to release some tension in him and he just slowly sank to the ground like a balloon losing all its gas. He just shook his head and said, "How can you manage to do all this and live with yourself?"

Then I looked at him for a while and said. "It certainly does not get any easier, Uri. Never, ever start if you can get away with it. Mind, there is one thing I have found out tonight."

"What is that?" he asked.

"I cannot rely on you to cover my back, can I? In this type of thing I am on my own. It is time you and I had a talk, Uri, and on my terms this time. I want none of your being the big man and the hero from now on, Uri. We both now know the score on that point, don't we! What's more, I think it is also time we were long gone from here. By the way, if you don't want to die now, you can get rid of that device they gave you to carry."

He looked at me and his mouth hung open. Then I said, "You realise now you will have to go the whole distance with me, don't you? Once they find this little lot you will be in it up to your neck as they say. Now let us search them for anything we can make use of, and then let us be on our way."

It took us some fifteen minutes to clear the bodies of anything we thought might be of use to us. We then crammed the bodies into the crevice in the rocks, the one where we had been sleeping before it all happened. I had thought of taking a pair of boots from one of them, but then I thought they might give me blisters. So far I have not got any blisters from the boots Sharon gave me. So I changed my mind. As I searched the bodies I found a map and a compass on the first one I had killed. These I managed to get into my pockets without Uri seeing them. By now I was more confused than ever about him.

The longer I thought about the whole incident after it had all ended the more I came to the conclusion that perhaps he had not intended to kill any of them. Still, if that were so, why had he given me this bloody vicious knife? Did he think I wouldn't use it? Still, I was armed once more. I would rather have had my own weapon but a large knife and an assault rifle were not to be laughed at. When I was satisfied the bodies were well covered I suggested we make tracks to wherever it was he was now leading me. Then with one last look around we set off in a north westerly direction.

We had a very uneventful time for the next twelve hours. The going was not easy by any stretch of the imagination, but it was not too hard either. As we progressed, the weather got decidedly colder, and as we continued, it seemed to be getting worse. The severe cold was probably caused by the fact that the sky remained clear and cloudless for the rest of the day. It started to cloud over a little as the end of the day got nearer. I suggested to Uri that perhaps we might stop for a rest, build a good shelter among the pines and have a good night's rest. It was going to get very cold tonight, I thought. Perhaps we were going to have a heavy snow fall. I thought we needed to be in substantial shelter when that happened, and I was pleased when he agreed with me. Uri was not very talkative, I do not know if it was true, but he seemed to have lost a lot of his enthusiasm since I had killed those men. I wondered if they were his friends, or what game he was playing. He had certainly made an arsehole of himself in the fight. He gave the impression he knew what to do, but for some reason best known to himself he did not do it.

We soon found the thing we were looking for. These were my favorite items in the whole of Russia, I liked them. They were the fallen pine, with the branches forming a type of ridge tent. Because of the way they stand on their sides after falling, they are so easy to convert into warm windproof shelters out here in this wilderness. The one I picked was not too big, but just right to get two people in. Not too much room in there, should one person move the other would know immediately. There was no way I was not going to touch him, because I still needed him. He would have a lot of trouble getting at me in the situation we would be in when I was asleep. Any move he made would wake me up. So I should be able to get a trouble-free night's sleep. We had our usual porridge stuff which he had brought with him for our meal. Then I produced some of the tea which Sharon had given me and made us a hot drink. It all went down very well and we carried out our final ablutions and then settled down for the night. The wind had turned very blustery by this time but it was not long before I was asleep.

Some hours later I came awake in an instant; I was up and had Uri by his coat front. The knife he had given me the night before was now at his throat. The wind was roaring outside the little bivouac we were in and I sensed there was a blizzard raging outside. "What the hell are you up to, Uri?"

Because it was dark I could not see him properly, but I could smell the fear on him. "Quick," I said, "What are you doing?"

All For A King's Shilling

"I have to make a call of nature, I must go out."

Slowly I felt his arms and hands. Much to my relief he did not have a gun or knife in them, so he was probably telling the truth. With that I released him.

"Uri, you of all people must know, with the way the weather is out there, that if you go out you will be lost as soon as you step away from this bivouac. You will disappear out there, man. Only fools who are already dead are out in that stuff. You have a call of nature, then you sit on it. If you are desperate you do it, then poke it out through the side of the bivouac, alright?"

With that I lay down again and promptly went back to sleep.

The storm raged for three nights and two days. When it finally stopped we were covered in snow but we were as warm as I think I have ever been in this part of the world. We could not stay here for too long. Uri's call of nature was also warming up and getting quite rich. The bastard had not even poked it out of the bivouac. He just left it to mature along with its bugs inside the bivouac. As we were likely to be in this place for a day or two and, what was more, we did not have much food left, his leaving his shit in the corner was not going to be very healthy. I was not too keen to share what little we had with his bloody bugs either. So I packed up my few belongings, took a piece of dried meat Sharon had insisted I bring then, with a lot of pushing and prodding, I got Uri on the move again.

The going was getting very tough as it was all new snow. Although the top was frozen it would not take the weight of a man. So each step was a labour in itself, sinking up to the crutch each time you put a foot down. Still, I was on the move again and I was heading west, something which helped to lighten my load and also my heart. I had given a lot of thought to Uri's plan. I would give it a go, but we had already lost some time with the storm. So I told Uri that we had better get a move on, then we just might make it. I was a bit worried about Uri now because it looked as if he had lost all his confidence and fight. It had all come about since I had killed those Russians. If only I knew just what game he was playing. I was going to have enough trouble getting out of Russia myself without having to carry him at the same time and trying to keep an eye on him all the time. He always gave me the impression he could turn very nasty without any warning at all.

It took us a further five days and nights of hard going to reach the settlement at Cape Kanin Nos. Nothing untoward happened in that time. As time passed and fatigue took over, we stopped being so cautious. I had sworn so many times before I would not give in to tiredness and let my caution slip. Yet every time I reached the point of being so tired that I didn't give a damn. I just dropped my head and plodded on as if I were back on a map march on Dartmoor. Even so we did arrive without further incident.

We stood and looked at Cape Kanin Nos and I could hardly believe my eyes. I half expected to see Charlie Chaplin eating his boots in the first hut I looked into. It was like somewhere from the Alaskan Gold Rush. All the place consisted of was a group of wooden huts; they used wood for building just about everything up here. The wood, of course, is warmer than stone or concrete. I do not think bricks would survive up here in these temperatures. I had the impression that most of the inhabitants were out at sea fishing or they had left. There were hardly any people around at all.

William Atlay

We were standing on a small hill to the south east of the place. I say a small hill. It looked very much like an old mining waste tip which immediately put me on my guard. Mines in this area were worked by inmates of forced labour camps.

In the settlement there was a jetty sticking out into the sea. It was empty. The edge of the sea was frozen to about halfway along the jetty. I thought if Uri's boat had been, I had had it here, but if it hadn't, then I could soon be on my way. Then it would only be another couple of days until it would not get in because of the ice. As we took in the scene below us it was starting to get dark. I thought it was a bit early for that and then I thought we were in for one hell of a storm tonight by the look of it. At this point Uri nudged my arm and pointed. Just beyond the end of the jetty a small fishing boat was heading towards the jetty.

He said, "Come, this one is yours." I picked up my bundle and with all sorts of ideas crashing around in my head, I followed him down the slope and into the settlement. It did not take us long to reach the end of the jetty. It was completely dark by the time we reached it and the place looked to be deserted. As we started to move along the jetty a man came out from the rear of a small hut. It was obvious he knew Uri as he addressed him by his name. We stood there, the three of us. Uri and this man talked in low voices. From where I stood I could not make out what they were talking about, but I was a little concerned. As they talked the man kept looking in my direction. I felt glad I still had the assault rifle with me and tucked into my side. I was sure he could not see it.

After some short while Uri stepped over to me, "It's all arranged. You are to board the fishing vessel, then it will be sailing as soon as you are on."

"Great," I said, "but I've one small favour to ask of you before we leave, Uri. Would you come on board with me?"

"Yes, of course I will."

With that we all three moved off to the end of the jetty where the boat was moored with its engine still running. "Not for a quick escape, just because they can sometimes not be started again, because of the cold," the skipper told me as we clambered aboard.

As I climbed aboard I was looking at everything. I had thought it would be better if Uri stayed with us until the rendezvous with the Norwegian fishing boat, that is. It surprised me somewhat when he offered no objections to doing that. So it was we sailed off on what I hoped would be the last part of this horrendous journey I had undertaken all those years ago.

Chapter Sixteen
London With Katrine And Carl With A Score To Settle
Here we go again, Russia 1979

Good morning Mr Fisherman.
Good morning Sir said he.
Have you a Lobster you can give to me?

As long as I live I don't think I shall ever forget the night we set sail from the fishing settlement at Cape Kanin Nos, on the northern coast of Russia. It was the start of a storm, a storm which had been brewing since mid afternoon. At first it wasn't too bad, but the small boat we were on was rolling and pitching like a tin can. It had been some considerable time since I'd been to sea and I even doubted if I could swim any more. What I did know was that if I went over the side, I wouldn't survive for more than two or three seconds at best in these conditions.

Still, the weather we were suffering, which would have put your ordinary Western fisherman into port, didn't affect these men in any way whatsoever. When we eventually reached their fishing grounds, they just kept on putting their nets over the side, making a trawl and hoisting the catch inboard. Then repeating the sequence time and time again. It was relentless the way they pursued the fish. It seemed that in no time at all after they cast, they were hauling them in, always with rather large catches. I think some Hull or Grimsby men would have been rather jealous of these boys.

We had been at sea for some time and they had just cast their nets for the umpteenth time, when Uri's friend came and told us we should go to the bridge. I collected my bits and pieces together and I also took the assault rifle, which I hadn't let out of my hands, not since I took it from that poor Russian whom I had killed, along with the others, about a week ago.

When we arrived on the bridge of the boat (and I suppose to call it a bridge was a little bit over the top, it would be better described as a garden shed) it honestly looked as though they had just built a garden shed on the boat and then called it a bridge. This was obviously what a real Russian fishing boat looked like, not one of the de luxe type which we see trailing our Royal Navy around all over the world.

Mind, this hut cum bridge had some pretty sophisticated equipment in it. I saw sonar, a couple of radars and two very powerful radios. Once we had crammed ourselves into this hut, I was introduced to the Skipper. He was an old man; at least he looked as if he was in his seventies, or maybe more. Mind, when I next saw myself in a mirror I had my doubts as to how old he really was. The thing is, he took me to one of the radar screens and pointed to a small dot on the screen. "That is your next fishing boat."

I spent the next half hour being tossed and thrown about this hut cum bridge while the old man manoeuvered his boat towards the dot on the radar, something which he did very skillfully, I thought. He continued as if he was fishing, making runs in one direction and then back again. Sometimes he would sail away from the dot, and then he would turn and head back towards it. Each time he made a run, when he finished it, he was a little bit nearer to the dot which he had pointed out to me. From observing the movements of the dots as an untrained observer, I would have said it was doing the same. I just had the idea they were both doing the same; all the time moving closer and closer together.

I thought to anybody else who was watching on radar in the area they wouldn't look suspicious. Just two boats, fishing in these waters along with all the other boats; and it looked as if there were perhaps a hundred boats fishing here at the same time, so the boat the Skipper had pointed out on the radar and ours should not stand out too much. All the boats appeared as dots on the radar screen. The Skipper told me that one, or perhaps two, of the boats were not fishing, just watching the others. He said, "You have to be patient, my friend. In time and without raising any suspicions, I will get you to the other boat."

"What can I say? I only wish there was something I could do for you, Skipper. As it is I've nothing left to give, so I'll just get out of your way."

"You have nothing I need my friend, your getting away is gift enough for me, I'll have beaten the bastards again."

Turning to Uri I said, "I think we should go and get some rest, there is nothing we can do here. It looks as if it will take some time before these two boats meet."

"Yes," said Uri, "I think I'll stay here on the bridge; it doesn't smell as fishy as down there."

So I made my way back below alone. One thing had puzzled me all the time I had been on the bridge. How in the hell did the Skipper of this wreck know which fishing boat among all the others to make for? One thing I did know was that if I thought about that too much, I'd not make the jump when the time came. With that I just shrugged my shoulders, had a little shiver, and put it out of my mind.

The lad who acted as cook on this thing gave me a cup of what passed for tea; it was worse than some of the stuff we used to get in the camps. So I waited until he was out of the place and then tossed it into his gash bucket which was spilling its contents all over the place. Then I occupied myself with my bits and pieces. First I cleaned the assault rifle, unloaded the magazines and then reloaded them. When I had finished I put one back on the gun and the rest into my bundle. Once I had completed everything, I then rested against the bulkhead and tried to get some sleep. As I watched from under my eyelids every now and then different members of the

All For A King's Shilling

crew came and had a look at me. It seemed as if I was attracting a lot of attention, I thought.

I must have fallen asleep at last, because I was awakened by Uri who told me. "We should go back to the bridge now; the time for you to change boats is nearly here, my friend."

I didn't like him calling me his friend; I didn't like the sound of it one little bit. It sounded to me as if he was mocking me, playing with my hopes of escape, but I followed him to the bridge anyway. When I entered, the Skipper told me, "Go and have a look at that radar, Englishman," pointing to the one I had looked at earlier.

Immediately I could see we were on a course heading towards a dot which I could only presume was the one he had pointed out earlier. There was no way of my knowing this for certain of course, but I was forever the optimist. As I looked at it for a minute or so, I felt nothing. It was just a dot on a radar screen and nothing else, and then suddenly I felt a swell of excitement in my guts as I watched the dot on the radar. It was getting closer and I knew as it did so I was getting closer and closer by the minute to my final objective and that was escaping the clutches of the bloody Russians and their twisted way of life.

This was it I thought, the time had come, and soon I would be on my way home at last and for real this time. Soon at least I would be away from it all, one way or another I'd be away from it all. If the dot turned out to be a Russian watchdog, well I would be dead soon enough. If it was what they said it was, then I would be on my way to settling an old score.

I asked the Skipper, "On which side do you intend to pass?"

"The starboard side; I will only be able to make the one pass, though. I'll slow the boat if I can, but it will not be much in this weather; you appreciate I have to keep steerage speed, you know. You will have to make the jump between the two boats on your own and you'll only have the one chance. If you miss, nobody will be stopping to rescue you. If you don't jump, there is no way I will have you on board when we return to port. It is as they say the end of the line for you my friend. I will have you thrown overboard dead or alive, one way or the other, you will be leaving this boat in the next few minutes. Voluntarily, I hope, or later with the assistance of the crew."

For a full two minutes I looked the Skipper of the boat eyeball to eyeball. I could see the pity in his eyes, but I also knew his life and the life of his crew depended on them doing exactly as he had just said he would do.

"I understand, Captain, I'll go of my own free will but thanks anyway for getting me this far." Nodding towards Uri I said, "I'd watch that bastard if I were you, though." The Skipper just nodded and gave a little grin, then said, "I am glad you understand the situation and I hope to God you make it."

"Oh, yes, I understand only too well. There is just one thing, though, if you cannot get close enough for me to make the jump do you think perhaps you could throw me overboard nearer the Norwegian coast than the Russian one? I'm just the unlucky bastard who'd survive and get washed ashore; I'd rather it was Norway and not bloody Russia."

At this he burst out laughing and putting an arm around my shoulder, he said, "Yes, I may try and do that for you, English, I cannot promise that, but I may try. Whichever way it goes you will be going over the side. There is no way in which we will be taking you back to our 'Great Motherland'. We would all be shot, after a long period of pain and torture, as I am sure you know only to well. So if there is no transfer, then over the side you go."

I looked at Uri, who had been standing listening to all that was said and I turned to the Skipper and said, "What about our big friend here?"

To this the Skipper just grinned and I thought well, at least should things go wrong I wouldn't be alone when they threw me, to Davy Jones' Locker.

Then I turned to Uri, "Thank you for all the help you have given me, Uri. Mind, I do think you need to change your occupation. If you keep on talking as big as you do, the day will come again when you'll have to back it all up with actions. As you have heard the skipper say, from now on there's no way I'll be able to help you out anymore.

"One way or another, Uri, tonight I shall be free of this terrible land and its crazy system of protecting its citizens. Mind, Uri if I make a success of this jump, I may just send you a card from Piccadilly, via your KGB friends in the Kremlin. That will help your prospects no end, Uri."

He just grinned at me and said, "You still have to make that jump, my friend."

With that we both stepped out on to the deck on the starboard side of the boat. Once there, I propped the rifle against the back of the bridge and looked for something to tie my bundle to my side. There was nothing, so I wedged it between the bulkhead of the bridge and a hatch. When I had done that I looked out over the bows of the boat and I could just see the mast light of a boat bearing down on us. As I looked hard into the darkness, I had a terrible fright. The boat I was expected to jump on to looked to be a lot larger than the one I was now on. It meant I would not only have to jump across to it, but up to the deck as well. A vision of the horror of the last ship transfer I did in these waters flashed across my mind. I wasn't very happy right at that moment.

The more I looked at the fishing boat which by now was bearing down on us it looked to me as if the sea was rougher now than it had been a few moments earlier. I thought, God, I'm never going to make it and I'm going to die in a few minutes' time. If the two skippers went too close, well, I would have an easy jump, but then I and the crews of both boats could end up in the sea. In fact within the next few minutes we could all be dead.

Then I thought what the hell, I'd been officially dead for years, this would only put the record straight, there's no time to worry now. With that I hoisted myself up on to the side of the fishing boat's bridge. With one foot on the side window ledge of the bridge I managed to get a hold on the roof of the thing. Once I felt secure, I half turned and looked back at Uri; I called to him to pass me the rifle and my bundle of bits and pieces.

I had the feeling that bastard knew exactly what I wanted but he made out he couldn't hear me. When I turned to see how the two boats were doing, to my horror I saw the bows of the two trawlers were not more than a foot apart. Shit, I thought, we are going down and then the next moment they were ten feet apart and I looked open-mouthed at the gap. Oh God, I thought, I'm never going to make that jump. Once again I turned to look at Uri and I saw he had the rifle in his hands. Then I felt the rush of air as the sea dropped into a trough and the trawlers once more came together.

All For A King's Shilling

At that moment I thought this was it, it was now or never. In another few seconds they would be yards apart again and I would never make it. So with my heart in my mouth I reached up and out with my right arm. Somehow, I didn't know how, but somehow I managed to get hold of an upright stanchion of some sort on the passing trawler. Then just as I felt as if my shoulder joint was about to be wrenched from its socket, I stepped out and into space. The pain in my shoulder was so severe I screamed and as I did, I felt myself being swivelled around the stanchion by the force of the forward movement of the boat. Then I landed with both feet hard on the deck in the waist of the boat. Apart from the pain in my shoulder, it had been as easy as that.

Still holding on to the stanchion to steady myself, I turned to look at the trawler from which I had just landed. It had been my intention to wave at Uri in that world famous re versed, Churchillian salute. On my face I had a grin from ear to ear, for I could hardly believe my luck, but I could hardly believe my eyes when I saw Uri.

He was taking aim with the assault rifle at me and as I watched I saw his finger jerking as he pulled the trigger. Then, I saw the look of anger on his face as it did not fire. I just had time to hold up my left arm and show him the firing pin from the rifle as both he and the fishing boat disappeared into the darkness of the Arctic waters.

So that was the 'something' he was going to give me when we parted, I remember thinking, I didn't think I'd seen the last of you, old pal.

After that everything was a little hazy, to say the least. The next thing I remember was hitting my head as I collapsed to the deck of the boat just as a face I had not seen for years peered at me from a large fur hood. I just said, "Nice to see you, Carl." I did not know if it was the relief or what, but I felt the emotion and stress of the last few years drain out of me and at that moment I thought I had died. As it turned out, I had just passed out. The dying well, that was to come later.

When I came to some one and a half hours later I was in a bunk and had a lovely warm feeling all over me. At first I was a little disorientated, but I was sure I was free and as soon as I saw my surroundings I knew I was free. The cabin I was in for a start was clean, in fact the cleanest place I had seen since I had left Katrine that fateful day all those years before. As I looked around the cabin I started vaguely to recognise and remember things in it. Then after a few minutes it dawned on me. I knew I had been in this cabin before. The last and only time was when Carl took me to see the skipper soon after we left Newcastle upon Tyne all those years before.

As the memories started to flood back again it must have emotionally affected me; because I must have either passed out or gone to sleep again. The next time I looked around the cabin I saw Carl was sitting on the other bunk looking at me, he was grinning from ear to ear.

"How goes it my friend?" I said.

He just grinned and said, "Fine, better now it is you we have picked up. We had given you up for dead some years ago but I for one never doubted that we would see you again one day and now that day has arrived, my friend."

I looked around the cabin once more, to check we were alone. Then I said, "You haven't told anybody who I am, have you Carl, and what did you mean just now, when you said we?"

"Oh just myself and the crew. Why do you not want me to tell anybody who you are? The Skipper is the same one who brought you here those long years ago so he knows, but the rest of the crew, well, they are all new. The Skipper is all right though."

"Has the Skipper reported a pick-up yet, or not?"

"No. He'll not be making any reports until we are well and truly clear of the Russian coast."

"Good, will you please ask the Skipper not to report picking me up this trip? It is important nobody knows I'm still alive."

He frowned at me for a moment, then he said, "Sure, but the Skipper will want to know more. Is it to do with that one trying to shoot you as you came over?"

"I will explain everything if you take me to the Skipper."

"Later, did you know the big guy tried to shoot you?"

"Yes, Carl, I knew, but thank heaven I took the firing pin out of the rifle before I ever let it out of my hands."

"Has this anything to do with your rescue not being reported?"

"Yes, it does. I think I have been used ever since I came across Uri, that is the big guy's name. At least that is what he calls himself. I have a feeling he is KGB. I do not think the poor sods on that fishing boat will be free for much longer. Once they get back to port I think there will be a reception committee waiting for the poor so and so's. If the skipper has any sense at all, he will dump Uri over the side long before they dock."

Carl looked at me for a while and then said, "From what you say, I suppose we are in danger then."

"Oh yes, I think we are in a lot of danger. Uri may have been working one of his own little rackets but I doubt it very much. It's my belief that he hopes to impress his bosses with the uncovering of some great escape route out of Russia. What is more, Carl, I am certain he knows who I am. You see, Carl, as far as the GRU knows, I'm dead. They think I died out on the ice some time ago and I do not want anybody in London finding out that I didn't and that I have survived the ordeal. You see, Carl, I now know who it was who set me up, and I also know who the number one spy in the organization is. As to Uri, well, personally I think he is nuts, but you can never really tell with these people. You should know that by now, Carl."

"What about our people? Can we tell them you are out, or not?"

"No, Carl, it is better we tell no one. This ring could also have penetrated our people for all I know. Best we keep things quiet for a little longer."

Carl then left me and went off to see the Skipper. "I think I had better tell the Skipper this entire story, Bill. They may have vessels out searching for us right now."

"Oh, they will have, Carl, you can bet on it. Did you not know that there are two or more minders out with that Russian fishing fleet every time it puts to sea? It could be this boat they are really after, Carl."

"Well, Bill, we have suspected for some time now that they had somebody watching us, but we have never been sure. Still, if you say they have a minder or two, then perhaps we should alter our methods of operating. Now I think I should have a talk with the Skipper."

All For A King's Shilling

Once he had left the cabin I was too tired to think about it all anymore, so I settled down and went to sleep again, I felt so tired now, more tired than I had felt for years. I must be getting old and soft, I thought, as I drifted off.

I must have passed out like a light, for it seems I slept the clock round, and the storm out. When I came to, I got up and poked my head out of the door of the cabin and asked a young lad who was in the passageway outside, "Are there any showers on board?"

He never spoke, but just pointed to a small hatch at the end of the passage.

"Thanks." I said.

I then popped back into the cabin and looked around it and eventually found a towel in the locker at the end of the bunk. So I went to have a shower. After the first flush of water I slowly increased the heat and the force of the shower. It was as if I were trying to wash away the horrors of the last few years when I had been unable to clean myself in any way, or stay clean. At first I must admit, I was a little shocked to see myself in the shining piece of steel that passed for a mirror. I'd not realised just what an effect the last few years had had on me, but I soon accepted my new look, and I still felt great!

The main thing was that after my shower, for the first time for years I felt really clean. More than that, after all those years of degradation I felt like a million dollars. It was the greatest morale booster I think I had ever had. The realisation had sunk in that I was all skin and bone now, but I was free, and I really did feel great. Shortly after I had my shower Carl brought me some clothes to wear. He also brought some anti-louse powder with which to dust myself as I'd just showered away all the powder they had doused me with. As I was dusting myself with the stuff I caught some in my mouth and throat. This then set me off coughing and soon made me sick. Before I could stop myself I was retching on to the deck and it wasn't a pretty sight. After a little I managed to stop the coughing and that also stopped me retching. Carl had a strained look on his face as he watched me, but I was a little perturbed about the blood which I brought up as well as other consumptive-type stuff. Still, when I had regained some composure, I put on the clothes which he had brought me and to my surprise they fitted me quite well.

Then I told Carl, "I am now ready for a good old English breakfast."

He asked me, "Are you really ready for that kind of food? I think you should have something light at first."

"Don't be daft, of course I am ready for it, I feel great, I'll be all right."

At my insistence he got the chef to cook me an English breakfast, eggs, bacon, tomatoes and fried bread with lashings of good hot ground coffee! I was a little surprised they had such food on board and ten minutes later I sat and took one look at it.

All I said was, "Well, here goes, once round the buoy, my friends."

Then I tucked into it, as if there was no tomorrow. I think I got half an egg down, one rasher of bacon, and half a tomato, I drank a mouthful of coffee, it all tasted so great.

Then it happened, the whole lot, everything I'd eaten plus everything I'd had these last few days came out in one. I do not think I had ever been so sick in my life. I felt ill, I was ashen white and I had one of those instant sweats which soak you in millionths of a second. Far, far worse than seasickness could ever make you feel, and seasickness can make you want to die and I felt as if I had died.

I remember Carl carrying me to the cabin I'd been in before. All I could do was apologize for the mess I had made in the mess room. I kept telling Carl I should go back and clean it up. Also, in the back of my mind I thought he should not be able to carry me this easily.

We reached the cabin and I was feeling hazy; things were moving around and I did not think it was the movement of the ship or Carl carrying me which was doing it. Then I remember Carl put me on the bunk and proceeded to remove my clothes. By this time I was shivering uncontrollably and I could see the worried look on his face which didn't do wonders for my morale. He really was concerned about me. It was the first time I had seen somebody look at me in that way since I had last seen Katrine in the courtroom that lifetime ago now. It was then I thought I should never see her again.

Carl covered me with blankets and what looked like a large sleeping bag. He then took off out of the cabin. He turned in the doorway; I think he said he would be back in a minute, and with that he left.

Once again in my life I felt all alone. I also felt very tired and very, very ill. For the first time I now felt really ill, the first time since I'd been taken prisoner all those years before. Somehow I had managed never to succumb to illness in the gaols or camps, but I must have been ill during that time. Never anything like the illness I was suffering now, though, God but I wanted to die. The look on Carl's face at the doorway had not given me much hope at all.

As I lay there I was still shaking and shivering uncontrollably, my bottom jaw was chattering fifty to the dozen. Again I vomited, and I just managed to raise myself enough to get it over the side of the bunk. As I looked at it through bleary eyes as it lay on the floor, I could see a yellow-coloured 'thing' in the stuff which had just come out of me. It was the most horrible stuff I had ever seen; the smell was like death itself. Some time and a couple of retchings later, when two more of these yellow coloured 'things' had joined the first, I realised what they were. They were my bloody teeth which were falling out. Some other bits of the stuff worried me but even so, I was also very pleased to realise that the worst-looking yellow bits were in fact my teeth.

Carl returned at that moment with a man who was by no stretch of the imagination a fisherman. He came into the cabin, stopped to look at the mess on the deck of the cabin, grunted a bit, and poked a pencil in amongst it all. He then stepped over to me and took my pulse. Again he grunted, and this time he stuck a thermometer into my mouth. "Keep that in if you can, please," he said. I lay there, stifling an urge to vomit again, and I was worried in case I swallowed his bloody thermometer while I was trying not to be sick. All the time I was shaking like a leaf. At last he took the thing out of my mouth, looked at it, and grunted again. He then left the cabin with a nod to Carl.

When he had gone I said to Carl, "I am sorry for making such a mess."

"Do not worry yourself, Bill; I will see it is all cleaned up."

Just then the grunter came back with a bloody syringe the size of a bucket. He also had something in his other hand, which turned out to be pills. He handed me the pills,

"Swallow those with a drink of water." This I did, all the time watching the syringe in his other hand.

He then turned to Carl, "Hold him down while I do this. I don't want him to move."

He then stuck the damned needle into me; I don't know how he found enough flesh to stick the bloody needle into me anyway. Once he got it in though, he proceeded to pump me up with the damned syringe. Within no time at all I felt drowsy and everything went hazy. Then I just drifted off into what could only be called oblivion and I had no recollection of anything from then until I came round.

When I did come to, it must have been much, much later. The first thing I noticed was that the movement of the fishing boat had stopped. Secondly, I was in a nice clean bed and it was not swaying from side to side. With that I deduced I was no longer in a bunk on a fishing vessel. So I looked around, only to discover I was in a room. The room was panelled in wood and it was clean, but sparsely furnished. It contained the bed I was in, a set of drawers, a chair and some mats on the floor. It was about ten foot by fifteen foot and I was all alone in it. Now I was fully awake, it reminded me of a situation I had been in years before. The main difference was, I could not feel any pains anywhere this time and I was not shivering. Something which I seemed to remember doing the last time I was awake. Then I remembered how I was shaking while that bloke was sticking that great big syringe into me. I tried to remember where that was, but I could not.

So I just lay for a while, looking around the room and taking everything in. There was a small window in one wall and I could see that the sun was shining outside. As I had not seen the sun for some time I decided to have a look out of the window. Not only did I want to see where I was, I felt I should make a move and get up. With that decision made, I sat up, no great problem there. Next I slid my legs out of the bed and sat there on the edge of the bed for a second or so, still no great problem. When I looked at myself I nearly burst out laughing for I had on a long old-fashioned type of nightshirt. Once I settled down again and as I still had no ill effects, I stood up; all seemed well. Then I went to step forward, over towards the window. The next I knew I was looking at a spider on the floor. The problem was I was looking at him from the same level he was at, floor level. "Well, Mr Spider," I said, "I've no idea how you got here and I haven't the slightest idea in the world how the bloody hell I got here."

Just then the door opened and an angel of mercy was standing over me. She was in a clean and sweet-smelling dress and she was carrying a tray which hid the top part of her body. She put down the tray she was carrying and she came over to where I was lying and picked me up. Then she carried me to the bed. It was as she was putting me back into the bed that I saw her face for the first time. It was at that moment I just burst out crying, "Katrine! Katrine!" I just kept repeating her name between great sobs of joy. "Katrine, how did you get out and when?"

The relief I felt was beyond description. She had made it, she had got out. My emotional state was such that I lapsed into unconsciousness again. It was another couple of minutes later before I came round again. Katrine told me later that she had thought I was going to die on her.

When my mind had settled down again she looked at me and said, "It seems I have made it in a better condition than you, my dearest heart."

Then I managed to pull myself together. I must have lain still for ages as she cradled me to her bosom. Eventually I asked her, "How in the hell could you lift me as easily as you did?"

"Oh! I am better trained and better fed than I was the last time I saw you or even when we first met. You know you have been here drifting in and out of consciousness every day or so for the last two months."

"Two months, two months, God I have got to get out of here. If those sods in London know I have been here for two months they will be after me."

"Don't worry about them. They, like our Great Russian friends, think you have been dead for a couple of years now. When we brought you off the boat even the Skipper thought you were dead. So to the rest of the world the man who managed to escape died of exposure. He is now buried up on the side of the hill. You will be able to see it when you are better, and you can look out of the window."

I then lifted the sheets of the bed and looked at myself. I said to Katrine, "The last time I saw anything like this was when the first pictures were published of the prisoners as they came out of Belsen."

"Yes, I know, but we can soon get you better, now you have at last come back to the real world again. It will not take long now, we will soon have you as fit as a fighting cock."

I looked at her and said, "I have had all the fighting I want in my lifetime, Katrine, I am at last through with all of that. Except that is, for the one man with whom I have a score to settle. A score which only I can settle, I'm afraid."

"I know," she said.

She looked at me for a while, and then said, "Are you sure that you must do this thing?

"Oh! Yes, I am sure Katrine, we will never be able to live anywhere in the world as long as he is alive. I say us, Katrine, and I am assuming we will be together from now on. You do know that I love you and I don't know what I would do now without you."

She looked at me for a moment or two and then said, "You fool, what do you think has kept me going all this time. I have only been waiting for this day when we would be together again, but is it you who has to do this thing. Is it necessary to kill this person? Surely if you tell the authorities in London, they will arrest him and he will be tried as the criminal he is."

"No, Katrine, it is not like that. If they are on to him and they think he will be of use to them, they will turn him. Then they will use him and they will protect him and use him for as long as he is of use to them. No, Katrine, the only chance we have is for him to die. I'm sorry but it is the only answer. As long as he is alive there is always the possibility he could find out about us. It would only take a message from him to his masters, the KGB, and they would either come here and kidnap us, or kill us. They would do that no matter where we were. No, Katrine, I do not intend to have to spend whatever time we have left together looking over our shoulders. Forever looking just in case he is standing behind us, as he will be one day. It is possible he has the protection of both sides of the fence already. No, he must die."

"Yes, I see that Bill, but surely the people in charge of the police in England can help you."

"Katrine, you are forgetting one important thing; to the British authorities I am dead. What is more, I wish it to stay that way. You know for the first time in years I feel safe here, and free. Let us make sure we can live the rest of our lives together that way."

"I suppose you are right. Carl says you must do this last thing or we will never be able to live without fear of somebody from our past popping up at the least expected time."

With that she never raised the subject again, and in fact became a very active member of our team as we hunted the Major down. What I can say is, that it was from that moment on I started to get better. For the first time in years I'd a purpose in life. Once more I had a reason for living, but unfortunately I still had an appointment to keep in London. As time went by I started not only to get better but to feel better as well. That appointment then became an irritation and I would get round to it as and when I was ready; I had all the time in the world.

When I had recovered from the worst of my physical problems, and my humour and spirits were rising once more and while Carl was away on another of his trips, Katrine and I consummated our relationship. When Carl came back it must have been obvious; he just grinned at us when he first saw us together and said, "This is good, and it makes my heart happy to see you two together like this."

The next few months were some of the happiest of my life as Katrine and I really got to know one another. We spent the time just talking, walking and generally taking things easy. She told me about her time in gaol and how one day Carl had arrived to take her away from it all. She said some other women and she had been working on a railway, laying sleepers. Then this tall man had appeared at the camp with paperwork to transfer her to another camp for further investigation. She said he treated her roughly as the normal guards had done. They had travelled northwards; all the papers Carl had were in order, for nobody questioned them.

They eventually arrived in a small port on the coast of Northern Russia. She told me they boarded a small ship to go to one of the islands off the coast. At least that was what he told the authorities. Once the boat left, they headed for the island, but when it got dark the boat rendezvoused with another boat and Carl and she transferred to it. He then told her he was my friend and he had come to take her away from Russia. She thought she was going to see me, but Carl told her that if I was still alive, and he had reason to believe I was, then I would be somewhere in the prisons or camps in Russia. Unfortunately they had been unable to locate me; but they would keep trying. They had, he told her, lost all trace of me in the camps. He also told her he would keep going to all the places we had arranged as meeting points should I ever get away. The problem was I seemed to have disappeared in the system, and none of their contacts could locate me. Which meant I was either dead, or in some very bad camp in the far north.

She told me he had given up hope of ever seeing me again, and when I had stepped on to the deck of the boat that night, he did not at first recognize me. He had told her it was not until I spoke he realized who it was. She went on to tell me the crew had been told to pick up some Russian dissident. "Carl was speechless when he realized it was you. But I'm glad it was you," she added, and then laughed in the way only she could.

When she had finished her story she asked me, "What's Carl's real name?"

"Just Carl," I said, "You must have heard of the famous Norseman, Noggin the Nod, well he is descended from him. He is a right Noggin!"

She just looked at me and laughing her head off said, "You are mad, you know."

I looked at her and just said, "Oh! Yes, that I do know, but I'm only mad now I am once more with you."

Months had passed since I had escaped on to the boat and I was now feeling two hundred percent better. I was getting fit once more and I had started training again. Not too much at first, 'Five BX' to start with and then I started to jog. This I did when everybody else was asleep as I did not want to attract too much attention. It had been reported in the press that a fisherman's body had been found floating out at the fishing grounds. He must have fallen over the side of some boat and died within minutes of falling. No people had reported anybody lost overboard so the Norwegians had buried the body in the settlement of Tana on the North Cape. Both Katrine and Carl were sure the report would confirm to all interested parties should they still be on the lookout for me, that I was now dead for certain.

The main thing at the moment was to continue to get myself fit and well again. I used to jog up to the top of the hills overlooking our cabin and then come down as fast as I dared. Each day I got a little fitter, a little stronger. My muscles had wasted away because of the length of time it had taken me to get over the rigours of the camps. If it hadn't been for the expert nursing and help I'd received from Katrine I would never have made it this far.

Time was passing and my fitness was improving day by day. Soon now Katrine and I would have acquired our new identities, which Carl's sister Helga was arranging for us through her boss in Oslo. Once all was set, then and only then Katrine and I, accompanied by Carl, would start on the last part of my mission.

Carl had all the arrangements for our stay in London worked out. Through his contacts in London he had arranged several flats in different areas of the capital to be made available to us. Katrine at first was not too keen on the date we had set to travel, but when she saw the improvement in my well-being, she relented. Helga, who had kept at a distance from us since I arrived, now started to take a more active part in events. She told me one day, "Bill, the new identities which will be ready in a week or two show the two of you as native Norwegians. No government will be able to fault them." To the rest of the world we would be natural born Norwegians. Katrine was to be given a new identity and then a second one as well; she was also to become my wife. She got all coy about it and started talking about weddings and things. To which I told her it would be better if we waited until the problem in London was sorted before we got into all that. When I asked her if it really made much difference, to my surprise she said no.

Helga told us we would be able to travel anywhere in the world we wanted without question. The identities were, she said, the real thing issued by the Government. Later with tears in my eyes, when Helga at last gave me my papers, I told Helga and Carl, "It's like coming home for good."

"It's just great to have you home at last, Bill."

"What are you three talking about?" asked Katrine

"Well, Katrine, many years ago before I was born my family moved to Scotland from Oslo, on Government orders. You see although I was born in England my parents were Scandinavians. Not only have I worked for the English all these years, I also worked for Carl's organization."

Katrine was still looking at me a little strangely when I told Helga, "You had better not put Russia on that list of countries to visit. I have had a lifetime of Russia, thank you very much."

As time passed my health improved dramatically and I started to get restless about getting on with the task which I knew I had to do. It was at this time that Carl and I started to spend more time in close conversation with one another. I did not want to get Katrine involved with the problem.

After about a week of this, she suddenly said, "I know what you are planning to do. There is no way I am going to let you go and leave me here while you do this thing you feel you have to do. I'm going with you, and if necessary I shall serve time in prison, or die helping you do this job you are so determined to do. There is no way I am going to remain here in the north of Norway and perhaps never see the two of you again." She turned to me and said, "I lost you once before, I'm not going to run that risk again. So either I go with you or I shall follow you until you do relent and let me join you."

It was left to me to tell her there was no danger of us getting into trouble doing what we had planned to do. Her reply was simple, "If there is no danger, then there is no reason why I should not come with you then."

As I looked at her I knew instinctively I couldn't face leaving Katrine here, and I knew she would be leaving with us.

So it was that our plans had to be changed to cover the three of us. Not only was Katrine determined to come with us, but she was determined to take part in the whole operation. The planning and the lot; so with this change in mind the plans were at last finalized. So it was some three months after this that the three of us left on our trip to Britain.

Britain, Home of the Brave, Land of the Free. Or is that America, I forget.

Carl arrived in Britain in the manner best suited to him, by fishing boat. He docked in the Humber and then made his way to London. He left Norway some time before us. We knew the day he was due to dock, so on that day Katrine and I left our haven in Norway.

We took a truck ride to Tromso and it was one hell of a trip. It took us the best part of three days. We made it in the end without too much trouble other than a few bruises and without arousing any interest, which was the main reason for our mode of travel. Once there, we joined the Bergen Ferry and settled down for the journey. We had to share the cabin with another couple who were retuning to the south before the winter set in. We tried not to have too much conversation with them and I think they thought we were newly-weds and they left us alone.

Katrine saw Russian agents everywhere. It took quite a bit of persuasion to settle her down. She kept saying, "Everybody on the ferry looks Russian."

"Don't be silly, Katrine, they are bound to look like Russians in this part of the world. All of you are descended from the same ancestors; you are all bound to look alike."

It seemed to work. She eventually settled down. I think in the end she was more tired than frightened. I told her, "I'll get Helga to come to Bergen and take you back if you don't put a stop to the nervous way you are carrying on. You will be no help to us the way you are, Katrine. Remember how strong you were in Russia when I was in trouble, Katrine."

This seemed to settle her down. I do think the memories of her time in the Russian gaol she had been in were just coming to the surface. Anyway we passed the journey sleeping and just resting. It was then she started asking me about Britain. "What is London like?" she asked and I then spent most of the time telling her what London was like the last time I saw it. How it was a wonderful place to visit, but could be hell to live in. The most pleasing part of this time was we were alone for most of it.

When we arrived in Bergen I left the ferry first and headed for the Newcastle Ferry. Katrine, who seemed to have got completely over her attack of jitters, then made her way to the airport. She took a small plane to Oslo and then took a plane on to Newcastle. We had arranged to meet up again on the train from Newcastle to London.

The plan was that we were to sit together, as if we were strangers; we would make polite conversation and chat. Then I would leave the train at York. She was to check to see if anybody got off and followed me. If they did she was to signal me when I arrived at Kings Cross on the next train from York to London.

Well, what was it Robby Burns said about plans of mice and men? When I got to Newcastle I eventually found the carriage Katrine was in. The problem arose that there were no empty seats in the carriage at all. It was the first time I had been on one of the new full length coaches and I could see Katrine sitting by the window, about half way down the coach. She just gave a little nod and a sheepish grin and I just did the same. All the time I was dying to touch her, talk to her and do God alone knows what to her. Instead I had to stand at the end of the carriage and just look at her. Shit, I thought, I cannot take too much of this.

After the train had left and I was standing at the end of the door she came out and stood by me. I told her everything was alright and we would carry on as planned. I would stay where I was. If a chance to sit beside her came up I would take it, but otherwise we would just carry on. If I didn't get a chance to talk to her again I would be looking for her in London. When I arrived she could come to me as if she was waiting to meet me, if all was well. She then went back and reclaimed her seat. I stood there, disbelieving all I had said to her. I thought what a shit you are, so I signalled to her that I needed to talk to her. I didn't give a shit by this time who the hell was watching. She got up again and came to the end of the carriage. As she got to me I said, "I love you Katrine." "I love you, Bill," she said, then she went straight back to her seat. She was right of course, but I was mad as hell.

By the time the train had arrived at York I had memorized every face in the coach. As it pulled in I gave her a nod, which I hoped nobody in the train knew was directed at her. I remember as I was getting off the train I thought what a beautiful woman she was.

All For A King's Shilling

I scrutinized everybody who got off the train; I then made my way to the exit queue; at the last minute I turned as if I had forgotten something. Then I made my way to one of the platforms over the footbridge. When I got there, I turned and looked back at the steps of the footbridge but nobody had followed me. Then I made my way back to the exit and to the booking hall. There, I bought a ticket for London and made my way to the station cafe where I bought myself a pie and a cup of coffee. When the woman asked me for the money I nearly fainted at the till; I must have been away longer than I thought. Then I sat down in the furthest corner of the cafe I could find, from where I could see all the room and the platform outside. As I could see nothing untoward, I settled down to eat my pie and drink my coffee.

I took one sip of the coffee and thought it tasted nearly as bad as the stuff we used to get in the first camp I was in. When I took a bite of the pie, I nearly choked. It was putrid; I would have complained if I had not wanted to remain in the background. So I just put it back on my plate and forced myself to wash down the one bite I had taken with the rest of the coffee. Then I spent the next half hour watching everything that happened in that station. When at last I was happy, I made my way out to the platform for the London train. Within ten minutes I was safely ensconced in a corner seat at the back of the carriage with a view of the full length of it. So I settled down and then spent most of the time studying my fellow travellers. As I could discern nothing wrong with any of them, I felt quite satisfied with myself.

We arrived at Kings Cross Station in London just before six that night and I left the platform via the ticket collector's gate. From the gate I made my way to the middle of the concourse and I looked around to see if I could see Katrine. My heart sank a little when I could see no sign of her. I must admit it was the nearest I had come to panic since we left the north. I'd started to make my way to the exit when I spotted Carl. He made no sign of recognition at all and made his way to the station cafe, so I did the same. This time I took my time, first stopping at the newsagents to buy the Evening Standard.

When I entered the cafe some five minutes after Carl, I decided that I would try the tea here, having had the problem with coffee in York. When I'd been served I took my tea and sat down with my back to Carl. He said nothing at first and then he turned and asked me, "Have you a light?"

I thought he's mad, he knows I don't smoke; there was however a box of matches on the table which I can only presume he had put on it. Which I picked up and gave it a little shake, there were some matches in it so I handed them to him. "Don't worry," he said," as he started to light his pipe, "Katrine's train has been delayed for some reason, it should be here in about ten minutes."

"Good," I said, "I think I was clear at York, but until we talk to Katrine we won't know for certain, will we?"

"Don't worry, I shall meet her. It will be best if you make your way to the rooms I have arranged for you."

He gave me directions and the address of the flat. He told me to take the taxi to Canon bury Road and how to get to the rooms from where the taxi dropped me off. With that he gave me back the matches and I left the cafe. I knew that if anybody followed me now he would spot them.

After walking around the concourse for a couple of minutes I left the station and took a taxi to the place he had told me about. Now I was in for another shock; it seemed the taxis in London had developed to such an extent that they now ran on gold tyres. Anyway I was duly dropped off. I had not seen anything untoward on the journey. Still, I took no chances and I followed the route Carl had given me and I took my time. After all, the more quickly I got there, the longer I would have to wait alone inside for Katrine. I was starting to fret a little about her. I should never have left her on that bloody train.

Then I walked down the road in which Carl's contact had rented the rooms for us. Once I had identified the house I just walked on past it. Although I was looking ahead as I walked the length of the road, I missed nothing in the road. There was nobody observing the house which our rooms were in, there were no cars or vans parked which in my mind could have been used as observation points. As I returned along the road I took particular notice of the houses opposite the rooms we had; once again I could see nothing untoward. Next I left the road and did a circle of the rear of both sides of it. When I was satisfied all was well I slowly made my way to the house the rooms were in.

I was just about to enter the garden when a taxi drew up and out stepped Katrine. I think the relief on both our faces showed. I put my arm out to her and said, "I should never have left you alone on that train."

"Yes, Bill, I wish you had stayed on and not left me."

With that the door of the house opened and a rather thin-faced woman said, "Ah! you must be Mr and Mrs Johannson."

"Yes, we are. I understand you have some rooms for us."

"Oh! You speak English, although you have a funny accent."

I thought, not as funny as you think, Mrs, but instead of saying anything I just grinned and said, "Yah!"

With that we were shown to the rooms, three in all on the second floor. After she had shown us up to them she left, saying, "You can contact me in the basement if you need to know anything."

Once the door was closed I looked at Katrine and then for a long time just held her close to me. After some time she whispered in my ear, "I am starving."

"So am I," I replied. We had a quick look around the rooms and then went out to get something to eat. We did not have far to go; there was a small corner shop cum cafe two streets away.

As we walked along I saw a figure on the road opposite move out and fall in behind us. He was some distance behind us and moving more slowly than us. I knew by instinct it was Carl. I felt comfortable again for the first time since we had embarked on this trip. I missed the big lumbering so-and-so when he was not around.

Katrine and I sat down to have something to eat. We read what passed for a menu and settled for a couple of ham sandwiches and a pot of tea. "No pots, just mugs," I was told with a snigger by the man behind the counter.

We sat down at the back of the cafe and faced the door. Carl came in and sat just inside the door, in what could only be described as the window. All the time he was eating he was watching the movement of both pedestrians and vehicles outside.

All For A King's Shilling

Nothing untoward happened, and after we had managed to eat the sandwiches Katrine and I left. We made our way back to the rooms Carl had rented for us.

Carl stayed in the cafe as we left. I did see him out on the street some distance behind us as we made our way back.

Katrine and I had been back in the room for about half an hour when there was a knock on the door. When I opened the door a fraction, Carl was standing outside grinning at me through the gap. So I then opened the door fully and let him in. Katrine looked at him and said, "I'm starving, Carl, do these people live only on those filthy sandwiches, or do they eat proper meals?"

Carl just laughed at her and said, "Oh! Katrine, we will take you out for a proper meal just now."

He turned to me and said, "All is well. I have taken great care to see if we have aroused any curiosity, but nothing. So I think we can say we are clear. We will have to take great care once we start to hunt in the Ministry area. There just may be somebody who remembers you, Bill."

I looked at him. "You must be joking, Carl. With this beard and all these wrinkles from my troubles. God, there can be nobody here who can recognize me from the old days."

"Don't be too sure. Still, that is tomorrow."

"Or the next day. Tonight we take Katrine to the West End. Just to have a look around and maybe, just maybe, if she is good and not too excited, treat her to a good meal."

"I'm all for that. If you now have a look under the bed, there is a case with some clothes which I bought for you earlier. They should fit you alright. I'll be in my room getting ready, so I'll leave you two alone for a while. Shall we say an hour from now?"

"Okay, Carl, can you ring a taxi for us?"

"Yes, I'll do that," and with that he went to his own room which was on the next floor down.

Chapter Seventeen
Let's See The West End
United Kingdom 1981

Hold him down you Zulu Warrior.

We arrived in the West End of London later that night. Katrine had never seen anything like it before, or I think since. She was like a small girl in a Christmas toy shop for the first time. She was looking at everything, gasping first at this and then at that. The shops were too much and too many for Katrine to take in, in the little time we had available to us that evening.

I told Carl that "we had better get her into a restaurant as soon as we can. Otherwise with the way Katrine is going on we will have too many people staring at us." I also reminded him. "The last thing we want now is to draw attention to ourselves."

He agreed with me and we made our way down Oxford Street, and then turned into Regent Street. All the time the three of us were making our way towards the Ministry of Defence buildings, I wanted to see what if anything had changed. Katrine was too busy looking into shop windows to know which way we were guiding her or what it was we were doing.

After walking down Regent Street, we turned left into Beak Street, then right into Lexington Street. There, we found a small, but as we were to discover a very expensive restaurant situated in the lower part of a building which was halfway along the street, and we went in. Without too much trouble we managed to get a table at the rear of the restaurant. The meal in fact was very good and when we had finished it the three of us sat and talked for a while. All Katrine could talk about were all the beautiful clothes she had seen in the shops.

She kept asking, "Please, Bill, can I go back and get some of those beautiful clothes tomorrow?"

To which I replied, "It will only be possible and I mean it, Katrine, it will only be possible if we have the money to pay for them.

"Katrine, at the prices I have just seen, you will not be getting very much with the little money we have. If everything we have come here to do happens quickly, which I sincerely hope it will, then perhaps we might have money to spare, but not as things stand at the moment."

All For A King's Shilling

In fact, on second thoughts her shopping trip could possibly provide a good cover for Carl and me as we tried to locate our target. We would have to see how things went.

I had to admit to Katrine, as we continued our discussion in the restaurant, "The styles of clothing for both men and women have changed so much since the last time I walked these pavements. After looking at my reflection in a shop window or two, I think I too need a change of wardrobe, Katrine."

When we had recovered from the shock of the bill for the meal we had just eaten, excellent though it was, we left. Slowly we made our way towards Trafalgar Square and when we arrived in the Square, we stood outside the National Gallery for a while. At first, we just stood watching the traffic and the people go by. It was while we were standing there that a young well-dressed man sauntered up to Katrine, who was standing about two yards to our left. He then made some suggestion to her. She did not know what he was talking about and as she looked across at me, I could see the look of fear and fright on her face.

With that I immediately stepped up to her and told her, "I think you should go and join Carl, darling."

Then I turned to the young man, who was just about to start remonstrating with me. Before he could say anything, I asked him, "How old are you, young man?"

To which he said, "I don't see what that has to do with you or the proposition I have just made to the young woman."

I thought, you arrogant bastard, I have a good mind to knife you right now and it was with great difficulty I held on to my temper. Then looking him directly in the eyes, through clenched teeth I hissed at him, "My question has a lot to do with whether you reach your next birthday or not."

Then in my best Norwegian/English accent I went on to tell him, "If you ever make an immoral suggestion to my wife again, or even look at her, I will personally kill you."

He started to grin and was about to prolong the discussion when for some reason he started to lose colour around his mouth and then his cheeks. Then he started to shake and blurted out, "You are both mad, this is England you know. You can't say that to innocent men out in the street for an evening stroll."

With that outburst he turned and fled along the pavement in front of the National Gallery.

"No," I said, and to his back as he hurried away. "I'm not the one who is mad, but if you would care to step into this doorway then I'll repeat my threat to you."

It was at that point I turned to find Carl standing right behind me. What he had done, he never did tell me, but whatever it was he had really frightened the young man and all the time I thought I had.

We reached Katrine, who had walked a little way from us and was leaning on the wall. I took her in my arms and told her. "Don't worry Katrine, not all Englishmen are like him or even that stupid. He was just a flashy Cockney chancing his luck with what he thought was a lonely young lady."

All three of us agreed that it would be better if we moved on as we didn't want him calling the police. If he did and they then found us we would be asked questions which would be hard to answer. So we made our way across the Square towards Admiralty Arch.

As we strolled past I pointed out a part of the building to Katrine and told her, "If it had not been for a man in that building we would never have met."

"Some day I would like to meet that man," she said.

"That may happen one day, Katrine, but I sincerely hope that it doesn't."

We talked little as we walked down Whitehall towards the Houses of Parliament and past Horse Guards. Katrine could hardly contain her exuberance as she looked at the uniforms and the horses of the two Life Guards on duty.

I was going to tell her that some days the uniforms were different, but then thought that it might not be a good idea. So we just continued to saunter down the road as any tourists would. It was when we were opposite Richmond Terrace that I first saw the man across the street. I must admit my heart missed a beat as I looked at him.

There, large as life walking down the other side of the road was the man whom I had come to London to kill. He was the one man in my life I had vowed never to forget. The realisation of who he was set me off shaking uncontrollably. I had to fight hard to stop my body shaking like a lump of jelly.

Both Katrine and Carl by this time had continued down the road past me. By the time they turned I had recovered my composure and exercised my mind over the wobbly jelly into which my body had turned. I started to walk down the road again.

Carl looked at me and asked, "Are you all right, Bill? You look as if you have just seen a ghost."

"Yes, Carl, I have seen a ghost, he is over there." Nodding across the road to where he was walking down the pavement.

Carl then turned and looked across the road. The man was past us by now but he said, "Yes, it could be him, but are you sure?"

"Oh, yes, I am sure. That one I'll never forget, I saw his face which has haunted me all these years."

Katrine, who had wandered a little further on, turned and looked at me. She then said, "You have seen this man you are looking for, haven't you, Bill?"

"Yes, Katrine, yes, I have. I didn't think it would be this easy though and it has shaken me somewhat."

Then I said, "Let's not spoil our first night out, so let's just carry on and enjoy the rest of the night. We've plenty of time to worry about him. After all, I've waited years to get close to him. It is enough to know we are on the right track. Tonight is not to be spoilt by thoughts of him and why we are here, so let's go and see some of the bright lights of London."

With that we caught a taxi to Soho.

I could not get the thought of him out of my mind though while we were in the taxi. The more I thought about it, the more I realised that I should have gone for him there and then. He was alone, I knew I could have been over the road and done what it was I had come so far to do. The thought of extracting retribution from this man and so putting an end to such a despicable person as him had kept me going all this time. If it had not been for my all-consuming hatred of this man, I would have died years before in the camps, of that I am certain.

All For A King's Shilling

We rounded the evening off with a drive via taxi past Buckingham Palace. Then, after changing taxis again, we went back to the area we were staying in. Carl stopped the taxi about three streets away from our destination. Katrine and I alighted from the taxi on the corner of Upper Essex Road and Canonbury Road.

Carl then went off in the taxi around the next corner and into Northampton Street. He was to pay the driver off and then take a stroll back towards the flat from Canonbury Grove to see if anybody was watching the flat. Once there, he was then to walk the length of the street. First down one side, and then back along the other. When Katrine and I spotted him at the junction of Canonbury Street and Upper Essex Road, we would then start to make our way into the street. Carl was looking for any signs of people or vehicles with occupants in the street or anybody taking an obvious interest in our flat.

As we approached the top of Canonbury Street, Carl came round the corner and the three of us went into a huddle by the corner. He then told us, "As I walked back down the side of the road opposite our flat was when I spotted them. They looked like any courting couple in a car at first sight, but although they look to be just that – a courting couple, I'm not so sure."

"It's a bit of a dilemma for us, Carl. Are we being watched, or is it just that we were being too paranoid and cautious?"

"How can they know we are here, Bill?" Katrine asked. "I think it is probably nothing to do with us."

"Katrine could be right, Carl, perhaps we should walk the length of the street and see what happens. We will take it slowly to give you time to get to your room using the back street. Once in the flat you could watch the couple in the car's reaction as we walk past. Then if they are watching us, we can leave the place straight away."

Some ten minutes later, after having spent the time like a couple of young lovers ourselves kissing and cuddling at the end of the street, that is, Katrine and I took a steady stroll down Canonbury Street. Katrine spotted the couple in the car before I did and she told me, "They are watching us approaching, Bill."

As I looked towards the car I could just see them as they were starting to kiss and cuddle; therefore I did not get a very good look at them. So I guided Katrine across the road to the opposite side and them leaning back against the garden wall, I drew Katrine into my arms. As I nestled my head into the fur collar of her coat, I fixed my gaze on to the car.

My first observation started the alarm bells ringing in my head. First of all the car had two radio aerials, one aerial was of a type I had never seen before. Secondly, I noticed the woman in the car was in fact doing the same as I was, she was watching everything that was going on in the street. What was more, I deduced she was watching Katrine and me with a lot of interest. Then when I looked up at the first floor window of the house opposite I could just make out the shape of a figure behind the curtains. By now I had seen enough, I put my arm around Katrine's shoulders and led her into the house in which we had rented the two flats. I had no intention of taking any risks; not now, especially not now I knew my quarry was in London.

As we entered the hall, Carl was there waiting for us with our bags packed. He had packed them while he was waiting for us, after he had seen the couple in the car watching us before we even got anywhere near them. Realising what was going on, it had only taken him a few seconds to throw our stuff into the bags. Once we had our belongings Carl then led us out of the house into the back yard via the rear entrance through the way in which he had entered the house. He saw us into the back street and then he returned to the flats.

Katrine and I then made our way down the back street and out into Essex Road. We crossed Essex Road and as we did, much to our surprise for that time of night, a big red London double decker bus turned into it from Balls Pond Road. On impulse, more than anything else, I stuck my hand out and the damned bus stopped.

As we clambered aboard, I told the conductor. "We are late, we are trying to get to Paddington Station. We have to catch the next train to Bristol. We called a taxi hours ago, but it hasn't arrived. So we decided to start walking in the hope of stopping a taxi or bus en route."

"We don't go anywhere near Paddington, mate, we are on our way back to our depot. We finished our last run about half an hour ago."

He went to the front of the bus and talked to the driver through a small window behind the driver's cab. After a while he came back and said, "We will drop you at a place where the driver thinks you will be able to catch a taxi."

Thanking him for his help, I asked him, "How much do we owe you for the fare?"

"Forget it, I've already cashed up my money for today."

Later they dropped us outside Warren Street Tube Station. The conductor wished us the best of luck and the driver waved as they drove off.

Katrine and I then made a big show of heading for the taxi rank there. Once the bus had disappeared, we then made our way to the station entrance. We stood outside the entrance for some quarter of an hour as we waited to see if anybody was taking any notice or interest in us. When at last we decided nobody was, we then went into the station.

First we caught a train to Oxford Circus on the Victoria Line and then from there to Nottinghill Gate via the Central Line. From there, via the Circle Line, we eventually made it to Paddington. We were both a little surprised to see Carl, who was already there waiting for us when we reached the station concourse.

He went on to tell us what had happened back at the flat. He said, "It was all a storm in a teacup, but it was really just as well you left when you did. I don't think we brought any attention to ourselves, but it will perhaps be better if we keep on the move. We don't want to get caught up in any police operations, Bill."

"I have to agree with you on that point, Carl."

He than went on, "You could hardly have been out of the back street when the police arrived with all lights flashing and stormed into the house opposite the one we had been in. They kicked the front door in and went belting into the house. They dragged some rough looking characters out and carted them away. I just managed to get out of the street before the police closed it. It looked as if they were searching a few of the houses from top to bottom. That was when I decided to slip out the back way and join you two. I came here by taxi. Don't worry, Bill, I changed taxis a couple of times going back on myself, just to make sure I wasn't followed, which I wasn't."

All For A King's Shilling

"Well, Carl, it is time we made our way to the next flat you hired for us. It is getting near to morning now and we should be able to get some breakfast soon, then once we have eaten we can go and find our new base. Then perhaps we can catch up on some of our lost sleep."

"It's probably the best thing to do now. Katrine looks as tired as I feel."

We soon found a small cafe which looked reasonably clean and we went in.

Some two hours later we were once again on the tube train and heading for Finchley Road Station. After leaving Finchley Road Station, we walked to Heath Drive in West Hampstead. There were very few people about at that time in the morning and I was surprised that we didn't have to knock the landlady out of bed to get the keys for the flat.

The flat, which Carl had arranged to rent some time earlier, was the one which we had expected to use once the job which I'd come here to do was over. Before we left London altogether, that is. Carl would now have to find another place for that purpose. Still, that was another day, we were all tired and needed some sleep.

This flat in Heath Drive was very good. It had a good shower which Katrine and I ended up using together. When we had finished Carl and I went over the last evening's performance. We decided it was better if we got on with the job in hand.

I said, "I'm going to need your help in tracking our friend's movements, Carl. Then after deciding just where and when to take him out I shall go alone. I don't want either of you anywhere near when I do go after my man."

"I'm not too happy with that, Bill, I think I should help you. You are not the only one that animal has handed over to the Russians to be killed."

"I know, Carl, but I must insist that it will happen this way, just me."

Carl was not too happy about it all, but went and had a shower. Katrine made us both a cup of coffee and I must admit I felt in a better frame of mind once I had drunk it. I went into the bedroom which Katrine and I were using; she was already in bed. She was sitting up in bed as large as life waiting for me and I could see by the way she was patting the bedsheets that I would not be going to sleep right away. Stripping, I sat down on the bed wearing only my birthday suit and I knew at that moment had she said, "Forget this man and let us go home," I would have done just that, for I had known I loved her from the first time I had laid eyes on her standing in that old woodsman's hut dressed in her fur hat and coat, all those years ago. It was then I had made myself a vow that no way would I ever endanger her life or our relationship. If I had to kill to keep it I would, but also if killing this man I hated so much was to endanger our relationship, then I wouldn't do it. As I drank the last of my coffee, I looked into those eyes and surrendered myself to the heat of passion and ecstasy for how long I shall never know. Nor did I care how long, for eventually I slipped off to sleep, satiated and completely exhausted.

It was six o'clock that evening when Katrine chided me into waking by calling me the laziest man she knew as I'd slept the clock round. At last I arose, dressed and joined her in the kitchen. She had cooked a meal for us both and I asked her where the food had come from. She told me, "Carl and I went to the local shops and bought food for us all."

I asked her, "Where is Carl now?"

"He has gone out to have a look around the area to check on the tube train times."

I was not very happy about it, so I ate my meal, a meal which was far superior to anything we had bought since we started on this trip.

Katrine then started on about going shopping in Oxford Street. She reminded me that before we left Norway I had said she could go there.

I agreed to let her go; I could find no other way of shutting her up. I told her, "The first thing tomorrow we will all go shopping in Oxford Street."

Then I said, "I wish Carl had told me where he was going."

She said, "Don't worry, Carl is a big boy now and he can look after himself."

Even so, I was not too happy about him going off like that and when he did return about three hours later he told me that because he could not sleep, he had gone into the Whitehall area to have a good look around. He said he also wanted to get to know the area better, then he told me what he had seen.

He started, "I was standing across the road from Horse Guards' entrance, and I was just going to move off when I saw the man we are looking for. He had come out through the gate and headed towards the same place where you had seen him last night, Bill.

"So," I said, "I think it's odd he should follow the same route both during the day and again at night."

"Yes, Bill, I thought that as well. Anyway, I'm not a hundred percent certain, but I'm pretty sure the man was being followed."

With that bit of information we sat and looked at one another for a while. Finally I asked, "Who do you think the follower is – a bodyguard – or perhaps he has become that much more important to them?"

Carl thought for a moment and said, "No, the person doing the following was not a bodyguard, Russian or British."

"So, do you think they are on to us?"

"No, Bill, I don't think they are."

So, I thought, I wonder just what is going on here.

At that point Katrine came in from the kitchen with some coffee for us all. "Perhaps somebody else wants to get rid of your man," she said. "If so, I hope they get him before you do, then we can all go back home with clean hands."

I only wish that could be so, I thought. It would certainly save us three a lot of heartache and soul-searching, I was starting to think this whole episode was getting too uncomfortable. Something didn't ring true.

The next morning we rested and just took it easy. In the afternoon Katrine and I took a stroll around Oxford Street, as I had promised her we would. She was in another world, seeing all the clothes and other items she had been starved of all her life. It would have taken a fortune to have bought all the things she wanted. She was easily satisfied in the end; she settled for a pair of shoes. We returned to the flat at about six that evening and spent the rest of the evening watching TV. At about 8.30 Carl made the most obvious tired signs and yawning his head off he said he would go to bed. As Katrine and I watched this charade we could hardly contain ourselves as he then left the room. It wasn't long before we, too, retired to our beds though.

All For A King's Shilling

Next morning we all awoke very early and went about our preparations to go to the centre of Whitehall. We wanted to see if we could establish any routine my intended victim followed. We arrived at the bottom of Northumberland Avenue at about seven o'clock. Katrine and I went into a small cafe on the corner and I bought two cups of coffee. We then sat by the window watching the pavement, which by now was pretty crowded with people coming from Charing Cross Station. It looked as if they were all heading into the area of Whitehall. As we watched them, the man whose face I had vowed l would never forget came into the cafe. He walked up to the counter and bought a packet of Russian cigarettes and left. I was so surprised and taken aback that I just managed to cover my face with my cup and hand as he turned towards the door. I didn't think he recognised me. So as he left I arose, took Katrine by the arm, and said, "We are on, Katrine, the game's afoot."

She just looked at me and said, "You're mad! What do you mean, the game is afoot?"

I just grinned at her and told her, "Come on, Katrine, or we will lose him."

We left the cafe and set off to follow our target. He crossed the road and made his way along Whitehall Place into Whitehall. He crossed over the road then made his way towards Cockspur Street. It was there that I saw Carl following us on the other side of the road, so Katrine and I hung back a little. For some reason Katrine stopped, then she started looking around in her handbag for something. I stood facing towards Trafalgar Square as she did this, getting a little edgy in case we lost him. It was then I noticed the man who had been standing outside the cafe window. He had been fidgeting with his watch then. He was taking more than a natural interest in our target. It was at this point I realised that perhaps we might have a small problem.

Carl was now following our target but Katrine and I were still standing on the pavement near the entrance to Horse Guards. This unknown man was still following our target and I decided I had to resolve the identity of this other man. The question was, was the man alone or did he have accomplices?

Katrine asked me, "Is it all right for me to stop fidgeting in my handbag now?"

"Of course it is. Why have you stopped anyway?"

"Because there is a man over there watching us."

"Can you describe this man, Katrine?"

When she did, I then casually turned and looked at him. Sure enough he seemed to be watching us. I took hold of Katrine's arm and led her across the road to where this man was standing. At once he started to look a bit flustered as we approached him. What I had done was the last thing he had expected to happen.

When we were standing in front of him, I took a tourist map out of my anorak pocket. Then in half Norwegian, half English I asked him, "I believe we are lost, could you direct us to the National Gallery?"

In fact he looked somewhat relieved to tell us how to get there. Katrine and I thanked him very much and then made our way to the National Gallery in case we were being followed.

We then spent some time waiting for the Gallery to open, trying to see if we were in fact under surveillance. When at last the Gallery did open we paid our money and stayed in the place until nearly dinnertime. Then we made our way back to the flat, where Carl was waiting for us. While Katrine was making us some sandwiches

Carl and I mulled over the events leading up to the time I asked the man where the National Gallery was.

He said, "You shouldn't have done that, Bill."

"I had to do something Carl, the man was taking too much of an interest in us."

After some more discussion we decided we needed to disguise ourselves a little. After we had had our lunch of sandwiches, cake and coffee Carl and I set off to see what could be done about disguises. We both agreed that about eighty-eight percent of the people we had seen that morning were white-collar workers. So we reasoned it was obvious that we would need to be dressed as workmen if we wanted to stay on the streets and not attract attention. To anybody watching us, dressed as white-collar workers we would have to go to a set destination, whereas dressed as manual workers we could loiter on the streets for a longer time without arousing any suspicions.

When we returned to the flat later that afternoon we had blue boiler suits, donkey jackets and hats. Also, both of us had Andy Capp type cloth caps, baseball hats, and a pair of British Railwaymen's hats each. We felt that with our own clothes, along with those we had just acquired, we had a couple of alternatives from the way we had appeared this morning. Also, I had managed to get a British Rail worker's pass, something I was going to need more quickly than I thought.

We both changed into our working men's clothes and had some tea and sandwiches. When we were ready we left Katrine to man the phone. We would ring in whenever we had the chance and she was to pass on any messages we needed to pass to one another. Once we had started to tail our man and his followers we would be pretty tied up, but if anything happened the only contact we would have would be the telephone. So, with everything set we left Katrine in the flat and headed back to Whitehall.

Carl then went to Whitehall and I went to Charing Cross Station and waited just outside the entrance to the stairs. Carl was near to Horse Guards and waiting for the target and his followers if he had any to leave. When I saw Carl come round the corner, my first thought was that he had missed our man, but then I saw our target behind Carl. He was closely followed by the man Katrine and I had talked to that morning. By the time they passed me Carl had gone into the Station, so I then tacked on behind the man following our target. We then all ended up standing on the same platform for a while. I stood watching the other three. Then I made my way to Carl and as I passed him I said, "I'll take the same train as our target." He did not even blink his eyes, but I knew he had got my message.

By the time the next train arrived I had made my way to the centre of the platform. Once there, I waited to board the train after the target and his follower had boarded it, but I was quite surprised to see the follower did not get on. Because of his not boarding the train I was nearly caught out. He stood in the middle of the platform and waited until the train started to leave. As he stood watching the train pulling out of the station, I just managed to clamber aboard as it was starting to gain speed. The follower turned and left the station, as did Carl.

From my position in the doorway of the coach, I could see my target in the next carriage. He was sitting chatting to some person, a person who had obviously saved him a seat and they were chatting like long-lost buddies. There was no way I could tell what it was they were chatting about. Probably which sucker they could stitch up as they had done with me. The sight of him so infuriated me that I was on the point of walking into the carriage and blowing the bastard away there and then when a voice asked me, "How are you doing then, mate?"

I felt a shudder run through me as I started to turn. I had my hand on the short-barrelled Webley which I was carrying. Standing behind me, and now on the opposite side of the carriage and looking at me, was a British Rail employee. The relief flooded over me and I relaxed my hold on the gun.

There followed the most testing time I have spent while I tried to sound as if I belonged on the train. Eventually I said, "Look, I'm new here, this is my first week, I don't know if I am coming or going."

He just laughed and said, "You will soon get used to it."

We then talked about football, who would win the cup and so on. I was praying my target would get off, but he just sat tight.

Eventually my travelling companion got off at New Cross Gate, I think it was, and I breathed a sigh of relief. My target was still sitting there and some seats had become empty in the compartment, so I went in and sat down with my back against the end of the carriage. I could see him quite clearly from where I was sitting and I felt quite safe now. It looked as if it was all going well for a change.

By now the train was going through some sidings, which I learnt later was Hither Green. Once we had cleared the sidings the target started to get ready to leave the train. He came and stood by the door I had been standing against and he was so close I could smell the bastard.

When the train stopped at Grove Park he alighted and made his way to the entrance. At the last minute he turned and made his way back to the train. By then I had gone too far towards the exit barrier and the train was now leaving the station. As I left I looked back and to my relief he had not re-boarded the train. He was just standing on the platform talking to a woman. It was at that moment I decided to ring Katrine in the flat, to let her know what was happening. I entered a telephone kiosk outside the station and dialed the flat. Just as Katrine answered I saw the target and the woman, the one he had been talking to, leave the station and head off into Chinbrook Road.

Immediately I hung up just as Katrine answered the phone. As I was about to leave the phone kiosk and follow them, I saw a man get out of a car which was parked nearby. He turned the collar of his coat up and set off behind them. When he was clear of the station, I was about to follow him when I recognised the man in the car. He was the man who had followed our target to the station earlier and had not boarded the train. I was, to say the least, dumbstruck. It was at this point I realised we were certainly in a completely new ball game.

Again I rang Katrine and told her, "I'll be returning on the next train. Can you ask Carl to return to the flat as soon as he rings in?" Then I rang off and I just made it back into the station in time to get the next train leaving for Charing Cross.

When I eventually got back to the flat, Carl was already there, having returned about half an hour before me. He said, "I was a little worried when the tail did not get on the train, Bill. So I followed him. He got into a car which pulled up as we left the station, and I've no idea where it went."

"Maybe you haven't, Carl, but I bloody have. The bastard was waiting at Grove Park when our target and I arrived."

Carl just looked at me, "How can they get there that fast?" he asked.

"Search me, Carl, but I think we need a set of wheels, don't you?"

We decided that the next day, instead of following our target, we would go and steal some wheels. "What we need is a van of some sort, then we can really pose as workmen, Carl. That way we will have more freedom of movement."

According to Katrine I spent the rest of the evening being a real bore. My mind was in a turmoil and I was trying to figure out who the hell these guys following my target really were. Later that evening I mentioned to Carl, "Perhaps it will be better, once we have got some wheels, that we should try and follow the men who were following my target. We need to find out just who they are. Let's leave our Major for a couple of days; he is not going anywhere, is he?"

"Yes, Bill, we need to find out who these men are and just what they are up to. Mind, I don't think it would be safe to get too close to our target. Not until we have solved the riddle of just who these men are?"

With that settled, we all retired for the night. When we were alone in the bedroom Katrine suggested, "You should give it all up, Bill, and go back home. We will be able to live quite well there and they wouldn't find us."

As I looked at her and took her in my arms I said, "Katrine, please understand me when I tell you that as long as this man is alive we will never have a place we can call home. We would never know when somebody would knock on our door, then it would all be over for us. No, Katrine, we have to get rid of this man if we are to have any hope of spending the rest of our lives together. If you have doubts, Katrine, just remember it was because of him that you suffered in the camps the way you did, before Carl managed to find you and get you out. Your father wasn't the only one who died in agony because of him. Our lives and our future depend on this man being eliminated, Katrine, we have to do it. If we want to spend the rest of our lives together, that is. We also owe it to all the others who have suffered, Katrine."

She thought for a while and then nodded and said, "Well, Bill, let's start living a little now, shall we?"

"Katrine, you are incorrigible, is there no hope for you at all?"

"Not one little bit, not when I'm with you, anyway."

I looked at her, turned and put the bedside lamp out, reached back and took her in my arms once more. Body contact with her was living in another world, free from all the troubles and intrigues of the world we were involved in. It was bliss, or the nearest thing to bliss I believe any human can achieve. In a matter of minutes I had forgotten all about the bloody Major and his double life, I was so blissfully happy and for me that was all that mattered right then.

Next morning Katrine and I awakened to a flat minus Carl, he was not there. At first I was a little worried. Normally he did not go out, not without leaving a note to say where he had gone, that is. Katrine could see I was a little edgy and said, "Don't worry, Carl is a big man and he can look after himself, Bill."

We sat down to have coffee and toast for breakfast and we had just finished when Carl returned. Ignoring my look of apprehension he said, "Come on, Bill, we have to get moving or we will be late for our appointment with the good Major."

Without any more ado, I kissed Katrine with Carl telling me, "Come on, don't make a meal of her, Bill."

Forgetting my apprehension, all I said was, "Bugger off, Carl."

With that we were off and out of the flat. As I turned to head in the direction of the tube station, Carl said "No, this way, Bill," and he guided me off in the opposite direction entirely. We went round into another street behind the one the flat was in and as we walked along he stopped me by the wreck of a van, which turned out to be an old GPO van. You could still see the old GPO markings under the sloppy paint job that had been done on it. He produced a key from his pocket and opened the driver's door. We both got in the front seats and he said, "Well, what do you think?"

"How well does it run, Carl?"

To which he replied, "Like a bloody rocket."

I turned and look at him, "You have to be joking."

"Ah, well, you will see," he said as he started the engine.

With that we were off, heading for Central London, and I had to admit as we went the engine sounded quite respectable. Not that I'm any real judge of van or car engines. There were no noises coming from the engine other than the normal noises one hears from these kinds of vans and cars. It also seemed to drive quite well, but then I wasn't driving, so I just grinned at Carl.

He punched my shoulder and said, "See, you are feeling better already."

"Carl, I will feel better still once I know who these guys were who were following our friend, the Major."

"Maybe he has risen a lot higher in rank than a Major these days, Bill."

"Ah! yes, Carl, but whose Army has promoted him, Carl?"

Soon we arrived outside Charing Cross Station and I got out of the van just past the entrance. I made my way to the concourse and waited for things to happen and I stood looking around for a moment or two, taking in the scene all around me. Nothing seemed untoward and after I had been there about two or three minutes, I spotted one of the two men I had observed in the car at Grove Park. Taking a stroll to the newsagent's kiosk, I bought a *Daily Mirror* and then I went and stood just one yard away from him.

He was about twenty-five years old, clean-shaven and what is commonly referred to as cleancut. He was wearing a tweedy type of jacket and flannel trousers. Also he had on a non descript tie, not a regimental tie for this lad. The fingers on both hands were badly stained with nicotine and because of this I figured him to be a serviceman. Looking at him I guessed he was probably a Corporal or an Acting Sergeant. As I watched him I thought he would probably have a lot of time on his hands during the day, therefore the strong nicotine stains on his fingers. It crossed my mind that the palms of his hands were probably stained brownish yellow with nicotine as well. Of one thing I was sure, he was the one who had got out of the car the night before at Grove Park Station and followed the Major.

It was getting close to the arrival time of the train and of course of our target. The young man was getting a little edgy, his head swivelling like a 'tuppenny budgie' and I wondered why. It crossed my mind that they might know their man was in extreme danger and that was what was making this man edgy. Standing there waiting for the train to arrive I thought, I wouldn't like to be guarded by somebody as edgy as this one, no sir.

Then I decided it might be better if I got myself a head start on the two of them, as I knew where we would all end up anyway. So I left the station the way I had come in and I do believe the young man never even saw me. As I walked along the road, Carl pulled up alongside me and I took my donkey jacket off and threw it in the back of the van. As I did so, I told Carl in a not too quiet voice, "I'll see you in Trafalgar Square in about ten minutes, mate," and with that he drove off.

As Carl disappeared into the stream of traffic I took a slow and deliberate walk along the route we had followed the previous day. It wasn't long before the first cleancut young man passed me. Then the Major passed me; he never gave me a second glance. Then the young man whom I had stood next to at the station brought up the rear. Once all three of them had passed me, I increased my pace a little. Not enough to make it obvious I had started to follow them, but just enough to keep them all in sight.

The Major made his way straight to the same building he had entered the day before. Then the first cleancut young man who had passed me and had walked past the building stopped. To my surprise, he turned and watched the Major enter the building. The second one, the one who had been following, stopped short of the building and also watched the Major enter it.

Not having expected this to happen, I'd got caught out again like the evening before, so I went past the first of the two men and stopped and fiddled with a hydrant cover. Just as I did, the first young man then turned and walked back towards me. A little panic was about to set in when a uniformed doorman came up to me and said, "So you have come to fix the damned thing at last?"

Looking at him with what could only have been described as an idiot's expression, I said, "Yes, my mate is trying to get parked round the corner. Then we can get the tools and get this thing sorted for you."

"About bloody time," he said as he stalked back to his little room just inside a rather elegant looking doorway.

Because of the look he gave me as he left I hoped my English had not caused him any alarm. It was so long since I had had any real conversations in English, with a true English person, that is, that I was a little unsure of myself. In fact, I did not know if in my long absence I had developed an accent, having only spoken Russian and Norwegian for so long. Mind, I think he was probably too bloody arrogant to notice.

As I looked back to the corner, I was just in time to see our two cleancut young men chatting together as they rounded it. So I turned and followed them, I needed to know where they went from here. Keeping my distance I followed them across Trafalgar Square and into Whitcomb Street. There they turned right into Orange Street. They then went into a building behind the National Gallery. As they disappeared into the building I did wonder and I was also a little puzzled why the National Gallery should have a team of what looked to be undercover men following our old Major friend around?

I settled against the wall and reading my *Mirror*, I waited around for about ten minutes. Nothing untoward happened. No other people came or left. As I was about to leave and had taken about four steps down the street a black taxi stopped right outside the door through which the two young men had entered. A smart city type gent got out and without paying the taxi driver, or even speaking to him, got out and entered the building. The taxi then drove off, but I had a distinct feeling that although he was not looking at me directly the taxi driver was taking in everything there was to see about me. It was then that I had this urge that perhaps it would be best if I made myself scarce. So without waiting any longer I crossed the road and returned the way I had come.

As I approached Trafalgar Square I could see Carl on foot and he was looking past me. From what I could see of his expression I knew he was going to ignore me and I could also see in his face that my suspicions had been right. Somebody was following me. So I just kept walking and made my way across the Square and into Cockspur Street.

There, I turned to my right and as I did so I glanced to my right rear. Sure enough he was following me, another of those cleancut young men. This one was my tail all right and he wasn't one of those I had tailed earlier, but he was one of them. An effeminate looking man this one, which gave me an idea and I slowed right down until I was just sauntering along. He didn't realise it until it was too late and he had closed right up to me. Waiting until he was so close I could hear his footsteps right behind me and I judged it right, I turned to face him.

The surprised look on his face was a picture to see and I started into him right away, really aggressively. I had no intention of letting him get over his shock. First I asked him, "What do you think you are doing following me around?"

My voice was loud enough to turn the heads of some of the passers by. This encouraged me somewhat and I then shouted, "It's a bit early in the morning for queers like you to be molesting innocent workmen on the streets. Looking for a bit of rough, are you? You should be bloody locked up man, or are you not a man?"

Over the man's shoulder I could see Carl standing on the other side of the road and he was grinning from ear to ear. Getting a little carried away, I then started to lay it on thick. Half turning to a member of the public, and gesturing to the man who had tailed me, I said, "It makes me sick to see these queers on the streets, but to have them accost you in the morning when you are on your way to work, well, I ask you?"

The young man was going to defend himself and then he thought better of it, turned and fled back across the road. He was just unfortunate enough to bump into a man and rebound into Carl's arms. I was about to follow him and shout some more when I noticed the blue policeman's helmet heading my way. So I took off in the other direction, just as fast as the young man had gone the other way.

Carl, when the young man had bumped into him, had relieved him of his wallet and some keys at the same time, of course, before helping him on his way. The man had apologised profusely to Carl for bumping into him and took off again from whence he had come, not knowing he'd had his pockets picked. Carl also disappeared immediately with the small crowd which had gathered when I had been shouting. By now I was well on my way back to our flat.

When I arrived Carl was already there and he told me when I got in. "You weren't followed when you left the Square, Bill, and I watched you when you came into the street and I couldn't see anybody following you here."

"Good, Carl, I'm glad of that, but I think we should be looking for a move, tonight or tomorrow; this afternoon would be better. By the way, I'm sorry I picked up that tail, but I was just about to leave their location when a taxi arrived. The person who got out didn't pay and the driver didn't ask for any fare. I'm of the opinion that it was the taxi driver who tipped them off about me, he was the only one who could have spotted me."

Then I went on to tell him what had happened behind the National Gallery. When I had finished both of us looked at one another and shook our heads. Eventually I said, "I don't like this one stinking little bit. I am worried, I'm worried we may be getting involved in events which could destroy us. I'm also worried about Katrine. I think we should send her back, don't you?"

"Yes, Bill, I think you are right about Katrine. Perhaps it would be best if you were to send her home. By the way, I lifted that guy's wallet when he bumped into me."

"Oh! great and what gem does it contain, Carl?"

"Nothing much, except that he's an Acting Sergeant in the Army on protection duties, whatever that means."

I looked and I thought that all our work could now turn to shit. "I hope this Sergeant thinks that it's all a mistake. Maybe he is too scared to report he has lost his ID."

Katrine came in a little later and said, "I've just been to the shops to get us some food. By the way, Bill, did you know that a young man was following you?"

"No, Katrine, I think you are wrong, Carl was watching me when I arrived and he says nobody was following me."

"Well, he is the one who is wrong, Bill, I was in the shop when you came past and there was a man following you."

Both Carl and I looked at one another, dumbstruck. "Katrine, how do you know it was me the man was following?"

"Because I saw you walk past the shop and I was just going to rush out to shout at you when I saw a young man who looked as if he was following you."

"Just because he looked as if he was following Bill doesn't mean he was," said Carl.

"He was following Bill, Carl. Let me tell you. I was going to shout after you, Bill, when I first saw him. So I got my shopping together and followed him. He watched you go round the corner into the street and just before he got there, I ran forward and bumped into him. He said he was sorry for bumping into me like that as he helped me pick the groceries up. By the time we both got around the corner, Bill, you had disappeared from sight. He then asked me if I knew you to which I replied, "Know who?" Carl and I sat looking at Katrine in amazement.

"That's not all. After that he went to the phone box at the end of the street and made a telephone call. He looked a little agitated while he did that and he is still at the end of the street now."

Both Carl and I looked at one another and said in unison. "It's time we were out of here."

Katrine and I went to our bedroom and I got a razor from my bag. Then I asked Katrine to give me her scissors and I commenced removing the beard which I had worn since my days in the camps. I'd been reluctant to shave it off ever since my escape. Perhaps there was something psychological about being recaptured and sent back, but the main thing was that it was coming off now. It was important to change my appearance now and this was to be the first step.

Next I asked Katrine, "Can you see if you can borrow an iron from one of the other flats?"

"What do you want an iron for, Bill?"

"When I eventually get this beard off, Katrine, I'm going to press a suit, tie and shirt from my rucksack."

Katrine managed to get an iron from the flat below us so I set about my ironing, much to Carl's amusement. First I steamed my tie and set it to dry by the electric fire. All the time Katrine was looking at me. At last she said, "It is a long time since I looked at the real you without that silly beard." I looked at her for a moment as I pressed my trousers and she said, "It has made a vast improvement. I think I have fallen in love with you all over again."

We both laughed and I started to feel good again.

"I'd better get us something to eat," Katrine said and she then started to busy herself in the kitchen.

Carl and I decided that we had better keep a watch on the street. Even though they didn't know which house we were in, it would not take them too long to find out that bit of information.

While I finished my ironing Carl had a look in the street at the rear of the one we were in. He then spent a little time watching the front street while Katrine and I ate our meal.

Then, while Carl was eating his food, I watched the street. While I did this I made my plan. I had just completed it in my head when Katrine came to sit with me.

It didn't take long before we spotted the watchers. Two of them were sitting in a car at the end of the street, the same end that I had used when I came back and where Katrine had seen the young man. The annoying thing was that again it was Katrine who had spotted them first.

Once we knew where they were, one of us kept an eye on them all the time. Both Katrine and I were watching the two men in the car when we had a stroke of luck. It was after we had been watching for about an hour. Another car which we had not spotted at the other end of the street, suddenly pulled out and drove up to the first car. When it was alongside the first car it stopped and a man got out and got into the rear of the first car. They stayed that way for about five minutes, then another car turned into the street at the other end and hooted its horn. This broke up the conversation, the man returned to his car, and it drove off. I could not swear to it, but it looked very much like the car I had seen last night at Grove Park Station. The main thing was we now knew that we had one car at each end of the street; in effect we were cut off.

I could not help smiling as I watched these people at work. It reminded me of the sloppy outfit which had been at work in Singapore all those years ago. The outfit which had nearly got me killed. It was then I realised something I had been pushing to the back of my mind for years had now to be faced. That was that I'd known for years who had been behind this little lot all this time, the man who had been responsible for all those deaths and for the unbelievable amount of penetration of our forces by spies from the early 1950s. By God, I thought, they have a bloody cheek. Using taxpayers' money and Ministry Staff to infiltrate and protect themselves from being found out as the spies they are. No wonder the Ministry never seem to catch any Russian or any other bloody Soviet Block spies. Yet they continually lose all their own to the Russians, including me, only I've lived to tell the tale and I hope to do something about it.

While all this was going on, Carl had been on the telephone in the hall. He had arranged a new flat for us. My clothes were dry and all smart, shipshape and Bristol fashion. We had eaten our lunch in shifts. Once more, we were all full of hope. With enough cheek, I thought, I'm going to pull this off.

So, while Katrine kept watch on the cars, I finalised my plan with Carl. It was simplicity itself. First, I was to leave via a taxi from three doors up the street. Carl and Katrine were to leave at the same time, only if they could they would go from about three doors or farther down the street from the flat we were now in. Once the taxi arrived I was to haggle with the driver until I was sure they were at the end of the street. Then I would board the taxi and leave. If the car which we believed was watching for us followed, then I'd just keep going until I reached the Strand. If it did not follow then I would stop the taxi and pick them up.

We would then all go to the Strand. It was my intention to settle this job once and for all and I wasn't going to have Carl or Katrine with me. No way was I going to have them mixed up in the business which I knew I had to carry out. No matter how justified I felt, in the eyes of the law it was murder. Oh! I had thought long and hard about it. They were not going to be – and I had never intended for them to be – involved in the final act.

First I said goodbye to Katrine, shook Carl's hand and then I left the flat via the rear basement door. I was wearing my suit when I left, both of them wishing me good luck as I went. There was a tear in my eye as I made my way into the next door garden knowing I might never see Katrine again. Or Carl, for that matter.

As luck would have it, the way to the house four doors further up the street was easy. Without even having to go into the back street, I reached the house and then I waited in the hallway for the taxi to arrive. While I waited I knew that Katrine and Carl would be waiting, watching the street for the arrival of the taxi from as far down the street as they had managed to get. Before leaving I had asked Carl to take care of Katrine if it all went wrong, otherwise I would see them at the new flat.

It wasn't long before the taxi arrived. It was a black one and not one of those mini cabs. So if all went well, it would be easier for me to carry out the plan I had now formulated since leaving the flat. I waited a couple of minutes after the driver blew the horn before I went out as I wanted to give them plenty of time to get out of the street. When I thought they would be nearly out, I then stepped into the street. I asked the driver, "Are you my taxi?"

"If you're Mr bleeding Smith I am," he replied.

Out of the corner of my eye I could see Carl and Katrine had come out of a house which was nearly at the end of the street. I thought, thank God, they only have a few yards to go. So I took my time opening the door of the taxi and getting in. When I was settled I told the driver I wanted to go to the Strand. He then set the meter and we left. As we did I sat as far into the corner of the taxi as I could and watched the car at the end of the street. My luck was in. I could not believe my eyes. All I could see in the front seat were two newspapers. It looked as if they were perhaps doing the crosswords or checking the horses.

Then as the taxi rounded the corner, I saw both Katrine and Carl were standing on the pavement waiting for me. By this time I was tight into the corner of the taxi, and bent down so that I couldn't see them and they couldn't see me. Once we were clear of them I asked the driver, "Will it be any problem to be taken to Northumberland Avenue, driver?"

He just said, "No, but it will cost you a lot more. The traffic in that part of the city will be bad, as the Government staff finished earlier to day. God, they have it made, teabreaks all bloody day long and then finish work just after lunch on a bloody Friday. I'll tell you, they have it bloody good, they don't know they are born."

I just sat there thinking how lucky I was I'd not stopped the taxi to collect Katrine and Carl. I had decided in the hallway at the last minute that I'd be better off without them. As I sat there, I felt a tear run down my cheek. Also I had a feeling of deep foreboding that perhaps I might never see Katrine again. Still, I knew that Carl would have the sense to know I needed to do this thing alone. He would take her back to Norway tonight. He'd not let anything happen to her and he would look after her for me. He also knew that if it was at all possible I'd make it back to her. I had done it once and I knew he knew I'd do it again.

I alighted from the taxi in Northumberland Avenue and paid off the driver. Then I stepped back into a doorway to observe the street and as I couldn't see anybody following me, or for that matter taking any notice of me, I presumed things were going well. The traffic was quite heavy, more like five o'clock to six o'clock than half past three. As I watched the flow of traffic I noticed how it came in bursts as the traffic lights changed higher up the Avenue. It was then I moved a little farther down the Avenue and settled into a doorway just on the corner of Craven Street. From there I could see all I needed to see of Northumberland Avenue.

I didn't have too long to wait. After about five minutes there was my man coming down the road, full of beans, a lift in his stride. Looking forward to the weekend no doubt. I got myself ready and took the gun I had out of my pocket and covered it with my coat. Exactly how I was going to do the deed I just didn't have a clue, but shoot the bastard I would. When I saw the first of the protection lads pass him and dash across the road through the traffic, then I knew the Major would be crossing the road in the next break in the traffic. As I stood waiting, I could feel a slight tremble in my left leg.

The break in the traffic then came and it felt like an eternity as he crossed the Avenue towards me. If ever any of the events which had happened in my life had been in slow motion, this was it. He was getting closer and I could see the second protection man was going to be delayed by the flow of traffic from crossing the road. The traffic was leaving the lights en masse, as if it were in the start of a Le Mans twenty-four hour race. As he stepped on to the pavement, I thought this is it, now or never, and I stepped out from the doorway into his path. In a moment I stood right in front of him as he crossed the pavement.

The look of fear which came over his face as he stopped and looked at me eyeball to eyeball for the first time must have matched the fear in mine as recognition at last dawned on him. It was, I think, a moment in his life he never expected to face as he must never have expected to see me again. My brain was telling me to move, get on and kill the bastard. So I moved to raise my gun, but before I could lift my gun to aim at him, he suddenly turned and ran.

Everything happened so quickly from that moment on and I could do nothing. As he turned and ran, the first of the lines of traffic racing to the next set of traffic lights arrived right next to us. The Major stepped off the pavement right under the large front wheels of a London double decker Bus. In seconds it was all over. In the last minute of all my years of hatred I'd been cheated. Much to my surprise it was at that moment that all my hate and all the tension of those years of living hell just drained from me. As I looked at the heap of meat (all that was left) splattered all over the underside of the front wheel arch of the bus I turned to the wall and retched my insides out. While I leaned against the wall, in the fog of retching my guts out, I was certain he had shouted a name as he went under the bus. I'd no idea what that name was, but perhaps it was just a shout of fear as he saw the wheels of the bus start to roll over him.

While I was standing there a pair of hands took hold of my shoulders and pushed me, none too gently, into a large saloon car. As I got in, the hands which had a tight grip on my collar forced me to the floor of the car and a voice said, "Keep down and lie still." Funnily, I did exactly that, then a hand reached down and removed my gun. The voice then said, "I shall take that, you will not be needing it anymore."

The voice then said to the driver, "Go on and drive for God's sake, man." The car then moved effortlessly away and I was still lying on the floor of it. I must admit I was very apprehensive about what would happen to me now. I was looking at a pair of immaculately polished black shoes. A pair of black socks were sticking out of them and disappearing up into a pair of immaculately pressed grey pinstripe trousers. I wondered why it was these bastards always had highly polished shoes or boots on. They reminded me of a pair of highly-polished brown boots which had stood over me years ago, but I had no Nobby to step out and help me this time.

So I lay there and thought during the drive. It was all I could do; I had all sorts of emotions going through my mind. First I went over the years, the years since I had last seen the man who had just died. That was at my trial in Russia. It was a funny experience and I wondered what they could or would do to me. The more I thought about it the more I came to the conclusion there was not a lot they could do. They could throw the book at me, but after some more thoughts on the situation it occurred to me that they would not be likely to do that. The only charge they could bring against me was absence without leave and I thought that was very funny, as I believed there was nothing anybody could do about it. They would never know when I had made my escape, or how. They would know nothing of the men I had killed on my travels through the Soviet Union and I had not, after all, killed the man here in England. Oh, yes, I had set out to kill him, but fate had deemed it otherwise. Seeing me may have caused his death, but I had not done the deed myself.

Oh, yes, I had killed quite a few people while I had been fighting for my existence all those years in the camps. Also, while making my escape from that hell. Okay, some of the people I had killed might have been entirely innocent, but I could not afford myself the luxury of asking them, could I? So I reasoned these people in

England could not know any of that. As far as these people knew I had been executed years before in Russia. So, all in all I began to feel pleased with myself and I was convinced they would not be able to touch me so I started to relax. For the first time in years I really felt free! My only wish was that Katrine was with me at that moment.

The drive was long and I heard the sound of the rush-hour traffic get less and less. From this I deduced we were heading out of London. I was right, of course, and when the sound of traffic had settled to the continual flow which one only hears on a motorway, I think I dozed off to sleep. How long I was asleep for I didn't know, but I didn't think it was very long, for just after that I was prodded awake by a brown, brogue boot. Then I was allowed to get up off the floor of the car to join my 'saviour' on the back seat. Once I was up I asked, "Where are you taking me?"

"Keep quiet, all will be revealed in good time, lad, you never change, do you?"

Shit, I thought, I am now over forty and he calls me lad.

It was about two hours later when we arrived at a farmhouse. I was to learn later that it was in Lincolnshire. The house was old, about the seventeen hundreds I thought, but it looked well maintained. They took me into the house via the back kitchen and from there I was ushered into a room which I believed to be in the middle of the house, only because it had double doors at each end but no windows. It looked like a study or office with a desk, bookshelves and a couple of armchairs. As I looked around I noticed a copy of the *Farmers Weekly* lying on one of the chairs. After Brown showed me into the room, he told the driver to stay with me, which of course the man did. I wasn't too keen on that driver; he looked a nasty piece of goods. My old mentor then said to his driver, "Be careful and watch this one like a hawk. This one's a little wild, so be on your guard all the time," he added, as he left the room.

Looking at the driver I was about to start a conversation with him, then I thought better of it. So I looked around the room, taking a good look at it. Then I decided, if I were to make a break, I would need to know what was on the other side of both sets of double doors. Next I stood up, rather too sharply for the driver, who immediately started to adopt a defensive stance. As he did, I just grinned at him and stepped across the room and picked up the *Farmers Weekly*. Then I sat down again and started to read some of the advertisements in it. That was when I came across a rather interesting advert – Lot one, three bedroom farmhouse, ten acres of good pastureland for sale, vacant possession. Lot two, ninety acres of mixed arable land for sale. Property can be sold as one or two Lots. It then went on to describe the asking price and the general area of the country it was in. So I marked it and I then read a couple more advertisements in a similar vein and I was just starting to get really into it all when the door opened and my old mentor Brown rejoined us.

Looking at him, I said, "The time has come and I think it is time you told me what the hell is going on, sir?"

I thought if he says lad, or laddie I swear I will kill the sod right here and now, but he didn't, so I didn't. Kill him, that is.

All he said was, "All in good time. You will have to be debriefed and the debriefing will start later. First, you need a good hot bath; best way to wash away all your evil thoughts, pains and troubles. Then some good food inside you, a good night's sleep and then tomorrow you can tell us all about the tricks, wanderings and dirty deeds you have been up to since you disappeared without trace over the North

Sea. We want to know everything you have been up to, especially what you have been doing since we heard you had been executed."

As I looked at him I could feel all the hatred start to build up in me again. Apart from Katrine, Sharon, Carl and now Helga, of course, no person had shown me any thought or consideration since the day I had left Plymouth, all those lifetimes ago.

Brown then led me through one set of double doors into a well-lit dining room. A little gasp left my lips as already seated at the table and looking apprehensive were Carl and Katrine. At first I was speechless and I just looked at them. Then I managed to ask, "How the hell did you two get here?"

"We can discuss all these problems as we eat," said Captain Brown.

Carl gave Katrine a funny look and I thought, something is wrong. So I made my way round the table and sat down next to her just as the driver was making for that seat. He then looked at Brown who just shook his head in a negative sign.

Katrine and I started to talk in Old Lapp because we knew that Carl could understand but we assumed none of the others could. I whispered, "I love you Katrine, more than you could ever know, I was a fool to leave you behind."

"I love you too, dearest; it's all right now you are here, I feel better already. One of them told me you were dead."

"I think it will be better, Katrine, if we wait until we are alone, then we can tell one another all that has happened today."

She looked at me with a rather strange look and said, "Surely you mean this week?"

"Week, what are you on about, I only left you this morning?"

To which she said, "Yes! Darling."

I could tell by the way she said yes that she did not believe it. Brown then butted in, "Well, Johnston, I see you have busied yourself learning a new language. Whatever are we going to do with you now? You are technically still in the Service, but I think they will not be extremely pleased with you if you ever show up in a Royal Marines Barracks again."

"Will they not? Well, just what can I do now? Perhaps I could retire to a hill farm somewhere out of the way and miles from civilisation. That would need money though, still, maybe the Service could stand the cost of a small hill farm, to keep me quiet, that is. After all, Captain Brown, they must owe me a hell of a lot of back-pay by now."

I saw the look on Carl's face and gave him a half nod, trying to let him know that I'd realised we were in really grave trouble now and I meant grave in its worst sense. I didn't think anybody else saw it.

Brown suddenly said, "Well, now, that isn't such a bad idea, you know. At least we would know where to contact you and what you were up to, wouldn't we?"

"Oh! yes, but I might not like that. I might not like the idea of you knowing where I was. No," I said after more thought, "I am not keen on that part of it at all."

Katrine then said, "Perhaps we could go to America."

Before I could answer her, Brown said in his best sarcastic voice, "If you had wanted to go to America, my dear, you should have joined up with an American agent, not this blundering idiot."

All For A King's Shilling

At that point Brown's eyes and mine locked for the first time since god knows when and I said, "Oh, I may blunder, as you put it, but I am nobody's idiot. You may do well to remember that Captain Brown, I've got the measure of you and your part in all of this."

As I stared at him, I knew I would have to kill him, and I knew exactly what had been going on. For the first time I knew what had being going on and why Katrine and Carl had looked at me the way they had. I knew they had been surprised when they saw me and I could feel their thoughts with me now, willing me to realise what had gone on, but I was now ahead of them. The 'penny' had at last dropped, as they say.

At last I broke his gaze, looked at Katrine and said, "After that I think I would like to get a breath of fresh air, do you want to come for a walk with me, Katrine?"

I was testing Brown, I wanted to see what he would do. Carl, Katrine and I needed time, we needed time to get away from here. Also, I needed to see just how urgent Brown was about what he had planned for us. I was surprised he had not got rid of Katrine and Carl yet, which made me think there was still hope.

Brown then said, "Now, look Johnston, you've had a very stressful time since I last saw you. In fact you were so worn out that you passed out in the car. We have had you sedated for a few days, but on doctor's orders only I assure you. The doctor said he would not be responsible for your health unless you had complete rest and he said the best way to do that was to put you out for a few days."

"Oh! yes, and just how many days do you call a few?"

"A week," he hissed through his teeth.

"So how long have you two been here, Carl?"

"A week. They told us you had collapsed and were being looked after in the best of hands I seem to recall was what they said."

"I bet they did." I turned to Brown and said, "I take it you have no objections to my going out for a walk with Katrine, do you, sir?"

"No, but just don't leave the grounds will you, you are still unsteady on your feet, you know."

I thought I bet I'm bloody unsteady on my feet, you arsehole, but for God's sake stop telling me what I am, and what I'm not. All I said though was, "I've no intention of leaving here until my future has been settled, one way or another."

Brown and I just looked at one another again, then Katrine and I left the room. We made our way outside. As we did I motioned her to say nothing. So in silence we left the front of the house and walked along the drive, the drive along which I had come earlier that night. It joined another rougher track which looked as if it led to the farm buildings at the rear of the house. We stopped and had a look. In the darkness I could just make out three cars. There were also a couple of men, but there were no farm implements of any sort, which I would have expected. More importantly, there were no farmyard noises, no noises of any animals at all.

We then set off along the drive which led off through some fields. When we were some way from the house, not knowing if I were bugged in any way, I took a piece of paper from my pocket and wrote, "You haven't told them anything, have you?"

She nodded, indicating that she had not. She then pointed to the question I had asked her and looked at me. I nodded and shrugged my shoulders and said, "I do not know."

Then I showed her my arm. It was black and blue with needle marks on it.

Next I wrote, "You know he is the main man we want?"

She read it and then looked at me. She was about to speak so I put my finger to her lips, then shook my head.

She looked at me and I wrote, "We are, all three of us, in great danger here. If they do not kill us tonight they will do it within the next day or so. It's my belief I have been brought here so they can kill us all together. Once they know just what it is they think we know, they will do it, I can assure you."

Then I wrote, "They must still not have all the details they need or we would not be alive now."

Katrine read the last bit, and then I ate the paper. It tasted bloody horrible. Still, eating it was better than having them find it. When I had finished I leaned forward and kissed her long and hard. When our lips parted I looked her in the eyes and said, "We shall never be apart again, Katrine, of that I can assure you. No matter what happens here tonight or in these next few days, we will always be together."

She then whispered in my ear, "I know, Bill, I love you so much I could never live without you now." With that we turned and went back to the house, both aware of what we would have to do to achieve just that, and both fully prepared to do it.

When we re-entered the house, Brown and Carl were still in the dining room and when we walked in I said to Brown, "It has been a long day and I must still be feeling tired from the drugs your doctor has given me. So I think it's time I had a rest."

"No problem, your friend Carl will show you to your room."

"Don't worry, sir, Katrine can show me. After all we will be sharing the same room from now on."

Brown looked at me, and I could feel the hatred in the man. I just looked at him for a second, turned to Katrine and said, "Let's go to our room, darling."

With that we both turned and left the room. As I glanced at Carl I could see he had really enjoyed that little exchange.

Chapter Eighteen
It Seems They Don't Want The Killing To Stop
London 1981

There is a hell of a lot of Sprog Officers around these days

When Katrine and I entered the bedroom I crossed to the window and drew the velvet curtains. Once they were drawn I checked every inch of them, but I could see no listening devices anywhere. Next I had a good look at the ceiling light, but found nothing. It was then I noticed Katrine was checking the bedside lights and the small bedside cabinets on which they stood. We then checked the pictures hanging on the wall and both of us looked at the double bed. We gave a little laugh as we both knelt down one at each side and had a good look under it. Something or someone had disturbed her side of the bed so I moved around to her side and lay on the floor to get a better look under the bed.

As I was looking under the bed, Katrine knelt over me and started to tickle my chin. She then put her lips right alongside my ear and said. "Does this mean we can't, um, do you know?"

I turned and whispered to her. "You must be joking, Katrine."

At which she gave a little giggle. Next I took the device from the bed and went to the window and opened it. I put the device on the windowsill outside, and then I closed it.

Once I had done that I got a piece of paper and wrote, "There are certain to be more, at least one more. So be careful what you say, Katrine. I do not want to spend the rest of the night eating bloody bits of paper."

She grinned and wrote. "You have to be joking now." She then burst out laughing. What happened next was between Katrine and me, or maybe it wasn't.

Later that night we talked by whispering into one another's ears. I asked Katrine, "You are certain, aren't you, that the man we know as Captain Brown is the man your father told us about, all those years ago in your house in Murmansk?"

She said, "Oh, yes, I am certain of that and Carl is certain as well." She then continued, "Three men picked Carl and me up in London about three days ago, the same day you left to kill the man who was in that Russian court when we were found guilty and sentenced." She then told me. "They took us in a black taxi to Paddington, to a small terraced house near the station. Carl and I were going to Paddington anyway, while trying to lay a false trail.

"It was there that these three men, who looked like off-duty policemen, asked us, 'Just where do you two intend going?'

"Both Carl and I said that we were going to visit Bath before we left for home. It's the last place on our list of cities to visit."

Looking at Bill she said, "I thought they had bought our story at first. Then they arrested us and brought us to this farmhouse. Since our arrival they haven't asked us anything more about our visit to Bath or anything else for that matter."

"Did they at any time, Katrine, take you or Carl to a police station?"

"No, they brought us straight here, to this old farmhouse." Then she went on, "Do you think it is all over now?"

"Well," I said. "Yes, I think we are into the last act of this play; we will have to be very careful from this moment on, Katrine. I do not want to upset Captain Brown now."

As I didn't think it boded well for us I didn't mention my fears to Katrine.

She went on. "Since we arrived at this farmhouse they have left us to our own devices for the last two days. Oh, they fed us, they have looked after us well considering the circumstances we are in. We have not been able to leave the house, though.

"They started asking us last night what we were doing in London."

"What did you tell them, Katrine?"

"Just that we were on holiday and that we were tourists, but I am certain they didn't believe a word we had told them. It was on the second day that they showed us some photographs of the three of us," she said.

"Photographs," I asked, "what photographs?"

"They have some photographs of you and Carl. They also have some photographs of you and me and others of all three of us together. Remember that man who made that awful suggestion to me the first night? Well, they have a photograph of you, him and me," she said.

"Oh, shit. They must have known about us since we arrived in London. They may have had us under surveillance before we even got here."

Katrine then said, "They even have photographs of Carl and you in the workmen's clothes you wore that day."

It was then I think we both realised that these people knew more about the three of us than they were letting on.

"They had told Carl and me that you were well and would be joining us soon; which of course you have done."

"When I arrived here, Katrine, I believed at first that I had come straight here from London. It was only later, when I had a flashback, that I realised this was not so."

It was then I told her, "I believe they may have been using a truth drug on me. Similar to the one the Russians used before they put me on trial. I am not sure, but I would have to assume they had. I would also have to assume that I may have told them something, if not everything, about why we had turned up in London. Otherwise they would have questioned you and Carl earlier and in more detail."

Then I asked her, "Katrine, you are sure both you and Carl can account for all the time since they picked you both up in their black cab? You see, I am sure that something is wrong. I am certain they needed more information. Otherwise, they would have killed us out of hand by now. If they were certain they were in the clear then they would most certainly have shot us by now."

I thought, it could be because the Russians had reported me dead to Brown, who I was certain was working for the Russians. Discovering that I was not after all dead, he may have had to seek guidance from his paymasters about what to do next. It could be possible that Brown thought I was working for the same masters as himself. He would wait for information from his paymasters before eliminating me. Anyway we were going to have to have a plan of action if we were to get out of this little lot. The problem was that at the moment we didn't have a plan, or any thoughts of one.

I saw the way Katrine was looking at me and said, "We have to try and play for time, Katrine; we need time to plan our escape from this little mess."

She looked me straight in the eye and said, "You will get us out of this mess, Bill?"

"Well, Katrine, without any plan the three of us must be ready to react to whatever and any chance we get. We have to make a break. The longer we leave it, the less chance we will have of getting away. If you can talk to Carl, you must tell him to be ready at any time from this moment on. Tell him to react to anything I do, any move I make. Our situation is really that desperate, Katrine."

With that we both lay back and eventually went to sleep.

Next morning at breakfast I raised the subject of a small farm again with Brown.

He looked at me for a moment or so. "Well, you know, that is quite a good idea. Have you anything in mind?" he asked.

"There are certain to be some suitable places advertised in the Farmers Weekly."

"Alright, you and I will have a look after breakfast," he said.

The conversation then died. I looked at Carl and he gave the slightest of nods that he understood the situation. From that I took it Katrine had been able to talk to him. For some reason they had so far kept Carl and me apart. I had to be able to talk to him in private, or in public for that matter. So I would have to think of some way of having a chat with him.

When we had all finished breakfast the three of us took a second cup of coffee each, hanging on to see if they left us alone, but they didn't. So when we realised they had no intention of doing so, we all then moved into the room that I had first entered the night before, when I had first arrived at the farmhouse.

Once everybody had settled down, I asked Brown. "What do you have planned for us today, then?"

Before he could answer, I continued, "I would like to get this all settled as soon as possible. I have a lot of living to catch up on. Living which I had to forgo these last few years while I was incarcerated in the Arctic Gulags, perhaps at your request. Mostly being looked after by just such people as you have around you here, you and your 'Old Pals' Boys' Club'."

"I presume you have finished," Brown said. "You have got very bold in your old age. It looks as if your jailers have taught you some rather bad manners while you have been away. Then you always were a Bolshie bastard, weren't you?"

I looked at him for a second or so. His two thugs were by now getting a little edgy. So I just said, "Yes, you are right, sir! I have always been a Bolshie bastard as you put it. Only now I know I had a bloody good reason to be a Bolshie bastard."

He completely ignored my remarks and said, "These conditions you want will take time to sort out and settle; they just can't be rushed like that. No, what you are asking me to do can't be done at the drop of a hat as you seem to believe. My superiors will need to know just what it is you want. Then they need time to decide on how to comply with your request. They need to put their little bits of paper into the correct pigeonholes. Otherwise the bits and pieces don't fit together correctly, even you must see that is how it must be."

At that point I interrupted him and said, "Look, Captain Brown, I have had it with all these faceless wonders deciding about my health, future and what things are best for me. I'm the only one able to decide those issues from now on. It matters not one bit to me. I don't care how high up the bloody departmental ladder, or civil service ladder, or whatever bloody ladder they are. Or even whose bloody ladder they are up. They have never been up to their pretty little necks in blood, mud and shit the way the three of us have. So take your bloody decision-makers and stuff them. We three are the only ones who can make any decisions about ourselves from now on. Can you at least get that through your head, man?"

He looked a little taken aback and realising I had him off balance, I went on to add. "What is more, sir, I don't see that waiting for you and your chums to make your minds up is any reason to keep the three of us cooped up in this bloody farmhouse? So if you don't mind, I would like us to be able to go out and have a look around, and perhaps go for a walk or something."

Much to my surprise he did not object. So, without waiting, in case he changed his mind, the three of us left the room and set off for a walk around the local countryside.

At first I had in mind to do a bunk there and then, but without wheels we would not stand a snowball's chance in hell.

We didn't talk as we made our way around the lanes, we all had too much going on in our heads, but we did take notice of the lie of the land though, just in case we had to leave on foot in a hurry. The three of us knew we had to know just what was going on; I believed we all knew what was really going to happen to us. If we just sat back and let it happen, that is. There was now no doubt among us that they would kill us and they would kill us soon. Executed I think is the correct word for what they had planned for us.

Not if I could help it, though. I had the distinct feeling that we would not see much more of this Green and Wonderful Land if we did not make a move to defend ourselves, and damned soon! It was as we walked back in the direction of the farm that I told the others of my fears.

"I now believe Captain Brown to be the main traitor in the system," I said. "Somehow I do not think he has always been that way. He was not the Brown whom I had known so many years ago, when I first came into contact with him. It is my belief the Russians have turned him, or whatever it is they do. Also I think they did it long before I left on the fateful trip from which, with your help, I managed to return. Maybe I'm wrong, but I also think he is a very unhappy man. It is as if he has lost all the spark and verve from his life."

Katrine looked at me and asked, "Did you kill that man in London, as these men said you did?"

"Katrine, I didn't kill him. I was about to, but when he saw me he turned and ran. Unfortunately, he ran right under a double decker bus and it was a hell of a mess. Before I could get away or do anything, Brown picked me up in his bloody car."

I think Katrine looked relieved when I had finished.

Then I went on. "You must not underestimate Brown, though."

Katrine looked a little frightened.

So I told her, "He will still kill us all as soon as look at us. So we will have to be on our guard at all times from now on."

"Carl, you'll have to react to any move I make and I will do the same for you. We cannot make any plans at this stage, Carl, we will just have to trust each other, okay?"

"Do not worry about me, Bill, I will not let you down."

"No, Carl, nor will I let you down," I replied.

We had by this time arrived at a point overlooking the farm and we were all leaning on a field gate looking towards the house. While we looked at the house we were just chatting about our situation and what we could do about it, trying to come to some kind of plan, putting ideas forward and then rejecting them just as quickly.

Carl was the first to point out the activity going on at the farm. He pointed to the farmhouse and said, "They seem to have come to a decision about us, Bill. It looks as if they are loading their belongings into the boots of the cars out front of the house."

As we watched this going on for a few minutes we all came to the same conclusion, time for us was starting to run out.

I told Carl, "I have no ideas, and we will have to take our chance as and when it comes. There is one thing for certain, I will not go out without one hell of a fight. I haven't come through what I have done just to be killed by some non-combatant bum boys licking up to Brown, no sir."

With that, we looked at each other and I said, "Well, we have been good together so far, let us keep that going at least. Don't forget. When the shit hits the fan, then we all go and we all go together, we give them something they will never forget. Make them rue the day they ever tangled with us. The Three Musketeers," I said. "Shit, they won't know what hit them."

With that we linked arms and made our way back towards the farm, our step a lot lighter than when we left now the decision had been taken. By the time we arrived, all the loading of the cars had stopped. We went into the house and found them all waiting for us in the dining room.

When we entered the room, Brown told Katrine to wait in the bedroom. I immediately told her to stay where she was. Then I told Brown that Katrine was to stay with me, and whatever he had to say he could say in front of her. As I listened to my voice I thought, this sounds bloody terrible, all this high and mighty shit, but I could think of nothing else to say which would keep Katrine with us. Instinctively I knew it was important that none of us should be parted at this moment in time.

Brown nodded to the ape who had stepped forward when I had spoken, but I didn't think I had bought any time by insisting that Katrine was to stay with us. As we stood there, I could feel the hair on the back of my neck start to stand on end and I knew then that they had planned to kill us here and now in this bloody room. Brown then started to address us.

As he started talking I could see one of them start to twitch and I thought this one's frightened. He would not react fast enough so I would leave him for later in the first encounter, the encounter that I knew was about to happen. Brown was babbling on and on as he told us, "You, Johnston, have caused a lot of trouble with our people and you have interfered with my plans. You have caused the death of a very important agent and you have all made complete arseholes of yourselves. Also, not to put too fine a point on it, you have disgraced the 'Old Firm'."

I thought 'Old Firm' my arse. They are a cosy little nest of Russian agents if the truth was to be told. Ever since I had witnessed the death of my old friend with the highly polished brown boots I had believed this bastard Brown had to be a part of it. The way the bastard was trying to justify killing us here in this place pointed to him being one of the leaders, if not the head man of the whole bloody set-up.

It wasn't long before he got to the main point of his little talk. "The three of you have become such an embarrassment you will have to be got rid of. You have gone wild and are killing your own agents. I'm sorry and all that, after all the good work you have done for us over the years, but you have outlived your usefulness, Johnston. Ever since you teamed up with this man here and this obvious Russian female agent you have gone mad, so I have no option but to have you killed," he concluded.

I looked across at Carl, and I could see he was thinking the same as me. We would have to move very soon, and it would be touch and go, but for some reason I was reluctant to make the first move. I think Carl understood that I reacted better to their actions, rather than initiating them myself. There were five of them in the room, not including Brown. Most, if not all of them, were likely to carry guns. There could be more of them outside in the rest of the house, so it might be tricky. We would have to get the bloody lot, which we would be unable to do in one go; especially if, as I thought, there were others who were up and about in the building. We did not have a weapon between the three of us and they were armed to the fucking teeth. Oh! shit, but we were in one hell of a mess.

While I was trying to work out how we could get at them, I kept looking from Brown to Carl, but it didn't look as if Carl was having any inspirations either, he just looked back at me. I felt Katrine close to me – so close to me that I could feel her trembling. The air in the place was electric, the hair was standing up stiff as hell on the back of my neck by now and I knew it would all be over in a matter of seconds. As I stood listening and watching, I could feel my hands starting to shake and I came to a conclusion. In the next breath or two I would just attack the bastard who looked the nastiest and was nearest to me. That way, at least, it would get the show moving and stop this stupid game of charades in which we were taking part.

I was just about to say, "I am not listening to any more of this shit," and launch myself halfway across the room at the one I thought looked the most dangerous, when the telephone in the hall started to ring. It broke the ice and I just could not believe my eyes as they all relaxed at the same moment.

That was all I needed. Before the phone rang for a second time, I was across the room and had this big sod by the throat. I kneed him in the groin, and then head-butted him. As he started to double over I felt him going weak and he started to buckle at the knees. In a trice I took one hand from his neck and I had the gun out of his shoulder holster. Then as he went down, I brought my knee up again, only this time, with my hand on the back of his neck, I smashed his face into my knee. As I heard the bones breaking I remember thinking, I hope it is his face and not my bloody knee that has split open.

Then I turned to survey the room. There were two down. Carl had dropped the one next to him with a chop that had broken the man's neck. The others were going for their guns, but by the looks on their faces, none of them had done anything like this before; and Brown in his he-man role was grabbing at Katrine, who was fighting him like a wild cat. Next I turned towards a noise near me and shot one of them in the head as he came over the table at me, gun in hand. He was about to hit me over the head with the gun, not shoot me. That spoke volumes.

They had obviously been told not to kill us yet and that in my eyes gave us the edge because we were going to kill them. It was the only chance we had. As I turned to the door another gun roared in the room. I felt nothing and assumed it was not aimed at me. Therefore, I took aim at Brown as he was moving to the door with Katrine. She was still kicking and fighting like a wild cat. I held my aim as I heard Carl shout, "Watch out!" Once more I turned and shot another one who was making for me and trying to hit me on the head. Again, I turned back to face Brown at the door because I knew that if he got out of the room with Katrine, it would be the end for us. Once again I took aim. As Katrine turned in her fight with Brown, she saw me. It was then she fainted, and I remember thinking, good girl. Whatever it was she had done I didn't know, but she had become a deadweight in his arms and he started to let her slip lower as he tried to reach the door to open it. That was when I shouted, "Brown," at the top of my voice. He turned to look and I shot him in the middle of his forehead, the bullet embedding itself in the doorframe. I felt no emotion as I did it. I had no feelings of sorrow, no guilt or pity, nothing at all.

As I turned to the room again, I was just in time to see Carl shoot the last one of them, who I think was trying to surrender. Carl looked at me and I said, "I think we have given them a better fighting chance than they would have given us later considering that when we entered the room we hadn't a gun between us."

"I agree," he said, "but it is not over yet, Bill."

I could hardly believe it. Only a few moments ago, I had thought it would be we three who would be dead but now it was the others who were dead. It was then that I heard a ringing somewhere in the house. The telephone that had set the whole episode in motion was in fact still ringing.

I turned to Carl and said, "I think we had better answer that, don't you?"

He agreed with me so I opened the door gingerly as he checked the bodies, which were laid in grotesque positions all over the room.

The hall was clear, and I could see no movement at all in the rooms leading off the hall. I wondered if there were any more of them around, but I gingerly made my way to the telephone on the hallstand. When I reached the telephone I picked up the handset and put it to my ear, listened and then said, "Yes?"

A voice at the other end asked me, "Why have you taken so long to answer?"

"We are packing and loading the cars ready to leave, why?"

The voice then said. "That is alright, now get me Brown!"

I replied, "Brown is out at the moment with our guests and some of the men."

All the voice said was, "Good, so it is being done, then."

"Yes, sir, I think it's already happened." I replied.

With that the line went dead. As I turned I saw Carl going up the stairs and pointing to his lips to indicate that we should stay quiet.

Next I checked the front rooms of the house and then the remainder of the ground floor rooms. As I was coming back into the hall, I saw the back of a man who was going slowly and gingerly into the dining room. I was at the door behind him in a flash and as he turned to face me I saw he had a look of utter fear on his face. Why do they take on these frightened boys, I thought, as I laid him out with the butt of the pistol I was carrying. He did not utter a sound; he just kept that look of horror on his face as he went down.

I laid him in the hall and then went to get Katrine. She was sitting dazed and looking at me. So I said, "Come on, darling we have to go now. It is all over, but we must get away from here."

Then I took her by her hands and helped her to her feet and led her by the arm out of that room of carnage. Carl came down the stairs and said. "The upstairs is clear."

I told him, "I think we have accounted for them all."

Katrine got a glass of water from the sink and I told her, "Hurry up, Katrine, we do not have time to hang about here. We have to get as far away as possible, and as quickly as possible, before anybody realises what has happened."

Carl said, "There are still two cars parked out front. We should leave in one of them and disable the other."

"Yes," I said, "That would be best, but first we should make this a little more confusing for the police, don't you think?"

With that I told Carl, "You check the cars out, immobilise one and make sure the other has plenty of fuel in it."

To Katrine I said, "Go with Carl and I will be with you both in a minute."

Then I went back into the dining room. Once there, I then set about putting the men's guns into their hands, having first wiped then clean of mine and Carl's prints. Next I made sure the guns were clasped with hands around the butt and the trigger fingers on the triggers. Then I fired a round into the man I had first attacked, from the gun Carl had taken, and then another round from the gun of the man I had beaten, into the man whose neck Carl had broken; once I had done all that, I looked around the room at the carnage and satisfied that I had confused the situation somewhat I left.

As I went, I thought was it possible the police would never even see this farmhouse, let alone this room. So without doing anything else I went to the front of the house. There Carl and Katrine were already sitting in one of the cars with the engine running.

I got in the back with Katrine and Carl asked, "Where to?"

I told him, "Just drive towards North Wales. I need time to think."

All For A King's Shilling

He looked at me for a moment and said, "Why North Wales?"

"I will tell you later, Carl, just get us away from this place. I am sick of all this carnage."

I looked at him. He just nodded. "Okay!" he said. "You are the boss."

With that we left the farm. I knew now I had finished with all this world of mystery and misery that I had suffered so long. All I wanted to do was to get away and try and live a normal life with Katrine. As we left the farm drive, Katrine moved closer and laid her head on my shoulder. Then she reached down and took hold of my hand and then she gave it a tight squeeze that she did not relax for at least an hour.

Chapter Nineteen
So It Is All Out In The Open, Well Maybe Not!
On the run again in the UK this time 1981

All of this excitement and money too.

Carl had been driving for some time and I must have fallen asleep because it was starting to get dark when he announced he was stopping for petrol.

"Where are we?" I asked.

"Somewhere in North Wales," Carl said.

"Yes, but where in North Wales?" I asked.

"Well," he said, "you said drive to North Wales, and I believed you meant to say we should drive to the North Wales Coast. So here we are only a couple of miles from Bangor. I assumed we are either heading for Southern Ireland or some fishing port on this North Wales Coast."

"Nearly right," I said. "I think we will stand a better chance of getting away from them if we use this area rather than any other."

"I am starving," said Katrine. "Are we going to get something to eat or what?"

"We will eat at the first chance we get, Katrine." I said. "Then we will have to find accommodation for the night, or for even more than one night. I think it best if we split up, with Katrine and I in one place and you on your own, Carl."

We found a parking place in Bangor and parked the car. The only eating place we found open was a fish and chip shop, so we all had fish and chips for supper. Next we set off to find some place to stay. Carl went off to find a flat and Katrine and I did likewise.

We agreed to meet back at the car and we decided to approach the car from two directions. First, Katrine and I would stay a reasonable distance from the car park just to see if the car was being watched. Then when we were satisfied it was not, we would approach it. One thing we did not want was a repetition of the fiasco in London. Then we had been spotted right away.

Half an hour later Katrine and I arrived from one side of the town and stood in the shadows observing the car. Meanwhile Carl had come from the opposite side

All For A King's Shilling

and done much the same as us. Although we could not see him, we knew he would be there. Katrine and I eventually decided we had not been spotted, or aroused any interest, so we went and stood by the car.

Within ten minutes Carl came and joined us and said, "I have not seen anybody observing the car or you two, so I presume we are okay."

"I think so," I said. "Katrine and I have found a nice little bed and breakfast place. How did you get on, Carl?"

"Alright," he said, "I have got myself into a boarding house, one of these summer only ones. It is okay, nothing special."

After some discussion we agreed Carl should take the car to Holyhead. Once there, he was to leave it in a car park near the Ferry Terminal and return here to Bangor. We would all then meet the next day in the same place at about 9.30.

Carl left for Holyhead at about half past eight that night. He looked tired but said he would be okay. Katrine and I then went to our bed and breakfast lodgings. When we had both showered, I got dressed again. Katrine got ready for bed and we both felt more settled than we had for a while.

Once we were more or less relaxed, Katrine asked, "Tell me, what is in that small case you are carrying?"

"I don't know," I told her, "I found it in the room at the farm, the one we had all been in when the shooting started this morning. I noticed Brown was holding it in his right hand when he started his judge and jury bit about us. He dropped it when he made his grab for you. So when I went back to the room to check everything out, I saw it was still there, I thought there might just be something of importance there, so I brought it with me."

"So what is in it?" she asked.

"I don't know yet, Katrine, do I, but we are both about to find out, aren't we?"

With that I forced open the locks on the case and laid the lid back to reveal the contents. We were both speechless as we looked at it. The case was stuffed with bundles of money.

For a while we just looked and then Katrine said, "What is the matter with you?"

I said, "I have carried this case, Katrine, and it is too heavy just to have paper money in it."

Just then, Katrine lifted a bundle of notes out of the case. As she did, there was a flash of colour, a colour which has driven men and women wild since time began – 'Gold'. We just looked at each other in astonishment.

I said, "Katrine, I think most of our troubles could just about be over."

"Oh, I do hope so," she replied.

We spent the next half hour packing the stuff away into our own and Carl's bags. Katrine could hardly sleep that night but eventually she dozed off. I forced myself to stay awake. I remained dressed except for my shoes. This time I meant to be ready, just in case we had to make a run for it. At this time I considered perhaps we were at out most vulnerable now, the most vulnerable we had been since we had left Norway. I knew a lot of problems could be resolved for a lot of people should we be eliminated.

The night passed without incident. Katrine and I got ready to leave and then went down for our breakfast. Carl had arrived back in Bangor some time in the early hours of the morning. He had parked the car in a long-stay car park near the Ferry Terminal. He had booked the three of us on the next night's ferry to Dublin. After that he had then come back to Bangor on the local train.

Katrine and I met up with him in the same street where we had parked the car the day before. He told us he was certain he had not been followed. He did admit to being very tired now, and he thought a good sleep would put things right.

I told him about the find in the case I had brought with us from the farmhouse. Then I told him, "I have made some plans for our next move and hopefully our escape. We just can't amble along anymore, we have to get our act together if we are to get away," I told him. "We need to sort this out before you get any rest.

"Firstly, Carl, do you have any fishing friends in this area?" I asked.

"I am afraid I don't know anybody who fishes in these waters," he said.

"Good," I said. "The last thing we need now is to deal with anybody we know."

"Why is that?" asked Katrine, "I would have thought that friends are the people we need right now in our predicament."

"No, Katrine, they are the last people we need," I replied.

"But why?" she insisted.

"Because, my dear, people who know us will also be known to those who are going to try and kill us, that's why!"

Then I said to Carl, "We should be able to hire or even steal something. What we need is to get out of the country and then make our way back to Norway."

"Okay," said Carl, "But how about if we make our way to the North East Coast. At least we can meet up with some Norwegian or some other Scandinavian boats there."

"Yes," I answered, "it could be that that is what they think we will do. Don't you think they will be looking for us there anyway? After all, it is the shortest route home."

"Right, I'll buy that," said Carl, "Then how about we head for Merseyside? At least it is a bigger place to hide in than here."

"I must agree with you there," I said. "But it is not a fishing port, so getting away on a no questions asked outfit will be hard to accomplish there. We have got to get away via this coast though, don't you agree?" I asked him.

"Okay," he said. "Let us make our way to Liverpool and see what we can do from there."

So it was agreed. Carl went off to get some rest and Katrine and I spent the day wandering around the town of Bangor. Later we joined up with Carl. It was just after seven o'clock that evening and we had a meal in a small restaurant. Then we all went to a small public house and stayed there until nearly closing time. From there we made our way to the station and Katrine and I went in and bought tickets to Liverpool. Carl came in some ten minutes later and did the same. We waited at different ends of the platform and we left on the train some time later. When we arrived in Liverpool in the early hours of the next morning the place was deserted.

After we had alighted from the train from separate carriages, we made our way from the station out into Lime Street. The place was dead and both Carl and I thought it best we did not venture too far as we were the only people on the streets. The Liverpool Police have a nasty habit of stopping people on their streets in the early hours of the morning. Therefore we beat a hasty retreat back into the station. We made first for the washrooms, where we spent as long as was possible cleaning ourselves up. Later we met up with Katrine, who had been doing similar things in the ladies' washrooms.

By the time we had finished at least there were some more people around, so we judged it safe to have a look around and perhaps get some breakfast. Eventually we came across a small cafe, which was just opening and starting to serve breakfast. Two fried sausages, fried eggs, bacon and fried bread. All washed down with a greasy cup of tea. We tucked in and ate it all. We had not had any sleep and we had had very little to eat the night before. The amount of fatty food we seemed to be having this last couple of days was, to say the least, starting to have its effect on the three of us. I think all three of us were all starting to become a little spotty.

I said to them, "The sooner we can all get back to a reasonable diet the better. I had forgotten we English live on so much fatty food. I am starting to hate this place."

Carl said, "Oh, you will be alright once we get away. Besides, this fat will do you good after the diet you were on for the last few years."

I had to agree with him on that point. We finished our breakfasts and I went across the road to buy a paper. When I came out of the shop I stood on the street outside and read the paper from cover to cover. Still nothing about what had happened at the farm. I was starting to wonder what they were playing at. I had also been keeping a good lookout on the road as I read the paper. There was nothing untoward to cause us any excitement, so I rejoined the others.

We then paid our bill and made our way slowly to the main shopping centre. Once there we did some window shopping, then Katrine and I went into a ladies' dress shop. By the time we had left she had a couple of large carrier bags full of things she had decided she needed. I just smiled as she tried things on. The main thing was that she was fulfilling the wish she had had from her first day in London.

We rejoined Carl at about eleven o'clock. He said he could not detect anybody following us, so we made our way to the bars and cafes along Bath Street, Newquay and Strand Streets. It was about two or half past that we first had any luck. We met up with a middle-aged alcoholic skipper of a small coaster. The man looked as though he could use some money. It was Carl who first struck up a casual conversation with him in his deep Norwegian accent. Then Katrine and I joined him. He was quite taken with Katrine's beauty, so she played him along. He then asked us back to his ship to have a drink with him. Of course, we agreed, a little reluctantly to do this but we agreed. We all arrived on the dockside by taxi, alongside a real shit of a boat. I had my doubts about it, but Carl gave it a quick look over with his experienced eye and put his thumb up, which I took to mean it was okay.

The Skipper took us to his cabin. It stank to high heaven. Poor Katrine's face was a picture. She looked as if she was going to be sick at any moment. We settled down and he poured us a couple of drinks from a half empty bottle of some clear spirit. I learnt later it was poteen. All three of us managed to get rid of it. Katrine poured hers down the washbasin in the corner. Both Carl and I managed to spike our newfound friend's glass with ours.

I then asked, "Where are you headed from here, Skipper?" He seemed to like being called Skipper.

"We are off to Sweden," he replied.

I looked at Carl and asked, "Oh, and when are you sailing to Sweden?"

"We are leaving on this evening's high tide," he answered. "Why do you want to know?" he asked.

"Well," I said. "I have never been to Sweden. They tell me they have lots of girls there."

"Oh," he said. "They have some beauties, just like this one," as he made a lunge for Katrine.

Just as he got within two feet of her, she brought her foot up into his groin and he went out like a light. I looked at her and started to laugh. Katrine did not think it was funny and said, "He is a filthy pig. I will not stay on this disgusting ship, boat, thing any longer."

I took hold of her and said, "Wait, Katrine, we could get to Sweden on this 'thing' as you call it. Then in no time we could be back home."

She looked at me and said, "There is no way I am going to sail one metre on this stinking 'thing'. So get me off right now."

I looked at Carl and said, "I must agree with her, Carl. I don't fancy having to fight him off Katrine all the way to Sweden."

"Yes," he said. "You are both right. It is not worth it. He would also blab his mouth off to the first person who bought him a drink. No, it is better we leave now."

With that we picked our things up and left the ship. As we walked along the dockside a young man who was in his middle twenties approached us. I looked at Carl and moved Katrine slightly behind us.

When the lad was about ten yards away, Carl said, "It's alright, I know this lad."

The lad said in Finnish, "Hello, Carl, and how are you keeping these days? Surely your fishing boat is not tied up here?"

"No," said Carl. "We have been on a hiking holiday in Wales. We have spent all our money and are looking for a cheap trip home. You don't happen to know of anything going our way, do you?"

"Well, yes, I do," said the young man. "We are leaving tonight on the high tide. I am no longer working the fishing boats, Carl," he said. "I am now a fully-fledged deep sea sailor. Come and see my skipper and see what he says. By the way, who are your friends?"

I looked at him and said, "We are old friends of Carl's. My name is Willheim and this is Katrine, my wife." I thought, I am having no more of the type of trouble we have just had on the ship we have just left. I felt Katrine nudge me when I had finished talking.

The lad said, "I am pleased to meet you, Willheim and Katrine. I hope you have enjoyed your holiday with this old reprobate, Carl."

"Yes," said Katrine. "We have had a wonderful time."

With that the young man led us to a small, clean, well-painted and well-maintained coaster of about twelve hundred tonnes. We all climbed the gangplank and the lad took us to see his captain. After the introductions, the Skipper came straight to the point.

All For A King's Shilling

"It will cost you fifty pounds each, payable in advance. For that, you get a cabin for the three of you to share. You will be fed, and you will be put ashore before we enter Gothenburg. From there you are on your own."

I looked at him and said, "Fifty pounds, no way. It is cheaper by ferry. We only came to see you because we are broke."

"Well, get the ferry then," was all he said.

I looked at Carl and he said to the Captain, "As my friends say, we are broke. We can pay you once we get to Sweden. We could pay you the fifty pounds then, but we could only manage about thirty between us now."

"I shouldn't do this," the Captain said. "But you look honest, so I will trust you. Give me your thirty pounds and my lad will show you to the cabin you can use. You must pay me the balance as soon as we get to Gothenburg."

With that we duly handed over the money and a young boy showed us to a cabin in the structure which housed the bridge. When we were settled in the cabin I looked at the other two and put my fingers to my lips. Then I wrote on a piece of paper taken from the wrappings of Katrine's purchases, "I don't trust this Captain. I think he will sell us to the highest bidder."

They both nodded their heads in agreement. I then wrote, "We are going to have to be very careful from now on. We must all remain together. One leaves the cabin, then we all go, okay?"

Again they both nodded their agreement. So I wrote, "Let us all go and have a look round." With that we left the cabin and made our way on to the main deck. It was just your normal coaster, bow followed by one long hold with what looked like four covers. Then the superstructure including the bridge, living quarters and galley. We were all alone on the deck, the hatch was battened down, and we looked to be just waiting for the tide. Everything seemed normal and yet there was something about the Captain. Still, we would see. It might be I was getting paranoid about things. Mind, this paranoia had stood me in very good stead over the years.

We familiarised ourselves with the ship and then went back to the cabin. We stayed in there as the ship sailed out into the bay. Once we were at sea, I must admit it felt good. We all went on deck and just let the fresh sea air blow over us.

When it was getting late the young man who had brought us to the ship came up to us and started talking.

"I do not know what kind of work you are into these days, Carl," he said. "But I think I should warn you that the Captain is not to be trusted. I think he works for some intelligence organisation, or something."

I looked at Carl and said, "What did I tell you."

"I know," he said. "The thing is, what can we do?"

I turned to the young man and said, "How close to the coast do we get when we are sailing past the northern coast of Scotland?"

"Well," he said. "I don't know exactly, but it is not too far off when we round Cape Wrath. We do go in quite close."

"One thing more," I asked, "Is the boat on the stern the only one you have?"

"Yes, it is," he answered.

"Okay," I said to him. "You have been a good help. Just one point, at what time are we likely to round Cape Wrath?"

"Just after last light tomorrow night," he replied.

"Good," I said. "You have been a great help. Now will you help us launch the boat at some time tomorrow night?"

"Yes, I will, anything to help Carl."

With that we all went inside the superstructure. I presume the young man to his duties, and we went to our cabin. We were called shortly after that to have our supper in the galley. It was clean, and it was a good meal. When we had finished we took another stroll around the deck and then retired for the night. Carl and I took turns keeping watch, first having immobilised the lock on the cabin door.

The night was uneventful, but we still had to take care. We took turns during the day to get what rest we could, with Katrine keeping watch. By the time we were called for supper, it was starting to get dark. We could see the definite outcrop which we assumed to be Cape Wrath in the failing light. As we entered the small eating place in the galley Carl's young friend was in there. We had our meal while exchanging small talk with him.

At last he said, "I am trailing a large piece of meat behind us, just to see what I can catch."

"Sounds good," I said. "Have you ever caught anything that way? I would like to have a look at it, wouldn't you, Katrine?

She said, "Yes, I would."

Carl said, "I am going back to the cabin, I'll see you there."

With that Katrine, the young man and I made our way to the rear of the ship. When there we immediately started to get the lifeboat ready to launch. Carl returned with all our bags. Katrine was more interested in his not forgetting the dresses she had bought in Liverpool. Once we had everything in the boat, we climbed in.

I looked at the young lad and said, "I hope you are alright and we have not caused you too much danger."

He just looked and said, "Take good care of Carl for me."

"You bet," I said, and we cast off.

It was not the best of launches, but we did make it. In the bow of the boat was a long rope, not too thick, but long. When we were in the water and before we cast off, for some reason I tied this rope to a eyelet on the stern of the ship. We then cast off and as the ship started to disappear into the darkness, Carl tried to start the engine in the boat. There wasn't the slightest flicker of life in it. For the first time ever I saw Carl look frightened. He sat back in the boat and just looked at me. He was about to say something when the boat was pulled quite violently in the direction in which the ship had just disappeared.

I looked at Carl and said, "I am bloody glad I tied that rope to the back of that bloody robbing bastard's ship."

Carl broke out laughing and said, "You never bloody change, do you?"

"Nope," I said, "I never bloody do."

With that, while Katrine kept an eye on the stern light of the ship, Carl and I set about seeing what the hell was wrong with the motor in the boat.

It was not long before we discovered there was no fuel in the tank. After a good rummage around in the boat we came across some blankets and a small can of fuel. Not a lot but I hoped it was enough. We put it into the tank and then settled down in the boat to try and keep warm. It was one hell of a long night and we kept getting water over the bow every now and again. We did, however, manage to stay dry thanks to the blankets we had found.

At about 3.30 in the morning I reckoned we must be near to the Pentland Firth. I had seen a couple of boats ahead of us heading in a northerly direction and one heading across our course southwards. I told Carl I thought it would be wise to cast off now, or pretty soon. I also said it would be best if we did not leave this long line of rope hanging on to the stern of the ship. We then started the long job of hauling ourselves in on the rope until we were only a few yards behind the ship again. Once there I cut the rope and watched the ship pull away from us. All seemed quiet on board.

We let it disappear from view, and then started the engine. It burst into life straight away. I told Carl to steer for the shore, which we could just make out in the distance. At least we thought it was the coast. The lights did not seem to be moving. We did not make very good progress and it was ages before we seemed to be getting anywhere near the coast. At last we could make out the actual headland and made for it.

Eventually we made a landfall on the coast just to the east of Crosskirk. We managed to get ashore on to the rocks and once we had our kit ashore we cast the boat off, after first having pulled the bung and made a couple of holes in it. Once we reached the higher ground above the shore we sat down and had a look at ourselves.

We looked like a trio of people who had spent a rough night in the open. I figured it would not be an uncommon sight in these parts. I told Katrine, who was shattered, "You had better let me have your bags, Katrine, we are going to have to re-pack our kit. We cannot walk around with bags which have the names of Liverpool dress shops on them."

She gave them to me, saying, "Don't you dare damage any of those clothes."

"Would I?" was all I said.

Once we had everything re-packed to Carl's and my satisfaction we set off to get away from the coast. Then we took one last look and could see no sign of the boat we had just left. After walking a while we came across a road about a mile from the coast and set off in an easterly direction.

It was about two hours later that we arrived in Thurso. We did not seem to arouse any suspicions as we made our way to the harbour.

There was a ferry in the port and Carl said, "The ferry goes to Stromness from here."

"Okay, Carl, but where can we go from Stromness?"

"Well, we can then go to Lerwick and from there we can go by ferry to Bergen. We are nearly home then," said Carl, with a grin on his face.

I looked at Katrine. We both smiled and I took her in my arms and hugged her and kissed her as if there was no tomorrow.

So it was three days later we were in our hut outside the village of Kirkenes. We had just made ourselves a hot drink before retiring. Carl had left and was in his hut a little way away. We were all at peace at last with the world and I felt for the first time for years, since I walked into that recruiting office in Westmoorland Road in Newcastle upon Tyne, that I was safe, but now it is up to you Mr Watkins, as to what happens from now on. You know that if you make the wrong move it starts all over again.

There is only one thing I will say before I shut up for good. If it does start all over again you must remember that I am not alone; there are hundreds of us who have been shafted by the likes of you, your counterparts and political masters around the world. If it does blow you will find that the Third World War, which is about to end, will look like a kindergarten party compared with what we are capable of!

That night was a night which Katrine and I would never forget. Nobody could take the happiness and bliss of that night from us. It was as if all the restraints of our life had been lifted from us. Both of us just sank into the emotions and happiness that engulfed us and we were at last as one.

Chapter Twenty
Is This Really The End?
Northern Norway 1989

They say that all good things must come to an end someday.

It was then that Mr Watkins left Kirkenes on the north coast of Norway. Mr Larvidson took him away in the Land Rover which had arrived during the night. They had a long drive to Bardufoss, but then the authorities would not allow any foreign aircraft to land at Kirkenes unless it was an emergency. Mr Larvidson did not consider the Englishman, Mr Watkins, to be that kind of emergency.

Once everything had died down a bit it didn't take long for life to get back to normal; as normal as life could be for the four of us living in our circumstances with the cloud of retribution from both East and West hanging over our heads. The mink farm flourished and the next four years passed quietly with no problems for them. The remainder of the village went about its business as it must have done for years. The only troubles on the horizon were the fall in the fish stocks, which caused the local boats to go deeper into the Arctic for fish. This caused some friction with the great bear neighbour Russia. More important to Katrine, Carl and me was the trouble in the fur trade caused by the animal liberation groups, anti-blood people, in the West.

I believed it was a ploy by the Russians to capture the world fur market for themselves. Still, the money we had 'liberated' from the farm in England that night all those years before was still quietly growing in our bank account in Switzerland. So we all reasoned that if the worst came to the worst we could all go and live in Switzerland.

Katrine gave birth to a strapping nine-pound boy and we called him Carl, after our friend who had been so instrumental in helping us to escape from the Russians. In fact everything looked to be all right and after a year or so Katrine was talking about a sister or a brother for young Carl. Big Carl and Helga's mother were also talking along the same lines. Helga's mother had adopted young Carl as her own grandson. I think she had given up all hope of Helga or Carl ever producing a grandson for her, so she looked on young Carl as her own grandson. Our future was for the first time looking good, I was starting to believe that the bad days had passed. Now perhaps we were no longer being hunted by anybody and perhaps we could face a good future together, all in all, I felt pretty good.

The time passed so quickly in those days and in no time at all four years had come and gone since young Carl's birth. He was growing up into a fine boy now and if there was any truth in old wives' tales, he would grow to the grand height of six feet five inches by the time he was twenty-one. As I said, Katrine and I had christened him Carl in gratitude for all the help which our friend had given us over the years. Without his help neither of us would have been here today, we would certainly never have been in a situation where we could have even had a family life, let alone a son. In fact we both felt eternally grateful to him. His mother and sister were the only family either of us had now. All our bridges were now burnt behind us and we couldn't have gone back even if we had wanted to.

Our mink farm had flourished well these last few years, but now there was this cloud on the horizon, with all this animal rights stuff in Europe and America. It was certainly not doing the fur trade any good this year and we had still got quite a lot of pelts to sell. We might even have to kill off some of our breeding stock this year because the fall in demand for mink in the American market had been so dramatic.

Carl had just said the other day, "What would these people do if they knew their efforts to save a few baby seals were going to cause the death of thousands of mink up here in the North?"

"Yes, and I bet these people still stuff themselves with hamburgers each day. I wonder where they think that meat comes from?" Katrine had added.

"Well, Katrine, there is not much point in worrying too much about that. If they stop buying our mink, then we will just have to think of some other means of making a living. What say you, Carl?" I asked.

Before he could answer Helga interrupted him, saying, "You are probably right, Bill, there is no point worrying about it at the moment. Winter will be upon us soon, and we can all go to bed for the winter. Then you two can make a little sister for Carl so you can forget about all this other stuff until next year at least."

Looking down his nose at her, Carl said, "God, is there no hope for you, Helga, just who will you be spending this winter with then?"

Before another word was spoken we all saw the look on Katrine's face and the subject changed.

"What is more important Carl, what are we going to do about young Carl's schooling? We have to make arrangements to send him off for his education at some stage. Katrine doesn't want to send him away, but he will have to go soon. He cannot stay here and just make do with what little education we can provide here, now, can he?"

"You are right, but can't we just leave things as they are for another year at least, then perhaps we can all go south with him. If the mink trade ceases, then we may just have to move south."

"That's probably true, Katrine." said Carl. "Yet Bill is right when he says you must send him south, at least if you want him to get to university. He would stand no chance if he stays here. No, Bill is right; he will have to go south for his education."

"I don't know what all the fuss is about," piped up Helga, having overcome her embarrassment at Katrine's look. "We all know that our mother would jump at the chance to have him stay with her during school terms. What's more, he will always be back up here for the holidays. I wouldn't mind betting that our mother has already entered him for the school, the one where both Carl and I started our education. So stop being so morbid and will one of you fill my bloody glass, a girl could die of thirst here."

We all looked at her and burst out laughing together. Carl did the honours with the Schnapps, and we all sat quietly in front of the log fire for a while. I think all of us were content in the warmth of the company in the cabin, a very close group of people. More so now that winter was once more starting to put its icy grip on us.

A little later that evening when all the talk between long-standing intimate friends had passed, night was well established when Carl and Helga at last said their goodnights and left for the cabin which they shared. It also doubled as the Government outpost, and was situated on the edge of the village. Katrine and I went to look in on young Carl, who was sleeping as snug as a bug in a rug, as they say. We then settled into our own bed, which at this time of the year we kept close against the wall of the room which formed the back of the chimney of the fireplace in the living room. It wasn't long before we were both fast asleep.

Out in the woods above the village that night were two hunters. Neither knew of the other's presence; these two hunters were both settling in for the night. Each of them had picked a place in amongst rocks situated on the edge of the treeline over looking a clearing. The two positions were situated about three hundred yards apart. The positions they had picked overlooked a clearing which was about five to six hundred metres wide and was on the landward side of the ridge overlooking the small port of Kirkenes. The two of them had made very similar hides, which they had camouflaged with pine needles and twigs. They had both made holes in the front through which they had a good view of the clearing and the trees on the crest and also the other side of the clearing. Once satisfied with their handiwork, they got into their respective hides and prepared themselves to spend the night out in the cold, on the reverse side of the hillside.

It was at this point in the proceedings that the difference between the two, if they had but known of each other's presence, then became apparent. One of the two took some dried reindeer meat from his pack, along with some black bread and a bottle of cold black tea. The tea was not frozen simply because he had carried the bottle closer to his body than he had the rest of his food.

The other hunter took three tins and a small gas stove from his rucksack, which he then lined up on the little shelf. He had built the shelf by using a flat piece of rock in the side of his hide. He covered the hole in the front of the hide, next he satisfied himself that it was completely light-proof, and then he started to prepare his evening meal. First he took the gas stove which he lit and placed on the ground. He had also taken a knife, fork and spoon from one of the pockets, and from a chain around his neck he took an unusual little object which had a flat piece about an inch and a half long. At right angles to this was a smaller, pointed piece which swivelled on the larger piece, opening at ninety degrees to the first piece. With this object he deftly opened the smallest of the three tins which he then replaced on the shelf. He then repeated the action with the other two tins.

By the time he had completed these tasks the contents of the first tin, which he opened and exposed to the air, had expanded. There standing in the tin was an eight-inch long fresh bread roll. Next the man lifted the first of the other two cans and pulled a tab which was attached to the bottom of the tin. This he placed on to three pieces of slate he had arranged in a triangle on the shelf. A hissing sound had started to emit from the can when he had pulled the tab and it had started to heat the contents. After about four minutes the man picked up the third tin and repeated the process. Again the hissing sound started. Next he picked up the tin which had just stopped hissing and with his spoon, and occasionally dipping his bread into the tin, he ate his hot, thick cream of chicken soup.

Once he had completed his soup and finished eating his bread, he picked the last tin up and, lighting the one cigarette he allowed himself each day, he sat back and drank his tin of hot coffee. As soon as he had finished all of this, he dug a small hole amongst the rocks and after flattening the tins, he buried them. Next he took his sleeping bag from the rucksack and settled down for the night; his small stove had enough fuel for about twenty hours, so as he settled for the night he was warm both inside and out.

A little way off the other of the two hunters had finished eating his dried meat. His food, if anything, had made him colder than he had been when building the hide. Now he pulled his coat closer around his body as he felt the frost begin to bite at his very bones. Next he pushed his body as hard as he could against the rocks at the back of his hide, trying to gain what little warmth he could from the effort of pressing his body against the ground. Then he closed his eyes and tried to get as much sleep as he could; it was going to be a long, cold day tomorrow waiting for his prey to appear. Even then he might have to wait longer if the information he had received was not very good.

Bill arose twice during the night to restock the fire in the cabin, not that it really needed stoking up. It seemed to him that it had got a lot colder during the night, and he was having trouble sleeping. He said as much to Katrine next morning as they ate their breakfast. She didn't think so. All the same, she looked at him a little strangely, but not letting him see the concern on her face.

The morning passed, as all mornings passed in the village. Bill went to feed the mink, and Helga joined him a little later. First she had made her report to Oslo, and then she helped him clean out the mink cages. When all was done the two of them went back to the cabin, where Katrine had coffee waiting for them. Young Carl was down on the boat with old Carl and Roald. When the boat was in port young Carl had become just about part of the crew. Already he was doing little tasks with, and watched over by, the members of the crew.

Once they had finished their dinner Bill asked young Carl if he wanted to go for a trip into the woods to set a few traps. This he declined, much as Bill had expected he would, and said he would like to go back on the boat with Carl. Katrine said she would go with Bill to set his traps, and so it was that both Carls would go to the boat and Katrine and Bill would go and set some traps above the village.

Just after that Carl collected young Carl and left for the boat. Katrine and Bill headed up the hill with some traps. Round about the same time, Helga left to visit a young woman of a similar persuasion to herself, with whom she had become friendly and who lived about three miles along the coast.

Two and a half hours later Bill and Katrine had finished setting all their traps and had started on their way home. The weather was good, there was no wind and everything was dead still. There were clouds starting to build up in the distance over Russia. The lull before the storm, Bill thought as he looked at them, and his mind went back to the time those years before when he was trying to stay alive in the hunter's hut near the Gulag where they had tried to kill him behind the truck in the wastes of the Russian Arctic. He gave a little shiver and hurried along the trail they were on.

The two huntsmen had lain all day in their hides on the edge of the trees; the two men were still unaware of each other's presence in the area. As they lay there, they had both come to the conclusion that it was perhaps time to call it a day and move off to spend the night in more secure positions; perhaps tomorrow would be better. It was as if they were in unison, they both started silently to pack their equipment away and get ready to leave, making sure they did not disturb their hides; but removing all traces of ever having been near them. Then, as fate ordains these events, they both saw the elk arrive on the edge of the clearing on the opposite ridge from their positions, as he started pawing at the base of a tree. They both settled down once more into their hides and raised their powerful hunting rifles, sighting on the elk.

Katrine and Bill arrived on the top of a ridge which on one side overlooked the village and on the other a large clearing. They stopped for a moment to admire the view, and it was a breathtaking sight at this time of the year, especially in this stillness. Katrine nudged Bill and nodded towards a large male elk, which had stopped his pawing at the base of the tree from which he loosened lichen to eat. He stopped for a second, and looked at them. He was one of the best specimens of elk either of them had ever seen.

"What a magnificent beast, Bill," whispered Katrine as the animal eyed them both. They stood dead still as all three, the elk and the two of them looked at one another. Satisfied they meant him no harm, he returned to pawing the ground with his left front hoof.

The two supposed hunters were now taking aim with their rifles; and each was taking aim from the other side of the clearing. They were both (unbeknown to each other) slowly squeezing on their triggers, taking the first pressure. Then simultaneously they both took a deep breath and held it for a second; and then they released all the air from their lungs and took the final pressure on their triggers. The assignment for both of them was now overtime to pack up and go.

"Perhaps we should be getting back now, Bill, I feel a little colder," Katrine said as she felt a shiver of unease run down her back.

"Of course we should, Katrine, young Carl will be waiting for his supper; and God help us both if you have nothing ready for him when he gets in."

Then, as he turned to kiss Katrine, he felt as if an express steam train had hit him somewhere in his chest, and immediately he started to fall. As he fell forward he could no longer control his body. He fell towards some snow which was lying in a small hollow in front of him. He saw from the corner of his eye that Katrine was falling too. He tried to shout a warning to her, but he just could not get the words to come, and the pain in his chest was becoming excruciating. He then tried to move a little closer to Katrine, trying to protect her from whatever it was that was causing him so much pain. For the first time since he was a child his body would no longer do as he wanted it to, he had lost all his coordination, he just kept falling. He saw from the side of his eye that Katrine was now falling towards him. It took ages and he was trying to twist his body towards her, but to no avail; at last he landed on the small area of snow. Thank God, he thought, the small fold in the ground would at least give them some cover and Katrine would be safe now.

It was then he first tasted the sickly, salt taste of his own blood in his mouth, and when he looked down he could see the snow underneath his head turning a dark red. He managed with a supreme effort to turn his head and look at Katrine. Though his vision was by now getting very blurred, he could just make her out. She was crying and she was calling his name, "Oh, Bill, Bill, Bill," she cried out and again with a superhuman effort which he managed to rally from somewhere, he reached out and took hold of her hand, the hand which with agony etched on her face she was trying to reach out towards him.

At last their fingers touched, and then finally their hands locked in an iron-tight vice-like grip. At last she smiled and said, "Forever, darling." The effort to reach out and hold one another seemed to have drained the final drop of life from both of them!

As they lay there, forever entwined, the first heavy snows of the new winter started to fall. These flakes were real snowflakes, about an inch and a half across, the kind of flakes which don't melt, the ones which stay for the duration of the winter and sometimes beyond.

EPILOGUE

Bill and Katrine found themselves floating above their bodies now. They embraced each other as they watched the snow start to cover their bodies. I seemed as if all the pain and hardship of their lives had now left them forever. They smiled at one another as they watched the two hunters rise from their positions in the edge of the trees. They watched as the two looked for a moment towards one another, over the two to three hundred yards which separated them. Holding their rifles at the ready, they sized one another up. Katrine and Bill watched the two of them who, with a curt nod towards each other, slung their packs on their backs and their rifles over their shoulders. Then one of them headed off towards the East and Russia, while the other headed off towards the West and America. Bill watched the man heading West and said to Katrine, "I should have killed that bloody signaller in Borneo when I had the chance."

They just looked at one another, and then to where their bodies where now nearly covered by the falling snow. "Time to go now," Bill said, and with that they turned and drifted higher and higher on their way towards the bright light which was now shining on them through the falling snow. The light was now getting brighter as they got nearer to it, then all was darkness and gray once more.